By Fred Mustard Stewart

The Mephisto Waltz
The Methuselah Enzyme
Lady Darlington
The Mannings
Star Child
Six Weeks
A Rage Against Heaven
Century
Ellis Island
The Titan

by

Fred

Mustard

Stewart

THE
TITAN

SIMON AND SCHUSTER
New York

2   3   4   5   6   7   8   9   10

Library of Congress Cataloging in Publication Data
Stewart, Fred Mustard
The titan.

I. Title.
PS3569.T464T5   1985   813'.54   84-27568
ISBN 0-671-50689-7

Acknowledgments

I wish to thank my two dedicated and wonderful editors, Patricia Soliman and Michael Korda, for their help and suggestions on this book. I would also like to thank John Weitz for his assistance and suggestions in the sections of the book dealing with Germany in the 1920s and '30s.

Whereas *The Titan* is a work of fiction, it is based on historical fact. The events depicted in the Fuelsbuettel Prison were not invented by me, but were based on first-person accounts of victims of the Gestapo brutality of that time. When it comes to inventing sadistic tortures, few writers of fiction, including myself, can match the Gestapo.

FMS

I dedicate this, my tenth novel, to my beloved wife, Joan.

Arma virumque cano.
        —VIRGIL
("I sing of arms and the man.")

Prologue

DEATH
OF A TITAN
1963

THE killer stood on the Tunisian beach, looking through his binoculars at the largest private yacht in the world.

The owner of the yacht—the "legendary," as he was often called in the press, Nick Fleming—was in his luxurious stateroom. It was only seven-thirty in the morning, but visible on the deck of the sleek 190-foot *Seaspray* were two members of the crew, one swabbing the teak deck, the other polishing the brightwork. The *Seaspray,* the killer knew, was kept immaculate.

The killer thought it curious he was being paid so much money to murder a man in his seventies—after all, how many years did Nick Fleming have left? But the twenty-five thousand dollars had been deposited in his numbered Swiss account, and for that much money the killer didn't ask pointless questions.

Nick Fleming would not be easy to kill. There were two armed guards manning the decks of the yacht twenty-four hours a day when the owner was aboard. As if sensing that violent death was always near him, Nick Fleming traveled in bulletproof limousines or in his own private jet, and his five residences bristled with state-of-the-art burglar alarms. There were a lot of people in the world who would like to see Nick Fleming dead. But then, hadn't a good percentage of his billion-dollar empire come from violent death? A passionate Fleming critic had estimated—with perhaps more vitriol than veracity— that seventeen percent of the people who died in World War II had

13

been killed by bombs or bullets manufactured by the Ramschild Armaments Company, of which Nick Fleming was chairman and chief stockholder. That was a lot of deaths.

For years, the press had called him the Titan of Death. On the other hand, the killer knew there were many who would sincerely mourn his victim. The Fleming Foundation, with assets of almost a billion dollars, had funded medical and scientific research, as well as giving millions to ballet companies and symphonies; skeptics could call it whitewashing, but still the public had benefited enormously, and all this had come from the monumental fortune of Nick Fleming. Though only half-Jewish and by no means an unquestioning Zionist, Nick Fleming had given millions to build hospitals in Israel: the Jews would mourn him. The auction houses and art dealers would mourn him: Nick's collection of modern art was one of the best in the world, and his forty-two Old Master paintings, including the best privately held Vermeer in the world, were appraised at fifty million. Caterers and florists, however, wouldn't mourn him: Nick's chef had trained at Le Grand Vefour in Paris, and his private greenhouses provided flowers for his parties. But luxury merchants in New York, London, Paris, Hobe Sound and Beverly Hills would mourn him: Nick's princely life-style cost the incredible sum of ten thousand dollars a day.

Women, young and old, would also mourn him: Nick's love affairs had kept the typewriters of gossip columnists hot for decades. The killer was never hired to murder nonentities, but he reflected with some pride and excitement that Nick Fleming was undoubtedly his most celebrated "client." With a professional interest in obituaries, he speculated that Nick would get at least two pages in *The New York Times* and that his funeral would be attended by the Vice President of the United States and a not-too-junior member of the British royal family. Probably, mused the killer, this is the peak of my career.

But he had to kill Nick Fleming first.

His binoculars panned to the fantail, where one of the guards was sitting on a canvas chair reading a magazine, a rifle casually crossing his lap. If the killer's plan succeeded, it was the guard's last day on this planet, too.

The binoculars swept slowly back across the *Seaspray,* the killer's eyes registering and recording every detail of the magnificent yacht, an almost arrogant symbol of monumental wealth. The binoculars stopped at midship. A woman had stepped out of an entryway. She was tall, with blond hair and a superb, diet-controlled figure. She was wearing an elegant light-blue suit and a wide-brimmed hat. It was difficult to guess her age because her face, while beautiful, looked vaguely unnatural, as if it had been lifted; but she was probably in her fifties. The killer knew she was Mrs. Fleming, a woman known to leave her husband's side only on rare occasions. Today was one of those occasions.

The arrival of Nick Fleming's yacht off the coast of the small island of Djerba, near the Tunisian-Libyan border, had caused a good deal of excitement on the sleepy island, and the killer had kept his ears open. A generous tip to his hotel concierge on his arrival had gained him the information that Mrs. Fleming had a toothache and that within an hour she would be flown from the yacht to Tunis by helicopter, then by private jet to Rome where she had an appointment with her dentist, Dr. Gianfranco Spada, the favorite dentist of the superrich. Imagine going to Rome for dental work! marveled the killer. But it was a fortunate toothache for Mrs. Fleming.

Mrs. Fleming walked to the yacht's rail and leaned on it, drinking in the splendor of the morning. The killer kept his binoculars trained on her. Then he realized she was watching *him*. She straightened, turned and said something to one of the crewmen, who hurried inside. A moment later, he reappeared and handed a leather case to Mrs. Fleming. She pulled out a pair of binoculars and focused on the killer.

Keep calm, he told himself, lowering his binoculars. She doesn't know me. But it's time to get out of here.

He started walking up the beach toward his hotel.

But the killer was wrong. Mrs. Fleming did know him. At least she had seen his face long enough to realize that it seemed familiar to her. She was certain she had seen the man on the beach somewhere before.

Djerba is an island off the coast of Tunisia, basking placidly in the southern Mediterranean sun. A few hundred kilometers from Djerba, in the tiny desert town of El Djem, rose the second-biggest coliseum in the world, its tiers and arches preserved by the dry desert climate, for Tunisia had once been a part of the granary of the Roman Empire. In 1881, the French had "occupied" Tunisia, refinancing the debts of the corrupt Turkish Beys, and even years after Tunisian independence, French was still spoken everywhere. Olives, phosphates and seafood contributed to the Tunisian economy, but tourism was its mainstay. Developers were already speaking of Djerba as the next Costa del Sol.

The reason Nick Fleming's yacht was anchored off the Djerba beach was that Nick was considering investing in a resort hotel on the Tunisian island.

Crime pays: the killer had become a rich man through murder. He dressed well and always traveled first-class, not only because he liked to live well, but because he knew most people assumed incorrectly that a professional killer would neither wear Turnbull & Asser shirts nor check in at the Ritz in Paris or the Connaught in London. In a world mad for money, even the semblance of wealth conveyed the aura of respectability. Rich men might be murdered, but they would never commit murder themselves.

Thus, the killer had checked into the best hotel on the island. Born in Düsseldorf in 1925, the son of a German army captain, he now used a Swiss passport but spoke to the hotel staff in French. He used the name Louis Arneau, from Geneva, a dealer in textiles. Purpose of visit: vacation. His domed room with its private terrace overlooked the beach, on which that morning he had jogged two miles, sharing the sand with a Bedouin sheepherder and a young Tunisian fisherman. The food in the hotel was good, but that evening he stayed in his room and had no dinner, taking a Valium instead and lying down for a four-hour nap, setting his wristwatch alarm for eleven. When the alarm woke him, he stripped to his blue briefs and did forty minutes of exercises especially designed for him by an Austrian gymnast.

After showering, he took from his camel-skin suitcase a square rubber package. Unfolding it, he pulled out a black rubber frogman suit, which he put on. A pair of flippers and a face mask he would carry to the beach, along with his set of suction cups and a waterproof pouch containing a Browning .22 automatic and a silencer. For close-up jobs like tonight's, the killer eschewed exotic guns, which were easier to trace. A .22 was in any case the ultimate close-range murder weapon. A .22 fired into the head would not come out the other side; it would ricochet lethally inside the skull, reducing the brain to dog food.

The killer knew the hotel was almost deserted after ten at night: there was little to do on Djerba after dinner except go to bed and make love.

At one he turned out his lights, left his room, descended one flight

16

to the empty garden courtyard and walked out to the beach. It was early March, and the desert night was chilly. But there was no wind, and tiny Mediterranean waves lapped lazily on the sand. Clouds obscured the melon-slice moon; a few hotel night-lights and the distant running lights of the yacht were the only other illumination.

The killer put on his flippers, adjusted his face mask, then waded into the water. When he was hip-deep, he began the fifty-yard swim to the *Seaspray*.

The old man had toyed with his salad listlessly earlier that evening as he sat in his dining room. Nick Fleming had never killed time in his life, but time was killing him, and he knew it. But he didn't resent death. Seventy-five years on this planet was more than enough; he rather looked forward to death as satisfying the ultimate curiosity. If it turned out to be oblivion, as he more than half expected, it would be the quintessential pleasure. If the more orthodox religions were right and there was an accounting . . . well, his case would certainly be interesting.

What he did resent was the failure of his body while he was still alive. He still enjoyed sex, but a recent mild heart attack had caused his doctors to advise him to "go slow," which had taken much of the pleasure out of lovemaking. Sex wasn't much fun if you knew it could kill you—which was a pity, because Nick loved his third wife as much as he had loved his first. Nick had always loved as fiercely as he had lived.

At eleven, he climbed into the double bed of the yacht's master stateroom. He read for a while, then turned out the lights and tried to go to sleep. He missed his wife. His thoughts wandered back over the years, retracing their love affair, remembering his life, which had had so many more than the average man's moments of excitement and danger. The guns and bullets and tanks he had manufactured, which had made him rich and powerful, had placed him so often at the center of where the action of the twentieth century had been. Two world wars, the Korean War and now this monumental blunder, the Vietnam War . . . he had played an increasingly important role in all of them, had known many of the century's leaders, had been on the scene of many of the century's most historic moments.

The memories of his long life were becoming a blur now, mixing in his aging brain, ingredients in that rich bouillabaisse called Time.

But at the bottom of the soup bowl was one memory that remained stronger than all: that cold November morning at the turn of the century when his mother had taken him to the forbidding Victorian mansion in Pennsylvania, that dark house that held the secret to his existence.

That would never blur.

The killer swam the last ten yards underwater, then silently surfaced beneath the overhanging stern of the *Seaspray*. He cursed his luck: the clouds had moved away from the crescent moon, and now the pale moonlight made him more visible. But all was still, and the overhang kept him out of sight of anyone on deck.

He pulled the four suction cups from the pouch at his belt, strapped two to his knees and put the other two in his hands, then pressed them against the white hull of the yacht. Slowly, silently, he began crawling up the hull like a fly. He climbed on the diagonal, coming around the stern to the perpendicular port quarter. When his head was at the level of the main deck, he peered over the teak decking and looked around.

One of the rifle-bearing Greek guards was standing by the fantail pool, smoking a cigarette.

The killer grabbed one of the deck stanchions with his left hand to support his weight as he pulled his .22 from its waterproof pouch. He aimed it at the guard's left eye. The silencer made a slight noise. The guard crumpled to the deck.

Swinging himself onto the deck, the killer removed his flippers. Then, barefoot, he hurried forward. From watching the comings and goings of the crew and Mrs. Fleming, he had inferred that the master stateroom was forward on the main deck. Opening a door, he slipped inside a thwartship passageway that was illuminated by a dim nightlight. The passageway opened aft to the main salon, forward to the master stateroom. The killer slowly turned the knob of the door.

It was unlocked. He let himself into Nick's dark study. Crossing it, he came to the bedroom. Silently, he opened the door with his left hand, holding the .22 in his right. The stateroom was dark, but enough moonlight came through the ports for him to see the man in the bed. The old man who seemed still and frail.

To the killer, Nick Fleming was just a piece of meat.

He came to within four feet of the bed and slowly raised the gun.

He aimed it at the head of the sleeping old man.

18

Part I

ENIGMA
VARIATION
1900-1918

CHAPTER 1

THE twelve-year-old boy was beautiful, with thick black hair, big ice-blue eyes, a thin, sharp nose and razor mouth, and pale, unblemished skin that the autumnal wind was turning pink. He was poor, with patched corduroy pants, a black wool coat, torn mittens and a long red knitted scarf wrapped around his neck. He was also confused and frightened as his mother dragged him up the stone walk of the Fleming mansion.

"Momma, why are we coming here?" asked Nicholas Thompson, speaking Russian as he always did with his Russian-Jewish mother, Anna Nelidoff Thompson.

"You'll see," snapped the thirty-six-year-old woman who had emigrated from Kiev fifteen years before, in 1885. Years of marriage to Craig Thompson, a Welsh-born coal miner, and a lifetime of poverty had ravaged Anna Thompson's once radiant beauty. Her dark hair was prematurely gray, and her skin—once as flawless as her son's—was turning to crepe. Still, even in her shabby overcoat and straw hat, she was a woman men looked at twice. Right now, with determination and anger blazing in her eyes as she tugged her son up the stone steps of the mansion, a man might have looked twice and run.

"Momma, I'm scared!"

"There's nothing to be afraid of," his mother replied as she reached the double leaded-glass doors of the biggest house in Flemington, Pennsylvania. She tugged the bell. Clouds scudded across oyster skies as a north wind moaned around the turrets of the brick mansion, which had been designed in the full flower of Victorian ugliness. On this cold November morning in 1900, the high brick walls, the huge stained-glass window to the left of the porte cochère, the mansard roofs tiaraed with ornamental wrought iron, represented to the boy all the vaguely ominous power and wealth of Flemington's eponymous family, the Flemings.

The front door opened and an angry black butler glowered at Nick's mother.

"You tryin' to pull that bell off?" he snorted. "Don't you know they's a sick man upstair? What do you want?"

"To see sick man," declared Anna, her English mangled by her Russian accent.

The butler looked at the poorly dressed couple with scorn.

"Trash like you not gonna bother Cap'n Fleming, no sir! Now you scat!"

He started to close the door, but to his surprise, Anna pushed past him into the big entrance hall.

"Hey—what you doin'? You can't go up there! Wait a minute!"

But Anna was already halfway up the ornately carved wooden stairs, tugging her son after her. The astonished butler closed the door, then started after them.

"I'll call the police!" he said. "I will! I swear!"

Anna reached the landing, over which hung a life-sized gold-framed portrait of Captain Vincent Carlysle Fleming, the master of the house and chairman of the board of the Fleming Coal Company. The painting, done ten years before, when its subject was fifty and in his prime, portrayed a tall, powerfully handsome man with brown hair and a full beard, wearing a stylish gray frock coat and shiny boots. His left fist rested imperiously on his hip. Nick Thompson stared at the portrait as his mother dragged him by.

"Who's that?" he puffed.

"Your father" was the grim reply.

Nick wondered if his mother had gone crazy.

When they reached the top of the steps, Anna unhesitatingly turned to the left and strode down a dark paneled hall to a heavy door at the end. Nick, his child's mind almost feverish with the excitement of the drama, looked back to see the butler huffing after them.

He's going to kill us! he thought in English. The black man's going to kill us! Oh, my God, what *is* this? My father? My father was Craig Thompson. . . .

Now they were in the big bedroom and suddenly everything was still. Nick looked around, his blue eyes wide. It was a high-ceilinged room, its walls covered with homely paintings of grazing cows and prints of historical scenes. Dark-green velvet curtains had been drawn over the windows; oil lamps cast a sickly glow over the Oriental rugs and burgundy silk walls. Against the far wall was an elaborate brass bed. In it, half propped up against big down pillows, was a man in a nightshirt whom Nick recognized as the man in the portrait.

However, this portrait in the flesh had Dorian Gray-ed. His brown beard was white, his face sunken and cadaverous, the power so evident in the painting now withered by age and disease. The room stank of medicine.

The old man stared listlessly at the intruders.

"They say you dying," said Anna, her voice strident. "They say your heart no good. I'm *glad* you die, you son bitch! My husband die in your rotten stinking coal mine—I hope you got great pain! But before you die, you see your son!"

She released Nick's hand and gave him a shove.

"Go to the bed," she said in Russian. "Let him see you."

Nick hesitated. He had become aware of three other people in the death chamber: a stout nurse, standing by the head of the bed, who looked shocked by the intrusion; an elderly man in a black frock coat who looked like a doctor; and a tall, elegant woman at the foot of the bed who was staring intently at the boy.

"I tried to keep them out, Mrs. Fleming!" came the butler's voice from the door.

"That's all right, Charles," said the woman, her gray eyes still on Nick. She had fair hair, rolled in a chignon; she wore a black crepe de chine blouse and a black skirt; on her blouse was an oval cameo surrounded by small diamonds. Her face was pretty, with a tendency to plumpness. Nick was impressed by her bearing, by the soft voice that nevertheless gave the impression of command and authority.

"What is your name?" she asked.

"Nicholas Thompson."

She looked at Anna.

"And this is your mother?"

"And that's his father," said Anna, pointing at the man in the bed. "I used to work here in kitchen! That son bitch seduce me! Now he's dying, and he owe something to my son!"

Silence. Nick and the old man in the bed were eyeing each other. Now the dying man feebly motioned to the nurse, who leaned down, putting her ear to his mouth. Nick heard a rasping whisper. Then the nurse straightened.

"Captain Fleming," she announced, "says it's a pack of lies."

"Is *truth!*" yelled Anna.

She pushed her son aside and went to the bed.

"May you rot in hell!" she said to Captain Vincent Fleming.

Then she spat in his face.

As the nurse gasped, Anna turned, grabbed her son's hand and yanked him toward the door. Then she stopped, giving the people in the room a look of supreme contempt.

"I didn't expect nothing from you bloodsuckers," she said, "but you not hear end of Anna Thompson! I hire lawyer! That old son bitch give my Nick *something!*"

Then she pulled Nick out the door.

Nick's last memory was the gray eyes of Mrs. Fleming still watching him.

Flemington was thirty miles south of Pittsburgh, in the Appalachian Mountains. In 1804, Vincent Fleming's great-grandfather had bought a two-hundred-acre farm in the hills and two years later discovered that his land lay over rich seams of coal. For almost a century, the Fleming Coal Company had been exhausting those seams and enriching the Flemings. At first, the miners were all local men, descendants of the Scotch-Irish settlers who had come to the mountains in the eighteenth century. But after the Civil War, the European emigration brought even cheaper labor to the hills. Welshmen like Craig Thompson, who had mined coal in Wales under brutal conditions, were hired at wages that were low by American standards but better than what they had earned in Wales. Most of the miners lived outside Flemington in crude, tin-roofed shacks that were owned by the company. Flemington, with a population of five thousand, was a sleepy town living off, and dominated by, the coal company. A Victorian courthouse stood in the town square, its statue of Justice white with pigeon droppings. In front of the courthouse, Civil War veterans played checkers and gossiped. Sherman Street was the town's only paved thoroughfare, and it was lined with pleasant white houses, most of which were girdled with covered porches. Flemington snoozed into the twentieth century with little interest in what went on in the rest of the world. The town voted for McKinley in the recent election, but mostly out of Republican habit. Few citizens could remember the name of the Vice President, Theodore Roosevelt.

When Craig Thompson was killed in a mining explosion in 1896, his widow and eight-year-old son were evicted from the company shack. In a way, Anna didn't mind. She had hated the two-room dwelling that froze in the winter and baked in the summer. But at least it had been a home. Now she had nowhere to go, and her only capital was five hundred dollars insurance money.

24

She was resourceful. Two blocks from the courthouse she found a café whose owner had tuberculosis and was moving to Arizona. Anna took over his lease, painted the run-down place inside and out, thoroughly cleaned the filthy kitchen, hired a fat waitress named Clara, and reopened, calling it simply "Anna's Café." Included in the lease were two rooms above the café, into which Anna moved with her son. They were still in two rooms, but now they had indoor plumbing and a Stone Age bathroom, which was a big step up from the privy behind the company shack. Nick was introduced to a new luxury: toilet paper.

There was one other restaurant in town, the Courthouse Café, directly in front of the Victorian courthouse, and Anna ate several meals there to gauge the competition. As was to be expected in a small Pennsylvania town at the turn of the century, the food was simple and uninspired, but the restaurant had a brisk lunch trade with the local businessmen. Anna decided to lure this lunch business to her establishment. An excellent cook, she contrived a menu that included several Russian dishes from her childhood.

The business didn't come. Anna had underestimated the provincialism of the Flemington businessmen. They *liked* uninspired cooking and were used to the Courthouse Café. Furthermore, they distrusted foreigners, especially Jews: Anna had the distinction of being the only Jew in Flemington. The businessmen stayed away, and two months after opening the café Anna was almost wiped out financially.

Then there were the men in her life. Anna's reputation among the miners had been anything but saintly: she had been pregnant when she married Craig Thompson, and there had been persistent rumors that Craig had not been the father. Shortly after she opened the café, men started arriving upstairs at night. Nick was always put to bed in the small bedroom he shared with his mother, but the walls were thin: he heard the whispered conversations, followed by the soft moans. Most teen-age boys in small-town America at the time were ignorant of the facts of life. Nick, already precocious in his schoolwork, now became precocious about sex. He adored his mother and told himself nothing she did could be bad. When some of his schoolmates began making snickering remarks about Anna, even though it was obvious they didn't understand exactly what they were snickering about, Nick took them on. Nick was skinny, but wiry and tough. He could lick anyone in his class in a fair fight, but this wasn't fair: three boys ganged up on him. When he came home to the café that night with cuts, bruises and a loose tooth, his alarmed mother said, "What happened?"

But Nick wasn't about to tell the truth.

"I fell downstairs."

Anna knew he was lying and suspected the truth. But she didn't stop seeing the men.

She needed the money.

They came the evening of the day she had taken her son to the Fleming mansion.

There were four customers in the café when the sheriff walked in with two deputies.

"Mrs. Thompson?"

She had been forced to let Clara the waitress go and was serving one of the tables. Now she looked with suspicion at the heavyset sheriff.

"Yes?"

"You're under arrest."

"For what?"

"Prostitution."

She yelled and fought. They had to put handcuffs on her before they dragged her to the door. Nick, who had been washing dishes in the kitchen, heard the commotion and hurried into the front of the café.

"Momma!"

"Nick, get me a lawyer!" she cried as the sheriff pushed her out the door. Nick ran across the café and out the door into the night where he saw the deputies locking the rear of the Black Maria. He ran to the sheriff.

"What are you doing to her?" he said.

The sheriff looked at him.

"Sorry, sonny, but your momma's a whore."

The cold insensitivity of the remark could have psychologically destroyed many twelve-year-old boys, and it came close to destroying Nick. As he watched the wagon rattle down the street, his stomach became nauseous. Bending over, he vomited in the dirt. Then, crouching beside his puke, he covered his head with his arms and began sobbing. The worst was that he knew what the sheriff had said was true.

Then rage replaced hurt and shame. He knew it was no coincidence that his mother had been arrested the same day she had taken him to the Fleming mansion. That dying old man—his father!—must have telephoned the sheriff and told him to "get" Anna. How could his father be so cruel? Or was it that he had genuinely feared Anna's threat of legal action? His father . . . Captain Fleming . . . *I* am his flesh and blood! Damn him!

His face still streaming with tears, he began running down the street toward Sherman Street, at the end of which, on the biggest lot in town, stood the Fleming mansion. I'll kill him! Kill the old bastard. . . . No, no, *I'm* the bastard. . . . Still, I'll kill him! KILL HIM!

In later years, he would admit to the few intimates to whom he told the story that he probably wouldn't have killed old man Fleming, that the thought was the result of the shock of seeing his mother man-handled and arrested mixed with rage and boyish bravura. Yet in his heart he thought that was a lie: he remembered the rage and knew that he very well might have killed his own father. As it was, when he arrived panting at the doors of the big house and began banging on them, the butler told him his father had died two hours earlier.

Nick stared at the black man.

"Then let me see his body!" he said.

"You get outta here! You caused 'nuff trouble this morning, you and that trashy woman—probably caused the Captain's heart to stop. Git! Go on!" He slammed the door.

As Nick wandered slowly back to the café, his rage draining, he began to realize he had nowhere to go.

He was twelve years old and alone. Self-pity and shame flooded him. As much as he adored his mother, the knowledge that she was a prostitute—and that everyone knew it—made him cringe. His shame for his mother, coupled with the shocking revelation that he was a bastard, left a deep and lasting scar on his mind. As an adult, his many detractors would accuse him of monumental hypocrisy, of bedding beautiful women while maintaining strict, almost Victorian standards of conduct for his family. The key lay in that horrible November day of his youth.

To Nick, family became all-important because he had barely had one.

CHAPTER 2

ANNA'S threat of legal action against Captain Fleming was a fantasy. There was no money for lawyers. The judge, who was a friend of Captain Fleming's, threw the book at her: two years in the county jail. It was the maximum sentence for prostitution, and since Anna had no prior record, there was no doubt in Nick's mind that the judge had been carrying out Captain Fleming's orders to get Anna Thompson out of town.

His fury at the injustice done his mother was matched only by his anger at being able to do nothing about it. The ruthlessness and greed he would be accused of in later years were born in that feeling of terrible helplessness he experienced in the courthouse. The law was for the rich and powerful, not for the poor and weak. Justice was as stained with pigeon shit as the statue on top of the courthouse.

On November 16, 1900, Nick was sent by the court to the County Orphanage for Boys, an institution that housed not only orphans but "wards of the state," as the judge had termed Nick. The orphanage was a three-story brick building that had been put up in 1856. It sat in the middle of a fifty-acre farm that the boys worked during the summer, growing vegetables for themselves and the state prison system. Nick was delivered by one of the sheriff's deputies, who led him through the front door into a high-ceilinged hall at the end of which were wooden stairs.

"Wait here," said the deputy, pointing to a bench. Nick sat down, clutching his bundle of clothes, as the deputy went through a door into an office. Nick looked around. The plaster walls were cracked and in need of painting. Above the one ancient radiator, dirt was smudged on the wall and someone had made an X mark with his finger. There was a large wood-framed photograph of President McKinley and, in a corner, an American flag that moths had lunched on.

"You can go in now," said the deputy.

Nick stood up and went into the office. It was a large room, with tall windows looking out on the brown lawn. Tall, glass-fronted bookcases filled with heavy volumes marched around the room; they

28

seemed to groan with the weight and boredom of the *Official History of Van Buren County, Dictionary of Childhood Diseases,* and the *Criminal Code of the State of Pennsylvania.* Behind an uncluttered desk sat a man Nick judged to be in his forties. Thin and neatly dressed, with sandy hair, he had a pleasant face. He smiled as he looked at Nick.

"Welcome to the orphanage," he said, cheerfully unaware of any irony in the remark. "I am Dr. Hilton Truesdale, the director of this institution. Please take a seat."

Nick sat in a wooden chair in front of the desk. Dr. Truesdale opened a file and studied it a moment. Then he looked at Nick again. He spoke precisely in a soft voice.

"Your mother has been convicted of prostitution," he said. "Do you know what that means?"

Nick shifted uncomfortably. "Yes."

"Yes, *sir.*"

"Yes, sir."

"Were you aware of your mother's profession?"

"I knew . . . that men came to see her."

"Did you know they paid her to use her body for immoral and disgusting practices?"

Nick stiffened.

"Please answer me, Thompson."

"I guess I knew."

"You 'guess'? Did you or didn't you know?"

"Yes, I knew."

"Yes, *sir,* I knew."

"Yes, sir, I knew. But it wasn't immoral! My mother's a good woman!"

A wintry smile appeared on Dr. Truesdale's thin lips. "I'm sure *you* think so, Thompson. Unfortunately, society thinks otherwise. You must understand that I am in charge of eighty-four boys here. Eighty-four *innocent* boys, I might add. It is my duty to protect these unfortunate orphans, both physically and morally. Which is why I am forced to ask you some rather unpleasant questions. Did you at any time witness what your mother was doing with her . . . shall we say 'customers'?"

Nick turned red. "No."

"No, *sir.* But you know what she did? You understand why she was being paid?"

"Yes, sir."

"Then you understand the facts of life? What decent people consider the baser, animal side of human nature?"

"Yes, sir."

"Did your mother ever caress you?"

Nick stared at him. "She kissed me."

"Yes, but did she ever do anything more than just kiss you?"

"I . . . don't know what you mean."

"It's very simple, Thompson. Your mother is a prostitute. These women of depraved character often indulge in perversions to satisfy their lusts. I have known several cases where prostitutes have made love to young boys—even committing incest with their own sons."

Nick was so stunned he could barely speak. "Mother," he whispered, "would never do *that.*"

Dr. Truesdale stood up. "Nevertheless, the possibility exists that your mother had contracted a social disease. And, living as you did with her in some intimacy, the possibility exists that she may have infected you. For the safety of the other boys here, I will have to examine you." He had gone to the window behind his desk. Now he pulled down the black window shade. "Please take off your clothes, Thompson."

"My clothes?"

"Yes. All of them. Strip naked."

He turned on his desk lamp, then went to the other windows and pulled down the blinds over them. Nick sensed something strange was happening, yet he didn't know what else to do but obey. He stood up and started undressing.

"My shoes too?" he asked, beginning to feel clammy.

"Please."

When Nick was naked, Dr. Truesdale stood in front of him, running his eyes over his body.

"Mm. I see you are well into puberty. Your penis seems quite large for your age. Do you masturbate?"

Sweat was trickling down Nick's ribs.

"Do I what?"

"Do you play with yourself? Do you 'whack off,' as it is vulgarly called?"

"No . . ."

"No, *sir.* And you are not a convincing liar. There is not a boy in this institution who doesn't indulge in this unhappy vice. Now, don't be nervous. I have to examine your organs for syphilitic lesions. This won't hurt."

As Nick tensed, **Dr.** Truesdale knelt down and began fondling his penis and testicles. Nick held his breath as the doctor gently squeezed them. Then the doctor released him and stood up.

"Well, you *seem* to be clean. But of course the infection can lie dormant for years. I'll have to give you periodic examinations, for your own safety as well as the other children's, of course." He smiled and put his hands on Nick's shoulders. "Don't be frightened. I want you to think of me as your *friend.*" He looked into Nick's terrified eyes and added softly, "You're a very handsome young man, Thompson." He walked back to his desk. "You may get dressed now."

As Nick pulled on his clothes, he realized in a panic that if he stayed in the orphanage very long, something horrible was going to happen to him. He didn't know exactly what it was, but he knew Dr. Truesdale was no "friend."

"This is not a prison," the doctor said as he sat down again at his desk. "On the other hand, it is hardly a private school for the rich. The boys here work hard and play hard. If their attitude is one of cooperation and cheerful, Christian fellowship, they are rewarded. If their attitude is not cooperative, they are punished. Those boys who cooperate with me *personally* are given certain . . . privileges." He smiled at Nick. "I hope *you* will cooperate with me, Thompson!"

As Nick buttoned his shirt, his blood ran cold. This new nightmare, piled on top of the seismic shocks of the past few days, was devastating. Aside from the vague menace of Dr. Truesdale, the accusation that he had ever had sexual relations with his mother was a blast out of hell. "Incest" was a word that would always disgust Nick Fleming.

"Lunch is at twelve-thirty and supper at six," said Head Proctor Sykes as he led Nick up the wooden stairs to the second floor. "Study hall is from seven to nine, lights out at nine-thirty. We wake you at six-fifteen, breakfast is at seven, classes and work programs start at eight. Saturday afternoons are free, as is Sunday except for chapel." Let me out of here! thought Nick. Let me *out!* . . . "Any questions?"

"No, sir."

"It's not as bad as it sounds. You'll get used to the routine."

They had reached the top of the stairs where a long corridor bisected the second floor.

"There are four dormitories on this floor: A, B, C, and D, with twenty boys to each. You've been assigned D dorm. The state installed indoor plumbing three years ago. We're quite pleased with our

31

showers, though the hot water's a bit unreliable. Dr. Truesdale has installed the most modern equipment. All boys are required to change their clothes every other day."

The heavyset head proctor rambled on until he reached the end of the corridor, where he opened a door marked "D." He led Nick into a large, cheerless chamber containing twenty iron cots. At the foot of each was a wooden chest. From the ceiling, bare light bulbs hung on long wires. There were no pictures on the wall, no rugs on the floor—nothing. The orphanage might not have been a prison, but it was giving a good imitation of one.

"This is your cot, number four. You will make it each morning before breakfast—Haines will show you how, he's your dorm captain. I'd advise you to get along with Haines, by the way. This is your locker at the foot of the bed. You'll keep all your personal belongings there."

He pulled out a gold watch and checked the time. "Lunch is in twenty minutes. The dining room is downstairs, in the rear. Meet me down there and I'll assign you a napkin ring and your table. Are you hungry?"

"Yes, sir," said Nick truthfully.

"You'll find the food here nourishing," said Mr. Sykes, rather sadly. "Dr. Truesdale has studied nutrition." He lowered his voice. "Unfortunately, it's not very good."

His chubby face wrinkled dolefully, then Mr. Sykes waddled out of the dormitory, closing the door behind him. Alone, Nick sat on the edge of his cot.

I *have* to get out of here, he thought. But where can I go? For a moment, he started to give way to tears of despair. Then he thought, No, dammit! Tears never got anybody anything. I've got to *think* my way out of here.

It was then he saw the "Fire Door" sign at the end of the dormitory. Getting up, he carried his belongings to the door and looked out. A fire escape led down to the lawn. All he had to do was open the door, climb down and walk away to freedom.

To hell with laundries and "nourishing" food and that weird Dr. Truesdale, he thought, opening the door.

As he scrambled down the fire escape, he suddenly knew where to go.

Edith Phillips Fleming was the daughter of the president of the Ohio Central Railroad, a small Midwest carrier that had for years bought

32

its coal from the Fleming Coal Company. Edith's father, Tom Phillips, and Captain Vincent Fleming had been friends, if not cronies, for years; and when, in 1892, the recently widowed Captain Fleming had asked Edith to be his wife, the twenty-three-year-old girl had accepted without much hesitation. Vincent Fleming was old enough to be her father, and had three children by his first marriage. But Vincent was handsome and rich and possessed one of those powerful personalities that seemed to sweep all opposition before the juggernaut thrust of its will. Edith was more than half in love with him, her father heartily approved of the match, and the wedding took place in Youngstown, Ohio, with great pomp and ceremony. Vincent took his young bride to London and Paris for her honeymoon, and when, after three months abroad, they returned to Flemington, Edith was happier than she thought possible.

Then the trouble began.

Vincent's eldest son, twenty-eight-year-old Barry Fleming, who had seemed affable enough at the wedding, began to show signs of hostility toward his new stepmother. Barry, who was married and had two sons, was second-in-command at the company, and Edith assumed the good-looking young scion of the Fleming fortune was becoming nervous about his future. It was obvious his father was infatuated with his new wife, and the Captain was still in his prime, certainly able to father a new son by Edith. Edith, who had no desire to jeopardize her stepson's career, went out of her way to be nice to Barry; but it seemed she could do nothing right. At family dinners, he was barely polite to her. And after two years, the situation was becoming so tense and unpleasant that Edith began to think her marriage was a mistake.

It was then that Captain Fleming suffered the first of a series of strokes that made him a permanent invalid. With the old man bedridden and obviously incapable any longer of siring children, Barry's hostility melted away and Edith found, to her delight, that her former enemy was becoming her friend. As the years dragged by and the ugly mansion became more and more a hospital, Edith began looking forward to Barry's visits—at first with his wife and then, more frequently, alone. Edith told herself it was his companionship she enjoyed, because her existence had become a lonely one, surrounded by nurses and doctors. But as time passed in the small, sleepy town, she began to admit there was more to it than companionship. Barry's presence excited her physically. Even worse, it was becoming increasingly obvious that her presence excited Barry.

Eight months before Vincent's death, Barry had tried to make love to his stepmother. To Edith's dismay, she almost gave in.

Now, three days after Vincent's funeral, his son was in his widow's front parlor.

"I'll divorce Barbara," he was saying. Edith, seated on a horsehair sofa before the heavily carved marble mantel, looked beautiful in her mourning dress.

"Barry, don't say these things!" she exclaimed. "It's impossible, and you know it. The scandal would . . ." She gestured helplessly. "The town would never forgive either one of us."

"To hell with the town!" he exploded, sitting next to her and taking her hand. "We own it anyway—what can they do to us? Darling, you don't know what hell it's been, being near you all these years, wanting you but not being able to touch you . . . and now . . ."

He pulled her into his arms and started kissing her, hotly. For a few moments she put up no resistance. There was an intense physical attraction between them, and Edith had not made love for six years. Once again, she *almost* went to bed with him. Once again, the consequences stopped her. She pushed him away.

"No," she whispered. "This is absolutely *wrong—totally* wrong."

"I don't understand you! We're in love with each other!"

"What's love have to do with it?" she said, getting up from the sofa. "Would people believe it was 'love'? You know what they'd say—that Vincent Fleming's son had been his wife's lover all those years he was an invalid. And what about your children? What would they think of me—and you, for that matter? No, it's all wrong, and we have to put an end to this now, before it's too late."

"It's the money, isn't it?" he asked softly.

She looked surprised.

"What money?"

"You inherited half of Father's estate—two million dollars. You're thinking I'm after the money, that if I marry you, it'll come back in the family."

"That's absurd."

"I'm willing to make a prenuptial agreement. You can keep all the money in your name."

"Barry, *stop* it!" she almost screamed. "I don't want to hear any more about this! I suppose it's my fault. . . . I probably encouraged you, or at least I didn't put a stop to this a long time ago when I should have. But I'm stopping it now."

34

He got up from the sofa and came to her in front of the fireplace.

"It won't do any good avoiding the truth," he said. "We love each other. Whatever you decide, I'm seeing my lawyer in the morning and starting divorce proceedings."

"Barry, you mustn't! It's unfair to Barbara!"

"Don't be so damned noble. And there's nothing you can do to stop me."

He left her, crossing the big room to the sliding double doors.

Edith groaned. "The idiot!" she said aloud.

Edith Fleming was a basically decent person, but right now she was feeling, for the first time in her life, dirty.

Forty minutes later, she was seated by herself in the cavernous walnut-paneled dining room with its palm-filled bay window. She had just begun to sip her consommé when Charles, the butler, came in.

"Miz Fleming," he said, "I'm sorry, but they's a boy at the front door who say he won't leave till he sees you."

"What boy?"

"You 'member the day Cap'n died an' that trashy Thompson woman done charged in here with her son? Well, it's *that* boy. Now I yelled at him an' threaten to call the police, but he just set down on the walk an' say he won't move till you see him. You want me to call the sheriff?"

Edith wiped her mouth, remembering the frightened boy. "No, Charles. Bring him in."

The butler looked surprised. "In *here?* I doubts that boy seen bath water for a month!"

"In *here,* Charles."

"Yes, ma'am. Whatever you say."

Shaking his head, Charles left the room. A few minutes later, Nick came into the dining room, holding his cap in his hand. He looked at the elegant woman seated at the end of the long, highly polished table. He knew this was one of the most important moments of his life.

"You wanted to see me?" said Edith.

"Yes, ma'am. Is it true Captain Fleming was my father?"

Edith put down her soup spoon.

"I don't know," she said. "Please sit down."

She gestured to the chair at her left. Nick came to the table and sat down.

"You look hungry," she said. "Would you like some lunch?"

He didn't answer, but she knew. She rang the silver bell. Charles appeared. His eyes bulged when he saw Nick seated at the table.

"Bring Mr. Thompson some lunch," Edith said. "Some of the lamb from last night."

"Yes, ma'am." Charles left, again shaking his head.

"I say I don't know," Edith continued, "but I certainly won't deny that my late husband had a reputation with women. It's certainly *possible* he was your father." She studied Nick's face a moment. "Yes . . . your eyes . . . Yes, there's certainly a resemblance to Vincent around your eyes."

She said she didn't know, but in fact she was almost certain the boy was correct.

"Do you know what they've done to my mother?" Nick continued.

Edith frowned slightly. "Yes, I know."

"Is it true Captain Fleming ordered her arrest?"

So he had guessed the truth! Edith felt guilt creep over her.

"I won't deny it," she said. "I tried to talk him out of it, but he was insistent, and how can one say no to a dying man? But I feel terrible about what's happened. Really terrible. Can you ever forgive us?"

"I don't blame *you,* Mrs. Fleming," he said truthfully. He sensed the woman's guilt.

"And what about you?" she asked. "Where . . ." She gestured rather awkwardly, embarrassed to ask point-blank where he was living.

"They put me in the County Orphanage, but I ran away. I'm smart, Mrs. Fleming. I can make something of myself if I have a chance—I *know* I can. But I need to get out of this town. I need an education." He hesitated, gulping with nervousness. Then he took a deep breath. "If I'm *really* Captain Fleming's son, then his family owes me something. I'm not talking about trying to get you or his children to give me some money. But would you *loan* me enough for me to get an education? I'd pay you back later on—honest I would. With interest. I'd work hard and make you all proud of me. I *know* I can be something! But I need help."

She looked at the boy. Maybe this is the answer, she thought. Maybe this is the way to stop Barry. . . . But do I *want* to stop him? Yes, I must. It's impossible. If I were *really* smart, I'd get out of this town myself. There's nothing here for me but trouble. And God knows, we owe this poor boy something. Maybe he's the answer for both of us.

36

"Would you like to come to New York with me?" she asked quietly.

Nick stared. "New York? Why?"

"To find you a good school. The best schools are in the East, you know. And New York's an exciting city. You'll love it."

"You mean . . . you're going to New York?"

"Yes, I'm moving. I'll put this house up for sale. It's a dreary place anyway, filled with unpleasant memories for me. New York is just what I need."

He looked incredulous. "When did you decide this?" he asked.

"Just now." She laughed. "The best decisions are made on the spur of the moment—I've always believed that. So, what do you say? Yes or no?"

He needed no prompting to grab the chance of a lifetime. "Yes!" he blurted out. "YES!"

"Well, I think this *is* exciting, don't you? A whole new life for both of us!"

Nick smiled.

"I *knew* something good would happen if I came here!" he said. "I *knew* you'd be fair!"

"Good for *both* of us."

Goodbye, Barry, she thought. I've got something new in life.

A son.

He couldn't believe how she had aged. In a little over a year, his mother had become an old woman. Now as she lay on the bed in the prison hospital, Anna knew she was dying—the cold she had caught in the poorly heated jail had quickly developed into pneumonia—but as she looked up at her son, who had grown an inch since she had last seen him, she told herself not to show any fear.

"So Mrs. Fleming's being nice to you?" she whispered.

"She's been wonderful to me!" he exclaimed. "And Momma, she's bought this beautiful house in New York . . . they call it a town house . . . and I have my own room on the third floor and a bathroom all to myself!"

"A bathroom," echoed Anna, trying to keep her frail strength from ebbing. "That's nice. And she's put you in a private school?"

"Yes, St. Nicholas."

"Sounds Catholic." She began coughing.

"No, it's mostly Episcopalians and Presbyterians."

"Are they rich kids?"

"Most of them, I guess."

"Are they stuck-up?"

"Not to *me!*" Nick grinned proudly. "They're afraid of me, because I beat them up."

She closed her eyes. "Mustn't be a bully," she whispered. "But it's good to have people afraid of you. Life is . . ." She started to say "hard," but her lips only half formed the word.

Suddenly she was still.

"Momma? Momma, don't go to sleep till they make me leave. . . . Momma?"

He reached over and touched her hand. Suddenly he knew.

"Nurse!" he yelled. He slowly got up from the stool, staring at his mother's lifeless body. Anna looked at peace at last.

By the time the ward nurse hurried up to the bed, the bully of St. Nicholas was crying silently. Anna might have been a convicted prostitute whom Edith Fleming preferred not to mention, but Nick loved her with all his fiery Russian soul—a soul that Edith Fleming and the schoolmasters of St. Nicholas were doing their best to Anglicize.

The football sailed through the crisp autumn air and was caught by the Princeton end, who managed to run fifteen yards before he was tackled by the burly Yale guard. The crowd of over a thousand well-dressed Yale and Princeton undergraduates, parents, relatives and girl friends cheered with well-bred exuberance, the Princeton side cheering the successful pass, the Yale side cheering for the tackle. The score in the second half of the Yale-Princeton game of 1908 was still 0–0, but Princeton, now on Yale's twelve-yard line, seemed poised to make the first touchdown. Edith Fleming, looking stylishly regal in her cartwheel hat and mink-trimmed coat, watched from the Princeton side with interest. Edith had become a football fan when Nick made the varsity team his sophomore year. Nick had yet to play in this game, but now, as the Princeton end was helped to his feet by his teammates and a bowler-hatted doctor hurried onto the field, Edith realized the player had injured his ankle. With a charge of excitement, she watched Nick run out on the field to substitute as left end. Edith began clapping.

Then, suddenly, she stopped.

She realized she was the only person on the Princeton side who was applauding Nick.

And—even more appalling—there were a few scattered boos.

. . .

"But I don't understand it!" she said that night as she sat opposite Nick at a table in a small restaurant near Nassau Hall. "Why would they boo you?"

Nick at twenty had grown into a tall and strikingly handsome young man with straight jet-black hair. Now he shrugged his shoulders as he forked his mashed potatoes. "Don't pay any attention to them, Mother," he said. Over the years he had drifted into calling Edith "Mother" out of affection, if nothing else.

"But how can I *not* pay attention? It's so . . . so *unfair* to you! And after all, you *did* make a touchdown."

"And I got some cheers for that."

"But you're evading the point. Obviously, *something* has happened. . . . What is it?"

He put down his fork. He had wanted to avoid this subject, not only because it was miserably embarrassing to him but because he had not wanted to upset Edith. Now she was forcing him to tell her.

"Do you remember Arnold Fleming?" he asked.

"Of course. Barry's oldest son. He's a freshman here in Princeton now."

"Yes, and he told everyone on campus about me. Or, more to the point, about my mother . . . and what she was. There are a lot of snobs here who didn't like me in the first place because I don't have the 'right' New York accent or the 'right' social connections. Well, I didn't particularly care about that, but now . . ." Again he shrugged, trying to cover his acute embarrassment with a show of nonchalance. "Well, now there are a lot of guys on campus who think Princeton shouldn't be 'represented' on the football field by the son of a convicted prostitute."

Silence as she stared at him.

"I can't *believe*," she finally said in a soft voice, "anyone could be that narrow-minded."

"Well, they can. But don't worry about it. I used to get into fights about my mother when I was a kid, but I don't now. I just ignore it."

She had come to know him well enough to understand he had to hide his sensitive nature beneath a façade of cool toughness, and she could almost smell his hurt. Edith was by nature a champion of the underdog, and this coupled with her guilt over the Fleming family's continued persecution of Nick led her to make a decision she had been considering for some time. She knew that Barry Fleming's passion for her had turned to sulking dislike when she rebuffed him by leaving Flemington for New York with Nick. If hounding Nick was

Barry's nasty way of getting back at her, then a stop to it had to be made.

"Whatever your mother did," she said, "she was only trying to survive and take care of *you*. I don't approve of what she did exactly, but I can understand why she was forced to do it. And certainly Barry Fleming—or any of the Flemings, for that matter—has no right to try to ruin *your* life over something that happened so long ago." She paused. "I've never regretted for a moment my bringing you to New York, Nick. You've become very dear to me. I suppose you're the son I've never had. I want to do everything I can to help you. I want to give you a sense of security, of *belonging*. If these silly snobbish adolescents think you're not good enough for them . . . well, we'll show them they're wrong."

Nick looked confused.

"What do you mean?"

"I'll give you all the money you need to 'keep up' with them. You'll have the best clothes—the best of everything! *And,* since you're better-looking than the law allows, there's no reason why you can't have the pick of the crop of the New York heiresses. We'll show them, dear Nick. I won't have any pimply-faced snobs looking down their noses at *my* son." She smiled as she reached across the table to squeeze his hand. "And that's what you're going to be: my son. I want to adopt you officially, Nick. I've been thinking about it for some time, and now is the time to do it. We'll shut the Flemings up. They won't be able to say anything about you if *you're* a Fleming. But even aside from them, I want to adopt you. You've become my son, dearest Nick. Now I want to give you my name."

The former orphan stared at the woman he had come to adore. Numbly, he realized she was handing him the world on a silver platter.

"Well?" she said, smiling. "Will you let me be your mother?"

"Of course," he gulped. "You are anyway. I mean, I've always thought of you that way . . . but . . . thank you. It seems I'm always saying thanks to you, but I really mean it."

"There's only one condition," she said. "You must always make me proud of you."

There were tears of gratitude and joy in his eyes as he said, "I'd rather kill myself than ever do anything you wouldn't be proud of."

Edith Fleming felt as happy as she'd ever been in her life.

CHAPTER 3

ON a windy, snowy March day in 1912, a Pierce Arrow limousine pulled up in front of a handsome Belle Epoque stone town house on East 64th Street in Manhattan, and a chauffeur in a yellow uniform with glossy boots hurried around the car to open the door. Holding her feathered hat so it wouldn't blow off in the gusty wind, Edith Fleming got out of the limousine and walked up the steps of her town house to ring the bell. A moment later, her English butler, Gladwyn, opened the elaborately grilled door, and Edith hurried into her marble foyer, accompanied by a swirl of snowflakes.

"Is my son in?" she asked as Gladwyn took her sable coat.

"Yes, madame. He's upstairs in his room."

"Tell him I want to see him immediately in the library."

"Very good, madame."

Gladwyn was aware that Mrs. Fleming was in a frosty mood.

Edith had bought the four-story town house in 1901, shortly after moving to New York, paying ninety-five thousand dollars for what was considered one of the most handsome houses on the Upper East Side. Now she walked into the library, closing the doors behind her. She was wearing a well-cut gray suit with a hobble skirt and a white silk blouse. She went to her desk and took a Turkish cigarette from a malachite box. Edith still didn't smoke in public, but when she was angry she smoked in private. And Edith Fleming was angry.

Nick came in. "You wanted to see me, Mother?" he asked. He was wearing a tailor-made dark-blue suit. Twenty-four-year-old Nick was not only one of the best-looking young men in New York, he was also one of the best dressed.

"I've just been with Max Fleetwood, my lawyer," she said. "Do you know a young woman named Myra Stilson?"

Trouble, thought Nick. "Yes. I met her at a party a few months ago."

"Then I think you'd better start going to better parties. This Miss Stilson—who I believe has a tenuous connection with the motion-picture industry—has told my lawyer she is carrying your child. She said you promised to marry her."

"That's a lie!"

"Perhaps. But she says unless I pay her five thousand dollars, she'll sue for breach of promise. Is she telling the truth?"

"I made love to her, but so have a lot of other men. I don't think she could prove I was the father."

She stubbed out her cigarette in the malachite ashtray.

"Do you think I invested a considerable amount of money in educating you so you could make love to cheap actresses? I *seem* to recall a young man telling me he'd work hard and make me proud of him if I'd give him a chance. Well, you've had the chance, Nick. Oh, have you had the chance! I've given you the best of everything, and what have you done? You've become an indifferent stockbroker on Wall Street who runs up debts *I* pay, who hangs around with some of the most disreputable young men in New York, who has absolutely no morals with women, and who now has impregnated some poor girl who probably was foolish enough to fall for your fast talk! Am I supposed to be proud of that, Nick?"

"No," he said.

She sighed as she sat down.

"Well, I'm being too hard on you, I suppose," she said. "I've spoiled you, and I know it. I gave you too much money and encouraged you to spend it and become 'charming' so your friends wouldn't look down their noses at you, and of course it all went to your head. You've become *too* charming! Oh, I'm furious at you, but I'm furious at myself too."

He came over and put his arm around her, kissing her cheek.

"Don't be," he said. "You were only trying to help me, which was wonderful of you. And I know I've been a disappointment to you. I've been a disappointment to myself, as far as that goes, but I've got some good news. . . ."

"Now *don't* change the subject!" she interrupted. "Let's get back to this Stilson girl. I'll pay her the five thousand dollars—I don't want your name and mine dragged into the newspapers because of some tawdry legal action. But it's the *last* time I'm going to bail you out. From now on, you're on your own financially. Before, I gave you too much money and spoiled you. Now you're going to have to pay your own way, and maybe it'll give you some character. You can continue to live in this house, of course, but you'll have to pay for your own clothes and whatever else. And *no more actresses!*"

He got up, put his hands in his pockets and went to one of the two windows overlooking 64th Street. He knew he owed everything to Edith. "You're right," he said. "From now on I'll pay my own way. How much do you figure you've spent on me these last twelve years?"

"That's not the point."

"It's *part* of the point." He turned and looked at her. "I asked you for a loan and told you I'd pay you back with interest. Well, you were generous with me—extravagant, really—and I've taken and taken. . . . I guess I was trying to forget what I was by having fun. And I've had a *lot* of fun. Maybe too much."

"I don't begrudge that, Nick. I *want* you to enjoy life! But I want to be proud of you, and I think I have that right."

"Of course you have. At any rate, I'll pay you back everything within three years."

"Oh, Nick, don't be such a child!" she exclaimed in exasperation. "I don't *want* the money in the first place, and in the second place you shouldn't make such wild statements! I don't want you doing something foolish on Wall Street, trying some crazy gamble to make a killing."

"I'm quitting the Street."

"What?"

"Did you ever hear of the Ramschild Arms Company?"

"Of course. It's in Connecticut somewhere."

"Well, Alfred Ramschild is a client of my firm, and I've made some stock suggestions that turned out well for him—I'm not a *complete* washout—and he's taken a liking to me and offered me a job. A *good* job, as a salesman for him. Five thousand a year plus commissions. That's a lot more than I'm making on Wall Street."

"But you don't know anything about guns."

"I can learn. And it'll get me out of New York." He smiled. "You're right when you say I've got no character. Well, New York's the last place to get character."

"But you'll have to think this over . . . this is a big step."

He laughed as he came across the room to her. "I seem to recall a very lovely lady telling me once a long time ago that the best decisions are made on the spur of the moment." He gave her a hug and gently kissed her cheek. "Wouldn't you be surprised if I turned out well after all?" he said.

She looked at him and bit her lip. "Damn you," she said, pulling a lace handkerchief from the pocket of her blouse.

"Why? What's wrong?"

She smiled as she wiped her eyes. "I'm going to miss you like the very devil, and I *shouldn't*. I should be thrilled to get rid of you."

"Oh, you haven't seen the last of me. I'll be back, like the proverbial bad penny." He kissed her again. "I'll miss you too. You're the best thing that ever happened to me."

Edith Fleming knew he meant it. Exasperated as she was with her charming son, his openhearted love more than made up for all her disappointments.

"You know," she said, her characteristic good humor beginning to return, "this may be a good idea."

"Of course it is! But if I'm going to be a salesman, I'll need a car."

"Oh, Nick," she sighed, "and for one *crazy* moment, I actually thought you'd reformed!"

"It doesn't have to be a fancy car. A Model T will do."

She looked at him, shook her head and laughed. "My God, I'm such a fool for you! Will I ever learn? Yes, I'll buy you the car. And you can pay me back when you become a munitions tycoon."

"Now, wouldn't you be surprised if I did?"

Nick had no way of knowing it, but he couldn't have picked a better time to get into the armaments business. In just over two years after he went to work for Alfred Ramschild, Archduke Franz Ferdinand and his morganatic wife, Sophie, were assassinated at Sarajevo, and Europe was plunged into the first of the two great wars that were to change the world. Not that Alfred Ramschild had ever failed to turn a handsome profit in the years of the long Victorian peace. There had always been colonial wars, and in 1901 he had made millions selling the Ramschild A-16 rifle to the army of the Sultan of Turkey. There was always a steady market for hunting rifles too. The company that had been founded during the Civil War by Alfred's father was a steady profit machine, but the World War was making Alfred Ramschild a multimillionaire.

He was a strange man to be an arms king. He hated blood sports and forbade hunting on his eighty-acre wooded estate outside Fairmount, Connecticut, even though the estate teemed with game. He thought wars were abominations, and he quieted his conscience by saying, perhaps too frequently, that the only reason he manufactured guns was that if he didn't, someone else would, and why shouldn't he make a legitimate profit? His two passions in life were painting and chamber music: he was a bad amateur painter but a good amateur pianist. His thirty-room pseudo-Tudor mansion had not only two Steinway grands, but a harpsichord, a pipe organ and a collection of fine stringed instruments including an Amati and a Stradivarius. Alfred's idea of the perfect evening was to host a lavish dinner, then lead his guests to the big, low-ceilinged music room where he and a violinist and cellist would play Beethoven trios for two hours. The guests might nod and doze, but Alfred was happy, lost in the music that obliterated all images of bloody battlefields, of wounds and amputations and gangrene and death caused by the bullets and shells his factory turned out by the millions.

Nick worked hard at Ramschild. He was a natural salesman with his glib tongue and boundless charm, and he was driven by a fierce determination to succeed after his dismal performance on Wall Street. He liked his new life. After the confining office of the Wall Street brokerage firm, traveling around the country in his Model T selling shotguns and hunting rifles proved a lark. In one month—April 1916—he had earned two thousand dollars in commissions, an achievement that warmed the heart of Alfred Ramschild. In fact, Alfred liked Nick a lot, and Nick took pains to ingratiate himself with his boss. Aware of Alfred's passion for chamber music, Nick even contemplated taking violin lessons in the hope of getting an invitation to Graystone, the Ramschild estate, to join in a trio or quartet. He decided this might be a bit obvious—aside from the fact that he had a tin ear—but what baffled and frustrated him was that, despite Alfred's friendliness toward him, the longed-for invitation was not forthcoming. Other employees were invited, often. But Nick wasn't.

Then, finally, in June 1916, Alfred called Nick to his office and said, "My wife and I are giving a dinner tomorrow night at our place, Nick, and we'd like you to be there. Can you come?"

Nick looked at the big, full-bearded man whom someone had once called a "fat Smith Brother" and repressed a desire to whoop with joy. "Yes, sir, I'd be glad to," he replied.

"Good. Be there at seven. Oh, and Nick"—he hesitated, and Nick thought Ramschild seemed flustered—"my wife can be a bit, well . . . *formal*. Don't be put off if she strikes you as a trifle cool at first. I'm sure she'll warm up to you as she gets to know you."

It was a curious remark. Nick had heard on the grapevine that Mrs. Ramschild was a snob. But he had acquired enough polish and self-confidence to figure he could handle her. And yet, Alfred Ramschild wasn't a man to waste words.

"By the way," Alfred continued, "my daughter will be there—she just graduated from Vassar. I'm eager to have her meet our star salesman."

Nick rented two rooms in a boardinghouse in Fairmount because no better accommodations were available in the tiny town, and the next night he put on his dinner jacket, slicked his hair, looked in the mirror and smiled with the confidence of the young and the beautiful. I'll charm the shit out of old lady Ramschild, he thought. And since Poppa seems interested in my meeting the daughter, well . . . who knows?

The drive to Graystone led him past the ugly brick Ramschild factory, squatting on the west bank of the Connecticut River, three miles upstream from where it debouched into Long Island Sound. Nick knew the factory dumped tons of waste into the river and that its tall chimney fouled the air, and though there was nothing he could do about it, he disliked it. But past the factory, the road led into the beautiful Connecticut countryside where handsome Colonial farmhouses with their red barns and flocks of Holstein turned the clock back to another, preindustrial era. And twenty miles from Fairmount, a heavy stone-and-wrought-iron gate with an attached stone gatehouse gave grudging welcome to the visitor to what a writer in the pacifist liberal magazine *The Masses* had called "the house that death built"—a comment that had caused Alfred Ramschild to attempt unsuccessfully to get the man dismissed.

Nick navigated the curving driveway through a half mile of woods that, on this June evening, were bursting with life, swarming with mosquitoes and midges and deer and squirrels, and noisy with peepers. Then the drive made a final turn, the woods gave way to lawns and flower beds, and Graystone loomed in all its fake Tudor massiveness. Alfred had built the house in 1897, instructing his architect to design something "Henry VIII would have liked." The result was a house that bristled with elaborate brick Elizabethan chimneys, had a timber-and-plaster main façade and brick wings and huge leaded windows. Whether Henry VIII would have liked it was questionable, but Alfred Ramschild loved it.

So did Nick Fleming.

After parking his Model T among the other grander cars, he walked to the carved wood front door where a butler admitted him. Passing a suit of armor, Nick went into the high-ceilinged main room with its huge stone fireplace. Alfred came to greet him, all smiles; but

46

when he was introduced to Arabella Ramschild, Nick thought "formal" and "cold" had been feeble adjectives to describe an iceberg of a woman. Tall, stately, well dressed and handsome, Mrs. Ramschild shook Nick's hand and managed a resentful "Good evening" with all the enthusiasm she might have exhibited to a leper.

What the hell have I done to *her?* Nick thought, as Alfred hurriedly moved him away from his wife and around the room to meet the dozen other guests.

"And this is my daughter, Diana," Alfred finally said.

She was a softer version of her mother and a beauty. Nick was six feet two, and Diana was only four inches shorter—she was tall, like her mother. She had honey-blond hair done in the currently fashionable Grecian style, striking green eyes and a perfect nose. She wore a white dress with a pink silk sash.

I'm not only looking at a lot of money, Nick told himself—but also at a lot of woman!

"So I've finally met the famous Nick Fleming," Diana said to him after dinner as they walked on one of the terraces.

"I didn't know I was famous."

"Oh, my father talks a lot about you. He says you're bright and ambitious and are going to be somebody someday."

"I think I'm somebody right now."

"Oh? Modesty, thy name is Fleming."

"Your mother thinks I'm somebody pretty rotten. During dinner, I saw her looking at me, and if looks could kill, I'd be at the undertaker's right now."

Diana paused by a big stone jardinière filled with pink geraniums. "I apologize for Mother," she said quietly. "She's really very nice, except for one thing—and she's totally unreasonable about that."

"Which is?"

She hesitated. "Mother's a terrible anti-Semite. When my father told her you were half-Jewish—which he shouldn't have done—well, she said she didn't want to invite you here. Father's been fighting with her for months, and finally she gave in. But I knew she'd act horribly to you, and I feel terrible about it. Will you accept my apology for her?"

"I'll accept *your* apology," he said after a moment, "but someday I'll make *her* apologize to me."

"I hope you can. But I wouldn't count on it."

"Want to bet? Ten dollars says I can make her like me—or at least *talk* to me—before the evening's out. I'm about the most charming half-Jew who was ever born."

She laughed. "You are modest! All right, you've got a bet. And it's one I hope I lose."

"Let's go back in, so I can start working on her."

She took his arm and returned to the house with him. Diana Ramschild found she liked the "famous" Nick Fleming. And his slim, broad-shouldered, dark good looks excited her more than she liked to admit to herself.

The guests were taking their seats in the music room where Alfred was at the Steinway and his string players were tuning up. Nick walked to the sofa where Mrs. Ramschild sat enthroned. As she eyed him coldly, he sat down next to her. He smiled as she glared.

"I wanted to compliment you on that dessert, Mrs. Ramschild," he said. "That was the best *crème renversée* I've ever eaten, with the possible exception of one I had at Mrs. Vanderbilt's."

Her icy eyes widened slightly.

"Which Mrs. Vanderbilt?" she asked crisply.

"Reggie's mother" was his casual reply. "I play poker with Reggie at Canfield's. That is, we *used* to, before I moved up here. But that was a *terrific* dinner."

"Thank you."

"Mr. Ramschild told me they're playing some Mozart tonight. I like Mozart a lot. My roommate at college, Bayard Phipps, used to play a lot of Mozart. Of course, he wasn't very good, but still . . ."

Again, the stare.

"You roomed with Bayard Phipps?" she asked.

"Yes, at Princeton." He looked around the room. "I like your house a lot. It's so comfortable and human-sized—not big and showy, like The Breakers."

"You've visited The Breakers?"

"Yes, with Reggie. But I didn't like it. It's too big. All those places in Newport are too big. But *this* house is perfect. And your taste in furniture is wonderful."

Again, he smiled. To his amusement, Mrs. Ramschild smiled back slightly.

"How did you *do* it?" whispered Diana as she gave him the ten dollars on the terrace. "I watched you and Mother . . . I think she actually likes you!"

"I dropped a lot of names of society people I've never met," he said, grinning. "And I flattered her. Laid it on with a trowel. It always works."

"You're *awful!*" she giggled.

"By the end of the summer, I'll have her speaking Yiddish."

"I think you just might."

"Will you have dinner with me tomorrow night?"

"I see you're a fast worker."

"That doesn't answer my question."

She looked at him in the moonlight. He's a slick one, she thought. But he *is* funny. And charming. And handsome as the devil.

"All right. But don't be *too* fast with me, Mr. Fleming. I don't like men who are *too* fast."

"Oh, I'm very slow," he announced innocently. "Safe, slow Fleming. And my friends call me Nick."

She smiled. "All right . . . Nick."

Something told her this cocky young man was a force to be reckoned with.

Nick's love life in freewheeling Manhattan had been active to the point of near legal prosecution; but his move to Connecticut had severely curtailed it, forcing him to "get character" whether he wanted it or not. Traveling-salesman jokes notwithstanding, small-town America was anything but a hotbed of vice, and Nick could count his amorous conquests on one hand—a hotel maid here, a waitress there. His sex drive being as fierce as his ambition, he was in a constant state of ruttiness; and while he didn't think Diana Ramschild was the sort who could be seduced, in the back of his mind was the ever-hopeful "maybe."

He picked her up at Graystone, and as they drove out the drive he said, "Did you tell your mother you were going out with me?"

"Yes."

"Was she upset?"

"Well . . . a little."

"Uh huh." He pulled a ten-dollar bill from his jacket pocket and handed it to her.

"Here's your ten dollars back," he said. "I lost the bet last night after all. I thought about your mother a lot. She's too smart to be taken in by a lot of my fast talk. Oh, she melted a little last night, but she still doesn't like me."

"You have to give her a chance."

"Of course I'll give her a chance, and I'll do everything I can to be nice to her. But it's not going to work. I can feel it in my bones."

Diana decided the less said about her mother the better.

He drove her back to the Connecticut River where, overlooking the Sound, there was a good seafood restaurant. They were taken to a table on the covered porch and ordered steamed lobster and a bottle of Muscadet. The June sun was still an hour from setting, and the Sound, with its sailboats, was a Boudin seascape.

"Tell me all about yourself," he said, staring intently into her amazing green eyes. "Do you have any beaux?"

"Oh, lots. But no one special yet."

"Then there's hope."

"Ah, ah, not too fast."

"I've got all summer."

"All summer": suddenly, they seemed the two most beautiful words in the language. She started to tell him she was going to Martha's Vineyard with her mother for July and August, but changed her mind—for a reason she didn't quite understand.

"I envy men," she said, breaking the silence that had become a bit embarrassing.

"Why?"

"Oh, there are so many things you can do. Like business. I think it would be fascinating doing what you do—or what Father does. I'd love to run a company like Ramschild."

He was barely paying attention to what she said, he was so enthralled by her. He was fantasizing making love to her. He was *always* fantasizing making love to women, but this time he was feeling something different inside. "Really? I guess selling guns is more interesting than selling insurance, but the fun is selling. I know you think I'm too fast, but do you like me at all?"

She looked surprised. "Yes, I think I do. Why?"

"Because I want to do everything I can to make you like me a lot."

"Why?"

"I know you'll think this is schmaltzy, but I think I'm falling in love with you."

She was amazed at how excited the words made her feel.

"But you *couldn't* be in love! We've only just met."

"But that's how it happens!"

"In novels and plays."

"No, in life! People meet and they fall in love. Don't you think love's the most important thing in life?"

50

She was taken aback by his intensity. The intensity in his eyes. She had never met anyone even remotely like him before.

"I . . . I think it might be if one felt a truly great love . . . if a person were lucky enough to feel that. But I don't think many people ever feel *that* kind of love. I think most people just"—she hesitated, feeling suddenly awkward—"just get married."

"If I believed that, I think I'd just as soon die."

"Now you really *are* sounding foolish."

"It sounds foolish to say you're only young once, but it happens to be true. I'm young and I want to experience everything I can—most particularly love. And it's happened to me." He broke into the most wonderful smile she had ever seen. "I'm the happiest man in the world!"

Suddenly, she was happy too.

"Mother, I don't think I want to go to Martha's Vineyard this year."

Arabella Ramschild put down her orange juice, looking at her daughter. They were sitting in the sun-drenched breakfast room of Graystone.

"Then where do you want to go?"

"Nowhere. I mean, I want to stay here to work on my French."

"Work on your French at the Vineyard."

"No, I get too lazy there."

Arabella looked down the table at her husband. Alfred shrugged. Then Arabella looked back at Diana.

"It's that Fleming boy, isn't it?" she said. "Diana, I hope you're not getting serious about him."

"I *told* you I want to work on my French."

"No one in the history of the human race has given up Martha's Vineyard to work on French. Don't insult my intelligence."

"All right, what if it *is* Nick?"

She was so suddenly defiant, her mother told herself to go carefully: Arabella knew her daughter was a fighter.

"Might I ask you just what is going on?"

"Nothing is 'going on'—but, Mother, he really is the most extraordinary person! You yourself admitted he's charming."

"In a glib, superficial way. I didn't believe half what he told me, and I trust you won't either."

"But he feels things so intensely! I don't think I've ever met anyone who's so full of life!"

"Well, I daresay he's full of something—'applesauce' is more likely the word. I won't tell you what you can or can't do. If you want to stay here this summer, that's your business. But remember: Nick Fleming is a Jew, and if ever I've seen a young man on the make, it's he. Don't be so blind as to think he's not got his eye on our money."

Diana threw down her napkin and stood up from the table.

"Mother, sometimes you make me want to throw up!"

She turned and stormed out of the breakfast room.

"Arabella," Alfred said, "that wasn't fair. Nick's one of the finest young men I've ever known."

"Would you want him as your son-in-law?" she fired back.

"Yes," Alfred said coolly.

Arabella shook her head in disbelief.

Nick was in love with all the fiery passion of his half-Russian soul, which had almost been put on ice by years of restraint drummed into his head by the Anglophilic masters and professors of the series of posh schools Edith Fleming had sent him to. They had given him education and the manners to maximize his natural charm. But now he was in love, the first love of his life, and everything else seemed trivial. Diana Ramschild consumed him, and when he wasn't with her, life seemed banal. He even lost interest in making money, and for a young man as ambitious as Nick, that was a serious sign. They began going out together every night. At first, Diana went as much to defy her mother as anything else. But by the end of the first week, she realized, with a sense of almost giddy rapture, that she didn't give a damn about her mother: she was as much in love with Nick as he was with her.

In his campaign to conquer her, Nick was careful not to go too fast sexually: he guessed Diana was physically innocent. But on their third date, when he kissed her for the first time, he was surprised at the passion in her response. It was obvious that behind her cool Greek-goddess façade, Diana Ramschild burned as hotly as Nick.

They spent their first Saturday afternoon together walking barefoot on a deserted stretch of beach on the Sound.

"Mother's going to the Vineyard tomorrow," she said, "but I'm not going with her."

"If you'd gone, I'd have followed you," he said.

"Yes, I think you would."

"I suppose your mother's mad at me?"

"She thinks you're after my money." Be careful, she thought. "Are you?"

52

"Before I met you, I thought it might be nice to catch the boss's daughter. Any man would, and he'd be lying if he didn't admit it. But now that I know you, I wouldn't give a damn if you didn't have a nickel."

She stopped, threw her arms around him and kissed him. "I was *hoping* you'd say that!" she exclaimed. "Oh, Nick, you were right: love *is* the most important thing in the world! You've taught me that, and I love you for it."

It was the first time she had used the word "love" and it sounded sweet.

"I love you," he whispered. "We're going to have one of those great loves you said happen only to the lucky few."

He kissed her with all the passion in his soul, and she finally understood the word "ecstasy."

"We *are* lucky," she whispered between kisses. "The lucky few. . . . Oh, Nick, I want you more than life itself."

His instincts told him the time was right. Taking her hand, he said, "Come on!" and started running down the beach.

"Where are we going?" she panted.

"You'll see. A surprise."

It was no surprise to Nick. He knew the place and had had it in mind as a contingency in case the opportunity arose. It was a big, shingled house overlooking the Sound that had been up for sale for six months. When they reached the covered front porch, Diana ran her hand through her golden hair.

"Whose place is this?" she asked.

"Old Mr. Gerson, who died last winter. They're trying to sell it, without much luck. I looked at it a couple of weeks ago."

He had gone down the porch to one of the big living-room windows.

He reached behind a shutter and produced a key, which he held up.

"The real-estate agent's too clever."

She watched as he opened the front door. Then, putting the key in his pocket, he held out both hands to her.

"Come," he whispered.

She knew what was happening. She took his right hand and they went inside. There was no furniture in the house, only big, empty rooms and the faint musty smell of a house waiting to be loved. He led her into the living room, whose dirty windows looked out on the Sound. He took her in his arms and began kissing her tenderly.

"I love you, Diana," he kept repeating.

She was wearing a cardigan sweater, which he slipped off.

"I love you, Nick," she whispered back as he began unbuttoning her white blouse. It was her first time, and she marveled that she didn't try to make at least a pretense at modesty. She wanted him with a hunger that was almost terrifying, which made a mockery of the virtuous behavior that had been drummed into her head all her life. Diana, raised Episcopalian, now felt pure pagan.

When they were both naked, he made a makeshift blanket on the floor with his clothes, then knelt on it, looking at her. Her body was full as a ripe peach, her breasts firm, with large, soft nipples. Again, he held out his hands to her.

"We are the lucky ones," he repeated. "The special lovers. Our love will last for eternity."

"For eternity," she whispered, taking his hands and kneeling in front of him. She trembled slightly as she felt his flesh against hers, warm and solid. He was rubbing her back, kneading her flesh sensuously, as he kissed her mouth, her cheeks, her neck, her shoulders, her breasts. She moaned as he sucked her nipples. Her heart pounded as his strong hands moved down her sides, around her waist . . .

"Nick, Nick," she murmured. "My love . . . my eternal love. . . ."

He laid her down on the floor. His clothes were already a rumpled mess and her back was on the chilly, dusty wood floor, but she didn't care: the floor could have been a meadow of sweet clover. The room was dark, but she could feel the sweat on his smooth body as he began making love. She felt his hard penis inside her, thrusting until she almost screamed as it broke her hymen.

"Oh, God, oh, God . . ." she gasped, and then he began pressing slowly in and out. The thought flashed through her mind that he must have loved many women, but again she didn't care: all that mattered was the sweet ecstasy of his love that was inflaming her body, assaulting her mind with sensations she never dreamed existed. She didn't even care if he made her pregnant: she knew he would do the right thing. Their love was forever, for eternity.

She was groaning and panting like an animal. His nails dug into her flesh. "I'm coming," he gasped, which she didn't understand until she felt a flood of warmth inside her. She let out a shriek of pleasure as she experienced the first orgasm of her life.

Afterward, they lay in each other's arms watching the lowering sun shine through the dirty windows.

"It was so beautiful," she whispered, kissing his cheek. "God bless you for making it so beautiful."

He ran his fingers tenderly over her face.

Then he sat up.

"We have to have a secret sign," he said, smiling.

"What do you mean?"

"Well, your mother dislikes me so much, we have to have some sort of signal we can show each other when the old battle-ax is around."

"Nick!"

"All right: something when she's around to remind us that we love each other and not to listen to her. Like this."

He held up his right hand and crossed his fingers.

"Now you do the same."

She raised her right hand and crossed her fingers.

"Like that?"

"That's it. When we cross our fingers, no one else will ever know what it means except us. And it means our love. Forever."

She thought the idea, like the man, was delicious.

CHAPTER 4

DIANA was amazed at the intensity of her happiness, marveling at how empty her life had been without Nick. She was so happy she couldn't resist teasing her anti-Semitic mother, telling her she was actually thinking of converting to Judaism. It was unwise, because Arabella had little sense of humor about the subject, and she was genuinely appalled at seeing her daughter so passionately in love with a man she was coming to hate.

When they were together, Nick and Diana could barely keep their hands off each other, their relationship having become so intensely physical. On their tenth date, they went to see the Theda Bara production of *Carmen* (which had come out at the same time as Geraldine Farrar's *Carmen*) and necked shamelessly throughout the movie. When they left the theater, they walked to Nick's car hand in hand.

"How's my stock with your mother these days?" Nick asked.

Diana hesitated. "Oh, I think she's coming to like you," she lied.

Nick laughed. "Which means if she had the chance she'd strangle me fast rather than slow. No, I think we have to bite the bullet and make her truly apoplectic."

"How?"

"By getting married."

They had reached his Model T. Now she turned to him.

"I won't even *pretend* to think it over. Yes, yes, YES!"

And once again, they were kissing. He pulled a black box from his blazer jacket and squeezed it into her hand.

"This about cleaned out my bank account," he said.

She opened the box. Inside was a small sapphire-and-diamond ring. "Oh, *Nick!*"

"Let me put it on." He slipped the ring on her finger. "With this ring," he whispered, "I pledge my love forever, Diana."

"And I pledge mine to you."

They kissed.

The next morning, which was blisteringly hot, Nick was just screwing up his courage to go to Alfred Ramschild's office and announce his engagement when to his surprise he was summoned instead.

Alfred's office overlooked the Connecticut River. The paneled walls were hung with photographs of Ramschild's various products, and there was a display case holding rifles and side arms made by the company since 1862. Framed in elaborate gold, the founder, Alfred's father, stared into eternity with muttonchopped elegance from above the mantel as two electric fans droned, stirring the humidity.

"Have you been keeping up with what's going on in Russia?" Alfred asked after he eased his damp bulk into his swivel chair.

"I read the papers," replied Nick. "I get the impression the whole country is being run by that lunatic monk, Rasputin."

"That's partially true—and, by the way, he's not a monk. From the information I get, the Tsar is under the thumb of the Tsarina, who in turn is completely under the influence of Rasputin. Whether she's his mistress or not, I don't know. There are rumors the little boy, the Tsarevitch, has some strange disease that only Rasputin can cure. At any rate, the government's a mess, the Army has taken a beating from the Austrians and now the Germans—the Russian losses are in the millions, I'm told—and there's a lot of speculation that there may be some kind of *coup d'état* in the near future.

"Now, four months ago an agent of the Tsar placed an order with us for a hundred thousand of our R-15 rifles and ten million rounds of ammunition. A month later, he ordered one thousand machine guns, with two million rounds. The total order came to eighteen million dollars, half of which the Tsar paid up front, transferring gold out of his private account in the Bank of England to our correspondent bank in London, Saxmundham Brothers. We have filled the order, and it's now in San Francisco ready to be shipped to Vladivostok. But now the Tsar's agent tells us we'll have to accept the remaining nine million dollars in Russian government bonds, because the Tsar has used up all his gold reserves—by the way, *nobody* will accept Russian currency, because everyone knows they're printing rubles as fast as they can to finance the war and their inflation is going wild."

Alfred leaned forward on his desk.

"Now, Nick, I don't want nine million dollars' worth of goddamn Russian bonds when everyone's saying the Russian government won't last another six months. Those bonds wouldn't be worth toilet paper, and nobody else will touch them, so I couldn't discount them without taking at least a fifty percent loss. On the other hand, I have a contract with the Russians, and I don't want to screw them—they need the guns desperately. So I'm faced with a nine-million-dollar dilemma. And you're the answer to it."

Nick looked surprised.

"Me? Why?"

"I need someone to go to Petrograd and talk with the Minister of War. I need someone to get me nine million dollars' worth of *something*—gold coins, art works, maybe even jewelry—at which point I'll ship the order. There's plenty of money over there—the Tsar's supposed to be one of the richest men in the world, if not *the* richest—and if they want our guns, they can come up with the scratch. I want you to go for me, Nick. I trust your judgment, and you can speak Russian, which should be a big help. I won't hide the fact the trip may be dangerous. Just *getting* to Russia will be no joyride, and God knows what may happen once you're there. I can't tell you how to get the nine million in coins or jewelry or whatever out of Russia once you get it; you'll have to depend on your wits. But if you'll do it, Nick, and if you're successful, I'll pay you a five percent commission on the eighteen-million-dollar order, which will make you a rich man. And I'll promote you to vice president in charge of sales." He leaned back. "Take some time to think it over, but I'll need an answer by this afternoon."

Nick's head was swimming. Five percent—nine hundred thousand dollars! A vice presidency . . .

"Of course I'll go, Mr. Ramschild. I'd love to go! But first, I want to marry Diana."

Alfred didn't look surprised.

"So it's gone that far?"

"Yes, sir. We're crazy about each other."

"Yes, I've noticed. Well, Nick, I couldn't be more delighted. And going to Russia will make you financially independent, and, I might add, it will make my wife feel better about the whole thing too. In fact, to be perfectly frank, another reason I thought of you for the job was that I was half expecting you and Diana to team up. But there won't be time for you to get married before you go. Arabella will want a formal wedding, and that takes a lot of planning. We can have the wedding in September—you should be back by then."

September seemed a long way off, but Nick realized Alfred was right. And it was important to keep Arabella reasonably content.

"All right, sir. I'd rather get married now, but I'll wait."

"Good. I was assuming I could talk you into going, so I've already made the travel arrangements."

58

He opened one of his desk drawers and pulled out a manila envelope. "Here's first-class passage on an Argentine liner, the *Santa Teresa,* which sails from San Francisco for Vladivostok a week from tomorrow. From Vladivostok you'll take the Trans-Siberian Railway to Petrograd. There are three thousand dollars expense money and a letter of credit for ten thousand more if you need to bribe somebody, which you may." He tossed the envelope across the desk. "Now, you'd better go home and pack. You'll have to be in New York in the morning to catch the train for San Francisco. And Nick . . ."

"Yes, sir?"

"Don't get killed. We'd miss you."

"I'd miss myself. Can I threaten them? I mean, can I tell them we're ready to resell the order if they don't pay up?"

"Of course. I could sell the order tomorrow to the British or the French for twenty million more. And tell them I will. But use your charm too. You'll be dealing with Grand Duke Cyril, who's one of the Tsar's cousins, and I wouldn't think it's smart to bully a grand duke *too* much. There's a letter of introduction to our new ambassador over there, David Francis, who used to be the governor of Missouri. I hear he's a rich hick and the Grand Dukes despise him. If *you* were a hick, I wouldn't send you. One other thing: it occurred to me it might be useful to use code names in any cables you send, just to keep the Rooskis confused, so I dreamed up names for the Tsar, the Tsarina, Grand Duke Cyril, Rasputin and a few of the leading politicians. They're all on this card, which you should memorize. I was listening to Elgar's 'Enigma' variations the other night and decided you should be Enigma."

"Enigma," said Nick thoughtfully. "I like that."

He stood up as Alfred came around the desk to shake his hand.

"Good luck," he said. "You'll need it."

After the death of Captain Fleming, his widow assumed she would remarry someday, and when she moved to New York she began "receiving a few gentlemen callers," as she put it. Edith was still young and attractive; by almost fanatical dieting, she had kept her figure under control. She led a fairly active social life; still, love didn't come to her for almost ten years. But when it did, Edith told herself Van Nuys de Courcy Clairmont was worth the wait.

He was forty-seven, tall, skinny, intense, nervous and so nearsighted he had to wear glasses a quarter-inch thick. He had curly carrot-red hair and owned the Clairmont chain of twenty-nine newspapers in cities ranging from Portsmouth, New Hampshire, to Miami. Three weeks after receiving this particular gentleman caller, an impassioned Edith became Van's mistress. The widow Fleming and the powerful, liberal publisher were crazy about each other, but there was a problem. Van was a practicing Catholic who had a wife in perfect health. Edith realized there was little chance of her living openly with the man she loved, not for years, but with her usual pragmatism, she accepted the situation. She found that in a city the size of New York it was not too difficult to carry on a discreet love affair. She even began to think that the very secrecy spiced the relationship, making their love affair more intense than it might have been if they were married.

Edith had told Nick about Van. She knew that even though her love affair compromised her maternal moral authority there was no way she could keep Van a secret in the long run; besides, she wanted the two men in her life to like each other.

Unfortunately, they didn't.

Van, who wrote some of his papers' most fiery editorials, was extremely high-minded—an insufferable, hypocritical prig, said his enemies—and he took a dim view of Nick's character, scolding Edith for spoiling her adopted son, a charge she was in no position to deny.

Nick, realizing even *his* charm was getting him nowhere with his mother's lover, wisely avoided him. His move to Connecticut had improved things somewhat. Van grumpily admitted to Edith that *maybe* Nick was reforming. But Edith knew the man she loved was still no fan of the son she loved.

Van's wife, Winifred, lived with their daughter in a large Park Avenue apartment. She hadn't spoken to her husband for years, but never failed to send all her bills to the Clairmont Building, two blocks from City Hall, an ugly seven-story edifice that served as the headquarters for the entire newspaper chain as well as housing Van's New York paper, the *Graphic*. Van paid the bills, managing with moral legerdemain to overlook his own fault (for he had walked out on Winifred) and thus sparing himself the boredom of guilt. Van lived in an enormous apartment on Riverside Drive with spectacular views of the Hudson. He also had a sprawling house at Sands Point, overlooking Long Island Sound, where, on that hot July day in 1916, he had just finished his fifth lap in the pool when Edith hurried across the lawn.

"Nick's going to Russia!" she exclaimed.

Van pulled himself out of the pool. He had been pitcher for the Harvard baseball team, Class of 1886, and prided himself that he hadn't put on an ounce since. He kept his body firm by daily exercise—either squash, tennis or swimming. He was also a fanatical anti-smoker and never drank anything but an occasional glass of wine at dinner. His employees thought of him as less than human, but Edith knew he was very human indeed in bed, and that his superb health made him a superb lover. Now he groped blindly for the eyeglasses he had left on the diving board. "Why's he going to Russia?"

"He just called. Something about an arms deal. . . . Do you think he'll be safe there?"

"He'll be safe enough, I guess, but hungry. My correspondent in Petrograd, Bud Turner, tells me that even the upper classes are having trouble getting food now." He found his glasses and put them on, then picked up a towel and started drying his hair.

"Then you don't think I should worry about him?" Edith persisted.

"I'll cable Bud and tell him to keep an eye on him."

Edith smiled as she came to kiss him.

"You're a good man, Van Clairmont," she whispered. "No wonder I'm mad about you." Then her face became troubled again. "You know, Nick is good too."

"Is he?" Van Nuys de Courcy Clairmont's tone left little doubt about his real opinion of Nick Fleming.

"But we want to get married *now!*" Diana exclaimed angrily to her parents. They were in the living room of Graystone.

"Diana, Nick is leaving in the morning," Alfred said patiently. "It's totally impractical."

"This is a *trick!*" she interrupted, turning on her mother. "You dreamed up this trip to Russia to get Nick out of my life!"

"Don't be absurd," said Arabella. "And stop being so emotional. You're behaving like a third-rate opera singer."

"But Nick might get hurt in Russia! He might even be killed!" She turned to Nick, who was standing beside her. "Darling, don't go. *Please.*"

He took her in his arms to soothe her.

"Diana, I can't back out now. It's important to your father, and it's important to us. It's only going to be a couple of months, and I'll be all right. Really."

She was trembling with anger and frustration, an emotional time bomb. Impulsively, she hugged him, holding him tight to her.

"If ever I lose you . . ." she whispered, clenching her fists behind his neck.

Then she released him and turned on her parents, angrily.

"If something happens to him in Russia, it will be *your* fault," she shouted. "And I'll never let either of you forget it."

"Really, Diana," said Arabella, "you're hardly behaving like a lady."

Diana took Nick's hand and squeezed it.

"When Nick's concerned," she said softly, "I'm no lady."

There could be no question she meant it.

Nick tugged gently at her hand. She looked down and saw his crossed fingers.

Sighing, she crossed her fingers too. Their secret signal. Their love. Forever.

It would survive even Russia.

The *Santa Teresa* was a cargo ship with accommodations for twenty passengers, and as Nick climbed up her gangway he took one look at her rust-streaked white hull and knew that his nineteen-day journey to Vladivostok was going to be anything but luxurious. An Argentine steward in a dirty white jacket took him to his portside cabin, No. 9, which had a louvered door, two ports and a roach as big as the Ritz, which the steward casually crunched under his heel.

"Captain Rodriguez, he eenvite you to eat deener at hees table tonight," said the steward, smiling and scooping up the dead roach with some toilet paper. Nick wasn't looking forward to dinner. In fact, he thought that his trip on the roachy liner might be a good time to diet.

Moreover, he was missing Diana desperately. The trip to Russia, whatever its dangers, was exciting, and he was exhilarated by the opportunity to see so much of the world. But he was haunted by the green-eyed goddess, in whom he had aroused such a fierce passion and who had in turn aroused such a passion in him. He lay on his bunk, thought of their lovemaking and became almost embarrassingly aroused. He ached to hold her in his arms, longed for the sweet smell of her skin. True, in only a few months they would be together again, and if all went well he would be a rich man, which was also exciting.

But as the *Santa Teresa* eased out into San Francisco Bay, it wasn't money or gun deals or grand dukes or war he was thinking about.

It was Diana.

The passenger list on the *Santa Teresa* would have fascinated W. Somerset Maugham. There was a fleshily pretty woman named Señora Gonzaga who was traveling with her alleged "uncle," Señor Alba, a swarthy man in his sixties who claimed to be a cattle rancher but looked more like a white slaver. There was a forbiddingly prim English lady who was traveling to Tokyo to take a position as governess to a member of the Imperial family. There was a plump and decidedly decadent-looking Russian named Count Razoumovski, who had a streak of gray in his black hair, wore a monocle and had a perpetual oleaginous smile on his thick lips. There were two young American newlyweds en route to Manila where the husband was taking a post with the U.S. Army. There were two Japanese businessmen, a Peruvian wine dealer, two Mexican couples and a middle-aged American divorcée on her way to Honolulu who ordered a gin sling and was drunk by the time she weaved to the Captain's table for dinner.

"This ship's a rust bucket!" she slurred as she sat down at the Captain's right. "My cabin's got bugs!"

Captain Rodriguez, who looked like a pirate disguised as a ship's officer, ignored her with obvious boredom.

"My name is Count Razoumovski," the Russian said as he sat next to Nick.

"And I'm Nick Fleming." He remembered hearing one of the Beethoven Razoumovski Quartets at Alfred Ramschild's and asked, "Are you of the same family that helped Beethoven?"

The Count looked pleased. "I'm impressed! Yes, one of my ancestors was Russian ambassador at Vienna, and a patron of Beethoven's. We like to think of Ludwig as a member of the family—though a slightly boorish one. You're an American?"

"Yes."

"And where are you going?"

"To Petrograd."

"Ah, then we must become friends! I too am going to Petrograd. It will be a long journey, I fear. Nineteen days on this *soi-disant* liner, then two weeks on the *Trans-Siberian Express*. But what brings a young American to Petrograd in such difficult times as these?"

Nick had prepared a cover. "I'm with the Singer Sewing Machine Company," he said.

"Then you're a salesman?"

"That's right."

The Count removed his monocle to polish it on his napkin. "I will give you my card. I know everyone in Petrograd—*everyone!* I'm very well connected at court. Evgenii Nicolaevitch Razoumovski will help you sell hundreds of sewing machines."

"That's very kind of you, Count."

"This soup," announced the drunken American divorcée, "is greasy."

Captain Rodriguez shrugged.

Count Razoumovski replaced his monocle. He was wearing a well-cut dinner jacket, as were all the men at the long table except the Captain, who wore a short white uniform jacket.

"You may have heard," the Count continued, "that the Empress Alexandra Fedorovna is a German spy. This is nonsense. Of course, she was born a German and has many German relatives, including a brother in the German Army, but I refuse to believe she's a spy for the Kaiser. But"—he raised a manicured finger dramatically and grinned—"she *is* Rasputin's mistress! Of *that* I am certain. They have orgies in the palace and Rasputin communes with the dead!"

It occurred to Nick that he was traveling to an interesting country.

Aware of the potential danger of the trip, Nick had brought a small Ramschild .22 automatic, which he carried in a leather armpit holster. On the second day out from San Francisco, he had occasion to use it.

Returning to his cabin from a half-hour walk around the deck, to relieve his boredom as well as get exercise, he heard a noise inside. Tensing, he pulled the pistol from its holster and quietly opened the door.

Count Razoumovski was searching the drawers of his bureau.

"Looking to borrow my toothbrush?" said Nick, closing the door behind him, glad he had had the foresight to carry his papers on him.

The Count, pudgily natty in a white suit and a white hat, turned and straightened, his smarmy smile at the ready.

"My dear Fleming," he said, "you've caught me *in flagrante*. I apologize *mille fois*. I hope this doesn't destroy our budding friendship?"

"It doesn't do a helluva lot for it. What are you looking for?"

"I'm an incurable snoop, but it happens to be my *métier*—my profession. You see, I'm a member of the Okhrana, the Tsar's secret police."

His hand reached toward his coat.

"Keep your hands where they are," said Nick, waving the pistol slightly. He clicked the safety off, with a loud snap.

The Count looked surprised.

"My dear fellow, I'm only reaching for my wallet so I can prove to you my affiliation."

"I believe you—sort of. But why is the Tsar's government interested in an American salesman on a two-bit Argentine rust bucket? He must be desperate for information."

"Fleming, whatever your game is, you're a bit of an amateur at it. The Singer Sewing Machine office in Petrograd has been closed since 1915. So under the circumstances, the Tsar's government is *very* interested in you. Why did you lie to me?"

Nick hesitated.

"I don't see why I have to tell you a damned thing."

"You don't," agreed the Count. "But you can't stop me from trying to find out. Meanwhile, I believe it's almost lunchtime. Will you join me at the bar for a brandy and soda—on me, of course—as partial payment for this monstrous invasion of your privacy? There's no reason we can't enjoy each other's company even though we mistrust each other thoroughly. In Russia, *all* friendships are based on mistrust."

Nick slowly replaced his gun in its holster. Count Razoumovski was one of the most *louche* characters he had ever encountered. But he did fascinate him. Besides, Nick was bored.

The Count's perpetual smile broadened as he saw the gun vanish.

"Do you play poker?" he asked chattily as he preceded Nick out of the cabin. "I learned while I was in the States. Maybe we can get up a game. There's nothing else to do on this wretched ship except get drunk."

"And rifle other people's cabins."

"Ah," said the Count, smiling and adjusting his monocle. "But I've already done that."

For the next two weeks, as the *Santa Teresa* wallowed through the hot Pacific, Nick played poker with the Count; Señor Alba, the Argentine cattle rancher; Lieutenant Perkins, the newlywed en route to Manila; and other passengers who sat in. Count Razoumovski turned out to be a bad poker player but an amusing companion. He had a fund of jokes and gossip, and seemed obsessed by Rasputin, about whom he had dozens of hair-raising anecdotes. He claimed to know the *starets* personally (*starets* being a Russian word vaguely translated as "holy man"), having once been in charge of the section of the Okhrana that was responsible for guarding (and reporting the movements of) the Empress's favorite. At Rasputin's tacky apartment at 63–64 Gorokhavaya Street, directly opposite police headquarters, Russians of all classes flocked to beg favors from the man who had such a powerful hold over the Empress and her husband. According to the Count, who obviously relished telling these tales, society women begged for Rasputin's sexual favors. "He's the greatest lover in the world!" Razoumovski whispered, practically rubbing his hands with glee. "Many women have told me he transports them to an astral plane of ecstasy, that it is greater than sex—it's a religious experience! They say he's got the biggest penis in Russia with a magic wart on the end. They say the wart prolongs the orgasm for minutes!"

The other poker players laughed at this, but Razoumovski insisted it was true. Nick's opinion of the Count was that he probably was purveying gossip as fact and that the fat Russian had at best a nodding acquaintance with the truth. He drank all day long, but though he never seemed to get drunk, the vodka and brandy obviously took a further toll on his veracity. And from the casual way the Count admitted belonging to the Okhrana, Nick even began to doubt whether *that* was true.

Yet, easy as it was to write the man off as a bragging, boozing liar, Nick thought there was something more to Count Razoumovski than what he was allowing others to see. Genial as he appeared, there was something vaguely sinister about him. Nick told himself not to let his imagination run away with itself; and certainly, aside from invading his cabin, Razoumovski never did anything even remotely suspicious. He even lost over a thousand dollars at poker without exhibiting the least ill humor.

But Nick couldn't shake the impression that Razoumovski was dangerous.

CHAPTER 5

W HEN the *Santa Teresa* finally berthed in the four-mile-square
harbor of Vladivostok (in which were anchored two Russian
cruisers), Nick felt a strange sensation as he stepped ashore in the
country of his mother's birth. Despite his fluency in Russian, Nick
considered himself one hundred percent American, and he knew as
little about Russia as most Americans his age. Yet he remembered
the folk songs his mother had sung him and the smells of Russian
food, of *blini* and *pirozhki,* that she sometimes had cooked; and these
memories returned to give him an odd sense of what he thought of as
an inherited "homecoming."

The customs authorities were remarkably casual for wartime, reflecting perhaps the ineptitude of the Tsarist regime, but still Nick
had little time to sight-see in Vladivostok: the *Trans-Continental
Express* was leaving in an hour on its six-thousand-mile journey to
Moscow.

Nick was traveling first-class. The compartment, which he had to
himself, was comfortable, with mahogany paneling, ormolu work,
gilded decor, plush upholstery and red velvet curtains over the window. Promptly at 5 P.M., the wood-burning locomotive pulled the
eight-car train out of the station, and Nick watched as they rolled
through the bleak suburbs into the countryside, heading northwest
toward Manchuria.

At six-thirty, there was a knock on his door.

"Come in."

It was Count Razoumovski, smiling as usual.

"Fleming, dear fellow, join me for dinner?"

Nick had had enough of the Count.

"No thanks."

"Ah, but a *charming* widow is in the compartment next to mine, a
Madame Vyrushka, whose husband was a rich merchant in Vladivostok. She's dining with me. I'm sure you'd enjoy her company." He
lowered his voice. "She's *disponible,* as the French say. She could
make the journey much more enjoyable for both of us." He winked
lewdly.

"Thanks, but no thanks."

Nick was inches from outright rudeness, but the Count seemed immune to insult. "Well, dear fellow, if you change your mind. . . . She's got enough to go around."

He closed the door, his smile, like the Cheshire Cat's, seeming to linger behind.

The track was single-line and bumpy, causing the train to rock and shake violently, even though it was going only twenty-five miles per hour. Furthermore, every two hours the train stopped to let the second-class passengers off, as there were no toilet facilities in the wooden-benched second-class carriages. But there were compensations. An aged attendant at the end of Nick's car kept his copper samovar, with its onion-shaped dome and brass tap, permanently at the boil, so that tea was available anytime.

The dining car was palatial, with red-buttoned leather seats, mirrors, and on each table a brass lamp with a red silk, tasseled shade. The service was excellent, and there was sparkling glass, silver tableware and clean white linen. Despite the food shortages in Petrograd, the dining car seemed a cornucopia of highly seasoned borscht, stews, fresh sturgeon, roast bear, caviar and cranberry cake. The wine list was surprisingly good. To sit at one of the tables sipping a Crimean Pinot Gris and watching the vast reaches of Manchuria pass by was, to Nick, not only pleasant but a revelation. He had seen a good part of the eastern United States as a traveling salesman, but Manchuria was astonishingly vast and beautiful, a mysterious world apart.

On the second evening, after leaving Harbin, the capital of Manchuria, Count Razoumovski came into the dining car in the company of a remarkably good-looking woman. She was as tall as the Count, and with the smart satin toque on her black hair she appeared even taller. She had on a light-blue dress that showed off her smashing figure, and the embroidered hem was six daring inches above her shoes. She wore two strands of pearls as pink as her complexion. The Count, who was wearing a dinner jacket, brought her to Nick's table.

"Here he is," he said in Russian. "Our dashing young American." He switched to English. "Fleming, I'd like to introduce you to Nadeshda Ivanovna Vyrushka—the most beautiful widow in Vladivostok! Nadeshda Ivanovna, this is Nick Fleming."

Nick stood up to kiss her hand. He had expected the widow Vyrushka to be middle-aged, but to his surprise she could hardly have been thirty. "I'm delighted to meet you," he said in English. "Will you and the Count join me?"

"Alas, I'm having a slight *crise de foie*," said the Count. "Too much vodka, I fear. I shan't be dining, but Nadeshda Ivanovna would be pleased to join you. I leave you in excellent company," he said to Mme. Vyrushka. Then he added, in Russian, "Find out what he's doing in Petrograd."

Nick was glad he had never let the Count know he spoke Russian.

"Have you known the Count for a long time?" Nick asked, after the waiter had served the first course.

"Oh, no. I met him last night on the train."

A lie, thought Nick. But he was impressed by her excellent English.

"He seems most interesting," she continued. "And he thinks very highly of you."

"I'm surprised. I won three hundred dollars off him at poker on the ship."

"But money means nothing to him. He's immensely rich, you know."

"No, I didn't. And how did you know, if you just met him last night?"

She looked innocent. "The Razoumovskis are a powerful family in Russia. They own huge estates." The waiter refilled their wineglasses. She took a sip. "I find it curious that an American is going to Petrograd," she said. "Are you on business?"

"Well, it's government business."

"Oh?"

"I'm carrying a message from President Wilson to the Tsar."

He almost laughed at the way she tried to hide her excitement.

"Really? How fascinating. Then you must be very important."

"I try to keep modest. But I guess the *message* is important."

She looked out the train window, trying to feign disinterest. But he could hear her brain whirring over the metallic click of the wheels.

She knocked on his door at eleven that night. When he opened the door to see her standing in the corridor with an overcoat over a white satin nightgown, he wasn't surprised.

"I wondered if you had a cigarette?" she asked. "I've run out."

"Sorry," said Nick. "I don't smoke."

He closed the door in her startled face, then sat down, grinning.

Mme. Vyrushka was so obvious she was funny. The widow of Vladivostok had her charms, but he wasn't going to betray his green-eyed goddess. Nick was so much in love with Diana Ramschild, he was—for the first time in his life—even being faithful.

Whatever their game was, Count Razoumovski and Mme. Vyrushka kept to themselves for the rest of the long journey. When Nick *did* encounter them in the dining car, she was coolly polite, as if nothing had happened, and the Count was his usual affable, smarmy self. Nick reasoned that if the Count were in fact a member of the Okhrana, he would eventually discover Nick's mission anyway, through government channels. If he weren't, the less he knew about the Ramschild arms deal, the better. Meanwhile, Nick enjoyed the scenery of Siberia, the vast wheat fields, the fir forests, the occasional tiny peasant village, the sealike Lake Baikal. At Irkutsk, they changed to another, faster train that took them over the Urals into European Russia and, finally, to Moscow. There, he changed to the *Petrograd Express,* which brought him to the capital in twelve hours.

It was a warm August night, but eager as he was to see the fabled city, he taxied directly to his hotel, deciding he could sight-see in the morning.

The European Hotel, on the city's main street, the Nevsky Prospekt, was a large, ugly nineteenth-century building. Nick checked into a two-room suite on the third floor that boasted ornately carved furniture abounding with wooden grapevines and animals, including two crouching bears holding up a heavy desk. Nick flopped on the double bed and was asleep in minutes.

His last waking thought was how in God's name he was going to get nine million dollars' worth of loot out of Russia and halfway around the globe to America.

He was awakened by a phone call. "Good morning," said a raspy voice. "My name's Bud Turner, and I'm Russian correspondent for the Clairmont newspapers. Van Clairmont cabled me to look after you. I'm downstairs in the lobby. How about breakfast? They've got good *blini* in this joint."

"I'll be down in ten minutes."

Bud Turner was forty, skinny, a natty dresser and vain enough to wear an obvious hairpiece. Now he lit his sixth cigarette of the morning and said, "What do you want to know about Russia?"

"How do I get an appointment with the Minister of War?" Nick asked as he ate a tasty *blin* filled with rich strawberry jam.

"The Grand Duke Cyril? Better make the appointment through the Embassy. I can arrange it for you. Mr. Clairmont said you're with the Ramschild Company. I take it you're here to sell arms?"

"Something like that," Nick said evasively. "By the way, do you know a Count Razoumovski?"

"I know *of* him. He's a big wheel here—one of the richest men in Russia. He threw a big party the other night at his palace on the Fontanka Canal. All the swells were there."

Nick looked at him. "But that's impossible!"

"Why?"

"He was on the train with me."

"Must have been another Count Razoumovski."

"What's *this* Count look like?"

"He's about seventy. Has a white beard."

Nick laughed.

"What's so funny?" Bud asked.

"I've been conned by the slickest no-Count in Russia."

But, then, what the hell *was* his game?

Nick's appointment with the Grand Duke Cyril was made for ten the next morning, and he devoted the rest of the day to seeing the sights of the city Peter the Great had founded in 1703. Bud Turner was his guide, and Nick found him a good one; the slangy New Yorker knew the city and its history well. Peter had built what he had named St. Petersburg on marshland, forcing his serfs to drag millions of tons of granite into the watery environs of the River Neva to form the foundations of his capital. Two hundred thousand workers died in the process, but the city slowly rose, spreading across nineteen islands to become the Venice of the North. During the next two centuries, grand baroque palaces and government buildings were erected, designed by Italian architects, and Nick marveled at the pale blues and yellows, greens and whites of their elaborately decorated walls. They toured the Admiralty and the mammoth green Winter Palace on the south bank of the Neva; the grim brown Fortress of Peter and Paul on the north bank, which was the Tsar's prison; the lovely Summer Garden, the enormous Cathedral of Our Lady of Kazan, the handsome canals and broad boulevards. But though to Nick's eyes the city seemed calm, Bud Turner warned him otherwise.

"Petrograd's a powder keg," he said. "Ready to blow."

CHAPTER 6

THE Grand Duke Cyril Vladimirovitch was a giant, at least four inches taller than Nick, and one of the most impressive men the young American had ever seen. Impeccably tailored, slim, with a ramrod military bearing, he had a well-clipped gray beard, a handsome, wrinkled face, a commanding presence and elegant manners. Like most of the Russian nobility, he spoke excellent English, and he listened as Nick explained his mission, frowning slightly when he heard about the nine million dollars. Whatever his opinion, the Grand Duke was careful not to express it. "I'm seeing His Majesty this afternoon," he said. "I'll discuss the matter with him. Come back tomorrow morning. . . ." He hesitated. "No. Better yet, are you free this evening?"

"Yes, sir."

"My wife is giving a small party for my daughter. Would you like to come? It will give you a chance to see a little something of Petrograd life, and I can give you His Majesty's answer. I won't pretend we're not extremely anxious to get the shipment. I want to expedite this as quickly as possible."

Nick stood up. "Yes, sir, I'd be delighted to come. Where do you live?"

The Grand Duke looked surprised, as if everyone *knew* where he lived.

"On the Moika Canal. Ask any taxi driver. I don't think you'll have any difficulty finding it."

In fact, Grand Duke Cyril's palace was hard to miss. Situated on the handsome Moika Canal, next to the Yusupov Palace, its pale-yellow façade, graced by a stately row of Palladian columns, was far less flamboyant than the rococo and baroque architecture of many of the other buildings Nick had seen. Getting out of his taxi, he drank in the splendor of the four-story palace, illuminated by the soft late-summer sunset, thinking that Alfred Ramschild's estate looked like an outhouse in comparison. Then he went to the front door and rang. He was admitted by a bewigged, silk-stockinged footman who looked as if he had stepped out of the eighteenth century. As he was led up the mammoth marble grand staircase, a replica of the *Escalier de la Reine* at Versailles, Nick thought he *was* in the eighteenth century. The palace, built in 1790, had been meant to impress, if not stupefy, and the walls of the stairs soared some sixty feet to a magnificent ceiling fresco where gods and goddesses swarmed in mythological profusion against a cerulean heaven while the biggest crystal chandelier Nick had ever seen sparkled beneath them. At the top of the stairs, he was led into a red drawing room, its ceiling decorated with a delicate neo-Pompeian design in gold leaf; in the center of the gleaming floor there was a huge and beautifully intricate circular design made of marquetry. The tall doorframes were minor marble monuments, with columns and pediments, and the walls of red silk were hung with seventeenth-century Italian paintings. Nick's eyes widened as the footman led him through three more drawing rooms, each bigger and more luxurious than the last, each filled with furniture and art that any museum curator would have killed for. Strewn everywhere on inlaid wood tables and Florentine *pietra dura* tables were onyx, jade, malachite and chrysoprase bibelots, jeweled snuffboxes, Fabergé pillboxes and picture frames—Nick even saw an ivory dish filled with uncut diamonds and rubies. The magnificence was staggering, and, in view of the situation in Petrograd, arrogant.

As they passed through a huge rotunda, in the middle of which was a lovely marble nude Diana by Canova, Nick heard phonograph music that was distinctly twentieth century, a jazz band playing "Alexander's Ragtime Band." A half world away from New York, Nick almost whooped with joy to hear the familiar tune. The footman led him down a long corridor lined with more statues, and the music grew louder. But as he passed one door, Nick stopped and asked the footman in Russian, "What's that?"

"The theater, sir."

Through the door was a complete theater, its gilt balconies groaning with cherubs, a full-sized stage surrounded by a gilt proscenium, and enough silk-upholstered orchestra seats for one hundred and fifty. The theater, the whim of some early-nineteenth-century ancestor of the Grand Duke's, was so insanely extravagant it left Nick speechless.

"Before the war," said the footman matter-of-factly, "we used to have several performances a week during the season."

Nick nodded numbly. They continued down the corridor.

Now "Alexander's Ragtime Band" had been replaced by another record, a slow and rather melancholy waltz that was unfamiliar to Nick. Reaching the end of the corridor, the footman opened two white-and-gold doors and led him into a vast ballroom. By now "splendid," "magnificent" and "extravagant" were beginning to lose their meaning; but the ballroom shook him out of a sense of jadedness. A gently arched ceiling, decorated with gold ribbon work, sailed down a broad room perhaps one hundred feet long, illuminated by four vaguely Russian-style gold chandeliers. White-and-gold Doric pilasters punctuated the walls; between them were gold and crystal sconces. Above the pilasters and beneath the coving of the ceiling was an entablature decorated with a frieze of gold wheat and Russian flowers. Waltzing on the polished parquet to the sad, slow music were about a dozen young men and women; on a white-and-gold Louis XVI table sat a windup Victrola.

The Grand Duke Cyril, who was wearing a dinner jacket, was standing at one side of the room among several older people. Seeing Nick, he quickly came down the room to shake his hand.

"Mr. Fleming! I'm delighted you could come."

As he led Nick down the length of the room, he said quietly, "I spoke with His Imperial Majesty this afternoon. Our embassy in Paris is negotiating an eight-hundred-million-ruble loan from the French government—or about one hundred million American dollars. His Majesty instructed me to tell you that the nine million dollars will be paid to the Saxmundham Bank in London by the end of this week— in dollars. I trust this will be satisfactory?"

Nick realized, with a ten percent leap in his blood pressure, that he had just become a rich man.

"Yes, sir—very satisfactory! I'll send a cable to Mr. Ramschild in the morning."

"To save time, could the shipment leave San Francisco as soon as possible? I realize the end of the week is four days away, but if there were some snag in the payment—which I don't foresee—the shipment could still be stopped at Hawaii."

Nick realized the money wasn't in his pocket yet. "I'll request it in the cable. Mr. Ramschild might agree to that."

"Please impress on him that every day we save is of great value to our government. We're not fools here, Mr. Fleming. We realize the international financial community is, shall we say, 'suspicious' of our financial situation. Quite frankly, we've had difficulty buying arms from other companies besides Ramschild. Our allies have been reluctant to make us further loans—obviously, France and Great Britain are bleeding financially too. But we have been able to impress on the French authorities the fact that they *must* help us. The war is costing

Russia millions of lives. Without us fighting Germany in the east, the Germans and Austrians could concentrate on France and, in my opinion, wipe it off the map in weeks. So the French have finally agreed to continue to support us. I'm sorry you had to make this long journey, but perhaps it's important for an American to see firsthand what conditions here are like. And here's my wife. Darling, this is the young American I told you about."

Nick was presented to the Grand Duchess Xenia, who looked neither very grand nor very duchessy, but rather was a short, plump woman with a homely face and frizzy gray hair. She wore a frumpy dress, and Nick wondered what hidden attractions she must have had to capture her handsome and aristocratic husband. Whatever they were, the Grand Duchess had a good mind. She was also keenly interested in America. She asked Nick what Americans thought of Russia.

"Well, frankly, ma'am, they're not entirely favorable toward the Tsar's autocratic government."

"There!" exclaimed the Grand Duchess, turning toward the others. "It's what I've been saying for months! Nicky should abdicate. He's made too many mistakes, and we all know the English don't like us. We *need* world support, and we'll never get it with this medieval form of government we have now."

Nick was surprised at how calmly the others greeted this remark, which, coming from the wife of the Minister of War and a member of the Tsar's family, could only be viewed as heretical—not to say revolutionary. But the others, even the Grand Duke, seemed to agree with her. Nick thought that Petrograd must indeed be a powder keg if the court aristocracy was ready to abandon the Tsar.

The Grand Duke introduced Nick to the other older people. By now word had spread around the ballroom that the stranger was an American, and Nick quickly found himself surrounded by the young people as well. But they weren't interested in politics.

"Do you know the Grizzly Bear?" asked a cute, short girl in a white dress whom Nick guessed to be about eighteen.

"Sure," Nick said, relishing his sudden star attraction. "But that's old hat now in New York."

"Then what's *new?*" cried a half-dozen voices, and Nick realized with a touch of poignancy how cut off from the world these young people were.

"It's called the Castle Gavotte, and it's a variation on the Castle Walk. Would you like to see it?"

The "Yes!" was almost a roar.

"I'll demonstrate," he said, taking the hand of the short girl in white. "Will you be my partner?"

"I'd love to," she exclaimed. "Poppa, introduce us."

The Grand Duke Cyril said, "Mr. Fleming, this is my daughter, the Grand Duchess Tatyana."

Now he saw the resemblance to her frumpy mother. Fortunately, the daughter had inherited some of her father's better features, if not his height, but she would never be a beauty. Still, with her curly blond hair and vivacious blue eyes, she was attractive in a way that seemed more American to Nick than Russian.

"Put on 'Alexander's Ragtime Band,'" Nick said, leading her onto the dance floor. As the music honked out of the phonograph, he started showing her the fast, jazzy step. "First, we rock forward, you on your right foot and I on my left," he said, holding her hands outstretched to the front and rear. "Then we rock back on the other foot. Then we turn away from each other and swing around . . . then we come together and do a quick two-step. . . ."

Tatyana caught on quickly. Within ten minutes, all the young people were trying out the new dance.

"It's fun!" said the young Grand Duchess. "It's really fun! I'm so glad you came to Petrograd, Mr. Fleming."

"So am I! I wouldn't have missed teaching a grand duchess the Castle Gavotte for the world."

CHAPTER 7

H E had so much fun dancing that he stayed until after midnight. Then, thanking his hosts, he left the palace and, since it was such a pleasant night, decided to walk back to his hotel. He was jubilant. By a stroke of luck and timing, his mission was an apparent success, and he could almost feel that nine-hundred-thousand-dollar commission in his pocket. He looked up at the star-strewn Petrograd sky and remembered his helpless rage at the arrest and lonely death of his mother, his bitterness as he witnessed that mockery of justice. I'll never be helpless again, he thought. Never! I'm rich and I'm going to get richer. The world's going to hear about Nick Fleming!

He was so wrapped up in his thoughts he didn't hear the four-door black car coming slowly down the street behind him. When the car was a few feet from Nick, a back door opened and two men jumped out. When Nick heard the running footsteps behind him, he started to turn to see what was happening when something smashed down on his head. For an instant, stars flashed and pulsed in his eyes. Then the world went black.

When he regained consciousness, he was tied to a wooden chair in the middle of a dimly lit room, his wrists secured by rope behind the back of the chair, his ankles tied to the chair legs, and a foul-smelling rag gagging his mouth. His head throbbed with pain, and he began to panic. The room was small, with cracked plaster walls. Aside from the chair, there was nothing else in it except a low table on which sat a cheap green-shaded lamp. If the palace on the Moika Canal had been an eighteenth-century fantasy, this was a twentieth-century nightmare. He realized, mentally kicking himself, that despite his boast of never being helpless again, he was now totally at the mercy of his abductors. But who in God's name were they? And what the hell did they want?

Since the room had only one window, covered by a heavy shade, he had no idea what time it was. Minutes dragged into hours, or at least he thought they did. He kept telling himself to keep cool, that leaving him alone was a ploy to reduce him to psychological jelly; still, he was scared. And as time passed, the tight rope began to cut off his circulation so that his arms began stabbing with needles and pins.

Finally, he heard voices outside the door. Then the door opened and in walked the bogus Count Razoumovski followed by a hulking young man dressed in worker's clothes and a cloth cap. The Count had dropped his debonair pose. Gone was the monocle, as well as the natty clothes. Now he wore rimless glasses and a cheap suit that gave him the look of a minor bureaucrat. The young man closed the door as the Count stood in front of Nick.

"Untie his gag," he said in Russian, and the young man walked behind the chair. "May I introduce my colleague," the Count continued. "Rodion Grigorivitch Selivanov, which of course is not his real name. I assume by now you've probably guessed that I am not Count Razoumovski, either. You may call me Radix, which is the *nom de plume* I use in the underground newspaper I edit, *Pravda*. *Radix* is Latin for 'root,' and from it derives the English word 'radical.' And I am *very* radical, Fleming."

Rodion Grigorivitch had removed the gag. Now Nick said, in Russian, "Could you loosen the ropes on my wrists? My circulation's stopped."

Radix smiled as he lit a cigarette.

"So you speak Russian, Fleming? I should have been more careful. . . . Ah, well, nobody is perfect. . . . Now, I'll be brief, my friend. We know why you are in Petrograd, and we know the Tsar has agreed to pay the remaining nine million dollars to obtain the Ramschild arms shipment."

"How do you know?"

"Let's say we have sources in the palace. We have abducted you to stop that arms shipment from being delivered."

"Why?"

"We are revolutionaries. We have pledged our lives to overthrow the regime. In our opinion, this war is our greatest ally. The Tsar is losing the war, and the people of Russia are learning to hate him because of it. Not a village in Russia hasn't lost sons, husbands or brothers. It is to our advantage to hamper the Tsar's war efforts, which is why we do not want the Ramschild arms shipment delivered."

"And what makes you think kidnapping me will stop the shipment?"

"It's very simple. We have already passed a message to the American Embassy for Alfred Ramschild. If Ramschild ships the arms, we will kill you." He paused to let the effect sink in. "I'm delighted, Fleming," he continued, "that you haven't made the cliché remark that 'you won't get away with this.' Because of course we *will*. I realize the possibility exists that Alfred Ramschild is more interested in profit than your life, and might send the shipment anyway—in which case we *both* lose. But I don't think this will happen. Particularly since the American press lord Van Nuys Clairmont is sufficiently interested in your welfare to send his correspondent to your hotel to look after you."

"And how did you know *that*? Sources at the hotel?"

"Exactly. I don't think Ramschild will risk the bad publicity in the American press if he forfeits the life of his charming young salesman for an arms shipment to the autocratic and extremely unpopular Tsar of Russia. Therefore I think the chances are our little scheme is going to work.

"You, of course, are the somewhat innocent dupe in all of this. You were available to me as a weapon, and I'm using you. However, I have no intention of hurting you, *if* it can be avoided. Cooperate with us and there's no reason why your incarceration can't be reasonably pleasant. Rodion will be your chief guard. You look like a strong young man, but I can assure you Rodion is stronger. You will be taken tonight to a farm several hundred versts from Petrograd where you will be held. Even if you managed to escape—highly unlikely, of course—you could never find your way back to civilization. So my advice to you is to accept what has happened and regard the next few weeks or months as a profitable opportunity for philosophical reflection. If you are wise, you'll realize you are helping in one of the most important events in world history: the destruction of the tsarist autocracy. The first step, let us hope, in world revolution! Do you have any questions?"

"A lot. What were you doing in America?"

"Raising funds. You'd be surprised how many sympathizers we have in your capitalist country."

"And who is Madame Vyrushka?"

"She is, shall we say, a 'colleague.' And now, my friend, I must bid you farewell. And Fleming"—again that insolent smile—"no hard feelings, I hope!"

He left the room.

        . . .

Even if Edith Fleming hadn't become hysterical when she heard the news, Van Clairmont would have splashed Nick's kidnapping on the front page, because he had a newsman's nose for a scoop: his twenty-nine papers were the first to headline "Young American Kidnapped by Foes of Tsar!"

Since the note delivered to the Embassy in Petrograd had been mysteriously signed "The Committee of Six," no one was quite sure who the abductors were, although Van suggested in the editorial he wrote that they were undoubtedly part of the "radical underground" of Russian politics, possibly nihilists or Bolsheviks, scare words even to someone as liberal as Van. Edith's town house was besieged by reporters, but because the doctor had put her to bed under heavy sedation, they were turned away by the butler. The morning after the story hit the papers, she was calm enough to accept a telephone call from the White House, and was somewhat cheered when President Wilson told her he had been assured by the Russian ambassador that "everything would be done" to find Nick.

But, still, the fear haunted her that somewhere on the other side of the world her son could be killed at any time. Even more frightening was the possibility he might already be dead.

But if Edith required sedation, Diana Ramschild was outraged when she heard the news.

"I *knew* it!" she screamed to her father. "I knew if he went to Russia, I'd lose him!"

"Diana, you're jumping to conclusions! We don't know yet—"

"He's been kidnapped by terrorists—what more do we have to know?"

She sank into a sofa, sobbing. Her father stood in front of her, embarrassed and guilty. He knew his daughter's heart was breaking, and he had to admit it was his fault.

"Diana, I'm sorry . . ." he mumbled, awkward at apologies. He reached out and put his hand on her shoulder, but she pushed it away angrily, got up, ran upstairs, slammed into her bedroom and threw herself on her bed. She stared at her engagement ring, remembered Nick's touch, saw his face, and told herself it wasn't possible she'd never see him again, never touch him again.

She rolled over on the bed, hugging herself, racked with fear and burning with sexual hunger for her lost love.

Her fear was not only for Nick's safety. She had gone to a doctor three days before and found out what she had suspected was true: she was carrying Nick's child.

In the gilded salons of Petrograd's nobility as well as in the homes of its middle class, the kidnapping of "The American," as Nick quickly became known, was another cudgel to use against the increasingly unpopular Imperial family and its inept government. "Why didn't you assign him a guard?" asked the young Grand Duchess Tatyana of her father, Grand Duke Cyril. And the Minister of War was forced to admit lamely that he hadn't thought it necessary. Even in the most famous room in Russia, the Empress's mauve boudoir in the hundred-room Alexander Palace at Tsarskoe Selo, Fleming's kidnapping was cause for anxiety. "The Okhrana hasn't a *clue* where he is!" said the Tsar as he paced the room in which everything, even the Hepplewhite furniture, was mauve. Nicholas II was a delicately handsome man who always spoke to his wife in English. Now he paused long enough to stub out his cigarette. "Not a *clue*. And the damnable thing is, we desperately need those guns."

"I have spoken to Our Friend," said the Empress, a golden-haired granddaughter of Queen Victoria's. She was stretched out on a chaise longue beneath a portrait of one of her favorite historical personalities, Marie Antoinette. "Our Friend" was the way Alexandra Fedorovna referred to Rasputin. "Our Friend says we mustn't worry."

"*Damn* Rasputin!" snapped the Tsar. Even though the *starets* seemed to be able to stop his hemophilic son from bleeding to death, sometimes Nicholas wished he'd never met the smelly peasant who had so mesmerized his wife.

The Tsarina looked shocked.

"Nicky, we mustn't talk that way about Grigory! He is a man of God!"

The Tsar impatiently lit another cigarette. He sincerely believed in God, but lately it didn't seem as if God had much faith in the Tsar of All the Russians.

"Checkmate."

Rodion grinned. He had moved his white bishop three spaces, and Nick's black king was dead. Not that Nick had much hope against his chief guard, who had turned out to be brainy as well as brawny. They had played chess for four months now, and Rodion had won eighty percent of the games.

"Shit," said Nick.

"Another game?"

"Why won't you let me teach you poker? I'm sick of chess, and I'm sick to death of losing at it."

"Ah, my friend, poker is a capitalist game. I'm not interested in it. But chess! Chess is like beautiful music. Chess is not only good for the brain—it's good for the *soul!*"

Nick got up from the roughhewn wooden table and stretched as he went to the window to look out at the snow. Four months in this log cabin somewhere east of the sun and west of the moon. Four months! The guards had treated him with surprising kindness. He had even grown to like Rodion, who was a cheerful grizzly bear when you didn't cross him.

But Nick was going crazy.

His breath frosted the windowpane as he stared out at the snowflakes drifting almost wearily, as if forty-eight hours of continuous snowfall had worn them out. He wondered if he would ever get out of the godforsaken log cabin he had grown to hate. The guards were friendly, but the cabin was a prison.

The worst was not knowing what was happening outside, and the guards purposely kept him ignorant. Nick didn't even bother asking them questions anymore. The only "facts" he had learned in four months was that Rodion came from Moscow, had a university degree in metallurgy and could quote Marx by the boring ton.

For the millionth time, Nick contemplated escape. But Radix had been right: the cabin was in the middle of an endless forest. The guards had taken him on long walks for exercise, and he had seen that even if he evaded them, he would become hopelessly lost—or frozen, now that winter had set in.

"Come, Nikosha," said Rodion, using the Russian diminutive, as if Nick were one of the family—which he practically was. "I've set up a new game."

"I *told* you I'm sick of chess."

"Got anything better to do?"

Nick sighed, then returned to the chess set. His passion for Diana was still at the boil, pressure-cooked by his monastic seclusion. But during the long wintry weeks of imprisonment, he also had thought about the Ramschild Company and the armaments business. He had told Diana selling guns was like selling insurance, but of course it wasn't. The armaments business was the steel of any nation's strength. Nick knew that the present war—and Germany's aggressive foreign policy for the past half century—was directly tied to the giant armaments firm of Krupp. It had been Alfred Krupp, the "Cannon King," who had enabled the various nineteenth-century Kaisers to turn the small, bucolic and not very rich state of Prussia into the big, industrial German Empire. The reason he was a prisoner in this deserted cabin was because of armaments. Whoever controlled a gun company automatically wielded power—power to deal with the rulers of this earth.

It was an enticing thought.

Edith Fleming stood at the window of the library of her town house and stared out at the snowflakes drifting down on Manhattan. For the millionth time she told herself her adopted son *might* be alive, but she felt in her heart he was dead. She had felt it ever since Alfred Ramschild told her he was reselling the arms shipment to England. Alfred had convinced her that to resell the shipment was the best way to free Nick, for if he had been kidnapped to prevent the arms going to the Tsar, when his abductors learned they were going to England instead, they would no longer have reason to hold him. Edith had nervously agreed, and the deal had been made.

That was November. Now it was February. Not only had Nick not been released, there had been not one word from his captors. Edith was convinced they had killed him, perhaps for revenge, but more likely to prevent him from revealing to the Tsar's government the identity of "The Committee of Six."

She remembered the beautiful boy she had taken to her heart so many years before in Flemington, the boy she had adopted and loved—with all Nick's faults—as if he were her own.

She heard the door open and turned from the window. Van Clairmont had come into the library. He wore a trim dark-blue suit, and his thick eyeglasses were steamy after coming in from the snow.

"Van," she said, surprised to see him in the afternoon.

He took off his glasses and started wiping them on his handkerchief as he crossed the room toward her.

"Winifred's dead," he said quietly. "She died about an hour ago. The doctor told me that even if she'd survived the stroke, she'd probably have been paralyzed for the rest of her life. So it's probably better this way."

"Still, I'm sorry to hear it," said Edith.

He put his glasses back on, stuffed the handkerchief into his breast pocket, then put his hands on her arms.

"You know what this means," he said. "I'm free."

She said nothing as he pulled her into his arms and kissed her.

"We'll wait a week after the funeral," he whispered. "Then we'll go down to Hot Springs and get married. I adore you, Edith. I'd be a hypocrite if I said I'm sorry about Winifred."

If only Nick were here, she thought.

"*Will* you marry me?" he asked.

She smiled up at him.

"I'd be honored to."

Van grinned, happy as a schoolboy.

"What do you want as a wedding present?"

"My son."

As much as Nick had never been a favorite of his, Van understood how deeply Edith was wounded by his death.

"I only wish I could give him back to you" was all he said.

The small bedroom of the log cabin in which Nick had been spending so many long, boring, cold nights had had its one window boarded up before he was brought there. Nick had tried numerous times to pry the boards loose, but they were actually split logs, and ten-inch spikes had been used to drive them into the walls of the cabin; without a hammer, it was impossible to budge them.

Nick told himself there was no hope of escaping, but continued to dream of it nonetheless. Then he thought of the floorboards. He began testing them one by one, for he had seen on his guarded walks that the cabin had no foundation and there was a crawl space under it. On the second night, he found a loose board under his bed.

He pushed the bed away and pried up the board. The underheated room was already cold, but now he could feel the really intense cold beneath the house. He was working in the dark, because they allowed him no lantern. He began levering up the other boards.

When he removed two more, there was a big enough space for him to ease through. The question was, Did he want to do it? He had a bearskin coat they had given him, gloves and sturdy boots, but how long could he possibly last in the sub-zero weather? He had no food, no weapons and no idea where he was. The probability was that he would wander for hours, become hopelessly lost and freeze to death.

Yet he had to try. The imprisonment was driving him crazy. He put on his coat and gloves and slipped through the hole, dropping to the frozen ground. Then he crawled to the edge of the cabin and stood up.

It was a clear, freezing-cold night with a quarter moon giving enough light for him to see by—this was as good a time as ever. Wrapping his scarf around his head to keep his ears warm, he started walking through the snow.

Then he saw the sleigh tracks, and his heart leaped. Of course! The cabin was brought food and supplies twice a week by horse-drawn sleigh; the sleigh had to come from somewhere, probably the nearest town. All he had to do was follow the tracks and ultimately he would reach the town.

He started running along the tracks, wanting to yell with relief—he was free!

He ran for five minutes, then slowed to a panting walk. As his lungs gulped the icy air, the cold bit at his throat and nostrils. He trudged on through the endless woods, the moonlight flickering through the snow-laden branches of the tall firs. How silent it was! Silent and cold, heavy with a lethal beauty.

He heard a distant wolf howl and now the chill seeped into his blood. Stories he had read as a child leaped into his mind, stories of pioneers in the Wild West hunted down by wolves and Indians and bears. He was in the wild east where there weren't any Indians; but it was unpleasant to be reminded there were wolves. It was still not too late to turn back. But he kept going. He retied his scarf so that it covered his mouth and nose as well as his ears, and he kept going.

They found him the next morning, unconscious in the snow, almost frozen to death. He had walked three miles from the cabin. They took him back and Rodion revived him, feeding him hot soup.

"You were very foolish, Nikosha," chided the big Russian. "You almost died. We knew you would try to escape sooner or later, but there's really no point to it. Do you understand? Really no point."

Nick nodded numbly. He had learned the hard way.

But at least he had tried.

He knew something was wrong when the new guards arrived.

He was locked in his small room, sitting on his bed, a crude peasant bed with ropes for springs and a straw-filled mattress, the bed he had slept on for more than half a year. He listened to their voices in the front room, wondering what was going on. Then the door was unlocked and Rodion came in.

"We are leaving, Nikosha," he said, coming to the bed. "I've come to say goodbye."

He stuck out his hand. Nick stood up and took it.

"What's happened? Why are you going?"

"I hope you'll agree that we treated you well, under the circumstances?"

"You treated me all right, but what the hell's going on?"

To his surprise, the grizzly bear hugged him.

"We are friends, Nikosha. No matter what happens. We are friends, no?"

"What do you mean, 'no matter what happens'?"

Rodion released him and smiled slightly.

"Don't be afraid," he said.

Then he went back to the door.

"Don't be afraid of *what?*" Nick yelled.

Rodion opened the door and went out. Nick ran after him.

"Rodion, for Christ's sake, *tell* me what's happening!"

The door closed and the wooden bar slammed into place.

Nick pounded his fists on the door, yelling, "Damn it, somebody *tell* me something! *Tell* me!"

He yelled and pounded for almost a minute. Then he stopped. Useless. He went back to the bed and sank down, staring at the wooden floor.

He wondered if they were going to kill him, and if so, how.

He prayed it would be quick.

A half hour of silence ensued. Then he heard the whinny of a horse. He got up and went to the door again, pressing his ear against it.

Someone had entered the cabin. Now, footsteps were coming toward his door. Then the bar was slowly lifted.

Nick backed away and faced the door.

For Christ's sake, don't show them you're terrified, he thought. Die like a man. Otherwise, the sons of bitches will laugh over your corpse.

As the door swung open, he wondered if it hurt to be shot through the heart.

An old man with a white beard and a fur cap was standing in the doorway. "Are you the man I'm supposed to take to Petrograd?" he wheezed, his Russian heavy with a peasant's accent.

"What?" said Nick, confused.

"I was paid fifty rubles to drive an American to Petrograd. Are you American?"

"Yes, but . . . who paid you?"

The old peasant shrugged. "He just said he was a chess partner of yours, and that you'd be in the back room."

Nick started laughing. "You mean I'm *free?*"

"I told you, I've already been paid. Are you ready to start? My sleigh's out front."

Letting out a whoop of pure exhilaration, Nick ran to the old man and hugged him.

"Everyone's gone crazy," muttered the peasant. "Since the Tsar left, everyone's gone crazy."

"What happened to the Tsar?"

The old man looked at him.

"You didn't hear?"

"I haven't heard *anything!* What happened?"

"There was an uprising in Petrograd last week. The Little Father abdicated. They say Russia's a republic."

Nick just stared.

CHAPTER 8

O N a blustery, rainy late-March day in 1917, Nick rang the bell of the door of the palace of the ex-Grand Duke Cyril on the Moika Canal and wondered why the former Minister of War wanted to see him. In the two days since his return to Petrograd, Nick had received a certain amount of notice in the local press, but the mood of the capital and its newspapers was almost hysterically antimonarchial after the abdication of the Tsar, and there was little room in the press for anything but shrill denunciations of the former Empress and her husband, both of whom were now prisoners in their palace at Tsarskoe Selo. Cartoons of the Empress sitting in a bathtub filled with the blood of revolutionaries ran alongside accounts of wild orgies at the Palace before the revolution.

Rasputin, who had been brutally murdered the previous December, was now depicted as a sexual monster who had not only been the Empress's lover but had "deflowered" her four daughters as well. Unmuzzled, the press had become a wild dog, and the city was seething with hatred. Nick had seen bands of revolutionary guards, wearing red cockades in their hats, roaming the streets, openly defying the police and troops of the provisional government. After three centuries of autocratic rule, the Romanoffs were reaping the whirlwind; and to Nick, the rain-washed palace of the former Grand Duke Cyril looked as if it were already under sentence of death.

The door was opened by a young man who wore a plain workingman's suit with an open, dirty shirt under the shabby jacket; gone were the eighteenth-century perukes and silk stockings Nick remembered from only seven months before.

"You're the American?" he asked in a tone that, while it wasn't exactly surly, was anything but deferential.

"Yes," said Nick. "The Grand Duke telephoned me at my hotel."

"There are no more grand dukes. The man living here *for the time being* is Citizen Romanoff. Come in, citizen. And wipe your feet."

Nick entered the marble foyer, removing the wet raincoat Bud Turner had lent him and holding it out to the servant—or whatever he was. The man pointed to a corner of the hall.

"Put it over there on the floor with your umbrella."

"I take it," Nick said as he did what he'd been told, "that one of the things tossed out with the revolution was good manners?"

"There will be no more servants in the new Russia. Every person waits on himself. The family is upstairs in the Red Room."

"Don't bother to show me. I know the way."

"I wasn't *going* to show you."

"I know."

Nick started up the monumental stairway. He understood that the old regime—inept and outdated as it was—had to go. But if this was a taste of the brave new world, it wasn't especially likeable. Bud Turner had told him the Soviets were gaining power in the city and calling for a Communist government and a "dictatorship of the proletariat." This was definitely not Nick Fleming's style.

At the top of the stairs, he turned to enter the red salon where he found the Grand Duke Cyril and his wife and daughter. Cyril still looked imposing as he stood beside his seated wife, but the former Grand Duchess Xenia and her pretty daughter, Tatyana, struck Nick as somehow shrunk in stature, as if the destruction of their glittering world had forced them into a shell of confusion and fear. If they were no longer grand dukes, bolstered by a tradition of centuries of privilege and authority, then what *were* they? Nick could understand the fury of the mob, but he also felt a surge of pity for Tatyana, who right now looked like nothing more than a scared teen-ager. History might be sweeping her into the trash heap, but the crimes of the Russian autocracy were hardly *her* fault.

Nick crossed the room to shake the hand of the former Grand Duke, who greeted him warmly and congratulated him on his release. Xenia poured him a cup of tea and Nick sat down to tell them of his seven-month imprisonment. Radix—whose real name was Valerian Ivanovich Sazanoff—had emerged since the revolution as one of the leaders of the Bolsheviks, a close colleague of Lenin's and one of the party's most articulate intellectuals. This Nick had found out from Bud Turner when he arrived in Petrograd. Now, Cyril filled him in further on Sazanoff's background.

"His father was a well-to-do merchant in Nizhni Novgorod," he said. "Sazanoff was a brilliant student and as a young man wanted to become an actor-playwright. He studied with Stanislavski in Moscow, and even though his plays were never successful, he began to acquire a reputation as an actor, specializing, ironically, as 'wicked' aristocrats in drawing-room comedies."

"Maybe," said Nick, "that's why he posed as Count Razoumovski on the ship. I had the feeling he was putting on a bit of an act."

"Undoubtedly," said Cyril. "He's always been something of a ham. But he became radicalized in Moscow, started writing revolutionary columns for underground newspapers, and was arrested by the Okhrana. That was about five years ago, as I recall. He managed to escape from prison, spent two years in Switzerland with Lenin, then returned to become editor of *Pravda*. It says a lot about the efficiency of the Okhrana that they were never able to find him. But I doubt very much that you'll be able to prosecute him for kidnapping you. The provisional government is too afraid of the Bolsheviks to try to indict one of their most prominent leaders."

"I know that," said Nick, "and I'm not interested in prosecuting anyone. All I want is to get out of Russia as fast as possible."

"I understand you're going to Stockholm tomorrow?"

"That's right. Then I'm taking a Swedish ship for London."

The wife and daughter had so far remained mostly silent, interrupting Nick's narrative only to ask a few questions. Now, as if prearranged, the Grand Duchess Xenia stood up and said, "If you'll excuse us, Mr. Fleming, my daughter and I have to check on the laundry. One of the exhilarating pleasures of the new regime is that Tatyana and I have learned how to wash clothes. We may even open a laundry soon."

Her tone was dry, but Nick felt the homely woman was doing her best to adjust. He kissed her hand, then shook Tatyana's. The girl smiled a rather timid smile and said simply, "I'll never forget dancing with you, Mr. Fleming."

That was all. But as Nick watched the two women leave the room, he thought Tatyana's remark was one of the nicest—and, under the circumstances, the most poignant—he had ever heard.

When the women were gone, the Grand Duke took a seat next to Nick and lowered his voice.

"May I be frank with you, Mr. Fleming?"

"Of course."

"As a member of the former Imperial family, I think I am being realistic when I say that my safety, as well as my wife's and daughter's, is—to put the best face on it—problematic. The Bolsheviks are clamoring for what they call 'people's justice'—which means the extermination of an entire class—and while so far Kerensky seems to be keeping them under control, my instinct is not to put too much faith in him. Only a fool would fail to see the parallel between what

90

is happening here in Russia and what happened in France. The moderates are in control now. But how far over the horizon is the Terror? So I've decided to act now, while I still have some freedom.

"You may have noticed that our servants have left us, with the exception of Misha, the young man downstairs, who used to be one of our stableboys but has now promoted himself to majordomo. Misha is a Bolshevik, and I'm certain he's been planted here in the house to watch our movements. The frustrating thing is that I can do nothing about him. Legally, this property is mine, but what does the law mean in Russia now? Nothing."

He paused to sip some tea, then continued.

"I feel I can trust you, Mr. Fleming, because you're an American, and as you have been a victim of Sazanoff's, I'm certain you're no friend of the Bolsheviks. I tell you—in confidence, of course—that I am making arrangements to take my family out of Russia. We will go either to the Crimea within the week or, if that proves too risky, we'll try to cross Siberia into China. Unfortunately, all my personal fortune is here in Russia, and with the war on, there's no way I can transfer any of my liquid assets out of the country, even if Kerensky permitted me to, which he wouldn't. Obviously, my country estate and this house, with everything in it, are"—he paused to glance around the room, and for a moment Nick thought he saw this remarkably reserved man's eyes mist—"nontransferable. God knows what will happen to them."

His eyes returned to Nick's. "My wife has a large collection of jewelry, and we are sewing as much of it as we can into the linings of our clothes. Whether we get the jewels out or not is questionable. We may have to use them to bargain for our lives."

He made the remark without emotion, but the effect was chilling.

"I've been searching for a way to insure ourselves, so to speak, and I'm taking the gamble that you may be willing to help us."

"Anything I can do, sir, I'll do gladly."

The Grand Duke seemed to relax.

"Good," he said. "I appreciate that. Please wait here a moment."

He stood up and left the room, returning two minutes later. He pulled a small chamois pouch from his coat pocket and handed it to Nick.

"This bag contains a number of precious stones," he said, "mostly diamonds, though there is one Burmese ruby that was given to my great-grandfather by Tsar Alexander I during the Napoleonic War. The ruby is famous in jewelry circles. It's called the Blood Moon

Ruby, and was taken from an Indian temple in the eighteenth century by an English soldier who later sold it to an agent of the Tsar. Its weight is eighteen carats, and I'm told it's one of the finest in the world. It's difficult to calculate the value of gems at a time like this, but I'm sure that in New York the ruby alone would be worth one hundred thousand American dollars. Have a look."

Nick loosened the mouth of the pouch and stared at the stones. He pulled out a large, round-cut diamond and held it up. As it was growing dark, the Grand Duke turned on an electric lamp. The diamond flashed blue-white fire.

"What I'm offering you, Mr. Fleming, is the Blood Moon Ruby in return for taking this bag of stones with you tomorrow and depositing it in the Bank of England. When—and if—my family and I get out of Russia, I will ask you to turn the jewels back to me. The Blood Moon would be your . . . commission, shall we call it? This way, even if we lose the jewels we're taking with us, we'll have something to start our new life with—wherever that may be. Will you do it for me?"

Nick returned the diamond, found the large ruby and held it to the light. Its color was a pure pigeon-blood red.

"I'd do it without the ruby," he said. Then he grinned at the Grand Duke. "But I'd rather do it *with* the ruby."

For the first time the Grand Duke smiled.

"I assumed a young American businessman would respect a business proposition," he said. Then he stood up. "Then we are agreed?"

Nick stood up and shook his hand.

"We are. But shouldn't I put the account in *your* name?"

"No. It might be confiscated by the English. Leave it in your name. I trust *you* more than I do the British government."

"I'm flattered, sir."

"Now I think you'd better go. Needless to say, don't let Misha see the pouch. I don't think he'd give you any trouble, but one never knows."

Nick put the pouch in his right pants pocket. The jewels created a bulge, but he figured he could hide it until he got his raincoat on.

"I wish you and your family luck, sir," he said.

The Grand Duke looked around the room again. "I've lived in a beautiful world. Perhaps there's no room for beauty anymore." He shrugged. Then he added, "At any rate, it's not a good time to be a Russian grand duke."

And he forced a smile. Nick admired his guts.

He went back down the stairs, wondering if he would ever see this enchanted palace again. When Nick reached the foyer, Misha stepped out of the shadows beside the marble staircase. He was holding a gun.

"Citizen Romanoff thinks me a fool," he whispered. "But I know why he asked you here. He's given you something to take to America, hasn't he?"

Nick stuck his hands in his pockets, affecting a look of cool indifference. "No," he said. Then he walked toward the corner, where his raincoat and umbrella still lay on the puddled floor.

"Whatever is in this palace belongs to the people of Russia," said Misha, his voice rising. "I insist you let me search you!"

Nick turned. He pulled his hands out of his pockets and held his arms out to the side, holding the chamois pouch in his right fist.

"All right, search me," he said.

Confused by this tactic, Misha started toward him, still holding the gun, though Nick noticed it was trembling, suggesting the young revolutionary was a bit nervous.

"Citizen Romanoff is an enemy of the people!" he said defiantly. "All the Romanoffs are!"

"Yes, I know. Would you mind hurrying up? I've got to get back to my hotel."

"What's in that bag in your hand?"

"Marbles."

Misha was standing directly in front of Nick now, less than two feet away, pointing the gun at Nick's belly.

"Give me the bag," he said, holding out his left hand.

Nick swung his right fist around, smashing it and the pouch of gems with all his strength into Misha's jaw. Simultaneously, he slammed his left fist against the gun, sending it flying across the foyer, where it clattered on the marble floor and slid to the wall. Misha howled in pain as he stumbled back. Using the pouch as a blackjack, Nick plowed his fist into Misha's nose. He could hear the cartilage crunch. Misha fell to his knees, groaning as he held both hands to his face. Blood was oozing through his fingers. Nick ran across the room, picked up the gun, then hurried back to grab his raincoat and umbrella. Misha watched him, tears in his eyes, his hands still shielding his blood-gushing nose. Nick aimed the gun at his head. Shall I kill him? he thought. If I don't, this sure as hell will put the Grand Duke in a tight spot. But Jesus Christ, he's just a kid. . . . I can't kill a kid, no matter if he *is* a bastard Bolshie. . . . The Grand Duke will have to fend for himself. . . . I'm doing all I can to help him anyway.

He backed to the door, still aiming the gun at Misha, whose eyes were full of terror. Nick opened the door, winked at Misha and said, "Happy revolution."

Then he hurried out into the rain, jubilant.

The cable from Alfred Ramschild that he had received the previous afternoon had read: "Thrilled and relieved you are safe. Have notified your mother. Arms shipment resold to England, but commission still yours as reward your valiant service to company. Proceed to London, via Stockholm. Will meet you Savoy Hotel Sunday the fifteenth."

The seven long months he had spent as a prisoner in the log cabin were paying off spectacularly. Not only did he have nine hundred thousand dollars in the bank, he had a hundred-thousand-dollar ruby. As he ran down the Moika Canal in the rain, it occurred to him that when empires crashed, there were always opportunities for the smart and the lucky to pick a fortune out of the rubble.

The only thing that troubled him was that there had been no mention of Diana in the cable.

"Is something wrong with Diana?" he asked the moment they had been seated at the table in the Savoy Grill in London. Alfred Ramschild looked a bit nervous.

"What makes you think that?"

"Well, you didn't mention her in your cable. She *is* all right?"

Alfred took a sip of water.

"No," he said. "Now, Nick, the doctors say she *will* be all right."

"*Doctors*? Then she's sick?"

"Not physically." He lowered his voice, looking around the crowded restaurant as if half expecting the entire room to be eavesdropping. "Arabella and I had no idea you and Diana were"—he hesitated, as if saying the truth was excruciatingly painful to him—". . . had been making love. Quite a few times, according to Diana—and without taking precautions. That was foolish, Nick. I'm not going to moralize, because of what you've been through . . ."

"She had a child?" he exclaimed, delighted to have become a father.

"Ssh! Not so loud."

"Mr. Ramschild, nobody's listening. And I'm going to marry Diana anyway, so the baby will be legitimate. And no one can blame us—"

94

"There *is* no child," Alfred interrupted. "Arabella forced Diana to go to Cuba for an abortion."

Nick winced.

"An *abortion?* Good God, why?"

"I'm not defending my wife. I think she was wrong, too, but Arabella couldn't stand the thought of Diana having an illegitimate child. Remember: we didn't know if you were dead or alive."

"But dammit, you killed my child! You had no right to do that!"

Alfred held up his hand in a peace gesture.

"But it's *done,* Nick. Right or wrong, it's *done.* And we have to live with the consequences."

"What consequences?"

"Diana's a very emotional woman. She was devastated when you disappeared, and then the abortion . . . Well, I won't pull any punches. She had a nervous breakdown. A rather severe one. She's been in a sanitarium in Hartford for five months."

Nick stared at him.

"You mean," he said softly, "she's crazy?"

"No, no—just severely emotionally upset. She's much better now. Dr. Sidney thinks she can come home in a few weeks, or perhaps a month. But we want to be extremely careful with her. Any sudden emotional shock might be a setback. That's why the doctor doesn't want to tell her about you just yet—at least until he's certain she can take the news."

"But . . ." He was confused. "How bad *was* she?"

"She was hallucinating, and then she'd go into severe depression. But, as I said, she's over that now. We have every reason to be confident—as long as we're careful. Will you trust me to handle it?"

"Pardon me for being blunt, but I think you've handled things pretty rottenly so far."

Alfred nodded. "I suppose I deserve that, and I don't feel happy about what's happened. In fact, I feel rather guilty. But I want to make it up to you, Nick, and the nine-hundred-thousand-dollar commission was just part of it. I want to make you vice president in charge of sales, as I said I would."

Nick said nothing. He was thinking of his green-eyed goddess, now in a sanitarium! He was thinking of his dead child.

"What was the baby?" he asked.

"A boy."

A son. His and Diana's son. He remembered that horrible November day sixteen years before when he had found out he was illegitimate and his mother had been arrested for prostitution. What if his mother had aborted him? His life would have been snuffed out before he had a chance to live it, and now this was exactly what had happened to his son. He could barely control his bitterness and rage.

"I ought to tell you to shove your job up your ass—but I suppose it wasn't your fault. Just don't expect me ever to be civil to your wife. As far as I'm concerned, she murdered my son for no better reason than to stop gossip. Plus she sent Diana to a sanitarium. Your wife's never liked me, Mr. Ramschild. But by God, the feeling's mutual now."

"Nick, I understand how you feel. What I'm trying to do is be the peacemaker for all of us. Now, let's order some lunch, and when you've calmed down, I'll tell you what I'd like you to do."

"Jesus Christ, tell me *now!* And I hope you're not going to send me off to Siberia again!"

"No, I want you to stay here in London, at least for a while. You know America's in the war now?"

"Yes."

"I've got the plant working round-the-clock because we've got millions of dollars' worth of orders. We're not only outfitting the French and English now, but the War Department in Washington as well. I could use you in London for the next month or so. We have a lot of business here, and it would release me to get back to the company. Will you do it, Nick? I know I'm in no position to ask you for favors, but it would be a great help. I've booked you a suite here at the Savoy. Of course the company will pay all your expenses."

Nick looked slightly disgusted.

"Mr. Ramschild, why the hell do you bother even asking me? You've already booked the suite."

"Yes . . . uh . . . Now, let's discuss your salary, Nick. And by the way, call me Alfred."

"I might have called your grandson Alfred. And before we discuss *anything,* I want to go home to see Diana."

"You can't! I told you she's in a sanitarium."

"Maybe the reason she's there is she thinks I'm dead! Alfred, she *needs* me! I *have* to go to her! I *want* to! I want to see Diana! I've been holed up in Russia for months, and I want to see the woman I love!"

"Nick, it's impossible for you to go to New York now. Please believe me—the doctor won't let you see Diana *for her own good!* Don't

96

you understand, the last thing she needs now is another severe emotional shock."

Nick scowled, drumming his fingers impatiently on the tablecloth.

"I think you're wrong. . . ."

"No, I'm not," interrupted Alfred. "The moment Diana's ready to see you and know the truth, *then* you can come home. It won't be long—perhaps next month. Meanwhile, stay here and help me out. Now, I've arranged for you to meet Lord Saxmundham. He's helping me put you together with a young man I think you'll find fascinating."

"Who?" Nick asked dully, his mind far away, thinking about Diana, thinking about his dead son.

"Winston Churchill."

Nick's eyes slowly warmed with a look of interest.

CHAPTER 9

SHE was the granddaughter of a duke at a time when English dukes were still held in almost reverential awe. Her maternal grandfather was the ninth Duke of Dorset, whose ancestor had earned his dukedom by being the bastard son of Charles II. The ninth Duke owned eighty-seven thousand acres and Dorset Castle, a brooding, pseudo-Gothic fortress that overlooked the English Channel on the Isle of Purbeck. Her mother, Lady Lettice, had been one of the reigning beauties of the nineties and a member of that group of highborn pseudointellectuals called the Souls. Her father, the second Viscount Saxmundham, was one of the richest, most powerful bankers in England. She was twenty-one, a beauty and engaged to Lord Rocksavage, one of the most eligible bachelors in the land, who was fighting in France. Few would deny that the Honorable Edwina Thrax-Farquhar had been born with just about everything a human being could reasonably want. A lot of people called her wild and headstrong. Others called her crazy.

Lord Saxmundham owned, among other things, an imposing town house in Belgravia, a sixteenth-century castle in Scotland and a gem of an eighteenth-century house in the Chiltern Hills called Thrax Hall. Thrax Hall had an interesting history. Originally an abbey, it had been burned and sacked by Henry VIII, who then gave the property to one of his most loyal commanders, Colonel Sir Merivale Thrax, along with eight hundred acres. Sir Merivale was a brilliant soldier, but he had contracted syphilis (by buggering a sheep, according to one legend, though the family denied this) and died a raving lunatic. The property was inherited by his nephew, but neither he nor his descendants exhibited any interest in the ruin for over two hundred years.

In the 1770s, General Sir Adrian Thrax, who had made a colossal fortune in India, decided it was time he impressed the world with his wealth. Admiring the French style, he hired a Parisian architect who built him an eighty-room stately home on the foundations of the abbey. The stone walls and graceful pediments of the new house looked inevitably more French than English, but the beauty of the palace, its façade reflected in a 120-foot pool with a 60-foot jet fountain, silenced the Francophobe critics of the day.

Sir Adrian had one daughter, Ariel, who married Robert Farquhar, an enterprising young fortune hunter who had founded the prospering Saxmundham Bank, named after the town of his birth, in Suffolk. Sir Adrian died of gout, and Robert, who adroitly hyphenated his name to Thrax-Farquhar, inherited the property. Ariel died in childbirth (she was said to haunt the west wing), and the property passed down through four generations to Maurice, the second Viscount Saxmundham, the father of Edwina. When, at her engagement party to Lord Rocksavage in June 1917, Edwina drank too much champagne and went for a nude midnight swim in the reflecting pool, the rumor quickly spread that she had inherited the Thrax "madness," referring not only to the lunacy of Sir Merivale Thrax but to a number of other dotty ancestors, including Lady Laetitia Thrax, who, in 1832, convinced she was a bird, had hurled herself from the roof of Thrax Hall. Edwina, who reveled in her family's odd history, thought the rumor was "delicious."

She had soft auburn hair, a perfect English complexion, large blue eyes and a profile one rhapsodic suitor had called "Grecian," though it was pure Anglo-Saxon. When in the country, she rode every morning; and at nine o'clock one Saturday in 1917, she dismounted in front of Thrax Hall, handed her horse's reins to a groom, ran up the stone steps, let herself into the entrance hall and looked with approval at the handsome young man in the Savile Row dark suit.

"Hello," she said, closing the massive door. "Who are you?"

"My name's Nick Fleming."

She noticed he wore a wristwatch, one of the few unlethal inventions to emerge from the Great War.

"Oh, yes, Father's talked about you. I'm afraid I don't approve of you."

"Why?"

"Father says you're making a fortune selling guns to the government, and I think anyone who makes money out of this horrid war should be shot—with one of your own guns, preferably."

"Your father's making money out of this 'horrid war.' "

"I don't especially approve of Father either. Banking's a grubby business too. All those boring interest rates and loans. . . . Are you spending the weekend?"

"Yes."

"Then don't expect me to be civil. On top of everything else, I don't like Americans. You all have ghastly accents and are money-mad. Aside from that, I'm sure you're perfectly charming."

"You're the daughter they say is crazy."

"Oh, I'm barking mad. Inherited, you know. The family tree *drips* with maniacs."

"Well, I don't think you're crazy. I think you're rude and stupidly opinionated."

She smiled. "You're absolutely right. I'm rude and *hideously* opinionated. Do you ride?"

"No. I hate horses."

"Good lord. What *do* you do, then?"

"I play a little tennis."

"There's a court behind the stable. Meet me there in half an hour. Jerome will get you a racquet—he's the butler."

She started up the stairs.

"I have a meeting with your father in ten minutes."

"Bugger Father. Oh, sorry—I forget. You're American. Business before everything."

She liked the way his jaw tightened.

"I'll be on the court in half an hour," he said tersely.

She caught the anger in his voice. Good, she thought. He hates me. Smiling to herself, she hurried up the steps.

Edwina didn't know the meaning of the word "bugger." All she knew was that it shocked people. Edwina loved to shock, so she used it as much as she dared, either as a verb ("Bugger Father") or a noun ("He's a horrible bugger"). If she had known it meant the act of sodomy, she would have had to have "sodomy" explained to her. Edwina was much less sophisticated than she thought she was, but in 1917 "sophistication" meant wearing lipstick, which Edwina had begun doing despite the protests of her mother, Lady Lettice.

She met Nick on the tennis court, purposely keeping him waiting ten minutes, and won the first serve.

"I suppose you think men are automatically better athletes than women?" she said.

"At some games. Baseball, for instance."

"That's such a stupid, boring game."

Nick merely shrugged as he took his position to return her first serve.

She aced him. Then she proceeded to win the first set, 6–1. Nick said nothing.

"Had enough?" she asked, coming up to the net.

"I'd go another set."

"I will admit you're a jolly good loser."

"Thank you."

"I don't mean to rub it in, but you know you're *really* just a beginner, and this isn't exactly fair to you. Not that I'm *that* good, but I have been playing for years. I'm worried about your male pride."

"I've been told the best way to improve is to play with people better than you."

"Oh, that's true."

"So if it's not too much of a bore, I'd really like to play one more set."

"Well . . ."

"And to spur me on to greater efforts, why don't we put a bet on it? Say, twenty pounds?"

She hesitated.

"That doesn't seem fair. . . ."

"I know you're thinking 'candy from a baby,' but money-grubbing American that I am, I really do need to be motivated. It would really help me concentrate." He smiled. "And if I win, I'll donate the money to the Imperial War Relief Fund."

"In *that* case, you're on."

He beat her, 6–0.

She was furious.

"You *cheat!*" she yelled. "You cad, you beast, you . . . You *bugger!* You're *good!*"

What made her want to throw her racquet at him was his laughing at her.

Having rescheduled his meeting with Lord Saxmundham for later in the day, Nick took a stroll around the grounds of the estate. He decided he liked Thrax Hall as much as he disliked Edwina, whom he considered a spoiled brat. But he had much on his mind. It had been months since Alfred Ramschild had left him in London to return to New York on a neutral Greek passenger ship, and Nick was still waiting for word about Diana. With increasing irritability, he bombarded Alfred with cables urging him to move matters along, but the answers were always the same: Diana was "improving," but the doctor was still "cautious." It was so frustrating, Nick began to wonder if this wasn't another plot on the part of Arabella Ramschild to keep her daughter away from him. He would tell himself that was crazy, no mother could be that vindictive. Then he would remember the abortion and tell himself maybe it *wasn't* so crazy.

The killing of his son rankled; he was consumed by hatred for Diana's mother and contempt for her father. As he brooded about it, it began to sour his feelings for Diana as well. After all, she had gone along with her mother's wishes. Admittedly the social pressures against unwed mothers were intense, but Diana had put up little resistance to Nick when he made love to her in the beach house, so she was hardly the conventional type, at least when it came to having fun. Yet when it came to the responsibilities of motherhood, apparently she became a lot more conventional. If she had put up a fight against her mother, it obviously hadn't been a successful one. As Nick walked down the side of the beautiful reflecting pool in front of Thrax Hall, he wondered what kind of woman Diana really was.

Of course, he loved her—there could be no question of that—and to love meant to forgive. He felt sorry for her, really, and told himself perhaps he was overreacting about the abortion. And yet, and yet . . . he couldn't help but view his green-eyed goddess in a slightly different and less flattering light than before.

It was then he saw Edwina come out of the house. She stopped on the stone steps of the mansion, a slight breeze fluttering her tweed skirt.

She might have been a spoiled brat, but as Nick looked at her, he marveled at her extraordinary beauty.

Lord Maurice Saxmundham, the second Viscount and chairman of the Saxmundham Bank, had inherited none of his family's "madness." A handsome man with a white moustache and a thick head of white hair, Lord Saxmundham's only folly was his passion for collecting first editions, and his collection was one of the finest in England. He had a much-valued first edition of Richardson's *Pamela,* a complete set of the Waverley Novels autographed by Scott, treasures by Balzac, Stendhal, Trollope and Dickens, a crumbling first edition of *La Princesse de Clèves* and Poe's personal edition of *The Fall of the House of Usher.* He housed the collection in Thrax Hall's handsome library, where, on shelves protected by elaborate bronze grilles, the tomes dozed through the decades, seldom, if ever, read by their proud owner. Lord Saxmundham—which he was always called by everyone except his family and a handful of intimates—bought to own, not to read. He was like a passionate wine collector who never drank wine.

A graduate of Eton (Pop) and Oxford (Christ Church), Lord

Saxmundham was an ardent Imperialist and a staunch Tory whose political views matched nicely those of the archconservative Prime Minister of some twenty years before, the Marquess of Salisbury (though his favorite Prime Minister was Lord Melbourne). The liberal direction English politics had taken before the war had outraged him, and he thought the imposition of the income tax a crime against nature. That such a quintessentially Victorian Tory could have produced a daughter like Edwina, who had actually sympathized with the Suffragettes, was a fact of life Lord Saxmundham himself could never have begun to explain. But perversely enough, of his two daughters, Edwina was the one he preferred; and when she barged into the library without knocking an hour after her tennis game with Nick, he looked up from *The Times* and smiled.

"Good morning, my dear," he said in a voice many compared to vintage Malmsley. "Mr. Fleming told me he played tennis with you."

Edwina had put on a tweed skirt and a bulky knit sweater, but Edwina could have looked fetching in a suit of armor. Now she came over to her father's chair and perched on the arm. The pale November sunlight through the tall windows caught the highlights of her auburn hair.

"Mr. Fleming cheated me out of twenty pounds," she said coolly. "He's no gentleman. I think you should send him packing."

Her father put down the paper. " 'Cheated' you? How?"

"By pretending he couldn't play tennis well, then beating me. I think he's despicable, and I'm appalled you'd have anything to do with him."

"I don't know anything about his tennis ethics, but Mr. Fleming has cooperated marvelously with the government, and I think you should bear that in mind. His company also keeps an account of over a half-million pounds in my bank. But aside from that, I rather like the young man. He's bright, aggressive and full of energy."

"A pushy American," she sniffed.

"Perhaps. But he's my guest, and I'll expect you to be gracious to him."

"Oh, I will," she said, standing up. "I'll be revoltingly sweet." She started toward the door.

Her father eyed her suspiciously. "Edwina," he said, "none of your tricks, if you don't mind."

"Oh," she said innocently, "I wouldn't *dream* of it."

Lord Saxmundham looked worried.

.   .   .

103

Edwina's initial impression of "the American," as she thought of him, might have been unfavorable, but that evening she found out two things about him that impressed her. The first was that he had power.

Edwina might flippantly criticize her father's profession, but secretly she relished the fact that he was a power in the Empire, and she enjoyed the powerful people he invited to Thrax Hall for weekends. She knew that one of the houseguests that weekend was—or, perhaps more accurately, had been—one of the most powerful politicians in England, and was even now, after the debacle of the disastrous Dardenelles campaign of two years before, still one of the most interesting, if controversial, members of the Liberal government. Furthermore, Winston Churchill had several things in common with Edwina. He also was the grandchild of a duke, the seventh Duke of Marlborough, and had been born in Blenheim Palace, the interior of which covered the staggering space of seven acres. Like Sir Merivale Thrax, Winston's father, Lord Randolph Churchill, had died of syphilis, though Lord Randolph had not caught it buggering a sheep. Rather, as an undergraduate at Oxford, he had been the innocent victim of one of the cruelest university pranks in history. At a party at Merton College, Lord Randolph had drunk a stirrup cup of champagne drugged by his classmates. The young man woke up in the arms of a toothless hag of a prostitute—his friends' notion of a joke. Horrified, Lord Randolph hurried to a doctor, but it was too late: the spirochetes were in his blood. Victorian medicine had no cure for syphilis, and in twenty years the relentless spirochetes would destroy his health, his sanity, his brief but brilliant political career and finally his life. His son Winston vowed the only possible vengeance: to forge for himself a political career as brilliant as his dead father's.

To achieve this, Winston seized every opportunity to force himself into the public eye. His mother, the beautiful American Jennie Jerome, had many powerful lovers, including the Prince of Wales, who, in 1901, became King Edward VII; Winston harassed his mother to pull every string to advance his career. His daring escape from a Boer prison camp, which he wrote up in English magazines, turned him into a popular hero. He used his celebrity as a springboard into Parliament, where his wit and energy kept him in the public eye. He became one of the youngest Home Secretaries in English history, and then, in 1911, one of the youngest First Lords of the Admiralty. At the outbreak of war, in 1914, he was in charge of the British fleet, the Empire's first line of defense.

He was forty.

This cometic career was short-lived. In 1915, as an answer to the bloody stalemate in the French trenches, Winston championed a naval attack on the Dardanelles. Turkey had come into the war on the German side; if the straits could be opened, badly needed arms could be shipped through the Black Sea to England's ally, Russia, and badly needed Russian grain could be shipped back to England. Turkey, "the Sick Man of Europe," could be knocked out of the war, and a back-door approach to Austria-Hungary and Germany, up the Danube, would be available to the Allies. The idea was brilliant; its execution was bungled. The attack by the British and Australians on the peninsula of Gallipoli was aborted by the Turks under the command of a young genius, Colonel Mustapha Kemal. Allied losses amounted to a slaughter, and the debacle was blamed on the First Lord, Winston Churchill. He was forced out of the Admiralty, his previous popularity soured to widespread scorn, and it was generally agreed his political career was over.

But it was unwise to count out Churchill. After a brief military service in Belgium and France, where he comported himself with his usual energy and undeniable bravery, he was recalled to London to serve as Minister of Munitions in the first Lloyd George government. From his office in the fashionable Hotel Metropole, in Northumberland Avenue, off Trafalgar Square, Churchill commanded twelve thousand civil servants comprising fifty departments; his responsibilities were guns, ammunition, railroads, airplanes and tanks—the latter an invention he himself had fathered. Quickly, Churchill galvanized a department that had been virtually moribund. That such a vital ministry could have been lackluster at a time when English soldiers were being slaughtered by the hundreds of thousands in France spoke volumes about the efficiency of the British High Command.

Knowing this, Edwina suspected it was no coincidence her father had brought Churchill and his lovely Scots wife, Clementine, together at Thrax Hall with a young American arms salesman. Something obviously was in the air. But what surprised her that evening as they all sat down together in the palatial dining room was the way Churchill, a notorious nonstop talker, seemed to lavish most of his attention on Nick Fleming, almost as if he were wooing the young American.

"Of course, it's a whole new war, now that the damned Bolshies have taken over in Russia," he said over the soup, his voice rumbling like the bass pedal of a cathedral organ. "They're taking Russia out of the war, which means Hindenburg can move his eastern armies to the Western Front, which can mean disaster—disaster!" He shook his head despairingly. "Our only hope now is you Americans, Fleming. Our *only* hope. But you know about the Bolshies, eh? Didn't they make you a prisoner a while ago? I realize President Wilson welcomed the fall of the Tsar, but I imagine even *he* must be reassessing the situation now, with Lenin in power. They're not to be trusted! I feel it in my bones; this Lenin is a menace. Mark my words: the day will come when Nicholas II, with all his faults, will look good in retrospect."

Nick, remembering the apprehensiveness of the imperturbable Grand Duke Cyril and the quiet despair of his wife and daughter, could only agree. He wondered if they had escaped, and, if not, what had become of them. Certainly, no one had yet claimed the bag of diamonds he had deposited in the Bank of England.

Churchill continued his monologue, bemoaning the war situation in general and consuming a goodly portion of Lord Saxmundham's Château Latour '07. When finally there was a lull in the conversation, Nick broached the subject that was his reason for being at the dinner.

"In my opinion," he said, "the greatest mistake of the English High Command has been to undervalue the machine gun."

"Definitely!" thundered Churchill. "They thought it was a toy. Damned fools thought my *tank* was a toy till I proved them wrong in France!"

"I'm told," Nick continued, "that eighty percent of the Allied casualties are caused by machine guns."

"True."

"I'm told that three Germans with one machine gun can hold off a battalion of English and French."

"I believe it."

"*But,* Mr. Churchill," Nick went on, raising his voice slightly, and Edwina sensed that "the American" was not without his own flair for Churchillian theatrics. "What if there were a *portable* machine gun? One light enough for individual infantrymen to carry instead of a rifle?" He paused to let the idea sink in.

Churchill frowned. "Is such a thing *possible?*" he asked softly.

Nick knew he was nibbling. "Right now," he continued, avoiding a direct answer for the moment, "each soldier is carrying seventy pounds of equipment, which makes it impossible for him to move fast. He carries a bayonet, which is for all intents useless in this war— he never gets close enough to the enemy to use it. His rifle is useless against a machine gun. The moment he leaves his trench, he's mowed down. But what if *he* had a machine gun? One that weighed seven pounds and could fire fifteen hundred rounds a minute. He would be mobile, and he would have the same firepower as the enemy. What if *thousands* of your men had such a weapon? The Germans wouldn't stand a chance."

Again, he paused. Clementine Churchill, Lady Lettice, Edwina and Winston were all staring at him. Lord Saxmundham stroked his moustache.

"I repeat," said Churchill, "is such a thing possible?"

Nick smiled slightly. "The head of our research department at Ramschild has developed a model. I have one upstairs. We could have it in production in six months. We think we can keep the price under one hundred pounds."

Churchill pounded his fist on the table.

"You rascal!" he roared. "Bring it down! Why didn't you *tell* me? Show it to me! Why didn't you *tell?*"

Nick laughed as he stood up. "Drama is as much the secret of salesmanship as it is of politics, Mr. Churchill," he said, and to Edwina's surprise, he shot her a mischievous wink as he left the room. Even Lord Saxmundham smiled, and Edwina realized her father was in on the conspiracy.

Two footmen entered the dining room and walked to the end of the room where they slowly drew open the navy-blue brocade curtains that covered the French doors opening onto the terrace. Floodlights were turned on, floodlights that Edwina realized had been specially installed for this "performance"—and it was turning into a performance.

Six German soldiers were standing on the lawn aiming their rifles at the French doors and the startled dinner guests. Lady Lettice let out a cry and almost dived under the table until her husband said, "They're cardboard cutouts, my dear."

Nick appeared on the terrace. He carried a strange-looking weapon with a circular drum on its top. He aimed at the cutouts and fired. The screaming, lethal chatter of the world's first submachine gun shrieked through the quiet English countryside. Edwina watched with fascination as the cardboard Germans were sprayed, chewed and bitten with death. In less than a minute, nothing was left but the wooden supports that had propped them up.

Then, still holding the smoking gun, Nick slowly and dramatically turned toward the dining room and aimed it at Churchill, who had risen from his chair, rapt. Nick, slim and handsome in his dinner jacket, eerily illuminated by the floodlights, holding this awesome new weapon, suddenly looked like the Devil himself. For an instant, Edwina wondered if he might not fire.

She knew from the tennis game that he was tricky. She knew from Churchill's attentiveness that he must be powerful.

Now she realized, with a rush, that he was exciting.

CHAPTER 10

EDWINA assumed England was the best country in the world and that she, being the granddaughter of an English duke, was one of the anointed of the earth. She worshiped the past, particularly the eighteenth century. She had been raised by a nanny, Mrs. Philpotts, whom she adored and to whom she was in many ways closer than she was to her "Mummie," Lady Lettice. Country life was her standard of all that was good, and horses and dogs were of vital importance to her. She was a moderately good shot (her father had given her a Purdey when she was sixteen), and she loved hunt breakfasts and fancy dress balls. She adored Beatrix Potter, Peter Pan, Bulldog Drummond and the Scarlet Pimpernel. Edwina still slept with her teddy bear at the age of twenty-one.

Typical of her class as she was, Edwina was still enough of a rebel to become interested in someone as different as Nick Fleming. Superficially, he was everything she disliked. He was American, and he was, even worse, "in trade"—and the arms trade, at that. And yet, as she hugged her teddy bear that night in her doll-filled bedroom on the second floor of Thrax Hall, she began to rationalize. Actually, *someone* had to supply the guns to beat the Germans, who were seeming to be almost unbeatable. Edwina had dozens of relatives, friends and acquaintances who had been killed in their prime: her distant cousins, Lord Elcho and his younger brother, Yvo Charteris; their brother-in-law, Raymond Asquith, the former Prime Minister's son; Rupert Brooke, whom Edwina had never met but whose poems she loved. . . . Godlike young men, the flower of a generation, butchered in the bloom of their youth—and for what? No one seemed to know anymore, as the senseless war dragged on, a tragic nightmare that had left all of England numb. Surely, if Nick Fleming's strange gun could shorten the war, he was to be admired. Certainly Mr. Churchill had been as excited as she at Nick's Wagnerian demonstration. And he *was* an American, and Americans *did* love business. And there was something fascinating about the whole mysterious world of international arms dealers, people like the Byzantine Basil

Zaharoff (who actually had been born in the slums of Constantinople and pimped as a child for Turkish brothels). Edwina had heard that Zaharoff was the man who was *really* running the war, and there was something riveting about that.

She wondered just how powerful Nick Fleming was.

When she finally fell asleep, she dreamed of a slim, handsome man holding a long, smoking gun.

When Diana Ramschild stepped out of her father's car and looked up at the pseudo-Tudor walls of Graystone, she burst into tears as she realized she was finally home. Then she saw her parents looking at her anxiously, and she told herself to stop crying. The pain was in the past: now she must be strong. *Strong,* or they might send me back . . . *strong,* or they might think me still—unstable.

"Welcome home, darling," said her mother, smiling and taking her arm. "I redecorated your room while you were away. I think you'll love the new wallpaper."

Wallpaper? thought Diana as she climbed the steps to the front door. When my love is gone? My son destroyed?

She had lost twenty pounds in the sanitarium, but her appetite was returning. The butler served a Beaujolais with the roast, and the first alcohol she had had in months relaxed her. After the dessert had been served, Alfred and Arabella exchanged looks. Arabella nodded, and Alfred said, "Diana, we have some good news for you, and Dr. Sidney has told me we can tell you."

"*Good* news?" she said dryly. "Well, that's a change. What is it?"

"Nick is in London."

She stared at him.

"Nick?" was all she said.

"Yes. He was released several months ago. He's in fine shape and very anxious to come home to you. We wanted it to be your welcome-home present."

Nick was alive!

She looked at the engagement ring she had never taken off her finger. Don't cry, she thought. Don't make a scene. Stay calm.

"How soon can you bring him home to me?" she asked.

"Not for some time," said her mother. "Dr. Sidney doesn't want you to get emotionally taxed."

"Emotionally *taxed?*" exclaimed Diana. "Doesn't he realize I'm in love with Nick and that not being with him is emotionally taxing?"

"Diana, you must keep control of yourself or we'll have to send you back to the sanitarium."

"Is that a threat?"

"Of course not, dear. We would never threaten you. But we have to consider your health above everything—including your wishes. Besides, it's time you took a more mature attitude toward Nick Fleming. At my insistence, your father hired a private detective to investigate Nick's background. It turns out he's not quite what he appears to be."

"What do you mean?" said Diana softly.

"Did he tell you his mother is Edith Fleming Clairmont?"

"Yes. . . ."

"That's only partially true. Mrs. Clairmont adopted him. His real mother was a certain Anna Thompson, a Russian Jewess who died in prison."

"Prison?"

"Yes. She was a convicted prostitute." She paused to let this sink in. "Now, in light of this, and in light of the fact that Nick never had the courage and honesty to tell you these rather fundamental facts about himself, don't you think it's time you reconsidered your engagement to him? I know that his classmates at Princeton didn't like him—they thought he was no gentleman. He barely made a club! Now, this is not the sort of man *I'd* wish my daughter to marry, though to be honest, I'll admit your father doesn't share my opinion."

"I couldn't care less what his mother was. . . ."

"She was a *whore*," interrupted Arabella forcefully. "A common *whore*."

Diana looked a bit shaken for a moment. Then she stiffened.

"I *still* don't care. I love Nick with all my heart."

Very well, thought Arabella. We'll try another tack.

"I'm so glad you called me," said Edith as she poured tea in the drawing room of her New York town house, into which Van had moved after their marriage. "Nick has written me about Diana, and she sounds so enchanting I'm dying to meet her."

"That won't be possible for some time," said Arabella, who was wearing a handsome pearl-gray suit. "Diana's doctor has insisted she have total rest and quiet for the time being."

"Yes, of course," said Edith, rather surprised by the coldness of the woman's tone. She smiled as she handed Arabella the teacup. "Then

111

the next best thing is to meet her mother. We should have met earlier."

"Mrs. Clairmont, I don't wish to present myself here under false colors. I am no champion of your adopted son. In fact, the main reason for my visit today is that I hope to persuade you to help me break up this engagement that has already cost Diana so much anguish."

Edith stared.

"Well, you certainly don't mince words. But why should either of us try to break off their engagement?"

"Your son is a great deal more sophisticated than Diana. I'm not saying that Diana is entirely blameless in what happened, but a girl with more worldly experience might have been less susceptible to your son's seductive, New York ways. I'm sure Nick would be happier with a girl more . . . urbane than Diana."

Edith's reading dropped to zero.

"Diana seems to have been urbane enough to let herself be seduced," she snapped. "And I have no intention of meddling with my son's engagement. My impression from his letters is that they're very much in love."

" 'Love' is one word for it. 'Lust' is another."

"The two generally go together."

Arabella put her teacup on the satinwood table and stood up.

"I see there's little point in continuing this conversation," she said. "It's obvious you share your son's rather casual morality, which doesn't surprise me. I'm well aware of your relationship with Van Nuys Clairmont before you became his wife. Now, more than ever, I'm determined to keep my daughter from marrying into this odious family."

Edith rose to her feet, her well-bred features stony.

"You *insufferable* woman," she said quietly. "The butler will show you out."

As she left the town house, Arabella smiled to herself. If *that* doesn't break up the engagement, nothing will, she thought. Edith Fleming Clairmont will move heaven and earth to keep her son from marrying into *my* odious family!

When Nick received the letter from Edith, he was so outraged that if Arabella Ramschild had been in his hotel suite he probably would have slugged her. To insult his mother, the woman who had given him everything in his life, the woman whose unfailing goodness and generosity had so dramatically changed his existence! Arabella had committed an act of open warfare that was perhaps even more infuriating than the abortion. As he paced about the living room of his suite that overlooked the Thames, Nick struggled in his mind to figure out a way to coexist with the woman. But it was no use. He hated her as much as she obviously hated him.

If he married Diana, it would have to be with the understanding that she would have to keep her mother out of his life. Arabella was no mother-in-law joke: she was a mother-in-law nightmare.

CHAPTER 11

Nᴜᴄᴋ was sitting in the bathtub of his suite at the Savoy reading *The Times* when he heard the phone ring. Getting out of the tub, he threw on a terry-cloth bathrobe and dripped his way into the living room where he picked up the receiver.

"Yes?"

"There is a young lady in the lobby who would like to see you, Mr. Fleming," said the hall porter. "The Honorable Edwina Thrax. May we send her up?"

"Give me ten minutes to get dressed," said Nick, hanging up the phone and wondering what the Honorable Edwina Spoiled Brat wanted.

It had been four days since Nick's weekend at Thrax Hall. Winston Churchill was fighting the Cabinet to commit to an order for the submachine gun, but, to Nick's annoyance, he was meeting stiff resistance. Neither Lloyd George nor the Imperial Staff seemed interested in another of Churchill's "miracle" weapons, despite the success of the tank in France. To Nick, this was further evidence of the pedestrian minds that seemed to be running the war. The only man on the Allied side Nick had met so far who possessed an undeniably first-rate intelligence was Churchill, and he was out of favor, if not totally out of power. The sad lesson seemed to be that the world was run by mediocrities.

But as Nick got dressed, he thought of Edwina rather than submachine guns. Her sudden appearance at the Savoy intrigued him. He had disliked the arrogant girl as much as she had seemed to dislike him. On the other hand, he had noticed that she had seemed rather impressed by him at the dinner and dazzled by his bravura performance with the submachine gun.

When Nick let Edwina into his suite, she seemed nervous. He wondered if it was because she had come without a chaperon.

"I want to apologize," she said without bothering to say hello.

"Why?"

"I was rude to you last weekend," she said, taking off her mackintosh. "I was being bratty, and I shouldn't have. I've decided you're not half as bad as I made out. I've even decided you're some sort of hero."

"Me? A hero?" He laughed. "No chance of that. I'm too mean. I was about to order some breakfast. Will you join me?"

"Tea would be lovely. I like your room. It must cost a fortune."

"It does," he said, ringing for room service. "But why am I a hero?"

She was at the window, looking out at the Thames. "Because you may shorten this terrible war. Or your submachine gun may."

"Not unless Winston can talk the War Office into buying it. Which doesn't seem likely."

She turned to look at him. "You mean they don't *want* it?" she asked, awe in her voice. "I can't believe they could be that stupid!" Then, to his surprise, tears appeared in her eyes. She sank into a chair and started sobbing. Nick, who thought this arrogant heiress had an icicle for a heart, was amazed.

"What's wrong?" he said, crossing the room to her.

She shook her head.

"Can I get you something?" he said softly.

Again she shook her head. There was a knock at the door, and Nick hurried to let in the waiter, relieved at the presence of a third party. He was feeling more than a little embarrassed by Edwina's mysterious tears.

"Good morning, sir," said the waiter, looking curiously at the sobbing girl. "Breakfast?"

"Yes. Two poached eggs, bacon, toast and coffee. And tea for the lady."

"Very good, sir."

Nick closed the door behind the waiter and went back to Edwina. She was drying her eyes.

"George was killed in France," she said. "We found out last night."

"I'm sorry, but who's George?"

"My fiancé, Lord Rocksavage. He was young and dashing and not very bright, I suppose, but . . ." She sighed. "He's dead. What a waste. What a stupid, horrible waste." She looked up at Nick. "I was very much in love with him. At least, I *think* I was. And now he's dead. I just can't get used to the fact that he's gone, that I'll never see him again. He was machine-gunned. That's why I thought of you. Maybe if he'd had one of your guns, he'd have had a chance."

"Maybe."

"That's why I came to apologize to you." She hesitated. "No, that's a lie. I wanted to see you again."

"Why?"

"I honestly don't know. But the first person I thought of when I heard about George was you. Isn't that odd?"

He looked at her, seeing the human being for the first time.

"I'm very flattered," he said quietly.

And he meant it.

"What will you do now?" he asked as he buttered his toast. She was sitting on the opposite side of the beautifully laid table, sipping her tea in morose silence.

"I don't know," she said. "But I want to do *something*. I've thought about joining the war effort, perhaps becoming a nurse. Except I don't think I could bear seeing wounded men. I may look strong, but I really can't stand the sight of blood. But I *do* want to do something."

She put down her teacup, then tossed her head back defiantly.

"No, that's a lie," she said, her eyes daring him to say something. "I came here because I'm horribly lonely and I wanted to throw myself at you. There . . . that's the truth, and I don't give a damn what you think of me."

He continued chewing his toast, eyeing her with new interest.

"I suppose you think I'm some sort of vamp?" she went on. "An English Theda Bara?"

"Well, I don't know. Just what did you have in mind?"

"Making love, of course. I hope you don't think I'm a virgin!" She made the word sound like "leper." "George and I were going at it like dogs in heat before he went to France. And, frankly, I miss it like the very Devil. Something tells me you'd be a terrific lover." She paused, watching him. "Well? Do you want me to leave? Or should I go in the bedroom and get deliciously nude?"

He poured a cup of coffee. "Before I make this earth-shattering decision," he said, "I think you should know I'm engaged to be married."

"Oh." She looked surprised, then totally crestfallen. "You're in love with someone else?"

"Yes." Or *am* I? The thought swirled through his brain as he looked at this undeniably tempting girl.

"Oh, dear, I've really made a fool of myself, haven't I? And all for nothing. You won't tell Father?"

"Word of honor. But were you serious? Did you really want to go to bed with me?"

She studied him a moment and suddenly she looked very vulnerable.

"Yes, I was serious," she said simply. "Maybe it's the war. Life seems so cheap all of a sudden. Who knows who will be alive tomorrow? And I thought how exciting you were the other night, and I thought, Yes, I want him for my lover—if only for a moment. I suppose that's terribly decadent of me, isn't it?" She looked at him nervously. He was devouring her with his eyes.

"You know something? I think you *are* a virgin."

She looked shocked. Then, shamefacedly, she nodded yes.

He suppressed a laugh. She was funny, in a way, but she was also rather poignant. To his total surprise, he found he liked her; and he couldn't take his eyes off her. He felt momentarily ashamed at betraying Diana even in his mind. But then he remembered that Diana had betrayed him by killing his son, and he remembered Arabella's rabid anti-Semitism and her attack on his mother. Was Diana what he really wanted, after all? Yes, he had fallen in love with her, but that was a long time ago and it had been his first love. Could a first love be trusted? For that matter, was there any such thing as eternal love?

"You must think me a silly ass," she said, standing up. "I *do* apologize, and I won't take any more of your time." She looked at him a moment, then started across the room to the door.

"No," he said. "Don't go."

She stopped still. Then, very slowly, she turned.

He got up from the table and came to her. "This is probably a mistake for both of us," he said softly. "But I have an odd feeling it's one we're not going to regret."

He took her in his arms and kissed her. As with Diana, he felt an intense desire in her firm body. Then, suddenly, she pushed him away.

"Oh, my God, I *can't!*" she gasped. "Dammit, I don't have the nerve after all!"

And she ran to the door and slammed out of the room so fast he burst into laughter.

But when he stopped laughing, he realized he wanted the Honorable Edwina Thrax with every nerve end of his body.

"But *why?*" cried Diana Ramschild, and it was the cry of a wounded animal. "Why does he have to wait two more weeks?"

"Diana, he says it in the cable!" exclaimed her father. "The Cabinet has yet to make a decision on the submachine gun. It's a contract worth millions—"

"I don't *care* about submachine guns and I don't care about contracts! I want Nick!"

She burst into such violent sobs, burying her face in her hands, that Arabella and Alfred exchanged worried looks. The cable, which had arrived minutes before, had struck with the force of lightning.

"Diana, it's just *two weeks*," said her father. "You have to be mature about this. The war is taking millions of lives, and if this agreement can shorten it by one day, it's worth all Nick's efforts."

She straightened, wiping her teary face with a napkin. Suddenly she was calm again. Deadly calm.

"It's not the war," she said softly. "Something's happened. I haven't had a letter from him for two weeks. He's met someone."

Arabella's hopes soared.

"You mean you think there's another woman?" she said, feigning concern.

"It's been a year since I've seen him. I'm losing him. I can *sense* it." She looked at her father. "Father, you're going to London next week. I'm going with you."

"Don't be absurd!" said her mother. "Dr. Sidney would never let you travel. Besides, it's dangerous! There are torpedoes. . . ."

"It's a neutral ship, and you're not going to stop me, Mother. Nor is Dr. Sidney. I'm going to London to save my love."

She put down her napkin, got up from the table and left the room. If only she's right, thought Arabella. If only there *is* someone else!

Time was doing for Arabella what all her conniving and prayers had failed to achieve.

When Nick received the cable announcing Diana's imminent arrival, he was thrown into an emotional hurricane. By now, he knew the truth: the passionate love he had once felt for Diana he now felt for Edwina. A combination of events had killed his love for Diana—their long separation, the abortion, Arabella's viciousness—or was it simply that Edwina had intoxicated him? At the same time, he didn't want to hurt Diana.

"What in God's name can I say to her?" he asked Edwina as the two of them walked down the Thames Embankment through a November drizzle.

"I suppose you'll have to tell her the truth: that you don't love her anymore."

Nick groaned as the mist dripped off his hat's brim.

"Yes, that sounds so simple and easy. But I have an idea she's not going to take it so simply and easily."

"But engagements get broken all the time."

"So do hearts. This is going to hurt Diana, and I don't *want* to hurt her, but I don't know what else to do."

Edwina took his hand.

"You really *don't* want to hurt her, do you?" she said tenderly. "I think that's sweet. So many men would just say ta-ta and be off like a shot. But you really want to protect her."

"Yes, protect her against *me*. *I'm* the problem."

"No, *I* am," said Edwina, squeezing his arm.

In the past several weeks, they had been together a dozen times, Nick wining and dining her in London at all the best restaurants. They had kissed and petted as the relationship became increasingly physical. Nick had, in his opinion wisely, not tried to go further, remembering her performance that first day in his hotel suite. But they were wild about each other. The girl he had originally thought of as a spoiled brat he now found funny and fun, fresh and exciting. They both got a kick out of reading about themselves in the London society pages, where he was billed as a "young American munitions salesman" and she "one of the great beauties of her generation," which Nick wholeheartedly agreed with. As for Edwina, Nick filled her thoughts night and day.

"If you hadn't met me," she went on, "you'd still be in love with Diana, so let her hate *me*. And I don't feel the least bit guilty taking you away from her. In fact, judging from the way I threw myself at you, I must be brazen and shameless."

He smiled at her.

"I like you brazen and shameless."

"Anyway, darling, try not to agonize over Diana. I know what you must be going through, but life is a jungle, and I turned out to be the better hunter. *I* bagged the tiger!"

Again, she squeezed him. Big Ben above them bonged three. Yes, life is a jungle, he thought.

But he still dreaded confronting Diana.

He met Alfred and Diana as they got off the ship at Southampton. He was polite, and no bystander would have thought anything was wrong with the scene, but Diana knew it was *all* wrong. She knew when he kissed her: it was no lover's kiss, there was no passion in it. During the train ride up to London, Nick and Alfred talked business as Diana sat beside her father fighting back her anxiety and fears.

When they were finally alone in his hotel suite, she took his hand.

"Are you glad to see me?" she asked.

"Of course." He was still avoiding her eyes.

"What is it, Nick? Something's happened. I can tell. *Look* at me."

Now he turned his eyes on her.

"I should have sent you a cable, except it's not the sort of thing that sounds very good in a cable. As far as that goes, it doesn't sound very good saying it. But it has to be said. I've met someone else, Diana."

She closed her eyes, tight.

"Who?" she whispered.

"An English girl. Her name's Edwina."

"Lord Saxmundham's daughter?"

"Yes. I've fallen in love with her. Very much in love."

She opened her eyes.

"I seem to remember you were very much in love with *me*."

"Yes, I know. I'm sorry, Diana. Truly sorry. And I know nothing I can say can . . ."

"Was it the abortion?" she interrupted. "Nick, I didn't have any choice! They made me do it—Mother and Father—they terrified me! They said if you were dead, I'd never be able to get a husband! Oh, please, darling, forgive me! I went through hell! I love you, Nick, with all my heart! I want you! I *need* you! Oh, God, darling, don't hold the abortion against me. Don't not love me."

She looked pitiful, and his heart was aching.

"I don't hold the abortion against you," he said. "I was angry when I heard about it, but I suppose you did what had to be done. It's just that"—he gestured helplessly—"I've fallen in love with somebody else."

Her green eyes became feral.

"We're engaged to be married, in case you've forgotten."

"I haven't forgotten. I'll have to ask you to release me."

"My God," she said, "my mother was right about you after all! And what happened to our love that was supposed to last forever? Our *eternal* love? 'Oh, Diana, we're the lucky ones'—I remember you saying that, and I was stupid enough to listen! Stupid enough to *believe!* But along comes the first pretty face, and poor old Diana's out the window! Isn't that right, Nick?"

"Look, I'm not pretending to smell like a rose in this . . ."

120

"A rose? You smell like *garbage!* Like rot, you smell like the son of a *whore!*" He stiffened. "Oh, you never bothered to tell me about *that,* did you? Never told me the *truth!*" She was screaming now. "Son of a *whore!* You *act* like it! I hate you—hate you!" She started sobbing. "I'll pay you back for this. You'll never forget me! You'll pray you never *met* Diana Ramschild! I gave myself to you; I gave you my love. I trusted you . . . you garbage! You whore's son!"

"Diana . . ."

"Don't SPEAK!" she screamed. "Don't ever say another word to me! I never want to hear your lying voice again! But you'll *never* forget me. I promise you, Nick Fleming, I'll haunt you to your damned *grave!*"

Now she stopped crying. Suddenly, she was icy calm, her emotion freezing to pure hatred. She walked to the door and opened it. Then she turned to take one last look at him. "I'm photographing your face in my memory," she said. "How I loved it once. I thought it was the most beautiful face in the world. Now it disgusts me!"

She pulled off her engagement ring and threw it on the floor. Then she walked out of the room, leaving the door open.

Nick walked over, picked up the ring and looked at it. "Son of a whore" was still ringing in his ears.

He had hurt her, but she had managed to hurt him.

"How could you have done that to her?" yelled Alfred Ramschild ten minutes later as he charged into Nick's suite, his fat face red with anger. "You *knew* she's been in a sanitarium. . . . She came back to our suite in hysterics! I had to get the house doctor to sedate her! Damn you!"

"Alfred, I tried to be reasonable with her. . . ."

"I'm holding you to your obligation, Fleming! You're engaged to my daughter—you're not backing out now."

"You go to hell!" Nick shouted, his own nerves finally giving out.

"If you back out, you're fired!"

"I'm way ahead of you, Alfred. I quit!"

"I made you a rich man—"

"Now, wait a minute. You risked *my* neck sending me to Russia to save your fat ass! How about those seven months I was a prisoner? I could have been killed"—he snapped his fingers—"like that. So I don't want any more scenes, Alfred. I liked you, and I loved your daughter—*once.* I'm sorry for Diana. I know I've hurt her, and I accept full responsibility for being a bastard. I am—as she pointed out several times—the son of a whore, I'm no gentleman, I'm whatever. But it's over. I have other plans."

"Such as?"

"That's none of your damned business."

The fat man's face had been getting redder. Now, suddenly, he jerked his head back and started gagging. He put both his hands to his temples and clutched his skull.

"Alfred . . ."

Nick hurried over to support him, for Alfred had started to sway.

"My head," he was gurgling, "something . . . in my head . . ."

"Sit here—I'll get a doctor."

He eased him into a chair. Alfred's face was now turning white.

"Doctor with Diana . . ." he whispered.

"I'll be right back."

By the time Nick got back to the suite with the doctor, Alfred Ramschild was sprawled on the floor, dead of a cerebral hemorrhage.

Nick felt terrible about Alfred's death and even a certain amount of guilt—for the rage that brought on the lethal hemorrhage had been directed against him. He wanted to talk to Diana again, to try to console her; he didn't want their final moments together to be the bitter shouting match that had developed. But she refused his calls. The hall porter told him she was under heavy sedation, and that preparations were being made to ship Alfred's body home to America for burial.

For the next five days, he kept pretty much to himself, taking long walks through London as he thought out his life. At first, his spirits were low, weighted down by guilt and worry about Diana and his entire involvement with the Ramschild family. But as time passed, his natural high spirits began to reassert themselves. Maybe it was all for the best, at least for him. He was free now, free to try something new in life. He was still young and a millionaire. And he was in love. The past was over; the future was beginning to look rosy in his mind.

The day after Diana checked out of the Savoy to return to America, Nick drove out to Thrax Hall, where he had made an appointment with Lord Saxmundham. When he pulled his car in front of the eighteenth-century mansion, he saw Edwina coming out of the house. She hurried across the gravel drive to hug him.

"I missed you," she said. "Father told me all about Mr. Ramschild. I'm sorry about that, but how did it go with Diana?"

"About as badly as possible. She hates me now. I suppose she has good reason . . . I don't know."

"What do you want to see my father about?"

"A business proposition. Then I want to talk to you."

"I'll be in the Red Room."

The Red Room, named for its spectacular red Savonnerie carpet, was one of the four main reception rooms in Thrax Hall and had been called one of the most beautiful rooms in England. When Nick came in forty-five minutes later, Edwina was curled up in a chair leafing through a copy of *Country Life*. It occurred to Nick there was something childlike about her, which was part of her enormous appeal to him.

He came over to her chair, took her face in his hands and kissed her.

"Mmm," she said. "I liked that. What was this mysterious business proposition you made to Father?"

He pulled up a stool and sat next to her.

"I've decided to become a private investor in New York, working with my own money and bringing in partners on certain deals. I thought your father might be interested, and he was."

"What kind of deals?"

"Real estate. Stock. New York's a hot spot for investments these days."

"It sounds exciting."

"Well, it may not be as exciting as the gun business, but maybe it'll be a little less bloody. I also talked to him about you."

She looked stunned.

"You *did?*"

"Uh-huh. I told him I was going to propose to you. I told him everything about myself—all the warts, the works—so, on the wild chance that you might accept me, I wouldn't have a fight with him. To my amazement, it turns out he rather likes me."

"Well, why *shouldn't* he?"

"A lot of reasons. Anyway, here I am, and here you are. How about it?"

"Oh, I've never *heard* of such an uninspired proposal! You're *supposed* to do it on your knees, and you're supposed to tell me all sorts of romantic things, like how much you love me and how you can't live without me, and that if I don't accept you, you'll drown yourself in the Thames."

"All right." He knelt in front of her and clasped his hands to his heart.

"Fair Edwina, one of the *great* beauties of your generation, daughter of an ancient and noble house who has won my heart and love, wilt thou accept the proposal of this miserable American peasant for thy hand in marriage?"

She giggled.

"Rise, fair Nick, who is much too cocky for his own good. Even though you are an American, and even though you're making fun of me, I accept your proposal because I'm mad for you."

He got to his feet, took her in his arms and kissed her.

"And I'm mad for you," he whispered, and he meant it.

Diana's face flashed through his mind for an instant, then vanished. His first love was over.

They were married three weeks later at St. Margaret's in Westminster, the parish church of the House of Commons. There were four hundred guests, the vast majority friends and relatives of Edwina's family. Edith came from New York and was entranced with her new daughter-in-law, whose wedding present from her groom was a diamond necklace with the Blood Moon Ruby as its centerpiece. Winston and Clementine Churchill were wedding guests, along with half the Cabinet, the powerful of the financial community, three dukes, fourteen marquesses, twenty earls, and a pride of viscounts and barons. Edwina's bridesmaids included her younger sister, Louise, and five daughters of the nobility. The bride looked breathtaking in white satin; she carried a bouquet of orange blossoms. The reception was held in Lord and Lady Saxmundham's town house on Wilton Crescent, and fifty cases of Louis Roederer Cristal were drunk by the war-weary guests. Everyone agreed it was the wedding of the year.

Their honeymoon was a trip to New York, and they sailed that night from Southampton on the Swedish liner *Gustavus Adolphus.* The ship sailed at 10 P.M. in a heavy storm, and by the time they were ready to make love, the liner was pitching and pounding.

"I'm not going to be seasick on my wedding night," Edwina announced firmly as she went into the bathroom of their suite to change.

"I certainly hope not," Nick replied as he sat on the bed to take off his shoes. Then he got undressed and climbed into the big bed naked, sitting up, watching the bathroom door, fantasizing with anticipation what was about to happen.

When she came out of the bathroom, she was wearing a white peignoir.

"Take off that damned peignoir," he said. "I want to see you."

"You're about as romantic as a lumpfish. Mother gave me this for tonight, and she told me men like to be enticed."

"I'm enticed. Now, take it off."

She came up to the bed and unbuttoned the peignoir.

Removing it, she let it slide down her silky body. He watched from the bed as she moved toward him. He admired her long legs, her slim boyish hips, her long torso and beautifully shaped breasts. Her skin was Devonshire cream.

"You're lovely," he whispered.

She climbed in bed beside him, admiring his hairless chest. Her eyes traveled down to his muscular stomach. Just below his navel, a thin line of black hair began, leading down to something she had never seen in her life.

"Is *that* what it looks like?" she whispered, amazed. "It's huge! And it's rather ugly. . . . May I touch it?"

Nick, whose erection was throbbing, nodded. She reached out and gingerly caressed him.

"Ahhh . . ." he sighed, pulling her into his arms, beginning to kiss her passionately. She reveled in the warmth of his hard body, loving his broad shoulders and muscled arms and back.

She felt him enter her. It was a strange sensation, one she wasn't sure she was going to enjoy; but she was enjoying his hot kisses, enjoying his smell. There was an animal side to him that was arousing her own animal instincts. George, Lord Rocksavage, had been an animal too, a magnificent animal in appearance at least, but George had been too civilized ever to arouse in her this wonderful, mad rapture of the flesh. Suddenly, she was no longer aware of the screaming wind outside the ship, or the pounding of the hull against the waves. Suddenly she was aware only of him, her husband, her lover, who was awakening a million nerves inside her with his lust.

He was kissing her breasts now, sucking her nipples, which became stiff with desire as his tongue caressed them. Then he kissed his way up to her neck as he slowly pressed his hard stomach against her soft one, again and again with the rhythmic intensity of a slow dance.

"Lovely," she moaned. "Oh, Nick, it's lovely . . ."

Now his mouth was against hers again, open, his tongue exploring, probing. She wanted to lick every inch of his body.

And then, thought gave way entirely to desire as her body seemed to turn inside out with passion, and nothing else in the world mattered until she achieved that sweet summation her body was starving for. She dug her nails into his buttocks as it happened, and she shrieked with pleasure.

"Oh, my God," she gasped as he pulled out of her. "It's better than clotted cream!"

With which they both started laughing like happy, antic, naked children. The fantasy had become flesh.

"I'll pay him back some day," Diana Ramschild said. Both women wore black veils. They were returning to Graystone after burying Alfred in the family mausoleum. "First he jilted me, then he killed Father."

She spoke softly, but her black-gloved fists were clenched. "I'll pay him back—if it takes the rest of my life."

"The Jews" was all her mother said.

Part II

MOVIE
MADNESS
AND MAYHEM
1922

CHAPTER 12

For Edwina, the daughter of one of England's richest and best-connected families, to marry a young American of no particular distinction raised many titled eyebrows. It had become accepted for English peers to marry American heiresses (Churchill's mother was American); still, the reverse was something new. But the fact was that Lord Saxmundham not only liked and admired his son-in-law, he also saw him as a potential New York-based agent for the Saxmundham Bank, an idea actually suggested by Nick. By 1917, it was apparent to any English banker not afflicted with myopia or rampant jingoism that New York had replaced London as the world's financial capital. The scheme worked out by Nick and his father-in-law was that Nick would operate out of a small New York office, looking for attractive American investments that he would finance with his own money and the Saxmundham Bank's. During the next five years, this actually happened. While it's true that it's difficult not to make money when you have money, it's also easy to go broke. It was a tribute to Nick's astuteness that he made millions for his father-in-law's bank by investments in real estate, hotel deals and radio stock, quadrupling his own fortune in the process.

Meanwhile, he and Edwina became known as one of New York's most popular young couples. Nick rented a large Park Avenue apartment where he and Edwina entertained at fast-paced, fast-drinking parties. Edwina's beauty and Mayfair accent flung open the doors of Anglophilic New York society, and Nick's reputation as a hotshot deal maker, as well as his access to the investment millions of the prestigious Saxmundham Bank, attracted the Wall Street crowd in hungry swarms. Edwina, who had formerly been so contemptuous of "money-mad" Americans, fell as headlong in love with the jazzy excitement of postwar New York as she had with her dashing husband. And the first four years of their marriage seemed to be one long party, interrupted by three pregnancies. In 1919, their first child was born, a son they named Charles. In 1920, along with Prohibition and the vote for women, came a daughter, Sylvia. And in 1921, with almost clocklike regularity, a second son, Edward.

Along with the rest of the world, Edwina had developed a passion for the movies. She even toyed with the idea of acting in one, which Nick had laughed at, even though she began taking the idea more and more seriously. Thus in 1922, when Nick casually asked her if she'd like to go with him to California, she leaped at the idea. He was going to look at the Napa Valley, possibly to buy a vineyard, but he was also going to Los Angeles and promised to show his wife a movie studio, which sent her into ecstasies.

A week later, after a luxurious train ride across the country to San Francisco, they climbed into a rented limousine and were driven north to the Napa Valley where they had an appointment with an elderly Italian named Salvatore Gaspartelli, who was waiting for them on a hilltop next to his battered Model T Ford. Both Nick and Edwina were impressed by the beauty of the valley stretching below them, and which was, thanks to an unusually rainy winter, now lushly verdant.

"But it will be brown by June," Gaspartelli said. "From April to October—no rain at all. All dry, brown. But it's good for grapes. It makes them *strong*."

Nick nodded absently. He was wearing a Glen-plaid suit and a splendid *fino fino* Panama hat, of which he was justly proud. Edwina, who had abandoned her tweedy country look to become one of the world's best-dressed women, had on a Chanel suit and a broad-brimmed black straw hat.

"How many acres?" Nick asked.

"Seventy-five," Salvatore Gaspartelli replied. He was sixty-three and had come to California in the 1880s to plant his beloved vines. His vineyard had prospered until, three years before, passage of the Volstead Act had ushered in Prohibition. Now Gaspartelli, like many California wine makers, was broke, forced to sell at bottom dollar the land he loved so passionately. For Salvatore, this was one of the worst days of his life.

"The best vines grow on the hills," he continued, forced to make a sales pitch. "The vines in the valley not have to work. They get lazy, so they produce lazy grapes. Up here, it's tough for vines to survive. They work hard, grow strong, give the best grapes."

"The people in the valley say just the opposite," remarked Edwina.

"What do *they* know?" Salvatore growled. "*I* know grapes! I tell you, the best is up here."

130

Nick looked at the vines, all neatly cut back, climbing up the steep hill to the top under a lowering sky. Nick had read enough about wine growing to know the Italian was probably right. He also knew that the Gaspartelli Winery had some of the best soil in the valley, its Cabernet Sauvignon and Chardonnay grapes produced some of the best wine in California, and that Salvatore Gaspartelli owed the Bank of San Francisco six thousand dollars, which he had no hope of repaying. He was asking thirty thousand dollars for the seventy-five acres, which was a steal. Nick knew he could get it for even less. It took no genius to realize that ultimately Prohibition was doomed to failure. Some day this winery would be operating again and the land would be worth a fortune. Nick looked to the long run.

For the next hour, he walked the land with Salvatore as Edwina sat in the Rolls, reading *Movie World* magazine. Finally Nick returned, telling the chauffeur to head back to San Francisco. He shook Salvatore's hand, then climbed into the back of the Rolls next to Edwina. As the big, heavy car rumbled down the dirt road, sending up a cloud of dust, Edwina said, "Well? Did you buy it?"

"I'm still thinking about it."

"I have no idea why you'd want to buy a winery when it's illegal to make wine."

"That's the time to buy."

"Who drinks California wine anyway? Why don't you buy a château in France?"

"I may some day. Right now, I'm interested in California."

Edwina, having no interest in wineries, went back to her movie magazine. She paid little attention to Nick's perpetual deals anyway, business being a mystery to her. What interested Edwina were her children, shopping, parties, movies and making love. She could have been accused of being hopelessly superficial, but she was young and why not? To Edwina, life was a perpetual adventure. Like Nick, she wanted to try everything before she died, and it was this as much as anything that he loved in her.

They were almost halfway back to San Francisco when he said, very casually, "What if I told you your father and I have made an offer of two hundred thousand dollars for Metropolitan Pictures studio?"

She put down her magazine and looked at him. After four years of marriage and three children, she was still immensely attracted to him physically, although their marriage, like most, had been punctuated with fights. Nick, she had found, was an intensely—almost insanely—

jealous man. Though this had its appealing side, it also tended to be a bit stifling and was the cause of numerous quarrels. But right now, he looked beautiful.

"Oh, Nick, *darling!*" she exclaimed, throwing her arms around him and kissing him. "You madman! Why didn't you *tell* me?"

"It's your surprise birthday present. Happy birthday."

"What a perfect present! I *adore* it! And will you let me act in a film?"

"I could hardly say no to the wife of the studio owner."

She looked dazzled.

"A movie star!" she whispered. "Wouldn't it be marvelous if I became a star? And Nick, I know I'm good! I just feel it inside me that I'd be a wonderful actress. Besides, everyone knows me anyway. I mean, God knows we get tons of publicity already, and how many granddaughters of dukes go into films? Oh, Nick, it's going to be so much *fun!* I *adore* you!" She kissed him again.

"Then I think I'll buy the vineyard."

"Oh, go ahead—who cares *now?* Movies!" She batted her eyes and struck a movie-queen, Nazimova-style, pose. "All the men in the world will fall in love with me and it will be trashy and vulgar and *fun!*"

"And expensive, if your movies flop."

She stuck out her tongue. He laughed. No impartial observer could ever doubt that the Flemings were really madly in love.

It would have been unnatural if a man with the ambition, greed, sense of adventure, money and financial connections of Nick Fleming had not become interested in Hollywood, because by 1922 Hollywood was the undisputed film capital of the world, and movies were big business. This was not true a few years earlier. Before the Great War, Hollywood was merely one of many movie centers, competing with New York, New Jersey, Berlin, London, Paris, Rome and Stockholm. The lure of sunshine and evasion of the Patent Trust finished the East Coast film making, and the war finished European film making. After the Armistice, Hollywood suddenly found itself almost without competition, with a worldwide audience of avid fans seeking escape in its silent confections, which could be equally enjoyed and understood in Shanghai, New Delhi, Moscow or Podunk. Pickford, Chaplin and Fairbanks were gods earning millions of dollars, leading the life of royalty. Even a genuine aristocrat like Edwina had been dazzled by the reception given newly wed Mary and Doug when they arrived in England in June 1920. The normally restrained English went wild, almost tearing Little Mary's clothes off at a Chelsea garden party, forcing police intervention to save her. This was not the respectful adulation given the English royals: this was something new, wild, savage, exciting!

It was Edwina who first started nagging Nick to help her get into films. At first, he resisted, telling her that she knew nothing about acting, which was true. But soon the idea began to appeal to him. Nick was looking for new worlds to conquer. When he learned the film industry was grossing a billion and a half dollars a year, he began to share Edwina's dream of turning her into a star. What better way to express his love of his beautiful wife than to make her the queen of Hollywood? And what an adventure for him—and a chance to make more millions!

When he learned that Metropolitan Pictures was for sale, for a quarter million, he cabled his father-in-law in London and suggested making an offer of two hundred thousand dollars, fifty thousand of which he would put up in cash, the remainder to be financed by the Saxmundham Bank. Nick had quadrupled his fortune since the war, but even so fifty thousand dollars was a lot of money in 1922 and Lord Saxmundham realized his movie gamble was more than a frivolous whim: Nick was serious. On the other hand, he knew little about movies or the movie business. "Neither did Goldwyn and Mayer" was Nick's retort, which was true. Remembering Nick's dramatic demonstration of the submachine gun, Lord Saxmundham decided his son-in-law didn't lack theatrical flair. He agreed to the deal.

Ironically contradicting its name, Metropolitan Pictures had specialized in Westerns, also churning out action-adventure serials and an occasional horror film. Its tightfisted owner, a Hungarian-born ex-furrier named Alexander Potofi, had made a fortune and, three months earlier, had dropped dead of a heart attack. His shy widow, caring little about business, put the studio on Santa Monica Boulevard up for sale. It covered eight acres and had two indoor stages, but the price seemed steep and her timing was bad. The recent Fatty Arbuckle scandal had hurt the film business all over the country, Paramount stock had dropped from ninety to forty, and no one was interested in buying a second-rate movie studio. No one but Nick. His offer was the first, and Mrs. Potofi, glad to be free of the worry, accepted it. Nick Fleming was in the picture business.

The news of the sale was greeted by his fellow moguls with indifference at best, snickers at worst. "Fleming's a 'dilettante' and a schmuck," one studio head was heard to say, "dilettante" being a word he had learned from one of his writers. "He won't last six months." Delicious waves of *Schadenfreude* swept the movie colony, where the rule was that to achieve true happiness one not only had to succeed but everyone else had to fail. Nick had no doubt what his critics were saying, but as he walked through the Spanish-style wrought-iron gates of Metropolitan Pictures and looked at the shabby stucco building he had just bought, he didn't care.

Nick Fleming knew what he was doing and, as usual, he had an ace up his sleeve.

CHAPTER 13

As she entered the gates of the white marble Dolmabahce Palace, its terraces stretching a half mile along the shores of the beautiful Bosporus on the European side of Constantinople, Diana Ramschild thought of money, power, corruption—and, not least of all, revenge against Nick Fleming. The years since Alfred's death had been difficult for Diana and near disastrous for the Ramschild Company. Alfred had been grooming Nick to be his successor; thus Nick's defection and Alfred's death dealt the company a double blow, leaving management in disarray. Alfred's estate had been divided between his widow and daughter, the two of them owning fifty-seven percent of the common stock. Arabella assumed Diana would vote for the vice president, Arnold Hastings, to become the new head of the company. But to Arabella's surprise, Diana argued against him. Arnold was sixty-three, near retirement, and little more than a glorified accountant. The company needed someone young and dynamic. . . . "Like me," she announced.

"You?" said her mother. "Diana, this is no time for jokes."

But Diana wasn't joking. The double shock of what she considered Nick's treachery and her father's death had galvanized her. It was her "mission" to carry on in her father's footsteps. After all, she was a Vassar graduate. Why couldn't a woman run an armaments company? At least couldn't a woman *try?*

She finally wore her mother down to a compromise. Diana could become a vice president of the company, learning the business. Then in two years, on Arnold Hastings' retirement, if she still wanted the job and the board of directors thought she deserved it, she could have it. Diana accepted and threw herself into her new role with such enthusiastic determination that even Hastings, who had had deep misgivings about her at first, soon became Diana's greatest fan and mentor. Diana had poise, looks and intelligence—that everyone knew. The surprise was that she had inherited her father's and grandfather's toughness. Soon she became known around the factory as "the Iron Maiden"—though no one called her that to her face. And

135

in 1920, when Arnold retired, the board of directors unanimously elected Diana his successor. Detractors sneered that the board didn't have much choice, since Diana and her mother were the majority stockholders. But in fact the board was enthusiastic about Diana. She had proved herself a natural businesswoman and a tough administrator. And, more urgently, business was terrible. The Armistice might have brought peace to a war-savaged world, but it had wrecked the armaments business. Ramschild stock had plunged from 126 in 1917 to 30 in 1920. Orders were down to one-fifteenth of what they had been in the boom years. Diana cut staff, slashed salaries, including her own, and laid off a third of the work force. She also decided she was potentially the company's best sales representative and began to search the world's trouble spots for likely customers.

Which was why she was in Turkey.

The enormous Dolmabahce Palace Diana was entering had been built in the 1840s by the Sultan Abdul Mejid, whose sexual excesses in his harem had rendered him impotent, at which point he became a drunk. Abdul Mejid wanted the "biggest palace in the world," and he got it. At a time when Turkey had almost no industry besides rugs and was known as "the Sick Man of Europe," her Sultan lavished fourteen tons of gold to decorate his rococo-gone-mad palace. But Turkey had been cursed by rulers of dazzling ineptitude for centuries. The last twenty-five all-powerful Sultans of the Ottoman Empire plumbed the depths of depravity in the most spectacular manner the world had seen since the most decadent of the Roman Emperors. Sloth, drunkenness, mass murder, every sort of perversion, genocide, torture, fratricide, uxoricide, infanticide, gluttony—all vices had been worn out by the parade of Sultan-Caliphs who were known as "God's Shadow on Earth." Meanwhile, the vast Ottoman Empire of thirty million souls shrank as chunk after chunk was bitten off by the hungry European powers.

In 1908, this creaking empire underwent a revolution when a group of "Young Turks"—hence the phrase—threw out the last all-powerful Sultan, Abdul Hamid ("the Damned"), and made his brother a constitutional monarch. The new Sultan, Mahomet V, was a near-idiot whose proudest boast was that he hadn't read a newspaper in twenty years. Unfortunately, the Young Turks, led by a baby-faced killer named Enver Pasha, made the mistake of entering the Great War on the German side. In 1915, as a brilliant young colonel named Mustapha Kemal was holding off the British forces at Gallipoli, Enver Pasha and his co-rulers launched a bloodthirsty genocidal campaign against the Armenians, slaughtering an estimated six hundred thousand of them, bashing the skulls of babies against stone walls. They later had the gall to try to collect the Armenians' life-insurance policies from the British insurance companies!

Enver Pasha was up to his ears in corruption, and at the disastrous end of the war, he and his cohorts fled the country, leaving the thirty-sixth Sultan, Mahomet VI, virtually a prisoner of, and dependent on, the British and French (the idiotic Mahomet V had been deposed in 1915). It was at this point that the British Prime Minister, Lloyd George, abetted by his Foreign Secretary, Lord Curzon, made one of the stupidest blunders in British history.

To lure the Greeks into the war on the Allied side—the Greek King Constantine was pro-German and married to the Kaiser's sister—the Greek Prime Minister, Eleutherios Venizelos, was promised the city of Smyrna, on Turkey's Mediterranean coast. In 1919, Venizelos, who had complied with the Allied request, sent in his I.O.U. Lloyd George and Curzon both despised the Turks; furthermore, they had a romantic view of a Homeric Greece that was the birthplace of democracy. They backed Venizelos. With the Sultan a pawn in Constantinople and with no other viable national government, Turkey was helpless. Venizelos sent in the Greek Army and took over Smyrna, which, even though it had a large Greek population, had been indisputably Turkish since 1453 when Sultan Mehmet II conquered Constantinople. Smyrna's Turkish citizens were looted, raped and in many cases murdered by the Greeks.

It was then that Diana Ramschild decided that the Sultan of Turkey was a likely customer for a shipment of Ramschild rifles. To meet "God's Shadow," she wore a smart green Charmeuse dress— green was the color of the flag of Islam, no fool Diana—a matching fur-trimmed coat, white gloves and a white hat with a veil. She had bought the outfit in Paris en route to Constantinople. (Diana liked clothes: she had six Vuitton suitcases with her on the *Orient Express*.) She was staying at the luxurious Pera Palace Hotel in the European Quarter. She had arranged the meeting with the Sultan by offering the Minister of War a thousand-dollar bribe. Neither the French nor the British authorities had interfered with her. Diana had assumed they didn't know who she was, but she was wrong. They knew. They also knew she was wasting her time.

She was led by a Stambouli-coated and fezzed majordomo through the enormous salons of the three-hundred-room palace. She was impressed, although the garishness of the rooms with their heavy gilt

French furniture and tall windows overlooking the Bosporus tended more to vulgarity than grandeur. Though at one time the cost of running this palace with its hundreds of eunuchs, servants and odalisques had been two million pounds a year, now the building seemed eerily empty. Diana wondered, Where has everyone gone?

Finally she was taken into a tall room where a very short man in a frock coat was standing before a window. The majordomo announced her in French. Diana spoke hardly a word of Turkish, but her French was fluent and she knew that almost all educated Turks spoke French. Now the short man turned and came toward her as the majordomo retired.

"*Soyez le bienvenu,* Mademoiselle Ramschild," said the little man, who had a Charlie Chaplin moustache. He kissed her hand and smiled. "I am Babur Pasha, aide to His Excellency the Minister of War."

"I'm delighted to make your acquaintance," Diana replied in French.

"Unfortunately, His Majesty is indisposed this afternoon. But he has instructed me to inform you that his government is not interested in any arms purchases at this time."

Diana was amazed.

"But the Minister led me to believe that His Majesty was very eager to discuss an arms purchase."

The smile never wavered.

"Unfortunately, the budget does not have sufficient funds at this time."

Diana's anger sizzled. "I see. And the Minister knew this yesterday when he accepted my bribe."

" 'Bribe' is a harsh word, mademoiselle. If, however, you could see your way to making a contribution to a charitable fund *I* represent—a fund for the wounded Turkish war veterans at Scutari—perhaps His Majesty could be prevailed upon to see you after all."

"How much of a 'contribution'?"

"Say . . . a thousand American dollars?"

She looked into small, dark eyes glittery with greed.

"You can go to hell," she said. She turned and left the room, her heels clicking angrily on the parquet. She was furious, mostly at herself for having been taken in by corrupt bureaucrats.

Very well, she thought, if this damned seedy Sultan is broke, I'll go to the other side.

She wasn't thinking of the Greeks, who had bought heavily from Italian arms dealers. She was thinking of the hero of Gallipoli, who had torpedoed Churchill's career, and who was now heading a revolutionary army in the Anatolian hills, bringing the Turks together to defend their homeland against the Greek invaders. She was thinking of Mustapha Kemal, the Gazi, or Conqueror of the Christians.

The Sultan couldn't even pay his servants, but she had heard Kemal Pasha had money and needed all the arms he could get to drive the Greeks from Turkish soil. Moreover, Kemal was beginning to look like a winner, and Diana liked winners.

But the immediate problem was how to get to Mustapha Kemal.

CHAPTER 14

THE ace Nick had up his sleeve for the picture business was his stepfather, Van Nuys de Courcy Clairmont, who had developed an almost adolescent passion for movies and whose newspapers had been reviewing them seriously since *The Birth of a Nation* in 1915. After the war, Van had begun selling off a few of his less profitable papers in the East and expanded his empire into the Midwest, picking up dailies in St. Louis, Omaha, Kansas City, Tulsa and Des Moines, and even penetrating the Far West with two papers in California. The fiery prewar liberal had moved somewhat to the right, his political views having been jolted by the Russian Revolution and what he now considered the "Bolshevik Menace."

Also, Van's commercial instincts, ever sharp, had sniffed the value of popular features, and articles about the plight of the workers were being replaced by pieces on fashion, home-decorating hints, an etiquette column, *The Compleat Gardener,* and Rhonda Reeves's *Kitchen Guide.* But his stroke of genius was hiring an ex-actress and frustrated romantic novelist from Glen Ridge, New Jersey, named Harriet Sparrow. Harriet was a plump, pretty twenty-seven-year-old who dyed her hair flaming red, who wore loud print dresses and fussy flowered hats, who had an insatiable appetite for gossip and who believed wholeheartedly in Love. She began working for Van in 1918, writing a gossip column about Broadway. Her gushy style evoked roars of laughter from sophisticates, but they read her anyway because Harriet got the goods on the celebrities. By 1920, she was including movie gossip in her column, and Van syndicated her countrywide. By 1922, when the following column was printed, Harriet Sparrow's readership was estimated by Van to be over twenty million Americans.

THE SPARROW SINGS
BY HARRIET SPARROW

Well, folks, here I am in Hollywood again, the glamour capital of the world, and the big news in Sunny California is Metropolitan Pictures, its dynamic young owner, Nick Fleming, and his beautiful new star who just *happens* to be his wife, gorgeous Edwina Fleming. These two have been in Hollywood less than two months and already are the *talk of the town!* I knew them in New York, of course, and wrote about them there *so* often, so it was a real *thrill* to see them taking pictures so seriously and yet at the same time giving gay *madcap* parties that have the movie colony buzzing!

I interviewed Nick at his studio on Santa Monica Boulevard (which has a railroad track down the middle of it!) and found him still the dashing, handsome heartthrob he was in New York, except now he has a tan, which is *so* becoming! His office has been redone in the Tudor style, with beamed ceilings and an enormous English desk. Nick told me Edwina, who is the granddaughter of the Duke of Dorset and whose blood is *the* bluest in Ye Olde England, did the decorating herself, "to put a little touch of England out here in California" as Nick put it—*so* charming!

Nick told me Metropolitan has five pictures planned, but the *big* picture for him is the movie *everyone* in town is talking about, *Youth on Fire.* We all read the novel last year, and I know *I* swooned over the *torrid* love scenes that almost set each page *on fire!* Well, all this steam is being transferred to the silver screen, and something tells me theater temperatures all over America are going to *sizzle!* Are you dying to hear who's playing the part of Buck Randolph, the football hero whose love life almost tore apart the small New England town of Shandy, Connecticut? Hold on to your hats, girls: you guessed it, ROD NORMAN, America's Dream Man! Oh, I can hardly *wait* to see Handsome Rod in those love scenes! And who plays the part of Laura Hardy, the sweet co-ed whose reputation is almost *ruined* by Buck Randolph? It's a part any actress would *kill* for. Well, I won't keep you in suspense: Nick is giving *the* part to *his wife!* Yes, Edwina Fleming's movie debut may put her right at the top of the Hollywood heap!

I asked Nick if he might be a *teentsy* bit nervous having his wife make love to Rod Norman, even if it's only movie make-believe? He smiled that irresistible smile of his and said, "I trust Edwina." Oh, if you could see those two together! They're *so* in love, it just makes you feel *good all over!*

And I *did* see them together that very night because Nick, who's *so* sweet and generous, asked me to Casa Encantada for a *very* social party he was giving. Casa Encantada is the *huge* estate Nick bought in the Hollywood Hills. It was built ten years ago by Orange Juice King Walter Fitzhugh, and it's surrounded by the *most* lovely gardens and beautiful palm trees, and there are two tennis courts and a big swimming pool with a waterfall at one end and a *canoe!* Isn't that fun?

Casa Encantada means "Enchanted House" in Spanish, and from the moment you walk through its big double front doors, you can just *feel* the enchantment! Oh, this is a happy house. There is love in every square inch of the stucco walls—it's Spanish style, of course. You feel the love for Nick and Edwina's three darling children: little Charles, who's three and *so* cute; his little sister, Sylvia, who is a dream; plus baby Edward (they have an English nanny, Mrs. Drummond, who told me the only thing she doesn't like about California are the "creepy crawlies"—ugh!). And then, of course, the love of Nick and Edwina— they actually *held hands!* Isn't it wonderful?

Well, *everyone* was there. Doug and Mary, Charlie Chaplin, Sam Goldwyn, Clara Kimball Young, King and Florence Vidor, Lillian Gish, Gloria Swanson, Rod Norman and his lovely, talented wife, Norma Norman—the stars glittered! *Plus* titled Europeans! Lord and Lady Tremaine, the lovely Duchess of San Stefano, Prince Carl of Roumania and the suavely handsome Marquis de la Tour d'Auberge. *So* much dazzle your reporter, who's just a small-town girl, almost had to put on *dark glasses!* Yes, Nick and Edwina are the talk of the town. But unless my crystal ball has sprung a leak, *Youth on Fire* is going to be the *talk of America!*

Of course, Nick and Edwina howled. But Nick knew chirpy Harriet Sparrow had just sold a lot of tickets.

Rod Norman had broken into Westerns after the war by claiming he was a real cowboy who had grown up on his father's cattle ranch in Wyoming. The truth was that it was a sheep ranch, and Rod was so afraid of horses he had to have several belts of bourbon before he could bring himself to saddle up. This not surprisingly gave him a drinking problem, which Prohibition had done nothing to cure. Rod got his booze from a bootlegger named Marty Siegle, who catered to movie stars. Rod had become a bona fide star in 1921 when he broke out of Westerns to play Private Dirk Dean in the war film *Up Front.* American women, who rarely went to Westerns and hence had not seen him, took one look at his rugged face and broad shoulders and went into a collective swoon. Rod Norman fan clubs sprang up all over the country and soon this son of a Wyoming judge was getting fifteen thousand letters a week.

This dizzying instant fame was more than Rod's fragile ego could handle. He became a monster. Convinced every woman in America lusted after his muscular body (the chest of which he shaved for his films because body hair was considered repulsive to moviegoers), Rod decided he owed it to his fans to seduce every attractive woman he

142

met. Since Edwina was not only one of the most beautiful women he had ever seen but also the wife of the producer of *Youth on Fire,* Rod's booze-addled brain decided she was a challenge he couldn't resist. And after he read the shooting script of *Youth on Fire,* he thought, given the intimacy of the many love scenes between Buck Randolph and Laura Hardy, that even if he looked like the Hunchback of Notre Dame, he ought to be able to score.

On the first day of principal photography at Stage One, Rod broached the subject with characteristic subtlety.

"Do you like sex?" he asked Edwina as they waited for the first shot to be set up.

She looked surprised. "Yes, actually, I think it's lovely," she replied. "My husband's awfully good at it. He's also insanely jealous. If you make a pass at me, I wouldn't be at all surprised if he blew your brains out. He carries a gun at all times, you know. He has ever since the war. And he's a terribly good shot." She smiled prettily.

Rod Norman gulped, thinking that perhaps he might have to reconsider his priorities.

The director of *Youth on Fire* was an ex-war ace and stunt pilot named Rex Simpson. Rex and Rod were drinking buddies, and that night they were sitting at the bar in Rex's basement sipping bootleg bourbon.

"This picture's not going to work," said Rod sourly.

"Why?" asked Rex.

"Because it's all about sex, and Edwina Fleming's about as sexy as an avocado."

Rex, who sported a moustache, looked surprised.

"She's sexy to *me!*" he said. "Every time I look at her I get hard! And she has great tits."

"Yeah, but she's not sexy inside. Maybe it's the English accent, I don't know. Anyway, if I'm supposed to be Mr. Red-Hot Lover to her in this picture, it's going to be the greatest acting job of my career. Does Fleming carry a gun?"

"I've heard he does. He was almost killed in Russia back in '17. I guess it made him a little crazy."

"And is he a jealous type?"

"They say."

"Well, he's not going to have anything to be jealous of with me," said America's Dream Man with bourbon-soaked sourness. "She really frosted me today. Course, maybe I shouldn't have said what I did."

"What did you say?"

"I asked her if she liked sex."

Rex Simpson groaned. "You *jerk!* You don't say that to the grand-daughter of a goddamned *duke!*"

"Yeah, I guess not."

"It's not as if she's a dress extra! Christ."

Rex Simpson was an up-and-coming director, but *Youth on Fire* was his first big picture and he couldn't afford to have it flop.

He decided he'd better have a talk with Nick Fleming.

In 1921, an article appeared in *The New York Times* reporting that information from Russia confirmed that the former Minister of War for the last Tsar, the Grand Duke Cyril, had been brutally murdered by the Bolsheviks along with his wife and daughter, the Grand Duchess Tatyana. This had occurred in the summer of 1918 in the week following the assassination of the royal family at Ekaterinburg, when almost all the Romanoff relatives still in Russia were dispatched with barbaric savagery. When Nick read this, he remembered the sweet teen-aged girl he had met in Petrograd and felt sad at her fate. But he also had to address the problem of what to do with the bag of diamonds the Grand Duke had given him, which still sat under his own name in the vaults of the Bank of England. He consulted Sir Desmond Thorneycroft, his father-in-law's barrister. Sir Desmond advised him that, since the Russian Revolution had abrogated the tsarist legal system, including all the wills, and repudiated its foreign debts, there was no question that the diamonds were legally his. Furthermore, any attempt to locate any of the Grand Duke's surviving relatives would undoubtedly produce a swarm of fraudulent claimants and leave Nick open to numerous legal actions, whereas even if a genuine claimant appeared he would have no better legal right to the diamonds than Nick.

Cutting through all the legal double-talk, Nick realized that if any direct heirs of the Grand Duke could be found alive, he or she would have at least some moral claim to the inheritance. There were many members of the Romanoff family who had escaped the Revolution, and they were busy haggling over the alleged fortune that the Tsar was supposed to have deposited in the Bank of England, so Nick had no doubt they would pounce on him if they knew of the existence of the jewels. He could either divide them among dozens of titled second and third cousins who would probably blow the money in the south of France, or he could consider the jewels his own, as spoils of war.

He had them appraised by Garrard and Company, which put a value on them of six hundred thousand pounds, or three million dollars.

He dragged his heels about making a decision until he bought Metropolitan Pictures. Then the enormous costs of making films—as well as financing his high, wide and handsome life-style—made the decision for him. He sold the diamonds to Garrard and Company and deposited the three million in the Bank of America in Los Angeles just in time to pay forty thousand dollars for the movie rights to the best-selling novel *Youth on Fire*. Harriet Sparrow had been wrong: he hadn't bought Casa Encantada; he was renting it for the then-staggering sum of three thousand dollars a month. Maintaining a staff of eight servants and gardeners, paying Edwina's steep clothing bills, throwing several parties a week to dazzle the movie colony—all this added up to huge outlays of cash. Since Nick was paying himself only a thousand dollars a week as head of the studio, he was dipping heavily into capital to make a success of his movie ventures. Nick knew better than anyone else how important it was that *Youth on Fire* be a hit.

Thus, when Rex Simpson called to tell him Rod Norman was feeling "rejected" by Edwina, thereby threatening the flammability of the movie's love scenes, Nick's reaction was electric. As he hung up and started to climb the sweeping stairs in the entrance hall, he also realized he was in the unique position of having to convince his wife to be attracted to another man.

Casa Encantada was "Spanish" with a vengeance. The stairs had an elaborate wrought-iron railing, and from the ceiling depended a heavy iron-and-glass lantern bought from a Mexico City antique dealer who *said* it had once hung in the Viceroy's Palace on the Zócalo. As Nick reached the top of the stairs, he passed down a long, gloomy corridor hung with a series of prints depicting life in nineteenth-century Madrid, along with a huge and horrible oil painting of a bullfight. At the end of the corridor, a wooden door heavily carved in the Mexican manner led to the master bedroom suite, its double windows covered with wrought-iron grilles, as if the builder of the house wanted to protect his wife from some imagined vine-climbing Zorro. Edwina, in a black leotard, was going through a regimen of ballet-related exercises she had been taught by her dramatic coach, Wilhelmina van Dyke, a Dutch ex-actress who had once toured with Bernhardt and who had come to Hollywood in her sunset years to mine whatever gold she could out of film-struck neophytes like Edwina.

145

"Rex just called," said Nick, closing the door. "He says Rod is getting pleasantly plastered because you rejected him. What did you do?"

She stopped her exercises.

"He made a vulgar remark, and I told him if he made a pass at me you'd blow his brains out. You *would,* wouldn't you?"

"Look, this is Hollywood, not Windsor Castle."

"Yes, I've noticed."

"These actors are *insecure!* They have to threaten women."

She laughed.

"Him? A *threat?* Oh, really, darling, I know he's America's dreamboat, but he's just an overgrown child. He's no threat to *me.* I really don't understand what all these millions of salivating women see in him."

Nick felt mixed feelings of relief and irritation.

"Then you don't find him attractive?"

"Oh, yes, he's attractive. He looks a lot like you, after all, and you know I think you're the handsomest man in the world. But he doesn't make me pant with desire the way *you* do."

"But you have to *pretend* to pant with desire."

"I know that, silly. It's called acting. I'll be fine in the love scenes—you'll see." She started running in place.

"Will you stand *still!*" he almost shouted.

She stopped and looked at him. "Darling, you're cross! What's wrong?"

"We're taking an enormous gamble on this film—*both* of us! This is serious business."

"I know."

"A man can't make love to a woman if he doesn't feel she wants to make love to *him.* And I know this is a movie, but John Barrymore couldn't do a convincing love scene with an iceberg, and Rod Norman sure as hell isn't John Barrymore."

"What are you trying to say?"

He gestured with frustration.

"I'm trying to say give him a little encouragement! Not a lot, but a little. Be *nice* to him. Even flirt a little with him! Build up his confidence."

She shrugged. "Oh, all right, if you think it's important. But it's such a bore." She thought a moment, then smiled. "I know! I'll pretend he's *you!*"

"Yes, that's it. Pretend he's me." He took her in his arms and kissed her. "That way we'll get the hottest love scenes in movie history."

"Conceited ape." She hugged him and nibbled his ear, whispering, "But you're right."

The scene to be shot the next day was set in the high-school gymnasium in Shandy, Connecticut, where the hero, Buck Randolph, first met the heroine, Laura Hardy. Rex Simpson was going to great lengths to make every aspect of the film as up-to-date as possible, and the set looked like a real gymnasium; however, it was doubtful that a small New England high school could afford to hire a twelve-man orchestra led by a young man in a snappy tux. All the male high-school seniors also wore dinner jackets, further stretching credibility, although giving the scene the "classy" look Nick wanted. But credibility snapped altogether when Edwina emerged from her dressing room wearing a white fox-trimmed evening wrap that would have cost the entire town budget of Shandy, Connecticut. However, Nick wasn't as interested in reality as he was in presenting his wife to the public in the most glamorous way possible, and he hired Hollywood's most expensive costumier to dress Edwina to the nines.

Movie making in preunion Hollywood was fast, but even so, setting up a scene with over fifty extras was time-consuming, and Edwina had a half hour to kill before she actually stepped in front of the camera. Nick came up to her and squeezed her hand, unable to kiss her because of her heavy makeup.

"You look fabulous," he said. "You're going to knock them dead."

"Well, I doubt many high-school girls wear dresses like this, but it *is* stunning, isn't it? You know, I'm not as nervous as I thought I'd be. I suppose that's a bad sign."

"Not at all."

"There's Rod. Shall I go over and be sweet to him?"

"That's my girl."

She made her way through the extras, carpenters and technicians, stepping over the thick electric cables that snaked everywhere, to Rod's canvas chair. The star was drinking a cup of black coffee.

"Good morning," she said cheerily, sitting next to him in her own chair. "How are you today?"

"Hung over," he growled, and she saw his bloodshot eyes. "Thank God there won't be any close-ups till this afternoon. Is my face puffy?"

"Not at all. You look very handsome."

He was surprised. "Why . . . thank you. And if you don't mind my saying so, *you* look gorgeous. I'm not making a pass!" he hastily added.

She smiled. "I was a bit abrupt with you yesterday. I want to apologize. I hope you won't hold it against me."

"Oh . . . not at all."

"I am *so* looking forward to working with you. You have *so* much more experience than I, I hope you'll tell me if I'm being hopelessly inadequate."

Despite his hangover, Rod Norman practically glowed.

"To tell the truth, I'm just barely adequate myself," he said, and they both laughed.

She realized, with an anticipatory shudder, that he had terrible breath.

Nick spent the day commuting between his English-style office and the set. Despite the fact that Wilhelmina van Dyke had assured him Edwina had natural acting talent, and despite the fact that she had photographed wonderfully in her screen tests, Nick was understandably anxious: so much was riding on a complete unknown. But by the afternoon, when the first close-ups of Buck and Laura were shot, it was apparent to everybody that some sort of magic was happening between the stars. The script called for Buck to dance close to Laura and then, on the dance floor, kiss her—which, at the time, was tantamount to rape—after which Laura was to slap him.

The first two takes were fumbled, and not because of Rod's bad breath: he had taken the precaution of gargling.

But the third produced a kiss that seemed so passionate that Nick felt fireworks of jealousy as he watched, even though he kept telling himself she was pretending Buck was her husband. Then Laura pushed Buck away and slapped him. Sparks flew from the kiss and the slap. When Rex yelled through his megaphone "That's a print!" the entire cast burst into applause.

Nick applauded too. But he was thinking, Was it just acting?

Acting or no, he found himself hating Rod Norman. The son of a bitch is making love to my wife—and I'm paying him to do it!

But the most surprised person on the set was Edwina. Rod Norman's passionate kiss had electrified her.

CHAPTER 15

REALIZING she had been naïve about the extent of corruption in the Turkish government and misinformed about the state of the Sultan's finances, Diana Ramschild now took the precaution of finding out everything she could about Mustapha Kemal before setting out to meet him. Yet she discovered that even though he was rapidly becoming the best-known man in Turkey, not much was known about him publicly, undoubtedly because it was to the government's advantage to downplay his exploits in the press. He had been born in Salonika forty-one years before, the son of a ne'er-do-well customs official named Ali Riza and an illiterate but strong-willed Macedonian mother named Zubeida. When Mustapha was ten, his father died in a typhus epidemic, and his mother moved the child to an uncle's farm. Zubeida wanted him to become a *hodja,* or priest, but the boy, influenced by tales of the conquests of his ancestors, the fierce Osmanli Turks, determined to become a soldier. A brilliant student, especially in mathematics, he was admitted to the Turkish Military Cadet School where he amazed his instructors by his energy and his insatiable desire for learning. He devoured books on military strategy and read Clausewitz, Moltke and biographies of Napoleon. Despite the fact that at the age of fourteen he had taken up drinking, smoking and whoring, he was given a new name by his superiors: Kemal, the Turkish word for "perfection."

After graduation, he distinguished himself in various military campaigns in the Turkish Army and flirted with radical politics, which earned him a three-month stay in Constantinople's notorious Red Prison. After the Young Turks overthrew Abdul Hamid the Damned, Mustapha was sent to Sofia as military attaché where he taught himself French, flirted with high society, gambled, became something of a dandy, contracted a kidney ailment, drank *raki* and the sweet Roumanian brandy called *tsuika* to excess, and, it was rumored, bedded an occasional boy. And all the while he burned for glory and ranted against the backwardness of his beloved homeland.

The war brought him glory at Gallipoli, but it brought ignominious defeat to Turkey. After the Greek Army invaded Smyrna and the British and French occupied Constantinople, unrest broke out in the rest of Turkey. The Sultan, nervous on his shaky throne, decided he must send someone to quell the disturbances and reassert his authority. He chose Kemal. At the last moment, his advisers convinced the Sultan he had picked a traitor, but it was too late: Kemal was on a boat in the stormy Black Sea, headed east for the Turkish port of Samsun, where he landed May 19, 1919.

He immediately set out to raise an independent army and establish a new, democratic government in Angora. Overcoming horrendous difficulties, he accomplished both, defying the Sultan in the process. The Sultan raised a punitive expedition called the "Caliph's Army" to crush the "Kemalists," and the horror of civil war was added to the nightmare of the foreign occupation. An advance guard of the Caliph's Army intercepted a group of Kemal's officers at a town called Konya. The officers were stoned and beaten into unconsciousness, then revived by water. Lashed down, they had their toenails torn out, then were blinded by red-hot swords. In retaliation, the Sultan's officers, when caught by the Kemalists, were slashed to death and then were dragged through the streets behind horses. The Kemalists used flogging to extract information, then killed the informers. The Sultan's forces tortured their prisoners with the bastinado, hanged them, blinded them and even crucified them. The most savage dogs of war had been unleashed.

The Sultan's chief advantage lay with the priests, who preached from every mosque in Turkey to rally the faithful to the support of the Sultan-Caliph, the head of Islam. Kemal's advantages were that he was a military genius on a par with Napoleon, had a will of iron and was a brilliant orator who could thrill the Turks to his cause. Slowly, he beat the Caliph's Army into retreat. He defeated the Greeks in two major battles, earning the admiration of the outside world. But the Greeks still held Smyrna.

This, then, was the man to whom Diana Ramschild decided to sell rifles. But she had to get to him first, and Kemal was headquartered halfway across Turkey in a villa outside Angora called Chankaya. Between them were the Greek Army, bandits, and two hundred miles of rugged Anatolian mountains.

But Diana was nothing if not a child of her century. Within three days of her visit to the Dolmabahce Palace, she had located a young Turkish pilot named Kadri who owned a war-surplus Italian biplane and who was willing, for four hundred American dollars, to fly her over the Greek Army to Angora. Taking only one suitcase, but packing her best clothes in it (she was well aware of Kemal's admiration for fashionable women), Diana met Kadri at an open field three miles outside Constantinople at eight in the morning. Taking a nervous look at the woebegone biplane, she put on a goggled helmet and then climbed in the rear open cockpit.

Five minutes later the plane taxied down the field, took off, dipped for a terrifying second, then slowly climbed into the blue Turkish sky to head east toward the distant mountains.

It was testimony to the popularity of arms dealers with generals that within two hours of landing on the field outside Angora, Diana had received an invitation to lunch at Chankaya. She was driven to the villa in an open-top four-year-old Benz by Kemal's closest friend, Colonel Arif, whose conversation was unavoidably limited since he spoke neither French nor English. Diana spent the ride admiring the magnificent scenery. Though it was July, and Constantinople had been steaming, here on the Anatolian plateau, four thousand feet above sea level, the weather was pleasantly warm and the air was clean and pure. Puffy clouds drifted over the umber and green mountains in the distance; a few miles away, the red roofs of the small town of Angora—which Kemal had proclaimed the new capital of Turkey, and which he was already thinking of renaming Ankara—spilled down a gentle hillside. Chankaya was a twenty-minute drive from the capital, and as the Benz pulled up in front of the villa, Diana was struck by the beauty of its situation and the pleasant plum-tree-planted garden that surrounded it, though she was unimpressed by the look of the house itself. Built by a Levantine merchant, the two-story house was constructed of local stone and had an ugly, heavily carved porch surmounted by a small balcony, all painted an odd ox-blood color. The roof was slate and conical in shape, but everything was redeemed by the magnificence of the view down the hillside, with the high steppe beyond.

Colonel Arif, a fine-looking young man, led her to the porch where two of Kemal's elite bodyguards stood flanking the front door. They were Lazzes, the huge, wild mountaineers from the south coast of the Black Sea, and they wore their native costumes of black wool with long, slashed coats and high boots. As they saluted Arif, Diana noticed they carried German rifles.

Arif led her down an entrance hall that boasted a small ornamental fountain and a red leather sofa where visitors waited to see the Gazi in his study. Diana's heart was pounding with excitement, curiosity and not a little apprehension; the man she was about to meet had a reputation for murderous cruelty. He had hanged army contractors for skimming profits and had personally shot dead two of his officers for hoarding cigarettes. Here in the Anatolian highlands, thousands of miles away from safe, comfortable Connecticut, Mustapha Kemal Pasha was the law, commander in chief, all-powerful. The unpleasant thought occurred to her that she might be risking her life.

Colonel Arif led her into the study, a moderate-sized room with lion skins on the wall, a small upright piano, and a table in the center where Kemal reputedly held forth at his nightly drinking bouts. The Gazi was standing behind this table, studying a map. Now he looked up. The first thing Diana noticed were his eyes. She had read many novels where characters' eyes were described as "piercing," but here the adjective was unavoidable: Kemal's steel-blue eyes pierced in a way that was a little frightening. She had the feeling he was not only drinking in her appearance but trying to penetrate her mind as well. Then he straightened and smiled. He was of medium height, slim and wiry, with hair and moustache that were, surprisingly, almost blond. He was not conventionally handsome, but his face was nevertheless extremely attractive. He had high cheekbones and a thin gash of a mouth. Curiously, for a general, he wore a well-cut gray business suit.

"You are without a doubt the most attractive arms dealer I have ever met," he said in French, coming around the table to kiss her hand. "It would almost be a pleasure to be shot by one of your guns."

"I hope, Excellency, it is a pleasure neither of us ever experiences."

Colonel Arif was still by the door. Now a very pretty young woman in a black dress appeared. She looked curiously at Diana.

"Ah, Fikriye!" said Kemal. "This is Mademoiselle Ramschild from America. Fikriye is my cousin." And mistress, thought Diana, who had heard of the woman. The Gazi spoke to Fikriye briefly in Turkish, then said to Diana, "I told her to study your clothes because I see you are a woman with considerable taste. That suit is made by the famous Chanel, am I not right?"

"That is correct, Excellency. I'm impressed."

"Women's clothes interest me almost as much as women. That is, *European* women's clothes. My country is very backward, mademoiselle. Two years ago, Fikriye was still wearing a veil. I want my country to jump from the seventeenth century into the twentieth as soon as possible—and in *all* things, even superficial matters like fashion." He spoke to Fikriye again, and she vanished, along with Arif. "Fikriye

152

will bring us coffee, then we can talk guns. I have always said the quality I like most in women is availability, but you have something I like even better: weapons. By the way, there is no hotel in Angora suitable to a woman of your distinction. I trust you will honor me by being my guest here tonight?"

"The honor is mine, Excellency."

"Good, then that is settled. Let's sit down. I understand you were at the Palace a few days ago, trying to sell guns to the Sultan."

Diana sat in a leather armchair, Kemal taking a similar chair opposite her across a small octagonal table.

"How did you know that?"

"My dear Mademoiselle Ramschild, there is little of importance that happens in Constantinople that doesn't get back to me. Your experience in the Palace must have cost you a good deal in bribes."

"A thousand dollars. Babur Pasha asked for another thousand. I suppose I should have paid him too, except something told me that would only be the beginning. I'm not averse to a certain degree of corruption—in this business one will inevitably run into it, I suppose. But there's a limit."

Kemal smiled.

"Good. I like that. The court is corrupt beyond belief—the *system* is corrupt. The Sultan has placed a death sentence on me, which is like a prisoner condemning the jail warden. You will not need bribes to deal with me, mademoiselle. Nor will I lie to you. I need weapons, and I know the reputation of your company. We can do business. I think you will find your trip here profitable. By the way, I have never been up in a plane. Is it frightening?"

"Terribly." She smiled. "I *loved* it!"

His eyes widened. "I like you, mademoiselle," he said softly. "You have courage, you have brains—and all that in such an attractive package. I am glad you have come to Chankaya."

Fikriye came back in the room bearing an enameled tray with two exquisite coffee cups, a delicately filigreed pot, a jar of rose honey and a plate of sugar buns. Silently, she set the tray on the table, glanced briefly at Diana, then left the room.

Fikriye knew what was going to happen.

"You have never married, mademoiselle," he said that night as they dined together, alone in his study. The room was lit by oil lamps, and a pleasant breeze wafted through the open windows. They had been served by Fikriye. Kemal had drunk an astonishing amount of the fiery *raki,* but so far it hadn't seemed to affect his wits. "Have you never been in love?"

"Once," said Diana flatly as she cut her excellent lamb. "With a man I now hate."

"You fascinate me. I too am a good hater. Hatred, like love, can be beautiful. But why do you hate this man?"

"Because he made me fall in love with him, proposed to me, and then married another woman."

"This is good cause for hatred."

"He also caused my father's death."

"This is *better* cause. Did he murder him?"

"He might as well have. He made my father so angry he had a fatal stroke. I've vowed to pay him back, and some day I will."

"But why wait? For what this man has done to you, he has earned death. Every day you allow him to live is an insult to your father's memory."

She stared at him. He was peeling a peach.

"Well," she said, "I didn't mean I'd *kill* him."

"What other punishment is just? A life for a life. I have killed many men. Sometimes it's not pleasant, but it must be done. When you have known war as I have known it, mademoiselle, you realize just how cheap life is."

"Yes, but . . . everything else aside, in America you don't just walk in and kill someone. We have something called the electric chair, which I have no intention of sitting in."

"Dear mademoiselle, you are speaking like an amateur," he said patiently, as if explaining something to a child. "You hire a professional assassin to do the job for you. In Constantinople, that beautiful whore of a city, there are dozens of hired killers whose addresses I could give you. If you would pay their fare to America, for a reasonable fee they would be delighted to kill this man . . . What is his name?"

"Fleming," said Diana thoughtfully. "Nick Fleming. He lives in Hollywood now. He bought a film studio."

"Hollywood!" Kemal Pasha laughed. "For a trip to Hollywood, they would kill for *free!*"

He refilled his *raki* glass, tossed it off with one gulp, then got to his feet.

"I'm getting drunk," he announced matter-of-factly. "I must go to bed. Think about what I said. The great truth of life is that either you

154

dominate it or it dominates you." He came around the table to her chair, where he looked down at her. "I have bought many of your guns today, mademoiselle. I have been a good customer. I have never made love to an American. I would be honored if you came to my room tonight. It is at the end of the hall upstairs."

He raised her hand to his mouth and kissed it, his blue eyes searching hers. Then he released her and left the room.

A moment later, Fikriye came in and silently began clearing the table. She looked at Diana, making her feel rather uneasy.

Diana wondered what the silent woman in black was thinking.

Mustapha Kemal Pasha, one of the most powerful men in Turkey, sat naked on the edge of his bed, wondering if the American woman would come to his room. America to him was a myth and a mystery—he hated Woodrow Wilson, who had been Turkey's enemy at the Versailles Conference after the war, but he liked Charlie Chaplin's comedies. And he liked Diana Ramschild. She was not only coolly beautiful and sophisticated—she could hate. He had an idea she could also love.

There was a soft tap at the door.

"Entrez," he said.

The door opened. Diana came into the room. She was wearing a gauzy white negligee through which he could see her flesh in the soft lamplight. She closed the door and looked at his nakedness. He held out his hand and she came to the bed, unbuttoning her peignoir and dropping it on a chair. The room was simple, with rough wooden furniture and an old-fashioned brass bed above which hung a photograph of his formidable-looking mother sitting sternly in her peasant clothes glaring at the photographer. French doors opened onto the balcony over the front porch where the Laz sentries stood guard.

Kemal put his arms around her hips and buried his face in her belly, kissing her soft flesh as his strong fingers kneaded her buttocks. She kissed the top of his head, reveling in the strength of his arms. Gently, he pulled her down beside him on the bed.

"Janum," he said as he squeezed her breasts. "That means you are my soul, my love. Say it, *janum.*"

"Janum," she whispered, and the lovely word, fragrant as jasmine, suddenly summed up her thoughts. Mustapha Kemal Pasha was one of the most intriguing men she had ever met. The only man to attract

155

her since Nick. His power, his cynicism, his ruthlessness, excited her. They *were* alike. He might well be her soul.

When they had finished making love, she whispered to him, "I want the address of the best professional assassin you know."

He laughed as he kissed her cheek. "I knew you'd ask," he said. "I didn't know whether you'd come to my room, but I did know you'd ask for the killer. Because you, like me, are a killer."

She should have been insulted. Instead, the words made her tingle with pleasure.

In the next few days, her pleasure steadily intensified. She had never really gotten over the passion she had felt for Nick six years before. Often she dreamed she was back in that empty beach house in Connecticut where he had first made love to her. Now, as Kemal observed, her love had turned to an equally passionate hate, a lust for revenge for his rejection of her, and Kemal had convinced her the only logical and fit revenge for his crimes against the Ramschild family was death.

After her negotiations with Kemal were finished, she flew back to Constantinople to make the arrangements for the arms delivery, promising her new lover she would return when the shipment was made. She checked into the Pera Palace Hotel, and that afternoon took a taxi, giving the driver an address in one of the oldest quarters of the city. The address, given to her by Kemal, was that of the house of a man known as Bald Ali. "His father and grandfather were torturers for the Sultans," Kemal had told her. "And members of the family for generations have been assassins for hire. To them it is strictly business. When you pay them, they guarantee results. You hire them, and your enemy is dead."

The street was narrow and ancient, filled with donkey carts, pedestrians, peddlers and children. She told the driver to wait, then walked to the wooden door of the old house, which, from the exterior, looked nondescript. She rang a bell. The door was opened by a veiled crone who looked as old as the house. The crone glared with suspicion at the smartly dressed American woman. Diana handed her a letter Kemal had written for her. The crone mumbled something in Turkish and slammed the door. Five minutes later she reopened the door and beckoned Diana to enter.

She stepped into a room furnished in the old Turkish style with an exceedingly fine Ushak rug, ottomans and pillows everywhere. Though the house was in an unfashionable quarter of the city, obviously there was money in the assassination business. Diana followed the old

156

woman through two other rooms, savoring the smell of cooking lamb as they neared the kitchen. Finally, in the fourth room, the crone left her.

Seated on a divan was an enormously fat man whose head was entirely bald. He wore a sashed robe and red velvet slippers and was smoking a cigarette through a long black lacquer holder. He examined Diana for a moment with tiny pig eyes, then took the holder from his mouth and said in French, without standing, "I am Bald Ali. You are welcome in my house. Do you have a photograph of this man, Fleming?"

Over the years, Diana had cut out whatever references to Nick she came across in the press. Now she pulled a clipping from *The New York Times* from her purse and handed it to him.

Bald Ali examined it, puffing on his holder. Then he looked up.

"Mustapha Kemal has suggested a price in his letter, but it is too low. The price will be one thousand pounds sterling plus expenses. The price is nonnegotiable."

"What sort of guarantee do I get?"

"My word, madame, and the reputation of my family."

She hesitated. "How . . . will it be done?"

"There is no reason for you to know that. The point is, the man will be killed. Are we agreed?"

Diana remembered the rapture of her love, the ecstasy of Nick's kisses, her agony in the sanitarium, her rage and her hatred. She remembered photographing his face in her memory the last time she had seen him at the Savoy the day her father died.

"We are," she said.

CHAPTER 16

THE SPARROW SINGS
By Harriet Sparrow

All Hollywood is gossiping about the *torrid* love scenes being shot at Metropolitan Pictures' *Youth on Fire*. Stars Rod Norman and Edwina Fleming, wife of producer Nick Fleming, are said to be steaming the camera lens. Spouses Nick Fleming and Norma Norman laugh off suggestions this may be more than playacting, but where there's so much steam, can't there be a *teentsy* bit of fire?

EDITH Clairmont threw down the newspaper and said to her husband, "Van, how could you print such trash?"

Van put down his coffee cup. They were in the breakfast room of their Sands Point mansion.

"What trash?" he asked.

"Harriet Sparrow's column. She practically comes out and says Edwina is having an affair with Rod Norman. And *you* printed it! Think of Nick's feelings, not to mention Edwina's."

"It's all publicity, Edith. Nick is probably dancing a jig. Harriet Sparrow sells tickets every time she mentions the picture."

Edith, who was now fifty-three and whose hair had turned a becoming gray, didn't look convinced.

"That's extremely cynical, Van," she said.

"The picture business is a cynical business, and your son is not exactly a Boy Scout."

"But this publicity is so *undignified!*" Edith continued. Then she sighed. "Well, I suppose I'm old-fashioned. I was always taught you were supposed to stay *out* of the newspapers."

"Happily for my circulation figures, that no longer is valid."

She hesitated, then lowered her voice. "Van, do you suppose it's *true?*"

Her publisher husband shrugged. "Don't ask *me*," he said.

All America was asking the same thing.

Douglas Fairbanks and Mary Pickford were making twenty thousand dollars a week apiece. Gloria Swanson was making seven thousand dollars a week. Rod Norman, not quite in their league yet, was costing Nick five thousand dollars a week, and since taxes were negligible, Rod felt "really rich," as he drunkenly bragged to his friends. The year before he had bought a French château-style house less than a mile from Casa Encantada. The château had thirty rooms, including a round room at the top of each of its two towers, which Rod and Norma used as bedrooms. There were the requisite tennis court and swimming pool, and Rod had installed a workout room in his basement so he could keep in shape the physique he knew was his meal ticket. He owned a Hispano-Suiza touring car with wicker side panels, a blue Bugatti sports car, an ivory Isotta-Fraschini, twenty-seven custom-made suits, fifty-two pairs of shoes, and he donated his shirts to charity after he had worn them once (thus economizing on laundry bills, he joked). All this was breathlessly reported in the movie magazines, which had assumed tremendous importance in the country, and the fans gobbled up such trivia as if it were manna from heaven. One fan club in Tucson had written him a letter, signed by fifty-six girls, asking Rod for a clipping of his pubic hairs.

Norma Norman, who was six years older than her famous husband and a topflight costume designer at Paramount, was not a woman to mince words.

"Are you screwing her or not?" she said as she came down the steps to the basement workout room where America's Dream Man was chinning himself.

"Who?"

"Who else? Edwina Fleming. It's in Harriet Sparrow's column this morning. As your wife, I have a passing interest. And if one more jerk at Paramount asks me about you and Edwina, I'm going to throw up."

Norma, whose father was a Kansas City banker, had come to Hollywood in 1915 to break into the movies as an actress. She had the face and figure for stardom—she was a statuesque five feet eight with chalk-white skin and raven hair—but not much acting talent. She met Rod when they both had bit parts in a Western. They married, she quit the movies to take up designing, which she found she preferred to acting, and she kept him alive while he was struggling to make it in films. For this, he repaid her by flagrantly cheating on her. Norma's love soured from bitterness to contempt. The only reason she stayed with him was that there were obvious business and social advantages to being Mrs. Rod Norman, but America's Dream Man had feet of clay to his wife. Their marriage was about as chummy as

159

their separate bedrooms at the top of the château's two towers.

Rod dropped from the chinning bar and wiped his face with a towel.

"Well?" said Norma. "Are you answering or not? I'd like to know just so I can keep your score card up to date."

She was wearing a flowered smock that gave her an arty look. She held her black hair in place with a pink satin headache band. Rod wiped his shaved chest and said, "Of course I'm not doing anything with Edwina."

"As if I believe *that*."

"She's a lady, something you may not have heard of. For instance, she wouldn't say 'screw.' I sometimes think I married a stevedore."

"No shit! Well, I'll be glad when this stupid movie is finished. It's getting a bit embarrassing playing the poor, dumb cuckolded *wife*." She started back up the stairs, giving him a contemptuous glare. "You know," she said, "if you didn't have your looks, you'd probably be a garbage man."

"Thanks."

"Think nothing of it . . . *darling*."

And she continued up the stairs.

The publication the year before of *Youth on Fire* had caused a sensation all over the country and sold a million copies of a novel that was thinly veiled pornography. But to the new liberated woman of the time, Laura Hardy's passionate lust for Buck Randolph, who treated her in a manner that could hardly be called gentlemanly, struck a responsive chord. Laura Hardy hung on grimly to her virtue, but just barely, and this was what was on the mind of the Jazz Age, heyday of the flapper. The climactic scene of the book occurred in a whorehouse outside Hartford, where Buck had gone to relieve himself of his sexual tensions. Laura learns of his whereabouts, and to save him from a Fate Worse Than Death, this intrepid virgin goes to the whorehouse to bring Buck out. Buck, drunk and stripped to his shorts, is reeling around the house having the time of his life with the girls, and is in no mood for Laura's sermonizing. When he sees Laura, he brutally humiliates her, then attempts to rape her. Laura's virtue is saved only by the intervention of one of the whores, who just happens to have a heart of gold.

This was hot stuff in 1922, and the filming of the "bordello" scene, as it was primly euphemized, was the high point of the entire production. Usually, Rod would have looked forward to the scene, if for no other reason than that it would allow him to show off as much skin as

160

possible, and he knew from his thousands of fan letters this was what the women wanted. But when he arrived at the studio in his enormous Hispano-Suiza at six in the morning, he was tense and apprehensive.

The truth was that, despite all the gossip, so far in the film's shooting he had been a perfect gentleman and Edwina had been a perfect lady. Yet he could feel the excitement in Edwina when they kissed, and it wasn't just acting. Rod was nearsighted, though too vain ever to wear glasses, and the harsh Klieg lights then in use made him practically blind on the set. The one thing he could see fairly well were the women he kissed in his close-ups, and his staring, myopic eyes were one of the factors in his enormous success. As he held, and stared at, Edwina, he felt a sexual excitement that wasn't playacting either. True, the newly formed Hays Office limited screen kisses to ten feet of film, but those ten feet were inevitably sizzling. The sexual tension between them was mounting with each day's shooting, and the icy looks Nick was giving him were producing in Rod an advanced case of the sweats. He didn't *think* Nick would do anything so crazy as shoot him, but there could be no doubt that a former arms dealer knew a lot about guns, and Rod was taking no chances: he would continue to be a gentleman.

Apprehensive as he was, the steamy bordello scene was shot without incident. At the end of it, Edwina said to him, "By the way, Nick wants you to drop by the house if you could."

"Sure. When?"

"Whenever. On your way home."

"Is it about the picture?"

She smiled prettily. "I have no idea."

Then she went to her dressing room.

Rod thought nervously about guns, but told himself he had nothing to worry about. He had been a perfect gent.

When he pulled up in front of the big Spanish house, however, his nervousness reasserted itself. Something about the place seemed different, odd. Telling himself he was imagining things, he got out of the Hispano-Suiza, walked to the front door and rang.

The door was opened by Edwina, wearing blue satin lounging pajamas.

"Butler's night off," she said, smiling. "Come in."

Rod entered the big entrance hall with the heavy lantern overhead. "Where's Nick?" he asked.

Edwina closed the door. "In Santa Barbara," she said. "There's a closing first thing in the morning on a vineyard he bought."

He looked at her. "What's the gag?" he asked.

"Mrs. Drummond has taken the children to a birthday party, and I gave the other servants the night off. We have the place to ourselves."

Rod began to sweat. "Look, Edwina, I don't think this is a good idea. . . ."

She came up to him and put her hand over his mouth.

"I love my husband, and I've never cheated on him. But playing these love scenes with you is driving me crazy. I want to do it once—just *once*—to get you out of my system. No one will ever know."

"No one ever does it *once*. . . ."

"*I* will. Trust me. Please don't make me beg."

Again, he thought of guns. Then he sighed.

"Hell, I've been dying to do this for weeks," he said, and he took her in his arms and kissed her.

"Upstairs," she whispered. "In the guest room."

They started up the big staircase.

The filming of *Youth on Fire* ended on August 3, 1922, and Rex Simpson immediately began the arduous task of editing the film so it could pass the strictures of the Hays Office Code (although the unedited version could be released in Europe and South America, where the Code didn't apply; it was only the virtue of *American* moviegoers that had to be protected). Rod took a week's vacation at Lake Tahoe before reporting to Fox to begin his next assignment—*Trouble in Samoa*. He heard nothing from Edwina and began to wonder if it were possible she really *could* do it only once. Making love to her had been as exciting as he had anticipated, and when he thought that his first impression of her had been that she was a cold fish, he laughed to himself. Nevertheless, he wasn't going to suggest a second bout—he still respected Nick's gun too much for that. However, he wondered what he would do if *she* approached *him*.

But she didn't—until the week after Labor Day. Then he received a phone call in his dressing room.

"Rod, it's Edwina."

His heart pounded.

"Hi" was America's Dream Man's monumentally uninspired reply.

"You must come to the house tonight. Something *terrible* has happened."

"What?"

"I can't tell you on the phone!"

"Where's Nick?"

"He's staying at the studio tonight, looking at the final cut with Rex. Be here at eight. I've sent the servants packing."

And she hung up.

The Santa Ana wind had turned Los Angeles into an inferno. As Rod drove to the Hollywood Hills in his Isotta-Fraschini, the pepper trees that lined the streets (and ruined car paint jobs by dropping peppers on the roofs and hoods) drooped from the heat, and the homely bungalows of the Angelinos seemed to shrivel. But in the Hollywood Hills, where the mansions of the movie people began, it seemed to Rod it became a little cooler—or was it his apprehension? A dozen scenarios unreeled in his mind, but the worst was his confrontation with a coolly angry Nick, who would aim his gun at him and . . . Of course, he told himself, those things don't really happen.

But he knew they *did* happen. A half year earlier, film director William Desmond Taylor had been shot to death in the study of his apartment on Alvarado Street in Los Angeles' placid Westlake district. The murder, which had not been solved, involved and ruined the careers of stars Mabel Normand and Mary Miles Minter. Sexual hanky-panky and drugs had been dragged into the scandal, and a neighbor reported seeing a man who walked "like a woman" leaving the apartment after the fatal shots were fired.

Reality in Hollywood could be more lurid than the fantasies it filmed.

The sun was just setting as Rod pulled up in front of Casa Encantada, and the long shadows of the palm trees stretched across the lawns and gardens into the enormous pool. He went to the front door, which was opened by Edwina. The English beauty seemed cool.

"Thanks for coming," she said, admitting him, then closing the door. "Let's go into the library."

"What's this all about?" he asked, following her across the blue-tiled floor of the hall.

"Keep your voice down. Mrs. Drummond's upstairs with the children. I don't want her knowing you're here."

She opened the library door and went in. It was a small, comfortable room with a Mexican-style round stucco fireplace in one corner. Two tall windowed doors opened onto a terrace; Edwina went to them and closed the heavy red velvet curtains. Then she turned on the lights.

163

"I'm sorry to be so melodramatic," she said. "But I thought you *must* know. I'm pregnant. By you."

He sank into a leather sofa.

"By *me?* One time? Come *on.*"

"Darling, it *has* to be you. There's been no one else except Nick, and he's been using condoms since Edward was born because we don't want any more children for the time being. So it's *got* to be you."

"But . . . God, I need a drink."

"Of course. Let me get you one. Whiskey?"

"Bourbon, and plain water. Does Nick know?"

The library had one big bookcase. Now Edwina pressed a button and the bookcase wheeled a half turn to become a mirrored bar. She fixed him a stiff drink.

"Yes," she said. "I told him last night. He went into a really violent rage—it shook me a bit, I can assure you."

"Did you tell him it was *me?*"

"Oh, he guessed. And I could hardly deny it, could I?"

Rod groaned.

"Thanks. Now he'll shoot me."

"Don't be silly, darling."

"Silly? *You* told me if I made a pass at you, he'd blow my brains out!"

"Well, I was exaggerating. Here, drink this."

He took the glass and gulped.

"After a bit, he calmed down," she continued. "I mean, it's to all our advantages to keep this a secret, isn't it? With all the gossip about the love scenes and so on, if it got out we'd *really* been making love, the Hays Office would go berserk."

"Then what are you going to do? Have an abortion?"

She stiffened. "Absolutely *not!* I would never kill my own child! No, Nick and I decided we'll have the child, and he has very sweetly agreed to raise it as his own. But I insisted you know. I mean, I think it's only *fair* you know."

He pulled a handkerchief from his pocket and mopped his forehead. "Do you think we could have a *little* air in here?" he asked.

"Sorry. It is ghastly, isn't it?"

She went back and opened the curtains, and then the doors, allowing a slight breeze to enter.

"Well, I'm glad you told me," he said. "I *guess* I'm glad. And I guess this is the best solution. But . . ."

There was a knock on the door.

164

"Damn," muttered Edwina. She went to the door and opened it a crack.

"Yes?"

Rod heard a high-pitched English voice and guessed it was the nanny.

"Charles has started coughing again," she was saying. "I took his temperature, and he's got a slight fever. Should we call Dr. Travers?"

"Let me go up and see him."

She closed the door and whispered to Rod, "Stay here. I'll be right back."

Then she reopened the door and left the room. Rod lit a cigarette, poured himself another bourbon, then walked to the doors to look out at the sky across which the vanished sun had splashed a gorgeous palette of oranges and reds.

Edwina and Mrs. Drummond were at the top of the steps when they heard the shots. Three of them, in rapid succession. Then silence.

"Oh, my God," said Edwina. Then, saying to Mrs. Drummond, "Stay here," she ran back down the steps, crossed the entrance hall and opened the library door.

Rod was lying on his side in front of the open doors, his back to Edwina. She ran to him and kneeled, afraid to touch him.

"Rod . . ."

Nothing. She stood up and stepped over him. Now she could see the blood spreading over his shirt and pouring out of the hole in his forehead.

"He's dead," she whispered to herself, as if unable to comprehend the fact.

Then she realized the murderer might be standing behind her. Cold with fear, she turned and looked out on the terrace. There was still enough daylight left that she could see it was empty.

Then the horrible thought occurred to her: Had Nick done it?

THE SPARROW SINGS
By Harriet Sparrow

Hollywood, which has suffered through a year of shocking scandals, has now been rocked by yet a new one that may eclipse the murder of director William Desmond Taylor and the alleged rape-death of starlet Virginia Rappe by comedian Fatty Arbuckle. America's Dream Man Rod Norman was shot to death last night in the house of producer Nick Fleming, head of Metropolitan Pictures. Your reporter, who was alerted by contacts on the L.A. police force, arrived at the scene of the crime a little after nine-thirty. Casa Encantada, the huge Spanish-style mansion of mogul Fleming, was filled with policemen and reporters. Edwina Fleming, Nick's beautiful English wife and costar with Rod in the much-discussed film *Youth on Fire,* was upstairs in her bedroom, incommunicado. Apparently, Edwina had asked Rod to meet her at Casa Encantada, for reasons so far unknown. They were in the downstairs study when Edwina was summoned upstairs by her children's nanny. It was then they heard three shots. Edwina raced back down to the study to find Rod's body on the floor. The assailant must have been outside, either on the terrace or in the gardens, waiting. However, so far there has been no clue either to his identity or to a possible motive for the brutal slaying. Nick, who was at the studio with director Rex Simpson, told me he was "stunned" by the murder, which seemed to him "totally senseless." Rod's widow, lovely Norma Norman, was unavailable for comment.

"But *why* did you ask him here?" Nick shouted for the tenth time. It was four in the morning. The police had finally left, the body had been removed, the forensic photographers had taken their last photos, and Casa Encantada was, for the first time in hours, a house again instead of a sideshow.

Nick and Edwina were in their bedroom, Edwina on the enormous silk-sheeted bed in tears, Nick, in his satin-collared red bathrobe, pacing back and forth at the foot of the bed. He had been berating his hysterical wife for a half hour. Now she shouted back.

"Why did you kill him?" she sobbed.

Nick stopped pacing to stare at her. *"Me?* Do you think *I* killed him? I was a mile away at the studio, with Rex Simpson!"

"That could be a lie!"

"Ask Rex! And why the hell would I kill Rod Norman?"

"Because you were *jealous!*" she screamed, bursting into tears again. Edwina, normally composed and immaculate, was a mess—her movie-star face was tear-stained and puffy, and one strap of her white satin nightgown had slipped off her shoulder as she crouched in the middle of the bed like a cornered animal.

Nick came around the bed and grabbed one of her wrists. "Was he your lover?" he whispered. *"Did* I have something to be jealous of?"

She said nothing. He sat beside her and violently shook her.

"Was he your lover?" he repeated.

Silence.

"What was he doing here last night?" he shouted, shaking her again and again.

"All right, I'll tell you the *truth!*"

She pushed him away, sat up and wiped her eyes defiantly.

"I asked him here to tell him I was carrying his child."

"Oh, Jesus," he groaned. "Then it *is* true. . . ."

"Just *once!* I went to bed with him once, Nick. I swear it! I developed this passion for him during the rehearsals. It really surprised me, but it was driving me *mad!* So whenever it was—four or five weeks ago when you went up to Santa Barbara—I asked him to come here. He was terrified of you, afraid you might shoot him, but, well . . . he'd developed a passion for me too. We did it, and I'll admit I enjoyed it because he was a lot like you, darling, but he really wasn't as good as you."

"Thanks a lot."

"It's true, Nick. And at least I got him out of my system."

"You make adultery sound like taking an enema."

"Maybe it *is!* But the damnable thing was that that *one* time he made me pregnant!"

"Do you expect me to believe *that?*"

"It's true! *He* believed it last night when I told him." She rubbed her temples with both hands. "Oh, God, I've done a terrible thing. I've lied to you, I lied to him . . ."

"I thought you said you told him the truth?"

"I told him *half* the truth. But I told him you knew and you'd agreed to let me have the baby and that you'd raise it as one of your own children."

"Edwina, you amaze me! Why the hell did you tell him that?"

"Because I was desperate! I was *afraid* to tell you the truth, and I wanted to try it out first on Rod. . . . Oh, Nick, forgive me. Please. I know I've behaved hideously, but I've been under a terrible strain making the film and trying to be a success in it because I know you've committed *so* much to it and me . . . but please forgive me."

"And the way you relieve your strain is to go to bed with your leading man?"

"It was a *mistake!* I admit it! I never claimed to be perfect. But remember, you virtually threw me at him. If you loved me, you'd forgive me."

He looked at her, anger and disgust fighting in his mind with his genuine love for her. He had told himself to trust her. Now he knew his

167

trust had been misplaced, and it hurt. Hollywood was a town where adultery was becoming a way of life, but Nick had an old-fashioned attitude toward marriage: *his* wife must be different, *his* wife must be true. He knew he would forgive her; practically speaking, he had little choice. If there was a rift between him and Edwina, the press, and everyone else, would say she had been Rod's mistress. But he would never feel quite the same about her again.

"All right," he said, "you're forgiven."

"Oh, Nick, *darling!*"

She crawled over the sheets into his arms and began kissing him.

He held her at arm's length. "What about the child?" he said.

"We can still have it, can't we? No one will ever know except us, now that Rod's dead. . . ."

"Yes, I suppose so. It's crazy, but I guess it's the only way." He remembered his first son, aborted by Diana, and the bitterness and rage he had felt then. He could never consent to aborting another child, even if it wasn't his own. Edwina would have the child and he would raise it as his own.

"But no one must ever know the child isn't ours," he continued. *"I'll* be the father, not Rod. Is that a deal?"

She hesitated. "But what about the child? We'd have to tell him— or her—someday, wouldn't we?"

"NO," he said, his mouth tight, his chin muscles moving beneath his skin. He was remembering his mother, his horror and shame at learning he was a bastard. If they were going to play out this charade, then he would never inflict on the child what had been inflicted on him. To the rest of the world, the Fleming family must look serenely united, free of the taint of scandal. As a child, Nick had never had the security of "family." Now he would force it on his own family—if necessary by sheer willpower.

Edwina was in no position to bargain. "All right," she agreed, almost meekly. She kissed him again.

"But . . ." He started to say something, then stopped.

"But what?"

"Then who the hell killed Rod Norman? And why?"

She extricated herself from his arms and straightened her hair. "Do you suppose it was Norma?" she asked.

THE SPARROW SINGS
BY HARRIET SPARROW

All Hollywood mourned Rod Norman today. Thousands of his adoring fans lined Hollywood Boulevard to say farewell to the screen's great lover, and many of them were weeping openly, perhaps the greatest tribute to the dead star. Moviedom's royalty came to the Church of the Dell to pay their respects to Rod, whose murder three days ago still has the police baffled. Charlie Chaplin was there, Doug and Mary, Gloria Swanson, Anna Q. Nilsson, Rudy Valentino, Constance Talmadge, Rod La Rocque, Nazimova, Pola Negri—all came, saddened and subdued by Death, which has struck down in his prime one of the film capital's most popular personalities. Rod's widow, lovely and talented designer Norma Norman, emerged from her limousine swathed in black veils, which hid from the public her terrible grief; everyone was impressed by her wonderful composure. Nick and Edwina Fleming were there, solemn and sad. Oh, how I wish I could have read their thoughts! *Youth on Fire* will now go down in history as Rod's last film. Aside from everything else, Nick and lovely, aristocratic Edwina must be wondering how the moviegoing public will react to this film, now so terribly marred by real-life tragedy.

The darling little Church of the Dell was filled with flowers, moviedom's final tribute to the man who embodied so many romantic dreams. And there, in front of the altar, in a tasteful white casket, was the Dream Man himself. I took a last look at Rod. How handsome he was, in his beautifully tailored dark-blue suit! His hands were folded in the Peace of Death over a small Bible. His face (the bullet hole in his forehead having been skillfully disguised by the art of the mortician) ruggedly handsome in the Eternal sleep. When I remembered the many wonderful hours he had given us in his films, I couldn't hold back the tears.

Outside, the sun shone warmly in an azure sky, as if God were welcoming into His firmament a new star. . . .

CHAPTER 17

THEY rolled out of the Anatolian hills like thunder. In August 1922, the long-awaited attack of the Kemalist guerrilla forces against the Greek Army had begun. Like Kutuzov, the brilliant Russian commander in the Napoleonic Wars, Mustapha Kemal Pasha knew that one of his greatest allies was Time. He waited for the Greek forces to become bored and dispirited. He was brilliantly assisted by the commander of the Greek Army, the pudgy, dressy General Hadjanesti, who was, conveniently, in the process of going mad. As his men suffered from the cold and the heat, the dust, short rations and rank water, the General sat in the cafés of Smyrna drinking himself blind. On one occasion, he became convinced he was made of glass and went to bed for twenty-four hours, certain that if he got up his legs would shatter. With such inept leadership, it was no surprise the Greek Army was in an advanced state of demoralization. When they saw the Turks descending on them, they broke ranks and fled for Smyrna, leaving their weapons and ammunition behind.

Kemal gave them no chance to regroup. Leading his troops in person, galloping back and forth before his lines, he urged the Turks onward, shouting, "On to the Mediterranean!" until he was hoarse. It worked. The wearying Turks were galvanized. Within ten days the Greek retreat became a rout. It is 160 miles from Ushak, where the Greeks had been, to Smyrna and the sea, but within eight days, the fleeing Greeks were entering the Mediterranean port. In their wake they left a trail of death, for the Greeks took their revenge by murdering as many Turkish peasants as they could find. The Turks responded in kind. Kemal himself saw a Greek soldier crucified on the wooden door of a peasant hut, iron stakes driven through each palm, a bayonet through his belly, his face slashed unrecognizably. It was a sickening sight, but Kemal said to Colonel Arif, "Good. A dead enemy always smells sweet."

He spurred his horse and continued his gallop to the sea.

Following the Turkish Army in Kemal's aging, open-top Benz, chauffeured by a Turkish sergeant, were the Gazi's two "women," as they were dubbed by the troops: the beautiful, dark-haired Fikriye in her perpetual black; and the honey-blond Diana Ramschild, who was riding out the war in boots she had bought at Hermès in Paris, breeches from Miller's in New York, a white open-at-the-neck blouse from Saks in New York and a solar topee she bought at Henry Heath's on Oxford Street in London. Diana was having the time of her life. In more ways than one, she considered this "her" war, first, because the Turks were fighting with ten thousand Ramschild rifles she had sold Kemal and which she had had shipped to Beirut, then smuggled into southern Turkey on three fishing boats. This one sale alone had raised Ramschild stock five points.

But second, and more important in her mind, was that she was in love with Kemal, her *janum,* her soul. His victories were her victories. Despite the heat and dust, the fearsome stench of burning and rotting flesh, the horrifying sights of mutilated corpses that lay everywhere, Diana was as galvanized by Kemal, the general, as his troops were. He had awakened a capacity for hero worship in her she never realized she had. And though his time with his "women" was necessarily curtailed by the war (he had also forsworn drinking until Smyrna was in Turkish hands again, which, for a man of Kemal's alcoholic tendencies, was no mean feat), she was happy being a "camp follower," as she called herself. She thought with amusement that few members of her class at Vassar were turning their lives into the romantic adventure hers had become. This was a far cry from being a Connecticut housewife, or even the head of Ramschild, and she was loving every minute of it. Kemal's ruthless cynicism, his reduction of the complexities of life to the simplicity of the strong dominating the weak, had drastically altered Diana's own morality. As Kemal had told her, they were both killers.

What had surprised her was Fikriye. First, she had assumed she spoke only Turkish. But it turned out Fikriye had a halting command of French, and her previous silence appeared to have been caused more by shyness than linguistic difficulties. Secondly, Diana had assumed that the Turkish woman would have at the very least resented the American, if not hated her, for sharing Kemal's bed. But upon Diana's return to the villa two days before the outbreak of the campaign, Fikriye spoke to her for the first time in French, and the silent "mystery woman," as Diana had thought of her, began to reveal herself as a helpful friend. This puzzled Diana at first, because she sensed that Fikriye was as passionate about Kemal as Diana had become. But then she began to understand. Fikriye seemed to accept Kemal's philandering as normal. Kemal was removing the veil from Turkish women and attempting to improve their subordinate status; but the institution of the harem was still a reality for many Turks. Diana told herself that Fikriye considered herself and Diana as members of Kemal's harem. It was an amusing thought.

They lived off the land. Each night, Colonel Arif would commandeer a farmhouse or villa for the Gazi and his retinue. Diana was sleeping on straw mattresses, and one night shared a barn with two cows and a bat. There was no plumbing usually; the best she could do was wash herself from a well. Yet primitive as conditions were, she didn't complain. Being with the Gazi was more than enough.

He was driving himself to physical exhaustion, but some inner reserve of nervous energy kept him going. It was as if he knew these were the finest days of his life. For the first week of the campaign, he barely spoke either to Fikriye or Diana, his conversation at dinner by necessity concentrating on military matters. But on the eighth night, as they neared Smyrna, after dinner he dismissed everyone from his table but Diana.

They were spending the night in a rug merchant's villa near Sardis. The house was pleasant and cool, with an open verandah, and it contained the ultimate luxury: an ancient zinc bathtub. Fikriye and Diana had taken turns bathing, scrubbing each other's back. The two women giggled and joked like schoolgirls, the baths affecting them like champagne. Diana put on a clean dress and made up her face carefully, as if anticipating that the Gazi might seek her out that night. Whether her instincts were correct, or her changing out of her breeches into a dress for the first time in a week was working the magic, she neither knew nor cared. At last, she was alone with her *janum*.

"You look lovely tonight, *Hanim Effendi*," he said, addressing her in the Turkish fashion as he sometimes chose to do.

"Fikriye *Hanim* and I found a bathtub," she said, smiling. "Our first baths in a week! It was delicious."

"I know it's been difficult for you. It must be especially hard for an American, used to luxury. But you are not unhappy?"

"On the contrary. Never happier. I think if I'd been a man I would have been a soldier like you. And unless I'm wrong, I don't think you've ever been happier either."

He smiled, and she drank in his blond good looks.

"You are a wise woman, my Diana. Come, I must show you something beautiful."

He stood up and came around the wooden table to hold her chair. As she stood up, he put his arms around her and kissed her.

"My darling," she whispered, "I've missed you so."

"Tonight we will make love. But first you must see part of what I am fighting for."

He led her out of the low-ceilinged dining room through the drawing room, which was furnished with cheap Victorian furniture of an appalling ugliness, out to the verandah, where Fikriye, Arif and a half dozen of Kemal's top officers were lounging and smoking. Kemal led her to his dusty Benz and opened the front door for her.

"It's only a short ride away," he said as she climbed in. He got in the driver's seat. The keys were in the ignition (no Turk in his right mind would have dared steal the Gazi's car); he started it and drove away. It was a cool evening with a near-full moon, and the stars, in the pure Anatolian air, were brilliant.

"Look at the Milky Way," she said, pointing upward. "Isn't it beautiful?"

"Like your skin, my Diana," he replied with a smile. There were few men on earth who could get away with a line that corny. From Mustapha Kemal Pasha, with his soft, low voice, it was magic.

Twenty minutes later, he stopped the Benz by the ruins of the Greek temple of Artemis at Sardis. In the moonlight, the broken marble columns glowed with a special mystery.

"This is why the Greeks say part of Anatolia belongs to them," he remarked as he got out of the car and walked around to Diana's side. "When they built this temple to Artemis in the third century B.C., this was part of the Greek Empire. Which is as ridiculous as Signor Mussolini saying Anatolia belongs to Italy because once it was part of the Roman Empire, or that England belongs to Italy because it was once part of the Roman Empire. No, the Greeks may have built this temple, but it is part of our Turkish heritage today. I wanted you to see it."

He helped her out of the car, then for the next half hour gave her a tour of the moonlit ruin, astounding her with his knowledge of ancient history and Greek architecture. When he stopped to light a cigarette, she said, "You surprise me—more every minute I'm with you."

"Why?" he said, exhaling. "Because I can kill men in cold blood and at the same time appreciate beauty?"

"Something like that, yes."

"There are many men in every man, or at least every interesting man. In me, there is even some woman. At times, I feel more woman than man. I have even made love to boys. Does that repulse you?"

"It fascinates me."

"But when I am with you, *janum,* I am all man."

He dropped the cigarette on the mosaic floor, ground it out with his boot, took her in his arms and kissed her.

CHAPTER 18

THE next morning brought news Kemal had been waiting for. The fighting was over. General Hadjanesti had decamped to Athens with his top officers, callously leaving his troops to fend for themselves. Looting and murder by the Turks were breaking out in the ancient Greek Quarter. It was time for Kemal to make his triumphal entry into Smyrna and receive the plaudits of his countrymen and the world.

He was jubilant. He hurried to the second floor of the villa and burst into Diana's bedroom. She was sitting up in bed reading a three-day-old issue of the London *Times* that had been brought from Smyrna by a courier.

"It's happened!" he exclaimed, coming to her bed and sitting on it. He was so excited he hadn't even removed the dark-gray woolen *kalpak* on his head. "The Greeks are finished! I'm going into Smyrna tomorrow morning."

Minutes before, the news would have thrilled her. Now she was so numb with shock, she had to force her enthusiasm.

"Darling, that's marvelous. . . ."

Kemal was too wound up to notice. "You and Fikriye will stay here till I can set up my headquarters. It's going to be a bit dangerous in Smyrna for the next few days—looting has already started—so I'll feel better if you're here, safe. But when the city's under control, I'll bring you in and then we'll have the biggest celebration in Turkey's history! And I give you my solemn oath"—he grinned—"I'm going to get drunk as an English lord!" He hugged her. "My beautiful American will be Queen of Smyrna!"

"Kemal," she whispered in his ear, "I've just read something in the London *Times* that's made me sick with worry."

He released her and looked at her. "What?"

"An American film actor named Rod Norman was murdered in Hollywood four days ago."

"So?"

"He was shot in the library of Nick Fleming's house. He actually resembled Nick."

Kemal was frowning. "So?"

"I have a terrible feeling Bald Ali murdered the wrong man."

Kemal stared at her a moment, then threw back his head and laughed, slapping his thighs.

"It's not funny!" she exclaimed.

"Oh, yes, it is! The funniest thing I've ever heard! Bald Ali—that fat rascal—had the wrong man shot! It's wonderful! But don't worry. He'll kill Fleming no matter how long it takes. He has to. His professional reputation's at stake."

His reaction disgusted her.

"I've killed an innocent man!" she said angrily. "Don't you think that's on my conscience? And it's *your* fault! *You* talked me into it!"

She immediately realized she had made a dreadful mistake. The laughter drained from his face and the most fearful anger she had ever seen flamed in his eyes. He slapped her so hard that she fell back among her pillows.

"Whore!" he yelled. "Don't blame *me* for your crime!" He slapped her again. "Mustapha Kemal has no conscience, and those he honors with his favors are there to please him, not accuse him! How *dare* you, you presumptuous slut? I have half a mind to take you outside and shoot you! And I'd tell the American Ambassador *and* the world that Mustapha Kemal had carried out the people's justice against a whoring arms dealer who hired an assassin to murder this actor—whatever his name is!"

He stood up, breathing heavily, still glaring at her with those burning eyes. "Whore," he repeated contemptuously. Then he turned and strode out of the room, slamming the door behind him.

She stumbled out of bed, ran to a small wooden table and threw up in the porcelain washbasin.

The city of Smyrna was one of the most fortunate in all Asia Minor. It had a balmy climate and a lovely crescent-shaped harbor fronted by rows of imposing two-story houses; it was backed by a rich, fertile hinterland where trees groaned with fruit; and it was drenched by the fragrances of almond trees, mimosa and oleander. It had a cosmopolitan and wealthy population of Turks, Jews, Greeks, Armenians and Europeans, each living in their separate quarters, each mingling in the crowded streets in their native costumes, giving the feeling of a never-ending costume party. The seaport, whose trade exceeded that of Constantinople, was famous for its gambling and its beautiful women, its houseboats, gold and racecourses, its clubs and restaurants. Most Smyrnans spoke three or four languages with ease.

But on the Sunday morning of September 10, 1922, it was a city of dread. For days it had been rumored among the Greeks and Armenians that "the Turks are coming." Now the Turks were here, and their reputation for cruelty had set the Greek and Armenian quarters packing. The beautiful harbor was jammed with ships: freighters, passenger liners, caïques and twenty-two warships. There were two British battleships, three American destroyers, three French cruisers, and an Italian cruiser and destroyer mingling with various other smaller warships. The reason for the presence of this armada of the Four Powers was to protect their nationals. Otherwise, it had been agreed that the foreigners would not intervene with what was now considered an internal Turkish problem. But the attention of the world was certainly on Smyrna that morning.

Mustapha Kemal entered the city in an open French touring car and was given a hero's welcome by the rhapsodic, screaming Turks. The Gazi smiled and waved and, with his flair for the dramatic, fooled everyone by refusing to wear any symbols of rank on his uniform. The first day he did nothing. That evening, he walked to the best hotel to take his first drink of *raki* since the start of his campaign two weeks before, and to everyone's amusement was told by the headwaiter, who didn't recognize him, that there was no table free. Kemal turned to a table of rich and nervous Greeks who *did* recognize him and asked, "Did King Constantine ever come here to drink a glass of *raki?*" They answered no. "Then why did he bother to take Smyrna?" he asked, and everyone laughed.

Word began to spread around Smyrna that perhaps Mustapha Kemal Pasha was not the monster everyone feared.

Diana Ramschild leaned on the railing of the verandah of the villa outside Sardis and stared listlessly at the floor. She wore a simple white dress and brown-and-white shoes. She wore no hat, and her honey hair needed combing.

"He can be like that," said Fikriye, who was sitting in a wooden chair nearby. It was Tuesday evening, and the villa was nearly deserted as the two women waited for word from Kemal. "He can be loving and kind, and then he can be terribly cruel. He falls in and out of love in a moment."

"I've behaved like a fool," said Diana quietly. "I suppose I deserved what he said to me. If I had any sense, I'd go home."

"But you don't have any sense, because you love him."

177

"Yes, I love him," she sighed. "I'm beginning to think I'm not very good at love."

"I love him too," said Fikriye in her soft voice.

Diana looked at the Turkish woman and felt more than a twinge of guilt. She had never given a second thought to Fikriye's feelings. To be frank, she hadn't thought Turkish women had feelings to hurt.

"I'm sorry for both of us," she said.

A car appeared at the end of the driveway and drove up to park in front of the villa. Colonel Arif got out and walked briskly up the steps. Nodding to Diana, he spoke to Fikriye in Turkish.

Fikriye stood up, a smile on her face.

"He has sent for us," she said to Diana. "Arif will drive us to Smyrna."

Diana wanted to cry with relief.

Three hours later, they parked in front of a lovely white villa in the wealthy section of Burnava, in the hills above the city. Diana and Fikriye got out of the car as Arif signaled one of Kemal's numerous Laz guards to carry their luggage. Even though it was near midnight, the villa was ablaze with light. Diana followed Fikriye up onto the porch, then paused to check her makeup in her gold compact mirror.

"It may be too late," she said to Fikriye, rather wryly, "but at least I can look my best for my execution."

Fikriye apparently didn't catch the humor.

They went inside the villa, which was lavishly furnished with French antiques. In the large drawing room, with a spectacular view of the harbor below, Kemal was seated at a desk reading telegrams and smoking. His uniform tunic was open, revealing his smooth, bare chest. He looked up at the two women and barked an order to Fikriye in Turkish. Fikriye left the room; then he looked at Diana. His face was stony. Although previously he had always gone out of his way to behave with punctilious courtesy to her, she was not unaware that now he remained seated.

"I'm thinking of getting married," he said. "Does that surprise you?"

"It depends on whom you're marrying."

"Her name is Latifeh. She is the daughter of the owner of this villa, a rich shipowner who is in Biarritz with his wife. Latifeh is beautiful, a patriot, and was educated in Europe. She would be a fitting wife for me."

"Congratulations," said Diana, telling herself not to show him her emotions. She knew he was trying his best to hurt her.

He held up a fistful of cablegrams. "I have received cables of congratulations from leaders all over the world, so I hardly need *your* congratulations. The President of France, the Chancellor of Germany, King Alfonso of Spain, Mussolini—even your President Harding. They know that Turkey has risen out of the ashes of defeat. They know that I am a man to be reckoned with—a great man."

"Did you send a telegram to yourself?"

He smiled slightly as he put the cablegrams down. "You defend yourself with humor—a Yankee characteristic, I understand. Since it is late, you may spend the rest of the night here. Tomorrow, I have booked you a room at the Cercle d'Orient, which is the most exclusive club in the city. Thursday, the French liner *Ville de Paris* sails for Marseilles. I have booked you a suite. You will be the guest of the new Turkish government, which has paid all your expenses. It has been a pleasure to have known you, mademoiselle. Good night."

He ground out his cigarette in a heaped ashtray.

"Is that all?" she said.

"What more is there to say?"

"You were my *janum,*" she said softly.

He was quiet for a moment, examining her with those extraordinary blue eyes. "Enduring, romantic love—the kind one reads of in cheap fiction—is something I'm afraid I'm incapable of."

"Then what did you see in me?"

He lit another cigarette and exhaled. "I had never made love to an American. It was an interesting experience for which I thank you."

"You cold-blooded bastard," she said, spitting out the words. "I feel sorry for Turkey."

He watched her as she left the room.

She was enraged. For the second time in her life, she had fallen in love with a man and then been betrayed by him, humiliated by him. In the hall outside the drawing room, she saw an antique Ottoman scimitar hanging on the wall. In her fury, she started to reach for it, to take it back in and kill him. Why not? Hadn't he taught her life was cheap? Hadn't he encouraged her to hire Bald Ali to kill Nick? But then she saw one of the guards standing at the end of the hall watching her, and she knew that even if she managed to kill Kemal, the Lazzes would never let her leave the villa alive.

No, control your emotions, she thought as she climbed the stairs, or your emotions will control you. Still, she spent most of the night lying on her bed weeping her *janum* out of her heart.

In the morning, she was driven to the Cercle d'Orient, a compound surrounded by a six-foot-high white stucco wall. It was in the European Quarter, not far from the French Consulate, and it was an island of luxury and excellent food, with a swimming pool, tennis court and casino. The manager, an elegant Frenchman named M. Duval, greeted her with almost exaggerated politeness. "You are a guest of Mustapha Kemal," he said as he led her to her suite on the second floor. "We are highly honored, mademoiselle."

Diana said nothing, her opinion of Mustapha Kemal being radically different from M. Duval's. The suite was spacious and handsome, furnished with white wicker. Two ceiling fans hummed lazily, and it had a balcony overlooking the swimming pool. As the porters deposited Diana's two suitcases, M. Duval said to her, "I would strongly advise Mademoiselle not to leave the compound today. Here we are safe. We have the wall and our own guards. But outside in the streets, it is dangerous. I regret to say the Turks are behaving abominably. Mustapha Kemal has decreed the death penalty for any Turkish soldier harming a Greek or Armenian, but this morning I saw two Turkish officers hold up a merchant directly across the street from us, so obviously the Turks are not intimidated by the Gazi's threat."

"The Gazi, Monsieur Duval, is a thoroughly loathsome man."

He looked startled. "At any rate, we are hearing many ugly stories, mademoiselle. I don't wish to frighten you, but please, stay in the compound."

"Thank you, monsieur," Diana said. "I have no intention of going anywhere except home."

Geographically, the Turkish Quarter was farthest south in Smyrna, near Mount Pagus. Then, moving north, were the Jewish Quarter, the Armenian Quarter, the Greek Quarter, and finally the European Quarter. Everyone in Smyrna knew that each day, between noon and two, a local wind called the *imbat* sprang up, blowing from southwest to northeast. Shortly after noon on Wednesday, September 13, 1922, four fires broke out simultaneously on the southern edge of the Armenian Quarter. The *imbat* fanned the flames, driving the fire northward, away from the Turkish Quarter toward the Greek Quarter. Quickly, other fires broke out, all to the north of the Turkish Quarter. By two in the afternoon, the Armenian Quarter had become an inferno.

Diana, having lunch by the pool a half mile to the north of the fires, saw the distant smoke roiling to the sky and asked the waiter what was happening. "They say fires have broken out in the Armenian Quarter, mademoiselle," he said as he refilled her wineglass with an excellent Turkish rosé. "They say the Turks are starting them, to kill all the Armenians and Greeks. It wouldn't surprise me."

She looked alarmed. "But isn't someone stopping them? Where's the fire department?"

The waiter smiled and shrugged. "The fire department is Turkish, mademoiselle." He returned the bottle to the ice bucket, then moved on to the next table where the French Consul and his wife were sipping vichyssoise.

Troubled, Diana returned to her lunch. The pool area was almost filled with well-dressed Europeans. The scene couldn't have appeared more normal.

But fifteen minutes later, as Diana was sipping her Turkish coffee, M. Duval appeared. He looked nervous. He came to the French Consul's table and whispered something in his ear. The French Consul, looking troubled, signaled for the check.

At two-thirty, as she prepared to wash her hair in her bathroom, Diana smelled the smoke. Hurrying out to her balcony, she saw smoke drifting over the swimming pool. The stucco wall couldn't keep out smoke.

There was a knock on her door. She came back into the bedroom, threw on her bathrobe and went to the door. It was M. Duval. He looked anxious.

"Unhappily, mademoiselle, we are forced to ask everyone to leave. The wind is blowing the fire our way, and as a precaution we are abandoning the club."

"But where can I go?"

"Ah, Mustapha Kemal Pasha has sent a car for you. It is in the courtyard now, waiting for you. Shall I send the porters up in, say, ten minutes?"

"Yes, ten minutes . . ."

M. Duval bowed and hurried away.

The car was a heavy, black French touring car with two small Turkish flags on each front fender. It belonged to the local Turkish Governor, but had been commandeered by Kemal. As the porters strapped Diana's two suitcases on the rear luggage rack, she thanked Duval, who nervously kissed her hand, then she climbed in the back seat.

Fikriye was waiting for her, her beautiful face drawn, her large brown eyes, normally so soft, now strangely hard. Diana was surprised to see her.

"Kemal Pasha sent me to take you to the docks," she said as the soldier-chauffeur started the car, heading it around the circular drive toward the wrought-iron gate. "He says you will be safer on the ship. A launch is ready to take you out to the *Ville de Paris.*"

"Fikriye, why doesn't he stop the fire? The whole city may go up in flames!"

"Kemal Pasha says the fire is a purge. It will cleanse Smyrna of the foreign pigs."

Diana was shocked. Up till now, she had considered Fikriye totally apolitical.

"But people will be killed! And I heard at lunch that Turkish soldiers are looting. . . . Whatever Kemal's faults, and God knows I'm aware of them, he can't want to start his government with a massacre!"

Now Fikriye turned on her, her eyes blazing.

"What do *you* know about Turkey? How dare you tell *us* how to govern our own country? You came here to profit by selling your rifles to my Pasha, then you make love to my Pasha and *dare* to criticize him! Go back to America and leave us alone."

This angry outburst stunned Diana into silence. Was she seeing the real Fikriye for the first time, a woman who, though pretending to befriend her, had all along detested her? The "my Pasha" business was new and revealing.

The car passed through the iron gates of the Cercle d'Orient and Diana began to see what was happening outside her island of luxury. The store opposite the gates had not only been looted, but wrecked. It had been a *quincaillerie,* or hardware store, but the plate-glass window had been smashed and the store's merchandise thrown out into the street, which was strewn with hammers and screwdrivers. The street was empty of people except for one ragged boy who was urinating on a brick wall until he saw the car pull out of the Cercle d'Orient, at which point, presumably terrified by the Turkish flags on the fenders, he ran down the sidewalk and vanished around the corner. But Diana could see through the windshield that the next cross street, which led to the docks and the harbor, was thronged with people. As the car reached the intersection, the chauffeur began honking his klaxon—*oo-ga! oo-ga!*—as he turned right, inching the car into the sea of frightened humanity.

Many of them wore European clothes. But more were in native

Greek or Armenian costumes, carrying bundles in their arms or on their heads, or both. There were literally thousands. Diana saw bizarre sights: one old man carried a potbellied iron stove, another had two wooden coffins, presumably empty, strapped to his back.

"They opened an American grave in the cemetery this morning," said Fikriye, who was sitting calmly in the corner, watching the passing scene. "They pulled out the corpse and tore it to pieces."

Diana tore her eyes away from the windshield to look at the Turkish woman, who, as always, wore nothing but black, including today a black snood over her hair. Diana noticed that, for the first time, she was carrying a black leather, European-style purse, which she held in her lap, clutched by both hands.

Diana started to ask why they would profane an American grave, but realized the answer was obvious. Turkey and America had been enemies in the Great War, and now xenophobia, as well as flames, was sweeping the city. So she said nothing, turning her eyes back to the crowd in front of them.

It took them an hour to reach the docks. By now, the fire had spread from the Armenian Quarter well into the adjacent Greek Quarter, driving the entire population in front of it to the harbor. Ernest Hemingway, a reporter from the Toronto *Star,* was watching the scene through binoculars from the safety of the bridge of the British battleship *Iron Duke,* anchored in the harbor.

"The whole goddamned city's burning!" he said to one of the British officers standing beside him. "Look at that smoke! It's going at least a hundred feet in the air! And the dock's jammed. . . . You can't tell me you're not going to pick up *some* of these people!"

"Only British nationals," said the officer. "We have strict orders from the Admiralty not to intervene."

"But how do you know some of those people on the dock *aren't* British nationals?"

The officer said nothing.

The car had reached the point of no return. The dock area all along the crescent harbor was jammed with humanity: no vehicle could get through. Fikriye addressed the driver in Turkish, then said to Diana, "You must get out here. We can go no farther."

"*Here?* But where's the boat?"

"Find it yourself."

Diana looked out the side windows, then the back. The car was surrounded by the mob, many of whom were screaming out of sheer panic. She turned to Fikriye.

"This is ridiculous—I can't get out here! I wouldn't be able to move through that crowd. If you can't get me to my boat, then take me to the American Consulate."

Fikriye opened her black leather purse and pulled out a small pistol, which she pointed at Diana.

"Vous descendez ici," she said. *"Here!"*

Diana stared at the steel barrel, realizing that now she was seeing the *real* Fikriye.

"But I may be killed . . ." she stammered.

Fikriye smiled. *"Tant pis"* was all she said. She shrugged.

The chauffeur pushed his way out of the driver's seat and was shoving the crowd away from the back door on Diana's side. Now he opened it, grabbed her wrist and began pulling her out of the car. Diana screamed and grabbed the leather strap on the rear of the front seat. The soldier cursed her in Turkish as Fikriye slammed the butt of the pistol on her fingers. Diana howled with pain and fell out of the car, sprawling under the running board on her back. The soldier slammed the car door above her, then climbed in front and began backing the car. *Oo-ga! oo-ga!* sang the klaxon.

Diana, sobbing with fear, rolled under the car, not only to prevent herself from being run over by the heavy tires but because there was no room to roll away from the car. She couldn't believe this nightmare was happening, couldn't believe Fikriye's hatred could be so intense. Or was it just Fikriye? Had Kemal instructed her to do this to the American woman who had defied and insulted him? Kemal, the self-confessed killer? Kemal, who was proud of having no conscience? Kemal, who probably had ordered the fires started, and sent her to the Cercle d'Orient, knowing she would be in the path of the flames?

The car was backing slowly over her head. Diana realized her best—perhaps only—chance was to stay under the car. She started crawling backward over the dirty, hot cobblestones, her face inches from the pavement. It was painful, but it seemed to work, since the car could back through the shouting crowd no faster than Diana could crawl. This continued for twenty minutes. Then, just as her hopes began to rise, the car stopped. The noise from the panicking crowd now was thunderous as the conflagration continued to spread rapidly toward the docks. The air was fouling with smoke and people were moaning with fear as they coughed and hacked the acrid stench out of their lungs. But over the din, Diana heard the chauffeur shouting. Then she heard rifle shots. Screams of panic. She tried to discover what was happening, but she could see only feet and ankles, an ocean of shoes.

Then she saw boots. Someone grabbed her ankles and began pulling her out from under the car. She screamed and kicked, but the hands holding her were too strong. She realized either the chauffeur or Fikriye had caught on to what she was doing and had summoned help. Now she was behind the rear of the car. She was grabbed under her arms by two Turkish officers and jerked to her feet. She saw that she and the car had crawled back as far as the handsome villas fronting on the harbor. As she continued to scream, she was dragged through the crowd to the nearest one. She looked back to see the car finally break out of the crowd into a side street, where it began to turn. A few more feet and she would have been safe.

There were four Turks in all. One kicked open the front door of the villa, and Diana was dragged inside. The house, furnished in expensive bad taste, was apparently empty, its occupants having fled. She was pushed into the drawing room where she saw, hanging on the wall above an upright piano, a large photograph of a benign Queen Victoria. The four officers, laughing and talking to each other in excited Turkish, started tearing her clothes off. Screaming, she beat at them with her fists, but they merely laughed. First her Chanel dress was ripped to shreds, then her custom-made lace-trimmed slip was torn off, then her brassiere and panties. She was so hysterical now, she was almost oblivious to what was happening to her.

The youngest officer was unbuttoning his tunic. The other three grabbed her and spread-eagled her against the upright piano, the ivory keys biting into her naked buttocks. The officer threw his tunic over an antimacassared armchair, then unbuttoned his pants and dropped them. His chest and shoulders were matted with black curly hair. She was screaming, "No, no, please, no," as he shuffled up to her, dragging his pants, which were still around his ankles, over the Ushak rug. The other three were egging him on as he raped her. When he was through, the other three followed suit, dragging her to the sofa for variety, then finally on the floor. When they all were finished, she lay, semiconscious, in the middle of the room. She was half aware of their laughing and chattering. Then she heard something being splashed around the room. She smelled gasoline. Then *she* was splashed. The cold shock of the liquid and the strong fumes revived her. She forced herself to sit up. She saw the four officers filing out of the room into the front hall. One was carrying a two-liter tin can.

Then they were gone.

She got to her feet, dripping gasoline onto the gas-soaked rug, coughing from the vile fumes. She started stumbling toward the door.

Then something crashed through the window. The room burst into roaring flames. Diana Ramschild, Vassar Class of '16, the president of the Ramschild Arms Company of Fairmount, Connecticut, became a pillar of fire.

When the fire of Smyrna finally burned itself out three days later, it was estimated that a hundred thousand persons had either drowned or been burned or crushed to death.

It was the birth of modern Turkey.

CHAPTER 19

T HE world premiere of *Youth on Fire* was held at Grauman's Egyptian Theater on October 26, 1922, and Nick Fleming pulled out every stop to make it as spectacular an event as possible. Searchlights sliced the Los Angeles sky, and fifty policemen had been hired to hold back the crowd of thousands of fans who shouted with excitement as they recognized their favorite stars stepping out of the limousines in front of the theater marquee. Nick had feared that the murder of Rod Norman might have hurt the appeal of the film, but of course the exact opposite had happened. All the gory publicity had only whetted the public's appetite to see Rod's last movie. And sneak previews in Pasadena and Santa Barbara had assured Nick that he had a hit on his hands. The audiences had loved it, and the talk in the business was that the love scenes, severely edited as they were so as not to offend the Hays Office, would prove to be as steamy as Harriet Sparrow had predicted.

To celebrate the opening, Nick had bought Edwina a magnificent ermine coat trimmed with white fox that swept from her rhinestone-buckled black evening shoes up her body to form a high-standing collar behind her head. When Edwina climbed out of their new Dusenburg limousine, which itself was a splendid sight, the crowd ooh-ed and ah-ed, even though most of those behind the police lines didn't know who she was. Yet.

"They'll know you after tonight," said Nick as he led her down the red carpet to the theater's double bronze doors.

"A movie star!" said Edwina, smiling. "I asked for it, and you made me one. Is it any wonder I'm insane about you?"

Youth on Fire was a smash. Costing $650,000 to film, it grossed in three weeks the astronomical sum of $4,000,000. For the moment, at least, Nick and Edwina Fleming were King and Queen of Hollywood.

Three weeks later, Nick's secretary, Miss Rawlins, ushered into his office Detective Arlan Marshall of the Los Angeles Police Department. Detective Marshall, a short man who covered his baldness with a bowler hat, had been in charge of the Rod Norman murder case. After shaking Nick's hand, he sat down in front of the big antique desk.

"Mr. Fleming," he said, "did you ever know a Diana Ramschild?"

"Yes, of course. In fact, I was engaged to marry her a number of years ago."

"You're aware she was killed last September over in Turkey when they burned Smyrna?"

"Killed?"

Nick was still young enough that the news of any of his contemporaries dying would have come as a shock. But this contemporary's death was a blow to his stomach. As the detective droned on about Diana's involvement with Kemal, Nick's thoughts rushed back six years to his passionate affair with her, that first skyrocket love of his life that had ended so bitterly. He remembered his green-eyed goddess, so coolly beautiful and so hotly physical when they made love in the deserted beach house. And now she was dead—as dead as their son. Had he been wrong? Had he been unfair to her? Diana dead? It seemed impossible. . . .

His attention drifted back to the detective, who had lit a cigar.

"A curious thing happened yesterday," he said, exhaling a foul-smelling cloud. "I received a phone call from the Turkish Consul here, asking me to have lunch with him at the Ambassador Hotel. Well, I had no idea what a Turk would want to see me for, but I wasn't about to pass up a free lunch, so I went. He was very vague. I didn't know what the hell he was driving at for about fifteen minutes. He told me that sources high up in the Turkish government, which he wouldn't name, had instructed him to contact me about the Norman case.

"Well, when I heard Rod Norman's name, I started listening *hard*. What he was suggesting was that a professional killer from Constantinople, of all goddamned places, had been hired to come to L.A. to shoot you—but he shot Rod Norman by mistake."

"*Me?* Why in hell would a Turk want to shoot *me?*"

"Well, the Consul hinted that the killer had been hired by this Diana Ramschild woman."

Nick stared at him a moment, then got out of his chair and walked to the big leaded window that looked out over the studio grounds. Was it possible? he wondered. Did she hate me *that* much?

"Think there's any truth to it?" asked the detective, watching him intently.

Nick turned, a smile on his face. "It's the most preposterous thing

188

I've ever heard," he said. "Diana Ramschild was a Vassar graduate and a lady. Vassar graduates don't hire killers, for Christ's sake."

The detective scratched his chin. "It struck me as a little wild too. But on the other hand, why would an official representative of the Turkish government tell me a pack of lies? And she *was* in Turkey."

Nick shrugged. "Don't ask me," he said. "I'm no detective, I'm a movie producer." He laughed. "Come to think of it, it might make one hell of a movie."

Yes, it *was* a wild story, but in his guts Nick knew it was true—he was lying to the detective to save Diana's posthumous reputation. How strong her love must have been to have hated that fiercely. Fiercely enough to try to assassinate him! He marveled at the primeval force of her emotion as, at the same time, he sweated at the thought that only Rod Norman's resemblance to himself had saved him from the assassin's bullet. Nick didn't believe in the supernatural, but he could almost feel the force of Diana's love and hate reaching out to him from beyond the grave.

Diana, Diana . . . Those magnificent green eyes now closed forever. He owed her a memorial, at least. What could it be?

Her words out of their past drifted into his memory: "I envy men. . . . I'd love to run a company like Ramschild." Well, she *had* run Ramschild, and it had cost her her life. But she had probably enjoyed those years.

He had jilted her for Edwina, and he owed her something. Maybe that something was to buy the Ramschild Company and make it into a success in honor of her memory and of old Alfred's too. The armaments business was in terrible shape, and it would be a risk to buy the company. But knowing human nature, he doubted the last war had ended all war. Germany was crushed and in a state of near anarchy, but never underestimate the Germans. . . .

Yes, he would buy old Alfred's company and turn it into a monument to Diana. He owed at least that to her.

And he might even make some money in the process.

189

Part III

A DREAM OF EVIL

1927

THE castle rose out of the German forest, its battlements and towers silhouetted by spears of lightning violent enough to have satisfied Baron Frankenstein. The fierce wind of the autumnal storm bent trees and whipped branches, sending flurries of dead leaves whirling in the air as thick clouds scudded across the sky, obscuring the new moon. Rain beat at the ancient stone walls of the Schloss Winterfeldt, situated sixty kilometers southeast of Munich near the town of Bad Reichenhall, close to the Austrian border. But while outside the Wagnerian storm raged, inside, in the sixty-foot-high *Rittersaal,* or Knights' Hall, all was a drafty calm as the castle's owner, Count Alexander Georg Joseph von Winterfeldt, entertained his ten guests at a sumptuous dinner.

Nick Fleming, seated to the right of his hostess, Countess Sophia von Winterfeldt, listened with polite boredom as the Countess droned on about a Munich politician-cum-rabble-rouser named Adolf Hitler. It seemed the heavyset, gray-haired Countess looked down her nose at Hitler, whom she called a *"petit bourgeois* gangster," who bit his nails and dressed terribly.

Nick had read about Hitler and knew that his National Socialist Party had about fifty thousand members, most of them attracted to his rabid anti-Semitism, which was a frightening phenomenon. But at the moment, Nick was more interested in the beautiful Italian seated halfway down the long chestnut dining table on the opposite side. Raven-haired, white-skinned, with a long, thin nose that gave her profile the look of an elegant hawk, the Contessa Paola Algarotti was shooting languid, if curious, looks at Nick, of which Edwina, seated at the right hand of her host, was not oblivious. By now, Edwina was used to Nick's flirtations, if not his increasingly ill-concealed infidelities, and she had her own ways of coping with them. She was devoting more than polite attention to the extraordinarily handsome young man on her right, the son of her host, Count Rudolph von Winterfeldt. Rudi, a graduate of Oxford, was the pluperfect Aryan: hair so blond it was almost white, dazzling blue eyes, and the clean-cut features of a Viking chieftain. Rudi, who was twenty-three, had never sat next to a movie star before. And even though his family tree reached back seven centuries and he was related to Bavaria's former royal family, the Wittelsbachs, as well as to the Austrian Hapsburgs, the normally composed young man seemed flustered by the attentions of one of Hollywood's reigning love goddesses.

"I really don't know much about movies," he was saying in his excellent English, "though I did enjoy one of yours I saw in London several years ago—*Burning Youth,* I think it was called."

Edwina, who was wearing three thick Art Deco diamond bracelets, leaned closer to him so that her low-slung silver evening dress would offer an even more tantalizing glimpse of her beautiful bra-less breasts.

"Youth on Fire," she corrected. "But that was ages ago! Five years ago—it was my first film. I'm crushed that you haven't seen any of my others." She batted her mascaraed eyelashes. "You *must* come to Berlin to see the opening of my new film, *Desert Love.* But surely your father's invited you. It's going to be *the* film event of 1927 in Germany!"

Count Alex, who was Minister of Culture in the Weimar government, had arranged the gala premiere at Berlin's Gloriapalast Theater to promote the exchange of German and American films. Edwina smiled her most engaging smile at Rudi, at the same time throwing a visual dagger down the table at her husband. To her surprise, Nick was no longer ogling the Italian Contessa. Instead, he was staring at one of the four footmen who were passing the heavy silver trays of venison and wild boar. A crash of thunder shook the castle as the rain continued to lash the tall leaded window of the *Rittersaal,* the window that held twelve different stained-glass coats of arms of the Winterfeldt family. All the guests were spending the night at Schloss Winterfeldt, which was lucky, considering the weather. But Edwina reflected she would be more than relieved to leave the gloomy castle in the morning. The bloody place was straight out of a horror film.

"Yes, I was invited," said Rudi, looking uncomfortable. "But I can't go to Berlin. I'm working on my doctoral thesis."

"Oh?" said Edwina, instantly bored by any subject that didn't deal with herself. "And what is your thesis about?"

"Political science. You see, ever since we lost the war, Germany has been living through a period of intense political turmoil. . . ."

"But surely all that street fighting is over now. From what we read in the States, Germany's quite prosperous and stable."

"Things have improved greatly in the past two years, true. But Germany will never be stable until the Treaty of Versailles is rectified."

She stifled a yawn. "My dear Count, you're *much* too serious for someone as young as you. And, I might add, as handsome. You should be thinking of love and romance! You *must* have a sweetheart. Tell me all about her."

Rudi looked even more uncomfortable. "No, there's no one . . . for the moment."

He's frightened of me, she thought. How curious.

It was then she saw her husband lunge at the footman and heard the thunderclap and the screams. Except it wasn't thunder: the footman had fired a gun in the air. The guests were jumping to their feet as Nick wrestled the footman to the stone floor. Count von Winterfeldt was shouting at the other footmen in German. There was another shot and more screams. Then, as the other footmen helped Nick subdue the fourth, it was all over almost as quickly as it had begun.

"Ein Arzt!" shouted one of the guests. *"Schnell, ein Arzt!* A doctor!"

Edwina saw her husband get to his feet. Blood was streaming down his forehead.

"Nick!" she screamed, running down beside the table.

As furious as she was at him for his flirting, when she saw he had been shot, all of her old love rushed back in an all-forgiving flood of emotion. "He's shot!" She was becoming hysterical. "Nick darling!"

He was holding a handkerchief to his forehead.

"Just a flesh wound," he mumbled. "I'll be all right."

At which point he collapsed facedown on the long table, shattering two wineglasses.

They carried him into the adjacent library, a dark, paneled room bristling with staghorns mounted below the ceiling, and stretched him on a leather sofa. Countess von Winterfeldt took charge. She had been a nurse in the war. Now, with a calm that impressed Edwina, she called for hot towels and wiped the blood away from the wound.

"Your husband is lucky, madame," she said. "The bullet passed right over the top of his skull. There are powder burns and he may have a slight scar, but he'll be all right. Bring some cognac, Rudi," she said to her son.

Edwina, still trembling, sank down in an ugly Renaissance leather chair that creaked from her weight.

"But what happened?" she asked. "Who was the footman trying to shoot?"

"I believe," said Count Alex quietly, "he was trying to shoot *me*."

"His name is Misha," Nick said forty-five minutes later after the doctor had bandaged his scalp wound. "He was a Bolshevik I met in Petrograd back in '17 when he was guarding the palace of the Grand Duke Cyril. I thought I recognized him in the dining room when he was serving. Then he recognized *me* and I think he realized I knew who he was. Anyway, when I saw him reach under his jacket, I decided not to take any chances and jumped him. He had just pulled out his gun when I grabbed his wrist."

"Thank God you did," said the Count. They were all sitting in the library having coffee and liqueurs. "You undoubtedly saved my life, and I'm grateful to you, Herr Fleming. I have no doubt that this Misha will turn out to be an agent of the Comintern."

His wife, Countess Sophia, looked grim. "Those terrible atheist Bolsheviks," she said. "They have been behind so many political assassinations throughout Europe. They want to spread their disgusting Revolution all over the world. But . . ." She hesitated. "It seems curious they would want to assassinate my husband. Alex, after all, is only the Minister of Culture. There are so many others in the government one would think they would be after. . . ."

She stopped, looking at her husband as if trying to understand.

Nick stood up.

"If you don't mind," he said, "I'm feeling a little tired. I think I should go to bed."

"My dear Fleming, of course!" exclaimed his host, also rising and coming over to Nick. "And again, let me thank you for your bravery. I will never forget—never." He put his hand on Nick's shoulder.

"Well," said Nick quietly, "there *is* something I would like to discuss with you in the morning. Perhaps before breakfast?" He exchanged looks with Winterfeldt.

The Count was trying to read his thoughts. Then he said, "I will be at your disposal. Say, eight o'clock? Here in the library?"

Edwina wondered what her husband was up to. She had found, after knowing him for ten years, that on the chessboard of life Nick Fleming was always thinking at least three moves ahead. He continually fascinated her because he was so damnably clever. The only way to understand him was to watch what he *did,* or, more exactly, to watch the *results* of what he did. Then, in retrospect, one could understand the workings of his complex mind.

Right now, as she climbed the great stone stairs of the *Schloss* to the second floor, she began to wonder if there wasn't more to the little scene she had just witnessed than was intended to be shown.

Their bedroom was on the second floor of the castle. It had high stone walls covered with handsome tapestries, a huge stone fireplace in which a welcome fire was burning, and rather moth-eaten magenta draperies covering the mullioned windows. A giant four-poster bed, topped by a red plush tester on which the Winterfeldt coat of arms had been stitched a century before, was covered by a thick *duvet*. As Edwina started to undress at the fake Louis XVI dresser, she said, "Why do I have the odd feeling you're holding something back from me?"

Nick was sitting in a high-backed tapestried chair removing his patent-leather pumps.

"What do you mean?"

"Don't play Mr. Innocent with me," she said. "It wasn't *that* important for us to be at the premiere in Berlin. And I know you juggled our schedule like mad so we could be at this dreary, godforsaken place tonight. You're up to something, aren't you?"

Nick stood up, took off his dinner jacket and came over to her so she could remove his lapis-lazuli-and-gold cuff links.

"Can I trust you?" he said.

"Of course you can. I'm your wife."

Nick watched her as she removed the cuff links. In fact, he *did* trust her. Despite her fling with Rod Norman five years before, despite her outrageous flirting with other men such as the young Count Rudi (which Nick had spotted, as intended), he knew that Edwina was still crazy about him and faithful to him. Theirs was a curious marriage: she felt a compulsion to *seem* unfaithful—part of the game, he supposed.

Of course, another reason he knew she was faithful was that he had kept her practically permanently pregnant for the last five years, which had produced three new Fleming children aside from little Fiona, Rod Norman's daughter, whom Nick loved as much as his own children, rather to his surprise. Edwina's constant pregnancy had hurt her film career and caused screaming fights between them, but she had borne the children stoically enough; and as the Fleming nursery filled to overflowing, she took delight in her brood as she continued to curse her husband for increasing it. Nick's motive for generating so many offspring was also partially a result of the aftermath of the shock of Diana's aborting his first son. The psychological scars of his childhood and youth were still visible on the man.

Edwina fascinated Nick as much as he fascinated her. And he did trust her.

"All right," he said. "The assassin tonight is named Misha, and he *is* Russian. But he's not the Misha I saw in Petrograd ten years ago, and he's not a Bolshevik. In fact, he fled Russia in 1919 because he hates the Bolsheviks as much as I do."

She stared at him. "Then who is he?" she said.

"His name's Misha Bronski, and he's an out-of-work Hollywood actor."

She gaped. "I don't believe it! An actor? Then what in God's name is he doing here? And why did he want to kill Count von Winterfeldt?"

"He didn't. Winterfeldt just *assumed* he wanted to kill him—particularly when I told him Misha was a Bolshie. The whole thing was an act. Misha and I rehearsed it in Hollywood two months ago, though I must say the bullet wound wasn't in the script. I guess it lent it authenticity, though."

"You mean, you *staged* it?"

He grinned. "That's right. I paid Misha twenty-five thousand dollars cash to do it. And I promised him a part in a film."

She laughed. "I should have *known!* Oh, God, it's the funniest thing I've ever heard! You *are* insane! But . . ." She stopped laughing. "It's *not* funny really. This Misha person will go to jail, won't he?"

Nick was untying his bow tie.

"For about six months. The Weimar Republic screams and yells about the Bolsheviks and the Comintern's conspiracy for worldwide revolution, but in reality they don't want to upset Stalin or the Russian government. Of course, if Misha had actually *killed* Count von Winterfeldt, it would have been a different matter. But since he really didn't attack him—to which I'll testify—they won't have much of a case. They'll stick him in the pokey for a few months for attempted assault or carrying a concealed weapon, then get him out of the country. There's a nice part for Misha in the *Counterspy* script Bill Pardee's working on. Misha should be back in Hollywood about the time I'm scheduling production."

He handed her his three shirt studs, and she put them and the cuff links in her Louis Vuitton jewel case.

"Of course," she said, "none of this makes any sense. In the first place, why would the German government not want to upset Stalin?"

"Because, dear wife, what you and most of the world don't know but *I* do know is that those damned Russians are secretly rearming the German Army—which I think you *do* know is prohibited by the Versailles Treaty. The Germans want the rifles and tanks, and the Russians—despite their undying faith in Communism—want the German money. It's a sweet deal for both of them."

Again, she stared at him, trying to digest what he was telling her. "All right," she said, "if you say that's what's going on, I'll accept it. But I still don't see the point of this bizarre charade you put on tonight!"

"It's simple," he said, smiling. "I want a very influential member of the German government to *think* he owes me his life." He leaned down and kissed her. "That bed," he whispered, "looks like it hasn't been used since Bismarck. Shall we give it a workout?"

"Darling, you're an absolute Byzantine snake," she said, kissing the end of his nose. "You'll probably end up getting us both shot with your mad schemes and I should have left you *years* ago. But you know why I don't?"

"Of course," he said, grinning. "You adore me."

"You're right, damn you. Let's go to bed."

She stood up and he kissed her again, this time more passionately. Then she pushed him away.

"Wait a minute," she whispered. "You're *not* going to sell guns to the Germans? Is that the point of all this?"

He looked noncommittal. "Of course not."

"Oh, Nick, you bloody liar! Of *course* that's what you're up to! What else would be worth twenty-five thousand dollars to you to stage this charade? Tell me the truth, are you going to sell them guns?"

He said nothing, looking stony.

"Oh, God, you can't! Have you forgotten that little war they caused thirteen years ago? Darling, *really*. . . . And aside from everything else, it's illegal, isn't it? I mean, aren't American arms companies prohibited from selling to the Germans?"

"Yes."

"But you're going to do it anyway?"

Again, he said nothing. She looked at him, disgust replacing the love that had been in her face a moment before. She walked to the bed.

"I'm not in the mood for sex," she snapped, climbing into the bed. "Besides, these damned storms give me a headache."

She turned out the bed lamp, thinking of Raymond Asquith and Lord Rocksavage and Yvo Charteris and all the millions of other young men whose lives had been snuffed out by the guns of the Great War. When, five years before, Nick had begun maneuvering to buy the Ramschild Company, he was met with determined resistance by Arabella Ramschild, whose hatred of "that Jew," as she contemptuously called Nick in private, had turned into an obsession after the death of her husband, then her daughter. Even though the other stockholders were easily seduced into selling their shares at Nick's offered price of fifteen dollars higher than the market value (especially since the company was racking up staggering losses), Arabella held out, defiantly stating in public that she would *never* sell to "Mr. Fleming." Then Arabella conveniently died, and her heirs were more than happy to deal at Mr. Fleming's price. By the end of 1923, Nick—and the Saxmundham Bank, for Edwina's father had financed the take-over—was solidly in control of the Connecticut arms company.

She heard him climb into the squeaky bed beside her, then felt his hand on her thigh. She shoved his hand away.

"Bugger off," she growled.

"You're not being fair, darling. I can't tell you what I'm after. . . ." She sat up.

"Nick, I don't want to talk about it. You know I didn't want you and Father to buy that damned armaments company. Of *all* things to get into when everyone in the world is sick to death of war and killings, *my* husband buys a gun factory! Don't you read the papers? Don't you know what they call people like you? Merchants of death. Oh, I know—that's headline hyperbole. But still, you shouldn't have done it, and I *hate* Ramschild."

"I give you my word I'm not selling arms to the Germans."

She looked at him. After almost ten years of marriage, she still took pleasure in looking at him. "Is that true?"

"Yes."

"You're not just saying it to get me to shut up?"

"For Christ's sake, Edwina, give me *some* credit for decency. I don't want to start a war, and your father and I didn't buy Ramschild to become merchants of death. We bought it because it was a good investment—or at least it's turned out to be a good investment—and I know from personal experience during the war that staying *out* of the arms business isn't going to prevent a war. By owning Ramschild, if nothing else, I'm in an excellent position to know what's going on in the world, and if you want to know the truth, *that's* why I'm in Germany."

She looked at him, confused but impressed by what he had said. "Well, I don't understand what you're up to, but I take back what I said about selling guns to the Germans."

He put his hand on her thigh. "Then how about it?"

Her anger simmered down and she laughed.

"Oh, Nick, I can never win with you. You always get your way. I suppose that's why I love you. I can't beat you, so I might as well just"—she shrugged—"love you."

He ran his hand up her stomach.

"It hasn't been bad, has it? Our marriage?"

"It's been delicious, and you know it. Even the fights."

"No regrets?"

"I could stand a teentsy bit more fidelity. I saw you eyeing that Italian Countess—whatever her name is—tonight."

"And I saw you going after the Count's son."

"Merely keeping in practice. My fidelity record's a lot better than yours, darling. If half the gossip I hear in Hollywood is true, you're having a merry time on that leather couch I rather stupidly bought for your office."

"Don't believe anything you hear. They say that about every studio head."

She looked at him with affection. "Oh, Nick, you don't really understand. I don't expect you to be one hundred percent faithful, mainly because I'm not as insanely possessive about you as you are of me. I know you're seeing dozens of gorgeous young girls and you're bound to be tempted—God, I'd be bored with you if you weren't. I don't even mind if you indulge—*periodically.* I suppose what really irritates me is that you can't have that same attitude toward me."

He frowned. "You're a wife and a mother. . . ."

"Oh, God, *am* I! With seven kids—don't remind me! But I'm also a woman and a human being. I'm not looking for a lover, but if I found one I wanted, you couldn't cope with the situation, could you? You couldn't say to me as I say to you, 'Go on, have yourself an occasional fling.' "

He thought for about a second. "No."

"You see? It's that damned American double standard."

"I suppose in England it's different?"

"You know it is, at least among the upper classes. Everyone plays around like dogs in heat and no one minds as long as one doesn't talk about it. It's much more civilized."

"I allowed you *one* lover, Rod Norman."

"And it's taken you years to get over that. I don't think you've *really* forgiven me, if truth be told. I'm just saying, darling, what's sauce for the gander should be sauce for the goose—or is it the other way around? I never can remember."

He sniffed irritably. "But I love you! You're *mine!*"

"And I love you, and you're mine."

They eyed each other.

"All right," he said. "If ever you meet some man you *really* want to go to bed with, tell me about it and I'll think it over."

"Hah! As if I believe *that* one!"

"No, honestly. You have a sort of a point. I don't like the point, but I'm willing to concede it's a point. Just don't take a lover behind my back again."

"As you do behind *my* back."

Silence.

"Are we going to make love or are we going to argue?"

She kissed him. "We'll make love," she said. "But think about what I said."

And they made love.

The storm began to weaken at five in the morning, and by seven-thirty, as Nick came down the staircase of the castle, it had died completely, replaced by a thin fog that gave the forest surrounding Schloss Winterfeldt a mystical look, reminding Nick of the ancient Teutonic legends— of Siegfried and dragons and trolls lurking in the Hercynian forests even before Germany became an outpost of the Roman Empire. The entrance hall boasted a full-length gold-framed portrait of Kaiser Wilhelm II wearing a white uniform and a plumed helmet. For a moment, Nick studied the portrait of the former German ruler now living in exile in Holland. The presence of the portrait left little doubt where the Count's political sympathies lay. He, like almost all of the nobility, was *Kaisertreu,* loyal to the old dynasty, and the Junker class still had considerable power in Germany. A restoration of the Hohenzollern dynasty was not out of the question. Germany, used for so many years to an authoritarian monarchy, was still uncomfortable with democracy, and many Germans longed for a *Fuehrer*—a leader.

Nick proceeded across the stone floor into the library, where he was greeted by Count von Winterfeldt, wearing a double-breasted gray suit. The Count was a tall, trim man with military bearing and impeccable manners that reminded Nick of the Grand Duke Cyril. The prewar officer class, despite its many faults, had superficial qualities in common that one could only admire. When one compared the Count with the street-brawling Nazi thugs Nick had read about, the Count came out far ahead.

"Herr Fleming," he said, coming over to shake his hand. "Good morning. How is your head?"

"Well, it still stings a little, but it's not as bad as I expected."

"Good. Please sit down. I have talked with Herr Halbach, our local chief of police. He tells me that our fighting footman of last night is named Misha Bronski. To our surprise, he carries an American passport."

Nick sat down on the same leather sofa on which he had been treated the night before.

"Really? I've read that the Comintern has many agents in the States."

"Perhaps, though it seems somewhat odd that they would send an agent from America when it would be so much easier to send one from Russia. However, who can understand the mind of the Bolshevik, no? By the way, Halbach asked if you would be willing to testify as a witness."

"Of course."

"Good." The Count sat down next to the sofa. Through the big leaded window that stood behind the heavy oak desk, the fog embraced the castle with its clammy clasp. "Now, sir, you asked to see me. I hope you have a favor to ask of me. Since I owe you so much— my life—I am most eager to be of assistance to you in whatever way I can."

Which is exactly what I wanted, thought Nick. "I want to sell arms to Germany," he said. "Can you help me meet the right people?"

Look at his eyes light up! He's walking right into the trap. Wonderful!

"I will be honored to help you, Herr Fleming," said the Count softly. "But, as I'm sure you can appreciate, we must be discreet. *Very* discreet."

CHAPTER 21

I F landscape is character, then Rudi von Winterfeldt must have had a beautiful soul, because he had grown up in some of the most staggeringly gorgeous scenery in Europe. That afternoon, as he drove his white Bugatti sports car from Schloss Winterfeldt in the direction of Munich, he passed out of the foothills of the Bavarian Alps, with their breathtaking views of the Obersalzberg, through lovely green fields dotted with charming villages and, here and there, a gem of a baroque church. He passed the Herrenchiemsee, that lovely lake on an island of which mad King Ludwig of Bavaria had built his final unfinished extravaganza, a late-nineteenth-century version of Versailles, the staggering price of which had cost Ludwig his throne. Then the fairy-tale castle of Neuschwanstein perched dramatically on top of a fir-furred mountain. And everywhere cows and goats peacefully grazed on the rich green grass of the rolling fields.

The fog had burned off and the sky had turned a brilliant blue. It was unseasonably warm, a late-November Indian summer after the storm. As Rudi sped down the road in the open car, the crisp wind blowing his blond hair, his soul responded as always to the beauties of southern Bavaria, even though he knew the landscape by heart. This was *his* landscape, and its lushness never failed to thrill him. There was an artistic side to Rudi, and a dreamy side. Part of him loved beauty and loathed ugliness.

Which was why he wasn't overly fond of Munich. The Bavarian capital had its beautiful palaces and museums, true. Almost a century before, King Ludwig I had spent a fortune beautifying the city before he lost his heart to Lola Montez and his throne to the Revolution of 1848. But Munich was a city, and like all cities it had its slums and factories. Rudi always felt a slight depression when he left the countryside and entered the dreary outskirts of Munich.

Now he drove to the Thierschstrasse, an uninspired street in a lower-middle-class section of the city, and parked his Bugatti in front of a dingy building. The expensive sports car was almost an affront, if not a provocation, in the poor neighborhood, and as Rudi prudently put the top down so as to be able to lock the car, he was well aware of the envious stares of the ragged children playing in the street. But he knew the person he was going to visit took a perverse pleasure in having expensive cars parked in front of his down-at-the-heels apartment.

Rudi walked into the entrance vestibule and turned the bell. A few moments later, a plump, gray-haired hausfrau in a black taffeta dress with an old-fashioned long skirt peeked through the lace curtain, then unlocked the door. She smiled.

"Guten Tag, mein Herr," she said, admitting him to the narrow hallway with the dirty rose wallpaper. The hall smelled of boiled cabbage. "He is out right now, but should be back soon. You may wait in his room if you like."

"Thank you, Frau Reichert," said Rudi with just the right touch of condescension. Frau Reichert, like most older Germans, still adhered to the prewar sense of class: she expected a count to act like a count.

Rudi climbed the sagging wooden stairs, past the grimy glass gas lamps to the second floor where a narrow hallway bisected the building. Walking down the corridor, hung with cheap prints in dirty dark wood frames, he passed a battered upright piano and an ugly vitrine filled with out-of-date sentimental novels. At the end of the hall, he opened a wooden door that badly needed scraping and repainting and entered a narrow room no more than ten feet wide. A single window looked out over a rear courtyard. In front of the window was a brass bed. The bed was made, but rumpled: someone had been sitting or lying on it. Opposite the bed, bookshelves had been screwed into the cracked plaster wall.

As Rudi waited, his eyes roamed the spines of the books. The upper shelves held volumes on the Great War, German histories, *Vom Kriege,* by Clausewitz, a history of Frederick the Great, Houston Stewart Chamberlain's biography of Wagner, a collection of heroic myths, and the memoirs of Sven Hedin. On the lower shelves were out-of-date novels and *A History of Erotic Art.* On the floor was cheap yellow linoleum, at least twenty years old; where it was cracked, the linoleum curled.

"Rudi," said a soft voice, "it's so good to see you."

Rudi turned to look at the slim young man in the raincoat standing in the open door. He spoke with a slight Austrian accent, not too different from Bavarian German but still noticeable to Rudi. He came into the room and closed the door. His eyes blazed with excitement as he came to Rudi and took both his hands. His Charlie Chaplin moustache gave him a slightly comical look, but, unimpressive as his clothes were, he still had an imposing presence.

"Ruderl, *mein Liebchen,* I have missed you like the very devil," he whispered.

Then Adolf Hitler kissed the young Count von Winterfeldt on the lips.

Hitler was extremely careful to keep his sexuality a secret; thus, so as not to arouse the suspicions of kindly Frau Reichert (who was genuinely fond of her tenant, whom she described as a "well-behaved bohemian type"), Rudi and Dolf, as the Count called him, drove in the Bugatti to the Schwabing villa of Captain Waldemar von Manfredi. Manfredi had been one of Hitler's superior officers during the war and had become a proselytizing, zealous Nazi, convinced that his former corporal was the savior of Germany. Manfredi was also a homosexual, who had had a brief affair with Dolf in the trenches of the war, so he was only too eager to offer the Fuehrer a cottage in the garden of his walled villa for his clandestine amours. In fact, the inner circles of the Nazi Party were riddled with what the ostentatiously heterosexual Italian dictator, Mussolini, contemptuously termed "a bunch of perverts." And though Hitler thought himself immune from such gossip, the cabarets and *Bierstuben* of Munich and Berlin buzzed with tales of his twisted libido, and the rich imaginations of the German intellectuals and wits dreamed up spectacular perversions for Hitler that would have exhausted the energies of the Marquis de Sade or the Baron von Sacher-Masoch.

The villa, surrounded by a high stucco wall, was on a tree-lined upper-middle-class street; most of the spacious houses had been built at the turn of the century, and the predominant architectural style was a heavy Wilhelmine version of the French Belle Epoque. Captain von Manfredi's three-story house was stucco, with a red-tiled roof, and its wall-enclosed yard and back garden were as well tended as his neighbors'. Rudi opened the wrought-iron gate and drove into the short driveway. Then, closing the gate, he followed Hitler around to the back of the house where, in a rear corner of the garden, a doll-like stucco cottage with a red door squatted peacefully beneath a willow. Manfredi's mother, Ursula, had been a best-selling author of children's books in prewar Germany and had written a wildly successful series of books about a nauseatingly cute rabbit named Pupi. In

1906, she had built the cottage as her writing studio. When she died in 1920, her son converted it to more sinister uses.

Hitler opened the door, and the two entered. The cottage had three rooms: a large workroom, a tiny bedroom and an equally tiny kitchen in back. The chairs and sofas were upholstered in fading chintz, reflecting the Anglomania of the prewar era. On the rough plaster walls were framed illustrations of Pupi, done in an Arthur Rackham style. As Rudi closed the door Hitler scowled at the illustrations.

"I always hated rabbits," he muttered. Then he turned and smiled at Rudi. "My beautiful Siegfried!" he exclaimed. "I love to *look* at you."

Rudi was wearing a Harris Tweed suit. Now, as he began to take it off, Hitler went to a closet and took out a black Gladstone bag. Setting it on Ursula von Manfredi's former writing table, where she had penned so many cheerful adventures of Pupi the rabbit, Hitler opened the bag and began pulling out a strange assortment of objects. There were a leather dog collar, two pairs of steel handcuffs, a leather riding crop and an expensive Hungarian riding whip. Hitler began trembling as he ran his fingers lovingly over the riding crop. "It's been ten days," he said. "It seemed like an eternity. I can't live without you, Ruderl, my darling."

Rudi, now completely naked, came over to the table, tore the riding crop from Hitler's hands and brought it down hard on his right shoulder. Hitler groaned and sank to his knees.

"Who am I?" shouted Rudi fiercely.

Hitler looked up at him, tears forming in his eyes. "You are my master," he said, "Prince Siegfried, the beautiful blond superman of purest Aryan blood."

"And who are you?"

"Prince Siegfried, I am of an inferior race, with dark hair, the scum of the earth, possibly polluted and poisoned by foul Jewish blood."

Rudi stepped up to him, raised his right foot and positioned it a few inches before Hitler's face. "Abase yourself, Jew slave," he commanded. "Lick my foot."

"Yes, master."

Hitler stuck out his tongue and licked the sole of Rudi's foot. After a full minute, Rudi snapped, "That will do. Now strip naked, Jew slave."

"Yes, master."

Hurriedly, letting out little moans of pleasure, Hitler took off his cheap suit, throwing his clothes with wild abandon on the chintz chairs. When he was naked, he got down on his hands and knees like a dog. His skinny body had slightly wide, gynandromorphic hips, and his penis, though extremely tiny, was erect.

Rudi placed the riding crop on the table and picked up the dog collar.

"What are you, Jew slave?" he asked.

"I am a Jew slave dog."

"That is correct."

Rudi leaned down and strapped the leather dog collar around Hitler's neck, at first tightening it so hard Hitler gagged, then loosening it slowly and fastening it.

"Bark, Jew slave dog!" he commanded.

Hitler barked.

Rudi went back to the table and picked up the two pairs of steel cuffs. "Hold out your arms, slave!"

Hitler obeyed.

Rudi clapped a pair of cuffs on his wrists. "Roll over, Jew slave dog!"

Hitler rolled over on his left side. Rudi cuffed his ankles. Then he went to the table and picked up the whip. He snapped it twice, menacingly, then came back to the shackled Hitler and grinned down at him.

"You fear your beautiful blond Aryan master, don't you?"

Hitler, trembling and sweating profusely, looked up.

"I fear my master," he said. "But I also love him, because my master is superior. It is my cherished dream that someday my Aryan master will rule the world and cleanse the earth of all evil."

"And what is evil?"

"I, the Jew scum."

"That is correct, slave. Now, prepare to receive your punishment."

Hitler, with difficulty, rolled over again on his hands and knees. Rudi raised the whip and slashed it across Hitler's buttocks.

"JEW!" growled Rudi as Hitler screamed with pain.

"KIKE!" howled Rudi, and the whip slashed a second, then a third time.

"Oh," cried Hitler, "it's beautiful, master! More! More!"

Rudi willingly complied, whipping Hitler savagely until the future Chancellor of Germany ejaculated, his semen spilling all over the wooden floor.

Rudi, panting and sweating from his exertions, tossed the whip onto the table and sank down into the chintz sofa.

"Now it's my turn, Dolf," he puffed, wiping the sweat off his thighs.

Count Rudi von Winterfeldt might have grown up in a gorgeous landscape, but his soul was definitely not beautiful.

"Something strange happened at my father's castle last night," said Rudi that evening as he and Hitler sat in a corner booth at the Café Neumaier, an old-fashioned coffeehouse at the corner of Munich's Peterplatz and the Viktualien Markt. The wooden benches had cushions, which was fortunate, as both lovers' bottoms were sore after the savage whippings (Hitler enjoyed the role of master as much as he enjoyed being the slave in their psychosexual playlets). The long room of the café was paneled, and it was here on Monday evenings that Hitler regularly held court, trying out his latest political ideas on his cronies and followers. Tonight not being a Monday, however, the crowd in the café was basically apolitical, although many of the Bavarians recognized Hitler, who was sipping lentil soup, one of his favorite dishes.

"What's that?" asked Hitler, who was careful not to exhibit any signs of fondness for Rudi in public.

"Have you ever heard of an American arms company called the Ramschild Company?"

"Of course."

"Well, its owner, a man named Nick Fleming, was a guest of my parents last night."

"I've heard of Fleming. I've seen some of his movies, which I like. He's a Jew, I suppose? All those Hollywood movie people are Jews. The Jews always take over the means of mass communication—the press, for example. They control the world press!"

"Fleming is half-Jewish, I believe," said Rudi, eager to stop Hitler before he launched into one of his interminable tirades against the Jews. Rudi was a fervent anti-Semite, but even his eyes could become glazed when Dolf began one of his monologues. "At any rate, we were all having dinner when one of the footmen apparently pulled a gun, or *started* to pull a gun—I say 'apparently' because I didn't actually see it happen. Fleming jumped him and got the gun away from him."

Hitler looked interested. "Why did the footman pull a gun?"

"Well, my father assumed he was trying to assassinate him."

"Why?"

"The footman is Russian, and the assumption is that he's an agent of the Comintern. But the odd thing is, he turned out to have an American passport."

Hitler, who was trying to improve his table manners as he rose in the world, daintily wiped his mouth with his napkin.

"That makes no sense at all," Hitler said. "In the first place, why would the Comintern want to assassinate your father, who is of no particular importance in the government? In the second place, why use an American agent? And in the third place, if you're going to assassinate someone, why do it in a dining room when it's so much easier—and more efficient—to kill him in a car, for instance?"

"Exactly what I thought. The whole thing was extremely odd. Then, this morning, Fleming met privately with my father before they all took off for Berlin together, which also struck me as rather odd. My instincts tell me there's something going on I don't see. . . . I mean, the fact that Fleming is an arms dealer is suggestive."

Hitler thought a moment as he sopped up the remains of his soup with a roll.

"Is Fleming staying at the Adlon?" he asked.

"Yes."

"I'll have him tailed. We'll *see* what he's up to."

The naked light bulbs over the double doors in the plain brick building just off the Kurfürstendamm blinked jazzily as they spelled out CAFÉ BERLIN. The German capital held many attractions for the tourist aside from cheap prices: deluxe hotels like the Adlon or the Bristol; magnificent art collections and the splendors of the Pergamon Museum; a lovely opera house; the rather forbidding architecture of the Imperial era softened by thousands of chestnut and linden trees lining the broad avenues where trams clattered and gold-striped black taxis and multicolored motor buses competed for right-of-way, supervised by mounted policemen in pearl-gray coats; the sylvan tranquillity of the Tiergarten and the Wannsee. For tourists with more jaded tastes, there were thousands of prostitutes, transvestites sitting at sidewalk cafés with their skirts revealing hairy thighs, and at The Femina Nightclub, lesbians reeking of cheap perfume and sweat dancing the night away to the hot jazz of a Negro band. But the greatest tourist attraction in Berlin was the Café Berlin, not only because the most beautiful and successful whores made it their place of business, but because of its star singer, Magda Bayreuth.

"It's not her real name, of course," said Count Alex von Winterfeldt to his guests Nick and Edwina Fleming as they sat at their white-clothed table waiting for the show to begin. "Her real name is Ulrika Himmelfahrt, so you can understand why she changed it. Her father was a plumber and her mother is supposed to have been a prostitute, like the two ladies at the next table. By the way, as you can see, each table has a telephone. If you want to do business with someone at another table, you just dial the table number and *voilà!*"

"I've always heard the Germans were efficient," said Edwina, who, despite her Teutonophobia because of the war, was finding Berlin fascinating.

"At any rate, Magda is without question the most beautiful woman in Germany—present company excluded, of course. My wife doesn't approve of her act, which is why she wouldn't join us, but I think you'll find it most enjoyable."

"I'm looking forward to it," said Nick.

"Am I the only nonprostitute here?" asked Edwina, looking around the large, smoke-filled room.

"Probably," said Alex.

Despite the raffish atmosphere, the men all wore dinner jackets and the women wore elegant evening gowns, although many of the whores were too heavily made up, and much of their jewelry was cheap paste. The walls were lined with semicircular leather banquettes separated by elaborate etched-glass dividers. At one end of the room was a small stage with a red-and-gold curtain. A six-man orchestra was tuning up. Now they struck a loud chord and the curtain parted. Out onto the stage strode a tall blonde wearing the white summer uniform of a German naval officer. Her hands were in the pockets of her slacks, her cap was pushed back at a jaunty angle, and from her thin scarlet lips dangled a cigarette. As a movie producer, Nick had seen a lot of beautiful women. But—and perhaps it was the shock of seeing a woman in a man's clothes, or perhaps it was the expression of bemused contempt on her gorgeous face, or perhaps both—he had never seen a more excitingly beautiful woman than Magda Bayreuth.

She sang in a soft, smoky voice that curled around the eardrum, licking the libido, suggesting, suggesting, suggesting. She sang of the pleasures and sadness of love and desire. She sang for a half hour, hardly ever moving, mesmerizing the room. When the curtain closed,

211

the crowd went wild. Nick was on his feet, cheering and clapping.

"She's fabulous!" he yelled over the noise. "Fantastic!"

"Want to meet her?" yelled Count Alex.

"Yes!"

Oh, my God, thought Edwina. Here we go again.

Magda's dressing room was an unimpressive one for a star, with exposed drainpipes in the corners and an ancient iron radiator that gave off more noise than heat. She was wearing a dirty bathrobe as Alex kissed her hand and said, "I wanted you to meet two American friends of mine: Mr. and Mrs. Nick Fleming."

Magda's eyes widened as she looked at Edwina.

"But I am a great fan of yours!" she exclaimed. "I have seen all your films several times and am looking forward to seeing *Desert Love* this weekend."

"And I am a fan of yours," said Edwina, smiling frostily. "I enjoyed your singing immensely."

Magda turned to Nick. "And I must confess your coming to me has saved me a lot of trouble." She smiled.

"How so?" asked Nick.

"Well, I was going to arrange an introduction. You see, I, like so many other performers, get stars in my eyes when I think of Hollywood. And I wanted to ask you if you thought a German actress would have any chance in American films."

"I didn't realize you act as well as sing."

"I have appeared in four films for UFA. Nothing earthshaking, I'm afraid—very small roles, though I don't think I did too badly. But I love films."

Nick glanced at his wife and saw her eyes narrowing. Then he smiled at Magda.

"Why don't we have lunch tomorrow at the Adlon and we can talk about it."

"How charming," purred Magda. "Shall we say one o'clock?"

"How charming," snarled Edwina ten minutes later in the taxi. "Shall we say one o'clock?" She nastily imitated Magda's German accent.

"You're invited too," said Nick, sitting next to her as the taxi headed for the Adlon at No. One Unter den Linden.

"And cramp your style? No thanks."

"Edwina, I make movies! It's part of my job to be on the lookout for new talent. Maybe this Magda could be the next Garbo."

212

"Oh, Nick, spare me this drivel. I suppose I can't blame you. She *is* spectacular. I just think you could be a bit more circumspect in front of your wife."

She sulked. He took her hand, but she pulled away from him.

"Just remember," she said, "there are a lot of good-looking German men. So be warned. You may have to cope with the situation we were discussing sooner than you think."

Now it was his turn to sulk.

At nine the next morning, a bellboy came up to Nick in the high-ceilinged lobby of the Adlon and announced, "Your car is here, Mr. Fleming."

Nick tipped him, then went through the revolving glass door. A modest four-door black sedan was parked in front of the hotel. A man in a black bowler hat with a monocle in his right eye was in the driver's seat. Nick walked to the car and opened the door.

"General von Treskow?" he asked.

"Yes. And you are Mr. Fleming."

"That's right."

"Get in, please."

Nick climbed in the front seat. The General, a thin, small man with sandy hair, was wearing a dark-blue suit. He shook Nick's hand, saying, "Count von Winterfeldt has spoken of you in glowing terms, Mr. Fleming. We of course are delighted to have an American on our side, so to speak."

"Every country must have an army to defend itself," said Nick. "There are a lot of Americans like myself who feel that the Treaty of Versailles was a mistake."

"Excellent!" said the General, smiling. Then he started the car, pulling out onto the Unter den Linden.

"I am an old friend of Alex von Winterfeldt's," he went on conversationally. "Our families have known each other for generations. That's why I feel so sorry for Alex and his wife."

"Sorry? Are they sick?"

"No, they're in good health. It's their son, Rudi. You'd have no way of knowing this, of course, but Rudi's a Nazi, and a passionate one at that. His parents hate Hitler and all he stands for, as do most of the General Staff, I might add. So for their son to join the Party—and to become an intimate friend of Hitler himself—well, it's been a terrible blow for them. They try to pretend nothing has happened, but everyone knows. It's a tragedy, really, but one I fear will become increasingly commonplace in Germany unless someone can shut that madman up. Personally, I don't understand his appeal."

"You've heard him speak?"

"Yes, once in Munich. I suppose he knows how to stir up a crowd, but I've never liked shouters. And Hitler *shouts*."

"So I understand."

"Did Alex tell you where I am taking you?"

"No. He was very secretive about the whole thing. He just told me you would pick me up at the hotel at nine."

"Good. What you are about to see is known to only a handful of Germans and a few Swedes."

"The Bofors Company?"

"Exactly."

"I've heard from sources in the armament business that Bofors is secretly owned by Herr Krupp."

General von Treskow turned a corner. "Officially," he said, "I would say you are wrong. Unofficially, I would say you have good sources of information."

"May I ask a blunt question?"

"Please do."

"Why are you trusting me?"

"The answer is simple, Herr Fleming. We need you. And here we are: Number Four, Potsdamer Platz."

He parked in front of an ordinary-looking office building.

"It's on the tenth floor," said the General. "Unfortunately, there's no lift. We'll have to walk."

They entered the turn-of-the-century building and began climbing the stairs. When they reached the tenth floor, panting, the General led Nick to a door at the end of the hall. On the door was a small brass plate that read KOCH UND KEINZLE (E).

"The *E* stands for *Entwicklung,* or Development," remarked the General as he rang a bell. After a moment, an eye appeared at a peephole. Then the door was unlocked and opened by a man in shirt sleeves with a green eyeshade on his head.

"It reminds me of a speakeasy," said Nick as he followed the General into a small reception room.

The door was relocked, then the two men were led through a second door into a large room filled with drafting tables. At least two dozen draftsmen were at work; now the one nearest the door stood up from his stool and came over to the General to shake his hand.

"This is Hugo Pfeiffer, who's in charge of the project," said the

General. "This is Herr Fleming, the owner of the Ramschild Arms Company in America. Hugo will show you some of the things we're working on here."

Chubby Hugo, who looked more like a Santa's helper than a designer of death machines, led Nick around the room, showing him the work in progress. Nick saw detailed drawings for a tank of a startlingly advanced design, the tank being heavy-handedly disguised as a *landwirtschaftlicher Akerbau Trecker,* or agricultural tractor— this particular "tractor" being equipped with a 7.5-cm. cannon. There were drawings for eight different kinds of heavy artillery, howitzers and light field guns, and a new, mobile 21-cm. mortar. Nick was dazzled. It was obvious to him that an army equipped with these weapons would have a crushing advantage over any other in the world.

"This is a division of the Krupp firm," said the General when the tour was complete. "And these designs are, naturally, all Krupp designs. The Krupp firm, as you know, is severely limited in what it can manufacture in terms of weaponry, and these designs, along with dozens of others you haven't seen, are designs for future production. However, to be frank, Herr Fleming, a certain amount of production is already taking place in Essen in secret. And the Bofors Company in Sweden—which, of course, has no such limitation—is also in production.

"When Alex told me you were eager to sell weapons to the German Army, I immediately saw how you could be of great use to us. If you would assume the manufacture of some of our designs in your factory in America, it would be what I think you Americans call a 'swell deal' for both sides."

"I see what you mean," Nick said thoughtfully. "But there'd be a considerable risk in it for me."

"We are prepared to pay well for the risk, Herr Fleming. We are, happily, extremely well financed."

Nick looked around the room.

"I'll have to think about this," he said.

"Of course. Meanwhile, I hope you will be my guest at lunch?"

"Unfortunately—or, rather, fortunately"—he smiled—"I'm having lunch with Magda Bayreuth."

The General laughed.

"I've heard you are a fast worker, Herr Fleming. Apparently my sources of information are as good as yours."

She was wearing a vanilla crepe suit that showed off her smashing figure to full advantage. When she entered the dining room of the Adlon with Nick, every eye in the packed room was on her, ogling her from her smart white-and-black Chanel shoes up her sensational legs all the way to the black and white-trimmed cloche over her blond hair, ogling her with desire and envy and awe: when Magda Bayreuth came into a room, it was an event. Oskar, the maître d' of the elegant room, kissed her hand with a trace too much unctuousness.

"You are more lovely each day, Fräulein," he oozed. "I have reserved you the table by the window, Herr Fleming!" And he led them through the room to a table overlooking the Unter den Linden, pocketing the hundred marks Nick had discreetly slipped him.

"We have lovely Irish salmon," he said as he seated them.

"I'm on a diet," Magda said with a smoky smile. "Nothing but caviar and champagne."

"That's an expensive diet," Nick remarked dryly.

"Not for me. For you, yes."

He laughed.

"When I lunch alone," she went on, "I eat nothing but two crackers and a piece of lettuce. It's not every day I'm taken to lunch by a Hollywood producer."

She placed her small black purse on the table, then crossed her legs so the room could see them. Fascinating, thought Nick. She must rehearse every move in front of a mirror.

"So, Mr. Fleming," she said after the champagne had been poured in the slender crystal flutes, "I hear *The Jazz Singer* is a great success in New York. Does that mean that all pictures will start talking?"

"There's a lot of controversy about that in Hollywood. Some say it's just a fad."

"And what do you say?"

"I'm converting my studio to sound."

"I see you are a man of action who is not afraid of decisions. I admire that in men." She paused a moment, studying his face with a frankly suggestive look. "Then does that mean a German with an accent like mine could never succeed in Hollywood?"

"I frankly don't know. I think that when audiences hear a lot of their favorite stars talking with bad accents or squeaky voices, it's going to make a big difference to a lot of careers. But Americans might be intrigued by an accent like yours. And your English is quite good. Would you be interested in making a screen test for me at the UFA studios in Potsdam?"

"Oh, yes. Very interested."

216

Oskar came up to the table. "Excuse me, Herr Fleming," he said. "There is a Mr. Arthur Harding on the telephone for you."

"Thanks," said Nick, getting up. "Will you excuse me, Fräulein?"

"Call me Magda, please."

He looked at her legs for a pleasant moment, then thought of Edwina.

"All right, Magda."

He left the table. Magda lit a cigarette.

She had already learned something interesting.

He was just over five feet tall and weighed not much more than a hundred pounds. As a child, he had been racked by infantile paralysis, which left him with a deformed foot that exempted him from service during the Great War. Transferring to Heidelberg from the University of Munich, he was graduated in 1921 with a Ph.D. in literature. He spent the next few years writing a romantic autobiography—a *Bildungsroman* entitled *Michael*—as well as lyric poems and plays, keeping himself alive by working as floorman of the Cologne stock exchange and as a tutor. Formerly an impassioned Marxist, when Joseph Goebbels met Adolf Hitler, he met the hero he had searched for all his life. "Great joy!" he wrote in his diary. "He greets me like an old friend. How I love him! And those big blue eyes. Like stars. He is glad to see me. I am in heaven."

A brilliant editor and propagandist, if a third-rate novelist, Goebbels was just what Hitler needed, and his rise to power in the party was meteoric. Just a year before, he had arrived in Berlin to be Hitler's personal representative there. Despite his calflike swooning over Hitler, Goebbels was a highly libidinous man, a real skirt chaser. The skirt he had been chasing successfully since his arrival in Berlin was the well-tailored skirt of Magda Bayreuth. At six o'clock that evening, he limped into the lift of her ornate apartment building in the Grunewald and rode up to the third floor where Magda admitted him to her Art Deco flat. Magda, who was five feet eight, had to lean down for him to be able to kiss her mouth.

"Magda, darling, my gorgeous *Liebchen!*" he gushed, squeezing her buttocks through her skirt. "I'm hard already!" The inventor of twentieth-century political propaganda techniques then ran his hand up under her skirt and massaged her crotch.

"Joseph, act civilized," she snapped, pushing him away. "Let's at least have a cocktail first. Besides, I have news for you."

"You had lunch with Fleming?"

"Yes. He's quite charming and *very* attractive."

She crossed the white fox rug of her lavishly decorated living room and opened a black and crystal bar.

"Did you go to bed with him?" asked Goebbels, burning with erotic curiosity.

"No. He didn't even make a pass. Of course, he may later. But during lunch he was called away to the telephone, and guess who was calling him?"

"Who?"

"Arthur Harding."

"What? But why—" He started pacing around the room. "Wait a minute. . . . Yes—of course! It's beginning to make some sense! Harding is the Berlin correspondent of the Clairmont newspaper chain."

"And you told me Van Nuys Clairmont is married to Fleming's mother."

"Exactly! Oh, my God. . . ." He stopped pacing, his skull-like face turning white. "My man at the Adlon reported that General von Treskow picked Fleming up this morning and drove him to Potsdamer Platz."

He stared at Magda a moment, then started laughing.

"What's so funny?" Magda asked, carrying him his martini.

"The fools! The idiots! They don't see what he's up to, but I think I do!"

"Who's 'they'?"

"The General Staff, of course. Are their faces going to be red!" He stopped laughing and took a sip of the gin. "This Fleming," he remarked respectfully, "must be a very smart man. And a dangerous one for Germany. He has to be stopped."

"Joseph, don't be so tediously murky. What do you think he's up to?"

"I think he's probably convinced Treskow and the others that he'd like to sell them weapons, but what he really wants is to expose the secret rearming of Germany to the world. I don't give a damn about Treskow and the others on the General Staff—they're a bunch of horses' asses in my opinion—but that's going to be *our* army someday. Yes, Fleming must be stopped."

He went to Magda's silver phone and picked up the receiver.

After they had made love in Magda's black and crystal bed, Magda lit a cigarette and exhaled.

218

"Joseph," she said, "you must talk to the Fuehrer. You know I hear all the gossip in Berlin—and I mean *all* the gossip. Everyone is talking about Rudi von Winterfeldt. It's becoming a scandal. It could ruin the Fuehrer *and* the Party."

Goebbels sat up in bed, a worried frown on his face.

"I know," he said quietly. "The Fuehrer is such a great man, so above the frailties of the rest of us. . . . And yet this one young man . . ." He shook his head. "He's like a demon." He sighed. "I'll talk to the Fuehrer, but that's going to be one hell of an unpleasant scene. Something tells me the Fuehrer is not going to be happy with me."

"IT'S terrific stuff!" exclaimed Van Clairmont to his wife, Edith, in the bedroom of their Sands Point mansion. "Absolutely terrific! I got the first thousand words from Arthur Harding this afternoon. I guarantee you when we print this it's going to make headlines all over the world! Nick actually saw Krupp's secret plans for the German Army, and they admitted to him they're already in production at the Essen plant. Plus the Bofors Company in Sweden, which is secretly owned by the Krupp interests, is manufacturing guns for the Germans. It's dynamite!"

Edith purred with pleasure.

"*Now* will you admit Nick isn't so bad after all? For years you've been saying he was greedy and tricky."

"He *is* greedy and tricky," interrupted Van, who was putting on his dinner jacket for a party they were giving. "But he can be tricky for me *any* day. And I'll grant you he's got a lot of guts pulling this off. But I'm no fool, Edith. Don't think for a minute that I don't know why he's doing this. And you know too."

Edith ran her hands over her gray hair, checking her reflection in the mirror of her dressing table. Then she stood up and confronted her husband.

"Yes, I know," she said, "and I'm not ashamed to admit it. After all, he's my son, and I want him to inherit something from me."

Van finished tying his black tie.

"That 'something' being my newspapers, I suppose?"

"Is that so bad? He's a brilliant businessman—you've admitted that. He's been a success in Hollywood when everybody said he'd fail. The Ramschild stock has almost doubled since he took over. And of *course* he wants your newspapers! Who wouldn't? And there's no one else to inherit them except your daughter, and I hope you're not going to tell me *she* could run them or is even interested in running them, for that matter. She's not sober enough to *read* a newspaper, much less publish one."

Van winced. The alcoholism of his only child was a sore point. Edith came to him and kissed him.

"I'm sorry, darling," she said. "That was cruel of me."

"No, you're right," he sighed. "And I suppose you're right about Nick too. He probably would be a successful publisher. And he is your son." He kissed her.

"Then you'll think about it?" she asked.

He laughed. "Since you've been wheedling me for the past three years about writing Nick into my will, don't think I haven't thought about it a *lot*. I'll tell you what I'll do. When Nick gets back from Europe, I'll have a talk with him. Then if he's serious, I'll start teaching him the newspaper business."

Edith hugged him. "You are *the* most wonderful man," she said.

Van eyed her for a few moments through his thick eyeglasses. "I wonder," he finally said, "if you'll ever love me as much as you love Nick."

She stiffened. "Van! What a terrible thing to say!"

"No, don't get me wrong. I'm not implying anything incestuous. But I think Nick has cast a spell over you ever since that day he came to you as a lonely, needy child in Pennsylvania."

Edith considered this.

"You may be right," she said. "He's always intrigued me."

"And flattered and charmed you."

"And outraged me. I'm not blind to his faults, Van. I've always felt that underneath it all there was something fine in him. And I think what he's doing in Berlin proves it."

"Well, he's hardly motivated by altruism."

"I know. Still and all, he's some kind of hero. To me, at least."

Van smiled slightly. "With you, Nick Fleming could get away with murder."

Otto Reineke, the bellboy who was one of Goebbels' "men" at the Adlon, crossed the lobby to where Nick was sitting in a chair flipping through a French magazine.

"Your car is here, Herr Fleming," he said, giving a little salute to his red pillbox hat, which was kept on his youthful blond head by an elastic band under his chin.

"Thanks, Otto," said Nick, getting up and tipping him ten marks. He crossed the busy lobby, went through the revolving door and walked to the car, wondering why General von Treskow was driving a different-model car. Then, as the doorman opened the door and Nick looked in, he saw that it wasn't General von Treskow. Rather, it was a young man in a brown suit and brown hat. The man's nose was half smashed in.

"The General asked me to pick you up," said the man in extremely bad English.

"Where is he?" asked Nick.

"At Potsdamer Platz."

Nick knew that a meeting had been arranged for him with other members of the German General Staff at the "Development" room on the tenth floor of No. 4, so he climbed into the car. The driver shifted and roared onto the Unter den Linden.

It was five minutes before Nick realized they were heading in the wrong direction.

"This isn't the way to Potsdamer Platz," he said.

"This is a detour," the driver said. "They're working on one of the streets." He turned right into a narrow street. He was going 70 k.p.h., and his tires screeched on the turn.

Nick reached into his jacket pocket for his gun. He pulled it out and pointed it at the man's head.

"Stop the car," he said.

The driver didn't even look at him.

"I said, *stop the car!*" Nick shouted, jamming the gun against the driver's temple.

The driver braked, turned into an alley and screeched to a halt. A truck was parked in the alley, facing the car. Three men in shabby suits were standing beside the truck. They held guns.

Silence, except for the engine. It was a little after nine on a clear morning, but the alley was deserted except for the men, and the windows of the tenements were shuttered. Nick realized it was an execution alley, that someone had figured out his game and betrayed him. He broke into a sweat.

With all his strength, he punched the driver in his stomach, causing him to double over in pain. Then quickly reaching behind him he opened the door and pushed him out. As the guns began firing, he crouched down in the seat, shifted into reverse and jammed the accelerator. As the car backed out of the alley, bullets shattering the windshield, Nick reached his gun hand up and fired blindly. Now the car was out into the street. Klaxons were honking as Nick backed swiftly into traffic, not even trying to guide the car, just keeping his foot on the accelerator. There was a screech of brakes and something slammed into the back of the car, jolting and stopping it. Angry cries of German motorists and more horns howling.

Nick scrambled out of the car and ran to the back of it, seeing the taxi smashed into its right rear fender and the taxi driver climbing out, livid with rage. He saw the crowd gathering. He also saw the truck roar out of the alley. He dived to the pavement as the guns fired from the truck windows. Screams from pedestrians, who ducked and scurried. In the confusion, Nick looked up to see the taxi driver drop to the pavement beside him. His left eye was gushing blood where one of the bullets had entered his brain.

Then it was all over.

"You *missed* him?" shouted Joseph Goebbels on the phone. He was standing in the living room at the Haus Wachenfeld, the modest villa Hitler had bought on the Obersalzberg. While it was still Indian summer in Berlin, here, in the Bavarian Alps, a light snow was falling. "You idiots! How could he have gotten away? There were four of you!" Goebbels listened for a moment, scowling. Then he said, "This will go in your files!" and slammed down the phone.

He thought a moment, looking around the pleasant, rustic room. Outside, a verandah, festooned with heavily carved Bavarian gingerbread, gave on to a snow-dusted garden. Goebbels had requested an audience with the Fuehrer in his beloved mountain retreat to broach the extremely touchy subject of Rudi von Winterfeldt. Now, more bad news! Goebbels cursed the ineptitude of his Nazi assassins. When he had informed the Fuehrer of Nick's stratagem, Hitler had wholeheartedly agreed that the "Jew American," as he called him, must be killed. Hitler believed with messianic zeal that time was on his side and that, despite setbacks, within five years he would be the political boss of Germany. The Army was the key factor in his dream of conquest in Eastern Europe, and, like Goebbels, he already considered it in his mind the personal property of the Nazi Party. He had been just as swift as Goebbels to see the danger inherent in any publicity about its secret rearming and, like Goebbels, had railed at the stupidity of the General Staff in trusting Fleming.

Now Goebbels had to tell the Fuehrer his goons had failed.

Taking a deep breath, Goebbels walked across the low-ceilinged room to the wooden door of Hitler's office. He knocked.

"Come in."

Opening the door, Goebbels entered the small room with its lovely views directly toward distant Salzburg. There was a small desk facing the window at which Hitler was seated, writing. Goebbels passed bookshelves filled with the Wild West novels of Karl May, a popular author for boys whom Hitler, rather to Goebbels' surprise, loved.

Hitler turned as he put down his pen.

"Mein Fuehrer," Goebbels began nervously, "I have some bad news. My men failed in the assassination attempt on Fleming."

Hitler scowled. But to Goebbels' amazement, he didn't throw a temper tantrum. Rather, after a moment, he merely said, "Well, then, the fat's in the fire. At least we tried. Unfortunately, we don't have the power to punish this Jew American now. But someday . . ." He paused to bite a hangnail. "Perhaps our paths will cross again, and Herr Fleming will learn that I have an extremely long memory. Now, Joseph, just what is it you wanted to see me about?"

Goebbels cleared his throat. He had been lucky once. Would he be lucky twice?

"Mein Fuehrer, it's about young Count von Winterfeldt."

From the shocked and angry look on Hitler's face, Joseph Goebbels knew he wasn't going to escape a "carpet chewing" this time.

It was Christmas Eve in Connecticut, 1927, and the snow lay thick across New England, weighing down the boughs of the pine trees and bending the fragile white birches almost to the breaking point. Hungry white-tailed deer wandered around the ten acres of Nick's Greenwich estate searching for ever-rarer strips of bark to eat; but in this year of peace and prosperity, the deer were almost the only hungry things in America. It was a crisply cold night, with the temperature in the twenties, and above the stone-and-brick Jacobean-style mansion that Nick had bought two years before to serve as his eastern base of operations, a pellucid sky blazed with the full glory of the winter constellations. On the stony beach of Long Island Sound, tiny wavelets lapped contentedly; fifty feet up in the snowy, gently sloping front lawn, the lights in the majestic twin two-story bay windows glowed warmly, illuminating with ghostly beauty the heaps of fresh snow on the stone balustrades of the front terrace. A tall pine tree in front of the house had been decorated with tiny white lights and another string of white bulbs framed the handsomely carved front door. Smoke curled out of the four chimneys of the house, and if Santa himself had appeared over the roof, he could hardly have added to the picture of holiday peace, joy and beauty.

Inside the twenty-four-room mansion, the Fleming family was posing for a photographer in front of the twenty-foot-high Christmas tree that stood at one end of the two-story main hall.

"Smile!" said the photographer, whom Nick had had to pay a hundred-dollar bonus to come out on Christmas Eve. But Nick didn't mind. He was at the full flood of his prosperity and contentment, it was the happiest Christmas of his life, his family was in good health and spirits, and he wanted to record this Christmas Eve for posterity.

Seated before the tree, which groaned with baubles, bulbs and balls, were Nick in black tie and Edwina in a red sequined gown and many diamonds. Seated in Nick's lap was the youngest, one-year-old Victoria; seated in Edwina's lap was two-year-old Hugh. Standing beside Nick was four-year-old Fiona, Rod Norman's daughter, a ravishing child with dark-brown hair; beside her was eight-year-old Charles, the eldest, who had inherited his father's dark good looks. Behind Edwina was seven-year-old Sylvia, who had light hair that was beginning to darken to her mother's auburn color. The two remaining children in the group were three-year-old Maurice, named after his maternal grandfather, Lord Saxmundham, and six-year-old Edward. Flanking this handsome brood were Edith and Van Clairmont.

The bulb flashed, the photographer packed up, and the children descended on the mountain of presents beneath the tree, whooping and chattering like happy monkeys.

After the Nazis' unsuccessful attempt on his life, Nick had been warned by the American authorities in Berlin to get out of the country because his safety could not be guaranteed. Realizing his usefulness in Berlin was finished anyway, Nick checked Edwina out of the hotel. Taking the train to Paris, he told her the truth about his reasons for going to Germany. Though Edwina was skeptical at first, when the articles by Arthur Harding began appearing in Van's newspapers, causing an uproar at the League of Nations and in most of the capitals of Europe, her skepticism melted into outright hero worship of her husband. Nick, as susceptible to praise as any man, purred. And on their return to America, when Van told him he was seriously considering making him his heir, Nick's cup was running over.

For the first time in his career, Nick was emerging, to his family at least, as what Edith had called him, "some kind of hero."

Nick was showing Van and Edith two of his recent acquisitions—a Picasso and a Renoir—when he heard a scream. Turning to the Christmas tree, he saw his two eldest children, Charles and Sylvia, tugging at a big gift-wrapped box.

"It's mine!" Sylvia was yelling. "My name's on the card!"

"You changed cards!" Charles yelled back. "I checked this afternoon! It's mine!"

"Children!" exclaimed Nick, hurrying across the enormous room toward the tree. "No fighting. It's Christmas Eve."

Ignoring him, Charles slapped his younger sister so viciously that the room fell suddenly silent as everyone stared at him. As Sylvia burst into tears, Charles calmly jerked the box away from her and began unwrapping it.

"Charles, you horrid boy!" exclaimed his mother, coming to him and taking the box from him. "What a terrible thing to do to Sylvia! You apologize to her!"

Charles looked up at his mother defiantly. "No," he said. "It's *my* present."

"Nevertheless, you should never slap anyone—particularly your own sister. Now, apologize!"

"No."

"Then go up to your room."

Charles's handsome young face turned to stone. "No."

Edwina turned to her husband.

"Darling, you saw what he did. Take him upstairs and give him the thrashing he deserves."

Nick looked at the eldest son he adored. Charles knew his father adored him.

"Daddy," he said, "can't I stay down? It's Christmas Eve."

Sylvia was still wailing by the tree.

"You can stay down if you apologize to your sister," said Nick.

"But it's *my* present!" Charles said. "She tried to steal it from me."

"That's not true!" sniffed Sylvia. "Charles is a bully!"

"It's a pair of ice skates!" snarled Charles, turning fiercely on his sister. "I saw Mommy wrapping them. Girls don't get ice skates. They're for *me!*"

"You spied on me while I was wrapping the presents?" exclaimed a shocked Edwina.

"Yes."

"Charles, gentlemen do not spy. Nor do they slap people. Now go upstairs. You've done enough to ruin Christmas for everyone!"

"Now, wait a minute," said Nick. "What Charles doesn't realize is that Sylvia's getting a pair of skates too. So let's open this package and see whose skates they are. Then we'll find the other package."

As Nick opened the package, Edwina stared at him. "Darling, that's not the point!" she exclaimed. "Charles has behaved like a little beast and must be punished."

"Edwina, it's Christmas Eve. Kids shouldn't be punished on Christmas Eve. Here, Charles, see if these skates fit."

Edwina, shaking her head in disbelief, walked over to her mother-in-law.

"Nick's spoiling that boy rotten," she whispered to Edith.

"He remembers his own childhood," Edith replied. "When he had nothing. I suppose he can't resist spoiling him."

"Nevertheless, he's turning Charles into a monster."

She turned to look back at the Christmas tree.

Charles, ice skates in hand, was grinning triumphantly at his mother.

The man in the white makeup with rouged lips stood on the small stage of the Brasserie Sedan in Berlin and did a bad imitation of Fred Astaire singing "Top Hat, White Tie and Tails," the hit number in that year's Broadway smash, *Funny Face*. The cabaret on the Bismarckstrasse was jammed mostly with men, although a few women of dubious sexuality were present, smoking furiously as they watched Willie Kleinburg, the singer of dubious sexuality, strut back and forth on the stage tipping his top hat and beating rhythm on the floor with his gold-topped cane.

The man in the black suit and hat appeared in the doorway of the smoky cabaret and looked around the room, ignoring the stage routine. When he saw the blond young man in the dinner jacket sitting in one of the rear corners, he squeezed his way through the crowd until he reached Rudi von Winterfeldt.

"The Fuehrer wants to see you," whispered the man. "Now."

Looking surprised, Rudi followed the man out of the cabaret.

"The Fuehrer is in Berlin?" asked Rudi as they reached the sidewalk.

"Yes. There is a meeting of industrialists, and he is addressing them. I thought you were instructed not to go to places like this?"

"In Munich, yes. But no one knows me in Berlin. And I wanted to hear Willie Kleinburg sing."

"Get in."

The man in the black suit opened the door of the coupe and Rudi climbed in. The man slammed the door, then walked around the car and got in the driver's seat. He started the car and drove into Bismarckstrasse.

"Where is the Fuehrer staying?" asked Rudi.

"At Dr. Goebbels' villa in Wannsee."

They drove in silence for twenty minutes until they approached the large, lovely lake to the southwest of Berlin called the Wannsee. Here and in nearby Dahlem and Grunewald the new rich were building suburban villas on tree-shaded lots. In the summer, the Wannsee, along with the other lakes girdling the city, attracted thousands of Berliners who picnicked, swam and boated in its waters.

The car reached an imposing gateway and pulled into a long, dark drive. Rudi, who knew most of the Party gossip, was aware that Goebbels kept up a front as a respectable family man with his wife, Magda, and his brood of children, while he led a clandestine love life with similarly named Magda Bayreuth, among others. Rudi's own sadomasochistic relationship with Hitler didn't prevent him from sneering at Goebbels' flamboyant hypocrisy. But since he had never seen Goebbels' villa, he was curious to see what the Party funds were paying for. Goebbels and Goering had a reputation for living high off the hog, unlike their more modest Fuehrer.

But the car didn't stop at the villa. Rather, the man took the service drive down to the lake, where there stood a small, attractive wooden boathouse.

"The Fuehrer is staying in the boathouse," said the man as he climbed out.

Rudi followed him from the car to the deck of the boathouse, the top floor of which was a two-bedroom guest cottage. The man opened the door and Rudi followed him into a chilly living room, pleasantly decorated and hung with prints of sailing ships. The man closed the door as Rudi looked around.

"The Fuehrer," said the man, pulling the gun from his jacket, "says to achieve his dream for Germany, he must conquer his personal weaknesses. You are his last personal weakness." And he shot him twice through the heart.

He carried the body down the steps of the boathouse and dumped it into a motorboat. Then he climbed in the boat, started the motor and rode out to the middle of the lake. There he tied weights to the ankles of the corpse, then dropped Rudi von Winterfeldt into the cold, black waters of the Wannsee.

Part IV

THE LADY
OF THE VEILS
1930-1934

T HE long, black Mercedes limousine with its bulletproof glass, its double-armored steel plating and its two small Turkish flags on the front fenders drove through the outskirts of Istanbul heading in the direction of Scutari. The limousine was preceded and followed by motorcycle policemen whose sirens shrieked the traffic out of the way. Beggars, peddlers and pedestrians scattered to the side of the street and then turned to gawk and wave at the presidential limousine, in the back seat of which sat, in solitary splendor, the President of Turkey, Kemal Atatürk, the former Mustapha Kemal Pasha.

In the eight years since the great fire of Smyrna—now renamed Izmir—Kemal had tugged and kicked Turkey into the twentieth century, removing the veil from the women, abolishing first the Sultanate and then, to the horror of priests, the Caliphate, forcing the adoption of a Roman-style alphabet for the ancient Turkish tongue, force-feeding democratic institutions while at the same time maintaining a personal power that was as autocratic as that of the former Sultans.

There had been victims: foremost was his onetime closest friend and ally, Colonel Arif. When Arif, dismayed by Kemal's dictatorial powers, had turned against him and joined in plotting a coup, Kemal arrested him and signed his death warrant without batting an eye, pausing only long enough to put out his cigarette in an ashtray. Arif approached his hanging certain of a last-minute reprieve and went to his death convinced there had been a mistake, that his old friend could not have betrayed him. But even Kemal's harshest critics agreed that this one man, whatever his drawbacks, had created a strong modern Turkey out of a country that, a mere ten years before, had been on the brink of dissolution.

Twenty minutes outside Istanbul the procession pulled into the courtyard of a hideous four-story red-brick building erected seventy-five years before as a Turkish Army hospital during the Crimean War but since converted to a state-run insane asylum. It had recently been renamed, like so many other state institutions in Turkey, in honor of

Kemal Atatürk. Dr. Mendur Halavy, the bald, middle-aged director of the Kemal Atatürk Asylum for the Insane, stood waiting nervously in front of the building as the limousine stopped and the secret-service man hopped out of the front seat to hold the rear door as the President of Turkey stepped out into the blazing September sunlight.

"Excellency!" effused Dr. Halavy as he bowed to Kemal. "We are honored."

Kemal shook the director's hand and was introduced to the three senior staff members flanking him. Then Dr. Halavy took him into his first-floor office, where coffee was served.

When the two men were alone, Kemal said, "I find your story almost impossible to believe. Tell me the details again."

"Of course, Excellency. The woman was transferred here from Smyrna—pardon, Izmir—seven years ago. She had been a victim of the great fire, and large areas of her body and face had been badly burned. Quite frankly, we were amazed she was alive, but the doctors in Izmir had done a remarkably good job with her and she was lucky—the doctors knew how to apply the Ambrine technique, which was developed during the war for burn victims, and this probably saved her life. Still, as you will see, she was hideously disfigured.

"She was also in a state of near catatonia. She was totally mute, and it was obvious that the horrors she had lived through had severely damaged her mind. She was so traumatized that I believe even if she could have talked, she wouldn't have remembered who she was. Since we had no idea of her identity, we named her Sophie and put her in Ward Three. For almost seven years, Sophie has been a very docile member of our little community. She was given simple cleaning jobs and, since she didn't respond to any of our treatment, we assumed Sophie's true identity would remain a mystery till the end of her days.

"And then, six weeks ago, she suddenly began to talk. I was surprised, although there are cases on record where the brain has, over a long period of time, managed to reverse severe psychological damage. Apparently, Sophie was one of these cases. But I was amazed to discover she knew no Turkish but could only speak English and French! Fortunately, I speak French, so I began meeting with her every day, trying to help her crippled memory heal itself. At first she talked about America—for it turns out that she is, apparently, an American. She talked about her childhood in Connecticut and about her family, which she says was extremely well off. As she gathered her mental strength, she kept coming closer to the great tragedy that had traumatized her brain, namely, the Izmir fire. Finally, two weeks ago, the final veils were torn away and she was able to confront the horror.

"She became hysterical as she told me, and I was afraid she might slip back into the catatonic state. But she is a strong woman. What devastated her mind so cruelly was not only the pain of her burns, but the fact that before she was burned, she was cruelly raped by four Turkish soldiers."

Kemal frowned as he lit a cigarette.

"Go on," he said, exhaling.

"It was then she told me her name: Diana Ramschild. And she begged me to contact you. She said you would help her because she had once been your *janum,* your soul. Initially, of course, I thought this was the raving of a disturbed personality. But day after day she kept begging me to contact you until finally, out of pity, if nothing else, I sent the letter to your aide. I hope I did not do the wrong thing, Excellency?"

Kemal was lost in thought. "You did the right thing, Doctor." He stood up. "Take me to see her."

"I can have her brought down here, Excellency."

"No, I want to see her where she's been for the past seven years."

He stubbed out his cigarette and then followed Dr. Halavy out of his office. The entire staff of the asylum was on hand to catch a glimpse of the revered Father of the Turks, and they stared in awe as he and Dr. Halavy climbed the freshly scrubbed stone steps to the third floor of the building. In anticipation of the advent of the great man, the walls had been whitewashed, the naked light bulbs dangling on the long black cords from the vaulted brick ceilings had been dusted and burned-out ones replaced, and the sickly sweet cherry-gumdrop smell of freshly applied Turkish disinfectant permeated the atmosphere. On the third floor, Dr. Halavy and Atatürk walked down the center aisle of the third ward, watched by bug-eyed female inmates, one of whom was muttering incoherently to herself. The beds were all tightly made, and the inmates stood beside them in white hospital gowns and bare feet. The tall windows of the room were all open to let in a breeze, but still the place was stifling; and, though the room was clean, an occasional scream from the violent ward on the fourth floor gave a grim, Dickensian ambience.

She was standing by her bed halfway down the room. Her honey hair was streaked with gray, and the skin on her exposed legs, arms, and neck and the lower half of her face was mostly scar tissue. Only the perfect nose, the striking green eyes and the alabaster forehead remained undamaged; otherwise, Diana Ramschild was a horror.

He couldn't help but wince; even Kemal Atatürk was moved to pity as he stared at this wreck of what once had been a beautiful woman. But he admired the way she looked at him without flinching: the flames had not destroyed her pride or her guts.

"You have come," she said softly. "Thank you."

He stepped up to her and embraced her. "If only I had known."

It was then that her pride gave out, as the warmth of his arms and body brought back a flood of memories of the past, a past that her shell-shocked mind had blotted out for seven long years. She sobbed in his arms as he stroked her hair.

"I will do everything in my power," he whispered, "to put your life back together again."

He turned to Dr. Halavy. "Miss Ramschild," he said, "will return with me to Istanbul."

He put at her disposal a suite of rooms in the Dolmabahce Palace— the same palace on the Bosporus where eight years before she had refused to bribe Babur Pasha—and instructed the Palace servants to treat her "like a Sultana." He brought Istanbul's leading couturière, Mme. Rosa, to the Palace and told her to design a new wardrobe for her that would veil her scars. "I have taken the veil off the women of Turkey," he told Diana, "but I will put the veil on you." He behaved to her like a lover, and rumors began sweeping the gossip-mad city that Atatürk was indeed having a love affair with a "monster," adding delicious new spice to his already legendary love life.

In fact, he *was* rather in love with her. As he had once been attracted by her fresh American beauty, now her scars attracted him in a different way, even as, at the same time, they repulsed him. Since physical lovemaking was out of the question, he became like a knight of old, courting an inaccessible princess. There was a romance to their relationship that was lacking in his affairs with the easily accessible women of Istanbul and Ankara, even if the romance was partially fueled by pity and guilt over the behavior of the Turkish soldiers who had raped her. He told her, truthfully, that he had had nothing to do with what had happened to her on the docks of Izmir, that Fikriye, whose satanic jealousy had finally forced him to commit her to an asylum in Germany, must have told the soldiers to kill her. Diana believed him. She wanted to believe him, because all she had now in life was this man, a man she once loved so passionately and whom now she found she loved again, perhaps even more fiercely than before.

Just how little she had in life she learned on her third night in the Palace when he came to dine with her in her rooms. She was wearing a floor-length dress of pale-blue chiffon that Mme. Rosa had delivered that afternoon, and since it was the first dress she had worn in eight years, her joy was almost indescribable. She was wearing—and would wear for years to come—elbow-length gloves to cover the scars on her arms and hands and a veil across the lower half of her face. Atatürk had sent the hairdresser from the Pera Palace Hotel, so her honey-and-gray hair was attractively coiffed, again for the first time in years. As Atatürk came into the room, he was truly dazzled.

"The veils," he said softly. "The veils have made you beautiful again." And he kissed her gloved hand.

"I will wear them the rest of my life," she said. "I will be the Lady of the Veils, and if it's true that beauty is half illusion, then perhaps I truly *will* be beautiful. I thank you, my pasha, for all you've done for me."

He led her to one of the huge gilt sofas and sat down beside her, unable to take his eyes off her. The knowledge that beneath the beautiful veils lay hideousness intrigued him.

"I have bad news for you," he said after a moment. "I received a cable from my ambassador in Washington this afternoon. Your mother died seven years ago."

She said nothing for a moment.

"I knew it in my heart," she finally whispered. "When my memory came back, and I realized how many years had passed, for some reason I knew my mother would be dead." She turned her green eyes on him. "Then who inherited the company?"

"No one inherited it. And since you are legally dead, I must tell you you would have absolutely no chance of making a claim on the stock."

She looked confused. "I don't understand. What do you mean 'no one' inherited it? I have cousins whom I assume my mother would have willed her stock to."

"That's true. But they sold out to an entrepreneur I think you may remember."

Her eyes widened. "You don't mean Nick Fleming?"

He nodded.

She let out a scream of rage that was like a blast from hell. She stood up, howling, then ran across the room and began pounding her clenched fists against the ornate boiserie of one of the walls. Then, just as suddenly, she stopped. Slowly, she turned and looked at him, her eyes blazing.

"Now I have something to live for again," she said.

"Revenge?" he said, with a slight smile.

"I'll destroy him. If there is a God, I swear to Him I will destroy Nick Fleming. I will cause him to suffer as much as I have suffered. I'll make him wish he were *dead*. And I'll do it *myself*. No more hired assassins!"

He stood up and walked across the gleaming parquet to take her gloved hands. "You are magnificent!" He smiled. "I told you once that hate was as fascinating as love, and it's still true. How will you destroy him?"

"I don't know yet," she said softly. "But the time will come, and it will taste sweet."

"Magnificent," he repeated, kissing her gloves. "You excite me, oddly enough now more than before."

CHAPTER 24

As the shadow of Depression began to eclipse the peace and prosperity of the planet Earth, Nick Fleming, like millions of other Americans, found himself hard pressed, though he was hardly reduced to selling apples. He was, after all, a millionaire many times over; and although he had suffered losses in the Wall Street crash, since he had never been a heavy speculator in the market, the losses had merely wounded him. Then too the movie business continued to prosper, if sporadically, and Metropolitan Studios continued to return a profit. On the debit side, Edwina's film career had been slipping for some time, her name no longer the box-office draw it had been in the mid-twenties. In 1929 she had made her last film, *Affair in Madagascar,* which, while filled with "sizzling scenes of passion," as the ads put it, died a horrible, gurgling death at the box office. Edwina, concealing her genuine hurt, announced that she was quitting movies as capriciously as she had entered them. Nick, who had watched her films go from mediocre to worse, privately heaved a sigh of relief. But the loss of her considerable income put a further strain on the family budget. The money Nick had been paying her now went to other stars.

However, the cornerstone of the Fleming empire—and the press was already beginning to refer to it as an "empire," which pleased Nick—was the Ramschild Arms Company, and while Nick had managed to pump life into the company during the twenties, mainly through substantial arms sales to South and Central America, by the early thirties the spread of the worldwide Depression was hurting the gun business. As a matter of business, Nick had always contributed heavily to the coffers of the Republican Party, but with the advent of the Depression and the widespread unpopularity of Hoover, Nick, basically politically amoral, began contributing to the Democrats as well; so after the Democratic sweep in the 1932 election, important doors were open to him in Washington, particularly the door to the office of the new Democratic Senator from Connecticut, the Honorable Harrison Ward. Ward, a bright, young New Dealer, had an obvious interest in full employment at the Ramschild Company, and it was at Ward's invitation that Nick addressed a group of influential senators at the Metropolitan Club in Washington in February 1933.

"Ever since the Great War," Nick said from the dais, "it has been the policy of the United States government to maintain what I call a minimal Army. The reasoning behind this is that the last war was the last great land war, that any future war—in particular one with the Empire of Japan—would be fought on the open seas. But, gentlemen, I have disputed that for years, and recent events in Europe make me dispute it even more strongly. True, I am a manufacturer of armaments and it is in my private interests to sell guns and ammunition to the United States Army. But, gentlemen, three weeks ago Adolf Hitler became Chancellor of Germany. I have personally experienced the brutal methods of the Nazis, and I can assure you that Hitler is doing everything in his power—which is now considerable—to build up the military strength of his country. If we Americans do not match this military buildup—and I would remind you that now our Army is ranked only twelfth in the world—the day will come when we will rue our lack of preparedness."

The senators gave him faint applause. A half dozen of them had fallen asleep.

In fact, Nick's timing was off. Aside from the Reichstag fire, the first few months after Hitler's accession to power were relatively uneventful, and the new Chancellor applied the soft pedal in his public speeches. The press and the governments of the world assumed that, now in power, Hitler had become respectable.

Nick, remembering the Nazi gunmen in the Berlin alley, knew better.

The two heavyset women with braided hair and unfashionable evening gowns sat facing each other at the keyboards of the two bow-in-bow Bechstein grand pianos pounding out a two-piano version of "The Ride of the Valkyries" as most of the international and diplomatic set of Istanbul mingled in the main reception room of the former Imperial German Embassy (which now served as the German Consulate, the seat of the Turkish government having been moved to boring Ankara, much to the dismay of the diplomats). Jewels flashed, rich Turkish women having an inordinate fondness for big diamonds and rubies; the men wore white tie with orders, their colored silk ribbons diagonally slashing their stiff white shirts. The British Ambassador wore his full-fig diplomatic dress coat, heavily embroidered with gold-thread leaves. The occasion was a reception honoring the new German military attaché to Turkey, General Ernst von Treskow. The small sandy-haired General with the monocle had been transferred to Turkey because he was one of a number of General Staff officers whom Hitler mistrusted. He was sipping the Louis Roederer Cristal and chatting with the German Ambassador, Baron Ulrich von Greim, when Atatürk was announced. Baron and Baroness von Greim went to greet the President, then introduced him to the guest of honor.

Two hours later, as Atatürk waxed eloquent on his beloved *raki*, he took General von Treskow aside and said in a low voice, "After the reception, you will be my guest at a private supper. I want you to meet the most fascinating woman in Turkey."

Treskow realized the President of Turkey was well on his way to getting drunk, but Atatürk's love of alcohol was no secret in diplomatic and governmental circles.

Besides, it was impossible to say no to Kemal Atatürk.

Forty-five minutes later, the presidential limousine, bearing Atatürk, Baron von Greim and General von Treskow, drew up in front of a lovely terraced villa on the east bank of the Bosporus.

"I call this our unofficial state guesthouse," Atatürk said with a grin as he stepped out of the huge Mercedes. "Of course, Greim knows it well—eh, Baron?"

He winked at the German diplomat, who, at the age of sixty and weighing almost three hundred pounds, had the grace to look embarrassed.

A black butler wearing the billowing white pants of the ancient Ottoman Turks and a short, sleeveless jacket over his muscled, naked torso was awaiting them at the beautifully inlaid double doors. "Welcome to the House of Veils," he intoned, bowing low. General von Treskow had seen some curious sights in Berlin, but this was like walking into an Arabian Nights' fantasy.

Inside the white marble octagonal entrance hall stood a large lead statue of a nude woman from whose nipples two jets of water squirted. The General ogled it as the butler led the party into a glass-roofed atrium filled with ferns and fruit trees and exotic birds, then into a large salon filled with fine French furniture. In the center was an ornate, marble-topped table on which rested a large golden bowl filled with melons, pears, oranges and luscious grapes. Flanking the table were two of the most beautiful girls the General had ever seen. They wore gossamer harem pants and, like the butler, short, sleeveless jackets of intricately filigreed silk that offered tantalizing peeks of their full breasts beneath. They were barefoot and wore gold anklets and dozens of thin gold bracelets on their bare arms. Now, as harp music began playing in the next room, the girls bowed and said together, "Welcome to the House of Veils." Then, leaving the butler behind, they led the party into the next room.

Here, the German General dropped his monocle.

The room, which was filled with incense, had walls of gold leaf, large French doors opening onto a terrace overlooking the moonlit Bosporus, a pink marble floor and ten blue silk gilt divans on each of which reclined a beautiful woman, totally nude. In one corner, another nude woman sat playing a harp; the scene was like an uncensored version of a Busby Berkeley production number. Standing in the center of the room, wearing a long pale-green chiffon dress, long white gloves and a veil over the bottom of her face, was Diana Ramschild.

Atatürk came up to her and kissed her glove.

"Good evening, my beautiful Lady of the Veils," he said, smiling. "I have brought the new German military attaché to share your Turkish delights. Baron von Greim you know, of course. And this is General Ernst von Treskow."

The Germans kissed her glove.

"You are welcome, gentlemen," said Diana.

"This villa belonged to a brother of Sultan Abdul Hamid," said Atatürk. "We confiscated it for the state after the royal family left Turkey, and I have rented it to my dear friend, Miss Ramschild— who has turned it into an extremely profitable business!"

"Ramschild?" said Treskow. "That's an unusual name. Are you by any chance connected to the family that used to own the Ramschild Arms Company in the United States?"

"My grandfather founded it."

"Then you must know Nick Fleming?"

Atatürk cleared his throat.

"That's a name we don't mention in front of Diana," he said.

"That's all right," she said. "I take it you know Mr. Fleming?"

"Yes. I met him six years ago in Berlin. He was pretending to be interested in selling weapons to the German Army, and we foolishly trusted him. It turned out what he was really interested in was exposing our secret plans to the world press. The Fuehrer has never forgiven me for making the mistake."

Two black men, dressed in the same costume as the butler, entered the room carrying silver trays bearing champagne and caviar.

"Then we have something in common," said Diana to the General.

"We have both been deceived by Nick Fleming. Enjoy the pleasures of my house, General. Then perhaps we can talk further about Mr. Fleming."

Treskow couldn't take his eyes off the naked houris on the divans. "I wish we had something like this in Berlin," he said wistfully.

"Perhaps I'll open a branch," Diana remarked.

Atatürk laughed.

"If you are serious," remarked Baron von Greim, "I would be delighted to make the proper introductions for you. Field Marshal Goering would *love* to have a place like this in Berlin!"

She looked at the fat, red-faced diplomat.

"Perhaps I *am* serious," she said quietly.

CHAPTER 25

EDWINA was restless, bored and over thirty. In that hot summer of 1934, most women would have sold their souls to be Edwina Fleming. Although her film career was over, she *had* been a movie star, and she was still beautiful, rich and famous. Her clothes were made by Vionnet, Schiaparelli, Molyneux, and she had mansions in Greenwich and Beverly Hills, a twelve-room Park Avenue apartment, a fleet of six cars at her disposal, jewels and furs, a clutch of beautiful children and a husband who loved her.

But the superficiality of her past life—the shopping, the parties, the fun—was beginning to pall. She admired the current First Lady, Eleanor Roosevelt, who had thrown herself so wholeheartedly into the problems of the Depression poor. But while Edwina contributed time and money to "worthwhile" charity projects, she wasn't a social activist. She wanted to commit her life to something more important than clothes and furs, but helping out at soup kitchens struck her as vaguely hypocritical unless she was willing to give up her wealth, which she wasn't. The role model she saw more suited to herself was Nora in Ibsen's *A Doll's House*. Nora had walked out on her husband in the play over a half century before, but her act of defiance, no matter how hotly discussed by the theatergoing public since, hadn't seemed to have much changed the institution of marriage. Edwina didn't want to walk out on her husband and children. But the idea of making some sort of defiant statement to Nick appealed to her as much as jumping naked into the pool at Thrax Hall had in 1917.

As the age of thirty-eight loomed before her, Edwina wanted to rebel. She just wasn't sure exactly how to do it.

She was planning the menu for a Fourth of July pool party she was giving the next Saturday when she heard the front doorbell ring. Moments later, her English butler, Sherman, came into the morning room of the Greenwich estate. "It's a Mr. Hill, madame. He was sent by Mr. Fleming for some papers."

"Who's Mr. Hill?"

"He works for your husband."

"Oh."

She got up from her escritoire and walked to the entrance hall. The young man in the gray suit was looking around the imposing hall. When he turned and Edwina saw his face, she almost gasped.

"Is something the matter?" he said.

"No. . . . I'm terribly sorry, it's just that . . ." She ran her hand through her hair, trying to silence the buzzing in her ears. "For a moment, I thought you were someone I used to know. You look so much like him, it gave me a bit of a shock."

The young man smiled. "I hope he was someone you liked."

"He was my fiancé, an Englishman named Lord Rocksavage. He was killed in the war."

The smile faded. "Oh, I'm sorry."

She looked at his face again. It was a remarkable resemblance. Memories momentarily flooded her mind, then ebbed away.

"I'm Mrs. Fleming. You work for my husband?"

"Yes. I'm Chester Hill, one of his vice presidents. Didn't he ever mention me to you?"

"No, but I don't discuss my husband's business with him—at least *this* business. I don't entirely approve of the weapons business."

He looked amazed. "You don't *approve?* Why, it's the most exciting business in the world!"

"Perhaps for you. You look awfully young to be a vice president."

"I may be. But I'm good at what I do."

"And what *do* you do?"

"I design those weapons you don't approve of. That's why I'm here. Mr. Fleming left some working drawings I gave him yesterday. They're pretty important, which is why he sent me. They're in the safe. He said you know the combination."

"Yes, I do. But since I really don't know *you,* I'll have to check with my husband first. You *could* be a spy from another company, after all."

He laughed. "Or an enemy agent." The phone rang. "That'll be Mr. Fleming. He said he'd call you. Do you think I'd make a good spy?"

She looked him over. He was more than six feet tall, with dark hair and the rangy good looks she had always been susceptible to.

"I don't know how good a spy you'd make, but with those looks you could get a job in the movies, if all else fails."

"Say, you were in the movies once, weren't you? Before the talkies . . ."

"Oh, I even made a talkie."

"That's right—I saw it! *Affair in Madagascar*. It was a stinkeroo."

"You've *made* my morning, Mr. Hill," she said, lowering the temperature twenty degrees.

"Oh, God, I put my foot in my mouth, didn't I?"

"Such a big foot. And such a big mouth. Yes, Sherman?"

"It's Mr. Fleming, madame."

"Excuse me, Mr. Hill."

She left the entrance hall. Chester Hill scratched his cheek and thought, You dumbbell! Insult the boss's wife—how *not* to succeed in business. She's one cool customer . . . and a beauty too. I wonder if I should apologize? No, something tells me movies are a sore subject. . . .

Five minutes later, she returned to the hall with a manila envelope. "I believe this is it?"

She handed him the envelope. He pulled out the drawings, looked at them, then put them back.

"Yes. It's a new gun we're working on. We hope to get a big order from the Army."

"Mr. Hill," she said, "you were right about *Affair in Madagascar*. It *was* a stinkeroo." They looked at each other, and she laughed. "I'm just not used to anyone being *quite* so blunt about my movie career. I did make some good films, you know. Back in the dark ages."

"Why did you stop?"

"Pride, I suppose. Once you've been on the top, it's rather ghastly to realize you're sliding down the greasy pole, as Disraeli might have put it. At any rate, I'm sorry I was so snappy a moment ago."

There was an awkward silence as they looked at each other.

"Why don't you ever come out to the factory?" he finally asked.

"Why in the world should I? Factories are ugly places, and I'm sure gun factories are hideous."

"But you're wrong! Why don't you let me give you a tour?"

She stared at him. She started to say no, then, to her own amazement, changed her mind. "What a lovely idea!" She smiled. "Wait till I get my hat and coat."

Why in God's name am I doing this? she thought as she went to the coat closet.

But she knew why.

Edwina, you nit, are you letting yourself in for something stupid?

The Ramschild factory was over a two-hour drive from the Greenwich house, which would have made for a disastrous commute if Nick had spent much time there, which he didn't. Nick's life had become an almost constant whirlwind of movement: weekly trips to New York to work with Van Clairmont, for Van had designated his stepson the heir apparent; trips to Washington to lobby the War Department; trips to the Coast to keep his hand in at Metropolitan Studios; and frequent trips abroad to make arms sales. All this activity was orchestrated by his efficient secretary, Frieda Gottschalk, and left Nick little time to be at the factory, which was run on a daily basis by the executive vice president, Edgar Flint. Nick had little interest in factory management, which some of his critics said was his greatest weakness as a businessman. Nick, the born salesman, loved the excitement and drama of the deal. And, since most of his customers were governments, he knew he had to go to them rather than vice versa.

Since Nick rarely talked business to his wife, it had never even occurred to Edwina to visit the factory, and the idea that Chester Hill could be so enthusiastic about it fascinated her. Yet as he drove his Buick sedan into the parking lot and she looked at the huge, ugly redbrick buildings, she sensed the power they represented—ultimate power of life and death.

"I wonder how many people have been killed by the products of this place?" she said as he led her to the executive wing.

"Ah, well, you have the liberal, sentimental view of the arms business, which I can easily understand. Believe me, I'd just as soon design cars or refrigerators or Coke bottles instead of howitzers, and if all the arms companies in the world went out of business, I'd be delighted. But that 'if' is never going to happen, at least for a long time. Critics say armaments kings like Mr. Fleming goad governments into making wars for their own profit, but I think that has very little truth to it. The truth is that *governments* make wars, and if private companies didn't arm the governments, they'd arm themselves. If the people of this world want to put an end to wars, they shouldn't go after us, they should improve their governments. But the sad truth is, in my opinion, a lot of the people on this planet *like* wars. It makes no sense, of course, but people like patriotism and jingoism. They like to get themselves worked up over a cause and go out and prove their manhood by getting themselves blown up. . . ."

"Wait a minute," she interrupted. "You say 'people.' Make that 'men' and you have a point. It's men who have to prove themselves heroes. Women have better sense."

"All right, I'll grant you that."

"If men would ever grow up and stop thinking like little boys playing soldier, the world would be a better and infinitely more peaceful place."

"But meanwhile, *someone* has to build the guns. And here we are, in the Kingdom of Darkness."

He opened the door and led her into the entrance hall past two security guards and then through a side door into the factory itself. He showed her with obvious pride the enormous fifteen-thousand-ton press, standing twenty-five feet tall, which made the cannon barrels; he showed her the blast furnaces, the rifling machines, the ammunition assembly lines where thousands of bullet and shell cases traveled on belts; he took her into the powder room to show her how the explosives were made; he took her into his private kingdom, the design room, where, on dozens of drawing boards, lethal improvements were devised for already-lethal weapons. The tour lasted over an hour, and when it was finished she was exhilarated and at the same time depressed. The place was as ugly and hot and smelly as she had imagined, and everywhere was the feeling of death. And yet, what he had said was at least partially true: barring Utopia, *someone* had to make weapons, and Edwina could feel the excitement of the giant guns. She also felt *his* excitement.

"Well?" he asked as he led her back into the executive offices. "What do you think of it?"

"I still wish my husband manufactured bicycles, but I'll admit there *is* something exciting about the place. Thanks for the tour."

"I still can't believe you've never been here. If I were married to Nick Fleming, I'd ask for a job here."

"If you were married to Nick Fleming, I don't think *anyone* would hire you."

Because he looked so embarrassed, she laughed.

"You're a funny man, Mr. Hill, but I think it's rather sweet that you're so enthusiastic about your work. Now if you'll take me to my husband's office, I'll talk him into driving me home."

"I can take you. . . ."

"No, that's silly. It's too long a drive. Do you live near here?"

"Yes, in Old Lyme."

He led her up a staircase lined with framed *Harper's Weekly* prints of Civil War battle scenes.

"And are you married?"

"I was. My wife and I were divorced last year."

"I'm sorry to hear it."

246

"I'm not."

He said it in such a clipped fashion, she decided the divorce must have been a bitter one.

At the top of the stairs, he led her down a long hallway lined with frosted-glass doors bearing the painted names of the officers and their titles: "Mr. R. M. Welles, Vice President Sales"; "Mr. Arthur Ten Eck, Vice President Personnel" . . . then, at the end of the corridor, a sleekly modern solid walnut door with raised brass letters reading "Mr. N. Fleming, President." Suddenly, Edwina was curious to see her husband's office, the heart of his far-flung empire. It occurred to her she had made a mistake never coming here before, that if Nick had remained something of a mystery man to her with his incessant scheming, it was because she had never seen him on his home turf—and her instincts told her this *was* his home, perhaps more than the Greenwich mansion or the Park Avenue apartment or Casa Encantada. A great part of Nick was, after all, his business. As Chester Hill opened the door, Edwina even felt a slight surge of jealousy. Suddenly, a line from her Church of England childhood flashed in her mind, a line from the beautiful William Blake hymn, "Jerusalem." "And was Jerusalem builded here/Among those dark Satanic mills?" Here was the quintessential "dark Satanic mill." Had her husband built his private Jerusalem on the banks of the Connecticut River in his factory of death?

The reception room, totally redone by Nick in 1928, was large and sleekly Art Deco, a far cry from the spittoon-and-fustian decor of Alfred Ramschild's day. The walls were paneled in honey wood with a waist-high horizontal stripe of inlaid darker wood and, below the ceiling, an inlaid Greek key design. Edwina had met Frieda Gottschalk many times in Greenwich and New York; Edwina knew heavyset Frieda would never be a threat to her or a temptation to Nick. Now she looked up from behind her kidney-shaped desk and gaped.

"Mrs. Fleming!" she exclaimed. "What are *you* doing here? Is something wrong?"

"Not at all, Frieda. Mr. Hill simply convinced me it was time I saw the factory. Is my husband in?"

"He's on the phone to London. I'll tell him you're here."

She got up and hurried through the double doors to the inner sanctum. Edwina went to the big plate-glass window and looked out over the factory, its eighty-foot chimneys wafting smoke over the Connecticut River, smoke that was cleaned by filters Nick had installed shortly after taking over the company. Was the moral of the factory

power? she wondered. Nick had power. She had once had an ephem-
eral type of power as a movie star, but that was gone now. Power, the
ultimate aphrodisiac. . . . Was power what she missed in her life?
No, she didn't think so, at least not Nick's kind of power. She didn't
really want to run businesses—businesses bored her. But she did *resent* Nick's power. For all the brash independence of her youth, for
all the wild things she had done in her life—not the least of which
having been to go into films—the total of her existence seemed to be
that she had ended up a wife and mother, living an admittedly en-
viably luxurious existence in the reflection of her husband. She was a
planet; *he* was the star. While that would be enough for most women,
was it enough for her, who had once been a genuine star earning vast
sums of money? The thought occurred to her: In a showdown, what
would be more important to Nick: his wife or his business? Dangerous territory, she realized; but wasn't it the very heart of the matter?
And wasn't perhaps this extremely good-looking Chester Hill the tool
she needed? Suddenly, Edwina knew how she wanted to rebel.

She turned to look at him, realizing he had been watching her.

"Mr. Hill," she said, "my husband and I are giving a Fourth of July
picnic Saturday—we're roasting hot dogs, there'll be a fireworks display . . . all sorts of amusing things. Would you like to come?"

He looked surprised. Nick rarely invited even the top Ramschild
executives to his home. While it was well known he lavishly entertained people he was wooing to make deals with in his varied enter-
prises, his own employees he kept at a respectful distance socially.

"Well . . ."

"There'll be some interesting guests," Edwina prompted. "Including an old acquaintance of ours from Germany, Count von Winterfeldt, the Minister of Culture. I think you'd have a good time. Unless
you have other plans?"

"Oh, no. I have nothing planned."

"Then you'll come?" She smiled prettily.

What's going on? he thought. What the hell is going on?

"Well, sure. I'd love to. Thanks."

"Good. Be at Graystone at noon. And bring a bathing suit. The
forecast is for hot weather, and you'll want to swim in the pool."

It doesn't matter whether I go to bed with him, she thought. The
important thing is Nick's reaction when I tell him I *want* to.

"You did *what?*" exclaimed Nick an hour later as he and Edwina
raced back to Greenwich in the back seat of his Cadillac limousine.

"I invited Chester Hill to our picnic Saturday," she said casually.

"Why the hell did you do that? You know I have a policy against mixing with my people socially!"

"Now, darling, calm down. It's all very simple. You remember I told you years ago in Germany that I resented the double standard in marriages? And that if someday I met a man I wanted to go to bed with I'd tell you? Well, I've met the man. I want to go to bed with Chester Hill."

He looked apoplectic.

"Edwina, be *serious!* I mean, besides everything else, he works for me! He's one of my vice presidents!"

"I know that. That's what makes it so much more interesting."

"Dammit, I don't know what craziness has gotten in your head, but you can forget *this.* I absolutely forbid it."

"Oh? So all that talk was just talk? You make love to your actresses—who are in *your* business, by the way—but I can't make love to one of your vice presidents?"

"The comparison is silly."

"To you perhaps. Not to me."

"Besides, I've been faithful to you."

"And pigs have wings."

"I *have,* dammit! And, Edwina, no matter how *you* look at marriage, the way the rest of America looks at it is that wives don't play around."

"Now *you're* being silly. I know plenty of wives who play around, including lots of our friends. Want a list of names? Sally Winston, who's been sleeping with the tennis pro at Piping Rock. Elvira Nesbitt, who's been sleeping with her lawyer, of all people! Dorothy Dunlop, who's taken on half the male population of Palm Beach. Agnes de Witt . . ."

"I'm not interested in them. I'm interested in *us*—you and me and the kids."

"I'm not talking about breaking up our family, and this has nothing to do with my love for you. It's a matter of principle. I think I have a right to take an occasional lover if I want to, and if you had any respect for me as a human being and not just your wife, you'd give me that right—just as I've given it to you over the years *in spades.* God knows, I could have done it behind your back dozens of times, but I don't want to sneak. I want to do it with your knowledge and approval."

"If this is a joke, it's a rotten one!"

"It's not a joke. I'm deadly serious."

"Well, the answer is no, and that's final. And I'm warning you, Edwina, if you play around with Chester, I'll fire him. And you won't just be hurting a young man's career, you'll be hurting the War Department of the United States, because Chester is working on some highly technical stuff—"

"Oh, we bring in the flag, do we?" she interrupted hotly. "Of all the gall! What's more important, my rights as a woman or some damned gun for the Army?"

"I'd say some damned gun for the Army, without any question!"

"Then our priorities are a lot different. But I knew it would be like this, Nick. I knew if I ever presented you with this situation, you'd worm out of it one way or another, though I'll admit waving the flag gets some sort of award for originality."

She looked out the window at the passing countryside.

"Well?" he said after a moment. "What are you going to do?"

"We'll see."

"Edwina, I love you. We've had a damned good marriage so far. Let's not mess it up now with some screwball scheme of yours."

"It's not screwball. And as I've told you, it has nothing to do with our marriage."

"Oh, yes, it does."

He said it softly, and she knew from experience that he was most lethal when he was soft. She turned her head to look at him, and there were tears in her eyes.

"Damn you, Nick," she said. "The most irritating thing about you is that you refuse to see how important this is to me."

"Important enough to risk my love for you?"

She looked at him a moment without answering. Then she turned back to look out the window again.

She really didn't know the answer to that one. How far was she willing to take the rebellion?

Four thousand miles away, at two in the morning, the Chancellor of the German Reich, Adolf Hitler, wearing a leather coat, climbed into a three-engine Junker 52 piloted by his favorite pilot, Hans Baur.

Baur took off from the airport at Bad Godesberg and flew to Munich, landing the plane in rainy weather at Oberwiesenfeld, a military airport. A few Nazi Party officials and army officers were on hand to greet the Fuehrer; Hitler, in a dark, explosive mood, greeted them by snarling, "This is the blackest day of my life. But I shall go to Bad Wiessee and pass severe judgment."

Bad Wiessee was a resort on the beautiful Tegernsee, a lake at the gateway to the Alps forty kilometers south of Munich. It was in this lovely setting that Ernst Roehm, one of Hitler's oldest confederates and head of the Sturmabteilung, or S.A.—the Brownshirts—was taking a rest cure with some of his top-ranking S.A. officers. For weeks rumors had been circulating in Germany about a possible eruption between the S.A. and the German Army—or even a *Putsch* on the part of Roehm against Hitler. The Brownshirts had begun as Hitler's personal army, and their rowdy tactics and ruthlessness had earned them the hatred not only of the German Jews but of many non-Jewish Germans as well. The S.A. considered themselves an elite, the driving wedge of pure National Socialism whom Hitler was selling out to gain the cooperation of the German Army. Despite veiled threats from Hitler, Hess, Goering and Goebbels, Roehm had stayed serene in his *pension* at Bad Wiessee. The previous evening he had played tarok, a three-handed Bavarian card game, received a neuralgia shot from his doctor, then gone to bed. Though he was a notorious homosexual, he had gone to bed alone.

At 6 A.M. two staff cars drove down the side of the lake to Bad Wiessee and pulled up in front of the Pension Hanselbauer. In the first car, driven by Hitler's chauffeur, Erich Kempka, was the Fuehrer; all told, there were less than a dozen men in the two cars. As the sun began to break through the dawn mist over the lake, Hitler led his party into the hotel, the ground floor of which was deserted except for the landlady, who looked amazed to see Hitler himself in her *pension*.

"Where is Reichsleiter Roehm?" snapped the Fuehrer.

"Upstairs," gulped the landlady. "Room Three."

The party climbed the stairs, their jackboots thumping ominously on the steps. Hitler pounded on the door of Room Three. He held a pistol. When the yawning Roehm opened the door, Hitler said, "Ernst, you are under arrest. You are a traitor to me and to the Reich. Get dressed."

"But . . ."

"Get *dressed!*" Hitler roared. "Or I'll have you shot on the spot."

"And then all the S.A. men in the hotel were rounded up at gunpoint," said Count Alex von Winterfeldt four days later as he sat beside Nick Fleming's pool in Greenwich, Connecticut. He was talking privately to

Nick at an umbrella table as the Fleming children and three dozen guests splashed in the pool under the blazing July sun or milled about the tree-shaded lawns of the lovely estate. "Many of the S.A. men were in bed with their chauffeurs," continued the Count, lowering his voice. "They were a rotten bunch—everyone in Germany knew it. They were taken back to a Munich jail and summarily executed, though I think Hitler gave Roehm the opportunity to commit suicide—at any rate, he's dead. The reports I'm getting by phone from my friends in Munich and Berlin say that perhaps as many as two hundred people were executed without trial. It's the final straw, Herr Fleming. Hitler has given himself license to murder. Germany is being run by criminals!"

Nick sipped his Cuba libre through a straw.

"Surely this doesn't come as a surprise to you?" he said.

The Count shook his head. "No. I'm convinced Hitler murdered my son seven years ago, though I'll probably never know the truth. The surprise is not that Hitler is an amoral monster, but that as the legally elected Chancellor of Germany he would have the gall to commit these mass murders in the face of world opinion! Can any other government deal with Germany now?"

"They deal with Russia, and Stalin has certainly killed more people than Hitler. Mussolini has murdered people, for that matter. Pardon me for saying it, but your attitude strikes me as naïve."

The Count sighed. "Perhaps. But you're not a German—I am. It is repugnant to me to think that my government—of which I am a part, admittedly—could behave in this manner. Which is why I wanted to see you."

Nick saw Edwina crossing the lawn toward them and signaled the Count to keep quiet.

"We'll talk later," he said.

"Darling, lunch is served," she said, looking smashing in her one-piece green bathing suit. "Can you help me get the children out of the pool?"

Chester Hill was the fourth son of a distinguished, but poor, Episcopalian minister whose family had inhabited the charming northwest Connecticut town of Salisbury since the 1740s. Chester had grown up in a rambling eighteenth-century farmhouse that until 1921 had had neither electricity, plumbing nor central heating. His boyhood memories of sitting in a freezing privy were still vivid in his mind. Chester had won scholarships at the nearby Kent School, then Yale, where

the raccoon coats, Stutz Bearcats and big spending of his rich classmates had intensified his sense of poorness and honed his hunger for
money to swordlike ferocity. He had grown up in a home where grace
was said before meals and his father read from the Bible each evening
for a half hour. In his sophomore year at Yale, he became an atheist.
He decided his fastest ticket to riches was his good looks and began
dating the sisters of his richest classmates. Unfortunately for this
scheme, he impregnated the daughter of his physics teacher and was
faced with the Hobson's choice of making an honest woman of her or
being kicked out of Yale, losing his scholarship. He married her,
acutely and bitterly aware she was almost as poor as he was. The
five-year marriage produced two children, endless fights and an expensive divorce.

Now, as he climbed out of Nick's pool to dry himself off for lunch,
Chester looked at the imposing mansion, the distant tennis court, the
beautiful landscaping—and envied his employer to the bottom of his
soul. The irrational side of him wanted to strike out somehow at all
this wealth: seduce Nick's wife, burn down the house, kidnap one of
the children. The rational side of him told him that Nick was a good
employer, he enjoyed his work, and he was making seventeen thousand dollars a year, a handsome salary in 1934. As he pulled on his
polo shirt to go eat lunch, Chester Hill was an emotional powder keg.

The barbecue had been billed as "one hundred percent All-American," but that had to be translated as All-American Rich. A betoqued
chef was grilling the hot dogs and hamburgers on the brick barbecue
while three white-jacketed servants manned the long outdoor buffet,
serving salads, fruit, pickles, deviled eggs and homemade strawberry
ice to the guests, half of whom were preteen-age friends of the Fleming children. The kids standing in line at the buffet in their bathing
suits were talking and laughing, typically ignoring the adults. But
when Chester joined the line, he noticed one girl who was not talking
to her peers but, rather, was watching him.

It was Sylvia Fleming, Nick's oldest daughter, who, now fourteen,
had grown into a dark-haired beauty. The look she was giving Chester
was so intense, so unabashedly adult, that he almost looked away to
avoid embarrassment.

It was then the idea popped into his mind.

Edwina had seen Sylvia's look also and realized with a jolt that she
wasn't the only woman interested in Chester Hill. For a number of
months now she had realized that her daughter was manifesting an

interest in the opposite sex that was as lively as hers had been at that early age. Since Edwina considered herself a "modern" woman totally liberated from the stuffy views of her parents' generation, she was surprised how much Sylvia's coquettishness—if that slightly stuffy word could convey the high-voltage look Sylvia had thrown Chester—upset her. In fact, her instincts were to drag her daughter inside the house and spank her. But a sense of guilt held her back. Hadn't the same scheme been in the back of her mind—to seduce Chester?

And it was then she realized a shattering truth about herself. For all her attempts at being shocking and madcap, for all her pride in her "mad" Thrax blood, for all her taunting Nick about her right to take a lover if she chose, for all the logic of her arguments, the harsh truth was that she couldn't bring herself to carry them into action. The plain truth was she adored her husband and her family and wasn't about to jeopardize her marriage by tossing her cap for a man she had nothing but a physical interest in.

My God, she thought, almost laughing out loud, I'm a conventional woman!

"When I found out how you tricked all of us seven years ago," said Count Alex von Winterfeldt to Nick, "I was frankly furious at you. Is it true that so-called footman was a Hollywood actor?"

"Yes." Nick laughed. "He's doing quite well in Westerns now."

The two men were sitting on the afterdeck of Nick's sixty-foot cabin cruiser, the *Sea Nymph,* as Nick's two-man crew cruised Long Island Sound in front of Nick's estate.

"Of course, the government and the General Staff were outraged when the articles were printed," the Count continued, "but in retrospect I now admire what you did. We had no way of knowing then that the German Army would become the personal toy of that madman, Hitler. I can't impress on you enough, Herr Fleming, how things have changed in Germany. To give the man his due, I'll admit he's brought us out of the Depression. Germany is more prosperous than the United States. But the price of prosperity has been personal freedom. You've undoubtedly read about the concentration camps, but all Germany is becoming a concentration camp. Hitler *has* to be stopped."

"I agree," said Nick, "but I don't know who's going to stop him."

"I am," said the Count, and Nick looked at him with surprise.

The Count eyed the bridge where the two crewmen were.

"They can't hear you," said Nick. "The engines are too loud."

254

The Count turned back to him. "I don't know what you may have heard about my son back in '27," he said.

"I heard that he was a Nazi and an intimate friend of Hitler's."

The distinguished man's face looked pained.

" 'Intimate friend' is a nice euphemism," he said. "My son was Hitler's lover. Rudi was mesmerized by Hitler, like all Germany today. Exactly when they became lovers I don't know, nor do I want to know; the point is, the gossip about them was beginning to hurt Hitler's political chances. I'm convinced that's why he had Rudi killed."

"Was there an investigation?"

The Count shrugged. "Yes, but nothing was found. I don't even know where his body is. You must realize that even then Hitler had extremely powerful friends in Germany. He got away with murder then, as he is getting away with mass murder now. I believe in an eye for an eye, Herr Fleming. That's why I now intend to pay Hitler back for what he did to my son."

"Excuse me, Count, but there's one thing I don't understand. If you're such an implacable foe of Hitler's, why did he reappoint you Minister of Culture last year? And why did you join the Nazi Party?"

"You must try to understand Hitler's psychology. He was in love with my son. I think probably to make the decision to kill him required a great act of will on his part and caused him genuine agony. Now he feels guilt, which is why he offered me the post in his government."

"Also perhaps to shut you up?"

"Yes, that too. As far as my joining the Party, I had to to keep the government post. There are many Party members in Germany now who don't believe in Fascism: they join to protect themselves, to function. My being in the Party and the government gives me freedom to maneuver and some protection. But what I'm involved in carries great risks, needless to say."

"And just what are you involved in?"

"I'm not alone in believing Hitler is a disaster for Germany and must be removed. Many of the big industrialists—Krupp and Thyssen, for example—back him, but there are others who don't. More to the point, many of the senior army commanders are anti-Hitler."

"Why?" interrupted Nick. "He's increasing arms expenditures and building the Army's strength."

"And for what purpose except another war? Oh, I know he talks peace in public, but in private he talks war, and any responsible German knows that another war for Germany would be a calamity. That's why the group I represent feels Hitler must be stopped now, while President von Hindenburg is still alive. Hindenburg is the only obstacle to Hitler's assumption of total power. But the President is an old man—he can't last for long. We must organize the coup *now,* so Hindenburg can hold the nation together until a new government can be installed."

"So you're planning a *Putsch*?"

"Exactly. Key elements in the Army will capture Hitler and the other top Nazis—either dead or alive—and hold new national elections."

Nick whistled.

"That's some ambitious scheme! What if it fails?"

"We're all dead men, Herr Fleming."

"Well, I admire your guts, Count. And I wish you every possible success. But I don't quite see where I fit in."

"We need guns, Herr Fleming—guns from outside Germany. We have key army regiments in all the major cities—Berlin, Hamburg, Frankfurt, Munich—which we control and which will carry out the *Putsch*. But they represent only a fraction of the Army as a whole. We are counting on the rest of the Army going along with us when the top political leaders have been removed, but of course we can't be sure of this happening. To back up our troops, we are organizing volunteer squads all over the country, and we have to arm them— secretly, of course. We decided the only way was to order arms from abroad, and remembering your ingenuity, I recommended contacting you. Naturally, the fact that you manufacture one of the best rifles in the world counted heavily as well. We are interested in ordering three million dollars' worth of guns and ammunition. I sincerely hope you are interested in filling that order."

"Of course I'm interested! But how could I deliver the guns to you without tipping off the Nazis?"

"You will make the delivery in Denmark. We will be responsible for getting them into Germany."

Nick looked at the dark clouds beginning to form in the west. It was four in the afternoon, and the July heat looked as if it was about to be broken by thundershowers. He got up and walked forward to the bridge.

"I think we'd better head in," he said to Tom Rydale, his thirty-year-old skipper.

"Right, Mr. Fleming."

Nick returned to Count von Winterfeldt and sat down again on the white canvas cushion.

"Can you tell me who some of the officers involved are?" he asked.

"Why do you want to know?"

"Most of my sales are made to legitimate governments, although I won't deny that I've made sales to certain antigovernment groups in South American countries I won't name. But most of my business is legitimate, and I want to keep it that way. If I go illegitimate—and this, from my government's viewpoint, would be an illegitimate sale, even though it's for a good cause—I like to know whom I'm dealing with. It's not that I don't trust you, Count, but you *could* be selling me a bill of goods."

The Count stiffened. "My dear Fleming," he sputtered, "if anyone is to be mistrusted, it is *you!* Seven years ago, you deceived me and the General Staff! What possible reason would I have for lying to you? Don't you realize that if this conversation were known to Hitler, I would be in front of a firing squad within half an hour?"

"Don't take offense, Count. It's just that in my business I have to be cautious—and I like to know whom I'm dealing with."

"I cannot reveal their names without their consent. However, if you come to Berlin, I can probably arrange for you to meet some of the principals involved."

"Would it be dangerous?"

"Not for you. You have an American passport. Of course it will be dangerous for us, but we are very cautious. Perhaps it will be better for you to come to Berlin anyway, because we will not be able to communicate with you from Germany—even a code would arouse suspicion. We can work out all the details there. What length of time would you need to deliver?"

"After I receive one-half down payment, I could deliver in a month."

"Excellent. Then are we in business?"

The boat bumped gently against Nick's dock.

"Let me think about it," Nick said, standing up. "I'll give you my answer in the morning."

"But, Herr Fleming, how could you possibly refuse us? You made it abundantly clear in your speech at the Metropolitan Club in Washington last year that you regard Hitler as a menace to world peace!"

"That's right, Count. But you are a member of Hitler's government and a card-carrying Nazi. You outline to me a scheme for a coup that in my opinion has a less than healthy chance of succeeding. That's why I want to meet the others involved and that's why I want to think about it. Shall we go up to the house? I hope the rain doesn't ruin our fireworks."

He helped the Count out of the boat. What he was thinking, but didn't say aloud, was that he tended to trust Count von Winterfeldt because the man was avenging the murder of his son. Nick was too cautious to understand taking the monumental risks Winterfeldt's group were submitting themselves to. But vengeance he *could* understand.

CHAPTER 26

THE threatened thundershowers did not materialize, and the heat, well up in the nineties, continued to sizzle until sunset, so that everyone stayed in their swimsuits, jumping in and out of the sixty-foot pool to keep cool. As the sun finally slipped out of sight, outdoor lights were turned on, attracting ten million bugs; but the more active adults, fueled by an afternoon full of beer, wine and liquor, and the kids, fueled by energy, kept using the pool until, at nine, Nick announced the fireworks. Chester Hill, realizing he had drunk too many rum punches, took a final dive in the pool to sober up, then climbed out and dried himself off as he walked down the lawn to the water's edge where the fireworks were to be set off. Most of the guests were already seated in the grass, slapping midges and mosquitoes, as Chester sat down to the rear of the group.

A moment later, Sylvia Fleming sat down on the grass beside him.

Sssssss-BANG!

The first skyrocket shot up in the air and exploded in a burst of blue and white sparks. The kids screamed with excitement and applauded. Sylvia was silent.

"Blue and white are Yale's colors," said Chester, keeping his eyes on the Sound but intensely aware of the girl's presence beside him. She was wearing a tight white bathing suit that showed her young body's every curve, the not quite fully matured breasts. He sneaked his eyeballs to the right and looked at her long, smooth legs stretched in the grass beside him. Only fourteen, but already the legs of a woman. The rum pumped in his veins and he repressed a desire to reach out and run his hand up one of those gorgeous legs.

"Did you go to Yale?" she said.

"Yes, Class of '28."

"Were you an athlete? Your body is very . . . muscular."

Sssssssss-BANG!

Up went another skyrocket, exploding a shower of red sparks. More squeals and applause. Sylvia was silent.

"Yes, I played third base. And I swam."

"I play field hockey at Miss Porter's. There's a mosquito on your back."

He felt her fingers run slowly and lightly over his right shoulder blade, brushing away a mosquito he hadn't felt. This is crazy! he thought. She's only fourteen, dammit! And yet the bulge in his swimming trunks began to expand embarrassingly.

Fzzzzzzzzz . . .

A pinwheel hissed and twirled and sputtered, throwing off dazzling sparks.

Sssssss-BANG!

Another skyrocket. The kids cheered and clapped.

"Daddy told me to tell you to spend the night," said Sylvia. "We have tons of extra rooms, and it's ridiculous for you to drive all the way back to Old Lyme tonight."

"Well, I didn't bring a toothbrush . . ."

"We have toothbrushes. I'll show you your room after the fireworks."

He stiffened as he felt Sylvia's upturned fingers slip between his right thigh and the grass. They gently massaged his flesh for a moment, then slowly pulled away.

Jesus H. Christ! thought Chester Hill, the sweat pouring down his ribs, his swim trunks about to explode.

Sssssss-BANG!

But she's only *fourteen!*

The idea he had had that afternoon had been simple enough. Sylvia was beautiful; Sylvia seemed interested in him. Perhaps, if he played his cards right, in six or seven years he might marry her and become Nick Fleming's son-in-law. Perhaps Sylvia would be the heiress he missed snagging at Yale.

But Sylvia was putting his plan into dangerous high gear.

"My older brother, Charles, is a spoiled monster," said Sylvia matter-of-factly. It was an hour later. The fireworks display was over, and the guests were leaving the estate. Sylvia was leading Chester up the painting-lined staircase to the second floor. Both were still in their bathing suits.

"That's not a very nice thing to say about your brother," said Chester, who was tense with repressed excitement. As he followed Sylvia up the steps, he watched her tight buttocks in front of him and kept saying to himself: Watch out! You're in a minefield.

"Charles isn't a very nice brother," she replied.

"He seems very nice."

"That's just an act he puts on. I think he's a potential ax murderer."

And she giggled. Chester thought she had a peculiar sense of humor.

As erotic as his thoughts were, Chester couldn't help tearing his eyes away from Sylvia's teen-age derriere to look at some of the paintings on the staircase wall and in the upstairs corridor. He knew enough about art to realize that at a time when most millionaires were still collecting Old Masters, the smart money was moving into modern art. Nick was smart money. The gilt frames on his walls contained some of the most jarring canvases Chester Hill had ever seen: Kokoschka, De Chirico, Kandinsky, Léger, Dali . . . He had no idea what the bizarre paintings were worth, but assumed that with every tick of the clock they became more valuable. You might marry into all this someday, he thought—but not if this teen-age time bomb explodes prematurely. But, oh, my God, what a lovely ass!

At the end of the hall, she opened a door and led him into a pretty room whose walls were covered with yellow flowered paper. She turned on the lights, then went to the windows and closed the curtains.

"Don't do that," he said. "I sleep with open windows."

She turned and looked at him.

"Close the door," she said.

Beginning to sweat again, he obeyed.

She crossed the room to him. "I think I'm in love with you," she said softly.

"Don't be ridiculous. You hardly know me. . . ."

"That doesn't matter. Love has to happen fast, and when I first looked at you today I knew we were destined for each other."

"Sylvia, you heard that line in a bad movie."

"It was in one of Mummy's movies."

"That's what I mean."

She was standing in front of him. Now she closed her eyes.

"Kiss me," she whispered.

He couldn't tell whether she was playing a childish game or was serious: perhaps a little of both. But, game or no, she was incredibly tempting.

"Kiss me," she repeated, "or I'll tell my father you tried to seduce me and he'll fire you."

He was sweating, more from apprehension than the heat. A minefield, a minefield . . .

He took her in his arms and kissed her rather tentatively. She kissed him back passionately, rubbing her hands over his back. He knew instinctively she was no virgin, but the reality astounded him. What astounded him more was that she was starting to pull down his swim trunks.

He pushed her hands away.

"You've got a very advanced technique for a fourteen-year-old," he said.

She looked at him defiantly. "I've made love over a dozen times," she said. "I've counted."

"With whom?"

"That's my business."

"Well," he said, wiping the sweat off his forehead, "I think you'd better get out of here before you get us both in a lot of trouble."

"You're afraid of my father."

"You're damned right I am."

She smiled and reached behind her, starting to unzip her bathing suit.

"If you don't make love to me, I'll start screaming," she said. "Then everyone in the house will know what you've done."

He stared at her. Go ahead and screw her, he was thinking. Why not? Maybe it's the best way . . .

The door quietly opened.

"Sylvia," said her brother Charles, "go to bed."

She rezipped her bathing suit, pouting. Charles came to her and took her hand, giving her an icy look. Then, holding her hand, he dragged her to the door.

"I'm sorry, Mr. Hill," he said, deadly serious. "She's done this before. The full moon and all that stuff. Good night, sir."

He shoved her through the door, then left, closing it behind him.

What a screwy bunch of kids! Chester Hill thought. Real nut cases! And yet he only wished that Charles hadn't interrupted them.

When the guests had all left, Nick and Edwina took a final dip in the pool together.

"You know I told Sylvia to ask Chester to spend the night," said Nick as he floated near his wife.

"Yes, and I don't think Sylvia was the smartest choice to deliver the message."

"Why?"

"You didn't notice? She was making the most outrageous goo-goo eyes at him all day. It was positively indecent."

"Sylvia's only fourteen!" he sputtered.

"I know. When I was only fourteen I was having the naughtiest thoughts about men. Something tells me Sylvia takes after her mummy."

He hesitated.

"Are you still having naughty thoughts about men? One man in particular?"

She swam over to him and wrapped her arms around him.

"Yes." She smiled. "I'm having naughty thoughts about *you*."

"And what about Chester Hill?"

"Oh, *him*," she pooh-poohed. "Dull as dishwater, in my opinion. He's interested in nothing but weapons—it would be like making love to a howitzer."

"That isn't what you thought the other day."

"I know, but I changed my mind. I decided I have a very lovely husband and I'm happy just the way I am. Sometimes talking about having a mad affair with another man is more fun than actually *having* one."

He looked at her and smiled. "You know something? You're crazy."

"Oh, it's much more serious than that, darling. The horrible truth is, I'm quite boringly normal." She shrugged and sighed. "Edwina Fleming, dull hausfrau, so hopelessly dotty about her husband, she can't even cheat on him. Isn't it awful?"

He kissed the end of her wet nose. "I think it's nice," he said softly and tenderly. "Let's go upstairs."

They swam to the edge of the pool, climbed out and started walking toward the house holding hands like two teen-agers in love.

"You have just made love," he said an hour later as they lay next to each other in their huge double bed over which hung one of Monet's paintings of water lilies at Giverny, "with the man who may help put Adolf Hitler out of power."

She sat up, turned on the light and looked at him.

"What do you mean? Is that why Alex von Winterfeldt was here?"

He nodded. "He tells me he and some high-placed German generals are organizing a *Putsch* to get rid of Hitler, and they want me to arm them."

"Are you going to do it?"

"I have reservations, but, yes, I'm going to. I'm not much of an altruist, but if I could help rid the world of that anti-Semitic madman, I'd feel damned good about myself."

She hesitated. "Is it . . . dangerous?" she asked.

"Well, there's a degree of risk involved. . . . I'll have to go to Berlin next week . . . but I can take care of myself."

"Darling, you're sure?"

"I'm sure. Don't worry, it's going to be fine."

She leaned down and kissed him. "You know, I'm *desperately* proud to be your wife," she said.

And she meant it. Edwina's rebellion was over before it had begun.

CHAPTER 27

IN 1934 the *Normandie* and the *Queen Mary* were still being out-fitted for their maiden voyages, so the "Big Three" ocean liners of the transatlantic run were the *Berengaria,* the *Aquitania* and the *Mauretania.* Ad writers waxed poetic about the beauties and social *ton* of each ship, but it was generally conceded that the "younger set" preferred the *Mauretania.* The *Berengaria* was for millionaires in the "international set," and the *Aquitania*? Well, in the snooty words of a travel brochure, "The *Aquitania*'s passenger lists tend slightly toward Burke and Debrett. The country-family sort of atmosphere predisposes in her favor people of social consequence, people of title . . . people you might meet at an important Thursday-to-Monday, when blood and achievement both count."

Edwina might have "kissed with wild abandon" her several leading men in her hottest movies, but she had never lost her Mayfair accent nor forgotten she was the granddaughter of a duke. So when she and Nick sailed for Southampton the following Wednesday, they went on the socially impeccable *Aquitania,* Frieda Gottschalk having booked them the prestigious Gainsborough Suite, which not only boasted a reproduction of *The Blue Boy* but a private dining room as well. With them went all seven children, for it had been decided to give the kids a vacation with their English grandparents, Lord and Lady Saxmund-ham; twenty pieces of Hermès luggage; a nanny and two maids. The tab for the six-day crossing was four thousand Depression dollars, but to Nick and Edwina, who always traveled deluxe, the wonderfully courteous English crew of the luxurious liner was worth every penny. The ship's accommodations were the finest afloat: the Pompeian swimming pool, the Turkish baths, the trellis-walled Garden Lounge for elevenses, or tea, the paneled Carolean smoking room where, in the words of the PR man, "The power of the *Aquitania*'s smoking room can be felt by the least erudite," thus putting the peons in their proper place. Though the liner was billed as a "temple of Taste in general and Anglo-Saxon art in particular," the first-class dining room was decorated to give the impression of being at Versailles, "the palace itself being visible in the distance through a colonnade of flower-decked Doric columns."

It was here, the first night out, that Nick, Edwina and their children made their appearance, to be guided to their silver-and-china-laden table by the tailcoated maître d'. Nick, who was as vain as the next self-made millionaire, relished the stares his handsome family attracted from the well-dressed crowd, and Edwina, who was looking fabulous in a white Vionnet evening gown with diamond-and-ruby eardrops and matching clips and four thick diamond bracelets, was pleased to see that many of the diners remembered her from her movies and whispered, "That's Edwina Fleming!" As the sleek four-stacked ship sliced through the July-calm Atlantic, the black sky above studded with blazing stars, as if a gigantic popcorn machine had exploded, they dined on rare roast beef, Stilton cheese and a ghastly trifle, which no one but Edwina liked.

In such sybaritic surroundings, it was easy to forget that twelve million Americans were on the dole. And, for the moment at least, they forgot.

But Nick didn't forget Count Alex von Winterfeldt, who was sailing for Hamburg on the *Bremen*.

Nor did he forget Adolf Hitler.

England gasped and sweltered in ninety-degree heat, which for the English was a heat wave of tropical proportions. But, after years of living in California, Edwina was used to heat. Her father had sent two of his Rolls-Royces to meet them at the dock at Southampton, and now, as the majestic automobiles pulled up in front of Thrax Hall, Edwina felt a rush of nostalgia and excitement.

"Oh, Nick, isn't it beautiful?" she said, holding his hand as she looked out the window. "Isn't England beautiful? I never realize how much I miss it until I come back home."

Lord Saxmundham, looking, in his white suit, unruffled by the heat and immensely distinguished, came down the stone steps to greet his family. England was being devastated by the worldwide Depression, and in India a barefoot Gandhi was bringing the British Raj to its knees, but one would never have suspected it looking at Maurice, Viscount Saxmundham. Still prodigiously rich, rising above the buffeting storms of the twentieth century, the courtly nobleman, now in his late sixties, gave the impression that Queen Victoria was still on the throne and all went well with the Empire.

After greeting Nick, Edwina and his numerous grandchildren, Lord

Saxmundham led them into Thrax Hall as the footman began hauling the luggage from the cars. Lady Saxmundham was upstairs in her bed, prostrate from the heat, but she promised to come down for lunch.

"Let's take a walk," said Charles to his sister Sylvia, and they went out the front door to head across the spacious lawns toward the woods that surrounded most of the estate.

"You would have gone to bed with Chester Hill, wouldn't you?" Charles said after they entered the woods.

"Oh, Charlie, will you shut up about that?" She sulked. "That's all you've been saying for *days*. It's none of your business anyway."

"What if Mom and Dad knew? They'd chew you out."

"I didn't *do* anything."

"But you were *thinking* of doing it. You're going to grow up to be a real slut."

"Will you keep quiet?"

"What if I told Mom and Dad?"

"You wouldn't."

"Maybe."

She looked at him. "I tell you I didn't *do* anything!"

"But you did something with Eddie Clinton, and don't try to pretend you didn't. I've kept my eyes on you."

"Well, keep them on somebody else."

They walked in silence for a while. Charles, who loved Thrax Hall and knew every square inch of the estate, was not wandering aimlessly: he had a goal in mind. Within ten minutes, they reached it, a lovely pond surrounded by lush trees.

"Look, a deer!" whispered Sylvia, pointing to the opposite side of the pond where a doe was drinking. Hearing the children, she bounded away into the forest.

"Let's take a swim and cool off," said Charles, loosening his tie.

"We don't have any swimsuits," said Sylvia.

"So what? We've seen each other naked a thousand times."

"Well, it's a little different *now*."

"Okay, *don't* swim."

She watched him undress for a moment, then started taking off her clothes.

When they were both naked, they looked at each other's slim young body.

"You're beautiful," Charles said softly.

"So are you."

He looked at her breasts and her flat belly and her smooth skin and her flame of pubic hair, then he turned and dived into the pond. She climbed on a rock and dived in after him, her body arching gracefully in the air, then slicing into the cool water. She swam underwater for a while, reveling in the coolness, then surfaced near her brother.

"Oh, it's *wonderful,*" she said.

He said nothing, watching her.

For a while, they paddled around in the water. Then Charles climbed out, standing and stretching beside the pond. She watched his lithe, almost hairless body and became frightened by her thoughts.

"How will we dry off?" she called.

He didn't answer.

She swam to the shore, then came out of the water and shook her rich dark auburn hair. Charles was watching her, a few feet away. She saw his long penis begin to rise.

"You're disgusting," she whispered. "I suppose you're going off in the woods to play with yourself."

"No," he said, coming up to her. They stood, inches apart, looking into each other's eyes.

"Charlie," she whispered "we *can't.*"

He put his hands on her arms.

"No one will ever know but us," he said. "It'll be our private, beautiful secret."

His right hand moved over her breasts, then down her stomach. He softly rubbed her pubic hair.

"I've wanted to do this for a long time," he whispered.

He wrapped his arms around her and pulled her body against his, beginning to kiss her mouth. Then, gently he pulled her down on a mattress of dead leaves. She put up no resistance, amazed at how much she suddenly wanted her older brother, terrified at the implications of what she was doing and yet unable, and unwilling, to stop.

Now he lowered himself on top of her. "No one will ever know but us," he repeated as he began making love to her.

Sylvia was terrified, but had to admit she had never been so sexually excited in her short life. Taboo, taboo, she thought as he kissed her; but the taboo *was* the thrill.

A squirrel in the tree above them looked down at the two white bodies, stared curiously at Charles's narrow buttocks as they moved slowly up and down, then scampered away.

"Do you like it?" Nick asked Edwina two mornings later as he helped her out of the back seat of one of her father's Rollses. Edwina looked at the L-shaped house with the thatched roof. The long arm of the L was a three-story Tudor structure, built of white plaster with wooden beams, while the short arm was mellow, almost pink brick. The many windows were leaded, and the five chimneys were elaborate brickwork. Before the house was a garden, blazing with summer flowers.

"Oh, I love it—I always have," said Edwina. "This is Audley Place. I used to play here as a child. Mother tells me old Lady Audley died last month."

"Yes, and guess who bought the house?"

"I have no idea."

"We did."

She stared at him as he took her arm and led her toward the brick path bisecting the garden.

"I asked your father the other night if there were any good properties around here for sale, and he said this had just come on the market and was a steal. So I came over yesterday to take a look and fell in love with it. Old Alfred Ramschild had a fake-Tudor house in Connecticut, but this is the real thing. It was built in 1565—I saw the original building contract."

She was stunned.

"But, Nick, we don't *need* another house."

"Of course we don't. But I saw how happy you were to be back in England, and I decided we should have a home here. Of course, it needs a lot of work—rewiring, central heating, new bathrooms and so forth. But I thought while I was in Berlin, you could start looking for an architect."

She looked at the house as they neared the front door.

"It has a little under fifty acres, and we can buy it freehold," he went on. "There's five hundred feet of frontage on the River Avon, with fishing rights, and an eighteenth-century millhouse we could turn into a guest cottage. Of course, if you don't want it, there's still time to back out. I haven't signed anything yet."

"No, I *do* want it . . . it's just that, as usual, you've taken me by surprise. How much is it?"

"Twenty thousand pounds."

"Well, they're not exactly *giving* it away."

They had reached the wooden front door. Now Nick turned and confronted his wife.

"I wanted you to have a place near your parents in case something happens to me," he said quietly.

Her eyes widened.

"Nick, you *said* there was no danger," she whispered.

He took her hands.

"I don't want you to worry," he said. "But there is a *little* danger. Anything can happen in Germany these days."

She looked at him, fear coming into her eyes.

"Then don't go!" she exclaimed. "For God's sake, Nick, don't go!"

"I have to."

"But why?"

"You know. The possibility of getting rid of Hitler. . . ."

He pushed open the heavy door, which squeaked on its ancient hinges. "There was a murder in the house in 1803. The owner went mad, strangled his wife, then hanged himself in the kitchen." He winked. "They say his ghost still haunts the kitchen."

He led her inside.

CHAPTER 28

Nick and Count von Winterfeldt had arranged that Nick would fly to Berlin, check in at the Adlon, then wait to be contacted by a person who would identify himself with the word *"Sommerwein,"* or "summer wine," to which Nick would reply *"Winterwein."*

It all seemed far too simple to interest a spy novelist, but the Count pointed out that the best security was maintained by keeping arrangements as unelaborate as possible, and Nick thought he probably had a point. The next day, Nick flew from Croydon Airport outside London to Tempelhof Airport in Berlin, checked into a lavish suite at the Adlon, then went downstairs for lunch. The hotel lobby was, as usual, filled with an international crowd, many businessmen, some still wearing winged collars with their suits, a few German army officers, a sprinkling of glamorous and not-so-glamorous women. Nick went into the dining room, where the maître d' recognized him and led him to a corner table. Nick ordered a grilled sole and a half bottle of Muscadet, then sat back to watch the people, wondering if, during lunch, someone would come up and say *"Sommerwein."*

Twenty minutes later, Magda Bayreuth came into the room. Nick knew that Magda had risen to the top of the German movie heap, not only because of her sensational beauty but also with the help of the increasingly powerful Dr. Goebbels. Now she made an entrance that was almost quintessentially movie starish. Unlike England, Berlin was chilly and damp; but Magda was again wearing her favorite color combination, white and black, this time a beautifully tailored white suit with long black kid gloves and a black beret with two white feathers shooting out on the diagonal. Her legs, nature's miracles, tapered down to white and black-laced shoes. On her jacket she wore a huge diamond-and-cabochon-ruby brooch. All eyes in the dining room were on her as the maître d' led her to a table. As she passed Nick, she spotted him and stopped. The look she gave him was all somnolent sex and, again, half-mocking suggestion.

"Mr. Fleming," she said as Nick stood up. "You can see I have a good memory. You are lunching alone?"

"Yes."

"May I join you?"

"I'd be delighted."

The maître d' seated her next to Nick.

"To show you how good *my* memory is," he said, "are you still on your caviar-and-champagne diet?"

"Yes. It's full of vitamins."

The remark, so empty of meaning, became by the suggestive lilt of her voice at the same time funny and lewd. Nick was again dazzled. After he had ordered, she said, "I should have snubbed you, you know. Seven years ago in this very room, you promised me a screen test. And then, poof! You vanish from Berlin. Is that any way to treat a lady?"

"I was called away unexpectedly on business. I apologize."

She smiled.

"The mysterious Mr. Fleming, arms king and multimillionaire, who operates in secret with all the heads of government of the world. I find it fascinating. And what brings you to Berlin this time?"

"I came for a rest."

She laughed.

"Ah, yes, calm, relaxing Berlin. A perfect place for a rest. Well, since you're on vacation, why don't you come rest with me? I'm giving a little party tonight at Berlin's most interesting *boîte*, the Villa Hubler, out in Wannsee. Frau Hubler, the owner, is a woman you *must* meet. Will you come? Most of my guests will be movie people—you may even know some of them. I think you'll find it amusing."

While Nick was in anything but a relaxed mood, he was not averse to a little relaxation with this dazzling woman. Besides, Magda, who had become Hitler's favorite movie star (along with King Kong), would provide a convenient cover for him while in Berlin.

"Thanks," he said. "I'd be delighted to come."

"Bravo! I'll pick you up here at the hotel at nine this evening. We'll have a light supper and then . . . entertainments."

The way she insinuated the last word suggested a wide variety of debaucheries.

He loved Edwina passionately, but her arguments about the marital double standard had never made much impression on him.

The Villa Hubler, situated in the center of a lovely two-acre garden, had been built six years before in the now officially-out-of-favor Bau-

272

haus style (one of Hitler's first official acts after coming to power was to disband the Bauhaus group, which had been founded by Walter Gropius after the war), and the two-story white stucco villa was sleekly modern, in strange contrast to the lumpy Wilhelmine style of most of the buildings in Berlin. Magda's white Benz limousine pulled up in front of the villa at nine-thirty. Her white-uniformed chauffeur got out to hold the door for the star, who emerged in a slinky black evening dress with a white boa, followed by Nick in a dinner jacket.

"Frau Hubler was badly burned in an accident a number of years ago," said Magda as they walked to the front door. "So she wears veils to cover her scars. She's known in Berlin and in other cities as the 'Lady of the Veils.' Do you speak French?"

"Passably."

"Good. She knows no English."

"Just what kind of a *'boîte'* is this?"

She smiled. "How cosmopolitan you are! It's a *maison de passe,* of course, but a very exclusive one—the best in Berlin. Field Marshal Goering is a frequent visitor, though that is kept very—how do you say it?—hush-hush."

The front door was opened by a hulking black man in a tight-fitting tuxedo who stood back to admit them. The entrance hall was severe and devoid of furnishings except for a floor-to-ceiling lamp that looked like a series of ever-diminishing steel coolie hats piled on top of each other to provide concealed lighting, and a steel-and-glass table on which stood a Chinese vase filled with white gladioli. Magda led him down the hall to an open archway that gave into a large living room overlooking the lake. The room was furnished with the *dernier cri* of white and chrome and steel modern furniture and was, in its cold, metallic way, attractive. Two glass doors to a terrace were open; standing in them, her back to Magda and Nick, was a woman in a flowing white chiffon dress, a white veil over her head, white kid gloves on her hands and arms.

Otherwise the room was empty.

"Frau Hubler," said Magda, *"c'est mon ami,* Nick Fleming."

Slowly, the woman turned. Although the veil covered her entire face, Nick could feel invisible eyes on him. For some reason, Nick felt suddenly cold.

For a long moment, she said nothing. Then the Lady of the Veils said in a hoarse voice, *"Enchantée."*

She looked at him a moment longer, then walked out to the terrace and vanished.

"A strange lady," Nick remarked dryly as he turned to Magda. "So warm and welcoming. Where are the other guests?"

Magda smiled as she put her hands on his shoulders.

"There are no others. After lunch, I called Frau Hubler and reserved the entire villa just for you and me. As your lovely American song puts it, 'I'm in the mood for love.' "

She waved her right hand and the lights in the room dimmed to a romantic glow. The black man in the tuxedo appeared holding a tray with two flutes of champagne.

"We'll have some bubbly, then go upstairs to the Room of the Veils," whispered Magda, adding, "Are *you* in the mood for love?"

Nick grinned. "I could be talked into it," he said. "In fact, I think I already have been."

They reached for the champagne.

The Room of the Veils was exactly that: a medium-sized square room with a high ceiling and gauzy white curtains. Over one wall, where open windows admitted a breeze from the lake, the veils billowed dreamily, creating an almost surreal effect. There was a large bed, itself surrounded by veils. Otherwise, there was no furniture in the room, the soft light coming from floor fixtures behind the curtains. The ceiling was mirrored; on the floor was a white Moroccan rug.

"This is my favorite room here," said Magda, dropping her boa on the floor. "It's also Goering's favorite."

"Don't spoil the mood," said Nick.

She smiled as she parted the curtains to sit on the edge of the bed.

"Don't underestimate Hermann," she said, crossing her legs to remove her shoes. "He's clever as a fox—and savage as a wolf. It's a fascinating combination in a man."

He put Goering out of his mind as he watched her take off her black high-heeled shoes, then slowly start to unroll her silk stockings. Every move rehearsed, he thought, but what a wonderful act! And what legs!

When her stockings were off, Magda stood up again and slowly unzipped the back of her dress, her eyes on Nick. Then, with the languid expertise of an ecdysiast, she pulled down her shoulder straps and stepped out of the dress, letting it slide down her body to the floor. Nick watched avidly as he took off his dinner jacket, pulled off his suspenders, then began unbuttoning his fly. Now Magda was pulling down her white lace panties, slipping them slowly over her thighs,

274

then dropping them and stepping out of them. Finally, the lace brassiere. She dropped it and turned to face him, smiling, naked and as radiant as a Botticelli Venus. Nick thought he would explode. She parted the veils of the bed and climbed on it, disappearing to a vague shadow as the veils fluttered back in place.

Nick almost jumped out of his underwear. Then, naked, he went to the bed, parted the veils and looked. She lay on the bed, one arm thrown casually back on the pillows, one leg half upright, her pale-pink skin in the pale-white light perfection, her body a triumph of diet, exercise and nature. He was hard with desire. In a career of bedding many beautiful women, including the cream of the crop of Hollywood starlets, he had never encountered such a superb embodiment of feminine sensuality. He kneeled on the bed, straddled her, then eased himself down into her open arms.

"My God, you're beautiful," he whispered.

"Unoriginal," she said, smiling, "but heartfelt, I think."

He kissed her lips. Her breath was sweet, and her skin and hair smelled of subtle perfume. Nick's heart was thundering; he hadn't felt such passion in years. He started caressing her breasts and nipples, causing her to moan softly. Slowly, he licked around her breasts, then down her stomach, reveling in her taste and smell. He licked the velvet skin of her inner thighs, sniffing the heady perfume of her vulva.

"Your tongue," she whispered. "I love your tongue."

Suddenly, he heard the door to the room open, then footsteps running toward the bed. As he looked up, the bed curtains were jerked apart by Frau Hubler, a Frau Hubler who had removed the veil from her face—the lower half a mass of scar tissue, the upper half somehow familiar. Her green eyes blazed in triumph as four black-uniformed S.D. men appeared beside her, grabbed his arms and legs, and pulled him off the bed onto the floor. As Nick howled and struggled to fight them off, one of them jabbed a hypodermic needle in his left buttock. Then, one guard holding each of his arms and legs, he was picked up and carried, roaring, out of the room.

Magda Bayreuth got off the bed and smoothed her hair.

"Darling," she said to Diana Ramschild in English, "you might have given me a few more minutes. He *is* a terribly good lover, after all."

Diana raised the veil over the lower half of her face.

"Do you think," she said, "I would have let that bastard enjoy an orgasm?"

She walked across the room, stopped to pick up Nick's underwear off the floor, then savagely ripped it to shreds.

"I don't envy Nick Fleming," she said, tossing the bits of cloth back on the floor.

Then she walked out of the room.

CHAPTER 29

HE came to finding himself spread-eagled, stomach down, on a low iron cot, his wrists and ankles manacled to its frame. He was naked, and his head still throbbed from the drug the Gestapo men had injected six hours before. As his brain swam to the surface of consciousness and his memory became unscrambled, bringing back the shock of his sudden seizure by the Gestapo, panic exploded in him. He strained his neck to see where he was. It was a prison cell, about ten feet long and five feet wide. The walls were filthy brick and obviously ancient. A heavy steel door with no window was at one end; at the other, a disgusting toilet with no seat. Almost seven feet above the toilet was a narrow, barred window, its glass shattered, through which sunlight streamed. The heat of England had reached Germany, and the cell was unbearably hot. The iron of the cot seared the skin of his stomach and thighs, and his sweat dripped through onto the stone floor. Normally fastidious, he was repelled by his own stench.

He tried to understand what had happened to him. Obviously, Magda Bayreuth had been sent to set him up, lead him into the trap at the Villa Hubler—but why the trap? And who was the hideous Frau Hubler? How could the German government dare do this to an American—an influential American, like Nick Fleming? The Nazis might be gangsters, but they tried to put a civilized face to the world. This was madness. When Nick got out, Van Clairmont would scream this atrocity in headlines all over America. . . .

Then it hit him. They didn't *intend* to let him out. When he had been captured by the Russian revolutionaries eighteen years before, they had been outlaws, at least until the Tsar abdicated. Now his captors were the legitimately elected government. As long as he was their prisoner, he was defenseless. Nick was a brave man, but he knew that the so-called fearlessness of heroes was bullshit. He was terrified.

Hours passed. He heard occasional shouts in German outside his window. A huge roach ran up his leg, over his buttocks, up his spine and over his face, making him almost vomit. He told himself not to scream, for that was what they wanted to hear, but finally he could no longer bear it.

"Let me out! I'm an American, goddammit! Let me *OUT!*"

His echoes mocked him.

They came at three o'clock that afternoon.

He heard their jackboots clumping down the corridor, the banging of rubber truncheons striking steel cell doors, then the jangling of keys. He turned his head to watch the door. It was opened by a pimply-faced blond youngster in a Death's Head black uniform. Behind him were three others. The first grinned and said: *"Sommerwein!"* And they all started laughing.

They crowded into the cell and unlocked his manacles. Nick knew little German, but he burst out, *"Ich bin ein Amerikanischer—verstehen Sie? Ein Amerikanischer!"*

Pimples said, *"Du bist ein Amerikanischer Jude!"*

And they all laughed again. They roughly manacled his wrists behind his back. Then two Germans grabbed each of his arms. They dragged him out of the cell into the corridor, past steel doors to a barred door at the end, which another guard unlocked. Down another corridor, up a flight of stairs to yet another corridor to yet another steel door marked, ominously, *"Fragenzimmer."* They opened the door and pulled him into a white-painted room, perhaps twenty feet square with a large, barred window at one side whose glass was frosted. Four green-shaded lights glared from the ceiling. A number of steel chairs stood around the walls. In the corner, a sink. In the center of the room, a steel operating table with leather ankle and wrist restraints. They shoved him down on the table. Panicking, he tried to struggle free. One of the guards beat him on the shoulders and chest, and Nick stopped; it was useless.

They unchained his wrists and strapped him, face up, on the operating table. Pimples went to a steel hospital table, opened the drawer and pulled out a leather gag. Returning to Nick, he strapped it over his mouth. Then, grinning, they left the room, giving him a sardonic salute and saying, *"Auf Wiedersehen!* Bye-bye!"

Then the steel door slammed shut, and he was alone.

Twenty minutes later, a guard opened the door and the Lady of the Veils came in. Nick stared at her as the guard stepped out, closing the door behind him. She walked to the table and looked down at him with those cold-deadly-beautiful green eyes. She clutched a small black purse with both gloved hands.

"You have no idea who I am, do you?" she asked in English.

Sweating, he shook his head no.

"I'm Diana Ramschild."

A flood of memories surged through him. Diana? It wasn't possible! Yet those green eyes . . . his green-eyed goddess of so many years before. . . .

"I know what you're thinking," she went on in a calm voice, although her own emotions were a cyclone. "I'm supposed to be dead. But I didn't die in Smyrna. I was burned . . . horribly, the way you see me now, but the doctor managed to save my life and I . . ."

She stopped, unable to speak. This moment, her supreme moment of triumphal revenge—the moment she had lived for for so many years—wasn't going at all the way she had planned. Far from savoring Nick's humiliation, she was beginning to feel sorry for him.

And then she saw him raise his right hand as far as the leather wrist restraint would permit, and he crossed his fingers.

The small gesture, so meaningless to anyone else in the world, had the effect on her that the dipped Madeleine had had on Proust. Suddenly, the grim *Fragenzimmer* vanished from her sight and she was once again with Nick in the empty beach house on Long Island Sound where they had made love that magical summer so many years before. Far from hating him, she found herself remembering her love of him—that first, fierce love of her life. His body, now naked and defenseless on the torturer's table before her, had once been the object of the most intense desire she had ever known. No matter how inured she had become to physical cruelty in Turkey, now the sight of him in this room was suddenly as repugnant and loathsome to her as the savage rapes that she had been subjected to in Smyrna. There, violence had almost ended her life. Did she *really* want the same for this man she had once loved so passionately?

Suddenly, she realized how wrong she was. How wrong Mustapha Kemal was. Hatred *wasn't* stronger than love. Those crossed fingers— no matter what he might have done to her in the past—symbolized the sweetest days and nights that she had ever known. What had he done to her? Abandoned her for another. What had she done in return? Hired an assassin to try to kill him, and now collaborated in his arrest by the Gestapo. It was a monstrous imbalance.

Had she been mad?

"Oh, my God, Nick," she whispered, "what have I done?"

She began to panic. They had allowed her only five minutes to see him, five minutes to gloat. Then Captain Schmidt, the Gestapo's most notorious torturer, had, as he had termed it, his "appointment," and she knew what they would do to him.

"Listen, there are only a few minutes . . ." She was talking rapidly, disjointedly. "They know all about the *Putsch* . . . Goering told me himself. You were a fool to deal with Winterfeldt; they've never trusted him . . . they arrested him when he landed in Hamburg last week . . . he's here, in this prison, awaiting execution. . . . Oh, my God, I hated you, but I shouldn't have done this . . . I'll get you out, Nick . . . I'll use my influence with Atatürk; they don't dare cross him. . . . Oh, my God, this is all my fault! I wanted to hurt you because you hurt me . . . I was so hurt, Nick. . . ."

She was crying, buffeted by wild storms of emotion, of wounded love, of years lost. . . . How little she had known her own heart! Yes, they had planned to arrest him anyway, but she had convinced Goering to let her stage the arrest *her* way. She had sent Magda Bayreuth to the Adlon, knowing Nick would be unable to resist her spectacular beauty, planning to have the Gestapo take him in the act of love. . . . She had behaved like a woman possessed, which she was.

She heard the door behind her open, and turned to see two guards enter the room. One carried a heavy black suitcase, the other a portable Victrola and a stack of records, which he carried over to a steel medicine cabinet.

"The time is up, Fräulein," said the first guard in polite German.

She turned back to look at Nick again. He was shivering with fear, covered with sweat.

"I'll get you out," she said in English.

Then she hurried out of the room.

A moment after the guards left the room, a man in a black Death's Head uniform came in, closing the door behind him. He walked over to the operating table, removing his cap and tossing it onto a chair. Then he looked down at Nick. He was about thirty-five, with thin blond hair and an extremely long Germanic face that had high cheekbones and small blue eyes set too close together. He reminded Nick of a greyhound.

"I am Captain Schmidt," he said in excellent English that had a

British accent. "You are charged with a serious crime: abetting an insurrection against the Reich." He began removing his gloves; Nick marveled at his professional manner, as if he were a dentist rather than a torturer. Now he put his gloves on the table next to the Victrola, then returned to Nick and took the gag out of his mouth. Nick, still reeling from the shock of seeing Diana Ramschild, realized that she—despite her engineering his arrest—still represented his best chance of escape. But he fully intended to defend himself as best he could.

"Captain Schmidt," he said, forcing himself to sound as calm as possible, "I'm an American businessman with a valid passport. I insist on speaking with my ambassador."

Schmidt looked at him curiously. "My friend, you're in no position to 'insist' on anything. You're a prisoner."

"But I've done nothing!" Nick shouted, his rage erupting.

Schmidt pounded his fist into Nick's solar plexus so hard Nick almost vomited.

"You will not shout!" screamed Schmidt. "You will be civil to me; you will speak only when spoken to—you understand? You are Jewish shit—you understand?" He grabbed Nick's testicles and squeezed them so tight Nick howled with pain. Then he released him and lowered his voice.

"We have known that Count von Winterfeldt was treasonous vermin all along, but we gave him free rein until we could determine the extent of his conspiracy. We know he visited you at your home in America; we know you came to Berlin to arrange the sale of a shipment of arms to him. The question before you, my friend, is whether you cooperate with us and tell us all you know of this conspiracy, in which case you will get off with a relatively light sentence of twenty years' imprisonment; or whether you don't cooperate with us, in which case you will be executed. Do you understand?"

Nick looked at him numbly. "Yes."

"Will you cooperate with us?"

"You already know everything I know."

"That is not an answer!" Schmidt screamed.

"But it is! I came to Berlin to find out more!"

"Which generals were involved in the coup?"

"I don't know! Winterfeldt wouldn't tell me!"

Schmidt glared at him. "Very well," he said quietly. "You choose the difficult path." He walked over to the cabinet. "Do you like Cole Porter?"

The question was so monstrously inappropriate, Nick wondered if one of them—or possibly both—had gone insane.

"Huh?"

"I said, do you like Cole Porter? 'Night and Day' is one of my favorites. We might as well get to know each other, we're going to be together a long time, my friend. I love American music. I love even Gershwin and Irving Berlin, even though they are Jewish scum. Let's see." He was looking through the records. "Ah! Noel Coward—so deliciously effete and decadent, like all the English. I read English literature at Oxford from 1929 to '31, and we used to go down to London to see Coward's shows. Ah! 'Mad Dogs and Englishmen'—perfect!"

He put on the record, and Noel Coward's fluty voice began singing to a piano accompaniment:

> *"In tropical climes there are certain times of day*
> *When all the citizens retire to tear their clothes off and perspire."*

Schmidt came back to the table, smiling.

"Music to be tortured by," he said almost merrily. Then he turned a knob at the edge of the table. The table tilted forward, swinging Nick to an upright position. Schmidt retightened the knob, then opened the big black suitcase. Nick saw, with a sinking sensation, a gruesome collection of whips and knouts. Schmidt pulled out a short dog whip, walked to the sink in the corner and turned on the tap, sticking the whip under the water.

> *"Mad dogs and Englishmen go out in the midday sun;*
> *The Japanese don't care to, the Chinese wouldn't dare to, . . ."*

Schmidt came back to confront Nick. The whip was dripping.

"Wet leather hurts more." He smiled.

The whip slashed across Nick's face like liquid fire. Then his shoulders, his chest, his stomach, his groin—which blinded him with pain—his thighs, his legs. Schmidt was savage, like a wild animal. Nick was screaming. The pain was beyond belief.

> *"Hindus and Argentines sleep firmly from twelve to one,*
> *But Englishmen detest a siesta."*

"Who are the others?" shouted Schmidt. "I want names!"

282

"I don't know," Nick moaned. "Believe me, I don't know."

Again, the whip ripped the air. A whining sound as it cut the air, and then a sudden burst of pain that pierced his brain. It bit across his throat, was torn free, then savaged his chest, slashing even more deeply than the first time.

> *"In the mangrove swamps where the python romps*
> *There is peace from twelve to two.*
> *Even caribous lie around and snooze*
> *For there's nothing else to do."*

Then the stomach, again the groin, the thighs, the legs. Blood was oozing from a dozen cuts. Nick, barely conscious, was sagging in his leather restraints, his body wet with sweat and blood.

"JEW!" Schmidt screamed. "I want the truth!"

> *"In Hong Kong they strike a gong*
> *And fire off the noonday gun.*
> *But mad dogs and Englishmen go out in the midday sun."*

"I don't know, I don't know," Nick gasped.

"Very well, my friend, it's the *Kaschumbo* for you. First on the thighs, then we'll turn you over and give it to your kidneys. You'll piss blood for a thousand nights."

He began slashing Nick's thighs: once, twice, three times, four . . . by the tenth slash, blood streamed down Nick's legs. The pain was a volcano in his brain. For the first time in his life, he longed for death. Edwina flashed through his mind, and his children. Then he sank into oblivion.

The last thing he remembered was the antic music playing and Schmidt screaming, "JEW!"

CHAPTER 30

T HE majestic black Rolls-Royce lumbered through the right-hand grilled gate of Buckingham Palace, then proceeded around the palace to the inner courtyard. A footman opened the door, and Edwina stepped out. She was wearing a black suit and hat; she looked pale. Behind her came her father, Lord Saxmundham, wearing a black suit and bowler and carrying a tightly furled black umbrella. An equerry led them into the palace, up long red-carpeted stairs. From the walls, generations of British monarchs stared at posterity from enormous portraits swirling with ermine robes of state; every stone of the palace reeked of history. Edwina, who had been there once before when she was presented at court, forgot for a moment her fear and warmed with pride at her English heritage.

The equerry led them down long corridors until they reached the office of the King. When they were ushered into the big room, King George V got up from his desk and came around to greet them. As Edwina curtsied, she thought that the King looked much older and more tired than he did in his photographs.

After greeting them, the King offered them chairs, then sat down facing them.

"The Prime Minister has apprised me of the situation," he began. "I am shocked and outraged, Mrs. Fleming, by the arrest of your husband. The Kaiser did many foolish things when he was on the throne, but I don't believe even he would have permitted such an outrageous breach of civility."

"Thank you, Your Majesty," said Edwina. "Has the Prime Minister been able to find out where he is?"

"Yes. He is in Concentration Camp Fuhlsbuettel, which is on the northern outskirts of Hamburg, near the airport. It's an old prison that was about to be torn down when the Nazis came to power. Since they have plenty of use for prisons these days, they turned it into a concentration camp. I am told there are hundreds of Communists there, as well as Jews." He hesitated. "I know why your husband went to Germany, but didn't he realize the danger?"

284

"Yes," said Lord Saxmundham. "I warned him before he left that he was taking a terrible risk, and he said he understood that. But he felt it was such a tremendous opportunity to get Hitler out of power, he had to take any risk to help the men planning the *Putsch*. He asked me not to tell my daughter of the danger, so as not to upset her. But he knew, Your Majesty."

"Well, I admire Mr. Fleming," said the King. "He did a great service to England during the last war, and if he had managed to get rid of Adolf Hitler, he would have done an even greater one. I wanted both of you to know that the Queen and I extend our every sympathy to you, which is why I asked you to come to the palace today. And needless to say, my government is doing everything possible to secure Mr. Fleming's release."

"What chance *is* there, sir?" asked Edwina quietly.

"Of course your husband is an American, and, as you know, he has high political connections in Washington. The American Ambassador told me yesterday that Washington has lodged a strong letter of protest to Berlin. Whether that will work or not is too early to tell. The German position is that your husband was abetting an internal insurrection—which happens to be true, so it seems they are within their rights to try him."

"But surely he has a lawyer? Or we can get him one?"

"The Germans say *they* will provide him with a lawyer when he comes to trial."

"He might as well have Hitler for a lawyer," said Edwina bitterly. "Then is there no hope?"

"There is *always* hope," the King said diplomatically.

It was a crumb, but Edwina was relieved to get even a crumb.

Every night for four nights he had been manacled to his cot, face down and naked, and the long, black hours of immobility were almost as horrible as his frequent beatings by Captain Schmidt. He had been fed nothing but a daily bowl of rancid potato soup and a piece of rotting bread, so raging hunger added misery to the constant pain of the beatings. Nick was in his prime, in excellent health, but he wondered how long even *his* body could hold up. He was not allowed to wash, and since he was given no toilet paper, he was foul from his own excrement.

As yet, he had seen nothing but his cell, the Interrogation Room and the corridors in between; though he thought the prison was full, as yet he had seen no other prisoners. He heard them, though, as they were cursed at by the guards outside his window. To add to the nightmarish atmosphere of the place, the guards amused themselves by firing occasional rifle shots through the windows of the cells, which was why his window had no glass. Everything Nick had read and heard about Nazi Germany should have prepared him for this prison. Nothing prepared him for its reality. There seemed to be no routine to the place; everything was done at random, so that he never knew what to expect, which entailed its own special terror. He had been dragged out of his cell in the middle of the night to be beaten, and the previous day he had been left alone for almost twenty hours, seeing no one but the guards who brought him his soup and chained and unchained him to the cot.

But the worst was that he was allowed no communication with the outside world. He had lived through this horror once before when he was a prisoner in Russia, but there at least he had been treated civilly. Here, in this outpost of hell, he felt as if he had dropped off the planet. He had no idea if any effort was being made to rescue him. He was worse than dead.

On the fifth morning, he heard the boots of the guards and the banging of the rubber truncheons on the cell doors. Then the jangling of keys, the rattle of the lock being opened. Four of them came in and unchained him. As he sat up, almost pitifully glad to move after hours of being spread-eagled, he saw Captain Schmidt standing in the door—something that had not happened before. He was holding a pair of filthy, torn pants.

"You have been assigned grave detail," he said, throwing the pants at him. "Here, put these on."

He marched out of the cell. Nick was jerked to his feet by the guards and forced to step into the pants, which were four sizes too big and had no belt. Grabbing his arms, they dragged him out of the cell. He stumbled to keep up, frantically trying to hold his pants up. For the first time he saw other prisoners, who were also being taken from their cells for the grave detail. They looked like the living dead, much worse than even he, and he knew he looked disgusting, his face and body a surreal crossword puzzle of whip scars and bruises.

They were marched outside to a large courtyard, and for the first time Nick saw the exterior of the prison—for that matter, he had no idea he was in Hamburg. The prison was predictably ugly, consisting of four huge brick cellblocks, four stories high, surrounded by bare yards. Around the yards was a high brick wall with guard posts; inside the wall was a barbed-wire fence carrying signs in four languages proclaiming: *"Warning! This fence carries a lethal charge of electricity!"* Whatever hopes Nick had had of escaping were dashed to shards of despair. A plane flew low overhead, coming in for a landing at the nearby Hamburg airport. Nick squinted up at it. How tantalizingly near the outside world seemed, and yet, of course, how agonizingly far.

Twenty prisoners had been assembled, with ten armed guards. Now the prisoners were assigned shovels and ordered to dig a trench six feet deep and six feet long. It was a job two men could have done well, but twenty men inevitably botched, getting in one another's way—which was what the guards wanted, since it gave them an excuse to shout insults at them and pound their truncheons on their skulls and backs. When the guards weren't doing this, they sang anti-Semitic songs:

> *"Wenn's Judenblut vom Messer spritz,*
> *Dann geht's nochmal so gut,*
> *Dann geht's nochmal so gut."*
> (When Jewish blood squirts under the knife,
> Then all is well,
> Then all is well.)

And:

> *"Armer Jude Kohn, Kleiner Jude Kohn,*
> *Hast ja Keine Heimat mehr. . . ."*
> (Poor Jew Kohn, little Jew Kohn,
> You have no home anymore. . . .)

Nick was in the middle of the crowd trying to shovel with one hand while he held up his pants with the other. Two of the guards shoved into the crowd, howling at him, pounding their truncheons on his head.

"I don't speak German!" Nick cried. *"Ich spreche kein Deutsch!"*

"They're telling you to use both hands on the shovel," said a sad-eyed man next to him.

"But I can't! My pants will fall down!"

The old man translated to the guards, who barked back in German.

"They say they will beat you if you don't use both hands on the shovel, but they will also beat you if you let your pants fall down."

"Tell them their mothers slept with pigs," Nick spat out.

"No, my friend, I won't tell them that, for they would kill you. But it's the truth."

"My friend." When Schmidt called him that, it was twisted and sardonic. But from this elderly, anonymous man, the two words suddenly took on a special beauty. All the prisoners were his friends, as he was theirs. And he didn't even know who they were.

He bent over in a ludicrous stoop, holding up his pants with his elbows as he grabbed the neck of the shovel handle and began digging, almost as if he were at the beach with a toy shovel. In this manner, he managed to defy the guards, but he was miserably uncomfortable, the heat of the sun baking him and his stooped posture placing his face so much nearer the dirt that he inevitably inhaled dust, causing him to choke. But if he was pitiful, the other prisoners were even more so. Most of them looked well over fifty years old and some of them were in their seventies, like the old man who had translated for Nick. For men of their age to be shoveling earth under such brutal conditions was a terrible hardship.

It took almost an hour to finish digging the hole. Nick was the last prisoner to be pulled out of the grave by the guards. When he reached the surface, still holding on to his pants, he heard a drum roll. He and the other prisoners were called to attention by the guards. Then four guards marched out of the prison, each pair carrying a litter that held a corpse. The guards brought the corpses to the grave's edge and rolled them onto the ground at the lip of the hole. Nick winced as he saw that one of the naked bodies—a thin, middle-aged, bearded man—had his genitals mangled. The death must have been horrible; the look on the dead man's face, with its mouth open in an eternally silent scream, was one that wrote the definition of agony.

The other corpse was riddled with bullet holes. Nick was shocked when he recognized the dead man as Count Alexander von Winterfeldt.

Captain Schmidt strode swiftly out of the prison past the two drummers, who now stopped their drum rolls, and approached the line of prisoners.

"This man," said Schmidt, pointing to the corpse with the mangled genitals, "correction, this *Jew!* was a race polluter. He committed one of the foulest crimes possible in our country today. He made love to a German girl, an Aryan girl of purest German blood. The girl was impregnated by this Jew, but happily the monster was destroyed in the womb. Yesterday, this Jew paid the price for his race pollution.

As you can see, his genitals were clubbed to mincemeat, and the Jew died."

He had addressed this in English to Nick. Now he repeated it to the others in German. Next, he turned back to Nick, pointed to Count von Winterfeldt's corpse, and reverted to English.

"You know this man, I think, my friend. You know his crime. He betrayed the Fuehrer. You see his punishment. The firing squad! You have helped dig his grave this morning. My patience with you is wearing thin, my friend. I would suggest you consider cooperating with me, or in the very near future, others will be digging *your* grave. Now, push the traitor's corpse into the grave."

Nick was staring at the corpse. He had never fully trusted Winterfeldt, mainly because the man had joined the Nazi Party, and had risked helping him principally because he believed his story of wanting to destroy Hitler in order to avenge his son's murder. Now, the proof of the Count's honesty lay before him in the burning sun. Here was a good German, a noble German, who had died trying to preserve a Germany he could be proud of.

Slowly, Nick came up to the corpse and kneeled beside it. For a moment, he placed his right hand on the elderly nobleman's left cheek, combining a plea for forgiveness of his suspicions with a loving *envoie* to the next world. Then, gently, he rolled the corpse over the edge of the grave and watched it fall to the bottom.

"That could be you, very soon," said Schmidt, who had been watching Nick intently. "Stay at the edge of the grave," he added. Then he started shouting in German to the other prisoners. To Nick's surprise, they began shuffling around to the side of the grave opposite him. The guards tossed the second corpse into the grave. Then Schmidt came over to Nick and stood beside him. There was a sneering smile on his greyhound face as he said, "I have told the other prisoners you have been chosen to receive their punishment for them."

"What punishment?"

"The punishment to all Jews for race pollution. Your punishment is that you will drop those ridiculous pants you have on and masturbate your Jewish semen onto these two corpses. While you do this you will shout over and over, 'I am a race polluter!' "

Nick stared at him, unable to believe what he was hearing.

"You see, I have told them," Schmidt continued, "that you, a Jew, had the gall to marry an English Gentile, whom you polluted by siring seven children. This crime has gone unpunished in England and

America, which are effete democracies, but it will *not* go unpunished here. I might add," he said gently, "either you do it yourself, or I will force *all* the prisoners to do it. And, as you can see, many of them are old men. The choice is yours."

The two men, torturer and victim, looked into each other's eyes a moment, Nick's burning with rage and hate, Schmidt's ablaze with triumph and excitement: he was proud of what he had dreamed up. Then, as Schmidt stepped back, leaving Nick alone by the grave, Nick hesitated. After a moment, he let go his pants, which dropped to his ankles.

"Say it!" called Schmidt. "Say 'I am a race polluter'!"

Nick closed his eyes tight. "I am a race polluter," he said.

"Louder!"

"I am a race polluter."

"That's better. Now, masturbate. Go on! Masturbate into the grave!"

Slowly, he reached his right hand down to his genitals.

It is possible the heroes of history are generated in response to history's villains. Without Adolf Hitler, Winston Churchill might have died a failed politician, a footnote in history instead of the subject of dozens of biographies. Without Adolf Hitler, Franklin Roosevelt might have ended as a two-term President whose vaunted New Deal failed to stop the Depression. Without Adolf Hitler, Nick Fleming might have been just another self-made tycoon. But as he stood at the side of the grave, saying over and over "I am a race polluter" as he tried to stroke some life into his limp and uninspired penis, feeling utterly debased, his soul fused with hate into something new. If I ever get out of here alive, he thought, I'll do everything in my power to rid the world of this monstrosity—and by Christ, I've got the power. . . . I swear to God I'll kill these Nazi bastards. . . . I'll kill them. . . . I've got the newspapers to wake up the world to this evil, and I'll sell my guns to the other governments. . . . If I ever get out of here alive, these fucking bastards will *PAY* for what they're doing . . . PAY for this evil . . .

When a few drops of his sperm finally ejaculated into the grave, the guards clapped and jeered. Then two of them rushed Nick and pushed him into the grave. He fell onto the corpses. Then, to Nick's horror, Schmidt shouted an order in German and the prisoners started shoveling dirt on top of him. Nick struggled to his feet as clods of dirt pounded on his head and shoulders. Keep cool, he thought with all the

290

will at his command. They're not going to bury me alive; they're just trying to frighten me. . . . Keep cool. . . .

He managed to claw his way out of the grave, and the fact that the guards didn't try to push him back in proved his assumption was correct. They were just heightening the terror. He lay on the hot earth by the hole, exhausted and humiliated.

But as weak as he was, it was a new Nick Fleming who climbed out of that grave—and spiritually the new Nick was stronger than he'd ever been in his life.

CHAPTER 31

I F Adolf Hitler was a genius of evil politics, if Joseph Goebbels was a genius of evil propaganda, then Hermann Goering was a genius of pure evil. His father had been a judge and Reichs Commissar for Southwest Africa. Hermann, the seventh of eight children, was an indifferent scholar; but the advent of war in 1914 brought him the chance to prove what he was, namely, a man of action. Dashing and handsome, he became an ace pilot and was the last commander of the famed Richthofen Flying Circus, for which he was awarded the highest military decoration, the Pour le Mérite.

After the war, he became a pilot for a Swedish airline and became engaged to the daughter of a Swedish nobleman. But the urge to help wipe out the disgrace of Versailles and the shame of defeat led him to return to Germany, where he enrolled in the University of Munich and where, in 1922, he met Hitler at a Party meeting at the Café Neumann. Reminiscing years later, he quoted Hitler as having said, " 'You've got to have bayonets to back up your threats.' Well, *that* was what I wanted to hear. He wanted to build up a party that would make Germany strong and smash the Treaty of Versailles. 'Well,' I said to myself, *'that's* the party for me! Down with the Treaty of Versailles, God damn it! That's my meat!' "

Twelve years and a hundred and fifty extra pounds later, the former dashing air ace was now a corpulent bully, the second most powerful man in Germany, a man who had amassed a personal fortune and vast art collection from the wealthy Jews he persecuted, a man on whose hands lay the blood of thousands of innocent human lives.

On the evening of the day Nick Fleming was pushed into the grave, Field Marshal Goering, resplendent in a white summer uniform of his own design, stepped out of his Mercedes limousine and waddled into the Villa Hubler, where he was greeted at the door by the *patronne,* the Lady of the Veils. Kissing her gloved hand, he then followed her into the main room of the villa, where the gorgeous naked ladies on the divans smiled prettily at him. Goering smiled back as he remarked to Diana, "The Fuehrer hopes you still plan to be at the

Chancellory tomorrow evening for the reception for your friend President Atatürk."

"Of course, Herr Feldmarschall. I wouldn't miss it for the world."

He turned to her. "I feel in the mood for Gutrune tonight."

"She will be honored."

She signaled the girl in question as the black butler presented two flutes of champagne. Goering and Diana took the glasses and clinked them.

"To the strengthening of German-Turkish ties," Goering said. "The Fuehrer is extremely pleased about the state visit tomorrow and asked me to thank you for your help in arranging it."

"You overestimate my influence with Kemal."

"No, we don't. But we don't underestimate it either. Will you be returning to Istanbul with him?"

"Yes. My work in Berlin is finished for the time being."

Goering chuckled as he sipped the Pommery. "Schmidt called me from Fuhlsbuettel this afternoon. He says he's giving your friend Herr Fleming a merry time. This morning he forced him to masturbate into Winterfeldt's grave in front of a bunch of his fellow Jews. The high and mighty Herr Fleming must have enjoyed that."

Diana was appalled.

"Masturbate?" she exclaimed.

"Yes. We're using it as a new technique in several of the camps. We call it sexual humiliation, and I find it highly effective. Of course, Fleming has no idea what we're after yet. We're satisfied he knows very little of the Winterfeldt conspiracy, but that line of interrogation has been useful in softening him up. You must understand that the secret of interrogation techniques is to intimidate and brutalize the victim until he gives up all hope and will agree to anything. I think that's where we've got Fleming now."

"I don't quite understand, Excellency. What is it you're after if not the Winterfeldt conspirators?"

"*Gnädige Fräulein,* how often does one get an international arms manufacturer in one's power? Fleming has a brilliant young designer named Chester Hill who works for him at the Ramschild factory in Connecticut. Hill has designed a sophisticated new howitzer we would like to get our hands on, and our intelligence tells us he's developing a radically different new tank for the United States Army. After a few more days with Captain Schmidt, we will offer Fleming a proposition he will be eager to accept. If he gets us those designs, we will give him his freedom."

"But what if he doesn't agree?"

Goering shrugged as he drained the champagne flute. "Then we'll lock him up until 1954. Of course, whether he would live to see 1954 is another question." He laughed.

"You realize you're being savaged in the American press," Diana said, her anxiety about Nick causing her to throw discretion to the wind. "Nick Fleming's stepfather is Van Clairmont."

Goering scowled. "We know that. Do you think we give a damn what he says? He already gives us a terrible press!"

"*Yes,* and why? You do terrible things! The opinion of the world is that you're a bunch of gangsters! If you were smart, you'd let Nick go. . . ."

The Marshal's beefy hand slapped her, hard.

"How *dare* you talk to me like that!" he shouted. "How dare you call me a gangster? I thought *you* were the one who wanted us to torture Fleming!"

"I was wrong," she whispered, holding her stinging cheek. "I didn't realize how wrong I've been all along."

Goering's face was red and his little pig eyes glared with anger.

"Fräulein," he said, "if you were not a friend of Kemal Atatürk's, you might find yourself in prison with your friend Herr Fleming. Good night. I find that I am not in the mood for romance after all."

He turned sharply and waddled out of the room.

"Get dressed," she said to her girls. "I'm closing for the night."

She walked out on the terrace and leaned on the balustrade, looking at the moonlight reflected in the waters of beautiful Wannsee.

Like most non-Germans, Diana had turned a blind eye to the increasing ugliness of the Nazi regime. But now she realized, with a jolt, that Goering—and undoubtedly Hitler—was planning a war. Why else go to such lengths to get American arms secrets? Diana now owned a chain of four highly profitable bordellos in Istanbul, Rome, Budapest and Berlin, and she was planning to open a fifth one in Paris. Her "nightclubs," as she euphemized them, had made her a rich woman, and she enjoyed the business—her clientele included some of the most powerful men in Europe. But international woman that she had become, she was still at heart an American. What role could an American woman in Europe play in case of a war? Should she perhaps go home? But where was home? Certainly not America anymore. Her past had been obliterated. Oddly, all that was left of it was Nick Fleming.

She marveled at the love she still felt for him—the love that had rekindled in the Gestapo prison. How could she feel any tenderness for him? And yet she agonized over the torment she knew he was experiencing. Perhaps she had been stupid to antagonize Goering, but at least she felt better about herself for having done it. She knew how to handle Atatürk. When he arrived on his state visit would be the time to convince him to use his influence with Hitler. In the meantime, Nick would have to remain in Fuhlsbuettel.

As she stood on the terrace, looking at the moon, she thought that what she wanted more than anything else in the world was for Nick to make love to her. Then she put her gloved fingers to the scars on her face and moaned softly.

He had once said to her the most important thing in life was love, and he had been right. Diana's tragedy was that love, although it had made her a millionairess, was the one thing in life she could never have.

In the 1820s, the dining room of Thrax Hall was decorated in the then-fashionable neo-Gothic style, and for over a century nothing else was done to the room except occasional repaintings. The ceiling soared in cathedrallike arches, with elaborate fan-ceiling white stuccowork filling almost every square foot of space with delicate tracery. The effect was beautiful, and the light blue of the walls and ceiling contrasted with the white stuccowork to give an almost Adamesque impression. Tall windows filled the long room with gloomy light as Lord and Lady Saxmundham, Edwina and her seven children sat down to lunch. The dining room of Thrax Hall might have been beautiful, but the lunch was as glum as the rainy weather outside.

Charles Fleming, normally so cocksure, was suddenly torn with doubt and insecurities. He had always regarded his father as a man of great power and wealth, and the realization that this godlike parent could suddenly vanish into a prison, perhaps never to be seen again, shook Charles's confidence to its roots. He didn't have much of a conscience, but nervously he wondered if this catastrophe might not be some strange form of divine retribution for the sin he had committed with his sister. No one in the family was saying much about the disaster; his grandparents and mother were keeping as stiff an English upper lip as they could manage. But all the children had heard Edwina sobbing in her bedroom, and they had seen her red, swollen eyes. For their normally composed mother to be this devastated said more about the gravity of the situation than any words, and Edwina's fears were contagious. Charles had always assumed someday he would inherit his father's empire. Now, as he sipped his cucumber soup, he wondered if there would *be* any empire to inherit. He had exploited his father's fondness for him for as long as he could remember, but this did not mean he didn't love Nick in his cold way. He wondered if he would ever see his father again.

Sylvia was even more guilt ridden than her brother. She too wondered if God had not struck down her father because of her sin of incest. If Charles's love for his father was cold, Sylvia's love was hot, and the thought that she might be somehow responsible for Nick's imprisonment had made her physically ill. Was it possible, she wondered over and over, that the sins of the *children* could be visited on the father?

Nor had Edwina been immune to torturous guilt. As she thought back over her long marriage, remembering her criticisms of Nick's business, her infidelity with Rod Norman, her many fights and spats with Nick, even her jealousy of his power, she also remembered how her husband, despite his infidelities, had always stood by her in the end, had always given her everything she had ever wanted, including movie stardom, had pampered and spoiled her and, most importantly, had loved her. How critical she had been of his bad qualities, and how blind to his good ones! Had she been too spoiled, frivolous and self-centered to show him how much she really did love him?

Nick was undergoing the tortures of the damned in Fuhlsbuettel. But his family was undergoing another form of torment in the lovely setting of Thrax Hall.

The two youngest Fleming daughters, Vicky, eight, and Fiona, eleven, were extremely close—not unreasonably, given so many male siblings. They both loved their father and were as devastated by his disappearance as the rest of the family. Fiona was growing up to resemble her dead father, Rod Norman; but since Rod had borne a resemblance to Nick, Edwina knew that Fiona could undoubtedly go through life without anyone ever questioning her parentage—which was what Nick wanted. But Edwina felt differently. She was aware of the risk of telling a girl so young that the man she had considered her father all her life really was not. But Fiona seemed a well-adjusted girl with strength of character, and Edwina had for a long time been convinced she had a right to know about her real father. Now, in her misery over Nick's imprisonment, Edwina resolved to tell Fiona the truth. She might not have admitted it to herself, but in so doing Edwina was also expiating some of the guilt she felt about her one-time fling with the movie star. Rod Norman was now a half-forgotten legend. America, embracing sound with enthusiasm, had turned its back on the silent era, which now seemed as outdated as the Model T Ford.

But Edwina remembered Rod and, in her guilt, thought she owed it to him to tell his daughter. So the next morning, after agonizing the whole night, she asked Fiona to take a walk with her. The rain had passed and it was a cloudy-sunny day with a stiff breeze. The lovely green lawns were still wet as Edwina and her daughter walked across them, the mother wondering how to broach the subject in a manner least hurtful to Fiona.

"Did you ever hear of a movie star named Rod Norman?" she finally said.

"No," replied Fiona. "Who was he?"

"He was a very famous actor back in the silent days. He was very handsome and millions of women all over the world were in love with him. I was in a movie with him once. It was called *Youth on Fire*."

"Oh, yes—one of Daddy's pictures. Can I see it sometime?"

Edwina stopped walking. Of course! What better way to introduce her to her dead father than to see him alive on a movie screen?

"I think I know where I might find a print of it in London. If I can, would you like to see it tonight?"

"Oh, yes!"

Edwina hugged her. "You know I love you very much," she said tenderly. "And so does your father."

"I know. And I miss Daddy like crazy."

"So do I, my darling. So do I."

She called Metropolitan Pictures' representative in London, a man named Sam Barron, and was told there was in fact a print available. It was sent out to Thrax Hall by messenger and that night Edwina screened it for her children. Charles and Sylvia, the eldest, had seen a few of their mother's films, but since Edwina was anything but proud of most of them, she had never organized a private Edwina Fleming Film Festival. Now, as she listened to her children's muted giggles at the outdated dramatics on the screen, she swore she never would. The film was only twelve years old, but it was amazing how unsophisticated it seemed in the light of 1934. What had seemed sizzling and daring in 1922 now seemed merely funny. Still, such being the power of film, it held the attention of the children till the final fade-out.

As the children went upstairs to their rooms, Edwina took Fiona into the library and closed the door.

"What did you think of Rod Norman?" she said, sitting beside her daughter on an enormous red velvet sofa.

"Dreamy-looking," said Fiona. "It's kind of hard to tell how good an actor he was in those funny old movies. Where is he now?"

"Dead. He was shot twelve years ago by somebody who was never found."

Fiona's eyes widened. "He was murdered?"

"Yes."

"Oh, the poor man. He looked so nice."

"He was." She took her daughter's hand. "Fiona, I'm going to tell you something that may . . . bother you a little, although it really shouldn't. You know your father and I love you just as much as your brothers and sisters."

"Oh, I know."

"And you will always, *always* be just as important to us as Vicky or Charles or Sylvia or Maurice. You know that, don't you?"

Now the eleven-year-old's eyes narrowed slightly. "Momma, what are you trying to tell me?"

Edwina took a deep breath. "Your real father is Rod Norman."

Fiona stared at her uncomprehendingly. "Then . . . then who's Daddy?"

"Daddy is your daddy. But he's not your father. Rod Norman and I . . . we made love once, and the result was you. I think you should know. But no one else in the family knows, and they never will unless you want to tell them. And really, there's no reason why you should."

There was a long silence. Edwina could see Fiona's eyes fill with tears. Oh, God, was I wrong to tell her? she thought.

Then Fiona threw herself into her mother's arms, crying. Edwina hugged her for almost five minutes, rocking slowly back and forth as the girl cried her heart out. Then Fiona sat up and dried her eyes.

"I'm glad you told me," she sniffed. "Did you love him?"

"I liked him very much—but not the way I love your daddy. . . . Not the way I love all of you."

"Was he really very famous?"

"Very."

"Then I'm going to find out all about him."

"I have a lot of press clippings in my scrapbook. We'll find out about him together."

"It'll be fun. But Daddy's still my daddy—right?"

"Forever," said Edwina, giving her a kiss.

That is, she thought, if he ever gets out of Fuhlsbuettel.

He had lost count of time, but was under the impression he had been in this hellhole seven or eight days. The monotony, the pain of his beatings, the excruciating boredom of the long hours chained to his cot, the stench and hunger . . . it was all beginning to crumble his defiance. The insidious thought kept gnawing into his consciousness: Give them what they want. Lie to them, make up names—anything! Just get out of here! Or get to a trial so you can make contact with the outside world! Then he would tell himself that if he named a name, it was tantamount to a death sentence for the man. True, that might be one way of decimating the German officer corps, but Nick was sophisticated enough to know that what Count von Winterfeldt had told him was true: many of the top German generals were anti-Hitler, and if they were removed they would undoubtedly be replaced by rabid Nazis. So he was caught in a dilemma.

But he told himself it was a test of his will against Schmidt's. Nick was no martyr: if he could have lied or tricked his way out of the camp without endangering innocent men he would have. But since he couldn't, then let it be a struggle to the death. He had no illusions it would be *his* death; but he would go out defiantly, like a man.

Then he told himself this was self-congratulatory bullshit. There was just so much pain the human body could withstand, and Nick was almost at the threshold. Schmidt knew it and was sufficiently professional at his lugubrious trade that he could undoubtedly make Nick do anything he wanted, given enough time. So that thought of heroic third-act curtains was self-deluding theatrics.

Then what alternatives were left him? If he couldn't tell them what they wanted and couldn't resist the torture much longer, what was left?

As he listened to the rain beat at the prison walls through the long night, the answer came to him with chill succinctness: death. He, Nick Fleming, in the prime of his life, was going to die.

He told himself not to cry, but he couldn't stop the tears.

The irony, which seemed so obvious until now, when he was finally experiencing it, was that despite his family and his friends, despite his wealth, power, houses, cars, factories and movie studio, he like every other human being on this lonely planet, was going to die alone.

When the guards came the next morning, they were to his amazement almost polite. *"Guten Morgen,"* they said as they unchained him. He sat up, moving his stiff arms. "You take shower *Bad,"* said one guard in lacerated English. "You shave beard, get pretty."

Nick looked at him as if the man were nuts, but in fact they led him to a clean bathroom, gave him soap and a towel and shaving equipment, left a clean, new prison uniform on a stool with a pair of leather sandals, then locked him in alone. What this new ploy meant, Nick had no idea. . . . Perhaps they wanted him to commit suicide with this razor. . . . If that was their idea, they'd picked the wrong customer: Nick Fleming sure as hell would not give Schmidt the pleasure.

His spirits rising, he shaved himself, then luxuriated in his first shower in over a week. Fresh-smelling and clean, he put on the uniform, which fit reasonably well, then knocked on the door. The guard who had become the smiling Nazi opened the door.

"Nice," he said, smiling. "No smell. No beard. Pretty. Nice."

"Sorry, my dance card's filled."

"Bitte?"

"Forget it."

They took him to Schmidt's office instead of the *Fragenzimmer.* Schmidt, standing behind his desk, the windows behind him overlooking the prison yard, was almost smiling.

"Good morning, Fleming," he said cheerfully. "How much better you look. Would you like breakfast?"

Nick bristled with suspicion. "Yes."

"But not that bilious soup we've been giving you, eh?"

"You mean the soup that won the cooking prize in 1920?"

Schmidt laughed.

"You have a sense of humor! Very funny. You're right, the soup is terrible. I wouldn't feed it to my dog—just my prisoners. But we have something more appetizing this morning."

He pressed a button. A door at the side of the office opened and a guard rolled in a table. The table had a white cloth and was set with silver and china.

"Room service," chirped Schmidt cheerfully. "Just like at the Adlon. Sit down, my friend. Eat breakfast, then we talk."

"Talk about what?"

300

"Oh, many things. Ships and shoes and sealing wax."

The guard had pulled a steel chafing dish from under the table. Now he opened it to pull out an English hunt breakfast of fried eggs, sausages, sliced ham, broiled mushrooms and tomatoes. He put this on the table, along with a silver rack of toast, creamy butter and three varieties of *confitures*. As Nick stared ravenously, the guard poured café au lait, then held a chair.

"Please, be seated," said Schmidt, gesturing at the chair.

Nick sat down. The smell of the food was erotic. Not giving a damn whether it was poisoned or not, he began wolfing it down.

When he was stuffed, Schmidt said, "Good. The National Socialist regime has its cruel side, but it also has its kind side. You have experienced the cruel side. We see no reason why you cannot enjoy its kind side from now on—if you cooperate."

Here it comes, thought Nick.

"And what does cooperation mean?"

"The Fuehrer wants to have good relations with America. He wants good relations with all the world, but especially America. National Socialism does not receive a good press there. It receives an especially bad press from the newspaper chain owned by your stepfather, Van Nuys Clairmont. In the interests of German-American relations, the Fuehrer is willing to drop all charges against you and grant you your freedom if you agree to a few conditions—one being that you would use all your influence on your stepfather to change his editorial policy vis-à-vis National Socialist Germany."

That's an easy one to get out of, thought Nick. Agree to it.

"I couldn't guarantee I could change Van's attitude," he said. "But I'd agree to *try*."

"Yes, we understand. The intent would be satisfactory to us. Our second condition is that you contribute one million dollars to the German-American Fund. Your contribution would be made *before* we grant you freedom, and the funds would be deposited in a German bank. The gift would be anonymous. We wouldn't want you subjected to criticism from your fellow American Jews."

Blackmail, thought Nick. I should have known. What the hell, agree. It's only money. Agree and get out of here.

"What are the other conditions?"

"That you make a further contribution of one hundred thousand dollars to the Hermann Goering Foundation."

"What's that?"

"A charitable foundation set up by the Field Marshal."

"What makes me think that the number-one charity benefiting from the foundation is the Field Marshal himself?"

For a second, the amiable expression on Schmidt's face was replaced by the murderous look so familiar to Nick. "My friend," he said, "I don't want to be forced to give you another lesson in etiquette. . . ."

"All right," Nick said. "I can agree to all the conditions you've mentioned. They're outrageous, but I'll agree to them."

"Excellent," Schmidt said, pulling a sheet of paper from the pocket of his uniform. "As well as I've come to know you lately, I assumed you would be reasonable. This, then, is the final condition. I have a list here, obtained by our intelligence agents in Washington, of eleven weapons projects your research-and-development department is working on for the American military."

He came to the table and gave the paper to Nick. He looked at it. It was official Abwehr stationery. Nick was surprised that even crack Abwehr intelligence agents could penetrate the War Department. He was even more surprised when he saw the list. The eleven weapons on it were Ramschild's top-secret projects for the Army, Navy and for their Air Corps arms.

"What we want are copies of your plans," said Schmidt. "When they have been delivered to Berlin and verified by our engineers, you will be liberated."

Nick looked at him.

"You realize, I assume, that if I did this—aside from being a traitor—I'd be putting myself out of business?"

"Not necessarily. The American command need never know."

"They'd know when they found out your Army had the same weapons."

Schmidt shrugged. "Blame it on our excellent Abwehr. These concerns are your problems, not ours. You have twenty-four hours to make a decision. If you refuse, then you will be brought to trial, and whether you get twenty years or the death penalty will be at the whim of your judge. There will of course be no question of the verdict. Think it over, my friend. Since I've grown rather fond of you, I hope—sincerely—that you make the mature and intelligent decision."

"I don't need twenty-four hours," said Nick. "I accept right now."

Schmidt's face lit up.

"Excellent!" he crowed. "Good show, old chap! I can't tell you how delighted I am you've made the right choice."

"Come now, Captain, you know as well as I do there's no choice at all. Twenty years in a Nazi prison is not my idea of a choice."

"Of course not, but I thought you might be tediously patriotic about the weapons plans."

"I'm a businessman, not a patriot. As you point out, I'll blame the whole thing on German spies. Now, what do you want me to do?"

Schmidt, beaming like a schoolboy, hurried around his desk. "On the chance you might be cooperative, I had a letter typed up to your vice president in charge of design, Chester Hill. . . ."

"No, no, a letter's too slow. I want *out* of here, Captain! Besides, a letter could get both of us in a hell of a lot of trouble with the American government. Let me call him. I'll tell him what to do over the phone."

"Oh." The obvious thought of a phone call had apparently never occurred to Schmidt. He checked his wristwatch. "But it will be three in the morning in Connecticut. . . ."

"What do I care?" said Nick, getting up from the table and going to the desk. "So I'll wake him up—I'm the boss, after all, and I want to get this ball *rolling* so I can get the hell out of here. Let me write down his number for you."

"Yes, of course. . . . Here's a pad and pencil. I suppose this is the better way. And I can't tell you *how* delighted I am you're cooperating with us. Confidentially, Fleming, I believe this will mean a promotion for me!"

Again, he was beaming. Nick scribbled a number on the pad, then tore off the page and handed it to him.

He turned his back to Nick and reached for the phone. There was a round paperweight on his desk. Nick picked it up and smashed it down on the back of Schmidt's head. The torturer grunted and fell on his desk, facedown.

Nick took Schmidt's service revolver from his black leather holster. Hurrying around the desk, he went to a closet and opened it. Thank God! he thought. Inside was hanging an extra S.S. uniform, complete with glossy black boots and a snappy, if evil-looking, black cap. Moving quickly, Nick kicked off his leather sandals and climbed out of the prison uniform, stuffing it onto the closet shelf. Then he took the uniform off its hanger and put it on, along with the boots. The uniform was too big—Nick estimated he had lost ten pounds during his week at Fuhlsbuettel—but wearable.

By the time Nick put on the cap, Schmidt was moaning. Nick ran to the desk, grabbed Schmidt's arm and jerked him upright, jamming the gun into the middle of his forehead. When Schmidt opened his close-set eyes, there was a look of almost comical terror on his long face as he focused on the gun barrel.

"Now, *my friend*," said Nick softly, biting the two words, "fuck your rotten deals. You're going to get me out of this shithole, or you're a dead man. And if you don't think it would give me the greatest pleasure in the world to splatter your brains all over the wall, you're a dumber Gestapo shithead than I thought. Where are we?"

Schmidt was trembling and sweating. "In Concentration Camp Fuhlsbuettel."

"Where's that?"

"In Hamburg."

Hamburg? thought Nick. Jesus Christ, I thought I was in Berlin! "What's the airport near here? The Hamburg airport?"

"Yes."

"Does it have military flights?"

"Yes."

Nick released him and stepped back, still pointing the gun at his head.

"All right, *my friend,* you're going to call for a staff car. When it gets here, you and I are going to walk out of here and get in it. If you try any tricks, I'll shoot you dead. It doesn't matter if I get killed in the process, because I don't have much of a future in this place; so just keep concentrating on *your* life. Understand?"

"Yes."

"You will also order a military plane to stand by to fly us to Copenhagen. We will drive in the staff car to the Hamburg airport, get in the plane and fly to Copenhagen. If anyone asks you who I am, tell them I'm your new assistant from Berlin and I have a bad sore throat, so I can't talk. That'll cover up my lousy German. Got all that?"

"Yes." Schmidt was sweating.

"All right, get on the phone. And remember, *no tricks.*"

Schmidt, trembling, picked up the receiver.

"Talk in your normal manner," Nick whispered.

Schmidt nodded. After a moment, he began barking orders in German. When he was through, he hung up and looked at Nick.

"The staff car will be downstairs in five minutes."

"Then let's go. And I'm right behind you. My hand and the gun are in my pocket. Just remember, *your* life. Move."

Schmidt came around the desk.

"Wipe the sweat off your face," Nick said. "Look *normal.*"

Schmidt obeyed, watching him fearfully. When he reached the door, he hesitated, looking back at Nick.

"Schmidt, remember one thing," said Nick softly. "I'm one race-polluting American Jew who's *eager* to kill. Now, open the door and let's go."

Schmidt stiffened slightly, then opened the door.

When they came out of the prison, Nick squinted at the glare of the sun, but he could see the staff car waiting for them. So far, so good, he thought. Schmidt saw a Nazi major climbing the steps of the building and saluted him. Nick, slightly behind Schmidt, also saluted. The Major stopped a moment and said something to Schmidt in German. Schmidt glanced a moment at Nick, then replied in German. The Major nodded curtly, then hurried up the steps. Schmidt and Nick climbed into the back of the staff car, the door held by the Sergeant chauffeur. The chauffeur closed the door and then hurried around the rear of the car.

"What did you tell the Major?" Nick whispered.

"He asked if I'd finished a report for him, and I said I'd have it for him in the morning."

"Smart man."

The chauffeur climbed into the front and started the car. Nick was sweating with tension, but he realized the German respect for military uniforms was working in his favor: in a Gestapo uniform, he was as good as invisible to German eyes. Just as the car started up, another captain hurried out of the prison, shouting at the chauffeur as he ran down the steps.

"What's going on?" said Nick, pressing the barrel of his gun into Schmidt's side.

"I don't know."

The Captain was talking to the chauffeur.

"He wants a lift to the airport," whispered Schmidt.

"Tell him no."

But it was too late. The Captain, a heavyset man, climbed into the front seat. The chauffeur started the car again as the new passenger turned and started speaking to Schmidt. Schmidt answered him. The car was nearing the prison gates as the two officers continued to converse. Nick's eyes darted back and forth between the two faces, straining to detect any secret sign from Schmidt or suspicion from the fat Captain. It was a nightmare not understanding what they were saying. Schmidt could be telling him anything. At one point the Captain addressed a remark to Nick. He pointed to his throat and whispered a hoarse *"Bitte,"* then coughed. The Captain looked a bit confused, then continued his conversation with Schmidt until they reached the prison gates. They passed through the gates without incident, and Nick relaxed a little as the car sped toward the nearby airport. The two officers said nothing more to each other, and Nick decided Schmidt had been too frightened to tip off the other Captain.

The chauffeur let the fat Captain out in front of the airport. As he got out of the car, he said, *"Danke,"* looked briefly at Nick and then started into the low main building.

"Get us out to the plane—fast," Nick whispered.

Schmidt barked an order to the driver, and the car drove around the building onto the grassy field where a twin-engined Stuka waited, its motors already started. The car stopped beside the plane and Nick and Schmidt climbed out.

"What happens to me?" asked Schmidt.

"You're going with me. Get in the plane."

Schmidt hesitated. Nick saw his eyes looking at the airport buildings. It was then Nick saw the armored car pulling out of one of the sheds. It was heading toward them at top speed.

Nick turned the gun on Schmidt.

"I didn't tell him!" he screamed. "He guessed—"

Nick fired twice, hitting him in the chest. As Schmidt fell to the grass, Nick ran to the plane and climbed in. It was an eight-seater, and the pilot was the only occupant.

"Go!" yelled Nick, slamming the plane door and locking it. *"Gehen Sie!"*

To his amazement, the pilot obeyed. He revved the engines and started taxiing down the field. Simultaneously, Nick heard the chatter of machine guns. He threw himself to the deck of the cabin as bullets ripped through the starboard side of the plane. The Stuka bounced into the air. Nick crawled to a window and looked out. Below him, the armored car was dwindling in the distance as the plane gained altitude. Soldiers were still firing at the plane, but Nick knew he was safe.

"Schmidt told Dolfuss who you are," yelled the pilot over the noise of the engines. "On the way to the airport. They radioed me from the tower not to take off."

Nick made his way to the cockpit, surprised that the pilot spoke good English.

"Then why *did* you?" he asked.

306

"We've all heard about the Winterfeldt *Putsch*—or the would-be *Putsch*. The Nazis tried to keep it a secret, but word leaked out of the prison. A lot of us think Winterfeldt was right. We know what goes on in Fuhlsbuettel—the torture and the shit they give the poor Jews. So when they told me from the tower you were Nick Fleming, I decided this was a good time for me to move to London."

Nick eased into the copilot's seat.

"You're leaving Germany for good?"

"I'll come back when they get rid of the Nazis. By the way, my name's Arndt Siemens."

He held out his right hand, and Nick shook it.

"Arndt, I am *mighty* glad to meet you," said a relieved Nick. "Can we make it to London?"

"I'm heading for the Dutch border. You told Schmidt you wanted to go to Copenhagen, so they'll be looking for us to the north. I think we'll be all right. The ride may be a bit bumpy—there's some rough weather to the west—but the clouds will help hide us. Did you kill Schmidt?"

"Yes."

"Good. That bastard deserved it. Hang on—here come the first bumps!"

And the little plane dived into a big cloud.

Atatürk had had built for himself a presidential train, constructed by the firm of Linke-Hofmann-Busch, the chief glory of which was a full-sized marble bathroom with an enormous marble tub. And the same day that Nick escaped from Fuhlsbuettel, the Turkish dictator's train slid into Berlin's Schlesische Bahnhof to be greeted by the Fuehrer himself and all the top Nazis, an honor guard, and a band playing the Turkish national anthem and the Horst Wessel song. Then the motorcade rode through Berlin to the Chancellory, at the Wilhelms Platz, where, on the second-floor balcony Hitler had installed shortly after his accession to power, the two dictators emerged to wave to the genuinely enthusiastic crowd below. Many Germans might have been shocked by the Roehm purge of that summer, but there could be no doubt that Adolf Hitler was still worshiped by the vast majority of the German public.

At the Chancellory reception that evening, to which all the diplomatic corps and *tout*-Berlin were invited, Diana Ramschild was talking to the French press attaché, waiting for a chance to talk to Atatürk alone about Nick. The chance came sooner than she expected.

At nine o'clock, the Turkish dictator, resplendent in a white uniform, made his way through the medal-and-jewel-bedecked crowd to the woman to whom he still had a peculiarly romantic attachment, though Diana had for some time been as much a business partner to him as anything else.

"I have news for you," he said, taking her arm. "Over here we'll get a little privacy on the terrace, and I can have a smoke."

He led her through French doors out onto a terrace. Hitler was a fanatical antismoker and his guests lit up at their peril, so the Chancellory rooms were free of tobacco fumes; but still the cool evening air with the promise of rain was refreshing.

"I'm afraid the news won't please you," he went on, lighting one of his Turkish cigarettes and exhaling with relief. "Hitler and Goering are furious. Nick Fleming escaped today from Fuhlsbuettel."

"He *escaped?*" she said softly.

"Yes. You don't seem to have much luck with that man—either that, or he's got the luck of the devil. Bald Ali's hired killer hits the wrong target, and even the Gestapo loses him. I'm sorry."

She started laughing, and he looked confused.

"You find this *amusing?*" he said.

"No—I'm laughing from relief! I was going to ask you to use your influence with Hitler to get him *out,* but he got out on his own. Thank God!"

"Diana, sometimes you're a difficult woman to understand. I thought you hated Nick Fleming?"

"I thought I did too, but I don't." She shrugged helplessly. "It turns out I'm still in love with him. I think I always *was.*"

He took her gloved hand and kissed it.

"Women," he said. "Endlessly fascinating. But I must say I feel a little jealous of this Nick Fleming. He must be an extraordinary man to have kept your love all these years."

"Yes," she said, looking at the moon over the linden trees, "he is extraordinary. At least, to me."

A wild idea was forming in her brain. Was it somehow possible for her to rekindle that hot love that she knew once had burned in Nick for her?

Part V

A WORLD AT WAR
1939-1942

IN May 1939, the big news in the society columns was the impending coming-out party of Sylvia Fleming, who was as much the glamour girl of 1939 as Brenda Frazier had been of 1938.

Photos of Sylvia appeared everywhere, her breathtaking, svelte, auburn beauty enhanced by fabulous evening dresses, sports clothes and swimwear. She was photographed at the Stork Club with society beaux, at the theater, at the races, at polo matches on Long Island, sailing on the Sound, riding in Connecticut. It seemed a Depression-hounded public couldn't read enough about this society beauty, and details of her coming out caused society writers to salivate. On May 15 a column in the *Herald Tribune* gushed:

The "it" debut of the year will be "it" deb Sylvia Fleming's, to be held three weeks hence at the St. Regis Roof. Great-granddaughter of the Duke of Dorset, daughter of Silent Film Queen Edwina Fleming and munitions magnate Nick Fleming, gorgeous Sylvia's curtsy to society is guesstimated to cost her Daddy Warbucks $60,000, give or take a case of champagne. Sylvia's a big fan of Glenn Miller's, but since his band is on tour, the swing and sway will be under the baton of society maestro Meyer Davis. Two hundred invitations have gone out to the *crème de la crème,* and those miserables who didn't receive one had better plan to hide out at the movies on the Big Night. Sylvia will have ten official escorts at the bash, but rumor has it that her heart belongs to dashing Ramschild Arms Company V.P. Chester Hill.

Being neither insensitive nor fools, Nick and Edwina had questioned the wisdom of hosting such a lavish affair in a world so racked by depression and strained by the ever-increasing tensions of possible war. They remembered Barbara Hutton's coming-out party eight years before, which had turned the dime-store heiress into the press's favorite whipping girl. But Barbara Hutton seemed to have pulled the sting of public disfavor, and Sylvia wanted the party so much—almost desperately in fact—that her parents crossed their fingers and gave in.

But when Nick and Edwina pulled up in their limousine in front of the hotel on the night of the gala, Nick knew he had made a terrible mistake. The sidewalk was jammed with demonstrators carrying placards reading "Down with Fleming, the Titan of Death!" "America Wants Peace, but Fleming Wants War!" "America Wants Peace with Nazi Germany, not a Fleming War!"

In the five years since his escape from Fuhlsbuettel, Nick had mounted an intense campaign in Van Clairmont's press—as well as in congressional offices—trying to alert the American public to the menace of Nazism and urging America to arm itself. He had written an account of his capture, which Van had published, describing in full detail the horrors of his torture. The result of the report was a storm of abuse and cries for censorship. It seemed the American public was more shocked by his use of the word "masturbation" in print than they were by the brutality of the Nazis, which many jeered was nothing more than sensationalism on Nick's part.

As for his anti-Fascist campaign, while some more sophisticated segments of the public applauded his efforts and agreed with him, the vast majority, from the Palm Beach rich to the Bowery poor, pooh-poohed him as a rabble-rouser who was only trying to scare America into buying his munitions.

For Nick, who had vowed a personal crusade against Nazism in the slime of Fuhlsbuettel, his failure to arouse the public to anything but personal abuse was maddening and frustrating. By 1938 he had come to the realization he was doing more harm than good and decided he would have to let the international gangsterism of the Nazi regime itself turn America against it. But the harm to his own personal image had already been done and, in a backfiring public-relations nightmare, he had been turned into a titan of industrial evil, manipulating America's defenses for his personal profit. Now, as he sat in the limousine watching the picketers outside the St. Regis, he clenched his fists with rage.

"The stupid bastards," he muttered. "Is Hitler going to have to bomb Times Square before they wake up?"

Edwina squeezed his arm. "Ignore them, darling," she said. "Someday they'll say you were right."

Nick had his doubts about that. But as he climbed out of the car, he did his best to ignore the catcalls, which commenced the moment he was recognized.

"Hey, it's the warmonger!" yelled one young man with red hair, and a roar of boos and whistles went up.

"When are you starting the next war?" howled an old man who wore an American Legion cap.

"Did you pay for tonight's champagne with bullets?" shouted Red Hair.

Nick had almost reached the hotel door, but this was too much. Before Edwina realized what he was doing, he had pushed past the cops holding back the crowd and slugged the red-haired man. Two women screamed and started beating him with their placards as Nick and Red Hair punched it out. Cop whistles blew as two policemen separated the fighters. Nick had a bloody nose, but he didn't care. Holding his handkerchief to his left nostril, he walked into the hotel.

It gave him some degree of satisfaction that the crowd, though no less hostile, was now at least silent.

"You heard about the mess downstairs?" said Chester Hill two hours later as he Lindy Hopped with the "it" deb of the season, Sylvia.

"Of course, and it made me furious. My father practically gets killed by the Nazis, and when he gets home he gets picketed and called all sorts of names. Those idiot jerks downstairs ought to be shot. Anyway, I'm not going to let it ruin my party."

"That's the spirit. And it's some party. And you're some deb. And I'm about to die, it's so hot in here."

"Isn't it? But I'm having fun, so I don't care."

The orchestra segued into the slower, dreamier "And the Angels Sing," the big hit song of the year, and Chester and Sylvia started dancing cheek to cheek.

On the other side of the dance floor, Charles was dancing with Kimberly Radnor, another deb that season.

"Damn," he muttered.

"What's wrong?" asked Kimberly, who was a horse-faced blonde from the North Shore and whose father owned the Radnor Shipping Line.

"Nothing," Charles lied. But he had seen Chester and Sylvia dancing, glued together as if they were making love. He had seen the blissful look on his sister's face.

Charles Fleming hated Chester Hill.

As Nick's numerous children matured, he had been forced to find a bigger apartment, and in 1938 he moved into a truly enormous triplex at 770 Park Avenue. By now every child had his or her own bedroom, though the younger ones shared baths; and at four-thirty the next morning, Sylvia, more than a little giddy from all the champagne she had drunk at her party, collapsed into one of the pretty chintz armchairs in her bedroom, taking off her shoes to rub her feet.

"Did you enjoy it, darling?" said her mother, who popped into the room looking as fresh as if she had just gotten dressed rather than hostessing an eight-hour extravaganza.

"Oh, Mummy, it was lovely. I had a *terrific* time! Thanks so much!"

Edwina came over and kissed her. "Well, your father and I were proud of you. You looked scrumptious."

"Poor Daddy. Is he feeling awful?"

Edwina straightened. "He was hurt, naturally. But your father's a strong man. It takes more than a pack of hoodlums to get him down."

After Edwina left the room, Sylvia got out of the chair to start undressing when Charles came in, without knocking.

"I wish you'd learn to knock," growled Sylvia. "And if you've come in here to tear the party apart and try to ruin the evening for me, don't. I'm tired and want to go to bed."

"On the contrary, I thought the party was a smash." He closed the door and leaned against it, watching his sister with that look of slight arrogance that had earned him the nickname "Cobra" from the girls he dated. "But you danced too much with Chester Hill."

"Why shouldn't I?" said Sylvia, removing the small diamond earrings her father had given her for her last birthday. "I'm crazy about him."

"Then you're a jerk. He's just after your money."

"That's *your* opinion, and one I wish you'd keep to yourself."

He crossed the room to her. "Take off my cuff links for me, will you?" he said.

"I'm not your slave."

"Come on . . . be nice." He held out his hands. She looked at him a moment, then started undoing his gold-and-diamond links.

"Of course," said Charles softly, "there's one way we could test Chester. I mean, to see whether he's after your money or not."

"Now what's going through your icky little brain?"

"I could tell him about you and me."

She glared at him. He smiled.

"If he's after your money, he'd marry you anyway. But I don't think many men would want to marry a girl who'd made love to her brother."

She slapped him, hard.

"We did it once—*once!*" she whispered. "And it was stupid of us to do it. But you're *not* going to hang that over my head the rest of my life!"

"Why not? You enjoyed it, and so did I."

"It was *wrong,* Charlie. Do you know what the word means? And I know you're jealous of Chester. . . ."

"I'm jealous of *any* man who looks at you," he interrupted. He grabbed her and kissed her hard. She pounded him with her fists, but he held on, kissing her.

There was a knock on the door, and Nick entered.

"Sylvia, I . . ."

He stopped, staring. Charles quickly released his sister, stepping back. Pulling his handkerchief from his pocket, he wiped the lipstick off his mouth. Then he smiled at his father.

"Hi, Dad. I was demonstrating my lover-boy technique on Sylvia. She doesn't believe me when I tell her I'm a lady-killer."

Nick said nothing, still staring at them. Suddenly, Sylvia burst into tears and ran into her bathroom, slamming the door behind her.

"She's a little sloshed on the bubbly," said Charles, sticking the handkerchief back in his pocket as he sauntered across the room to his father. "That was a great party tonight, Dad. Best coming-out do I've ever been to. Well, good night."

He walked around his father and out into the hall.

Nick didn't move for almost a minute. Then, slowly, he turned, left the room and walked down the art-lined hall to his bedroom. All he could think of was that long-ago horror at the Pennsylvania orphanage when Dr. Truesdale had accused him of having sexual relations with his mother. The scene still seared his memory, and the idea of incest made his flesh crawl. He reached his bedroom and opened the door. Edwina was already in bed, sitting up beneath the magnificent Seurat Nick had bought the previous year in Paris. He closed the door softly, then came to the enormous bed and sat down on it next to his wife. She had never seen him look so stunned before.

"Darling, what's wrong?" she asked.

"Were the Nazis right?" he whispered incredulously. *"Am* I a race polluter?"

"Whatever are you talking about?"

He looked at her, his face white. "Just now . . . in Sylvia's room . . . I came in and Charles was *kissing* her."

She frowned. "What do you mean?"

"What do you *think* I mean? He was kissing her on the *mouth.*"

It was Edwina's turn to look shocked. "Nick, it had to be some sort of game. . . ."

"It was no game! Shit."

He stood up, put his hands in his pockets and started pacing around the room, fighting back the tears in his eyes. "My son," he said bitterly. "Could my son do *that?* Christ, I can't believe it. But I *saw* it! No, it's impossible. Sylvia wouldn't let him. But then she burst into tears. . . . Goddammit, *something's* going on between those two. . . . Damn!"

He stopped pacing, sat down in a chair, buried his face in his hands and started crying. Edwina got out of the bed and hurried across the room to hug him.

"Darling, darling," she soothed, "he's *my* son too. If they've done something wrong, don't blame it on yourself. It's probably *my* crazy Thrax blood. . . . God knows half my ancestors were dotty, if not barking mad. . . ."

"This isn't being 'dotty,' " he said. "I'm talking about *incest.*"

They stared at each other, shocked into silence by the ugly word. Edwina stood up.

"Do you think they've . . ."

"I don't know. I'm not sure I want to know." He wiped his eyes with a handkerchief. "It's my fault," he said grimly. "I've spoiled him rotten. You always said it, and you were right. I've raised a son and heir who's arrogant . . . twisted . . ." He stood up and started pacing again.

"What can we do?" said Edwina.

"We get him away from Sylvia *fast,*" said Nick, talking quickly. "We'll send him . . . I don't know . . . England! We'll send him to Oxford. . . . He's got terrific grades at Princeton, he could get in. . . . Anything to get him out of here! Then we'll get Sylvia married . . . *fast.* Chester . . . my son-in-law . . . Oh shit, shit, shit! My *son!* I can't believe it . . . my *son!*"

He stopped pacing and looked at Edwina. Suddenly, he was all icy calm. "If he doesn't straighten out," he said softly, "I'll disinherit the bastard."

Edwina knew he meant it.

CHAPTER 33

Less than ten weeks later, Hitler invaded Poland and launched a general European war that most people assumed would be short. When, to the amazement of the world, Hitler's *Blitzkrieg* knocked Poland out of the war in a few weeks, most people assumed it would be a short war that Hitler would undoubtedly win. Nick, who had preached the evils of Nazism for years to mostly deaf ears, now assumed that, if nothing else, he would be vindicated, and Americans would be eager to join England's and France's cause morally, if not as outright allies. To his amazement and chagrin, the attitude of most of the press (Van Clairmont's newspaper chain being an outstanding exception) was to become even more stridently isolationist. The Ramschild Company tripled its munitions production as a flood of orders came in from England, but this only served to make Nick increasingly unpopular.

He could do nothing right. When he donated a million dollars to the British government, it was taken by the American press as further proof of his complicity in the escalation of the war. When he donated a quarter million to the International Red Cross, he was denounced as a monster of hypocrisy. In the spring of 1940, when such American heroes as Charles Lindbergh were praising the Nazi regime, and Joseph Kennedy, the father of the future President and then Ambassador to the Court of St. James's, was telling everyone who would listen that the British were finished, a poll was taken by a Chicago newspaper of the ten most hated men in America. To Nick's fury, he was Number Three. When Edwina pointed out that Number One on the list was President Roosevelt, Nick became even further depressed.

He was achieving power and wealth beyond his wildest dreams, but he was one of the most controversial public figures in the country, and hated every moment of it. He even toyed briefly with the idea of selling Ramschild, and getting out of the arms business, which was causing him such widespread odium—but then he would remember Fuhlsbuettel, and his hatred of the Nazis would squelch that thought.

His most powerful weapon against the Nazis were the weapons his factories were mass-producing.

"So you're the third most hated man in America?" beamed Franklin D. Roosevelt as he shook Nick's hand in the Oval Office of the White House. "Well, I'm the *most* hated man in America and damned proud of it!" At which the President of the United States burst into an infectious laugh. "Sit down, Nick. Some coffee?"

"No thanks, Mr. President. I'm nervous enough, being so hated."

"Oh, to hell with them. Those damned isolationists can't spot a good war when they see one, and if *any* war can be called 'good' it's this one. If Hitler isn't a first-class villain worth licking, I don't know who is. Unfortunately, most of the country doesn't share our opinion. Which is one reason I asked you to come to the White House."

He paused to fit a cigarette in his long holder and light it with a brass lighter from his cluttered desk. Though Nick had met him several times previously and had contributed to his campaigns, he was somewhat skeptical of the New Deal. Still, he liked the man and was susceptible to his famous charm. And he was flattered to be invited to the White House. He reflected that he had come a long way from the mining slums of Flemington, Pennsylvania.

"The Army Air Corps tells me," said the President, exhaling, "that your son-in-law has designed a bombsight that's even better than the Norden."

"Chester's improved the accuracy. The Air Corps has ordered five hundred of them."

"I know. At ten thousand dollars apiece. No wonder the taxpayers hate you." He paused again to puff on the cigarette. "Nick," he continued, "you know a lot of top people in England—in the government, the armed forces, industry and the financial world. What do you think England's chances are in this war?"

Nick hesitated. It was not an easy question. "No one admires the English more than I do," he finally said. "As you know, I'm married to one of them. I think the English misjudged Hitler in the past, but probably Hitler's misjudging them now if he thinks they won't fight. A lot depends on the German Air Force. If the Luftwaffe's as good as everyone thinks it is, then England will be in for a tough time of it. But I'm not sure that Germany can ever really *beat* England, even if Hitler invades. On the other hand, I'm not sure England can ever really *beat* Germany unless we come in on her side."

"What do you think is the worst that can happen? A stalemate?"

"That or a negotiated peace, which in my opinion would be a victory for Hitler. But you have to remember I've had rather unpleasant personal experiences with the Nazis. I suppose most Americans would heave a sigh of relief at a negotiated peace."

"Oh, no doubt about it. And of course it's no secret to you that I'm walking a tightrope here in the White House. I want to help the British and French as much as possible, but if I go too far, the country will have my scalp. Naturally, there are ways for me to operate that the country doesn't have to know about—which brings me to you.

"I know you're a busy man, but I'm also told you don't involve yourself too much with the day-to-day operations of Ramschild. Is that true?"

"Yes, sir."

"Then you could be away for a certain amount of time without interfering with Ramschild's production, which is extremely important right now?"

"Well, as long as I could be reached by phone or cable, yes, I could be away."

"Good. What I want to do is appoint you to a special commission, the purpose of which is to go to London and negotiate with the British to standardize American and English weapons. As I'm sure you're aware, it's absolutely ridiculous that the standard American rifle caliber is .30 inch and the British counterpart is .303. Three-thousandths of an inch difference completely bars any interchangeability between us, and this results in tremendous waste of time and material. It's amazing! This was a problem in the last war, and nothing has been done about it. . . . The other members of the commission are Generals Laughlin and Billings and Rear Admiral Howland.

"But the commission is really more of a cover, particularly for you. What I want from you is *information*—gossip, even! I want your opinion—because I trust it—of what England's going to do. I want you to do as much as you can, short of outright lying, to bolster the English, at least to give the impression that we're behind them. Our ambassador, Joe Kennedy, is such an outright defeatist that in my opinion he's doing serious damage to English morale, and I'd like to do everything I can, short of recalling him, to counteract that. Of course, Joe doesn't want a war because it'll depress the stock market. You, on the other hand, are well known for your anti-Nazi views, and even though you're as popular as a skunk here, in England I understand you're something of a hero. So you could be of real service to me and to the country if you'd take this job. I'm afraid I can't offer you much more than my gratitude, travel expenses and a per diem allowance of fifteen dollars. But I'm told you can get a suite at Claridge's for four dollars a day, so it shouldn't be too bad. Besides"— he winked—"I understand your business is booming."

Nick smiled. "You might even say it's exploding, sir. I'd be glad to take the job, and I'll do everything I can to help."

"Excellent! I'll have Missy reserve you a seat on the first Clipper to Lisbon."

"Can you ask her to reserve two, Mr. President? I'd like to take my wife—at my expense of course. Edwina's anxious to see her parents. And then our oldest boy, Charles, who was at Oxford, has enlisted in the R.A.F."

"Bully for him, as Cousin Ted used to say. Of course—Missy will handle it. Missy handles damned near everything in this place." He flashed his dazzling smile. "Glad to have you on the team, Nick. We hated men have to stick together."

Nick got up to shake the President's hand.

He was beginning to feel less depressed about his unpopularity.

Her name was Lena Pfeiffer, she was forty-eight years old, was fifty pounds overweight, had graying blond hair and had been the cleaning lady for the executive offices at the Ramschild factory for three years. Since the company was now operating two eight-hour shifts a day to cope with its enormous backlog of orders, Lena came on duty at midnight when everyone else (except the security guards) was leaving. At 2 A.M. two nights after Nick visited the White House, Lena pushed her cleaning cart down the hallway of the deserted executive wing to the service elevator. Getting in, she descended to the first floor, then pushed her cart out and headed for the factory. Bill Ziegler, one of the security guards, was dropping a nickel in the Coke machine.

"How ya doin', Lena?" he asked as the machine released a bottle.

"Can't complain."

"Did you hear *Amos 'n' Andy* tonight? A funny show."

"Nope. My radio's busted. Got to take it to the shop tomorrow."

"You sure got no luck with machines. Didn't you tell me last week your washing machine broke?"

"Yep. If I had any luck, do you think I'd be a goddamn cleaning lady?"

She winked at him as she pushed her cart through the double doors, then headed past the giant fifteen-thousand-ton press for the drafting room. At the door to the drafting room, she stopped, pulled out her keys, selected the correct one, unlocked the door, pushed her cart inside, turned on the lights, then locked the door behind her. She reached into the cleaning cart and pulled out a small camera. Moving with surprising speed, considering her weight, she went to the safe, turned the dial right 18, left 26, right 40, then 0. (She had learned the combination by bringing in an electromagnetic listening device two weeks before to listen to the clicks of the dial. The device, the latest development of Siemens Elektrogerate Aktien Gesellschaft, had been given to her by Dr. Ignatz Theodor Griebl, the chief New York spy for the Abwehr, the German intelligence organization.) When the safe opened, she pulled out the final sheets of the Hill bombsight designs, put them on Chester's desk, lighted them by tipping the shade of his desk lamp, then began photographing them.

Tonight she would finish the entire set of drawings, which had taken her ten nights to photograph.

"I *hate* this house!" screamed Sylvia Fleming Hill. "I hate, hate, HATE IT! It's tiny and crummy and it STINKS!"

She flopped down on what she considered the hideous green sofa in the living room of the three-bedroom Cape Cod-style house her husband of eight months, Chester, had rented on the banks of the Connecticut River.

"Give it a chance, will you?" Chester yelled back from the kitchen, where he was opening a can of beer. "Christ, we've been here three days and already you're bitching! This is the fourth house we've lived in in eight months and I'm getting sick of moving!"

He slammed the door of the refrigerator and came out of the kitchen he thought was charming, walked through the dining room he thought was pretty into the living room he thought was cheerful. Sylvia glared at him from the sofa she loathed.

"I can't help it," she said. "Do you want me to lie to you? Do you want me to say, 'Oh, Chester, sweetie, this is the most wonderful little housie in the world'? I say nuts to that. God! Last year I was the most glamorous girl in America, with my picture on the cover of *Life*. What am I now? Harriet Hausfrau in this godforsaken town in Connecticut."

"You wanted to get married!"

"My *father* wanted me to get married—you know that as well as

I do! He practically *pushed* us to the altar. And here I am, nineteen years old and *stuck*."

He put down his beer and came to the sofa, putting his hands on its back and leaning over her.

"You don't mind being stuck in bed," he said in a leering tone. He leaned down and kissed her mouth.

After a moment, she pushed him away. "No one likes sex more than I," she said, "but you can't do it all day long. When you're not here, there's nothing to do. *Nothing!*"

"Find a hobby!"

"What? Tiddledywinks? Knitting? I listen to the damned soap operas till I think I'm going crazy."

"You're just spoiled."

"Of *course* I'm spoiled! My father spoiled me rotten. I'm *glad* I'm spoiled. I wish *you* spoiled me a little!"

Chester told himself to hold his temper. Sylvia's tantrums and sulks were becoming more and more frequent and less possible to live with—at times he wanted to strangle her. But he had to keep her happy, because her father was boss.

"What do you want?" he sighed.

"To fly to Europe on Friday with Mommy and Daddy." To see Charlie, she thought. It frightened her how much she missed her brother.

"Well, your father said no to that. So what else do you want?"

"I don't *know*. But I hate this house. Why don't we build our own house? Something screamingly modern that will shock everybody in this hick town?"

Chester considered this a moment. He had so far fought her urge to build because he didn't want to spend the money. He might be the son-in-law of one of America's richest men, but he was still making only twenty-five thousand dollars a year, the raise being one of his wedding presents from Nick. On the other hand, maybe building a house would shut Sylvia up, and he could hit her old man up for a loan.

"All right," he said. "Let's build a house."

Her sulky expression swept away like clouds before the sun. "Oh, Chester!" she exclaimed. "You *are* going to spoil me!"

He eased himself on top of her and began making love, repressing yet again that disquieting urge he was having more and more frequently lately.

The urge to murder her.

Chester's attitude toward his father-in-law was an uneasy amalgam of envy, awe, admiration and fear. Since the wedding, Nick had insisted his new son-in-law call him "Nick," but still their relationship was anything but chummy. So the next morning, as Chester entered Nick's office to ask for a loan, it was with considerable trepidation.

Nick's office was as sleekly Art Deco as the reception room, but there was no Rich Man's Power Play in its decor. It was simple and uncluttered, with only a series of large original Audubon bird prints on the wall to serve as a reminder that Nick was passionate about art (although Chester thought the birds were perhaps as much a psychological ploy to defuse Nick's image as a "Titan of Death"). Nick, as usual, was genial to his son-in-law, shaking his hand and offering him a chair.

"I've been getting a lot of last-minute stuff out of the way," said Nick. "As you know, we're leaving on the nine o'clock Clipper in the morning, and God knows when we'll be back, so Frieda's piling the paper work on me. Now what did you want to see me about?"

Chester knew this was Nick's not-so-subtle way of saying "You've got five minutes."

"It's about Sylvia," Chester began.

"More tantrums?"

"Yes. I don't mean to saddle you with my problems, but she's getting worse. In a way, I guess I can't blame her. She's been used to everything—excitement and glamour—and now she's 'stuck,' as she puts it, in Old Lyme. . . ."

"What does she want?" interrupted Nick.

Chester squirmed. "She's been after me to build a house. I've been putting her off because I didn't want to take on that kind of expense, but . . . well, I'm beginning to wonder if I've been wrong."

"And you want to borrow money from me?"

Damn him, thought Chester, he always reads my mind.

"Well, I wanted to ask your financial advice. . . ."

"My answer is no. No, I won't loan you money; no, don't borrow from a bank; and no, don't build a house. You're earning a damned good salary, Chester, and the stock options I'm giving you should make you a rich man in your own right in a few years. *Then* build your house with your own money. Meanwhile, make Sylvia taste a little reality for a change—it'll be good for her. And the worst thing that can happen to your marriage—believe me—is if she knows you came to me for a loan to give her some trinket, or build her a house. Then she'll have nothing but contempt for you, and she'll be sending you off to 'Daddy' every ten minutes. I've been expecting this to happen, knowing my daughter. Frankly, I'm impressed it's taken you eight months to give in to her. But don't. Go back to her and kick her in the ass. I love Sylvia, but I know how spoiled she is. My biggest failure as a parent is that I've spoiled my children. I sure as hell don't want my son-in-law doing the same thing."

It irritated Chester to admit his father-in-law was probably right.

But that wasn't going to make life with Sylvia any easier.

"I know that woman," whispered Nick to Edwina as they took their seats in the Lisbon Clipper at La Guardia Airport. "I swear to God I know her."

"Which woman?" asked Edwina, who was wearing a comfortable suit for the long transatlantic flight (with stops at Bermuda and the Azores).

"She's on the other side of the plane, two seats back. She's got gray-blond hair and has on a white hat with a veil."

Edwina turned to look back. "There isn't any woman," she said. "Oh, wait a minute—she's getting off the plane."

Nick turned to see the woman in question just leaving through the rear door. He frowned.

"That's odd," he said. "Why's she getting off?"

"Maybe she changed her mind about going to Lisbon."

"But it's taken us a week to get seats on this plane, and we have government priority. . . ." He turned back in his seat, his frown deepening. "Who the hell *is* she?" he mumbled. Then, suddenly, light dawned. "It's my cleaning lady!" he blurted out.

"Your *cleaning* lady?" said Edwina. "What's *she* doing flying to Lisbon?"

Nick was out of his seat. "That's what I'd like to know. And how's she paying for it?"

He was running down the aisle. The stewardess was in the process of closing the door.

"Wait a minute!" Nick yelled. "Don't shut that door!"

The stewardess looked confused. "Sir, we're about to take off. . . ."

"I know, but you'll have to wait. This is an emergency."

Pushing her aside, he shoved the door open. Lena Pfeiffer was halfway across the runway to the terminal.

"Lena!" he yelled. "Lena, wait!"

She started running.

"Stop that woman!" he yelled at an airport security guard. The guard looked confused, but did nothing. The plane's ramp had already been removed. Nick pulled his gun from his armpit holster and fired over Lena's head. The passengers in the crowded plane began screaming. The stewardess grabbed his arm.

"Mr. Fleming, give me that gun!"

Nick shoved her away and aimed again. Lena was almost at the terminal door. He aimed at her right thigh and fired. She fell to the ground, clutching her leg.

More screams. Now the guard pulled his gun and aimed at Nick.

"That woman's a *spy!*" Nick yelled, praying he was right. But why else would his cleaning woman be on a plane to Lisbon, the notorious clearinghouse for Nazi spies, and why else would she leave the plane the moment she saw him come on?

"Search her!" he shouted. "She'll have classified material on her!"

Christ, if I'm not right, there'll be hell to pay. . . .

Just then, he was pinioned from behind by the pilot. "Take his gun," the pilot shouted. "The cops are on their way."

Nick put up no resistance, giving the gun to the copilot. When the pilot released him, Nick pulled out his passport case.

"I'm accredited by President Roosevelt," he said, showing the official document. "I don't blame you for calling the cops, but I'm telling you that woman out there is a Nazi spy."

The pilot looked skeptical.

"Shoot-out at Airport!" screamed the headlines of the afternoon papers. "Arms Titan Shoots Elderly Woman!" "Fleming Firepower Panics Pan Am!"

Nick's lethal reputation with the press again served him up on a skillet of hot-headline innuendo. Only farther down in most of the articles was it revealed that the "elderly woman" was indeed found to be carrying films of classified material. Unfortunately for Nick, the Hill bombsight was so top secret the Army refused to reveal to the press exactly what Lena Pfeiffer had stolen. Even Van Clairmont's papers—pro-Nick as they were—carried the headline "Gun Magnate Shoots Nazi Spy," and while at least providing a more accurate account of the incident, still retained a certain sneer with "gun magnate."

Nick and Edwina had remained in New York long enough to see

Lena Pfeiffer booked for espionage by the F.B.I. Then, by presidential order, they were flown in an Army Air Corps bomber to Bermuda to rejoin the Clipper flight.

"Darling, you did the right thing," Edwina comforted as Nick scanned the newspaper headlines. "I'm proud of you."

Nick said nothing, but the bad publicity rankled.

CHAPTER 34

IN April 1940, just as Nick and Edwina landed in Lisbon to transfer to a London flight, the *drôle de guerre* or *Sitzkrieg* or phony
war that had lasted through the fall, winter and early spring was
suddenly and dramatically ended by the Nazi invasion of Denmark
and Norway. By noon, April 9, nine thousand Wehrmacht troops occupied the five principal Norwegian ports—Narvik, Trondheim, Ber-
gen, Stavanger and Kristiansand—and had captured Oslo, in each
case after scarcely firing a shot. While German bombers kept the
British Navy at bay, the Wehrmacht then swiftly gained control of
all the major airfields, including the most important one at Sola, outside Stavanger. It was one of the quickest, most daring and bloodless
military occupations of all time, and Hitler had reason to rejoice as
he turned his attention to his next targets, Belgium, Holland and
Luxembourg.

Thus, as Nick and Edwina motored out to Audley Place, their
Tudor country home Edwina had completely refurbished after Nick's
escape from Fuhlsbuettel in 1934, whatever faint hopes the English
might have had that Hitler was bluffing were dashed by the reality of
the Norwegian invasion. The Germans were as apprehensive as the
English and the French. When their beloved Fuehrer had invaded
Poland in September, the outbreak of war was greeted by silence and
empty streets in Berlin. The brilliant early successes of the German
Army created enthusiasm, but in the collective heart of the nation
lurked the suspicion that Adolf Hitler, the new Napoleon, might be
leading them down the path to ruin.

But the weather was so glorious that April day that not even the
lugubrious news from Norway could dampen the spirits of Nick and
Edwina as they pulled up in front of Audley Place.

"Isn't it beautiful?" said Edwina as she climbed out of the Rolls.

"Yes, and you did a beautiful job fixing it up," said her husband,
putting his arm around her and kissing her. "By the way, have I told
you today that I love you?"

She smiled. "No, but I love to hear it."

He took her hand and they started toward the front door.

"Now that I'm getting seriously middle-aged," he said, "I think I should take up gardening, like any proper English squire. Shall we plan a garden together and try to forget this damned war for at least a few hours a week?"

"Oh, Nick, that would be lovely. We'll do a garden together!"

"And bore each other silly." He grinned.

She laughed and kissed him. "You're never boring, darling. Infuriating, yes, but never boring. And I hope you're not so 'seriously' middle-aged you're going to lose all interest in lovemaking."

"They say life begins at forty, and I'm almost fifty-two and feeling mighty frisky for an old geezer."

He opened the door and they went inside to a spacious entrance hall with a sagging Elizabethan wooden staircase. Mrs. Dabney, the plump housekeeper and cook, was hurrying in from the kitchen.

"Welcome to Audley Place!" she said, beaming. "And isn't it a lovely day?"

But the smell of war was in the April air.

The garden was planned and planted, but Nick had little time to spend in the country. First, there were his duties on the Standardization Commission, as it was called, although as Roosevelt had hinted these duties were light—all the more so since neither the British nor the American military men showed the slightest interest in standardizing anything. Because of his connections, Nick was invited everywhere in that nervous London of 1940 and, in accordance with the President's wishes, he listened and took copious notes, which he sent on to the White House. He had booked a suite at Claridge's, a few blocks from the American Embassy, in Grosvenor Square, and he entertained there a cross section of London society, ranging from the American-born social leaders Lady Cunard and "Chips" Channon to his old friend Winston Churchill, now back at the Admiralty. Nick and Churchill had kept up a correspondence over the years, one that had increased in length and frequency as Hitler rose to power. For as Nick was warning about the Nazis in America, Churchill was doing the same in England, meeting with about as much success as Nick. Churchill liked the energetic American, and the common ideological ground they had shared in the past was a bond. Nor was Churchill oblivious to, or forgetful of, Nick's generous gift of a million dollars to the British government. Now Churchill asked Nick if he would address a joint meeting of the Admiralty and the Imperial General

Staff, giving his estimate, as an arms manufacturer, of the relative strength of the German and French armies. Nick had sold millions of dollars' worth of material to the French over the past three years and, being at the very heart of the arms business, was extremely well informed about the condition of *all* the major armies of the world. He gladly consented.

April gave way to one of the loveliest Mays in living memory, and the world waited tensely to see what the master of Germany would do next.

On May 10 the world found out. On the same day Winston Churchill replaced Neville Chamberlain as Prime Minister of Great Britain, German armies invaded Belgium, Holland and Luxembourg on their way to the French border.

The phony war was over, and the real war, which was to be the greatest bloodbath in human history, was on.

"Haven't I seen you someplace before?" the stockbroker asked the beautiful girl sitting next to him at the bar. She wore a tilted black hat and a silver-fox jacket over a smart black suit. She was on her second martini.

"Maybe."

"Wait a minute, you were on the cover of *Life!* You're the deb . . . Sylvia Fleming! Am I right?"

Sylvia gave the young man in the gray Glen-plaid suit a sultry look. "You win the jackpot."

"Hey . . . gee, this is fantastic! I've never met a cover girl before! What are you doing in a crummy bar like this?"

She smiled. "What are *you* doing in a crummy bar like this?"

"Trying to forget my wife."

"Well? I'm trying to forget my husband."

"Want to tell me about it?"

"What's to tell? He bores me. And he's a cheapskate. What's your wife like?"

"She's always complaining, always nagging me. 'Buy me this, Charlie,' 'Buy me that.' . . ."

"Charlie?" she interrupted. "Is that your name?"

"Yeah. Charles Wells."

She looked at him as she drained her martini. "I have a brother named Charlie," she said softly. "Charlie, my wicked brother." She smiled rather boozily at the young broker. "And I'm the wicked sister." She hiccoughed. "Charlie's over in England with the R.A.F. *My* Charlie, that is. My brother. My beautiful, wicked brother."

Charlie Wells saw the tears in her eyes and wondered if she was a crying drunk. She seemed so young, so innocent, he couldn't believe she'd be sitting in a near-empty Madison Avenue gin mill getting sloshed on martinis at two o'clock on a Wednesday afternoon. He wondered if she wanted to get laid. She certainly *looked* like she wanted to get laid.

"Can I buy you another drink?" he asked.

She laughed. "Oh, if I have another martoony I may get drunk and do something awful."

"Like what?"

"Who knows? Maybe go to bed with someone named Charlie."

She looked at him, but was seeing instead her naked brother stretching beside the pond in the woods near Thrax Hall. Her sin, their private secret. . . . Except, *was* it private now? Had her father guessed? Was that why he had hustled her into marrying Chester? The idea had haunted her for almost a year now, just as the shame— and the sexual thrill—of that one incestuous afternoon had haunted her for years. As the gin shimmied her brain cells, the tears rolled down her still-smooth cheeks. The hideous pain was that she had never enjoyed sex so much since. Even with Chester, who was good in bed and to whom she was magnetically attracted. It was maddening, but she wanted her brother again. And yet, she could never have him.

Charlie Wells was staring at her, hardly able to believe his luck. "We could go to the Biltmore," he whispered. "It's only two blocks away."

She smiled. "Charlie," she whispered. "Make love to me, Charlie. Make me happy again."

Charlie Wells, sweating with anticipation, signaled the barman for the check.

Like a mighty juggernaut, the German Army Group A, under the command of General Gerd von Rundstedt, rolled across the Meuse River into Belgium and northern France, the Fourth Army under Kluge attacking Dinant, Hermeton and Givet to the north while, to the south, the 19th Panzer Corps under Guderian attacked the French city of Sedan, where, exactly seventy years before, Louis Napoleon's Second Empire had met defeat before the superb Prussian Army of Moltke. What seems obvious in retrospect then took the French by surprise: namely that the German armies merely went around the Maginot Line, on which the defense-oriented French Army had placed most of its bets. Within four days, the battle of the Meuse was over, the French troops were in retreat, and the government in Paris was beginning to panic.

By May 16, when Churchill flew to Paris to assess the situation, the officials of the Foreign Ministry were already burning the state papers in a huge bonfire in the courtyard of the ornate palace on the Quai d'Orsay. The French Premier, Paul Reynaud, begged Churchill for more British planes to stem the German flood, while his mistress, the attractive and power-hungry Countess de Portes, was in their apartment on the Place du Palais-Bourbon busily packing suitcases for a quick getaway. Reynaud, a staunch anti-Nazi, was no defeatist; but his mistress, after years of maneuvering to attain supreme power in France, now, with maddening lack of consistency, was doing everything in her power to convince her lover to capitulate to the Germans.

Mme. de Portes wanted out—fast.

Within a few short weeks, Edwina had fallen more in love with Audley Place than she had ever been with any of her more lavish residences in America. It was simple, and yet to her it had everything (of course, "simple" was a relative term to Edwina: Audley Place had over twenty rooms). The Gallery, which was what she called the living room, was a seventy-foot room with a low, beamed ceiling and three brick fireplaces. In the sixteenth century, the Gallery had been a dairy barn. Now, two long oak tables, piled with books and back copies of *Country Life,* stretched down the center of the room, illuminated by lamps made out of large nineteenth-century Chinese vases. Around the room were comfortable sofas and chairs covered in cheerful chintzes, curtains of which also hung in front of the leaded windows. The other rooms in the house were less grand but equally comfortable: a paneled dining room that could seat twelve; a paneled library with double doors opening on to the garden; a billiard room, a flower room, butler's pantry, immense kitchen and four servants' rooms completed the ground floor. Upstairs, there was a master bedroom and bath, and four other bedrooms and baths, the bathrooms all installed by Edwina during the restoration of 1935.

The master bedroom was her favorite. She had had it painted in a faint heliotrope, filled it with delicately feminine French and Regency furniture, and hung on the walls handsome old prints. (She wondered if one reason she adored Audley Place was the absence of any modern art, which she loved much less than her husband did.) She and Nick were lying in the bed in each other's arms, having just made love, when the phone rang. Edwina kissed her husband's forehead, sat up, turned on the light and picked up the phone.

"Yes?"

The many windows in the room were open, and through them a cool June-night breeze fluttered the curtains as, outside, the silver shield of a full moon hung low in the heavens.

"Darling, it's for you. It's the Prime Minister. I'm impressed," she whispered, handing Nick the phone.

He sat up to take it. "Hello?"

"Nick, it's Winston," boomed the familiar voice. "Can you fly with me to France tomorrow? We're going to make a final stab at talking Reynaud into staying in the war. I've talked to President Roosevelt, and he's agreed to loan you to me. I want you to tell Reynaud that American industry can outproduce Germany, and that you can get the French enough weaponry to beat Jerry—if they'll just *hold out!* Lie to them; I don't care *what* you tell them—but we have to convince them to hang on! Will you come with us?"

Nick didn't hesitate. "Of course, sir."

"Good. Be at Hendon at ten-thirty in the morning. We'll fly from there to Tours. The French government's already fled Paris and they've commandeered a pride of châteaux on the Loire—by God, it's like the days of Francis I! We'll be lucky to find which château Reynaud's in. . . . He'll probably have that damned Hélène de Portes with him. . . . Maddening bitch of a woman! Well, see you tomorrow. Ten-thirty sharp!"

And he hung up.

"What did he want?" asked Edwina, pulling the heliotrope satin sheet up to cover her nakedness.

"I'm flying to France with him tomorrow. We're going to try to talk the French government into staying in the war."

Edwina remembered Fuhlsbuettel and the wreck of a husband who had returned to her six years before.

"There's no danger, is there?" she said. "I mean, I assume you'll be safe with Winston?"

"I certainly hope so. If Jerry catches Churchill, the war's over." He turned over on his side to go to sleep.

"I love you," he muttered sleepily, filling her with contentment tinged with anxiety.

He might be going with Winston, but still they were flying to France, a country in chaos.

The danger was there.

That "maddening bitch of a woman," the Countess de Portes, had been born the daughter of a wealthy contractor and shipping magnate in Marseilles named Rebuffel. Bright, attractive, energetic and ambitious, she married Count Jean de Portes, son of the Marquis de Portes and the Duchesse de Gadagne. The bridegroom promptly went to work for his new father-in-law. The Countess, bored by Marseilles, took off for Paris to conquer the capital. There she met Paul Reynaud, who was twice her age. When the Countess realized his political star was on the rise, she promptly became his mistress.

Ironically, another titled woman was the mistress of Reynaud's chief political rival, Edouard Daladier. The Marquise de Crussol, born Jeanne Beziers, was the daughter of a Nantes businessman who had made a fortune canning sardines. Jeanne married the Marquis de Crussol, a grandson of the Duchesse d'Uzès; he at one time had courted Hélène de Portes. Soon Parisian wits were referring to the upwardly mobile Marquise de Crussol as *"la sardine qui s'est crue sole"* (the sardine which took itself for a sole), a play on words in French, *"crue sole"* having the same pronunciation as her name. When she met Daladier, a widower of ten years, the politician was living in a gloomy apartment in the Rue Anatole-de-la-Forge with his sister and two sons. The Marquise became his mistress and introduced him to the fashionable salons of *tout*-Paris.

The two titled mistresses became rivals, conniving to further the political careers of their lovers with a vicious gusto that would have been amusing if France hadn't been sliding into the abyss. Both became mistresses of premiers of France, thus achieving their ambitions; but if their hope had been to emulate their illustrious predecessor, the Marquise de Pompadour, who virtually ruled France as mistress to the King for twenty years, they were to be severely disappointed: governments came and went too fast in prewar France. And Mme. de Portes was to have the misfortune of achieving power just as her lover, the Premier, was about to preside over the funeral of the French Republic.

No one could quite believe it was happening. France had fought valiantly in the previous war. The French Empire was second only to the British in size and importance. France was rich. The French

Army had its faults, but as Nick had reported to the English General Staff, its weaponry was equal to the German Army. And yet, in a few short weeks, the French Army was in flight before the Germans. By June 9, one day short of a month since the start of the German offensive, word reached Paris that there was nothing to stop the German Army's approach. Millions of French from the north who had already fled the Germans to Paris for safety, thinking the capital would never fall, were now forced to continue fleeing southward. They were joined by over four million Parisians, terrified at the thought of falling under German control. By June 10, eight million French were jamming the roads to the south, pillaging, fighting, and begging for food and water. This chaotic exodus was creating excruciating hardships for the terrified French people; conditions were made worse by the Luftwaffe, which sent occasional planes overhead to strafe the refugees with machine-gun bullets.

The roads were so jammed that at midnight on June 10, when the Premier of France climbed into an automobile with the lanky General Charles de Gaulle to transfer the government of France southward to the Loire Valley, it took them six hours to reach Orléans, only 160 miles away.

And this was the most important automobile in France.

CHAPTER 35

I$_T$ was a hot June day in the Biltmore Hotel, and an electric fan droned lazily on the dresser in Room 418, stirring the air over the two naked, sweaty bodies making love on the bed.

"Charlie, Charlie," moaned Sylvia Fleming Hill, her eyes closed tight, her head pushing back into the pillow as she reveled under the hairy, muscled flesh of Charlie Wells. It was two on a Wednesday afternoon, the fourth consecutive Wednesday they had met in the hotel. The temperature was ninety-three degrees, and the sweat poured off Charlie's body as he thrust in and out of her.

"Charlie, it's happening, it's happening. . . ."

"I'm coming," he panted. "Oh, Jesus . . ."

"Charlie, Charlie, I love you. Charlie, Charlie . . ."

"CHRIST!"

After the explosion, he collapsed beside her on the bed.

"It's almost too hot to fuck," he puffed.

"I love it sweaty," she purred. "It makes it more . . . I don't know, animallike. I think sex should be sort of dirty."

"Yeah, I know what you mean. It sort of surprises me to say it, but the dirtier the hornier. But right now, I think I need a shower."

He got off the bed and went into the bathroom. She heard the shower turn on, then heard him humming to himself as he got in. She liked this casual, almost anonymous sex. She knew little about him except that he lived somewhere in New Jersey, had a wife and two kids, and commuted to work in a midtown brokerage firm. That was all she wanted to know. He was her sex machine. When he made love to her, she thought of her brother Charlie and it was almost as good as that rapturous idyll by the pond at Thrax Hall so many years before.

She heard a key turn in the lock, and the door was opened by a fat man in a seersucker suit and a straw hat who was smoking a vile-smelling cigar. As she scrambled to pull the bedspread over her naked-ness, her husband appeared in the door.

"This your wife?" said the fat man with the cigar.

Chester was icy. "Yes."

335

"Look, lady, this is a respectable hotel. I'm the house detective, and if you come here again, I'll make sure you don't get a room—understand?"

Chester slipped him a ten-dollar bill. "I'll make sure she won't bother you again," he said.

"Thanks, Mr. Hill. Much obliged."

The detective bowed out, closing the door.

"Get dressed," Chester said. "I'm taking you home. And there'll be no more of this bullshit about coming into New York on Wednesdays to shop." He crossed to the bathroom. "I figured out what you were shopping for was men."

"You go to hell!" she yelled, throwing a pillow across the room at him. She missed.

Chester pulled a Ramschild .22 from his coat pocket, stepped into the bathroom, jerked open the shower curtain and aimed the gun at a terrified Charlie Wells.

"I . . . don't kill me," blubbered the stockbroker, whose hair was a mass of lather.

Chester reached in and turned off the water.

"Get out of there," he said.

"Who . . . who are you?"

"I'm the husband who works in a gun factory."

"You . . . you wouldn't . . . I didn't do anything. . . ."

The poor man was almost comical in his fear. Chester shoved him out of the bathroom into the bedroom.

"Get going," he ordered.

"Yes, yes . . . I'm going . . . just let me dry off and get some clothes on. . . . I'll be gone in a minute. . . . I didn't mean anything. . . ."

Chester gave him another shove.

"You're going like *that*."

"I can't! I'm naked!"

"That's your problem. *Go.*"

Chester, still aiming the gun, opened the door. Charlie Wells looked even more horrified at appearing naked in public.

"I *can't!*"

Chester grabbed his arm and practically flung him out the door. As Charlie stumbled down the hall to find a hiding place, Chester slammed the door and confronted his wife, who started laughing.

"Oh? So you think it's funny?" he snapped.

"No, but . . ." She tried to choke back her laughs. "Charlie . . .

all covered with suds on Madison Avenue. . . . Oh, my God . . ."
She gave way to uncontrolled howls. Chester came over to the bed
and slapped her, hard.

"You *bastard!*" she yelled.

"You slut. Get dressed. I'm taking you home."

"No! I don't want to go back! I'm happy here!"

"Being a slut?"

"Yes, being a slut!"

He slapped her again. She burst into tears.

"Get dressed," he repeated.

"I want my daddy," she sobbed.

"You'll have to settle for me."

"Oh, Chester." She looked up, her eyes streaming. "I want to be
happy with you, but I'm so goddamned *bored* in Old Lyme . . . can't
you understand? Can't you try to understand me a *little?* There's
nothing for me there—nothing!"

"There's me."

"It's not enough!"

He watched her a moment, fuming, telling himself not to explode.

She's right, dammit, he thought. I'm not enough. I've got to give
her kids—that'll tie her down. And a house. Shit, I wish her old man
hadn't been so damned sanctimonious and loaned me some money.

If *only* I had some money. . . .

There were many reasons Churchill invited Nick to accompany him
to France, not the least being that he liked and admired him. He also
knew that Nick, at considerable personal risk, was defying the American Neutrality Laws, which proscribed American manufacturers selling weapons to any of the belligerents in the European war. Nick was
shipping via Canada thousands of tons of ammunition, thousands of
rifles, artillery and antiaircraft guns to England, which the beleaguered
island desperately needed. Churchill knew Roosevelt was about to
rescind the arms embargo, but this didn't lessen Nick's personal risk
in defying it.

But most important, Churchill realized listening to Nick at the
meeting of the Imperial General Staff that the arms titan had a detailed knowledge of the world's armies far superior to anything
Churchill had ever received from England's intelligence sources.
Churchill was getting a daily report from his Washington Embassy
of arms movements in America, but he valued Nick's knowledge as
highly. And the idea had occurred to him that Nick's forceful Ameri-

can presence might stiffen the spines of the wilting French leaders.

Thus, the next morning at ten-thirty, Nick joined the Prime Minister, the Foreign Secretary, Lord Halifax, Lord Beaverbrook and a number of other high-ranking officials to climb aboard the two twin-engined Flamingos for the flight to France. It was a beautiful morning, though bad weather was forecast later on.

The plane landed at Tours at 2 P.M. to find the recently bombed airport almost deserted. To Nick, it was a scene out of *Alice in Wonderland:* the Prime Minister of Great Britain having to hitch a ride to meet the Premier of France. But then it seemed all of France was something out of *Alice.* Certainly its government was. After fleeing Paris on the night of June 10–11, government officials had inched southward in cars and trucks, making their way as best they could through the hundreds of thousands of refugees until they reached Orléans. There, they scattered to various châteaux south of the river from Briare on the east to Tours on the west.

The châteaux were undeniably charming, but they were woefully ill equipped to house the twentieth-century government of France in a time of national crisis. The plumbing was, if adequate at all, adequate for a single family, not a ministry. Worse were the communications. There was at best one telephone per château and the telephone system was antediluvian and unreliable even under ideal conditions. No one had thought of—or had time to—string extra lines, and the local operators were still taking two hours off for lunch. The result was chaos. The President of France, housed in the impressive Château de Cangé, was entirely isolated and knew virtually nothing of what was going on with the government of which he was head.

It took Churchill's car two hours to get from Tours airport to the Château de Chissay, situated above the River Cher near Tours, because of the congestion on the roads. It was at the Château de Chissay that the Premier of France, Paul Reynaud, had installed himself with his aides and his mistress. As Churchill's car pulled up, a curious scene was taking place. The courtyard of the château was jammed with trucks and cars trying to find parking space at what had now become the center of the French government. Standing on the front terrace was a short woman in her thirties with curly brown hair and an oversized mouth smeared with garish lipstick. She wore a red silk kimono over white pajamas and was gesticulating and bellowing at the truck drivers, telling them in excited French where to park.

"There she is!" guffawed Churchill. "The power behind the throne of France: *Mme. la Comtesse de Portes elle-même!*"

It was certainly a bizarre sight. As the British delegation piled out of its commandeered staff car, Mme. de Portes started yelling at them until she recognized Churchill. Then, with a startled look on her face, she disappeared inside the château.

"She not only runs the government," said Nick, "it looks as if she's got the parking concession too."

He made Churchill smile.

Inside the château, all was confusion as officers, diplomats, aides and secretaries milled about the high-ceilinged rooms trying to determine where they were supposed to be, what they were supposed to do, and getting very little information on either point. Others just stood around, staring listlessly out tall windows, smoking Gauloise after Gauloise. No one seemed aware of the presence of the English delegation until the Premier himself, presumably alerted by his mistress, hurried out of the main salon to greet his ally. After introductions were made, Churchill, Beaverbrook and Halifax retired with Reynaud.

"Wait out here," Churchill whispered to Nick. "I'll call you in when I need you. And remember, lie if you must, but we *have* to keep France in the war!"

An hour passed. Then one of the aides, Colonel Forbes-Taylor, came out of the room and said to Nick, "We're getting nowhere. Reynaud keeps saying the only way he'll stay in the war is if we send him more planes. The P.M. says for you to take a walk in the garden. It'll be at least an hour before he needs you."

"Right."

Nick wandered out the rear doors to take a stroll through the rather uninspired garden, which was dotted with puddles after a recent rain. At first, he thought he was alone, until he turned into an *allée* of chestnut trees and saw a French officer sitting on a bench, smoking a cigarette. Nick had noticed him earlier inside. He was a captain, about thirty, a tall man with a thin black moustache, thick black hair under his kepi, very white skin and burning brown eyes. Nick remembered having thought the man seemed upset. Now, as Nick came up to him, he noticed him almost surreptitiously wiping his eyes, as if trying to conceal the fact that he was crying.

Nick addressed him in French. "Good afternoon. It looks as if you and I are the only people around here who know what to do—which is nothing."

The Captain looked up. "You are American, no?" he said in heavily accented English. "The arms king, Monsieur Fleming?"

"That's right. I came over with Mr. Churchill to try to talk your government into staying in the war."

The Captain threw his cigarette to the ground. "You are wasting your time. These people"—he gestured angrily at the château—"they are quitters! They don't want to fight; they want to get out and save their necks! It makes me sick to my stomach. Why do you think I come out here and cry like a boy? Because I see my country sold—no, not even sold! Given away by this bunch of *poltrons,* these cowards! *Merde, alors.* Oh, well, I suppose no one gives a damn. It's just *France,* the most beautiful, the most civilized country in Europe. Maybe we're *too* civilized. I don't know. Too civilized to fight."

The man's honest shame and rage moved Nick. "What can be done?" he asked.

The Captain shrugged. "I don't know, but you don't give up and run. The Boches are good fighters, but they're not supermen. We are good fighters too, but the generals and the politicians . . ." He made a face. "They're all—how you say it?—shit."

"What are you going to do?"

"Try to go to London. Other friends of mine are there already. Maybe we can fight back from England or join the English Army. We can do *something.*"

Nick removed a card from his wallet and handed it to him.

"If you make it to London, look me up. Maybe I can help. I've got a score to settle with the Nazis myself. I'm staying at Claridge's."

The Captain looked at the card, then stood up to shake Nick's hand. "My name is René Reynaud," he said.

"Reynaud? Are you . . ."

"The Premier is my uncle," said the Captain, nodding toward the château. "He's the bastard who's giving away France. Now you see why I cry, my friend?"

And he lit another cigarette.

Nick had his chance to speak to the French officials shortly after six that evening, and he made an impassioned plea to them to stay in the war, citing impressive statistics to prove that America could keep the French Army in sufficient weapons to continue the struggle. But even though he thought he had spoken well, it was useless.

Whatever dim hopes Churchill had had of bolstering his French allies were quickly dashed. Defeatism had drenched the generals and politicians of France like the heavy rains of Normandy. The next day the delegation flew back to London. Nick said nothing, because the mood of his English colleagues was so savagely gloomy. Churchill sat huddled in his seat, smoking his ubiquitous cigar. He didn't need to say anything. Everyone knew. Now that France was out of the war, England stood alone.

After the plane landed, the delegation disembarked. Before getting into his official car, Churchill turned to Nick and shook his hand.

"I want to thank you for what you did for us," he said.

"I only wish I'd been more effective," he replied.

"None of us had a chance, but you spoke well, and you spoke from your heart. I appreciate it. How would you like to be a general?"

"I beg your pardon?"

The Prime Minister grinned. "I'm going to recommend to Franklin that he give you a temporary commission in the American Army and keep you posted here as an attaché. I want you around, and a man's going to look like a spy or a pacifist in London if he's not in uniform. Besides, you'd look good in uniform. You won't mind if I recommend it?"

Nick was stunned. "I suppose not. . . ."

"Good. You'll like being a general. It's a damned sight more fun than being a private. Safer too."

He climbed into his car, still chewing his cigar, and was driven away to No. 10 Downing Street.

CHAPTER 36

Roosevelt was leery of the inevitable publicity if he made Nick Fleming—one of the most hated men in America—a general. But he figured he could make him a colonel without causing too much uproar. Roosevelt was aware of the value of Nick's almost daily reports to him. It was without a doubt England's darkest hour. With France out of the war and Italy now in it as Germany's ally, few neutrals gave England a chance to withstand the German invasion almost everyone assumed was inevitable. The reports the President was getting from his ambassador, Joe Kennedy, were increasingly pessimistic. Roosevelt wanted to help the English, but his hands were virtually tied, at least until the presidential election was over the following November. Thus, he was glad to read Nick's cables, which, unlike Kennedy's, praised the English for their unity and determination while at the same time not minimizing the danger confronting them.

Nick knew Churchill was banking on American help and Nick did everything he could in his dispatches to urge the President to come to the aid of the English, reminding him that if Germany came to dominate England through a Vichy-like pro-Nazi government in London, the United States would confront the world power of Adolf Hitler alone. And if Hitler got his hands on the British fleet—as he was trying to do with the French fleet—America would be extraordinarily vulnerable. "For us not to send arms and assistance to England," he cabled, "is like a man refusing to lend a fire extinguisher to a next-door neighbor downwind whose house is on fire."

The harsh fact was that, aside from good wishes and moral support, America had done practically nothing to help England, and the war was almost a year old. Finally, in the middle of August, as Luftwaffe bombers began to attack England, Roosevelt authorized a shipment to England of World War I rifles. It at least was a beginning, and Nick liked to think his cables had helped influence the President.

Nick did not exaggerate in his reports: the unity of the English was remarkable, near miraculous when compared with the apathy, the appeasement of the prewar years, which had led Hitler to write the English off as effete. Now the island was experiencing in its darkest hour what Churchill called its finest hour, and the excitement and defiance were contagious. Nick was not English, but he felt it. Edwina and her family not only felt it but were moved to action. Lord and Lady Saxmundham loaned Thrax Hall to the government for the duration to use as it saw fit. Since the bombing raids on London and other cities were intensifying, it was decided to turn the eighty-room mansion into a home for children orphaned by the bombs.

Edwina, the former silent-movie vamp and fashion plate, volunteered to work at Thrax Hall in whatever capacity the government chose.

The Spitfire, with "Sylvia" lettered on its fuselage, barreled off the runway at Harwell Airport near Oxford. With its throttle full out it climbed through two layers of clouds to ten thousand feet.

Flying Officer Charles Fleming, R.A.F., had been told by Control that he should find a Jerry bomber cruising somewhere over the southeast coast of England at about that ceiling. In two months on active duty, Charles had already made a name for himself as an ace with six kills to his credit. Now, as he leveled off and looked down at the enormous expanse of white clouds below him covering most of the east of England and the Channel, Charles keenly anticipated his seventh kill.

His colleagues in the R.A.F.—they could hardly be called "friends," much less "buddies"—had nicknamed Charles "Killer." They admired his cool, ruthless nerve as much as they disliked his conceit, enjoyed his openhanded way with money as they envied his wealth, laughed at his braggadocio with women as they cursed his amatory conquests. None of the English liked Killer Fleming, but they all admitted he was a "bloody character." He was also a stuck-up son of a bitch, but during wartime you took what you could get.

After ten minutes, Charles spotted a break in the clouds. He peeled off, headed for the break and winged through it. His radio sputtered.

"Look lively," warned Control. "Jerry knows you're up there."

Just then, Charles spotted a speck. He straightened the Spitfire out and took another long look. It was a Junkers 88, the two-engined medium bomber for which he was hunting.

"I've got him, and I'm closing," said Charles to Control.

His adrenaline pumped as the chase began. The sky became a battlefield, with flaming death the stakes. But Charles had trained himself never to think of *his* death. He only thought of *their* deaths, of killing. Charles loved the game.

At eight hundred yards, the Junkers' upper-turret guns opened up. Charles continued closing. At six hundred yards, he gave the Junker his first burst of fire. The bomber was firing at him from every port except the upper-turret guns, and Charles assumed his first burst had killed the gunner.

Another burst and the bomber's starboard engine exploded into flames. Jerry went into a spin. Charles, now as close as fifty yards from the bomber, kept firing, raking the fuselage with bullets. Both planes were diving now, both spinning, flying almost in formation in a dance of death as they hurtled through the second cloud layer. Charles, so intent on firing at the Junkers, suddenly saw the waters of the English Channel less than one hundred feet ahead of him. Panicking, he kicked the rudder and prayed. He was going so fast he knew it would be close.

The Spitfire shuddered as it came out of the dive. Charles's eyes bulged as he saw how close the water was—he figured twenty feet. Then he started climbing again, heading for the white cliffs of Dover. Off to his port, he saw the Junkers 88 crash into the water.

Charles had his seventh kill.

The R.A.F. rules for reporting enemy casualties were:

1. The enemy pilot must be seen to abandon his plane in the air.
2. Or the aircraft must have been seen to strike the ground or the water.
3. Or the plane must have been shot to pieces in the air.

Charles's kill qualified under Rule 2.

But three of the kills he had reported were only "probables."

Charles Fleming lied.

Charles Fleming lied about a lot of things in life, but there was one indisputable truth about him: he loved the war, he loved the excitement of it, the danger and the thrills. And he loved the fact that Ramschild arms—his weapons, as he thought of them—were playing such a conspicuous role in the war. Never mind the fact that many of his fellow pilots—American and English—ragged and in some cases attacked him for being the son of Nick Fleming, the "Titan of Death." He didn't mind being "Son of Titan," as someone had dubbed

344

him. Someday Ramschild would be *his.* Someday *he* would hobnob with generals and admirals and presidents and prime ministers, just as his father did.

But meanwhile, Charles was—as he wrote on the postcards he sent his sisters back in the States—"having a wonderful time."

Fiona Fleming had told none of her siblings the secret of her real father, Rod Norman, for almost a year. But by that time, she had become so intrigued with him—had amassed such a vast collection of old fan-magazine articles and photographs of her glamorous father— that she couldn't resist sharing the secret with her younger sister and best friend, Vicky. Vicky was initially amazed that *her* best friend, Fiona, was a half sister instead of a full one, but such was the strength of their bond, it made no difference, and in fact Vicky quickly came to share Fiona's obsession with the murdered silent-screen star.

Of course, Rod's mysterious death was the subject of endless speculation between the two girls, as was Edwina's infidelity to Nick—an infidelity that Fiona had not quite understood at the time her mother confessed it to her, but which, as she learned the facts of life, assumed a shocking clarity. Curiously, neither of the girls held it against their mother: the "illicit" romance that had produced Fiona only added a further sheen of glamour to Edwina, who was already glamorous to her children.

But Rod's murder had to have an explanation, and finally Vicky convinced Fiona she had to ask her father about it. If *anyone* knew, it was he. And it was in this way that Nick found out Edwina had told Fiona.

His first reaction was outrage. But when he saw that, far from being psychologically disturbed by the truth of her parentage, Fiona was truly fascinated by Rod Norman, he accepted the situation. As to the murder, he would only tell the girls that he believed the murderer had meant to kill him instead, which merely tantalized them all the more.

But the chief result of Fiona's Rod Norman cult was that she realized she had greasepaint in her blood from her father as well as her mother, and, clearly, her destiny was to become an actress. Certainly her looks were no drawback. All the Fleming children were beautiful, but Fiona's beauty had a smoldering quality that hinted at potential stardom. Now seventeen, she tried out for a school production of

Romeo and Juliet at Miss Porter's. She won the role of Juliet and broke the audience's heart.

Vicky, fourteen, was also at Miss Porter's. She was a pretty, cheerful, uncomplicated girl whose main enthusiasm was for horses. Unlike the elder Fleming children, Charles and Sylvia, who were developing some unpleasant characteristics, the two young Fleming girls were liked by everyone.

Nick adored them.

CHAPTER 37

C HURCHILL was right. Nick would have looked out of place in civilian clothes, for by September, with the beginning of the heavy bombardments of London and other cities that quickly became known as the Blitz, hardly a man was not in a uniform of one sort or another, and many women were as well, so Nick felt more comfortable in his uniform of an American colonel. Other changes he observed in London were:

The clubs had waitresses instead of waiters.

Most people carried gas masks and everyone had to have identification and ration cards.

In restaurants, one was served a single lump of sugar, a thin flake of butter, and few cheeses.

Since paper was in short supply, the newspapers had only six pages.

Iron railings were being torn down for scrap.

Lights were cut off or shaded after dusk on pain of heavy fines or a month's imprisonment.

Barrage balloons hovered over the city; the parks were strewn with barbed wire to prevent enemy parachutists from landing; there were pillboxes at road junctions and concrete barriers at intervals.

No radios were allowed in cars.

And yet life went on in the city with a defiant insouciance that would have enraged Hitler, who expected the British to be begging for peace on any terms. The hotels were jammed at lunch and the few theaters open played to capacity houses. Nick found it as incredible as it was inspiring. He was in love with London, thrilled to be in a city where he was liked and admired rather than New York, where he was constantly cudgeled by the press.

He had been "adopted" by many of the high-ranking officers on the General Staff, and it was at a cocktail party, given by a certain General Haddington-Smythe at his flat in Belgrave Square, not far from Lord Saxmundham's town house, that he met her.

The flat was jammed with men and women in uniform, all smoking and drinking, so the air was practically unbreathable, when the air-raid sirens went off. With the calm indifference of people grown used to—and bored by—the almost nightly raids, the guests filed out in orderly fashion, many taking their drinks with them, and went to the nearest tube-station air-raid shelter, where they resumed their interrupted conversations. Nick had noticed her at the party: an extremely attractive woman, perhaps twenty-five, in the trim uniform of a sergeant in the Women's Auxiliary Air Force. She had brown hair, blue eyes and a lovely pink complexion, and was at least five feet eight and slender. Her face was animated and intelligent. As the bombs and the ack-ack guns boomed above, Nick made his way through the crowd to her side.

"Mind if a lonely American sits out this air raid with you?" he asked.

"Not at all. You were at the party, weren't you?"

"That's right. My name's Nick Fleming."

Her eyes widened. "Not *the* Nick Fleming?" she said. "The arms tycoon?"

"My reputation precedes me."

"But this is terribly exciting. I've never met an American millionaire before. Is it lovely being so rich?"

He laughed at her frankness. "Not at tax time."

"Oh, but I should think it would be great fun for a day, anyway. My conscience wouldn't allow me to enjoy it for more than that. But on that one day I'd go into Harrods and buy everything in sight. Then I'd go to Fortnum's and buy all their chocolate and eat it till I blew up."

"I take it you like chocolate?"

"*Mad* for it. It's a wonder I'm not fat as a pig, and covered with spots. My name's Margaret Kingsley, by the way. I'm secretary to Major General Farnley at the War Office."

"Yes, I've met him. Seems nice."

"He's a sweetie, but he smokes too much. Put him in his grave, I tell him, which he doesn't like to hear."

"I can imagine. When this raid's over, I don't suppose you'd like to have dinner with me at Claridge's?"

Her expression cooled slightly. "Oh, dear," she sighed. "You Americans are so predatory. Just like in your films. I think you should know, Mr. Fleming, that I am very happily married, and my husband's a lieutenant in the Royal Navy, and I'm not about to upset his morale by being seen in expensive restaurants with a dashing American millionaire. So thank you, Mr. Fleming, but I have some leftover kidney pie in my flat, which will do very nicely—even without steak."

"I wasn't being predatory. I'm happily married too. I just"—he shrugged—"was feeling lonely."

There was a tremendous explosion over their heads. The lights in the station dimmed a moment, and some dust fell from the ceiling. Margaret, suddenly pale, looked up.

"That one nearly dropped right down the tube stairs," she muttered. "It would be nasty to think Jerry's getting *good* at this game."

"I like kidney pie," he prompted. "Even without steak."

She looked at him with a fleeting nervousness. "Seriously, you're not trying to start . . . something?" she asked.

He smiled. "Maybe a friendship."

She hesitated, looking into his eyes. "My flat's a mess," she said. "And even when it's clean, it's no prize. I won't have you snooting down your millionaire's nose at me, mind. And I hope you're not allergic to cats. I won't be putting Maybelle out for anyone, much less an arms tycoon."

"Do you hold it against me that I'm rich?"

She laughed. "Well, of course I do! I'm a bloody Socialist."

He looked surprised. "Oh. Well then, maybe . . ."

"Oh, no, you don't," she interrupted. "You can't back out *now*. I'm going to drag you to my dreary working-class flat, give you a bloody-awful working-class meal and bore you silly about the evils of capitalism."

Good God, what have I gotten into? he thought.

It had never occurred to Nick Fleming that Socialists could be sexy.

She lived in Earl's Court, and her flat was neither dreary nor working class. It was on the second floor of a red-brick building put up, Nick guessed, in the 1880s, and over the front door was carved, in heavy Victorian letters, "Chatham Mansions." After she had pulled down the blackout blinds she turned on a lamp, revealing a high-ceilinged room Lady Mendl would have scorned but which was, in its way, cheerful and cozy.

"There's my Maybelle!" she cooed as a large, sinister-looking black cat meowed loudly, scampered across the room and leaped into her waiting arms. "Isn't she beautiful? You'd best be nice to her. If Maybelle doesn't like you, she can cast a spell on you. Maybelle, this is Mr. Fleming. Say hello."

Maybelle meowed.

Nick was looking around the room, which was filled with ancient middle-class furniture, including a sagging plush sofa piled with magazines and books. The walls were covered with a cheerful, cheap rose wallpaper, badly soiled. At one side of the room stood a battered upright piano, its top piled with scores. There was also a framed photo of a handsome young man in naval uniform.

"That's my Johnnie," she said, letting the cat out of her arms. "Isn't he absolutely breathtaking? I met him last year at the London School of Economics in a course on trade-union history and fell madly in love. He's on a destroyer now, though I'm not supposed to say where."

"How long have you been married?"

"Two months," she said casually. "As you can see, I'm a hopeless housekeeper. My father was a vicar in Lincolnshire, compulsively neat like my mother, and I grew up in a vicarage where there wasn't even a pin out of place. This ghastly, slovenly mess is my rebellion. That, and Socialism. Would you like a drink? I have some Italian red wine that will dissolve your intestines."

"Sounds good."

He watched her as she went into the tiny kitchen. One drink and I'll get out of here, he thought. She's gorgeous, but as wacky as this flat.

She returned with the bottle and two wineglasses.

"Wasn't that a lovely party?" she said, pouring the wine. "And of course, Adolf had to ruin it with his damned bombers. Can you beat the cheek of the Nazis? Cheers." She held up her glass, took a sip and made a face. "God, it's bloody awful. Tastes like sheep-dip." She flopped into a frayed, overstuffed chair. "Where's your wife?"

"In the country. Her parents have lent their home to the government and Edwina's helping take care of the children. They're kids orphaned by the Blitz."

"Well, that's a nice thing for her to do. But we all have to pitch in." She hesitated. "I looked at the kidney pie. It's looking a trifle . . . well, elderly. I don't even think I'd feed it to Maybelle. Can you forgive me?"

Thank God, he thought.

"Of course. I'll eat at the hotel."

"I can make us an omelet! I really *do* make good omelets."

"No, really—I'll just finish the wine and go back to the hotel."

She laughed as she got out of the chair.

"You poor man—I drag you all the way to Earl's Court and then no dinner. I'll cook the omelet in a jiffy . . . and since I'm being such a rotten hostess, I won't say one word about capitalism."

"There's hope for the evening yet."

"You can set the table. Just toss all that rubbish on the sofa." She indicated a round wooden table in front of the blacked-out windows, then went into the kitchen.

Nick picked up the magazines from the table, noting that they were mostly about the music world. "Are you interested in music?" he called as he dumped them on the sofa.

"*Mad* for it. When I was a girl, I dreamed of being a concert pianist. Playing great, crashing concertos at the Albert Hall, thunderous applause, and all that wonderful romantic nonsense."

"What happened?"

She appeared at the kitchen door with two white china plates. "It turned out I have a *terrible* memory. I mean, really terrible. I play for people and go positively blank. So goodbye to the concert stage. Here's some plates."

The omelet was excellent, properly *baveuse,* and throughout the meal she chattered cheerfully and interestingly, asking him questions about America. He decided she had a first-class magpie mind, interested in a vast range of subjects, and was a true bohemian in that what were high in the priorities of most women—marriage, housekeeping, etc.—were low in hers. He really had never met any woman quite like her, and he found he was enjoying himself despite his trepidations.

When they had finished the omelet and the wine, he said, "Play me something."

"Do you like music?"

"I don't know much about good music, but I'd love to hear you play."

She hesitated, then got up and went to the upright. "It'll have to be something soft. Mrs. Clark, my landlady, lives downstairs and she doesn't like music after nine. I know, the thirteenth Mazurka. It really is one of the most romantic things Chopin ever wrote, and it's as beautiful as the Nocturnes, which get played to death."

She took one of the scores from the top of the piano, opened it on the music rack, then sat down on the bench. She rubbed her fingers for a moment, then began playing. The soft opening chords were moonbeams. Then the melody, so astringently elegant, with its lovely arabesques like gossamer cobwebs, washed his eardrums with magic. He was enchanted. Halfway through the short piece, he got up from the table and silently moved to the side of the piano to watch her. Her face was transformed, her concentration in the music having

351

dispelled all the cheerful eccentricity of her personality, leaving nothing but poetry on her exquisite features.

As she finished the Mazurka, its final *perdendosi* chords losing themselves in silence like tiny diamonds sinking into black water, she was still for a few moments. Then she looked up at him. Like the violinist in the perfume ad, he wanted to lift her off the piano bench into his arms in a passionate embrace. Moreover, he had the feeling she wanted the same thing.

"You'd better go now," she said quietly. "Music does odd things to me. I don't want to do something I'll regret in the morning."

It was then the air-raid sirens went off.

"Blast!" she groaned. "Two raids in one night? Doesn't Hitler realize he's a bloody bore?"

She was getting up from the piano bench when the bomb exploded across the street. Chatham Mansions rocked as the glass in her windows shattered. She screamed.

"Get down!" he yelled, grabbing her and throwing her to the floor. Another bomb exploded in the street. The lights went out.

"We're going to be hit!" she screamed. "We're going to be killed! Oh, my God—"

He hugged her to him, covering her with his body, half expecting the flat to go up in explosive death. The blackout blinds had been torn off their rollers by the blast, and he could see the building across the street blazing like an inferno, a direct hit. Now fire-engine and ambulance sirens could be heard, along with the thunder of the bombs, twentieth-century music blotting out Chopin's Mazurka. She was trembling with fear, and he could feel her hot breath on his cheek. He kissed her mouth. She responded, fear dissolving into desire. For almost a minute they lay in each other's arms on the floor, kissing hotly as the light of the flames from across the street licked angrily at the cheap rose wallpaper.

Then she pushed him away, sitting up and straightening her hair.

"This is obscene," she said. "We can't make love during an air raid."

"Why not?"

"It doesn't seem . . . I don't know . . . patriotic."

"We'll do it for England. Come on . . . where's the bedroom?"

He got to his feet and took her hand. She looked sheepish for a moment, then stood up.

"Well, you *can't* go out during an air raid, can you?" she said, and she led him across the room to the door opposite the kitchen, opened it and went inside. The single window of the small bedroom had also been shattered by the blast, and the light of the fire across the street revealed a room so littered with clothes that a bomb might have gone off inside as well. Silently, they took off their uniforms. Then, naked, they looked at each other. The light of the flames licked the skin of her tall, slim body, illuminating two surprisingly large breasts. He came to her and took her in his arms, rubbing his strong hands over her back.

"It's properly Wagnerian, isn't it?" she whispered. "Bombs, Valhalla going up in flames . . . it's really rather exciting."

"*You're* exciting," he whispered as he eased her down on the unmade bed.

"I forgot to feed Maybelle."

"To hell with Maybelle."

"She'll put a curse on you. She's got magic powers."

"So do you," he whispered. "You've bewitched me."

And he began kissing her breasts.

CHAPTER 38

PETER Chadwick was ten years old. Peter's father had been a long-shoreman working London's East End docks. Peter and his family had lived in a three-room slum flat in the East End, not far from the Prospect of Whitby Pub where, three centuries earlier, Samuel Pepys had quaffed ale before going home to write his diary. On the night of September 20, 1940, Peter's mother, father and two younger sisters had been killed when their building had taken a direct hit during one of Goering's most devastating air raids. Peter had escaped only because he had been outside in the privy when the bomb hit. Orphaned and penniless at ten, he had been sent by the government to wait out the war at Thrax Hall.

Of all the forty-three orphans at Thrax Hall, Peter Chadwick had touched Edwina most. All of them were sad, of course, but somehow Peter's wan, angelic face melted Edwina's heart. Using her own money, she had bought all the toys she could get her hands on for the children, converting the billiard room into a playroom. When she found out Peter had a passion for balloons, she bought him a huge red one. He was so delighted with it that for the first time since he had been delivered to Thrax Hall she saw his face light up in a smile of pure joy, and the experience gave her one of the greatest pleasures of her life. The former silent-movie queen had finally found herself. Gone were restlessness and boredom and her sense of rebellion. The war, which was bringing out the worst in so many people, was bringing out the best in so many others, and Edwina belonged to the latter category. She felt useful and needed, and she threw all her considerable energies into making the lives of her forty-three charges as happy as possible under the circumstances.

Without officially being appointed by the government, she had taken over the direction of Thrax Hall: there was simply no one else available. She hired a dietitian, placed all the orders for food and supply, supervised the housing of the children in the dozens of rooms in the magnificent eighteenth-century mansion, organized a daily schedule, arranged for local, mostly retired schoolmasters to give lessons, taught one class herself, organized play periods and picnics and horseback rides—in short, she became Mum to forty-three kids. It was exhausting, but she loved it. She ate most of her meals with the children, tucked them in at night, often told them bedtime stories, then, at ten, would bicycle the three miles to her home at Audley Place where she would collapse into bed, setting the alarm for six the next morning. Her only "normal" life was on weekends, when Nick would come out from London. Even then, she spent several hours each day at Thrax Hall.

Nick never failed to bring her a present from London: a hat, or a new book, or a tin of caviar he had bought from the management of Claridge's—while staples like butter, sugar and coffee were in short supply, there was an astonishing wealth of luxury items available in wartime London. He brought them because he loved her and was proud of her, not because of any guilt over his new liaison with Margaret Kingsley, which, with Nick's convenient domestic morality, he considered a legitimate release from the stress of the Blitz. If Edwina suspected, she chose to ignore it. By now, Edwina had accepted Nick's one-way morality as a fact of life. She loved him despite it, and was so happy to see him on weekends she wasn't about to spoil things with a fight she knew she was doomed to lose anyway.

On the third weekend of October, Nick brought her a different present: her son. Charles had been given a three-day pass, had dined with his father at Claridge's, and with his father had driven out to Audley Place. Nick had mixed feelings about his son and heir. He was understandably proud of Charles's record as a war ace. But the memory of that night in the New York apartment still rankled. A hundred times since then he had asked himself if his suspicions had been right or wrong. Either way, the father lost, because if there *had* been an incestuous relationship between Charles and Sylvia, then two of his children were guilty of what Nick considered a heinous crime. If there *hadn't* been, then Nick had disrupted both of their lives needlessly, and while Charles seemed to have loved Oxford, Nick was well aware that Sylvia's marriage to Chester Hill was far from ideal. The problem was that Nick didn't dare probe for the truth for fear of finding it; and he often wondered if he was destined never to know it.

Charles, dashing in his R.A.F. uniform, was full of war stories. A born raconteur, with the added spice of little interest in unadorned facts, he regaled his mother and father with stories of his squadron and his heroic battles in the sky. With the exuberance of youth, he babbled through the cocktail hour, hardly letting either Nick or Edwina get a word in edgewise. Then, as they went into the dining room for dinner, he segued from war stories to his love life, which Charles was never modest about.

As Mrs. Dabney served her excellent soup made from vegetables grown in the garden, Charles launched into the seduction of his second barmaid.

"Charles, *really,"* said Edwina, half amused. "I'm sure you're God's gift to women, but can't we be spared the graphic details?"

"Oh, but, Mother, wait, you haven't heard the best yet." He smiled down the table at Nick. "Father will get a kick out of this one. I've got a girl friend in London too. She's a sergeant in the W.A.A.F.'s and is a smashing brunette. Her husband's off in the Navy, but that doesn't stop her from having fun. She's got a flat in Earl's Court."

Nick almost choked on his soup.

"She works at the War Office for Major General Farnley, and her name's Margaret Kingsley. Ever run into her, Father?" He smiled.

Nick stared at him. The son of a bitch *knows!* he thought.

"Afraid not" was all he said.

"Father, could you lend me a thousand quid?" Charles asked an hour later as he strolled into the library with a cigar and brandy. "We've got a pretty hot poker game going at the barracks, and I'm afraid my luck's not been too good lately. I've run up some debts I'd like to pay off."

Nick and Edwina, who were drinking coffee, exchanged looks. Then Edwina turned to her son.

"Darling, do you think it's a good idea to be gambling for such high stakes?"

"Oh, come on, Mom, we're under a lot of pressure! Poker takes our minds off the war, and God knows we could use some escape."

"I know, but still, a thousand pounds! That's five thousand dollars, which is a lot of money to lose at cards. And I'm sure there are a lot of those boys who can't afford losses like that."

"That's their problem. *I* can afford it. Or at least Father can. Everyone knows Ramschild's coining money out of this war—right, Father? Your dividends must look like Fort Knox."

Nick gave his smiling son an icy stare.

"I'm making money, yes," he said evenly.

"Well, then, certainly you wouldn't begrudge me a thousand pounds play money? Let's say that's about one hundred fifty quid for each of

356

the Jerry planes I've shot down, which seems cheap enough." He laughed as he warmed his brandy.

"I'll let you men discuss this," said Edwina, getting up from the sofa. "I'm exhausted. Good night, darling," she said, kissing her son's cheek. "We're terribly proud of you, but I really don't think you should use your war record as a bargaining point with your father. It doesn't seem quite . . . proper."

"Oh, it's just a game, Mother." He laughed. "The whole war's a game, as far as that goes."

"It's not a game to my children at Thrax Hall," she said coolly. Then she left the room.

"Mom's doing a terrific job with those kids, isn't she?" said Charles when she had gone. He sat down in a chair, swirling his brandy. "I'm really proud of her, aren't you, Father? Of course, you're doing some pretty terrific stuff too. In London, I mean. Margaret told me you practically saved her life the night the building across the street from her flat got blitzed."

"Are you trying to blackmail me?" asked Nick quietly.

"Oh, come on, Father, blackmail's such an ugly word." Charles smiled. "I'm your son. I wouldn't blackmail my own father—why should I? I just think it's an amusing coincidence we've ended up with the same girl friend." He drew on his cigar.

"Why didn't Margaret tell me?" Nick said.

"She didn't know we were related. She was just telling me how she'd run into this very romantic arms tycoon when I said, 'Hey! That's my old man!' She about fainted. Margaret's a nice girl. I guess she goes for the Fleming style." And he chuckled. "Anyway, don't worry. I can be discreet. And I admire you—you've got terrific taste in women. I only hope when I'm your age I can wow the girls the way you do. Of course, Mother might not share that opinion." He sipped his cognac.

Nick crossed the room, grabbed the brandy snifter from Charles's hand and splashed the cognac in his face.

"Hey!" Charles yelled.

Nick grabbed his son's jacket and half jerked him out of the chair. "Now, listen," he said softly. "You're my son, and I love you. But I don't like you at all, Charles. You've got a rotten streak in you a mile wide, and I don't give a damn *how* much of a war hero you are. You probably go up there and take crazy risks just to get back at me, don't you?"

"That's not true!"

"The hell it isn't, or you wouldn't pull this blackmail stunt on me—and that's what it is, blackmail. And *I don't like it*. Why do you hate me?"

"I don't! You're my father—I love you! I admire you! I . . ." He started crying. "I want to be like you . . . I think . . . except . . ." He started gagging on his sobs. Nick released him and he fell back down in his chair.

"Except *what?*"

"Except you don't know what it's like being the son of a man all the papers call a 'merchant of death.' " He looked up at his father with bloodshot eyes. "There are guys in my squadron who won't even *talk* to me because they think you caused this war!"

"*I* caused it? Who the hell was trying to get America to wake up to the Nazis for the past six years? *Me!*"

"But they don't know that! They hear all this stuff from the American fliers over here. I *have* to be a damned hero to live you down!"

Nick stared at him. "If it means that much to you," he said, "I'll sell the company."

"NO!" Charles exclaimed. "*I* want it! I mean, someday it's going to be mine! It's just that right now, it's . . . *hard* being Nick Fleming's son."

He pulled out a handkerchief and began wiping the brandy off his face.

"It's not so easy being Charles Fleming's father," said Nick. "All right, I'm going to level with you. You say you want Ramschild. Fine, then I'll keep it for you. But *if* I keep it, I have to know something about you, Charles—and I never thought I'd have the guts to ask. Did you ever touch Sylvia . . . sexually?"

His son's face contorted with rage. "So *that's* what you think!" he almost shouted. "What a *disgusting* insinuation—and coming from *you*, who's screwing Margaret Kingsley behind my mother's back! You can go to hell with that lie—and it *is* a lie! I never did anything with my sister—*never!* But don't think I don't know that's why you shipped me off to Oxford, because you've got a filthy mind! And *that's* why I hate you! It's a *LIE!*"

He was screaming, almost manic. Nick choked back his nausea. He walked back to his burled walnut partner's desk, sat down and pulled out his checkbook.

"I'll do better than lend you a thousand pounds, Charles," he said, taking his fountain pen from its malachite holder. "I'm going to write you a check for two million dollars. Then I never want to see you again."

Charles looked amazed. "Why?"

Nick gave his son a deadly look.

"Because," he said quietly, "you protest too much. And what you did to Sylvia disgusts me."

Charles got out of the chair. "Father . . ." he whispered. "Don't do this to me. . . ."

But Nick was already writing the check.

"I'll tell Mother about Margaret Kingsley!" he shouted. "I'll tell her what a two-timing bastard you are!"

"She already knows," said Nick, signing the check. "And don't bother telling her about Margaret Kingsley. I'm telling her myself. Right now."

He tore out the check, got up, crossed the room and handed it to his red-faced son. "Goodbye, Charles," he said.

Then he left the room.

"Nick, you *can't!*" Edwina exclaimed five minutes later. Nick had gone upstairs to their bedroom, where he told her what had happened. "Charles is our son! No matter what dreadful things he's done, we brought him into the world, and we can't just hand him a check and say goodbye. He's our *son.*"

"Edwina, do you think I *wanted* to do it? But he's turned into a conniving monster. He tried to blackmail me—*me, his father!*"

Edwina, in a pink nightgown, was sitting on the edge of the bed. "Was it this woman he was talking about?" she said quietly.

Her husband, who had been pacing the bedroom, stopped and looked at her. "Yes. I cheated on you, and he found out."

She turned her face away. He came to her, sat beside her on the bed and put his arm around her.

"I'm sorry, my darling," he said softly. "I've always loved you, but I haven't been the world's best husband. You used to complain that I had a double standard, that I could cheat on you but you couldn't do the same with me, and it wasn't fair. Well, you were right—I admit it. And I apologize to you from the bottom of my heart. You've been a far better wife than I've been a husband."

She looked at him and sighed. "Well, at least you've admitted it, after all these years," she said, forcing a sad smile. "I suppose that's some sort of minor victory for me. But it's a Pyrrhic victory, if we lose our son."

"Edwina—"

"Wait a minute. I'm not making excuses for Charles. I suppose he's everything you say he is, which isn't much credit to either of us. But what in God's name is this horrible war being fought about if it's not . . . families? Oh, I know that's simplistic and there are all sorts of world issues involved, but when I work with the children at Thrax Hall, all the war means to me is families that have been destroyed, broken up by stupid bombs, children who'll never see their parents again. We can't break up *our* family, can we? Just because our son isn't what we hoped he might be? So far we've been lucky: no one's been killed. But what if Charles were shot down next week—which is certainly possible? How would we feel then?"

"He committed *incest!*"

"How do you know?"

"I *know*. When I accused him of it, he went crazy denying it. Edwina, I know, as I know I love you, that he's guilty. And I don't want to have anything more to do with him. Christ knows, I'm no saint—all you have to do is read my press coverage to see that. But what *he's* done . . ." He shook his head.

"Nick, if you love me . . ."

"There's no 'if.' "

"There's *always* an 'if' in a marriage. I cheated on you once a long time ago, and it took you a long time to forgive me. Well, I've overlooked your infidelities and I forgive you for them, because I love you more than . . . more than myself, I suppose. But now I'm putting it on the line. If you love me, you'll give Charles another chance."

"Dammit, I can't!"

"He's our *son!*"

"If our son were a murderer, would you still love him?"

"Yes, I'd have to."

He stood up, again shaking his head with frustration. She watched him as he went to the window and looked out. After a moment, he said, "I'll think about it. Only for *your* sake, Edwina. I'll think about it."

For a while they remained silent, lost in their thoughts. Then she got off the bed, came to him, took his hand and kissed his cheek.

"It's been a wonderful life with you, my darling," she whispered.

He looked at her still-beautiful face, cast in soft chiaroscuro by the bed lamp. As torn with rage and anguish as he was about his son, he had never loved his wife more than at that moment. He took her in his arms and hugged her tightly.

"And you've given me the best moments of my life," he whispered in her ear as he kissed it.

"It's a damned lie!" Margaret exclaimed hotly, two nights later. "I *never* made love to your son! What a nerve he's got saying that!"

"What *did* happen?" asked Nick. They were drinking tea in Margaret's flat, its windows now replaced.

"I met him at the Air Ministry when he was delivering some papers for his squadron. Then we met again at lunch and he asked if he could sit with me, and I said yes. It was two days after you had been here, and since he was American I asked if he knew you. Of course I was amazed when he said you were his father—I hadn't caught his last name—but I certainly didn't tell him you and I had made love, and I certainly didn't make love to *him*. I do love my husband, after all, and just because I made a fool of myself with you doesn't mean I've done anything with other men. But I could bloody well strangle your son!"

"Then he guessed we were lovers," Nick said. "And used the guess to blackmail me."

"*Blackmail* you?" She sounded surprised.

He nodded.

"My son's not exactly an Albert Schweitzer type. A lot of it's my fault—I spoiled Charles rotten when he was a kid. And I don't know if I've done the right thing, kicking him out of my life. My wife's sick about it and doing everything she can to bring us together again . . . except he's done something I can never forgive."

"What?"

He shook his head. "I can't tell you. I'll never tell anybody. But it's there, in my mind, and it's killed all the love I had for him. And I *did* love him."

He stopped, and she could see he was fighting tears. She came to him and took his hand.

"I'm sorry," she said.

He looked up at her and tried to force a smile.

"I didn't mean to unload all my troubles on you," he said. "Except I had to talk to you. I had to find out the truth about Charles and you."

"Well, your son's attractive, but not half so attractive as his father." She leaned down and kissed his forehead. "Do you want to spend the night?"

He looked at her and shook his head. "No. I wasn't lying when I said you'd bewitched me, but I think I have to break the spell. There's your husband, and there's my wife. I've cheated on Edwina a lot in the past and always managed somehow to rationalize it. But I don't want to cheat on her any more. I suppose that sounds odd, doesn't it?"

"Not a bit. I think you're in love with her."

He smiled slightly. "I've always been in love with her, but now . . . having lost my son . . . I think I *need* her for the first time in my life."

She squeezed his hand, then released it. "I'm glad this has happened," she said quietly. "I won't pretend I haven't been feeling guilty myself. But you'll always be a lovely memory." She smiled. "I came terribly close to compromising my Socialist principles by falling in love with a capitalist."

He stood up and put his hand on her cheek.

"This capitalist," he said, "has never met a lovelier or more enchanting Socialist."

CHAPTER 39

PETER Chadwick was running after the new red balloon Edwina had bought him when Edwina spotted the airplane zooming in low over the trees. It was January 1942. America was now in the war and, to Edwina's despair, Nick was soon going to return to Washington to help coordinate the massive weapons effort at the newly built Pentagon.

"Elvira," she said to her twenty-year-old assistant, "get the children inside—quick! That's a German plane."

The homely redhead squinted. "What's it doing *here?*"

"I don't know . . . maybe the pilot's lost. *Hurry!* I'll get Peter."

As Elvira began herding the children inside Thrax Hall, Edwina ran across the huge open lawn behind the house, calling, "Peter, come back!"

But Peter, who was at least two hundred feet away from her, had no intention of losing his beloved red balloon. He kept chasing it.

"Peter!"

The plane with the big black cross on its fuselage roared over his head. He heard the chatter of machine-gun fire. He stopped and turned. The plane zoomed over Thrax Hall, seeming to skim its chimney tops, then dwindled into the distance toward the Channel.

Suddenly, everything was very still.

Peter, forgetting his balloon, began running across the vast lawn toward the beautiful woman he had come to love. He couldn't understand why she was lying so still on the grass.

"Mrs. Fleming!" he called.

When he came up beside her, panting, he kneeled down and took her hand. Then he saw the red blood oozing out of the holes in the back of her white dress.

"Mrs. Fleming," he began crying. "Wake up. *Please* . . . wake up. . . ."

Peter Chadwick had lost his second mother.

Edwina's senseless killing drove Nick mad with grief. That an innocent woman, miles from any target of military value, had been machine-gunned from the air as she ran across a lawn to save a ten-year-old boy struck him as the height of barbarity, and his hatred and detestation of the Nazi regime, ignited six years before in the Gestapo's interrogation chambers, now exploded in his brain. When he went to the local morgue to look at her body, he broke down and wept like a child. Her face, so beautiful in death, conjured up a thousand memories. His first seeing her at Thrax Hall so many years before during that first savage war, their tempestuous romance, their giddy years together in Hollywood, their fights and their joys, their lovemaking and their brawls . . . they had spent almost a quarter of a century together, and now she was gone. Quickly, brutally, needlessly.

As he pressed her hand to his mouth, his hot tears fell on her cold skin and he thought his heart would break.

The stirring strains of William Blake's hymn "Jerusalem" filled the small eighteenth-century stone chapel two days later, sung by the boys' choir and the congregation. By Nick's consent, his wife was to be buried with the other members of her ancient family, who had worshiped in the chapel in the nearby village with varying degrees of devotion and piety for over two hundred years. Lord and Lady Saxmundham were there, looking suddenly very old indeed. The Duchess of Kent was there, representing the royal family. Clementine Churchill was there, though her husband had sent his regrets. Lady Blake, Edwina's sister, was there. Perhaps most poignant, Peter Chadwick was there, along with forty-two other orphans who had lost their beloved Mrs. Fleming.

"Till we have built Jerusalem," sang the choir, "in England's green and pleasant land."

Charles was there. He had slipped into the chapel just after the service began. Now he sat in the rear pew in his R.A.F. uniform listening as the Reverend Dr. Cadwallader eulogized the woman he had preached to when she had been a little girl in a safe, long-ago time that now seemed as far away as the Land of Oz. Then the final prayers and the final hymn, and Edwina's coffin was lowered into its crypt.

Outside the chapel, Charles came up to his father. It had been over a year since they had communicated. "May I talk to you?" he asked.

Nick looked at him numbly and nodded. They walked to the side of the chapel. It was a cold, raw day with a moaning wind and gray skies. Charles pulled a piece of paper from his jacket and handed it to Nick.

"You know I never cashed the check," said Charles.

"I know."

"I want to be your son again. I . . . ." He gulped. "What you accused me of is true, and I know I did a terrible thing with Sylvia. I'm ashamed of it. But I'm going to ask you, for Mother's sake, if nothing else, to try to forgive me and give me another chance. I really *want* to make you proud of me." He hesitated. "I'd even like you to *like* me a little."

Nick closed his eyes and heard Edwina's voice in his mind. "Charles is our son!" she had said. "No matter what dreadful things he's done, we brought him into the world, and we can't just hand him a check and say goodbye." For the last year of her life, Edwina had struggled with her husband to bring about a reconciliation with their son. Now, as he looked at Charles, Nick regretted his stubbornness and the pain it had caused his wife. He opened his arms. The two embraced.

"I loved her *so*," said Charles.

"So did I," said Nick. "More than I ever realized."

He tore up the check and the wind scattered the two million dollars over the face of the earth.

"We'll start all over," said Nick as they walked back to the Rolls-Royce. At least he had his son back.

He was about to climb into the long, black car when young Peter Chadwick came up to him. The boy's face was angelic, but Nick could see from his red eyes he had been crying.

"Mr. Fleming," he said timidly.

Nick knelt down and put his hands on the boy's arms.

"You're Peter, aren't you?" he said. "You were with her. . . ."

The boy nodded.

"She had given me a beautiful red balloon," he said. "I'll always remember her for my balloon."

The middle-aged American and the young Englishman looked at each other, united by the death of someone they both had loved. Now Peter pulled something out of his coat pocket.

"These fell from the plane," he said. "I saw them fall out of the sky. I thought"—he hesitated—"you might want them."

He held out his hand, as did Nick. The boy put three brass cartridges into Nick's palm. Nick looked at them. From anyone else except this child, the cartridges would have been a ghoulish gift. But somehow from Peter, they seemed right.

"Thank you," he mumbled, staring at them.

Then his blood ran cold.

He saw the tiny engraved initials: "R.A.C." and the bin number "479." He instantly recognized them. A silent howl of fury raged through his brain as his hand closed over the cartridges that had been manufactured by his own company.

"R.A.C." meant "Ramschild Arms Company."

Three days later, Nick, having flown the Atlantic in an Air Corps cargo plane, confronted the fifteen top officers of his company in the paneled boardroom overlooking the Connecticut River.

"Gentlemen," he said, "my wife was shot by a German pilot. But she was killed by American bullets. *These* bullets." He pulled the three cartridges from his pocket and tossed them onto the polished board table. "These bullets, which were manufactured right *here,* in this factory."

He paused to let the shock of this announcement sink in.

"Now, gentlemen," he continued, "one or more of you present in this room must know how our ammunition is getting to the Luftwaffe. I am going into my office. If, in one hour's time, one of you hasn't come to me and confessed, you *all* are fired, without severance or pension, and I will notify the F.B.I. to investigate *all* of you for possible treasonous activity. Gentlemen, I am furious, I am outraged, and I am *deadly* serious. One hour."

He walked out of the room, leaving fifteen of the most stunned-looking men in America.

Ten minutes later, there was a knock on his door.

"Come in."

The door opened, and Chester Hill came in.

Nick winced. "Dammit," he said, "I *knew* it was you."

"Nick," said his son-in-law, who was ashen and literally trembling with fear, "I had no idea the stuff was going to the Luftwaffe! Honest to God . . ."

"Who'd you sell it to?" he roared.

"A Swede!"

"Who the hell did you think a Swede was buying ammo for?"

"He *said* it was for the Polish Underground. . . ."

"The Polish Underground doesn't have airplanes."

366

"It was for machine guns, for Christ's sake! I didn't know it was going on a plane!"

"Bullshit!" roared Nick. "Listen, Chester, you're no fool. You either knew there was a damned good chance the ammo was going to Germany, which is buying up all the black-market ammunition it can get its hands on to keep the Luftwaffe operating, or you conveniently ignored the fact. Besides, the government has made a list of *all* countries we can sell to, and Sweden is definitely *not* on it. And don't pretend you don't know *that*. How much commission did he pay you to make the deal?"

Chester sank into a chair and broke down. "Nick, I *had* to have the money!" he sobbed. "Sylvia's been driving me crazy . . . you don't know how bad it's been with us. . . . She was going into New York and picking up men in bars, for Christ's sake. . . . I *had* to have some money to build her a house . . . I had to. . . ."

He buried his face in his fists, rocking with agony.

"Sylvia's been picking up men in *bars?*" said Nick, his voice somewhat lower.

"Yes! Like a real slut. . . . She's used to living like a goddamn princess, and I haven't got enough money to keep her happy. . . . Christ, I know I made a bad mistake, but can't you understand a little? It's been *hell* living with your daughter!"

Sylvia, his beautiful, beloved Sylvia, a slut? He had always assumed Charles had been the aggressor in the incestuous affair with his sister, but now, perhaps, it could be seen in a different light. Was it possible Sylvia had led Charles on? At least, what might have been painfully obvious if he had ever been able to consider the situation dispassionately, Sylvia hadn't exactly fought her brother off. His children! Oh, God, his children—they seemed to be the source of half his woes. Was it all, ultimately, his fault for having spoiled them? Was it, in some twisted way, his fault Edwina had been killed, rather than his sniveling son-in-law's fault?

"Nick, I'll do *anything* to make it up to you!" Chester burst out.

"How do you make up for Edwina's death?" was the cold reply. "How much did the Swede pay you?"

"Thirty thousand dollars. Enough to start the house. . . ."

"You sold out me, this company and your country for a down payment on a house? Jesus, Chester, your marriage may be hell, but you're a contemptible son of a bitch."

"It's *Sylvia's* fault!" he yelled defensively.

"Yes, and maybe it's *my* fault for spoiling her, but Sylvia didn't sell ammunition to a Swede, and neither did I. Oh, no, Chester, you're hung with this one. Now the question is, what the hell do I do with you? If I report you to the F.B.I., you're in a helluva lot of hot water. You may go to prison—which I'll admit I don't want for Sylvia's sake."

"Please, Nick," he blubbered. "Can't we just do nothing?"

"And how do I explain that to the rest of my executives? Nick Fleming's son-in-law gets off scot-free? No, it won't wash. Sweet Jesus, you've put me in one helluva position. You stupid, contemptible bastard. Damn! If my life has any meaning, it's to help wipe the Nazis off the face of this earth, and what happens? My son-in-law sells them the ammunition they use to murder my wife. Oh, no, Chester, maybe *I'd* let you off. But not Edwina. Her blood's on your hands." The sweat was pouring down his white face.

"Then what will you do?" Chester whispered.

Nick stared at him for almost a full minute, his mind searching for a way out. There was none.

"I have no choice," he finally said, reaching for the phone. "I'm turning you in to the F.B.I."

"NO!" Chester screamed, jumping out of his chair and throwing both hands over the phone. "Please! Give me a chance! Think of Sylvia!"

"I have thought of Sylvia. It can't be helped. You've committed a crime. You've got to pay for it."

"Nick, please. . . . I'll leave the country . . . go to South America! You'll never see me again . . . please . . . anything but prison. Christ, you can't send your own son-in-law to *prison!*"

"Can't I?" he said. He jerked the phone away. "Frieda? Get me the Federal Bureau of Investigation."

Chester backed away from the desk, rubbing his hands in agony. "You cold-blooded bastard," he finally said. "I'll pay you back for this. *Some* day. I'll pay you back."

Nick just looked at him and said nothing.

Chester Hill got five years in Lewisburg Penitentiary.

For the second time in his life, Nick Fleming thought seriously of getting out of the arms business. The murder of his beloved Edwina by bullets he had manufactured struck him a devastating blow. Time and again the thought swept over him that perhaps his critics were right: perhaps there was something inherently evil about the arms business. It had corrupted Chester Hill; perhaps ultimately it would corrupt everyone connected with it. God knows, he had had tempting offers over the years to make sales to shady governments. Now was Edwina's murder some sort of sign for him to get out of the business? He remembered Edwina's first remarks to him when they met so many years before: that he was making money from death. The years of bad publicity continued to gnaw at him—he hated being called the Titan of Death.

And yet, how could he sell the company *now,* with the world at war? He couldn't quite bring himself to do it. But the seed, planted in his mind earlier, was beginning to grow.

Of course, Edwina's death affected her many children also. Vicky, the youngest, who had adored her mother, was almost inconsolable. Fiona, who had never known her real father, now had lost her only other real parent. She too was devastated. But having lost both parents seemed to reinforce her determination to become a great actress—now not only for the memory of Rod Norman but for his costar of that long-ago silent film, Edwina Fleming.

Edward Fleming, the third Fleming child, who was twenty, left Princeton to join the Army. But unlike his older brother, Charles, Edward had no taste for war and no love of the arms business. The death of his mother was vivid proof to him that war was no path to glory but rather a vicious, senseless bloodletting. Edward made up his mind to become a writer. Perhaps he would write the great American war novel that would end all wars, and avenge his beloved mother.

Part VI

BEAUTY AND THE BUTCHER

1944-1947

CHAPTER 40

O<small>N</small> the third of January, 1944, Nick was back in the Oval Office at the White House with a haggard-looking President Roosevelt and Major General William J. Donovan, the head of the O.S.S.

"It's good to see you again, Nick," said the President, shaking his hand. "And I think you know Bill Donovan?"

Nick had met Donovan several times at capital social functions, for since Pearl Harbor and America's entry into the war, Nick had spent almost half his time in Washington working with the Pentagon sending arms shipments all over the world. Now, with Hitler's collapse merely a matter of time, Nick felt satisfied that he had done everything in his power to help destroy the enemy he hated so much. He shook Donovan's hand, then the two took seats in front of Roosevelt's desk.

"Nick," the President began, "Bill here has gotten a rather curious communication through underground sources from a lady in Paris named Diana Ramschild. I believe you know her?"

"Very well," replied Nick. "I almost married her a long time ago. Because I married someone else, she hired a Turkish assassin to kill me, and when that backfired she engineered my arrest by the Gestapo ten years ago."

The President laughed.

"Hell hath no fury like a woman scorned, but she seems to have gone a bit overboard."

"A bit. Except I think she forgave me. When she showed up at the Gestapo prison, I think she came to gloat, but changed her mind. At any rate, she *told* me she'd get me out by using her influence with Atatürk, but then I got out on my own, so I never knew whether she went to Atatürk or not. I haven't heard anything from her since. So she's in Paris now?"

"Yes. She owns a very successful nightclub there called Semiramis where she gets all the top Nazis drunk and 'entertains' them. I'll leave it to your imagination how."

"I have an idea."

"Now, the story she sent to us—and Bill's agents in Paris have confirmed it as true—is that one of her girls, a blond beauty named Laure Ducaze, has become the girl friend of General Friedrich von Stoltz, who is second-in-command in Paris, and a very important man indeed. Stoltz has a wife and two daughters in Baden-Baden, but apparently he has gone middle-aged gaga over Laure and gives her the moon—money, furs, champagne. She even has available a chauffeur-driven car with unlimited gasoline, and from what I hear, that, in Paris, is the ultimate luxury. Stoltz also tends to get stumble-down drunk with Laure and has told her some very indiscreet things about the war. If I were Hitler—which thank God I'm not—I'd have the man shot, but apparently the Fuehrer is so preoccupied with the Russian Front, he doesn't have any time to pay attention to Paris, so Stoltz has gotten away with it—at least so far.

"Now, all this would be of minor interest to us except for two words Stoltz mentioned to Laure, who passed them on to her boss, Diana, who has passed them on to us. The two words are 'heavy water.' "

Nick looked blank. "Excuse me, Mr. President, but I don't get it," he said.

Roosevelt shifted in his chair. "We'll have to provide you some background, Nick, or you'll be completely in the dark. But I must warn you that this information is top secret. Under *no* circumstances is it to leave this room."

"I understand."

"We are presently developing a revolutionary new type of bomb. If it works—which is a big if—it will make every other weapon in the world obsolete. It will be a bomb of unbelievable destructive power. When I tell you that one of these bombs could obliterate a city the size of Chicago, for instance, you'll probably think I've gone crazy, but that happens to be the truth."

"One bomb could destroy Chicago?" said Nick, stunned by the implication.

The President nodded. "It's frightening," he said. "And it was a terrifying responsibility for me to give the go-ahead on the project. However, I was assured by our top scientists that the bomb was not only feasible but probably, given the state of modern physics, inevitable. And that if *we* didn't develop it, Germany might. Which left me little choice. And which brings me back to heavy water.

"The development of heavy water is a necessary step in the bomb's production. Now, if General von Stoltz in Paris is talking heavy water,

374

that, in our opinion, can mean only one thing—the Nazis are working on the same bomb we are. Hitler has lost this war. But if he succeeds in manufacturing this bomb before we do, he can achieve the most dramatic turnaround in history. He can *win*. I don't have to tell you we're damned nervous about it."

"With good reason."

"Which brings me to you. Needless to say, we want to find out what Diana Ramschild knows about heavy water, but she refuses to tell us. She's told Bill's agents in Paris she will tell what she knows to *one* person, and that person is Nick Fleming."

"Me?" he exclaimed, stunned yet again. "Why me?"

The President spread his hands. "Well, Nick, I think the lady's still in love with you. Apparently, she has a serious illness and doesn't expect to live much longer. And she told our agents she wants to see you before she dies. It's really rather touching."

"Touching if true. But with Diana's track record on trying to get me killed, I wonder how true it is."

"You said she'd forgiven you."

"I said I *thought* she'd forgiven me. I have no proof of it. Everything she told me in prison might have been an act. *She* certainly didn't get me out. I got myself out! If you're asking me to go to Paris to get this information from Diana, you could be sending me into a deathtrap. Diana knows the Nazis would string me up on piano wire if they got the chance."

The President looked at Donovan, who said, "In fact, we *are* asking you to go to Paris for us. It's vitally important."

Nick squirmed uncomfortably. The memory of his torture in the Hamburg prison was still vivid. The scars on his body had long since healed, but the scars on his mind still gave him nightmares. Now he tried to focus his memory on that brief meeting he had had with Diana in the dreaded *Fragenzimmer*. He remembered the look in her green eyes, those green eyes he had once loved. He remembered her words, "Oh, my God, Nick, what have I done?"

At the time he had felt her remorse was genuine, but could he be sure? After all, her hatred of him had been so intense she had hired an assassin to kill him. And now he was being asked to trust her with his life! And for what? Two words, "heavy water," which still meant nothing to him. Yet, what little they had told him about this super-bomb left little doubt about the importance of the mission. How weirdly ironic that it all hinged on the unstable emotions of a woman he had seduced and abandoned more than a quarter of a century before! And how right he had been: in his life, at least, love *was* turning out to be the most important thing.

"We realize this is no minor decision on your part," said the President. "Take your time to think about it. At least, take a few days."

Edwina. Edwina, now dead three years. Edwina, whom he still missed achingly. Physical love was no problem for a multimillionaire who was still youthfully handsome, but the love of his life was gone forever. He had built her a memorial: he had endowed with a million pounds the Edwina Fleming Home for children orphaned by the war, and her name and memory would live on. But her brutal murder still infuriated him. Chester Hill was paying in prison for his complicity in her death, but the Nazis were still in power. And then, there were the rumors that were now pouring out of Europe of the monstrous culmination of Hitler's madness, the death camps, where it was said a whole race—a race whose blood Nick shared—was being exterminated. . . .

"I'll do it," he said quietly. "I'll do it for a lot of reasons, but I'll do it mostly for my dead wife. I still owe the Nazis for that."

The President and Donovan looked relieved.

The near-naked show girls at Semiramis, Diana Ramschild's hugely successful nightclub on the Place du Tertre in Montmartre, paraded down the steps of the stage dressed in spangled G-strings, high-heeled, ankle-strap Joan Crawford shoes, plumed headdresses and nothing else as Laure Ducaze, the breathtakingly beautiful blond star of the show, sang at a microphone center stage the theme song of the show, *"Paris bei Nacht."* A hundred and fifty sweating, half-drunk German officers ogled the naked breasts of the show girls in near-comical silence as Laure sang, in German and then in French, the atrocious lyrics of the song, which translated roughly as:

> *"Are you lonely?*
> *Are you thirsty?*
> *Do you want to meet a girl?*
> *Take a velo*
> *Or a bike*
> *And give Paris a whirl!*
> *Paris by night,*
> *Lovely, gay Par-ee!*
> *Paris by night,*
> *Where love is never free!*
> *Kick a kike,*

Steal his bike,
And come to gay Par-ee!"

Unlike the show girls, Laure wore clothes, a white-sequined evening dress that shimmered in the smoky spotlight. The skirt was slit up to her thigh, revealing Laure's sensational legs, which the anti-Semitic, pro-German periodical *Je Suis Partout* had compared favorably to Betty Grable's. Taking the hint, Laure had piled her dyed-blond curls on top of her head, Grable-fashion. Unlike Grable, Laure's features were extremely fine, and her sea-blue eyes were an Aryan's dream. This daughter of the Mayor of Poitiers had spent five years in the ultra-conservative Convent des Oiseaux in Paris before deciding that the cloistered life was not for her. Running away, she got a job singing in a cheap nightclub a year after the Germans marched in. There she was spotted by Diana, who hired her away and made her a star. Diana, known in Paris as *"La Dame aux Voiles,"* knew talent when she saw it.

"Paris le soir,
Ville d'amour et du vin!
Paris le soir—
Mais pas pour les youpins!"

Laure sang.

"Paris by night,
City of love and wine!
Paris by night—
But not for the kikes!"

The audience gave her a standing ovation.

One German S.S. lieutenant named Werner Herzer had seen the show nine times and was almost a fixture at Semiramis. Nice-looking, blond, a former champion gymnast who had competed in the 1936 Olympics in Berlin, Werner Herzer was well known to the waiters, hatcheck girls and even to the owner, Diana herself. "He seems nice" was often said about him.

But everyone knew Sturmfuehrer Herzer was in charge of the execution squad at Fort de Vincennes. While the men on the firing squads were frequently rotated to prevent psychological damage, Herzer had held his job for a year.

He enjoyed his work.

Militärbefehlshaber in Frankreich, the German Military Governor in France, was General Karl Heinrich von Stülpnagel, a well-born intellectual whose heart was not in Nazism and who believed there were no political differences between Germany and France. He lived in the Avenue Malakoff, in the Palais Marbre Rose, which belonged to Mrs. Florence Gould, the heiress to one of America's greatest fortunes. (Mrs. Gould hosted a series of famous Thursday lunches throughout the Occupation where her guests included most of the German and French celebrities in the arts.) General von Stülpnagel had requisitioned the Hôtel Raphaël, on the Avenue Kléber, for his staff, and it was in a suite on the sixth floor that Stülpnagel's second-in-command in charge of Internal Security in Occupied France, General Friedrich von Stoltz, lived. Stülpnagel's passion was the history of Byzantium. He genuinely disliked any harsh methods of treatment for the French, and fought constantly with Berlin over the necessity of executing resisters and deporting Jews. Since he rarely won his fights, Stülpnagel sighed with resignation, went back to Byzantium, and turned the dirty work over to Stoltz.

General von Stoltz was the younger son of impoverished minor nobility in Saxony. Saxons were mockingly called the clods of Germany, and Stoltz lived up to his billing. Unlike Stülpnagel, who was a man of genuine culture, Stoltz's idea of "art" was getting drunk listening to Laure Ducaze sing her anti-Semitic ditties. Short, stocky, messy, with a fat red face, a W. C. Fields nose and thick rimless eyeglasses that made his myopic eyes look twice their size, Stoltz had all the military dash of a butcher. And in fact, the Parisians, who had nicknamed the slim, stylish Stülpnagel the "Nutcracker King," had dubbed Stoltz *"Le Boucher,"* The Butcher. This fifty-two-year-old alcoholic, who, like Hitler, bit his nails, was responsible for the execution in the dreaded ditches of Fort de Vincennes of over five hundred Frenchmen.

It would be as wrong to say that most Parisians were collaborators as it would be wrong to say that most Parisians were members of the Resistance. The vast majority merely tried to live their lives as best they could under unpleasant conditions—to get by from day to day. The rule seemed to be that the higher one stood in the social scale, the pleasanter the conditions and the chummier the relationships between the Germans and the French. Certainly the lives of the rich and celebrated were hardly inconvenienced. Picasso lived through the

Occupation well, as did Cocteau, Serge Lifar, the film star Arletty, Chanel, Colette and dozens of others. Louise de Vilmorin, a famous hostess, became so pro-German she was nicknamed "Lulu the Pomeranian." Many French women—and *tapettes*—found the well-behaved German troops ravishing. On the other hand, at Le Colisée, the most popular sidewalk café on the Champs Elysées, Paris's swinging youth, known as *Zazous,* wore long, greasy hair and blue-tinted glasses to show their contempt for the barbered German troops.

One could buy caviar at Pétrossian's, and luxury shops such as Hermès, Cartier and Boucheron were as well stocked as ever. Antique dealers enjoyed a boom. The leading auction house, the Salle Drouot, realized a record forty-seven million francs at the sale of the Viau collection in 1942, including five million francs for Cézanne's *Montaigne Sainte-Geneviève,* bought by a German. Celebrated restaurants like Lapérouse, La Marquise de Sévigné, La Tour d'Argent, Le Grand Vefour, Claridge's, Ciro's, Chez Carrère, Drouant and Maxim's, under the management of the Berlin restaurant Horcher's, all remained open to booming business. Diana Ramschild's greatest rival, Fabienne Jamet, the madame of the famous whorehouse at 122 Rue de Provence, admitted she had never been so happy or prosperous. Diana herself was netting over a quarter-million dollars' personal profit a year from Semiramis. Paris was the eye of the hurricane. Around it raged the storms of war; but in the beautiful French capital, under the well-polished boot of its German captor, aside from a few Allied air raids that damaged suburban factories and blasted a crater in front of Sacré Coeur Cathedral, life was relatively serene, relatively normal. The important modifier is "relatively."

The submarine surfaced silently in the inky sea beneath a black sky a half mile off La Rochelle, on the west coast of France. The hatch was opened and the skipper, Commander Warren V. Hickman, U.S. Navy, climbed out onto the slippery deck. Following him were his chief bosun's mate and two crewmen, who began inflating a rubber raft. Then out of the sub climbed Colonel Nick Fleming, wearing a black suit, black turtleneck sweater, black overcoat and knitted black seaman's cap.

The sea was like a sheet of steel, for there was no wind. The temperature was a numbing minus three degrees Centigrade. Nick pushed up the lapels of his overcoat and waited for the raft to be launched. He carried his gun and a thousand dollars in French francs. He was apprehensive, because he still believed there was a better-than-even chance Diana Ramschild was luring him into a trap. Nick believed in the power of love, yet how could Diana still be in love with him after all that had happened in the past quarter century?

And yet, he felt he had to take the gamble.

"Good luck, Nick," said the skipper, shaking his gloved hand. Then Nick climbed into the rubber raft, and the two crewmen began rowing him to the dark French shore. They were south of La Rochelle. Within fifteen minutes, they saw two flashing green lights and headed in that direction. Another ten minutes and Nick was transferring from the raft to a French fishing boat, where he was greeted by twenty-eight-year-old Nicholas Foucade, a member of the French Underground. As the raft returned to the sub and the fishing boat headed into shore, Foucade introduced Nick to another member of the Underground, who looked familiar.

"This is the man who will take you to Paris," said Foucade. "René Reynaud."

Nick was delighted to shake the hand of the young French Captain he had met in the garden of the Château de Chissay four years before when the government of France was collapsing.

"As you can see, Mr. Fleming," said the Captain, who had shaved off his moustache, "I found something to do for France."

"So did I," said Nick, smiling. "I'm glad we'll be working together."

"When I heard about your mission, I volunteered for the job. We may even pick up a few dividends at Semiramis, eh?" And Reynaud winked good-naturedly.

CHAPTER 41

IN every generation, a certain number of women are born with the special talent to enslave men, and Laure Ducaze was one of them. Aside from her spectacular good looks, she had a charm and calm self-assurance that made her irresistible. Because she was slightly hard-of-hearing in her left ear, she always maneuvered to sit to the right of any man she was after, because she had early discovered that by leaning close to hear what they were saying she gave the impression of being absorbed in their every word, which immensely inflated their vanity. And part of enslaving men, she knew, was inflating their ego. Privately, she held a certain contempt for the male sex, most of whom she considered power-hungry buffoons—which was not to say she didn't enjoy them in bed.

Or *some* of them. Stoltz's drunken attempts at lovemaking revolted her, but his mad passion for her was too valuable to forgo, and when he pushed her into bed, she gritted her teeth, closed her eyes and imagined he was Clark Gable, which took enormous powers of fantasy. Even though Laure included crude anti-Semitic gibes in her songs, she did it only to accommodate her audience. Personally, she had nothing against the Jews and had had a young Jewish actor as a lover before he went into hiding and joined the Underground. She had not told Stoltz this—it would have made him apoplectic—but the knowledge amused her.

One obvious advantage to being Stoltz's mistress was the luxuries he heaped on her. Whether he paid for them out of his own pocket or requisitioned them, Laure neither knew, nor cared. She liked her creature comforts, and at a time when many Parisians were finding it hard to heat their homes and fill their larders, due to strict food rationing, Laure was comfortably warm and so well fed from food Stoltz obtained from the German-dominated black market she had to diet to keep her figure.

Stoltz bought her jewels from Van Cleef and Chaumet, he bought her gowns from Nina Ricci and Balenciaga, he bought her a Russian sable coat and a Russian white-fox cape (displaying dubious patrio-

381

tism, since the Russians were slaughtering the German troops in the East). Laure loved it all. She loved the chauffeured Horch that was at her disposal, at a time when there were only seven thousand licensed motorcars in Paris, when a natural-gas-propelled car called the *voiture à gazogène* had been invented to circumvent the gasoline shortage, when two million Parisians were using bicycles, and a pedal-powered rickshaw called the *velo-taxi* competed with horse-drawn carriages from the last century for the lucrative taxi trade. And she loved the four-room flat he paid for on the Place Vendôme across from the Ritz, where Coco Chanel was holed up in her apartment with her own high-ranking German officer-lover. Laure told herself she was doing as well as Chanel, and that was no mean achievement.

But there was another advantage to being Stoltz's lover, and this advantage had been pointed out to her a year earlier by her employer, Diana Ramschild. Laure liked and admired Diana, who had her own luxurious flat on the Avenue Foch. Laure knew Diana was smart as a whip. Laure was basically uninterested in politics and the war, but Diana told her as early as the spring of 1943 that Hitler was losing, that it was only a matter of time before the Germans pulled out of Paris, and when the Free French returned, it was going to be rough going for *collabos* like Laure and herself. Therefore, Diana said, Laure should start listening to what Fritzy babbled in his drunkenness and then pass the information on to her. That way, they could play both sides of the fence. Diana had already made contacts with the Resistance, and by passing on military information, both of them could insure themselves against postwar retribution. Laure, who disliked the sound of the ominous word "retribution," readily agreed and started making mental notes. It was in the late autumn of 1943 that she began hearing about "heavy water." On the snowy night of January 18, 1944, she was to hear more.

Stoltz was drinking two or more bottles of Burgundy a night, though such was his oxlike constitution he would awake the next morning seemingly free of a hangover. On the night of January 18, he as usual watched Laure's last show at Semiramis, then took her to Maxim's for a midnight supper (where the headwaiter, Albert, fawned on Fritzy with embarrassing obsequiousness). By one, Stoltz, half loaded, ordered another bottle of La Tâche, then took it and Laure to the flat on the Place Vendôme, where he bellowed the Horst Wessel song as they rode the wrought-iron lift to the second floor. Laure was so used to the singing, she ignored it, though she knew her neighbors didn't. Letting them into her flat, she turned on the lights as Stoltz weaved to the kitchen to uncork the bottle. More often than not of late, Stoltz was passing out before he could get to the sex, which was a marked relief to Laure. Now she went into her bedroom to change into her latest gift, a matching blue silk-and-lace nightgown and peignoir he had bought her at the Galeries Lafayette.

Laure had good taste in clothes, but her taste in decoration was something else and her flat was frilly and froufrou to a fault, filled with pink bows on lampshades and *faux*-Hollywood modern furniture and dolls and stuffed animals on the chairs and sofas that were enough to induce nausea in anyone except Stoltz, who found all the kitsch adorable. When she returned to the living room, he was sprawled on one of the sofas, his boots and tunic off, his shirt half open, a hole in one of his white socks, tossing one of Laure's teddy bears in the air as his wineglass sat on the floor.

"Poupée," he belched—Stoltz spoke French and had nicknamed his mistress "Doll"—"do you want to go with me to Brittany this weekend?"

"Brittany? In *January?"* she growled. "Why not take me to Iceland?"

"Oh, it's nice in Brittany."

"Nice and cold. If you want to take me someplace, why don't we go south? I'd love to go to Rome or Naples."

"Poupée, there's a war on."

"So what? I thought the Italians were your allies."

"They are, but I still can't go to Rome for a weekend. Berlin wouldn't like that at all. Berlin won't like my taking you to Brittany, for that matter, but I'd miss my *poupée."* He smiled blearily at her. "We could eat Belon oysters. You like oysters."

She put on a Benny Goodman record. They both adored American swing.

"I don't like oysters enough to freeze in Brittany," she said, going into the kitchen to put on the kettle for a cup of black-market tea.

He appeared in the doorway, mammoth and drunk, his bloodshot eyes behind his thick lenses beginning to cross slightly as they did when he had too much alcohol in him.

"There's a fort," he slurred. "I have to visit it. It's where they're making that heavy water I told you about. But right down the road there's a château we can stay in. It's very beautiful, very nice . . . belongs to a rich banker who'll treat us well . . . very romantic. . . . Say yes, *Poupée*. Please. We'll have a good time. Say yes."

Laure was making mental notes. "Oh, well," she said, "if you really want me."

He smiled happily, came to her and took her in his arms. "That's my *poupée*," he muttered, giving her a kiss.

Laure closed her eyes and thought of Clark Gable.

Shortly after five on the morning of January 23, Charles Pepin, a farmer from outside Chartres, drove his horse-drawn wagon into Paris. The midnight-to-five curfew had just been lifted, and as he had done three times a week since the beginning of the Occupation, Charles was delivering a wagonload of firewood to Les Halles, where he would sell it at a handsome profit, firewood being precious in fuel-short Paris.

Although it was dark and cold, intrepid Paris housewives were queuing up already in front of bakeries and foodshops, waiting for as much as two hours for the shops to open to buy bread, ersatz coffee or rutabagas; before the war the French had fed the latter only to horses, but they had now become a staple of Parisian cuisine. When Charles reached Les Halles, the wonderful glass-and-iron central market of the city, he pulled his wagon up to the firewood stall, his and his horses' breath steaming in the cold. Charles climbed off the wagon, took note of the two German guards standing in the distance looking the other way, then knocked twice with his fist on the side of the wagon. A moment later, a false bottom opened beneath the wagon and Nick and René Reynaud climbed out of the cramped compartment they had traveled in from Chartres and hurried off.

Nick was impressed with the efficiency of the Resistance. He had been given a new identity—Jules Granet—and all the necessary forged documents in a farmhouse outside La Rochelle. Then he and René had taken the train to Chartres without incident. At Chartres, they were furnished with bicycles, which they rode to Charles Pepin's farm. And now, Paris.

They took the Métro to the south of the city. The subway car was almost empty, but at the second stop two German soldiers, the worse for wine, stumbled into the car—according to the somewhat peculiar rules of the curfew, one could sit it out at a bar. Nick tensed, but the soldiers sat down at the opposite end of the car and promptly fell asleep.

Nick and René left the Métro near the Porte de Versailles, walked a few blocks on the Rue de Vaugirard, then ducked into a narrow

384

side street where, in the middle of the block, they came to a four-story house marked "No. 5." An elderly concierge, wrapped in a coat and a blanket and wearing mittens and a stocking cap, looked at René and nodded. They hurried up ancient stone steps to the third floor, where René produced a key and unlocked a door. Inside was a four-room apartment overlooking a rear alley. The high-ceilinged rooms were furnished in comfortable bourgeois taste. At first, Nick thought the living room was empty. But after René had locked the door, two men emerged from behind a curtained doorway, replacing their guns in armpit holsters.

"Guy and Paul," said René, "this is Jules Granet—Nick Fleming."

Nick shook their hands. Then Guy went to the kitchen, returning with a pot of coffee and four mugs.

"This is *real* coffee," he said, grinning, "not that Kraut ersatz shit. We stole it from a train we blew up outside Lyons."

"That's the best news I've heard since I came to France," said Nick, who was freezing.

"Guy's a film director," said René, "and Paul's a writer."

"We're planning to do a movie about the Occupation, after the war," said Paul. "What we're doing now we regard as research."

"Nick owns a film studio in Hollywood," said René.

Guy and Paul looked duly impressed. "That means we *have* to keep him alive," said Guy, and they all laughed.

After they'd had some coffee, René said, "Diana Ramschild doesn't know yet whether you're coming to Paris or not. For obvious reasons, we've kept her in the dark. But now you're here, we'll contact her and set up a meeting. Don't worry, we don't trust her, and we know it could be a trap. She'll have to go to two separate places first before we bring her here. That way, if the Germans are following her, we can abort the whole thing."

Nick stirred his coffee. "I wonder," he said, "why she insisted on giving the information only to *me*. I know what she told your contact—that she's dying and wants to see me and she's still in love with me—but frankly, the more I think about that, the more it sounds like a lot of crap. There's something else going on."

"Well," said René, "we'll find out soon enough. The meeting's set for midnight tonight. Meanwhile, we might as well try to get some sleep. Four hours bumping around in that firewood wagon was not my idea of fun."

"Not exactly the *Orient Express*," Nick agreed.

"She's gotten rich from this war, this Diana Ramschild, this *'La*

Dame aux Voiles' as they call her," said Guy. "Whatever her motives are for helping us now, I'll never forgive her for making money while France suffered."

"Guy's a typical Parisian," said René. "He despises the poor, but he hates the rich."

"I hate *collabos*," said Guy quietly. "And this whore, Laure Ducaze, with her fat pig of a Boche general and her furs and jewels and car— I'd like to shove an Iron Cross up her cunt."

"Maybe, but you'll shut up about it," said René. "This isn't one of your movies, with good guys and bad guys. If Laure Ducaze can help us, I'll pin the Cross of Lorraine on her and shove my prick up her cunt."

"Gentlemen," said Paul, with mock primness, "the conversation is degenerating."

He was surprised how beautiful she looked as she entered the room that night. She wore a floor-length mink cape of war-mocking richness. Over her now dyed-golden hair, beautifully coiffed, she wore a green satin turban that, with the light-green veil over her lower face, gave her an exotic harem-girl look that was strangely entrancing. Beneath the mink she had on an evening dress of silver lamé that shimmered in the candlelight (the electricity having been shut off at midnight). Her gloved hands clasped a jewel-encrusted gold purse from Cartier that Nick, who had once bought one for Edwina, knew carried a price tag of three thousand dollars. Almost arrogant in her display of wealth in war-pinched Paris, queenly in carriage, *La Dame aux Voiles* came up to Nick, looked at him with her still-striking green eyes and said, "We meet under slightly different circumstances from the last time."

Nick remembered the *Fragenzimmer*.

"I think that might be called an understatement," he said gently.

She looked at the three Resistance fighters who were standing at the side of the room holding pistols.

"I have acted in good faith," she said. "There were no Germans tailing me. Now you must do the same. I wish to speak to Nick Fleming alone."

René held out his hand.

"I'll have to check your purse," he said.

Diana tossed him the three-thousand-dollar bauble almost contemptuously. "I don't intend to shoot my old friend," she said. "There's nothing in the purse but mascara and change. Lipstick and rouge are a waste of time on *my* face." She turned back to look at Nick again. "Although I'll admit I *did* try to have you shot once, a long time ago. Did you ever figure out who shot Rod Norman?"

"The bullet was meant for me, wasn't it?"

"Yes. I hated you then. I deserved to hate you for what you'd done to me. But I stopped hating you when I saw you in that German prison. One thing you learn as life goes by is that hatred can become a bore. By the way, I wrote a letter to the assassins I hired asking for my money back, since they killed the wrong man. They never answered me."

"You'd waste your money hiring professionals to kill me now. There are a lot of amateurs who'd like to see me dead, my former son-in-law heading the list."

"Well, you can strike me off the list. It's very much in my interest to keep you alive—now."

René handed her back the purse.

"She's right, Nick. Nothing but mascara and change."

"Then you'll leave us alone?" said Diana.

René headed for the end of the room.

"We'll be in the kitchen," he said, and the three men left.

Diana sat down at a lace-covered round wooden table on which was a small radio, its cord plugged into a glass-shaded brass chandelier above it.

"Did you believe what I told them?" she began. "That I was dying and wished to see you?"

"Should I have?" he asked, sitting down opposite her.

"It all depends on whether you're still a romantic. Are you, Nick? You told me once, years ago, that love was the most important thing in life. Do you still believe that?"

"Yes."

"You also said our love would last forever. Your crystal ball was a bit clouded on that point."

"I assume you haven't brought me all the way to Paris to discuss our love life?"

"Oh, but perhaps I have. It was very important to me, Nick. You have no idea how many times you've been in my dreams. You've haunted me for years. I still am in love with you. Bizarre, isn't it? That one human being could have that much impact on another. We humans really are peculiar creatures." She hesitated. "Do I still have any impact on you, Nick?" Then she laughed. "No, don't bother to answer that one. My business has made me an expert in love. Men fall in and out of love. Only a woman can love a man forever. That's been my curse, Nick. And my weakness. I've loved you all these years—even when I thought I hated you. That's one reason I wanted you to come to Paris: to tell you that. I suppose you think it wasn't worth the trip?"

She had spoken quietly and convincingly. He was surprised at how touched he was.

"No," he said. "Perhaps it was."

"Were you happy with Edwina?"

"Very. You may be a little cynical about men, Diana. I loved Edwina the way you say you love me. She's dead now, but I still love her memory."

She played with the handle of her gold purse. "Well, then," she said, "it would seem we've been at cross-purposes all these years. I loved you, but you loved Edwina. But I suppose that's what makes life interesting: cross-purposes. Which brings me to the other reason I wanted you to come to Paris. You owe me something, Nick, and I intend to collect. Not out of bitterness or revenge—that's all dead now. But simply out of a sense of fairness."

"What do I owe you?"

"The Nazis vilify you in their press," she evaded.

"The Americans vilify me in our press."

"Dr. Goebbels calls you the 'Titan of Death.' He says you and Churchill caused the war. He claims you're making hundreds of millions from it. Is that true, Nick?"

"Of course I'm making money. There's hardly a manufacturer of anything except tiddledywinks who's not making money out of this war. And I'd say—judging from that mink coat you've got on—that you're not doing badly either. By the way, I'm amazed you'd wear that in public."

She shrugged. "Here I'm considered an exotic with a style of my own. The Parisians forgive anyone anything as long as they have style."

"They may not after the war, considering where your money's coming from."

"Ah, but that's one reason why I'm here tonight. I've milked the Nazis for everything I could, but I've never liked them. Goering can be charming when he feels like it, but underneath he's a brute. And then, too, I'm an American at heart. You may not believe this, Nick, but at the beginning of the war when the Germans looked invincible, I was really afraid they'd win—afraid for the States. So now I can help the right side, which makes me feel good. And I can ensure my future—with your help."

She's being very careful getting to the main point, he thought, but here it comes.

"I'm leaving Paris in a few months," she went on. "I'm going to Switzerland with as much cash as I can and sit out the rest of the war. I don't care what happens to my nightclub—if the Germans don't close it, the French certainly will when they come into Paris."

She paused, still not taking her eyes off him.

"You got my inheritance, Nick. You got the Ramschild Company, which was founded by my grandfather and would one day have been mine. I'm not saying you got it illegally, but you own it and I don't. I want part of my inheritance back. I want it because I think I'm due it, and because when I get to Switzerland I want to have a comfortable old age. And by the way, I lied about dying. I'm healthy as a horse."

"How much?" he said.

"I want five million dollars' worth of Ramschild stock deposited in a Swiss bank in my name."

"No."

"Then you won't get the information about the heavy water."

"I won't give you the stock. I'll deposit five million dollars in your name but not the stock. You're right, Diana. I owe you something, and I'm willing to pay. But not the stock."

Her eyes flashed green fire, and for a moment he thought there was going to be a fight. But then she shrugged.

"All right, I'll take the money. Then we have a deal?"

"We have a deal."

She reached her gloved hand across the table and they shook. Then she squeezed his hand.

"Dear Nick," she whispered. "How different our lives might have been!" She released him and stood up. "The best place for you to meet Laure is at the nightclub," she said. "Since the Nazis think Semiramis is a hotbed of *collabos,* they pay no attention to the place. And of course Laure has a special immunity, being Fritzy von Stoltz's mistress. You and your friends"—she nodded toward the kitchen—"be at the club at nine tomorrow morning. Laure will tell you everything she knows—and she found out a lot more last weekend when she went to Brittany with Fritzy."

Nick stood up. "We'll be there. And Diana . . ."

"Yes?"

389

"Thank you."

She looked at him rather sadly, he thought, yet with a trace of defiance, as if she had told him more than her pride would have liked. A magnificent woman, he thought.

"You're still a beautiful woman, Diana," he said.

She looked pleased. Then she opened the door.

"How will you get home?" he asked. "The curfew's on."

"I borrowed Laure's German car," she replied, her eyes mischievous. "No German soldier would dare stop General von Stoltz's Horch."

And she vanished into the night.

CHAPTER 42

So it was love, after all, that had brought him to Paris, he mused the next morning as he, René, Guy and Paul bicycled north across Paris to Montmartre. Love and money. Five million dollars was a lot to pay, but he thought of it as conscience money, because it was possible he had been unduly harsh on Diana so many years before, and God knows, she had suffered. So to guarantee her a happy and secure life was worth it. Besides, the secret of the heavy water was worth much more than five million. It was possible that the outcome of the war depended on it.

He wondered if his mission was now over. He certainly hoped so, because as they pedaled through the beautiful streets of Paris—now so oddly empty of traffic except for military vehicles, the *velo-taxis* and bicycles—he saw ample evidence of the German presence. Nazi flags fluttered from famous buildings and the top of the Eiffel Tower, and wooden signposts, spiky with German-inscribed direction arrows, were everywhere. The end of the Occupation might be drawing near, but the conqueror was still very much in control. The sooner Nick could get out, the sooner he would feel comfortable.

When they reached the Place du Tertre, where a German private had set up an easel on the sidewalk and was executing a watercolor of the famous square, they pedaled to the rear of the building housing Semiramis and leaned their bicycles against the wall near the stage door. "Lock it," said René, handing Nick a padlock. "Bicycles cost as much as a new car used to before the war."

The four men went to the stage door and knocked. It was nine sharp. The door was opened by an elderly man wearing two sweaters, a beret and a cigarette drooping from his lips.

"*Bonjour,*" he mumbled, stepping back. "*Madame vous attend.*"

He led them through the cramped backstage area of the club that had been three apartments before Diana gutted and renovated them in 1938, after the death of Mustapha Kemal. Reaching a door with a small star on it and a placard reading "Mlle Ducaze," the old man

391

knocked. *"Entrez."* He opened the door, and the four entered a smallish dressing room where Diana and Laure were sitting in white wicker chairs. Diana, as always, wore a floor-length dress, even though it was morning. But Laure was dressed in the height of Occupation chic: a white peasant blouse with puffy shoulders, a tight-fitting black skirt that showed to perfection her long, gorgeous legs, and a pair of black-market shoes. The dressing room was fussily decorated, with a screen in the corner pasted with French and American movie posters, but all eyes were focused on Laure. Nick had seldom seen a sexier blonde, and he had seen a lot of sexy blondes. Now he understood General von Stoltz's obsession.

"This is Laure," Diana said as the old man closed the door. "Nick, how's your French?"

"Passable."

"Good, since Laure's English is nonexistent." She switched to French. "Darling, tell them about your weekend."

Laure lit a cigarette and exhaled nervously.

"Last weekend," she began, "Fritzy—that's General von Stoltz—took me to Brittany with him. We went to a town on the north coast called Trégastel and stayed at the château of a banker named the Vicomte de Luchaire. It was all very plush, the Vicomte being a buddy of all the Nazi bigwigs. Anyway, the reason we went was because Fritzy had to go to this place where they're making the heavy water. It's a few miles away from the Vicomte's, right on the coast, in what I gather is a fortress built in the fifteenth or sixteenth century—I'm no good at dates."

"What's the name of it?" asked René.

"The Forteresse de Morlaix. Fritzy left after lunch and didn't come back till five-thirty. He was very hush-hush about everything while he was sober, but that night he got drunk as usual, and he told me they were moving the whole operation into Germany next week."

René looked startled.

"Why?"

"I think it's because they're afraid there's going to be an invasion."

"That doesn't give us much time," said Guy, looking worried.

"Now that we know where the operation is, why don't we contact London and have them bomb the fortress?" said Paul.

"Too risky," said Laure. "Fritzy told me they have one of the heaviest concentrations of antiaircraft guns on the west coast of France around the fortress. I don't quite understand it, but they consider this heavy water *very* important."

She stubbed out her cigarette. There was a silence that Nick finally broke.

"I have a plan," he said quietly.

Fritz von Stoltz really didn't *like* signing execution orders; it was, unhappily, part of his job. One reason he drank so much was to forget those forms, which, within hours, sent men to the shooting posts at Fort de Vincennes, where they were tied, blindfolded, then dispatched under the direction of Lieutenant Werner Herzer. The wine blotted all that out, blotted out the ghosts of his victims—for even a man as brutal as Stoltz could be haunted. Unfortunately, it seemed to be taking more and more wine to exorcise his ghosts.

Two nights after Nick, René, Guy and Paul had bicycled across Paris to meet Laure at Semiramis, Stoltz was sitting at his special table, drinking his beloved La Tâche, watching his beloved Laure sing the opening number of the club's new revue, called *"Frühlingszeit in Berlin,"* or "Springtime in Berlin."

"We'll wander hand in hand down the Unter den Linden," crooned Laure, who wore a clinging white satin dress with white spaghetti straps over her bare shoulders. Behind her, the near-naked show girls paraded, holding branches of fake apple and cherry blossoms. On the backdrop, two painted lovebirds twittered above a flower-twined swastika. Even some of the German officers in the club were snickering. But Stoltz, half drunk, watched Laure with spellbound, tear-filled eyes. Stoltz, remembering his youth in Berlin, thought it was all terribly romantic.

"We'll kiss in the Tiergarten," Laure sang in German. "And find love when it's springtime in Berlin."

Stoltz applauded vigorously, wiped the tears from his eyes and ordered another bottle of La Tâche.

"I *loved* it!" he burped an hour and a half later as he collapsed on his back on the sofa in Laure's Place Vendôme living room. "Especially that opening number you sang. 'We'll kiss in the Tiergarten,'" he warbled in his cracked voice, "'. . . when it's springtime in Berlin.' . . . Ah, *Poupée,* I'd love to kiss you in the Tiergarten. Berlin, Berlin! How I miss it."

Laure filled his wineglass. "There may not be any Tiergarten left to kiss in," she said. "There may not be any Berlin left, for that matter."

Stoltz waved his hand dismissively. "They can bomb Berlin, but they can't destroy it. And then, after the war, the Fuehrer will build a beautiful new city, with great broad avenues . . . even bigger than the Champs Elysée. You'll see. Things look bad now, but the Fuehrer is a genius. The Allies will get tired; there'll be a settlement of some sort. It can all be worked out. The Fuehrer"—his eyes closed—"is a genius."

She watched him, holding the wineglass and the bottle of La Tâche.

"Fritzy?" she whispered. She froze, listening to his heavy breathing. He had drunk a half bottle more than usual at Maxim's, so she wasn't surprised he had passed out so quickly.

She set the glass and bottle on a table, watching him. He started to snore softly. She came over to him and unbuttoned his tunic, exposing his undershirt. She waited a minute more to be sure he was drifting into a deep sleep. Then she tiptoed to her bedroom and silently opened the door.

Diana was inside, wearing her floor-length mink and a mink hat. Laure nodded to her. Diana went to the closet door and opened it. René Reynaud, wearing a leather jacket and a black knit cap, stepped out. Diana pointed to Laure, and the two moved to the door.

"He's asleep," Laure whispered—needlessly, since Stoltz's snores were now rumbling through the apartment.

The three tiptoed into the living room. René pulled a revolver from his jacket and twisted a silencer over its muzzle. As the two women watched, spellbound, he tiptoed to the couch and aimed the gun at Stoltz's heart, the silencer no more than an inch from his undershirt.

"Vive la France," he said in a soft voice and pulled the trigger. Stoltz's body jerked slightly, and the snoring stopped.

"Get a towel," René ordered.

Laure, who had closed her eyes to avoid watching the execution, now hurried to the kitchen, her face white. She returned with a dish towel, which she tossed to René. He stuffed it between the bloody undershirt and the fatal bullet hole.

"Now we wait a half hour," said René, untwisting the silencer. "Mind if I drink his wine? It seems a shame to waste good Burgundy."

Laure nodded. Diana walked to the sofa and stared down at the General's corpse.

"Now I know what they mean when they say 'dead drunk,' " she commented.

René raised the wineglass in a toast to the corpse. "Right now,

Stoltz should be having an interesting conversation with those five hundred people he executed. *Prosit,* Herr General—you fat fuck!" And he raised the glass to his mouth.

Laure hurried into her bathroom and threw up.

A half hour later, Laure, in her Russian sable, and Diana, in her mink, carried between them the dead General, his arms slung around the women's necks, out of Laure's building into the Place Vendôme where Stoltz's Mercedes staff car was, as usual, parked, the smart red-white-and-black miniature swastika flags springing at attention from each front fender. It was snowing lightly, and Reinhard, Stoltz's sergeant chauffeur, was asleep in the front seat, as Laure knew he would be. They had buttoned Fritzy's tunic in the apartment. Then, as René held the corpse up, they had put on his fur-collared overcoat and stuck his General's cap on his head. Laure, whose flesh crawled at the thought of touching a dead body, nevertheless rose to the occasion; Diana, who had seen many dead bodies in Turkey, didn't even flinch. The two women had bumped the corpse down the stairs, then out into the snow and over to the car. Laure opened the back door and they propped the General in a corner in an upright position.

"Reinhard, wake up!" said Laure, tapping on the glass partition. The chauffeur jumped as Laure slid the partition open.

"Fräulein! I'm sorry, I dozed off. . . ."

"That's all right. The General just got a call—he has to go to the Forteresse de Morlaix immediately. The airports are closed because of the weather, so we'll have to drive. Do you have enough gas?"

Reinhard was staring at the General, propped in the back seat. Diana was sitting next to him.

"Yes."

"Then let's go. As you can see, the General had too much to drink, so my friend and I will go along to take care of him."

"Yes, Fräulein. You should have called me to help. . . ."

"No, that's all right. How long will it take to get to Brittany?"

"Five, six hours. . . ."

"Well, step on it. This is an emergency."

She closed the door, stepped over Stoltz's boots and Diana's galoshes, and sat in the opposite corner as Reinhard started the staff car. She leaned forward to close the glass partition as the Mercedes, equipped with blackout blinkers over its headlights, roared into the night.

"So far, so good," she muttered to Diana.

Diana, who was carrying three cashier's checks totaling seven million francs in her evening bag—all her available cash—nodded agreement. She reached over and moved Stoltz's right arm slightly.

"He's starting to get stiff," she whispered.

Laure shuddered and looked the other way.

CHAPTER 43

Convict #50143 was led into the visitors' room of Lewisburg Federal Penitentiary by one of the guards and was directed to the third cubicle from the end. There, Chester Hill sat down on the wooden chair and looked through the wire screen at the beautiful woman in the black dress and smart, tilted black veiled hat sitting on the other side.

"You have ten minutes," said the guard, returning to his post by the steel door.

"Did you bring the photos?" asked Chester, who had lost fifteen pounds during his three years in Lewisburg.

"Yes. I gave them to the guards," replied his former wife, Sylvia. She had divorced him a month after his conviction.

"How is Arthur?"

Arthur was their son. What Chester discovered shortly after his arrest by the F.B.I. was that he had finally succeeded in impregnating his wife.

"He's fine," Sylvia replied.

Chester clenched his fists. "If I could only *see* him," he muttered morosely.

"Chester, you know damned well I couldn't bring a child here, and I wouldn't even if I could. I don't want my son to know his father is a convicted felon and a traitor to his country."

Chester winced. "I did it for *you*," he said.

"What's that matter? It was a stupid thing to do. God, and I thought you were so smart!"

"You bitch," he snarled.

"I didn't come here to be called names."

"Then why did you come? You haven't bothered to before! None of your damned family's come. I suppose all of you pretend I never existed! Or maybe you tell people I died? Anything but admit your ex-husband's serving time."

"Chester, I can understand why you're bitter, but after all, you *did* trade with the enemy, so don't take it out on us. My father treated you

397

pretty well, if you ask me. He let you keep your stock options, and he's continued to pay you royalties on all your inventions. You're probably the richest convict in America."

And getting richer every day, he thought. Rich enough so that someday I'll pay you *all* back. The irony was that Chester, who had never had enough money as a free man and who, in fact, went to prison because of his greed for cash, was now, in prison, becoming a millionaire because of his inventions and the brilliance of his stock-market investments.

"Anyway," she went on, "the reason I'm here is that I wanted to tell you personally that I'm remarrying."

"Congratulations," he sneered. "Did you meet the lucky groom in a bar? Or did you bump into him at the Biltmore?"

She told herself to keep calm.

"Neither, thank you. I met him at Piping Rock Country Club. He's very nice and very rich and very special. His name is Cornelius Payson Brooks, and he'll make a wonderful father for Arthur. He's even agreed to adopt him."

"*Adopt* him?" Chester almost jumped out of his chair.

"Chester, be practical. You're in *prison*! It wouldn't be fair to Arthur going through life with your name. Corny's family's been around since the Revolution. . . ."

"No!" he yelled, jumping up. "He's *my* son! You can go to hell, you whore! You and your goddamned war-profiteer father and that snake of a brother of yours! I'll make you pay someday—*all* of you!"

Two guards rushed him, but Chester was so crazed he fought back, punching one guard in the mouth. This was a mistake. He was put in solitary confinement for a month.

But during that month, his stock-market investments increased in value by ten thousand dollars. And as he sat in the dark, windowless, stinking cell, nursing his wounded pride and fanning the flames of vengeance, he conceived the idea of the invention that would one day make him one of the richest men in America.

St. Patrick's Cathedral was jammed with the notables of the press world for the funeral mass for Van Nuys de Courcy Clairmont, who, despite his years of rigorous exercise, had surprised everyone by dropping dead of a massive heart attack. The Vice President of the United States attended, as well as the Governor of New York and the Mayor, leaders of society and business and the arts. The power of Van's newspapers had affected all areas of society, and though he had been heartily disliked by many powerful people, even his enemies showed up at his funeral, if for no other reason, as one of them quipped, than to make sure he was really dead.

His widow, Edith, now seventy-five, was devastated by the loss of the man she had loved for so many years. Her only consolation, as she sat in the huge cathedral, was the knowledge that she had won her long fight with Van: her adopted son, Nick, would inherit the newspaper chain.

That is, if Nick came back from Paris alive. . . .

It had been a boring half hour for Flying Officer Charles Fleming.

"The Luftwaffe's let us down," he radioed from his Spitfire. He was flying over Norfolk on a cloudy day. "There's nobody up here."

"Then head for home," Control said.

"Roger. Wilco."

He started humming the song he had heard at a London cabaret the night before. The song, sung by a blond Hungarian knockout named Magda Kun, had convulsed the audience when she hit the punch line:

"I've got the deepest shelter in town."

It was then Charles spotted the Messerschmitt-109E off his port quarter, coming in fast, armed with two 20-mm. cannon on the wings and a pair of 7.92-mm. machine guns behind the propeller. Charles went into a dive, aiming for a cloud where he could maneuver into a better firing position, but it was too late. The Messerschmitt fired and a horrified Charles saw his engine go up in flames.

"Jesus!" he gulped, sliding open his bubble cockpit hood. The black smoke and flames from the engine were choking him. He was at an altitude of three thousand feet and diving fast. He waited till the plane fell into the cloud. Then he jumped, counting slowly to ten before pulling his rip cord. The great white chute blossomed above him and his free fall jerked to a float. He was still in the cloud, which was an eerie sensation, but Charles knew that once he floated free of his cover he'd be fair game for the Messerschmitt. Both sides considered a pilot parachuting to safety fair game. Pilots were harder to replace than aircraft. Charles had become known as a wild man of the skies whose daring amounted at times to stupidity, but right now, he was scared shitless.

He fell out of the cloud. He looked down and saw the farmland of Norfolk drifting toward him. How peaceful it looked, with the Channel in the distance.

Then he saw the Messerschmitt, a speck now but heading directly for him, an angry wasp of death. The moment Charles had resolutely refused to contemplate was now almost on him: his death. It wasn't his past that rolled through his mind, it was his future, what he would miss. Taking over Ramschild, becoming as important as his father, perhaps *more* so . . . not being Nick Fleming's son, Nick becoming Charles Fleming's father. . . . I'm going to miss it all, screamed through his brain as he stared at the oncoming Messerschmitt, its machine guns aimed directly at him. This is what death looks like, he thought wildly.

Below him, his Spitfire hit the ground and exploded in orange flame and black smoke.

The Messerschmitt swerved, passing him twenty feet away. Charles saw the German pilot giving him thumbs up.

Charles howled with glee, sending back two grateful thumbs up to the pilot, who waved back and then disappeared into a cloud.

He had read that near the end of the Civil War, as the South's cause was obviously lost, soldiers on both sides had begun to show mercy, refusing senseless bloodshed. Apparently the German pilot had exhibited the same gallantry.

Charles was doing a jig of joy in the air. The future was his after all!

He landed in a field of Brussels sprouts and broke his left leg.

Stoltz is *really* loaded tonight! thought Reinhard Kissler, General von Stoltz's chauffeur, as he looked in the rearview mirror at the General, who was still propped in a corner of the back seat next to Diana Ramschild. I've been driving five hours, and he's *still* stiff as a board! He's going to kill himself if he doesn't lay off the booze. . . .

By now it was almost six in the morning and winter dawn was beginning to break over the road that led along the rocky northern coast of Brittany. There had been almost no traffic the entire way, so Reinhard had made excellent time. They were only fifteen minutes from the Forteresse de Morlaix. Reinhard had been forced by the narrow, twisty road to reduce his speed to 65 k.p.h., but even so his tires were screeching on the turns. Now the road moved away from the coast and entered a short tunnel blasted out of the rock.

Bang! Bang! Bang! Bang! Reinhard jammed the brakes as all four tires blew. The Mercedes veered crazily, almost crashing into the wall of the tunnel, but Reinhard's expertise saved him. He managed to stop the car just before the tunnel exit. He jumped out with a flashlight to see what had happened. He had just spotted the shards of glass and curled barbed wire on the pavement when the three men with sub-machine guns ran into the tunnel yelling, "Don't move or you're dead!"

Reinhard turned and raised his hands over his head. Guy (whose real, non-Resistance name was Vincent Jolicoeur) took away his service pistol and handcuffed him as Nick opened the back door of the car. General von Stoltz's body toppled into his arms.

"My God, don't drop him *now!*" exclaimed Diana. "I've been prop-ping him up for *hours.*"

Nick pushed him back in the car. "Are you both all right?" he asked.

"The General is *dead?*" gasped Reinhard.

"That's right," said Guy, grinning. "You've been driving a corpse."

"Gott in Himmel!"

Four other Resistance fighters drove a horse-drawn wagon into the near end of the tunnel.

"Get the tires changed," yelled Paul (whose real name was Yves Lefebre). "Then load the car."

Nick was helping Diana and Laure out of the back seat.

"We've got a half hour to meet the sub," he said. "We have to move fast. Come on."

"I should have worn walking shoes," Laure moaned.

"They'd have looked a bit bizarre with your sable, darling," said Diana.

Nick went over to Guy. "Any problems?" he asked.

"Not so far."

"Then I think we're taking off. We'll watch the fireworks through the sub's periscope."

Paul joined them. Nick shook his hand.

"You've got guts," he said. "I admire the hell out of you."

Paul shrugged. "You figured out how to do it. France won't forget."

"France won't forget *you,*" said Nick, and he meant it.

"Boches!" yelled one of the Resistance fighters.

They turned to see the headlights approaching their end of the tunnel.

"Shit," said Nick. "This sure as hell wasn't in the plan. . . ."

"They've seen our lights—damn!"

"Don't fire till they get in the tunnel!" Guy yelled. "And keep working on the tires!"

"Somebody prop up the General! He's fallen over."

Diana opened the back door of the staff car and climbed in.

"Come on, Fritzy," she said, pushing his corpse upright. "Smile for Jerry. Look important. And don't look so goddamned *dead*." She turned on the inside light of the car so the General would be on view.

Nick had run over to Laure. "You speak German?" he said.

"Yes."

"Go tell them who you are. Tell them the General is on his way to the fort, but the Resistance blew up his tires! *Stall* them!"

"Yes, all right. . . ."

She started toward the end of the tunnel. By now the vehicle, a military bus, had stopped and a German lieutenant was emerging from the front door.

"What's wrong?" he called.

Laure hurried up to him. The young Lieutenant's eyes widened as he took in her sabled beauty.

"Who are you?" he asked.

"I'm Laure Ducaze, a friend of General von Stoltz's, in the car back there. Someone put broken glass in the tunnel—the Resistance, I suppose—and blew out all his tires. We had to get help from a farmer. . . ."

"Can we help?"

"No, everything's fine now. But thanks anyway." She smiled her prettiest smile. The Lieutenant's thoughts were so obvious, she almost laughed.

"Well, uh . . ." he gulped. "They'll have to move the wagon out of the way. I have to get my bus through. I'm delivering two dozen Jews to Drancy, and they have to be there by noon."

Drancy, the notorious camp outside Paris, near Le Bourget airport, was where French Jews were detained, waiting for deportation to the death camps.

"Yes," said Laure, "I'll tell them to move it." Again, she smiled. "And thanks so much for your help, Lieutenant. You're as gallant as you are handsome."

He turned red. She hurried back to the tunnel.

"The bus is full of Jewish prisoners going to Drancy," she told Nick, Guy and Paul. "He wants the wagon out of the way so he can get through. I think he believed me."

"Good work," said Nick. He turned to the others. "Clear the barbed wire and move the wagon—and don't shoot unless we have to! We don't want to kill the prisoners."

"If they're going to Drancy, they're as good as dead," said Guy. "I say let's kill the Boches."

"*Maybe* they're as good as dead," snapped Nick, "but they're not dead yet, and we're sure as hell not going to kill them ourselves! Hold your fire. And keep the guns out of sight."

Lieutenant Kurt Eigler climbed back into his bus and told his driver to move on as soon as the wagon got out of the way. Lieutenant Eigler was still dazzled by Laure's beauty, but it occurred to him the situation was rather odd. How could even General von Stoltz have gotten this many farmers to change his tires at *this* ungodly hour? And yet, there was the official staff car, and in the back seat—he must have nerves of steel to sleep through all this commotion—sat General von Stoltz. No matter how strange the situation, Lieutenant Eigler was trained not to question the authority of a superior officer—and certainly not a general!

When the wagon was out of the way behind the staff car, the driver of the bus shifted gears and started the vehicle toward the tunnel entrance. Thinking of Laure Ducaze, the driver started singing, *"Ich bin von Kopf bis Fuss auf Liebe eingestellt"*—"Falling in Love Again." Lieutenant Eigler, also thinking of Laure, joined in. The two were singing boisterously as the bus lumbered into the tunnel.

When Diana Ramschild had been freed from her years in the Turkish asylum by Mustapha Kemal, she had determined to exert all her willpower to steel her emotions against any further shocks in her life. She had been largely successful. Despite temporary setbacks, such as when she had seen Nick in the Gestapo prison, Diana had become known as a woman of iron control, tough and invulnerable. But now as she sat in the back seat of the staff car watching the bus approach, something happened that blew her self-control to smithereens. She felt the corpse of General von Stoltz next to her move.

The cadaver was slowly stiffening! Screaming in sheer terror, Diana opened the nearest door and jumped out of the car. Lieutenant Eigler and his driver stopped singing.

"Was ist los?"

The bus was next to the staff car.

"Stop!" ordered Eigler, looking at the back seat of the staff car where General von Stoltz was no longer visible. Eigler, pulling his service revolver, opened the bus door and climbed out to investigate. Diana had stopped screaming and the tunnel was suddenly eerily silent. Eigler hurried to the staff car and peered inside. The gases released by the corpse's decaying intestines had combined with its advancing rigor mortis to stiffen the body into a totally unnatural position. Eigler reached in through the open door to touch the General's face. But Eigler already knew the man was dead.

"Guards!" he yelled.

The back door of the bus opened and four German soldiers started climbing out. Simultaneously, the French submachine guns opened fire. Lieutenant Eigler's chest was ripped open by bullets, and he fell backward into the staff car on top of Stoltz's corpse. As the tunnel rang with the screech of the guns, the four guards also crumpled onto the pavement. Then, silence, except for the echoes of the gunshots ricocheting off the tunnel's damp walls and ceiling.

Nick ran to the rear of the bus, stepping over the dead guards, and looked inside. In the dim light, he could barely make out the prisoners crowded in the small bus, like Dantean shades.

"Come out," he said. "You're free! Come out!" No one moved. "I'm an American," he added, "and the others are Resistance. Come out. You have to hurry! We have little time!"

The shades began to move. Nick was joined by Guy, Paul and Laure.

"Get back to work," Guy yelled to the other men. As the Resistance men returned to changing the tires on the staff car, Laure watched the prisoners climbing out of the bus. Laure, who had blithely sung of "youpins" and "kikes" at Semiramis, now saw two dozen frightened human beings climb out of the bus, their hands tied behind them. Two teen-agers, a brother and sister perhaps, housewives, businessmen, an elderly couple, all climbed down the steps assisted by Nick, Guy and Paul. They looked more shocked and confused by their sudden change of fortune than elated.

> *"Kick a kike,*
> *Steal his bike,*
> *And come to gay Par-ee!"*

Laure Ducaze felt the nausea of shame.

"Can you take care of them?" Nick asked Guy.

"We'll have to. We'll find some place to hide them. Meanwhile, we're ten minutes behind schedule."

"I know. We'll have to start loading the dynamite in the car. Wait a minute!" Nick looked at the bus. "To hell with the car—the bus is better! And they won't spot the dynamite in it!"

404

"You're right." Guy yelled at the workers, "Forget the tires! Load the explosives in the bus! We'll use it instead."

Eight minutes later, the bus, loaded in the back with six wooden crates of wired dynamite—enough to blow up a city block—backed out of the tunnel, did a U-turn, then roared off in the direction of Forteresse de Morlaix. The driver, alone in the bus, was Paul, who had spent the previous day checking out the route to the fort and the fort itself through binoculars. He checked his watch: he had twelve minutes before the timing device detonated the dynamite in back. He hit a straightaway and jammed the accelerator. The speedometer climbed: 50 k.p.h., 55, 60, 65, 70, 75. Paul thought about his life, which now had nine minutes left, nine minutes to eternity. He remembered his childhood in the pleasant Paris suburb of Neuilly, his father, who was a doctor, his mother, who had written poems that were never published. He remembered his first love affairs, his years at the Sorbonne, his romance with the movies, his dreams of writing film scripts. . . . They had drawn straws the day before, and he had picked the short one. Now he would live a greater film script than he could ever have written.

The high stone walls of the fort loomed in the distance. Paul checked his watch again: three minutes. He checked the speedometer: 100 k.p.h. He was sweating. What would it feel like? Nothing. I will feel nothing, he told himself. Just sudden blackness. He was vain enough to tell himself he would be remembered as a hero. He was smart enough to wonder if, in twenty years' time, anyone would remember him at all. *N'importe,* he thought. I'm giving my life for something fine.

The two guards at the gate in the chain-link fence saw the bus hurtling toward them. They came out of their guardhouse, assuming the bus would slow down. To their amazement, it didn't. "Halt!" one yelled as they aimed their rifles. They fired.

A second later, the bus crashed through the horizontal pole and roared toward the gates of the fort. One guard scrambled to sound the alarm while the other continued firing at the bus. Like a thunderbolt, the bus crossed the drawbridge over the moat and crashed into the heavy wooden gates.

The explosion was heard as far away as the town of Morlaix, six kilometers to the south.

CHAPTER 44

"J ESUS CHRIST!" exclaimed Commander Warren V. Hickman, skipper of the U.S.S. *Starfish*. "It really blew! Take a look."

He stepped aside and Nick put his eyes to the periscope. Through it he saw the flames and smoke roiling up over the fort, which looked like an oil tank after it had been struck by a V-2 rocket. Somewhere in that smoke, he thought, is the soul of Yves Lefebre, alias Paul, the brave Resistance fighter. God rest his soul.

"I think we'd better get out of here," said Commander Hickman. He took back the periscope, took one final look at the fort, swung the periscope around to check the water surface, which was free of boats, then ordered, "Down periscope. Prepare to dive."

Nick climbed down the ladder to join Diana and Laure in the tiny wardroom. In the cramped machinery-choked confines of the sub, the women in their sable and mink looked wonderfully out of place.

"It's all over," said Nick, joining them at the table for a cup of coffee. "Thanks in part to both of you."

"And Paul?" asked Laure.

"He's dead."

"How was he picked?"

"They drew straws. He could have backed out, but he didn't."

Diana, whose feet were sore from the climb down the rocks to the beach where they were picked up by the rubber raft, and whose nerves were still frazzled by the shock of the moving corpse, looked at Nick.

"Commander Hickman says we'll be in London in time for lunch. I think we could all stand a good meal."

"At Claridge's," said Nick. "On me."

Laure took a sip of her coffee. When she put the cup down, she noticed that Nick was watching her.

She had seen him looking at her that way several times before.

Diana, who also saw the look, felt a twinge of jealousy.

. . .

Six hours later, they were finishing a lunch of sole Véronique in a luxurious corner suite on the third floor of Claridge's.

"What are your plans now?" said Nick as the waiter poured the second bottle of Puligny-Montrachet '38. "You can't go to Switzerland now without going back into France—which I wouldn't advise."

"I realize that," said Diana. "Now that I'm in London, I'll wait out the war here. I have enough money, I have a Turkish passport, and I have connections. I should be all right. Meanwhile, you'll be arranging the details of our little financial transaction. I may not be able to get into Switzerland, but your money can."

"I'll talk to my London bankers this afternoon. Don't worry, Diana. I don't go back on my word."

"Oh? You did once."

He nodded. "Touché. All right, but I won't renege this time." He turned to Laure. "How about you? What are your plans?"

She shrugged as the waiter put the bottle in the ice bucket and silently left the room. "I suppose I'll stay here too," she said. "I really have no other place to go."

"How about New York?"

She looked surprised. "New *York?*"

"Why not? I can set you up in a nice apartment and lend you whatever money you need."

"But I don't speak English!"

"Go to Berlitz."

She looked at Diana, then back to Nick. "Monsieur Fleming," she said, "I'll admit I let Fritzy von Stoltz buy me because life in Paris has been hard. But that doesn't mean *anyone* can buy me." She got up from the table. "Excuse me. I've had a very unpleasant night, and I'm very tired. Thanks for the lunch."

He watched her as she left the suite.

Diana sipped her wine. "She'll go with you," she said. "She's just playing hard to get. But you're a fool to get involved with her. She'll take you for millions before she's through." She put down her glass. "If you're smart, you'll find yourself another Edwina."

Nick frowned.

"Diana, I figure I've repaid my debt to you. I don't need advice to the lovelorn."

"Perhaps. I hope you're not thinking of marrying her?"

"Who's talking about marriage? I just think she's terrific-looking, and I admire the way she handled herself throughout this whole thing.

Why shouldn't I offer her a chance to go to New York? I'll offer the same to you, if you want it."

"No thanks."

She leaned back in her chair, her mind a bit woozy from fatigue and the wine. If only it were *me* he wanted! she thought. If only *me!*

But no, I'll always be the Lady of the Veils. And beneath the veils, those hideous scars. . . .

A memory jolted her, a memory of a conversation she had had with some German officers at Semiramis a month before. They had been talking about a plastic surgeon in London who had developed new techniques in skin transplants while working with burn victims of the Blitz. Word had reached even Germany of the miracles he was performing. What was his name? Dr. Tremaine, or something like that? She had been skeptical at the time, but now that she was in London . . .

She looked across the table at Nick. If I could remove the veils, she thought. . . . If I could be beautiful again—or at least presentable—I'd make him a good wife, the wife I always wanted to be to him. . . .

Oh, damn you, Nick, I still love you so! Maybe there's still a chance for me. . . . Oh, God, maybe there's still a chance!

Nick was tired. The strain of his time in France was catching up with him. True, they had knocked out Forteresse de Morlaix, and its threat to the outcome of the war, and for that he was proud and relieved. But he would be fifty-six years old next month. Even though he was still fit, by no stretch of the imagination could he be considered a young man, and in a few years he wouldn't even be a middle-aged man anymore. The realization of his mortality, which had begun with his fiftieth birthday, had increased with each succeeding year. Now he wanted no more of the war. Now he wanted peace and comfort and love. He wanted an infusion of youth.

He wanted Laure.

At six that evening, Laure was luxuriating in a hot tub in her room on the fourth floor when she heard her bell ring.

"I'll get it, luv," called the chambermaid who was turning down the bed for the night. Laure didn't understand her, but went on sponging. Then she heard the maid say, "But she's in the tub, sir! You can't go in there." And then Nick's voice saying, "Thank you. That will be all." And then the maid's voice, as she pocketed the pound note, "Thank *you*, sir. Good night." Then the door closing.

And then he was standing in the bathroom door, looking at her with those hungry eyes.

"You might have knocked," she said.

"The door was open. I've made an appointment for you and Diana in the morning at Adrian Pell's shop. The management tells me he's the hot new designer in town. Since you had to leave your clothes in Paris, you'll need a new wardrobe." He looked at her soft, pink shoulders, flecked with soap suds, at her full breasts barely visible beneath the sudsy water. "I told him to send the bills to me."

"Thank you, but I can pay for my own clothes."

"You didn't in Paris."

"If you're going to throw that up to me again, you can go to hell!" she shouted.

"I made a reservation for us tonight at Boulestin's. It's the best restaurant in London."

"I don't like English food!"

"It's French."

"I have a date with General de Gaulle!"

He started laughing.

"Well?" she growled. "How do you know I don't? Aren't I a heroine of the Resistance now? Maybe he'll give me a medal!"

"Oh, you deserve one. I won't argue with that."

"Didn't I get the information from Fritzy? Didn't I make it possible for you to kill him? Didn't I sit next to his disgusting corpse last night? Your great plan would have gone nowhere without me!"

"I agree. I admire everything you did. I think you're terrific. I also think you're the most beautiful woman I've seen"—he hesitated—"since my wife died."

Now he was serious. And now, *she* was serious. Wife? He was certainly handsome. And the way he had masterminded the attack on the fort had impressed her enormously: he was a man used to command. And Diana had told her he was one of the richest men in America.

America. . . . After four years in a Europe tearing itself apart with war, peaceful America seemed like a golden dream. . . .

"Is the food *really* French?" she asked in a softer voice.

At least, she thought, I won't have to close my eyes and think about Clark Gable. With M. Fleming, I'd keep my eyes wide open!

That night, after a superb dinner and a bottle of vintage Louis Roederer Cristal, they made love in his suite. After months of the drunken and repulsive advances of the Butcher of Paris, Nick's lovemaking was a concerto of lust after chopsticks. She reveled in his strength and smell and hunger and desire. As he thrust into her, slowly at first but with increasing passion, their clasped hands outstretched like two figures on a cross, the sweetness flooded her body and she forgot the war and Fritzy and death and remembered only love and life and joy. When they came in a perfect orgasm, they drifted into the afterglow of sweet satisfied desire.

"An hour ago," she whispered as she kissed his shoulder, "I'd have gone to New York for your money. Now I'll go for you."

The strong light hurt her eyes, but Diana sat uncomplaining as Dr. Kenneth Tremaine examined the scars on her face. The examination seemed endless. Finally, he turned off the light.

"I cannot guarantee results, Miss Ramschild," he said. "I *never* make guarantees, for that matter, and your face was severely burned. But certainly I have dealt with worse cases. If you are willing to take the gamble, I think there is a seventy percent chance that skin grafts could be successful. It would require several operations."

"What would I look like if it was successful?" she asked quietly.

"There would be very fine scars that makeup could disguise. I'm not saying you'd be a movie star, but you would not be disfigured. You could throw away your veils."

"What will I look like if the operations are not successful?"

"I won't deceive you. Massive skin transplants such as I am proposing are dangerous—or at the very least risky. There is a possibility of infection. To be frank, there is a possibility of death."

"I see."

She thought a moment. She could live to a comfortable old age as she was now, cushioned by Nick's millions. Or she could take this enormous gamble and perhaps have a chance for Nick. Or, if not Nick, at least the chance to stop being an "exotic," which was, she knew perfectly well, a nice term for "freak." Did she want love enough to gamble her life?

"When can we begin the treatment?" she asked as she placed the veil back over her face.

A week after V-J Day, Nick gathered his children together in the living room of the Park Avenue triplex. There was Charles, now twenty-six, who had been honorably discharged from the R.A.F. after being shot down over Norfolk. His broken leg had not mended well, and he would walk with a slight limp for the rest of his life. He was finishing his war-interrupted studies at Columbia and was considered one of New York's most eligible young bachelors.

There was Sylvia, twenty-five, whose marriage to Corny Brooks was having a rocky go of it—Corny, it turned out, was a mean drunk. Sylvia had left her four-year-old son by Chester Hill, Arthur Brooks, at home in Cold Spring Harbor to come into town to be with her father for the evening.

There was Edward Fleming, twenty-four, who had served honorably in the Pacific and was now looking for an apartment in Greenwich Village so he could begin work on his war novel.

Maurice Fleming, twenty-one, had served in the Coast Guard and was now re-enrolled in Harvard to finish his education.

Fiona and Vicky—the inseparable sisters—were sitting together on a couch. Fiona was trying out the next morning for a part in a re-staging of Mary Roberts Rinehart's venerable horror play *The Bat,* and was understandably nervous. She was twenty-two. Nineteen-year-old Vicky was in her sophomore year at Smith.

Finally, there was twenty-year-old Hugh, the family jock, who was Yale's star quarterback.

"I wanted us all to be together tonight," Nick began, "first, because we've been separated for a number of years and I wanted to see all your faces again. You all look mighty good to me."

"You don't look bad yourself, Pop," piped up Hugh, and his brothers and sisters applauded. Nick looked pleased.

"Second," he went on, "I wanted you to know what probably doesn't need saying. Namely, that you were all very dear to your mother."

The smiles faded as each child recalled his or her private memories of Edwina.

"And third, because all of you have an interest in the future of Ramschild, I wanted to tell you about some important decisions I've made. I'm reorganizing Ramschild, Metropolitan Pictures and Clairmont newspapers into a holding company called Fleming Industries. I'm looking very aggressively for new businesses to buy to bring into Fleming Industries, because I want to phase Ramschild out of the arms business. . . ."

"What?" exclaimed Charles, so loud that Vicky, who was near him, jumped. "You can't do that!"

Nick gave his eldest a cool look.

"I can do what I damn well please," he said.

"But why would you do it? If *any* company was responsible for winning the war, it was Ramschild! We've got dozens of citations from the government to prove it! Besides, the company makes a bloody fortune!"

"Charles, Ramschild caused your mother's death."

"That was Chester Hill, who was a traitor. It had nothing to do with the company!"

Nick sighed. "Let me put it this way: I'm tired of being linked in the public's mind with weapons and death. Besides, I think if a major arms company gets out of the business, it might have a beneficial effect on the whole world."

"Oh, come *on*. What effect? The other companies would just fight over our customers. When they forced Krupp out of the business after the first World War it sure as hell didn't stop the second."

Nick looked very uncomfortable. "It's possible I'm being optimistic," he conceded. "It's also possible the atomic bomb has put us *all* out of business."

"Has the Pentagon stopped placing orders?"

"They've cut back. . . ."

"Yes, because the war's over. But have they *stopped?*"

"No."

"And I bet they won't. And I bet the United Nations won't stop wars either. I'll bet things will go on pretty much as they always have because we're too *afraid* to use the atomic bomb. If we weren't, then we'd drop it on Moscow *now,* before the Russians get it. I'll bet it's going to be wars as usual and business as usual with arms companies, whether Ramschild is one of them or not. Father, you say you're tired of being called the Titan of Death. All right, let them call *me* that! I'd be delighted. All my life I've wanted to run Ramschild. You *can't* take that away from me now!"

It was an impassioned plea. Again, Nick hesitated.

"You're the boss now," Charles continued. "No one's denying that. But we're the future of the company. At least let us have some say in what's going to happen to it!"

Nick looked around the room at his numerous progeny, the children who were now growing up, looming ever larger in his own life.

"All right," he said finally. "I'm willing to put it to a vote. All those wanting to keep Ramschild in the weapons business, which Charles will eventually take over, raise their right hand. But before you vote, think. Think as I've been thinking since your mother died. The arms business is a business of death. Do we, as a family, want to stay in it?"

412

He paused. Silence.

"All right. Those in favor raise their right hand."

Up shot Charles's, followed by those of Maurice and Hugh and Sylvia. Abstaining were Edward, Fiona and Vicky.

"It's a majority!" announced Charles triumphantly. "Hot damn!"

Nick said nothing, but in his bones he knew he had made a mistake.

Diana Ramschild closed her eyes as Dr. Tremaine put the mirror in her hand and guided it to a position in front of her face. The hospital room was devoid of flowers because Diana had undergone the four difficult operations in secret, spending her recuperations in her apartment on the Quai de Mont Blanc in Geneva, Switzerland. Besides, Diana had few flower-sending friends. Kemal Atatürk was dead, Goering and the other top Nazis were either dead or awaiting trial in Nuremberg—the world she had inhabited for so long was turning to dust. She had sold off her chain of cabarets at a handsome profit in preparation for the long ordeal of the operations.

Now was the moment.

She opened her green eyes and looked in the mirror.

The scars were gone.

What she saw was the face of an attractive middle-aged woman who had had a skillful face-lift. With proper makeup, the face could be more than attractive.

"Doctor," she said in a soft voice, "you are a magician."

A week later, she was back in her luxurious apartment on the Avenue Foch. She was in the process of buying an entire new wardrobe from Christian Dior, who had just taken the fashion world by storm with his sensational "New Look." Diana was giving herself a new look: gone were the veils, the gloves, the long dresses to cover the scars. She was spending thousands on clothes, and all with one goal in view: to return to New York after all these years abroad and lay siege to Nick Fleming. She didn't know if she could catch him, but she had hope.

Her apartment had six rooms, wonderful airy high-ceilinged rooms from the Belle Epoque with French windows opening out on the fourth floor over the wide Avenue Foch. She had filled the rooms with furniture she had bought during the war at bargain prices in the little *antiquaire* shops she had come to know so well. Though she was now a resident of Switzerland, she regarded Paris as her home.

She was sitting at her dining-room table in a peignoir sipping her café au lait and orange juice made for her by Marie, her sixty-year-old maid. Diana had never had a weight problem, but she had decided to lose five pounds, so she was forgoing her usual brioche and *confiture*—she called the five pounds her "Nick pounds." She knew she would have to have every advantage on her side to have even a chance with him.

She was glancing over the pages of the morning paper when she saw the headline:

> Munitions Magnate to Wed Entertainer
> American Tycoon Nick Fleming
> to Marry Laure Ducaze, Former
> Chanteuse at Paris Nightclub

Marie was in the kitchen when she heard the sobs. She hurried to the door to see her employer sobbing heartbrokenly.

"Mademoiselle!" she cried, hurrying to her.

"Useless!" Diana wept, as she tore at her lace peignoir. "It's all been useless! The operations . . . everything . . . useless! He doesn't love me, he loves that *whore!*"

Part VII

LOVE AT TWILIGHT
1950-1951

I N 1949, Nick infuriated conservative New Yorkers by beginning the razing of a block of twenties-era luxury apartment houses between Park and Lexington Avenues in the Fifties, prime real estate he had bought personally for the then-staggering sum of ten million dollars.

But if conservative New Yorkers rightly howled at the beginning of the end for residential Park Avenue, architectural critics rhapsodized over the thirty-story office building Nick erected. Designed by Rolf Dietrich, a prize-winning Swiss architect who had been a pupil of Walter Gropius', the Fleming Building was a sleek and stunning glass-and-steel tower that was then innovative but was doomed to spawn a thousand clichéd bastards.

The building's purpose was to house Nick's empire, which he had reorganized into the giant holding company called Fleming Industries. Ten floors of the building housed Fleming Communications, the nucleus of which was Van Nuys Clairmont's newspaper chain, which Nick now owned. Van's chain had comprised twenty newspapers and two radio stations at his death. Nick had bought three more radio stations and two TV stations and had gone whole hog into the magazine field, buying such low-profile but high-profit publications as *The Home Mechanic* and *Knitting World* as well as higher-profile magazines like *Movie Gossip,* now edited by an aging Harriet Sparrow, and *High Fashion.*

Six floors housed the international offices of the Ramschild division, now under the supervision of Charles Fleming. Nick might regret his giving in to his children about getting out of the arms business, but he had nothing but admiration for Charles's running of the company. All of his good and bad qualities—his daring, his intense egocentricity, his insensitivity to anything but success, his forceful personality—made him an outstanding businessman, and the Ramschild profits were staggering, helped, of course, by the Cold War and now the Korean War.

Charles spent a hefty percentage of his time at the Pentagon and loved every minute of it. He had none of his father's philosophic qualms about the essential immorality of the gun business; far from it, he viewed himself as a patriot and Ramschild as Uncle Sam's "muscle." He had opened a huge new plant in Tennessee and was working on plans for one in Brazil. Nick went along with all this. But when Charles wanted to branch out into the military aircraft business, to his intense chagrin, his father said no and would give no better reason than that "enough is enough."

Charles began to view his father as a roadblock to his ambitions.

Four floors of the building managed Nick's real-estate holdings, bought bit by bit over the years, which included valuable chunks of Manhattan, Los Angeles, Miami, Dallas, Chicago and Indianapolis as well as his Napa Valley vineyard, a Texas cattle ranch that included six profitable oil wells, two thousand acres in northern Louisiana where they were exploring for natural gas, and Metropolitan Studios, now leased to independent production. Two floors of the Fleming Building were devoted to Nick's personal finances. His fortune, now estimated at close to a billion dollars, required a small army of accountants and tax-savvy lawyers. The bottom seven floors were rented to outside businesses.

But the top floor, the tower's crowning glory, housed the executive offices, where Nick's fifteen vice presidents worked in sumptuous, art-hung offices and where Nick reigned in a six-room suite that included a bedroom and bath, a private dining room, a private kitchen, a screening room, a mammoth reception room and Nick's forty-by-sixty-foot extravaganza of an office with spectacular views of Manhattan to the north and east.

Nick's wartime exploits in France, which were not revealed to the public until after Hiroshima, earned him the Distinguished Service Cross, which was pinned on him personally by Harry Truman in the Oval Office, and promotion to brigadier general. This, plus a postwar re-evaluation of his prewar warnings about the Nazi menace and a general euphoric canonization of American industrialists who had led the nation's amazing war effort, earned him a reversal of his public image in the press. And with the beginning of the Cold War and the anti-Communist hysteria of the late forties, Nick became if not exactly beloved, at least respected by most Americans. But to the radical fringe, he was still anathema. And the official opening of the Fleming Building in October 1950, while greeted warmly in the large New York dailies, generated new outbursts in the left-wing press against

Nick's alleged war profiteering, raking up the old chestnuts about his "dark ties" with warmongering foreign governments.

When Nick brought Laure Ducaze to New York in 1944, he had had no intention of marrying her. He installed her in a four-room apartment in a building he owned on East 56th Street, gave her a handsome allowance, opened charge accounts for her at all the best stores and made love to her, thinking this the best of all sensible worlds. He had never thought of her as anything but a glorious mistress. To his surprise, after six months, he found he was missing her when he wasn't with her. She was not only great in bed, she was the first woman he had met since Edwina died whose company he actually enjoyed. Two more months and he was convinced he was in love. He grappled with the question of marrying her. He was over twice her age, and would he look like a dirty old man, robbing the cradle? Finally, he decided he would have what he wanted and to hell with the rest of the world.

To his surprise, however, Laure wasn't in that much of a hurry to become Mrs. Nick Fleming. Nick, who had grown up in a world that assumed every woman wanted a wedding ring, was puzzled by Laure's lack of interest in legitimacy. She was happy as she was. She liked luxury, but Diana had been wrong. Laure wasn't an especially greedy person and had scant interest in Nick's fortune. She liked the freedom she enjoyed as his mistress and was reluctant—and a bit shy—to become stepmother to seven adults of her own generation.

But to Nick, the appearance of family virtue was always vitally important, and he wanted to legitimize the situation. He badgered her for two more years until finally, in 1947, she gave in.

Laure turned out to be a better stepmother than she—or her stepchildren—would have imagined. With the exception of Charles and Sylvia—who saw little of her anyway—Nick's children rather liked their new French stepmother, who was essentially easygoing with a streak of indolence. Lazy or no, when twenty-four-year-old Vicky announced her engagement in the fall of 1950 to Ross Harrington, Jr., the heir to a steel fortune, Laure took over the arrangements for what promised to be one of the biggest weddings of the year.

"What do you think, Laure?" Vicky asked as she modeled her wedding dress in front of the full-length mirror in her bedroom.

"It's lovely, Vicky," replied her French stepmother, who had learned to speak English, albeit with an accent that made her husband sound like "Neek" and Vicky "Veekee." "Truly lovely. You will be the *most* beautiful bride in the world."

Vicky smiled. She had inherited Edwina's English beauty, although her hair was darker than her mother's auburn. She was a tall girl, and the white satin wedding dress with its broad skirt made her look statuesque.

"Well, I don't know about the *world,* but it's beautiful. Should I show it to Daddy?"

"Oh, no, that's bad luck!"

"It's showing the *groom* that's bad luck. No, I want Daddy to see it. After all, he's paying for it. Come on—he hasn't left for the office yet."

The two women hurried out of the bedroom on the second floor of the Park Avenue triplex, down the hall hung with the Utrillos and Vuillards Laure loved and down the stairs to the mammoth reception hall, Vicky's long train fluttering behind her. Then into the dining room with its exquisite eighteenth-century Chinese wallpaper and its crystal chandelier. Nick was sitting at the end of the English yew table drinking coffee and finishing *The Wall Street Journal.*

" 'Here comes the bride,' " sang Vicky, " 'all fat and wide.' Ta ta!"

Nick put down the paper, looked at his youngest daughter and for a second saw Edwina.

"It just arrived," said Vicky, beaming. "You like it?"

He stood up, came to her and kissed her. "It's gorgeous, just like you."

"Oh, Daddy, I'm so excited!" she said, hugging him. "The wedding's going to be dreamy! I can hardly *wait!*"

"Ten more days and you'll be an old married woman."

"Ten more days and I'll be a young bride," she corrected, waltzing around the long table. "Mrs. Ross Harrington, who had the *most* lovely wedding of the year and then took off for Bermuda and Nassau for a glorious honeymoon with her dashing husband. Doesn't it sound marvelous? Sun, sand and sex! Yippee!"

Laure laughed. "It doesn't sound bad," she said, taking Nick's hand. "Why don't *we* take off for some sun, sand and sex?"

"We are," he said, kissing her. "I have to go to Rio after the wedding, and you're coming with me. And there's *lots* of sun, sand and sex in Rio."

"Rio!" said Laure. "I've never been. What fun! You see, darling," she said to Vicky, "life with your father is a perpetual honeymoon."

"If you're trying to make me jealous, you're wasting your time," said Vicky. Then she looked at her father and smiled. "But he *is* the most dreamy father in the world."

"And you're a pretty dreamy daughter," Nick said with a wink.

Of all his children, he had a special affection for Vicky, perhaps because she was his youngest, and most innocent, but also perhaps because she reminded him so much of Edwina. Nick loved Laure, but in his heart there would always be a special corner for Edwina.

"Are you Miss Vicky Fleming?" asked the young man with the pock-marked face. He wore a black chauffeur's uniform and cap.

Vicky had just been seated at a corner table at Pavillon where she was going to have lunch with her sister Fiona, who was to be one of her bridesmaids.

"Yes."

"I have a message from Mr. Ross Harrington, Senior. I'm his chauffeur, and I'm supposed to drive you out to Far Hills. Mr. Harrington said it was an emergency."

Vicky was alarmed. "Is something wrong?" she asked. "Is Ross sick?"

"I don't know, miss. All I know is that Mr. Harrington said it's an emergency, and I'm supposed to drive you out there right away."

"But I'm having lunch with my sister. . . ."

"He said right away, miss."

Vicky sighed. "I guess that means no lunch." She edged out of the banquette. "I'll leave a message with Monsieur Soulé."

"I'll be outside with the car, miss."

Three minutes later, Vicky, wearing a raincoat and hat, emerged from New York's finest restaurant, at the corner of 57th Street and Park Avenue. It was a windy, rainy autumn afternoon, and umbrellas were being turned inside out by the gusts. The chauffeur, who was of medium height but very muscular-looking, was standing by the black Cadillac limousine, holding a black umbrella. Vicky waited in the doorway for him to come to her with the umbrella, but since that didn't seem to occur to him, she decided he must be new to his profession and dashed across the sidewalk in the rain. He opened the door and she climbed into the back. Then he closed the door, got in front, started the car and headed west across 57th Street.

She noticed one of the ashtrays was full of cigarette butts. This guy's not going to last long in this job, she thought. She knew that her future father-in-law hated dirty ashtrays.

She didn't become alarmed until twenty minutes after they had left the New Jersey side of the Lincoln Tunnel. Then she opened the glass partition and said, "Excuse me, but this isn't the way to the Harringtons'. I've been there dozens of times. . . ."

"I'm not taking you to the estate, miss," he interrupted. "Mr. Harrington's at the hunting lodge."

"*What* hunting lodge? I've never heard of any hunting lodge."

"It's not Mr. Harrington's hunting lodge, miss. It belongs to Mr. Corbett."

"Who's Mr. Corbett?"

"A business associate of Mr. Harrington's, miss. There are four or five of them having a meeting in the lodge."

"But . . ." She frowned. "I don't understand. Has someone been shot by accident?"

"No, miss."

"Then why . . . I mean, this makes no sense."

He said nothing. She noticed him watching her in the mirror. There was something in his dark-brown eyes that frightened her. She sat back in the seat. They were traveling through woods now, passing an occasional forlorn shack, going seventy miles an hour over the bumpy road.

She sat forward again.

"What's your name?" she demanded angrily.

"Williams, miss. William Williams."

"Well, William Williams, I want you to let me off at the next house. I'm going to telephone the Harringtons and find out what's going on. I should have called them from the city."

To her surprise, he said, "Very well, miss. The next house."

She sat back, thinking perhaps she was overreacting.

They passed a farmhouse badly in need of a paint job.

"I said the next house!" she almost shouted.

"Sorry, miss. The *very* next house."

"Well, see that you stop! And I'm going to tell Mr. Harrington about your behavior!"

"Sorry, miss."

A minute later, he pulled into a muddy lane that might have been a driveway and roared the limousine into the woods.

"This isn't a house!" she screamed.

"Yes it is."

The heavy car lurched and bumped, splashing through puddles. Then, two hundred yards from the road, he stopped. She was trembling as he got out of the front seat. He opened the back door.

"This is the next house, miss," he said.

She looked at the sagging shack in the woods. "They won't have a telephone," she said.

"Let's go in and see."

"No! Take me back. . . ."

She stopped. He had pulled a gun.

"Get out, miss," he said quietly. "There's no one within a mile of here, so there's no point in screaming. If you do what I say, you won't be hurt."

She was terrified. The rain had slowed to a drizzle, and he had a black umbrella hooked over his wrist.

"Who are you?" she said, almost choking.

"Get out."

Starting to cry, she got out of the limousine.

"Let's go to the house."

"What are you going to do?" she sobbed.

He grabbed her wrist and pulled her forward. She started screaming, petrified by the strength of his grip. He pulled her up onto the front stoop and kicked open the door. Then he pushed her inside.

The shack was a squatter's desolate hideaway left over from the Depression. There were a sagging, filthy cot, two battered chairs and a rough wooden table with an oil lamp on it. Rain dripped through a dozen holes in the ceiling.

"Take off your clothes," he said, slamming the door shut.

"No . . . please . . ." She was backing away from him, trembling.

"Strip naked."

He closed the umbrella and placed it in the corner. Then he started unbuttoning his tunic. He still held the gun.

"I told you you won't be hurt," he soothed. "Just do what I say."

Her common sense told her to obey. She took off her raincoat and hat.

"Put them on the floor," he said.

She did. Then she took off her rain boots and her Delman shoes.

"Why are you doing this?" she whispered.

"You're very pretty, miss." He took off his boots, then unbuttoned his pants. "I want to fuck you, miss."

She was sobbing again. He dropped his pants, and she saw he wore no underwear. His body was hard and muscled, the body of a boxer perhaps.

"You're a pervert!" she sobbed.

"That's right, miss. I enjoy this. See how stiff my prick is? It's very eager, miss. It's telling me, 'Fuck the pretty lady. Fuck her *hard.*'"

"Oh, my God. . . ."

He put the gun on the floor beside the umbrella, then jumped her like a savage animal and tore off her Hattie Carnegie suit.

"I told you to *strip!*" he raged. "Get naked, you bitch!"

"Please . . ."

"Get *NAKED!*"

He ripped off her bra and pants, then stared at her nakedness. "Oh, my." He smiled. "The lady is *very* pretty, William. That's the name of my prick, miss. William Williams. He's my pet, and I have to feed him regular. Look at her nice big tits, William. And those nice hips and legs. And that pretty twat, just waiting for you, William. Oh, what a nice meal we'll have!"

He grabbed her and threw her down on the cot. She screamed and beat at him with her fists as he pushed himself on top of her.

"Don't get me mad!" he roared. "No telling what I'll do when I'm mad! See that umbrella! I could shove that into you if I'm mad! All the way up!"

"Dear God . . ."

"Lie *STILL!*"

She obeyed, too terrified not to. She could smell his sweat, acrid and foul.

"Now in you go, William. Nice and easy."

"Oh, God, oh, God . . ."

"Oh, she's so nice and warm and tight, William. . . . What's this? She's a virgin?"

She screamed as he rammed through her hymen.

"Daddy, please help me . . . somebody help me . . . Ross . . . somebody save me. . . ."

"In and out, in and out. . . ."

"Help me, help me!"

"Oh, it's so nice! Isn't it nice, William? Having a good time?"

"Oh, God, oh, God . . . Why is this happening to me? WHY?"

"Ahhh . . . Oh, it feels good." He was gurgling. "Coming, coming . . ."

He put his hands around her throat and started squeezing.

"Coming, coming . . . it feels so good . . ."

He crushed her windpipe. By the time he reached his orgasm, Vicky Fleming was dead.

. . .

Laure was having a facial at Elizabeth Arden's when the phone call came from Nick. It was four in the afternoon.

"Something's happened to Vicky," he said. "She was going to have lunch at Pavillon with Fiona, but when Fiona got there she was told a chauffeur had picked Vicky up to take her out to the Harringtons'. But when I called the Harringtons, they knew nothing about it."

"Then where is she?"

"I don't know. But I've notified the police."

"The *police?* You don't think . . ."

"I don't know what to think, but I'm worried. I need you, Laure. Can you come home?"

"Of course, darling. I'll be there as soon as I can."

She found him in his study on the phone and she waited till he hung up. She had never seen him look so tense. Even in the tunnel ambush in Brittany he had looked less concerned than now.

"The police got a description of the chauffeur from the waiters at Pavillon," he said. "They're sending it to the F.B.I. in Washington."

She came around his desk and kissed him. "Then there's still no word from her?"

"No."

"But what do you think it could possibly be?"

"I don't know. Perhaps a kidnapping. The police are going to tap our phones in case we get a ransom call."

She smoothed his hair, which was now silver-gray. She saw his fist clench, then unclench, then clench again.

"If anything happens to her . . ." he said softly. He didn't finish the sentence.

The members of the Fleming family who were in New York gathered at the apartment that evening for a glum dinner (twenty-six-year-old Maurice, Nick and Edwina's fifth child, was spending two years in London working at the Saxmundham Bank with his cousin, Lord Ronald Saxmundham, who had inherited his uncle's title and position at the bank when Edwina's father died at the end of the war). There was the eldest, Charles, now thirty-one, and still unmarried. His sister Sylvia sat opposite him next to Nick. Sylvia was separated from her second husband, Corny Brooks. Next to her was twenty-nine-year-old Edward, dark and broodingly handsome, who after his graduation from Princeton had flabbergasted his father by telling him he had no interest in business and wanted to become a writer. All the children had inherited substantial trust funds from Edwina, so Edward could afford to move to Greenwich Village, where he was struggling with his first novel and, unknown to his father, smoking "boo," which was what black jazz musicians called marijuana. In the Village Edward wore dirty khaki pants and sweaters with holes in them, but uptown he deferred to his father's conservative tastes and put on a suit and tie.

Across from Edward and next to Charles was the ravishing twenty-seven-year-old Fiona. Her dark good looks had won her supporting roles on Broadway and in television, and her agent had gotten her an offer for a three-year contract with M-G-M. But Fiona was in love with a stockbroker named Jerry Lord, who had told her he was divorcing his wife. So far, Jerry was more important to Fiona than Hollywood.

Sitting at Laure's right was twenty-five-year-old Hugh Fleming, who had been a star athlete at Yale and was now working for his father. Hugh already had the reputation of a playboy, but tonight Hugh, like everyone else, was thinking of one girl in particular: his beloved sister Vicky. Hugh's appetite was usually voracious, but tonight he merely picked at the roast beef and Yorkshire pudding.

Table talk was out of the question. Everyone ate in silence as the candles in the massive silver sticks cast a warm glow on the Chinese wallpaper.

Then the phone rang.

Everyone stopped eating, all watching Nick, all thinking the same thing: Was this the ransom call? A moment later, the butler carried in a portable phone. "It's the police, sir. Detective McGinnis."

He placed the phone on the table and knelt down to plug in the jack.

"Yes?" Nick listened as his family watched. He frowned. "Oh, my God. You're sure?" Again, he listened. "All right, thanks." He hung up.

"They've identified the chauffeur," he said, "or the man who pretended to be a chauffeur. He's an ex-convict named Willard Slade." He hesitated, a look of pain on his face. "He served ten years at Lewisburg for rape."

"Christ," muttered Edward Fleming.

Fiona, who was closer to Vicky than any of her siblings, got up from the table and ran out of the dining room, bursting into tears.

CHAPTER 46

THE elderly gentleman sitting in the bar on the Rue Cambon side of the Hotel Ritz in Paris had gentle blue eyes, white hair and a white moustache. He was wearing a well-cut gray suit and had the air of an aristocrat. When Count Aldo Pitti-Gonzaga saw the beautifully dressed middle-aged woman come into the bar, he stood up and kissed her hand as she joined him. Then Diana Ramschild sat down in the banquette next to the gentle Italian who had been her constant escort for two years. After they had ordered cocktails, Aldo said, "Something has happened, *cara*. I can always tell with you. There is excitement in your eyes."

"I got a letter from Nick," she replied. "I told you I wrote him when I read about his daughter being kidnapped. Well, he answered the letter. . . . It was terribly sad . . . he really sounds devastated, which is natural. But the letter was . . ." She spread her hands slightly. "He seems different. More mellow and thoughtful than the way I remember him."

"He's older," said the Count, taking some peanuts out of the dish on the table. "People mellow as they age, like wine—at least, if the wine's any good. When bad wine ages, it just turns sour."

"At any rate, he asked me to call him next week when I'm in New York."

"Ah, so *that's* why you're excited."

She looked sheepish.

"Is it *that* obvious?"

He smiled as he squeezed her hand.

"Dear Diana, Nick Fleming is like a disease with you. You've been infected by him all your life. I was conceited enough to think perhaps I could be the cure, but I can see I was wrong."

"No, perhaps you aren't wrong. Perhaps you *are* the cure. God knows, I realize I've behaved like an emotional baby about the man for most of my adult life. It's either time I forget about him and marry you, or . . . ." She paused as the waiter served the two martinis.

427

"Or," said Aldo, smiling, "make one final desperate attempt to get him?"

"No, there's no question of that. He's married to Laure. . . . I assume they're happy. It's just that I want to see him once more." She smiled at the gentle Italian she had grown so genuinely fond of. "And then I'll come back to you, my dearest Aldo."

The Count sipped his drink.

"If I were a betting man, which I'm not," he said, "I'm not sure I'd give very good odds on *that*."

Detective Frank McGinnis was thirty-four, twenty pounds overweight, chain-smoked Lucky Strikes and had three kids living in Queens. McGinnis had seen many corpses in his professional career: decapitated corpses, ghastly "floaters" from the rivers—mementos of the savagery that lay beneath the eggshell veneer of American civilization. Now as he stared down at the shallow grave behind the shack in a northern New Jersey woods, the body of the young girl didn't shock him, although it was decomposing.

It shocked and sickened the man standing next to him, though, because Nick Fleming was looking at what was left of his daughter.

"Is it Victoria?" the detective asked.

"Yes."

Nick turned away and walked back to his limousine, fighting back the nausea. For weeks he had clung to the dwindling hope that Vicky was still alive, somewhere. Now that hope was as dead as his beloved daughter.

He leaned on the front fender of the Rolls, staring at the dilapidated shack that squatted beneath cold, gray skies. Vicky, who had had everything in her young life, had died in this filthy place, only to have her body discovered by a stray dog. How rotten, how cruel, how unfair, how infuriating.

Detective McGinnis lit a cigarette and walked over to the limousine, leaving the grave to be photographed by the New Jersey authorities. The gleaming Rolls-Royce with its leather seats and custom-made bar in the back fascinated him. He was burning with curiosity to know what it cost. Forty thousand? Fifty? An inconceivable sum to Frank McGinnis, whose take-home pay was $125 a week. He had never met an honest-to-God tycoon before, but he had read all the press coverage of the case with the avidity of a minor actor devouring his press clippings. "Titan," "press czar," "billionaire"—the phrases flung about in print to describe Nick Fleming had an unreality to Frank McGinnis, just as the Rolls did. To own a million dollars, much less a billion, seemed unreal. Oddly, McGinnis felt more curiosity than envy. Nick Fleming was a human being, just like him. He went to the toilet, brushed his teeth, made love just like him—didn't he? And he grieved over his dead child, just as Frank McGinnis would grieve. Curiously, violent death had brought these two men from such vastly different worlds together, just as the Blitz had brought Londoners of different class together. Frank McGinnis was not much of a philosopher, but he wondered if the only thing that made men brothers might be catastrophe.

"It makes no sense," Nick said as the detective joined him. "I've racked my brain for weeks now, and the damned thing makes no sense. I've put myself in Slade's shoes, and it still doesn't add up. We know he knew who she was, whom she was engaged to, and that she was having lunch at Pavillon. But if he wanted to kidnap her, why do it the way he did? Why go into a famous restaurant where he's bound to be noticed by any number of people? Noticed and probably remembered. He must have known Vicky went around the city pretty freely. I'd think there would have been a dozen ways he could have picked her up less conspicuously."

"Maybe not. I mean, maybe not if he didn't want to arouse her suspicions. He had to fool her into going with him, and obviously—and unfortunately—his method worked. Your daughter wasn't going to hop into somebody's car for a joyride."

"I suppose not. But still, his way seems so risky. Either he was too dumb to think of the consequences of going into the restaurant—which somehow I doubt—or he didn't give a damn if he was recognized! He must know the F.B.I. has a file on him and the chances were he'd be identified. And what was his motive? If he's a psychotic thrill killer, why pick my daughter and go to such elaborate lengths to get her? He must have known there'd be tremendous publicity. Why wouldn't he have picked up some kid from a small town somewhere? I know that sounds cynical, but I'm trying to figure it out. If he'd demanded ransom, it would have made sense. But he didn't. This way it makes no damned sense at all!"

He pounded his fist against the car fender in angry frustration. McGinnis didn't know what to say, because it didn't make any sense to him either.

"She was a nice girl," said Nick. "A sweet girl. Oh, I mean she had a streak of the devil in her and liked to try to shock people every once in a while, but she was a good kid, a loving daughter. And now *this*. . . ."

He stopped, and McGinnis knew he was choking back a sob. Fascinating, he thought. Rich people have emotions.

"When they catch Slade," Nick went on, "and I know they'll catch him eventually, which is the only thing that keeps me from going crazy . . . when they catch that monster, I want to be there when they put him in the electric chair. I want to watch him die."

He climbed into the back seat of his car and slammed the door. For most of his life, Nick had managed to master events. Now he felt totally and maddeningly helpless.

As he was driven back to the city, he thought about his life. He had lost Edwina in a random act of wartime violence, and now he had lost Vicky in what seemed to be a random act of peacetime violence. All his life, violence had swirled around him, the violence of a violent century. The violence of wars, of revolutions, of Communists and Fascists, and now, apparently, the criminal violence of a single, twisted individual. He even admitted that his desire to watch Slade die in the electric chair was a violent wish, albeit a natural one under the circumstances.

Nick was an agnostic, but now he began to wonder if perhaps there was some sort of divine retribution involved in these deaths. He had had his chance to get out of the arms business, but had given in to his children. Were the millions of human beings who had been killed by the bombs, bullets, guns, howitzers and tanks his company had manufactured over the years—was this their vengeance on him? Nick didn't believe in the supernatural, but he was so shaken by that shallow, horrible grave, he couldn't keep the idea out of his brain.

But what could he do?

It was then the idea of the Fleming Foundation formed in his mind. He immediately saw that the cynical would call it a mammoth whitewashing of his millions, but to hell with the cynical. He could achieve something positive with his vast wealth in a world that seemed in love with negative violence. No foundation would bring Edwina or Vicky back to life, or the millions of war dead.

But it might be the best possible memorial.

430

CHAPTER 47

"D IANA!"

Nick held out both his hands and smiled as she came into the living room of his New York apartment.

"The reports I've heard are true," he went on as she took his hands. "You look beautiful. Congratulations."

"Thank you, Nick."

"I appreciated your letter about Vicky. It was very thoughtful of you."

"I was so shocked when I read about it. And I can imagine what you've gone through."

He shook his head slightly. "No," he said quietly, "I don't think anyone can imagine. It's been the worst thing since"—he hesitated—"Edwina."

There was an awkward silence. Then he forced a courtesy smile. "Sit down. Would you like a drink?"

"A martini, please. I allow myself two a day." She looked around the enormous living room with its first-rate Gauguin, its 1918 Picasso *Clowns* and its huge yellow Matisse. "Your apartment is spectacular," she said. "Did Laure decorate it?" She sat down in a cream sofa as Nick brought her drink to her.

"Laure? She has no interest in decorating. Besides, she admits she has terrible taste."

Diana smiled. "I remember her Paris flat. All those stuffed bears and ribbons and bows. Ye gods! Thanks." She took the drink..

Nick sat opposite her and raised his glass. "To us," he said. "We go back a long time."

"Amen to that."

They clicked glasses, then sipped.

"Where is Laure?" asked Diana.

"In bed with a cold. She told me to give you her love."

Diana smiled. "She doesn't want to see me, does she?" she said. "I imagine I represent a lot of things she'd like to forget."

"You're right. I shouldn't have tried to pull the wool over your eyes,

Diana. She really *doesn't* want to see you. She told me she wants to forget about the Occupation and Semiramis . . . and General von Stoltz."

"I don't blame her. I've done my best to forget it too. But you're happy with Laure?"

He hesitated. "Of course. How about you? Have you found someone? With your spectacular new appearance, I imagine you must have half of Europe at your feet."

"You flatter me. But I *do* have a charming Italian count. He's older than I, but he's a very special human being. He's gentle and kind and witty. We've been seeing each other for several years now. I've grown terribly fond of him."

"Good, I'm glad to hear it. How long are you in town?"

"Ten days. I wanted to do some shopping and look around . . . see the city. One misses New York, you know." She hesitated. "One misses America." She sounded rather wistful. Then she smiled. "You know, I haven't seen Rockefeller Center or the Empire State Building or the George Washington Bridge—anything! It's been over thirty years since I was in New York. I feel like a complete tourist."

"Would you like me to be your tour guide?"

"Oh, Nick, that's sweet of you, but I'm sure you're far too busy."

"No, I'm not. I'd like to show you around. It will take my mind off . . . Vicky. Why don't I pick you up at your hotel at ten tomorrow morning? I'll show you everything that's been done to New York since 1920, then we'll have lunch."

She laughed. "That sounds like a *very* crowded morning. But," she added warmly, "a delightful one. I'll look forward to it."

Their eyes met. She was thinking back over the years to a deserted beach house on Long Island Sound where she first made love with this man, where she became "infected," as Aldo had put it.

Her problem was, did she *want* to be cured?

"My God, it certainly *is* impressive," she said the next morning as she and Nick stood on the eighty-sixth-floor observation deck of the Empire State Building and looked down at Manhattan, shivering in the clear cold of an early-November chill that had brought frost to the suburbs. "I can see what all the excitement is about."

"You can't understand King Kong until you've been up here."

"Did you know *King Kong* was Hitler's favorite movie? That and a picture made back in '31 called *The Congress Dances*. Goering told me Hitler had watched it dozens of times and loved every frame. It was about the Congress of Vienna and a serving girl who has an affair with the Tsar of Russia. A giant ape who climbs the Empire State Building holding a tiny girl he can't possibly make love to, and a peasant girl who goes to bed with the Tsar. . . . I always thought those two movies told a lot about Hitler's mind."

"Yes, I think you're right."

"Well, the view *is* spectacular, but I'm beginning to freeze."

"Next stop Rockefeller Center. Then lunch. By the way, I asked my daughter Fiona to join us for a drink before lunch. I wanted you to meet her. She's an actress who's doing quite well. Her father was Rod Norman."

Diana turned sharply to stare at him as she hugged her mink coat to keep warm.

"You mean . . ."

"I mean that killer you hired killed her *real* father instead of me. She doesn't know it, and I have no intention of ever telling her."

"Does she know Rod Norman was her father?"

"Yes, Edwina told her. And then Fiona told Vicky, and Vicky told Hugh . . . the whole family knows it now. But no one knows who hired the killer."

Diana shivered slightly. "You make me feel so guilty," she said. "But Kemal made it seem so easy, so logical. . . ." She sighed. "Well, I paid. Seven years in a Turkish asylum, almost seventeen years wearing veils every day and every night . . . no lovers, few friends . . . terrified that people might see my face. I'm not trying to make you feel sorry for me, but I paid for what I did to Rod Norman—and tried to do to you. I'm not saying that makes it right, but I paid. Can you ever forgive me?"

He looked at her a moment, a thousand memories enveloping him.

"Yes," he finally said. "We hurt each other because we were in love. We must have been a lot more in love than I realized, because we hurt each other so much."

"I still am in love," she said.

A sudden wind whipped around the eighty-sixth floor.

She smiled. "I've embarrassed you," she said. "I can tell. I won't again. Let's go to Rockefeller Center. And, Nick, I'm having a *wonderful* time. Thanks so much."

She started for the door. Nick watched her a moment, thoughtfully, then followed her.

While Diana and Nick were touring Rockefeller Center, Laure was at a fund-raising lunch at the Plaza for a charity of which Nick and she were patrons. And that was when Laure met him. She had heard of Juan Alfonso Hernando Guzman y Talavera, the Marqués de Novara—who hadn't heard of him? The dashing Spanish nobleman–race driver had lit up the headlines of postwar Europe with his racing triumphs, his thrilling brushes with death in two accidents, his amateur exploits in the bullring and his amatory conquests, which, according to the papers, had left a trail of broken hearts across Spain, Italy and France and earned him the nickname "El Toro." Married three times, twice to rich women older than himself, Juan had just emerged from his latest divorce from auto heiress Sylvia Mainwaring with a million-dollar settlement.

"Laure, I want you to meet the Marqués de Novara," said Phillipa Wilson, another patron of the charity. "Juan, this is Laure Fleming, whom I've told you so much about."

As Juan raised her hand to his lips, Laure had to admit he was one of the most handsome men she had ever seen—at least six feet tall, with slightly wavy black hair, a tanned face with the chiseled features of a movie star. He had blazing blue eyes that pierced into hers and suggested "Aren't I gorgeous?" He was impeccably dressed in a dark-blue Savile Row suit, and he wore a striped Turnbull & Asser shirt with gold cuff links. He smelled slightly of an astringent cologne.

"I have heard the wife of the famous Mr. Fleming was beautiful," he said, speaking with a Ricky Ricardo accent. "Now I see with my own eyes that it is true. You are Parisian?" he added, switching to French.

"Yes. Well, I'm originally from Poitiers."

"Ah, like Diane. And something tells me you are as exciting as that exquisite creature."

It occurred to Laure that Juan was laying it on a bit thick, but she was charmed nonetheless.

"But of course!" he exclaimed. "I have seen you before. I saw you sing at Semiramis in Paris during the war."

"Oh?"

"Yes. You reminded me of Betty Grable then, with your hair up. Now you wear it down. I like it even better this way."

"And what were you doing in Paris during the war?"

"I was attached to the Spanish Embassy. I was a neutral." He smiled and she saw he had beautiful teeth. "You were neutral too?"

She stiffened. "I survived," she said coolly. "And I helped the Resistance."

"At the end. Yes, everyone helped the Resistance at the end."

Her thermostat dropped to zero. "I helped destroy Forteresse de Morlaix, which you may or may not have read about. I have nothing to be ashamed of, and I certainly don't have to be insulted by a neutral Spaniard who probably never came within a mile of a bullet."

"You are ravishing when you are angry."

"I thought lines like that went out with Valentino."

"Then you know my reputation?"

"Oh, yes. You're supposed to have the biggest penis in Western Europe and can keep it up all night."

He frowned. Then, suddenly, he laughed.

"It's true," he said. "And I'd love to prove it to you."

She looked at him. She was tempted. For the first time since she had married Nick, she was tempted by another man.

"No thanks," she said. "My husband keeps me very happy."

"You are a lucky woman—and an unusual one, from my experience. Most of the wives I meet have . . . shall we say, complaints? But since we are doomed to a Platonic relationship, how about lunch? I make terrific paella."

She hesitated. "You mean lunch . . . at your apartment?"

"Yes, why not? I have a little *pied-à-terre* on Sutton Place. I will make paella, we will share a bottle of Rioja, and it will be wonderfully exciting because nothing will happen. Very, very safe. Even your husband couldn't object."

"Well . . ."

"How about tomorrow at one?"

She said nothing. He pulled a Hermès wallet from his pocket and extracted a card.

"Twenty-seven Sutton Place. The seventh floor. Seven's a lucky number, you know. I'll be expecting you."

He kissed her hand again and walked away. She looked at his card. Well, she thought, *lunch* couldn't be dangerous.

Nick took Diana to lunch at a small Italian restaurant. A few minutes after they were seated in their booth, Fiona hurried in, her cheeks flushed from the wind. She came up to kiss her father, who introduced her to Diana.

"I can only stay a few minutes," Fiona said, slipping into the booth next to her father. "I have to be downtown in forty-five minutes for a reading. Father says this is your first time in New York in *thirty* years! It must seem terribly different."

435

"It's a whole new city," said Diana, admiring Fiona's beauty. As the girl chattered on, Diana also saw how close she was to her father, and how close Nick was to her. She began to understand how important his family was to him.

"Do you know Greenwich Village?" Fiona asked.

"No."

Fiona turned to her father. "Why don't you bring Miss Ramschild . . ."

"Diana."

"Yes, Diana. Why don't you bring her down one night this week and I'll fix you dinner? Would you like that, Diana?"

Diana was enchanted by the warm, unaffected, utterly beautiful girl. At the same time, she was being assaulted by waves of guilt over her involvement with the death of her father. How *could* I have done it? she kept thinking. How *could* I? "I'd love it," she said. "But I don't think your stepmother is overly eager to be in my company."

"Oh." Fiona looked uncertainly at her father.

Nick didn't even hesitate. "If Laure doesn't want to join us, she can stay home," he said, which Diana liked.

"Wonderful!" Fiona exclaimed, getting up. "Then how about tomorrow night at seven?"

"Fine."

"Do you like bouillabaisse?" she asked Diana.

"I love it."

"Then that's what we'll have. I make a *wonderful* bouillabaisse. Bye-bye. It was lovely to meet you."

She shook Diana's hand, kissed Nick and was gone.

After Fiona hurried out, Diana said, "She's an extraordinary beauty. Absolutely stunning. And she seems so bright and nice too. You must be proud of her."

"I am. She and Vicky were so close . . . Fiona was devastated when Vicky died. She seems to be coming back now, thank God. But her love life's a little messed up."

"Not unusual at that age," remarked Diana as the captain handed her a menu.

"Not unusual at *any* age," said Nick, and they both laughed.

"Tell me about your Foundation," said Diana after they had ordered.

"Are you really interested?"

"Of course. Why wouldn't I be?"

"The subject bores Laure to death."

436

"I don't mean to criticize your wife, but I knew Laure well and she's a bit of a scatterbrain. Or, to be more kind, a bit of a child."

"Yes, child," Nick agreed. "She's not interested in serious things, and the Fleming Foundation is serious. But it's also terrifically exciting. In fact, I'm more involved with this than anything since the war."

"You find giving away money more fun than making it?"

He looked surprised. "Yes. How did you know?"

She smiled. "I can see it in your face."

He thought a moment, looking at her.

"You were talking about Hitler this morning," he said. "Hitler did one positive thing in my life: he made me hate him, and that made my life in a way rather simple. I was motivated to do anything I could to destroy Nazism, and then when it was over and Hitler was dead, I didn't know exactly what to do with the rest of my life. Yes, you go on living, you enjoy life if you're lucky . . . but life has to have some larger purpose. Making more money wasn't a satisfying goal to me anymore because I have more than I can sensibly spend now. I even tried to get out of the armaments business as a sort of . . . gesture, I suppose you might call it, or maybe a protest against all the slaughter weapons have caused in this century, but I was voted out of it by my children, and I'm not sure I was right to let myself be. Anyway, what I'm trying to say is that for the last five years I've been looking for a focus for my life. And the Foundation is it." He hesitated. "Am I boring you?" he asked uncertainly.

"Not at all. I'm fascinated."

And she was. The "new" Nick Fleming she had sensed in his letter was unfolding to her: a much more sensitive, caring man than she had remembered. My God, he *has* mellowed, she thought.

I'm falling in love all over again!

On his part, Nick was delighted to be talking to a woman who was—unlike Laure—as intelligent as he. As the lunch progressed and he talked on and on about his dreams for the Foundation, he found himself having more fun than he'd had in years.

As he was paying the check he realized how much he'd hate to see Diana return to Europe.

CHAPTER 48

Barbara Bates, playing Phoebe, held the Sarah Siddons Award won by Eve Harrington (Anne Baxter) and stood in front of the triple mirror bowing her head to imagined applause.

"What a terrific movie!" exclaimed Fiona as she applauded enthusiastically. "Fabulous! If Bette Davis doesn't get the Oscar, everyone in Hollywood should have their heads examined."

"I know," said Jerry Lord, "but this is the third time we've seen it in two weeks. I'm getting worn out."

As they made their way out of the crowded Roxy Theater, where *All About Eve* had opened to rave reviews on October 14, Fiona went on and on and on about the movie whose dialogue she knew practically by heart. "I *love* the scene where Bette Davis and Gary Merrill have the big fight on stage and he throws her down on the bed . . . the look in her eyes! They talk about eyes that flash fire, but Bette Davis' really *do!* What acting! And what a part. God, what I wouldn't give for a part like that."

"You're a little young to play Margo Channing."

"You know what I mean."

"Still thinking about taking that movie offer from M-G-M?"

They were out in the street now, and she buttoned her cloth coat against the chill. Fiona had been given a mink by her father, but she rarely wore it. As an actress, she spent a good deal of her energies living down the fact that she was Nick Fleming's daughter. While most of her friends in the theater dreamed of fame and fortune, Fiona dreamed of fame and hid her mink in the closet of her Greenwich Village walk-up.

"Of course I *think* about the offer," she said as he hailed a cab. "I'd love to go to Hollywood. The movies are where all the excitement is. But I'd hate to leave my father right *now* . . . I mean, Vicky's murder has really shaken him, and all the rest of us, as far as that goes. And then . . . well, there's you."

She looked at him, and he averted his eyes as he always did when the issue of their relationship arose. A Checker cab pulled up and he opened the door, climbing in beside Fiona. "Forty-five Barrow Street," he said to the cabby.

As the taxi started down Seventh Avenue to the Village, Jerry Lord held Fiona's hand. He was a nice-looking man in his early thirties who covered his premature balding with a hat. Fiona often asked herself why she had fallen in love with him. She knew that with her looks and her money she could have had the pick of the lot, but she had fallen for a man who was neither spectacularly handsome nor spectacularly rich—and, what was worse, a man with a wife and two children living in Scarsdale. He had dated an actress friend of hers, which was how Fiona had met him, so his record of cheating on his wife was firmly established, which Fiona had first disapproved of. And yet he was such a wonderfully nice, sweet, decent man, despite his infidelity, that she had come to overlook his cheating and even, in time, to sympathize with him. Jerry Lord had had the misfortune to marry a really impossible woman.

Right now he was looking uncomfortable.

"When we get to your place," he said, "let's talk about me and you."

Fiona realized, with a bit of a jolt, that at long last Jerry was going to stop averting his eyes.

Fiona's fourth-floor walk-up constituted the top floor of a charming brick Federal town house on the West Village street and had a skylight and broad windows overlooking the rear garden. For the tall living room, tiny kitchen, bedroom and bath, Fiona paid fifty dollars a month, low rent even in 1950. Her friends, who knew she could have bought the block if she wanted to, thought she was crazy; but Fiona loved her cozy apartment, which she thought of as "bohemian," and she was perfectly happy with her framed theatrical posters of plays like *A Streetcar Named Desire,* her secondhand furniture bought for peanuts in junk shops, and her two mongrel cats, Eeny and Meeny. Her one extravagance had been to install a completely new bathroom to replace the apartment's dilapidated one. Fiona might hide her mink in the closet and downplay her family's wealth, but Fiona liked her bathrooms immaculate.

"All right, let's talk," she said as they took off their coats after panting up the steep stairs.

He took her in his arms and kissed her. "You know I love you," he said.

"And I love you."

"But you know what the problem is."

"Your wife."

"No. The *real* problem is your money."

She pushed him away. "My *money?*" she asked.

"Well, your father's money."

"What's *that* have to do with it?"

"Everything. Look, Fi, I make thirty-five thousand a year. If I divorce Marilyn, I'll have to pay her alimony and child support, and that's going to be at least fifteen thousand a year with two kids. That'll leave me peanuts to live on. I've been giving it a lot of thought, and I've realized I simply can't afford to marry you."

"I'm not expensive!" she said. "Look how I live!"

"Yes, but come on, Fi, this is all a sort of game to you."

"A *game?*" She was furious. "Do you think I'm *playing* at being an actress?"

"No, but I know damned well you know you can go back up to that Park Avenue triplex any time you want—and if you *don't* know that, then you're fooling yourself."

"You go to hell, damn you!"

"*Listen* to me! We're just too different. Your father's one of the richest men in the world. I'll be lucky if I make sixty thousand a year when I retire. It just makes no *sense,* the two of us."

"But we love each other!"

"Yes, we love each other. But you told me what happened to your sister Sylvia. She married someone like me, and he ended up going to the penitentiary trying to come up with money for a down payment on a house. I don't want that to happen to us."

"But Chester Hill was a criminal! You're not."

"How do I know I might not become one trying to make you happy? I have a bad, stinking marriage, and I'd give anything to divorce Marilyn and marry you. But to tell you the honest-to-God truth, I'm terrified of your money."

She started to cry. "But that's not *fair,*" she sobbed.

He took her in his arms again. "I know. But it's true."

"Are you saying we shouldn't see each other anymore?"

"No. But I'm saying I have to stop fooling both of us by talking about a marriage that would never work. And if you're not going to Hollywood because of me, then my advice is to forget me."

She hugged him tightly. "I don't *want* to forget you!"

"But you may have to."

She released him, biting her lip. "Let's make love," she sniffed, wiping her eyes.

"All right. But let's forget about marriage."

She shrugged. "Right now, all I want is love."

Outside, on Barrow Street, a large black man in a pea jacket stood under a streetlamp, looking up at Fiona's windows.

Juan Alfonso Hernando Guzman y Talavera's *pied-à-terre* on Sutton Place was the full floor of a handsome building dating from the twenties. As Laure, wearing one of her two sable coats, rode to the seventh floor in the paneled elevator, she told herself for the hundredth time she was not even contemplating deceiving her husband, that she was merely going to lunch. But in her heart, she knew it was a lie. The handsome Spaniard had kindled a fire hot enough to overcome all the common-sense objections to going to his apartment alone. Laure knew Nick was a jealous husband. She wasn't overly materialistic, but she liked being Mrs. Nick Fleming. Was the Marqués de Novara worth the risk of losing the incredibly luxurious life she led? No, no, no, she had told herself over and over.

And yet, here she was in the elevator. It was going to be an interesting afternoon.

Although it was in the thirties outside, when he opened the door she saw he was dressed like a Caribbean beach boy. He was barefoot and wore extremely tight white pants with flared cuffs and a blue-and-white-striped polo shirt. He flashed that infectious smile and said, "I knew you would come. Welcome, beautiful lady of the sables."

He kissed her hand, took off her coat, then whisked her inside the apartment, which was decorated as if Mies van der Rohe had redone the Cathedral of Toledo. Here and there were pieces of modern furniture, and on the walls hung an occasional "modern" painting. There were two large Salvador Dalis. There was also, in the living room, an enormous full-length portrait of Juan wearing his racing outfit, including a crash helmet. But everything else was heavy and Spanish with a vengeance. Doleful madonnas hung on the wall, wooden *santos* were everywhere, and on the floor stood tall wooden cathedral candlesticks. The windows, which gave a spectacular view of the East River and the wonderful Queensboro Bridge, were hung with dark-green velvet draperies that were vaguely funereal and that cried for Scarlett O'Hara to turn them into a dress.

"You like it?" he asked in English, extending his arms to take in the large living room.

"I didn't know you were so religious," said Laure carefully.

He laughed. "Oh, I am a good Spanish boy, despite my wicked reputation. Very, very safe, that's me. I confess all my sins to my priest."

"You must keep him busy."

"I give him an earful. Would you like a drink?" he asked, switching to French, which was fluent and less accented than his English.

"A glass of wine."

"Then we'll start on the Rioja. You'll like my bar. It's a little crazy, like me."

He went to one of the wooden saints and twisted its right arm. Immediately, a whole section of one wall slid noiselessly out and turned 180 degrees, revealing a chrome-and-colored-glass bar that looked like a jukebox. At the same time a phonograph was activated, and Edith Piaf started singing *"La Vie en Rose."* Laure couldn't resist laughing with pure delight.

"It's wonderful!" she said.

"Isn't it? I designed it myself. Everybody thinks I'm just a playboy, but I'm really very smart."

"And modest."

"No, not modest. I'm good and I know it."

He had gone to the bar, where he was opening the wine bottle.

"Do you always go barefoot at home?" she asked, sitting on a heavily carved Spanish sofa.

"I hate cold weather. So when I have to be in a cold climate, I dress as if I'm in Majorca or on the Côte d'Azur or the Caribbean. It makes me happy, so why not do it?" He carried the two wineglasses over to her, giving her one as he stood in front of her. "Cheers," he said in English, touching her glass. As she drank, she stared at the bulge in his white trousers directly in front of her eyes. My God, she thought, it must be true! Laure had slept with a lot of men in her life, but she'd never seen anything like that.

He sat next to her on the sofa, so close his thigh pressed against hers.

"Spanish red wines," he said, "can be like a beautiful woman, but Spanish white wines are like a witch: they are dangerous. So, tell me about yourself. You say you are a happy woman?"

"Yes."

"But you're a curious woman. That's why you came here, no?"

"Perhaps."

"And what do you think so far?"

She eyed him. "That you are a conceited little boy."

He shrugged. "That's partially true."

"That you try to 'conquer' women more out of pride and ego than out of any real sense of romance."

442

"Also partially true."

She stood up, putting down her wineglass. "And I think I'm going home."

"You're afraid?"

"A little." He held out his right hand. She looked at him curiously. "I really *must* go," she said.

"Give me your hand."

Slightly annoyed, she obeyed. Gently, he pulled her down toward him until she was forced to sit on his lap. Then he put her hand on his crotch. He leaned back in the sofa, smiling at her as he held her hand in place.

"Was that what you were curious about?" he whispered.

She felt it stiffening beneath her touch. He released her hand and watched her. She didn't remove her hand. Still smiling, he pulled the polo shirt over his head and threw it across the room. She stared at his torso, so muscled and tan and smooth.

"You're nothing but a whore," she said.

"Wasn't that what you were in Paris?" He pulled her down into his arms and began kissing her.

After a moment she pushed him away and stood up again. She was trembling and afraid—not of him, but of herself.

"I may have been a whore in Paris, but here I'm Nick Fleming's wife—his *faithful* wife."

"You don't expect me to believe that?"

"Believe what you want. I'm going home."

"No one's stopping you. Of course, you'll pass up a good lunch."

He started unbuttoning the fly of his white trousers. She stared at him, riveted. Slowly, like a striptease artist, he pulled the pants down his hairy legs, then kicked them off. All he had on was a dark-blue European-style brief.

"I have these custom-made for me in Rome," he said. They cost fifteen dollars apiece. I wear them once, then give them to charity. Or"—he winked—"I give them as souvenirs. Would you like a souvenir?"

He snapped the elastic band against his hip. She was still staring at him.

"Yes," she whispered.

He pulled the brief down, and she stared at the biggest male organ she had ever seen in her life. Now she knew why Juan Alfonso Hernando Guzman was called El Toro. He stood up, stepped out of the brief, picked it off the floor and totally naked brought it to her. He put his arms around her and kissed her as her hands began caressing his back.

"We'll make love before lunch," he said. "Then we'll eat paella. Then we'll make love after lunch. Then we'll have espresso—I have a machine I bought in Florence. Then we'll make love after espresso. You'll be amazed. I never tire." He kissed her neck.

Her head back, she closed her eyes and whispered, "Make me happy, El Toro."

CHAPTER 49

SHE discovered that his lovemaking secret was an Egyptian technique called *Imsak*. No matter how aroused he became—and she quickly discovered how aroused he could be—he didn't allow himself to complete the act. He told her that his joy came from the sense of control he achieved over his own body, and that by not wasting what he called his "body fluids," he was able to keep his desire at a peak and therefore excite the woman beyond control—beyond, as he put it, "the threshold of ecstasy," which sounded better in French than in English. "I must be the absolute master of the act of love," he said. "That way I give my partner the greatest pleasure. Most men want nothing but to rush to the climax—to get it over with, so to speak— but I disdain that. The pleasure is the aching for the climax, to remain in a state of sexual agony, so to speak. I once went a whole month without a climax, though I made love every day. Believe me, it was the most sexual month of my life. I was exhausted, *drenched* with desire.

"Sex, you see, must be an art, with perhaps a touch of religion. It is nature's greatest miracle, but at the same time, one of the body's simplest functions and yet in ways one of the most complex. Most men might as well masturbate. I, who have devoted my life to giving pleasure to women, have made myself a connoisseur of love, which is the secret of my great success. A connoisseur of wines never gets drunk. It is the same with me: I, as a connoisseur of love, very rarely ejaculate. When I do"—he shrugged—"I feel like I have a hangover."

Laure had never heard such a philosophy before, but she had to admit it worked: she had never had such an erotic afternoon in her life. Nick was an excellent lover, but even he was not in the same league with El Toro. Juan had made her feel almost mystically excited. She had reveled in pleasure, reaching a level of ecstasy she had never known her body capable of. When she left his apartment at five, she was exhausted, sore, in a bit of a daze—and avid for more.

He had put his pants back on, though he was still shirtless. As he held her sable for her he asked softly in English, "You felt pleasure, yes?"

She turned to kiss him. "You not only lived up to your reputation, you surpassed it," she replied.

"Good. I am happy when I have given pleasure. And the paella wasn't bad either, was it?"

She smiled. "I loved it."

"You will come again? Soon?"

She hesitated.

"It was too lovely not to be repeated," he prompted.

"Yes, I'll come," she whispered.

"Tomorrow?"

Oh, my God, she thought. "Yes, tomorrow."

He smiled as he kissed her. "Good. *A demain, chérie.*"

Nick picked Diana up at her hotel, then they started downtown to the Village in his Rolls.

"Is something the matter?" she asked. He looked grim.

"Did Laure have other lovers in Paris besides General von Stoltz?"

"Do you want me to be polite and lie, or do you want the truth?"

"I want the truth."

"Of course she had other lovers. Not when she was with Fritzy, though—or at least I wasn't aware of any. I think she was too careful to cheat on Fritzy. But I know she'd had quite a few boy friends before Fritzy. Why do you ask?"

He didn't answer for a moment. "Because she lied to me today," he finally said.

"Oh."

"She told me she was going shopping, but she didn't take her car. She went in a taxi, instead. No woman would take a taxi to go shopping when she has a chauffeur at her disposal. Am I right?"

"Absolutely."

"Now the question is, where did she go in the taxi?"

"Any ideas?"

"No, but I intend to find out."

He said nothing more on the subject, but Diana knew he was angry.

When they arrived at Barrow Street, which looked as if it could have been 1850 rather than 1950, they climbed the sagging staircase to the fourth floor.

"It's a good thing I gave up smoking," Diana panted.

"Fiona's having a love affair with poverty—mainly because she's never been poor. She's crazy about this place."

446

When they reached the top landing, a tiny dark area at the top of the stairs despite a skylight, Nick rang the bell.

"Can you imagine carrying groceries up those four flights?" he whispered to Diana. "At least she says the building is clean. There aren't any roaches."

"I'm glad to hear that—especially before dinner."

Nick laughed. "Sorry." He rang again.

"My second oldest son, Edward, lives four blocks from here. He's writing the great American novel—or so he tells me. But he's been working on it for five years, and so far I haven't seen a chapter, much less a novel. But I don't say anything to him. I had a lot of trouble with my oldest, Charles, so now I try to stay out of my children's lives as much as possible."

"Does it bother you that Fiona's an actress?"

"Not at all. She takes after her mother. I'm very pleased for her. I think she's wonderfully talented and has a real future."

The door was unlocked and opened by Fiona, wearing a pretty tartan skirt and blue blouse with a white apron over everything. She smiled at Diana.

"Welcome to New York's most glamorous penthouse. Hello, Daddy." She kissed Nick as he followed Diana into the skylighted living room.

"The bouillabaisse smells divine!" Diana exclaimed, looking around the apartment, which reminded her of Left Bank artist studios she had seen so often in Paris. Nick helped her off with her mink, which Fiona took to put on her bed.

"Yes, and I got a terrific wine to go with it," she said, disappearing into the bedroom. "A white Châteauneuf-du-Pape."

"I love it," said Diana, picking off a table a silver-framed photo of a man in profile smoking a pipe. It was a classic Hollywood studio portrait, and the man's dark hair was slicked down in the style of the early twenties.

"What a wonderful picture of you, Nick," she said. "Who took it?"

"It's not me. It's Rod Norman."

Diana almost dropped the photo. "Oh, my God," she whispered, replacing the picture on the table.

Again, she felt swamped with guilt. This charming, talented, beautiful girl who was her hostess . . . and she, Diana, was responsible for the death of her father. How could she have done it?

And then she remembered Kemal's cynicism and her ancient hate and the anonymity of hired killers and she remembered how she could have done it. Twenty-eight years ago it had seemed so easy and safe and simple.

Now, as Fiona returned to the living room, a cheerful smile on her face, Diana thought of her behavior as monstrous.

The ghost of Rod Norman was beginning to haunt Diana Ramschild after nearly thirty years.

"Nick, I know you don't like talking about Vicky's death," Diana said an hour and a half later as they drove back uptown in his Rolls, "but did it ever occur to you it wasn't just a random killing?"

He looked at her, her handsome face illuminated intermittently by passing streetlights and advertising signs.

"What makes you say that?"

"Because I went through such agonies tonight at dinner, thinking I was responsible for Fiona's father's death. I almost blurted out, 'I did it.' I felt so ashamed. And then I began thinking how, at the time, Rod's death must have seemed so senseless to everyone. I mean, it was a bolt from the blue!"

"Yes, that's true. I remember none of us had any idea why he'd been murdered. But what's that have to do with Vicky?"

"My point is, there's a reason for every crime, even ones that seem totally pointless, like Rod Norman's. And I'm wondering if there isn't a reason for Vicky's murder."

"I've racked my brain, but I can't think of one."

"I can. The same thing that motivated me to hire someone to kill you. Revenge. You're a very well-known man, Nick, and a very rich and powerful one. There must be a lot of people who hate you, as I once hated you. And what better way to vent that hatred than to kill one of your children? And—even more important—perhaps kill *others* of your children? It was being in Fiona's apartment tonight that made me think of it. How easy it would be for someone to break into that place and kill her. I know she loves her apartment, but if I were you I'd make her move to a building that at the very least had a doorman—or hire bodyguards for her. And maybe your other children too. I know that may sound alarmist, but look how pathetically easy it was to get to Vicky."

He didn't say anything for a moment.

"You mean," he finally said, "you think someone might be trying to wipe out my entire family?"

"I'm saying it's a possibility you have to consider. I *know* how easy it is to hire killers if you're emotional enough to forget your conscience and you think you can get away with it. Nick, I'm not trying to upset you, but I think Fiona is adorable, and . . . well, if I could perhaps save her life, maybe it would make up a little for what I did to her father."

The Rolls had stopped for a red light.

"Jesus Christ," he said softly. "Lewisburg. What a fool I've been! What a blind, stupid fool!" He turned to Diana, took her hand in both of his and squeezed it. "God bless you, Diana," he said fervently. "I think you may have just saved my daughter's life."

CHAPTER 50

THE tube that Chester Hill invented in 1946 shortly after he got out of Lewisburg was, like many moneymaking inventions, basically simple. But it so improved TV reception that soon all manufacturers were incorporating it in their sets; and as the television boom took off in the late forties, the royalties from the little invention were making Chester almost absurdly rich, one of the first multimillionaires of the Age of Television.

Still smarting from his years in prison, he lived quietly for a rich man on a farm in Westchester County and in a town house on Beekman Place. In 1948 he married his secretary, a pretty and intelligent woman named Betty Drew. Chester and Betty were rarely seen in public except when they went looking for antiques, because Betty had a passion for French and English furniture her husband came to share. Soon the farm, the town house and a Palm Beach villa they bought in 1949 began filling with truly beautiful pieces, some of museum quality. Betty and Chester had no children and few friends, but they could sit on a sofa that had once belonged to Marie Antoinette. As a convicted felon, Chester could never vote, but he could work on his inventions at a desk that had once belonged to Lord Melbourne. The stock ticker in his office with which he followed the fluctuations of his enormous holdings on Wall Street was, however, no antique.

Chester Hill was sitting at Lord Melbourne's desk reading the prospectus of a frozen-food company he was considering investing in when Betty knocked on the door and came in. She was a redhead with a good figure who dressed plainly for a rich woman. Right now, she looked surprised.

"There's someone here to see you," she said, closing the door. "It's Sylvia Fleming."

He laid down the prospectus.

"Sylvia?" He said it quietly, but Betty knew what he thought of his first wife. "What's that bitch doing here?"

"She's brought your son."

Chester looked stunned.

450

"Arthur? He's here?"

"Yes." She smiled slightly. "He's a handsome little boy. Well, he's not so little—he must be ten, isn't he?"

"Nine," corrected Chester.

"He looks like you."

"Does he?" Chester said in a flat voice. "That's news to me, since they've never let me see him. Tell her to go to hell."

"You mean you don't want to see your own son?"

"No. He's not my son anymore. They took him away from me, changed his name—he's a Fleming, he's not my son. I never want to see another Fleming in my life. Tell Sylvia to get him out of here."

"Chester, I can't believe . . ."

"Tell them to *GET OUT!*" he screamed, jumping out of his chair. "I *hate* those sons of bitches—hate 'em!"

He stopped, trembling, trying to control his emotions.

"I know, but, darling . . . your *son*."

He stood behind the magnificent desk for almost a minute, saying nothing. Then, quietly, "Does he really look like me?"

"Yes."

"Where are they?"

"Downstairs in the living room."

Another minute of silent indecision. Then Chester came around the desk and walked to his wife, whom he hugged.

"Five years in Lewisburg," he whispered, "and all because of the Flemings."

"I know, darling. I know."

"Five long years."

He continued hugging her for a moment. Then he released her. He straightened his tie and flattened his hair with the palms of his hands.

"How do I look?" he asked. He sounded nervous.

"Handsome as always." She smiled.

"I . . ." He gulped. "I want to make a good impression on him. I suppose that sounds foolish, doesn't it? He's a Fleming, but . . ."

"He's yours too. It doesn't sound foolish to me. And you'll make a fine impression, don't worry. Do you want me to come with you?"

He hesitated. "No. I'll see her alone."

He left the study, walked down the upstairs hall past the gilt Récamier that had belonged to Charles X of France, down the curved stairs hung with a set of magnificent eighteenth-century prints of the court of the Ch'ien Lung Emperor of China, across the entrance hall where a Languedoc marble jardinière from Versailles was filled with fresh lilies flown up from Florida . . . the poor minister's son from Salisbury, Connecticut, who had tried to marry rich and gone to prison as a result, had come a long way.

He went into the living room and looked at the woman he hated. She was still beautiful and still stylish, wearing an elegantly simple black suit with a small black hat. A diamond-and-sapphire brooch was on the lapel of her suit.

"Hello, Chester," she said.

He looked at the boy standing beside her. He was tall for his age and extremely good-looking. Chester saw a definite resemblance to himself, although he was dismayed to see there was something of Nick Fleming about his eyes. The boy was staring at him with unabashed curiosity.

"Chester, I realize I've been wrong about Arthur," Sylvia said. "I've explained to him all about you, and it's time you two met. Darling, this is your father, Mr. Hill. Go shake his hand."

The boy rather tentatively came across the room and extended his hand.

"How do you do, sir?" he said with an automatic politeness that was almost ridiculous under the circumstances.

Chester, staring at him with wide eyes, slowly reached out and took his hand. "I'm glad to meet you, Arthur," he said.

"Are you *really* glad?" he asked shyly.

"Yes. Very glad."

They looked at each other a moment.

"Now, Arthur, go out and wait in the car," Sylvia said. "I have to talk to your father alone for a few minutes."

"Gee, Mom, I just *met* him!"

"I know, but you'll see him again later."

Arthur looked at Chester. "Will I?" he asked wistfully.

Chester smiled. "Yes, of course," he said. "Now that your mother's beginning to act like a human being, I'll arrange for us to have dinner sometime soon. We have a lot of catching up to do, young man. I want to hear all about your school, and . . ."

"Would you take me to a football game?" Arthur interrupted eagerly. "I'm nuts about football!"

"There's a Giants game next Saturday. I'll get us tickets . . . that is, if it's all right with your mother."

Arthur turned. "It'll be all right, won't it, Mom?"

"We'll see. Go out to the car, Arthur."

"Oh, all right." He stuck out his hand to Chester. "It's been great meeting you, sir. And I'm really looking forward to next Saturday. It"—he hesitated—"it's been sort of tough not having a father all these years. I wish Mom had told me. . . . I mean, *I* wouldn't have cared if you'd been in prison. And . . . well, anyway, I'm really glad I've got you now."

The little speech, so ingenuous but obviously so sincere, almost cracked Chester's heart. Tears in his eyes, he hugged and kissed his son.

"I'm glad to have *you*," he said. "Really very glad. I've wanted to know you all these years. . . . It was so hard in prison . . . so hard . . ."

He broke down completely and started sobbing. He let his son go and just stood there, crying like a little boy as Arthur stared at him. Then, suddenly, Chester raged across the room at Sylvia.

"Why couldn't you have done this years ago?" he shouted. "Why did you have to *torture* me?" He turned to Arthur. "Did she tell you *why* I went to prison? Because I needed money to keep *her* happy! I bet she didn't tell you that, did she?"

Arthur looked stunned.

"Chester, for God's sake, pull yourself together!" snapped Sylvia.

"You shut *up!*" he growled.

"If you want to see Arthur again, *you'll* shut up!"

Chester pulled a handkerchief from his pocket and blew his nose. "I'm sorry," he said.

"Now, Arthur, leave us alone."

"Okay."

Looking frightened, Arthur hurried out of the room. Sylvia waited till she heard the front door close. Then she looked at her former husband.

"You know," she said, "there were times when we were married when I had the feeling you wanted to kill me. Oh, I know a lot of husbands would *like* to kill their wives at times, but I had the feeling you actually could have. Apparently, I was right. You really hate me, don't you?"

"What are you trying to get at?"

"Very simply, that my father has figured out who killed Vicky—and why. It was you, Chester. The tip-off was that Willard Slade did time at Lewisburg, your old alma mater. You must have gotten to know a lot of fascinating types at Lewisburg . . . rapists, murderers, thieves. It must have been a real education to you, Chester, much more interesting than Yale. Because you could hire your fellow alumni to kill for you."

"That's preposterous. Look, Sylvia, I don't have to take this absurd bullshit from you."

"Oh, I knew you'd deny it. But you're a throwback, Chester. You're out of some Renaissance court like the Borgias where people killed off their relatives so they could inherit the papacy, or something."

"How much did you pay Slade, Chester?" asked Nick as he walked into the room. Chester paled at the unexpected sight of the man he considered his nemesis. Behind Nick were two more of his children, Edward and husky Hugh. "It must have been enough to let Slade retire to South America for the rest of his life, because he obviously didn't give a damn who saw him. So what *was* the price for my daughter's life? A hundred thousand dollars?"

"What the hell are you talking about?" Chester sputtered.

"I've got seven children, so let's say you budgeted a million for all of them, making it about a hundred and thirty thousand a head. It would have been well worth a million to you, wouldn't it, Chester? Wipe out my family, one by one, at no risk to you. Then the sweetest revenge of all: *your* son, Arthur, becomes my sole heir. You must have been elated when you dreamed that one up, Chester. Oh, it's slick—I'll grant you that. Slick and lethal. But it's *not* going to work."

"I warn you, Nick, I've got the best lawyers in New York. I'm not the poor defenseless slob I was when I was your son-in-law and you railroaded me into prison."

"Railroaded?" said Nick. "You son of a bitch, you were lucky you didn't get the chair."

"Get out of my house!" Chester roared. "All of you! You fucking Flemings foul the air I breathe!"

Hugh started to charge at Chester, but his father restrained him.

"Calm down, Hugh."

"But he killed Vicky!"

"You're all crazy!" yelled Chester. "The bunch of you. . . . But I'm warning you, there are libel laws, and if you spread this nutty fable around, I'll sue you for every cent you've got!"

"Fine," said Nick softly. "You do that, Chester. Meanwhile, I'm taking this nutty fable, as you call it, to the district attorney. We'll let *him* decide how nutty it is. And I've hired bodyguards for my entire family. You won't be able to do to the rest of us what you did to Vicky. I loved that girl, Chester. And when they put you in the chair . . . They'll convict you, don't worry. My lawyers tell me you're not as safe as you think. When they pull the switch on you, Chester, I'll *smile*."

Chester was white.

"Let's get out of here," said Nick. He turned and left the room.

"You're pathetic," said Sylvia to her ex-husband. "And don't get your hopes up about my letting you see Arthur again. I brought him here so you could see what a fine son you have, but you have my word, you'll never see him again."

"God *damn* you!" he howled as he started running across the room toward her. As if Chester had been the Harvard left end, Hugh tackled him, bringing him to the floor. Then, as Chester struggled to escape, Hugh pulled him to his feet again.

"This is for my sister," he said. And he punched him in the jaw so hard that Chester literally flew back against the elaborately carved mantel that had once belonged to the London Rothschilds.

Then Hugh and Edward followed Sylvia out of the room.

His name was Paul Allen and he was called Big Paulie. He was black, six feet five and weighed 280 pounds. He had been born in Harlem thirty years before. He never knew his father. His mother was a cleaning lady who brought home to her roach-filled three-room slum sixty dollars a week to feed her six children.

His first arrest was at age fifteen: he got two years for car theft. At eighteen, he was sentenced to ten years for second-degree manslaughter: he had knifed a grocery clerk in a holdup on Tenth Avenue. Paroled at twenty-four, he was sent to Lewisburg a year later on a charge of stealing Social Security checks from the federal mails.

It was at Lewisburg that he met Chester Hill. Chester was the first Yale graduate he had ever met.

He had never heard of Yale until he met Chester.

Chester Hill had never been in Harlem until he met Big Paulie.

Now Chester climbed the urine-soaked stairs of the tenement on 110th Street between First and Second Avenues. A radio somewhere was playing Bessie Smith. It was a cold day, but the boiler in the building hadn't worked for three years and the two tenants in the five-floor granite house that had been built in 1896 didn't expect heat. Chester's breath steamed in the air.

When he reached the second floor, he knocked on the first door. After a moment, Big Paulie opened it. He was wearing a heavy sweater and a pair of jeans. He smiled.

"How you doin', Chester?" he said, sticking out his mammoth hand. Chester shook it as he came into the room that had once been the front parlor of a prosperous white family, but was now, fifty years after the whites had fled, dilapidated beyond repair. It was crowded with dozens of TV sets Big Paulie had stolen. Except for a battered sofa, a wooden table and a chrome stool, they were the room's only furnishings.

"You not talkin' to me, man?" Big Paulie said as he shut the door. "Cat got your tongue?"

"Something's happened, Big Paulie," he said. "I have to call off our deal."

"Call it *off?*" He laughed, putting his huge fist to his chest in a half-comic gesture of surprise. "Now, I *know* you got a weird sense of humor, Chester, but let's not fool 'round with a subject that is dear to my heart."

"I'm not kidding. I have to call it off. It's too dangerous. Nick Fleming figured out what I was doing. I'm scared, Paulie. I'm real scared."

He took off his hat and the naked light bulb above him cast curious downward shadows on his face.

"You mean," said Big Paulie softly, "you *don't* want me to kill his daughter?"

Chester shook his head. "I was crazy to dream it up in the first place, but I hated them so . . . hated the whole fucking family . . . I don't know. It seemed so wonderful at first, but now . . ."

He shrugged.

"You white mother fucker," whispered Big Paulie, moving softly toward him like a panther. "You *hired* me to do a *job* for you. I made all these *plans* for the rest of my life, man, sippin' rum punches on a Rio beach surrounded by a lotta lovely pussy . . . now you not gonna fuck up those plans, you understan'? If you turn chicken shit, that's okay, but you still gonna pay me the rest of that one hundred grand."

"You can keep the down payment. . . ."

"*Fuck* the down payment, Chester! Ten thousand is *shit,* man! I want it all!"

"I'm not going to pay you for not doing it! I tell you, the whole deal is *off!*"

"You mother FUCKER!" the black man howled. He grabbed a TV set with a nine-inch screen and raised it over his head.

Chester backed away. "Big Paulie . . ." he started to say, but the set crashed against his chest. He fell backward, sprawling in a field of TV sets.

"I had my life all laid out, all my dreams comin' true," the giant was raging as he tore the electric cord off a TV set. "Now you tell me they *ain't* comin' true after all! That makes me *mad*, Chester. Real *mad!*"

"I'll pay you the hundred thousand!" gasped Chester as the huge man advanced toward him, tensing the cord between his two fists.

"I don't believe you, Chester."

"No, no, I *will!* You can trust me! I'll send you a check in the morning. . . ."

"I don't believe you. You fucked me once, you gonna fuck me again." Big Paulie whipped the cord around Chester's throat. Chester screamed and tore at the cord with both hands, but his strength was no match for Big Paulie's. Chester fought hopelessly for breath as Big Paulie, a grin on his face, remorselessly tightened the cord.

When Chester's body limped into death, Big Paulie released it and it crumpled back on the TV sets. Then Big Paulie picked up the TV set he had thrown at Chester, leaned over and bashed the screen into Chester's face, twisting it around until the shattered glass had turned the face that had been voted the "Arrow-Collar-Man Face" of the Class of 1928 at Yale into a mess of bloody pulp.

CHAPTER 51

IT was snowing as they buried Chester Hill, whose body had been found in a dump in New Jersey. Though his face had been unrecognizable, his teeth had finally enabled the coroner's office to make positive identification. His widow, Betty, who had no inkling of her husband's plot against the Fleming family, collapsed with grief, assuming the murder was some horrible, irrational mistake. Nick, however, guessed something close to the truth: that Chester's hiring of killers had backfired. For what Chester had caused to be done to Victoria, Nick hated his memory. But he admitted Chester had paid for his crime.

But to Arthur, his father's murder was as mysterious as Rod Norman's had been to Fiona, and he asked Sylvia if he could go to the funeral. There were few people at the cemetery, even though the murder of the millionaire inventor had generated considerable publicity. But as Chester had been a loner in life, he remained a loner in death. Only a few cousins from Connecticut, his widow, his ex-wife and his son stood in the snow watching the coffin being lowered into the ground.

Afterward, as they were driving back to the city in the limousine, Arthur said to his mother, "He seemed like a nice man. I would really have liked to go to a football game with him."

His mother took his hand and squeezed it. "I'll find you another father," she said. "I haven't had much luck with the first two, but I'll find you a *good* father, I promise."

Arthur looked at her and forced a smile.

"I can't *stand* Nick!" Laure exclaimed two weeks later as she sat in the bathtub with El Toro. "Ever since Vicky's funeral, he's just moped around the house . . . it's like living in a mortuary! He's like an old man all of a sudden. And he hasn't even touched me!"

Juan, whose feet were on her stomach, smiled.

"You don't need him, you've got me."

"That's true. But it's still depressing. Of course he's badly shaken,

458

losing his daughter that horrible way, but life has to go on, doesn't it?"

"Yes, but perhaps not life with *him*."

"What do you mean?"

They were facing each other in the tub. Now he moved his feet and sat up, leaning forward so he could put his hands on her sudsy shoulders.

"I love you, my darling," he said. "I love you with all my heart. Divorce Nick and marry me. We will be so happy together! I will take you to Spain and show you my homeland. And I will make love to you all day and all night forever."

Laure considered being the Marquesa de Novara. "A divorce might be messy," she said. "And though I'm flattered you want me, Juan . . . well, not to sound heartless but I'd be giving up a lot if I left Nick."

"You mean money?"

"Of course."

"But he'd give you a huge settlement! You'd be a rich woman."

"Not necessarily. I'm sure he's been faithful to me, and I haven't exactly been faithful to him—needless to say."

"Get a smart lawyer. Use mental cruelty—it always works. Threaten him with a scandal. All the papers and TV would *love* to know you and I are lovers! It would be all over the country. He's already had so much bad publicity with the murder, he'll pay you to keep quiet."

He moved his hands down to her sudsy breasts.

"Yes, publicity," she mused. "You're right. He wouldn't want that."

"You haven't told me you love me yet," he said.

She looked at his handsome face. She wasn't sure she did love him, but she had become addicted to his lovemaking and wasn't sure she could live without it. What was confusing her was her feeling toward Nick. She had genuinely loved him for five years. Did she love him now? The murder had wrenched their relationship. And then there was damned Diana, with whom he seemed to be spending more and more time. She certainly couldn't love Nick with Diana in the picture!

"I love you," she finally said, "but I'm not sure yet if I love you enough to leave Nick."

He abruptly got out of the bathtub and put on a terry-cloth bathrobe he had stolen from the Plaza Athénée in Paris.

"I think you'd better go now," he snapped. "Go back to your precious Nick and his millions. Juan Alfonso Hernando Guzman y

Talavera does not waste his time on women who can't make up their minds."

"Darling, that's not fair! You're asking me to make a huge decision!"

"Please go. I have better things to do."

She got out of the tub, dripping water and suds all over the tile floor, and threw her arms around him.

"You've made me happier than any man I've ever known," she said.

"Well? Then why don't you love me?"

"I do! I couldn't live without you!"

"Then divorce Nick and marry me."

She hesitated, then kissed him. "All right," she whispered.

He smiled and opened his bathrobe, taking her nakedness in against his.

"That's better," he purred.

He figured her divorce settlement from a man as rich as Nick Fleming would be at least three million, and he could certainly peel one of those millions off for himself.

"So the detective was right," Nick said softly. He was sitting in the back seat of a taxi with Diana. The cab was parked across the street from El Toro's Sutton Place apartment building. Laure had just emerged from the front door, and the doorman was helping her into a cab.

"Who's her lover?" asked Diana.

"A Spaniard named the Marqués de Novara. He's a male whore with a title."

"I've heard of him. They call him 'El Toro' in Europe."

"Mm, I know. The great lover. Well, I hope Laure enjoyed it, because this little fling has cost her her marriage. The Fleming Building, please," he said to the cabby, then he settled back in the seat next to Diana. "I suppose it was inevitable she'd cheat on me, sooner or later. I had a feeling she was getting restless, and let's face it: she *was* a whore. Well, if not a whore, pretty damned close to one. I suppose I was a damned fool ever to have married her, but it was the classic story: older man blinded by sex. How many times has it happened?" He sighed.

"I suppose it's natural at a certain age," said Diana tactfully.

He took her hand and squeezed it.

460

"Life's crazy, isn't it?" he said. "Remember when I told you love's the most important thing in life?"

"I'll never forget it."

"I didn't know what I was talking about then. I thought sex was love or love was sex. When I fell in love with Edwina, I think it was mostly sex at the beginning. As I remember it, all I could think of at first was getting in bed with her. It was only after being married to her for a long time that I learned that love was friendship as well as sex. We fought a lot, but we really were friends as well as lovers. And the damned thing is, after I lost her, I forgot what I learned. Laure was basically just sex to me. I told myself I loved her, but we really never had much in common except sex and the things I bought her. It must be that, because now that it's all over I don't feel anything for her. Nothing at all. I just want to get her out of my life."

He looked at her. "The odd thing is, we've become friends, haven't we? After all the fireworks between us these past thirty-odd years, here we are, both getting older, and friends. I'm glad it's happened, Diana."

"So am I."

"I owe you something very precious," he went on. "You saved Fiona's life for me. I'll never forget that, Diana."

The taxi pulled up in front of the Fleming Building. He looked out the window at the shiny tower.

"Look at it," he said. "My empire." He looked back at her. "I sometimes wonder what the hell an empire means. I might have been happier being a dentist."

She smiled.

"I somehow doubt that, Nick."

He studied her face a moment.

"You've always had such beautiful eyes, Diana." He looked at her tenderly. "You said you still loved me. Is that true?"

"Can't you guess? Why am I here? Why do I keep postponing going back to Europe?"

"What about your Italian friend—the Count?"

"What about him?"

They looked at each other. Then he leaned toward her and kissed her mouth. Slowly, her hands reached out for him. His kiss became harder, the kiss she had waited more than thirty years for. Nick! Nick, my love.

He released her and whispered, "I think I've fallen in love with you a second time! Is that crazy?"

461

"Oh, my darling," she said, hugging him, "it's crazy-wonderful! I've been waiting for this for so long, I don't know whether to laugh or cry!"

"It *is* crazy, but it's true: I love you. My God, the first girl I ever fell in love with, and here I am years later, and I fall in love with her again!"

"And I never stopped loving you, my darling," she said, pulling his handkerchief from his pocket to wipe her eyes.

"Then why the hell don't we get married?"

"I don't know, why the hell don't we?"

"My God, we've had plenty of time to know each other's faults, haven't we? I certainly know yours: you tried to murder me!"

"Oh, darling, I was so wrong to have done that. . . ."

He laughed. "Wrong, hell! You'd do it again, wouldn't you?"

She shook her head as she blew her nose. "Never," she said.

"Well, I know you've got a temper. I'll just have to be careful with you. Shall we go to London for our honeymoon?"

"Mister," interrupted the cabby, "this is all very romantic, but I have a living to make. Would you pay me and take the lovey-dovey stuff somewhere else?"

They both laughed like love-struck teens.

Juan Alfonso Hernando Guzman y Talavera was practicing his putting in his living room when the doorbell rang. Since it was his servant's day off, Juan leaned his putter against one of his *santos* and walked through the big apartment to the entrance foyer to open the door. It was Laure, looking beautiful in her sable coat.

"Well, it's all over," she said, coming into the apartment. "The son of a bitch didn't even have the decency to say goodbye. He flew to London with Diana and left the dirty work to his lawyers. Can you *believe* he's marrying Diana? She's almost *his* age! My God."

Juan closed the door. "And?" he asked impatiently.

"And what?"

"How much are you getting?" He took her sable.

She walked through the apartment she had come to know so well. Juan followed her to the living room.

"I want to get away from New York," she was saying. "Everything about the place depresses me now. Take me someplace romantic, Juan. Someplace where it really *is* springtime."

"We could go to Majorca. I have a beach house there. You'd love it."

"Majorca! That sounds nice. We could wait there until the divorce is settled and then get married."

"But what *is* the settlement?" he insisted.

"A million dollars. I'm rich."

"A *million?* You settled for that?"

"I think it's a lot of money."

"You fool! You little fool—you could have held out for more! Nick Fleming's rich as Croesus! You should have asked for five and settled for three!"

"He knows about us. I don't know how he found out, but he knows, and his lawyers implied they were ready to get nasty if I didn't settle. So I took my million. It's plenty, and you're rich. How much money do we need?"

Juan was furious. "A million dollars isn't rich!" he shouted. "Do you think *I*, Juan Alfonso Hernando Guzman y Talavera, Marqués de Novara, sell my beautiful looks, my title, and my lovemaking genius for a mere million dollars? Well, you can forget Majorca. And you can forget the wedding bells. There are too many *rich* women around waiting to be plucked for me to waste my talents on *you*."

She slapped him, hard. He slapped her back, harder, so much harder that she fell back into a chair.

"You *bastard!*" she screamed.

"Look, Laure, just get out. I don't want a fight with you. We had some nice times together, so that's the end of it, okay?"

She got out of the chair, holding her cheek where he had slapped her.

"I should have known," she said. "You really are trash, you and your *Imsak* and your 'fabulous success' with women. I'm probably lucky you're *not* marrying me."

"Could be."

Swiftly, she grabbed his putter with both hands, swung it and whacked him in the genitals. As Juan howled, doubling over with pain, Laure dropped the putter on the sofa and started out of the room.

"Maybe it'll swell up and get even bigger, lover boy," she said, smiling.

"It hurts!" he wailed.

"Good."

And she left the apartment.

Six weeks later, Nick and Diana were married in a private ceremony in his apartment. The bride and groom held hands. And when Nick kissed her, Diana wept with happiness.

It had, after all, been a long time.

Chester Hill left half his fortune of seventy million dollars to his widow, Betty, and the other half to his only child, Arthur Brooks. Ironically, young Arthur became the richest individual member of the Fleming family in his generation, the heir to a father he had met for only ten minutes.

Neither Willard Slade nor the murderer of Chester Hill was ever found.

The cocktail pianist was rambling through "I'll See You Again" as Fiona slid into the banquette in the cocktail lounge of the small midtown hotel. She was wearing a simple black dress because she was still in mourning for her sister, but Fiona didn't need elaborate clothes to attract men's looks: her beauty was enough.

"I have exciting news," Jerry Lord said after he kissed her. "I've decided to hell with your money. I'm going to ask Marilyn for a divorce."

Fiona looked stunned. "Well, *that's* a switch."

"I know. But why should I go on being miserable married to Marilyn when I can be happy married to you?"

"A good question. A Coke, please," she said to the waiter. Then she turned back to Jerry. "And I have some exciting news for you."

"What?"

"I'm signing the M-G-M contract. I'm going to Hollywood—well, Brentwood, to be precise. My agent's found me an apartment there."

Jerry frowned. "What's that mean? I mean . . . for you and me?"

"It means don't divorce Marilyn for *me* because I don't want to marry you."

He looked so crestfallen, she felt sorry for him. She took his hand. "Jerry," she said, "when you have a rich father like I do, there's one thing you have to worry about: a man who's going to be more interested in your money than you."

"But that's not me! I *told* you, it's your money that's been the problem!"

"And when you told me that I realized you were more interested in my money than me. Oh, perhaps my money intimidated you rather than attracting you, but the point is I want a man who'll think of *me* first, not the money."

He pulled his hand away from hers, and his expression cooled. "Then I wish you luck, Fi. You'll need it."

"Don't be angry."

He shrugged.

"I'm not. But I think I'll have another Scotch."

He signaled for the waiter.

"So you're going to Hollywood?"

"Yes. I'm going to be a star." Just like my father was, she thought. And my mother.

"That shouldn't be difficult," said Jerry, "since your father owns a movie studio."

Her face turned to ice. "I'll make it on my own," she said through clenched teeth.

The waiter set down the Coke.

"Sure," Jerry said.

Fiona stood up, picked up the glass and poured the Coca-Cola over Jerry Lord's head. "I'm glad I found out about you *now*," she said, fuming.

"Maybe you *could* play Margo Channing," he remarked.

"And maybe I *will*."

She stormed out of the cocktail lounge.

"Darling," Diana said as she sipped her orange juice, "I want your children to like me. Do you think they will?"

Nick, who was sitting opposite her at the room-service breakfast table in their honeymoon suite at the Connaught in London, smiled and blew her a kiss.

"If they don't like you, I'll kick them in the collective ass."

"No, seriously, Nick, I really *do* want them to like me—and maybe even love me after a while. But I have an enormous sense of guilt about Fiona."

He reached across the table and squeezed her hand.

"You have to put all that behind you, Diana. Believe me, you saved her life—and the lives of all the others, as far as that goes. If you hadn't made me see what Chester was up to, God knows what might have happened."

"But it was Chester Hill who made me see what a horrible thing *I* did. Chester did the same thing I did almost thirty years ago. It all seemed so clear-cut and simple to me in Turkey: why not hire a killer? But *now* . . . now that I see how ugly killing is, how terrible it was to murder an innocent person like Vicky . . ." She shuddered.

465

"I want to tell Fiona the truth about her father. I won't feel right about her until I tell her I was responsible for his death. Can you understand that? I mean, I think she's one of the loveliest girls I've ever met, and I want our relationship to be an honest one, now that I'm her stepmother."

He thought about it. "I see why you want to do it, and I admire you for your honesty. But I think it's risky."

"Legally? I don't think Fiona would run to the police."

"No. I wasn't thinking about that. Fiona's an emotional girl, and she's made a cult of Rod Norman. She has four or five huge scrapbooks filled with clippings about him and his career, and hundreds of photographs. . . . If she knew you were involved in his death, she might not be able to handle it."

"But that's all the *more* reason for me to tell her the truth! It's *because* she's made her father so important in her mind that makes it so hideously difficult for me carrying around this burden, knowing that I caused his death! I'm willing to risk antagonizing her—though I hope to God I don't—but I *have* to tell her."

"Then tell her," said Nick.

"Will you help me?"

"Of course. Fiona's an intelligent girl. She'll understand." He hesitated, then added, "I hope."

Diana looked nervous. "God," she sighed, "the foolish things you do in your youth come back to haunt you. What a crazy woman I was then." She bit her lip. "But what if she *doesn't* understand? Oh, Nick, I don't know . . . maybe I shouldn't tell her, after all. I mean, if she came to hate me for it. . . ."

"No," he interrupted. "Tell her. It's the right thing to do. I probably should have told her the truth myself, years ago. I don't put much stock in burying family secrets. I did once, but I've come to change my mind. It's better to bring the truth out into the open, no matter how painful." He was wondering now if he could have staved off the incestuous relationship between Charles and Sylvia if he had brought it out in the open at once, rather than hiding from it. How differently things might have turned out if he had! "No, we'll both tell her. She may not be too pleased with *me,* as far as that goes, but she deserves to know the truth."

"You ordered his *assassination?"* gasped Fiona three weeks later. Nick and Diana were in the living room of her Brentwood apartment. "I

can't *believe* it! You hired some . . . Turk to come out here to Los Angeles and gun down my father?"

Diana looked uncomfortable. "I hired him to kill Nick, but because your father and Nick looked so much alike, he shot your father by mistake."

"Oh, that makes it all right, I suppose! What kind of woman *are* you, who hires killers? That's what Chester Hill did!"

"Fiona," Nick said, "it's hard for you to understand the situation then. Diana felt she had been rejected and betrayed by me. She was in Turkey, where they have a different attitude toward killing, and she was deeply upset. . . ."

"You're *defending* her?" she cried out. "You're defending what she did?"

"I'm trying to make you understand it. This all happened almost thirty years ago."

"What difference does that make? My father's dead! He's dead because this . . . this crazy woman you married *paid* someone to kill him!"

"Please, Fiona," Diana pleaded. "I only told you this because I wanted our friendship to be an honest one."

"*What* friendship?" she snarled. "Get out of here! As far as I'm concerned, I never want to see you again!"

"Fiona!" said Nick, shocked. "She's my wife and your stepmother. You apologize!"

"NEVER!" she screamed, bursting into tears and running out of the room. She slammed into her bedroom and threw herself on her bed, sobbing her heart out. Then she turned on her side and looked at the bureau and the wall, which were covered with dozens of framed photographs of the man she had become obsessed with, the father she had never met: Rod Norman.

Part VIII

END GAME
1953-1963

CHAPTER 52

THE old, white-haired lady lying in the big bed with the Pourthault sheets was frail and dying, but even eighty-four years had not been able to destroy all of Edith Fleming Clairmont's beauty. Two strokes, one minor and one not so minor, were killing her, but Edith had few regrets. Her bedroom in the 64th Street town house was filled with photographs of family and friends, and memories seemed to haunt every cubic inch of the high-ceilinged room.

Nick sat in a chair next to her bed, holding her hand. It was the autumn of 1953.

"Remember when you first came to me?" she whispered.

"I remember."

"So long ago . . . *so* long . . . You were afraid of me, I think, weren't you?"

"Yes, I was afraid."

"But you had the nerve . . . no, the guts . . . to say what you did. I'm glad you came to me, darling Nick."

He leaned down and kissed her hand.

"Everything," he said softly. "I owe you everything. I thank you from the bottom of my heart."

She smiled, her eyes only half open.

"We didn't do badly, did we?" she whispered. "Both of us did pretty well, didn't we? That's important. And I was always proud of you, my darling son."

They remained in silence for a while as the afternoon sun filtered through the old-fashioned lace curtains over the windows.

"Life goes by so fast," she finally said. "Suddenly you're old, and it all seems to have been a blink in time . . . your whole life. So curious . . ."

She closed her eyes and after a while Nick thought she had drifted off to sleep. Then she spoke again.

"Those horrible bombs," she said, her eyes still closed. "There seem to be more and more of them all the time. . . . Do you think there might be another war someday, Nick?"

"I hope not. But I fear there might be."

"If all of them went off, it could destroy everything, couldn't it? This beautiful earth? All the flowers and trees. . . ."

"And people," he said.

He felt strength surge through her as she squeezed his hand.

"You must try to stop it, Nick," she whispered. "A war . . . the ultimate war . . . You have the power and the money, you might be able to stop it. Will you promise me that, Nick? For all I gave you in your life, I ask only one thing in return: try to stop war. Try to save this beautiful earth. Will you promise?"

Again, he kissed her hand.

"I promise," he said.

"Good." And she seemed to be at peace.

He meant the promise, though he was baffled as to how to implement it.

Edith died the next morning.

As the years passed swiftly, the Fleming family, like most, chalked up a series of marriages, births and deaths. Unlike most families, its wealth continued to swell, thus proving, if anyone needed proof, that the rich get richer. In 1952, Charles married a rich socialite named Daphne Pierce. Sylvia, who still harbored a secret unnatural affection for her brother, loathed her new sister-in-law; and as if to thumb her nose at Daphne and Charles, she took off for England with her son, Arthur, where to everyone's surprise she managed to bag one of the most eligible bachelors in Europe, her cousin Lord Ronald Saxmundham, head of the Saxmundham Bank. Ronald had inherited Thrax Hall, which had been returned to the family after the war, so Sylvia became the new chatelaine of the ancient manor house, which gave her immense satisfaction and revived memories of her beloved mother, Edwina. Sylvia enrolled Arthur in Eton, quickly picked up an English accent and set about becoming a force in London society.

In 1955, Edward Fleming, the family bohemian, or "beatnik," as they were now being called, published his first novel, a strange tale of pot smokers in Greenwich Village that got good reviews but sold only three thousand copies (the enormous success of *The Naked and the Dead* had made him so envious, he abandoned his war novel). Edward was so enraged by the failure of his magnum opus that he borrowed a million dollars from his father and bought the publishing company, renaming it The Fleming Press. Nick, who had always taken a dim view of the writing profession, encouraged Edward to retire his pen and become a publisher instead, which Edward did. To his surprise, he enjoyed it. Having been a writer himself, he was generous with his advances and willing to gamble on innovative fiction. In 1956, he published a first novel called *Deep Space,* a science-fiction adventure set on a planet near the star Tau Ceti. To his amazement, the novel sold like hot cakes and The Fleming Press, for the first time, turned a profit. Nick, sniffing a winner, talked Edward into merging his publishing house into Fleming Communications. Stock was exchanged and Edward, rather to his embarrassment, because he had always prided himself on his lack of avarice, found himself richer than he had ever been.

Hugh and Maurice Fleming had both married and were working for their father. So in 1960, when Nick turned seventy-two, he told Diana, "I think I can finally retire. The boys have got things pretty much under control."

He was in for a surprise.

On the third of February, 1963, President John F. Kennedy said to his secretary, "Get Nick Fleming on the phone. He's on his yacht in the Caribbean."

"Yes, Mr. President."

The *Seaspray,* built in Holland the year before, was Nick's final extravagance. Sated by his many residences, disliking resorts because of the lack of privacy, but needing a warm climate in winter because of his arthritis, Nick had decided he wanted a yacht, and he and Diana had thrown themselves into the designing of the new toy, working with the shipbuilder and designer to come up with the dream yacht. And the *Seaspray* was precisely that. One hundred and ninety feet long, with a graceful white hull and a raked stack, the ship could make twenty-two knots and cruise four thousand nautical miles, propelled by four powerful diesels. There was a crew of twenty-five, including a French chef, a Swedish masseuse and a Canadian doctor, to minister to the needs of the magnate and his wife and guests. Nick had pledged most of his modern paintings to the Museum of Modern Art after his death, and, in the fifties, had started buying Old Masters. Thus, the yacht's paneled salon was hung with a choice Watteau, a Goya, and a Delacroix, while the dining room had a magnificent Rembrandt that had cost him over two million dollars. In the master suite, he and Diana could enjoy a Manet and two Greuzes, while Diana's dressing room had a lovely painting by Mme. Vigée-

Lebrun. After a life on the fast track, Nick thought of the *Seaspray* as life on the slow, luxurious track, and he and Diana had come to relish their time aboard it.

Nick and Diana were sunning by the swimming pool, the yacht anchored off Jamaica, when the call came through.

"It's the President, sir," said one of the stewards, handing Nick the phone. Nick sat up.

"Mr. Fleming," said John F. Kennedy, "how is it down there in Jamaica?"

"Couldn't be nicer, Mr. President," Nick replied. "It's eighty-eight and not a cloud in the sky."

"Well, I envy you. I just talked to your son Charles again. He tells me you still won't sell Ramschild equipment to us."

"That's right, Mr. President. And my reasons remain the same. This is a lousy, misbegotten war we're in over there in that damned country no one can even pronounce correctly. I'm too old to start being called a 'Titan of Death' again, and I don't even want to be involved with a war that's becoming more unpopular every day. But there's no point in my telling you this on the phone, because I know you read my papers, and if I've said it once I've said it a hundred times: Get out of Vietnam!"

He heard the President clear his throat.

"Yes, I'm well aware of your opinion on that subject. But whether you're right or wrong, the point is we *can't* get out now. . . ."

"Pack up your bags and leave!" snorted Nick.

"You know it's not that simple."

"The hell it isn't! Don't listen to what those generals in the Pentagon tell you! They love this war, and God knows I've known enough generals in my life to know their game. Don't listen to them."

"Well, I can see this conversation's getting nowhere, Mr. Fleming. The fact is we *need* your armaments. Can't I appeal to your patriotism, sir?"

"The last refuge of scoundrels, as Dr. Johnson called it? No, Mr. President, you can't, because my patriotism tells me this war's going to hurt this country more than help it, and waste a lot of lives in the process. What do we give a damn if Vietnam goes Communist? Let it go—who wants the damned place anyway?"

The President sighed.

"All right, Mr. Fleming. Enjoy the sunshine."

"No hard feelings, Mr. President?" Nick was grinning.

"Well, I'm not exactly loving you right now. Goodbye, Mr. Fleming."

The President hung up and said to his brother, the Attorney General, "That stubborn old fart, Fleming. I can't get him to budge."

Nick hung up and said to Diana, "Boy, is he mad! I'm having more fun *not* selling guns than I ever had selling them."

"When you can tell the President of the United States to go fly a kite, darling," said Diana, "that's what I call *power*."

"When Mother died ten years ago, she made me promise her to try to stop war, to try to get rid of the bombs. Well, that was a pretty tall order, but I think I've finally figured out how to do it. I just won't sell them. I wanted to get out of the arms business back in '45, but Charles talked me out of it. Well, he's not going to talk me out of it *this* time. This war's a stupid mistake, and I want no part of it."

She was full of pride. "You're absolutely right, Nick. But Charles *will* fight you on this."

"Let him. I'm still the boss."

He leaned back in his deck chair and closed his eyes to the Caribbean sun. He thought of his mother, and his promise to her.

He thought he had finally found the way to honor that promise.

An hour later, Charles Fleming met with his three brothers, Edward, Maurice and Hugh, in the boardroom of the Fleming Building in New York. Charles walked with a slight limp because of his war wound, but at forty-four he was still slim and relatively youthful-looking and, in his London-made gray pinstripe suit, still a commanding and handsome man. He was also an angry one.

"I just talked to the President," he said, sitting down at the head of the table as his brothers took seats flanking him. "He called the old man on the *Seaspray,* and it's still the same old story."

"No sales to the Pentagon?" said Maurice, who was thirty-nine and the father of four.

"No sales to the Pentagon. Now I'm fed up. We're losing hundreds of millions of dollars in orders because one senile old man on a yacht has the crazy idea this isn't a moral war."

"It isn't," said Edward, who was now a vice president of the book and magazine division of Fleming Industries. Edward, who was still a bachelor, might have joined the business establishment, but he still wore rather baggy tweed sport coats instead of business suits as a last-gasp act of aging beatnik defiance.

"The hell it isn't!" said Charles. "If we don't stop them in Vietnam, all Asia will go Commie! America has to be strong and powerful, and our father, who should know better—Christ, he was in Russia during the Revolution and was taken prisoner by the Commies—now goes soft in the head and wants to let them scare us out! America's always fought moral wars, and this one's just as moral as the Second World War!"

"Charlie, you're full of shit," said Edward. "We have no *business* in Vietnam. The old man's right. Frankly, I'm amazed he's taken the position he has, but I admire his guts."

Charles glared at him, but told himself not to lose his temper.

"All right, let's forget morality and whether the war's right or wrong," he said. "Let's talk money. *Our* money. We're not only losing a fortune in orders, we're putting ourselves on the Pentagon shit list. I've been told by more than one top-ranking general that if we don't play ball with them now when they need us, they'll never play ball with us again. Ramschild is one of the top armaments companies in the world and generates a fourth of the revenues of Fleming Industries. But if we're blackballed by the Pentagon, we might as well go back to making hunting rifles and BB guns. You're my brothers. We all have a big stake in this company. Do you want that to happen?"

There was an uncomfortable silence.

"What can we do?" said Maurice. "It's Father's company. He's the boss."

"Maybe he isn't," said Charles. "He's seventy-five years old now. Maybe we could have him declared mentally incompetent."

"Oh, get off it," pooh-poohed Edward. "He's as sharp as any of us—sharper—and you know it. You try that with him, and he'll have your balls for breakfast."

Charles drummed his fingers.

"You're right," he conceded. "But there's another way. There are approximately fifteen million shares of Fleming Industries Class A voting stock outstanding. Father's the biggest single shareholder with three and a half million shares he owns outright. He funded the Fleming Foundation with three million other shares, which are out of the picture in terms of voting. About two and a half million are owned by the general public. But each of us six children owns a million apiece. If we banded together with our six million shares, we would be the biggest voting bloc. We could *force* him to sell to the Pentagon."

"You're playing with fire," warned Edward. "The old man can

still rewrite his will, and if we tried to outvote him he could disinherit any or all of us. He could give the rest of his stock to the Foundation. Then *it* would be Fleming Industries and could toss us all out on our ass. Besides, you can count me out. I agree with the old man."

Charles glared at his obstreperous younger brother. "Damn it, Eddie, you've always been a rebel! First you go down to the Village to try to be some half-assed hippie, and now you're trying to torpedo the rest of the family. Don't you realize Wall Street knows we're not selling to the Pentagon? Look what's happened to the stock in the last six months! Fleming has been the bluest of the blue chips, but it's plummeted from a hundred and eighty-four to a hundred and nineteen. We're *all* taking a bath!"

"We can afford it," said Edward.

"Charlie's right," said Maurice. "Financially, the company's hurting. If Ramschild's not going to play ball with the government, then I think we *should* sell it off."

"Oh, no, you don't," said Charles. "Ramschild's my baby, and we know how much money it *can* make. It's a gold mine, but one we're not exploiting because of our father. Look, it boils down to the question of who's really running this company—we or the old man. Eddie's right—there's a certain risk if we take him on. But, after all, we're doing the work now. He hasn't been in this building for months. He and Diana are either on the yacht or off in Europe somewhere. He's not involved any longer. . . ."

"I think he's very involved," interrupted Edward. "Not in the day-to-day operations, but in the long-term interests of the company and us, the family. In the long term, if we stay out of this cockamamy war, we'll come out smelling like a rose."

"If there's anything left to smell!" said Charles. "I say we have to force the issue. The only thing Father respects is power, and if we show a little muscle I think there's a better than even chance he'll give in to us."

"Count me out," Edward repeated.

"I already have. How about you, Maurice? And you, Hugh?"

They hesitated.

"What about Fiona and Sylvia?" Hugh finally said. "We'll need them."

"Fiona will vote with me," said Charles. "She hasn't talked to Diana since she told her she'd hired that Turkish killer to assassinate Rod Norman—which was pretty dumb on Diana's part."

"And Sylvia?"

"I can handle Sylvia."

"If you can get Sylvia in on it, you can count on me."

"Good boy, Hugh." Charles smiled. "Maurice? How about it?"

Maurice, the most conservative member of the family, equivocated. "I'll think it over," he said. "You get Sylvia first, then I'll give you my answer."

Charles shrugged. "Fair enough. Tomorrow I fly to London to see Sylvia."

"You're all making a big mistake," said Edward.

Charles stared at him. "Maybe it's *you* who are making the mistake," he said softly and lethally.

The astonishing beauty was still in evidence, but it was fading fast before a combination of too much California sun, California wine and, lately, California drugs. Fiona's dream of becoming a great star like her father, Rod Norman, had turned into a nightmare. She had the looks for stardom and was a talented actress, but she lacked that indefinable something that made the public take her to its heart. After a series of minor roles in lackluster movies, her agent suggested she get her father to use his influence to help her flagging career. This offended her so deeply that she not only withdrew from films, she began to withdraw from life—or at least reality.

Her cult worship of her dead father, which had warped her into hating her stepmother, Diana, now led her into a druggy dream-world. Being astonishingly rich, she bought the run-down château that had been Rod Norman's in his heyday but had since become a two-bit apartment house, and she began to turn back the hands of time. She evicted the tenants and, at a cost of almost a quarter of a million dollars, turned the place back into as close a replica of what it had been in 1922 as research and money could achieve. Her favorite movie, which had been *All About Eve,* now became *Sunset Boulevard,* a print of which she bought. And, like Norma Desmond, she filled the great rooms of the old fake château with her vast collection of photographs of Rod Norman—pose after pose of the handsome star with his slicked-down, early-twenties hair—resting on tables, piano tops and bureaus. In Southern California, which thrived on eccentricity, Fiona's bizarre behavior raised few eyebrows; she was known as Fey Fiona, the nut case.

But as wave after wave of increasingly exotic drugs lapped the shores of the Los Angeles consciousness, Fey Fiona tried them all. With her small group of friends, hangers-on and casual lovers, she locked herself up in her Rod Norman dream house and went from pot to peyote and beyond. She owned a print of every one of Rod's silent films that had not disintegrated into oblivion or become lost, and she would screen them over and over as she tripped out on the latest chic drug. That lost, innocent world of the early twenties held enormous appeal for her: the flickery melodramatics that had once seemed so funny now seemed wondrously romantic and rich and safe. And there he was, on the silver screen, eternally alive, the conqueror of time, that wondrously handsome hero who would always be with her and would never fail her and could never possibly be after her money . . . Rod Norman.

Thus, when Charles called her and asked her to back him in his fight against Nick and Diana, Fiona—whose druggy brain had forgotten all the loving kindness Nick had lavished on her over the years and had turned him into a kind of collaborator in her father's death—said, "I'll vote every share I own for you, Charlie."

Charles, in New York, smiled.

"I knew I could count on you, Fi," he said.

CHAPTER 53

SYLVIA had loved England when her parents used to bring her over as a child in the thirties. She loved the soft green beauty of the countryside around Thrax Hall; she loved the peaceful villages with their thatched-roof cottages, villages that seemed to drowse undisturbed through the centuries. She also loved the excitement and glamour of London. Half-English through her mother's Thrax blood, she considered England as much her homeland as America. And thus, after her wretched marriage to Chester Hill and a not much more successful one to Corny Brooks, it was not only to turn her back on Charles and his new bride, Daphne, that she had gone to England: it was also to find a serenity she remembered from her childhood.

London was climbing out of the rubble of the Blitz and England was recovering from the devastation of the war, alive with the confidence of the new Elizabethan Age. Sylvia found it as exciting in its own way as New York. She had many family connections, but her cousin, Lord Ronald Saxmundham, took it on himself to help his American relative settle in. Ronald was in his late thirties, tall, railthin, with washed-out sandy good looks, rather shy—which some people mistook for stuffiness—and highly intelligent. He was also kind, thoughtful and, perhaps most appealing to Sylvia after her rocky marital record, solid. She liked him a lot. She decided he'd be the *good* father she had promised Arthur she'd find. For his part, Ronald was dazzled by her beauty, her sense of style and her capacity for fun. What most people first considered an unlikely couple soon became a prime example of the attraction of opposites. Their marriage was hailed in the press: England still remembered the Yanks with affection. For that matter, England still remembered Nick and Edwina with affection.

As Lady Saxmundham, the third Viscountess and wife of one of England's leading bankers, Sylvia found herself in an on-approval situation with the English Establishment. Two world wars might have cost England its Empire and shaken up the class system, but the heart of the Establishment remained fiercely conservative. Sylvia, after all, was an American, despite her mother, and one who, before the war, had been on the cover of *Life* as debutante of the year— something that was not quite "U" in English eyes. Sylvia was suspect.

To everyone's surprise and her husband's delight, Sylvia became almost more English than the English, *plus royaliste que le roi*. Always an accomplished equestrienne, she joined The Quorn, rode point-to-point, won a number of cups, and impressed everyone with her dash and verve. Good horsemanship is a sure route to English affection, but to many people Sylvia remained something less than loved. She had a short temper, a sharp tongue and a rather imperious manner that led her more polite acquaintances to describe her as "difficult." She also had an eye for men; and while she was careful to remain faithful to Ronald—she liked being Lady Saxmundham and was genuinely fond of her husband, if he wasn't exactly the grand passion of her life—she became known as a bit of a flirt, which didn't endear her to the wives of the men she flirted with. Sylvia became a successful hostess and cut a swath through the upper reaches of English society. But the English never took her to their collective heart.

She had borne Ronald a son, Perceval, in 1957, and a daughter, Penelope, in 1958; and it was after Percy's sixth birthday party at Thrax Hall that Ronald took Sylvia into the library, poured a brandy and told her, "Charles is arriving tomorrow."

As always, mention of her brother's name gave a quick little surge to Sylvia's blood, a surge of mixed guilt and still-not-quite dormant passion. Her relationship with her brother had always been what someone once called "testy intimacy": both the testiness and the intimacy were products of their shared secret.

"Why?" she asked. "Charles hasn't been over here for a year. I hope he's not bringing Daphne. Every time I have to be polite to that woman, I break out in a rash."

"No, he's not bringing Daphne. This is business, and rather sticky business, from what Eddie tells me. He gave me a call to warn me what Charles is up to."

" 'Up to'? You make it sound conspiratorial."

"It is. As you know, your father has put a ban on selling arms to the Pentagon. Nick disapproves of the Vietnam War, which I rather admire, even though it's a trifle suicidal in a business sense. Charles is trying to put together a sort of family bloc of you and your brothers to outvote him."

"Really? I'm amazed Charlie has the nerve. He's been terribly intimidated by Father ever since he almost disinherited him during the war." (She remembered a naked Charles stretching sensuously beside the pond in the woods adjacent to Thrax Hall. She remembered the excitement she felt watching him, the near delirium.)

"Yes, I know. But Charles is passionate about Ramschild. He likes the feeling of power it gives him, meeting with generals and admirals and whatnot—he's really a bit of a little boy about the whole thing. It doesn't surprise me he's willing to fight to save the company."

"But to take on Father? That's not something one does lightly." (She remembered his hot kisses, the warmth of his strong body, the thrill of breaking taboos.)

"Which is why I'm bringing this up," Ronald went on. "I think this is extremely ill-advised on Charles's part. I think it could tear apart the family and even tear apart Fleming Industries, if it went far enough. Nick Fleming is no King Lear. He's not going to give away his kingdom to his children without a fight."

"Yes, I agree. What about the others? How do they stand?"

"According to Eddie, Fiona will go with Charles, and Hugh and Maurice may if you join in. Eddie is adamant against it and would vote with his father. Personally, I think Charles is mad to try it at all. But the point is, it all depends on *you*. And as your husband, I strongly advise you to stay out of it. Don't antagonize your father."

"Don't worry, I have no intention to. I love Father too much to stab him in the back—which is what Charlie's trying to do. It doesn't surprise me, in a way. Not to wallow in cheap psychiatry, but Charlie's always held a secret grudge against Father. You know, it's the old immensely-successful-father-jealous-son business. I'll tell him to forget it—and that *he* should forget it too."

"Good. I thought you'd be sensible."

"But he's coming *tomorrow?* Does he realize we're giving the Thrax Ball tomorrow night?"

"Oh, yes. He's renting a costume."

"What's he coming as?"

"The Devil."

Sylvia laughed. "How appropriate."

(She remembered the ecstasy of their lovemaking, an ecstasy that still tingled even after almost thirty years. The Devil indeed.)

The Thrax Ball was first given in 1883 and had been an annual event at Thrax Hall ever since, with the exception of the war years. It was one of the major events in English society, and the invitation list had varied little in the eighty years of its existence, although, since the war, film and theatrical stars as well as business magnates had been added to a list heavily tilted in favor of Debrett. It was a costume ball, and because the English love to dress up in elaborate and sometimes silly outfits—as well as the attraction of the splendor of the setting at Thrax Hall and the gallons of champagne that annually flowed—it took death or a major illness to keep people away. In 1883, the then Lord Saxmundham had put up his guests and their numerous servants in the dozens of bedrooms, the servants being squeezed into the attic. Now only the elderly and those coming from far away stayed overnight; the rest were taken back to London in a fleet of chartered buses.

Since the rooms had all been allotted, Charles, a last-minute guest, was staying at Audley Place, which still belonged to his father and was used by various family members for infrequent summer vacations, the old Tudor house that Edwina had loved so much standing empty most of the time. But Charles's staff was efficient: they had alerted the caretaker and his wife. And after Charles had flown the Atlantic in one of Fleming Industries' corporate jets, he was met at Heathrow by a chauffeured Rolls and was driven to Audley Place, which was ready for him, the thermostat having been turned up to a toasty seventy degrees and fires lit in the many fireplaces to combat the bitter February cold outside.

But Charles, like any rich man, assumed his creature comforts. What was on his mind as he drank a stiff whiskey in front of the library fireplace was his father. He vividly remembered the scene in that very room twenty-two years ago when his father had thrown his drink in his face and jerked him out of his chair. He had almost disowned him then, and Charles had never forgotten or forgiven. What would he do now, when he learned of Charles's latest treachery? (For that matter, he probably already knew, because Eddie would undoubtedly have told him.) Charles had no illusions about his father's reaction: he would boot him out of Fleming Industries. The die had been cast. Either he or his father was going to win control of the empire.

But Charles had two aces up his sleeve. Three, if he counted Sylvia.

Sylvia. Everything depended on his mercurial, bewitching sister.

As he stared into the flickering flames of the fire, Charles also remembered that afternoon so long ago when he had committed incest with his sister.

Sylvia . . . Even her name still aroused dark passions in his blood. . . .

CHAPTER 54

EDWINA, like most of the English, had never really "taken" to modern art, and during the twenties and thirties, when her husband was building his impressive collection of contemporary canvases, her reaction to each new acquisition had been at best feigned enthusiasm and at worst a wince and some remark like, "God, darling, isn't it a bit ugly?" Her idea of good art was either a painting that "told a story" or a fine old family portrait, preferably by Gainsborough or Lawrence.

At first, Nick had written her lack of appreciation off to British provincialism, but as the years passed, he began to wonder if she hadn't been on to something after all. Certainly by the fifties, he had come to the conclusion that the modern movement, whatever excitement it had possessed at the beginning of the century, was now debasing itself into idiocy, if not downright fraud. Diana, despite the wildly adventurous life she had led, also held conservative attitudes toward art. So when they were married, both Nick and Diana embraced the past with a vengeance, aided by Nick's now enormous fortune.

The result was not only a change in the paintings that hung on the walls of their yacht and many residences, but a decision to make the yacht interiors "period," letting the twentieth century be reflected in the technological marvels of the ship itself. They didn't carry this to the ridiculous length of concealing air-conditioning ducts behind coromandel screens, but once aboard the *Seaspray,* there was little beyond the phones and TV sets and electric lights that had been made in the twentieth century. The master stateroom was a case in point. The walls were hung with panels of early-nineteenth-century wallpaper depicting views of London that Diana had discovered and fallen in love with and Nick had paid eighty-five thousand dollars for. The rug was a delicately hued antique Persian; the furniture was all eighteenth century, including a French desk, the price of which had made even Nick wince. The end result of this extravagant escape into a romantic past was probably the prettiest bedroom afloat. Diana loved it. She didn't give a damn what it cost. As Nick had said, "If we go broke, we can ram an iceberg and collect the insurance."

There were few icebergs in sight as the *Seaspray* sliced through the Caribbean at twenty knots, headed for the Bahamas. Diana had just finished dressing for dinner and was crossing the bedroom when Nick came in. She had never seen him look so apoplectic.

"Damn him!" he exploded, slamming the door behind him. *"God-damn* him!"

"Who?" she exclaimed. "What's wrong?"

"That son of a bitch, Charles! Eddie just called. Charles is trying to turn the family against me! What kind of a son . . ."

He stopped and clutched his chest with both hands, letting out a sound that was a mixture of a gasp and a moan. Then he fell onto the bed.

"Darling!" she cried, running to him.

"Get the doctor," he whispered. "Quick!"

Four thousand miles away, Sylvia was standing in front of a full-length mirror in her bedroom on the second floor of Thrax Hall examining *her* escape into a romantic past, namely her costume for the ball. She had toyed with the idea of dressing as Cleopatra, but had decided Thrax Hall was too chilly for that, so had decided on Eleanor of Aquitaine instead. Then she had looked in a costume book and decided she would look silly in a peaked hat, so she thought of her mother and went to the attic where many of Edwina's clothes had been stored after her death, carefully packed in mothballs. There, among a number of twenties and thirties dresses that evoked with the smell of camphor the glamour of those receding years, she found a white "flapper" dress that looked as if it had been made around 1925. Her instincts told her it would be perfect, and when she tried it on she found to her relief that her figure was still as good as her mother's had been. Now, as the first buses from London were pulling up outside, she looked at her reflection and decided she looked "super"— Sylvia was careful to keep up with the latest buzz words of the young. She had inherited most of her mother's fabulous jewelry, so to glitz herself up for the occasion she had put on four of Edwina's thick Art Deco diamond bracelets, two of her ruby-and-diamond brooches, a pair of dangling diamond earrings and the magnificent diamond necklace holding the Blood Moon Ruby that Nick had given her mother as a wedding present almost half a century ago. The dress's hem hit her knees in front, so that her fabulous legs were shown to advantage, and the thin shoulder straps showed plenty of satiny skin. She had had her auburn hair restyled in a twenties bob, with sharp bangs over her forehead, and she had used a slashing scarlet lipstick and heavy twenties eye makeup. Now she assumed a sexy silent-movie vamp pose and trailed her fingers up one arm.

"Irresistible," she murmured.

"The first bus is here," said Ronald, coming into the room. He was dressed as the Scarlet Pimpernel. Sylvia turned and smiled alluringly at him.

"Clara Bow," she said.

He never tired of looking at his wife, but tonight she was spectacular.

"Smashing," he said, smiling. "Absolutely smashing. You'll be the belle of the ball." He extended his arm. "Shall we go down?"

She crossed to him, took his arm and they left the room.

"Charles called," he said as they walked down the second-floor hallway toward the staircase. "He'll be a little late."

Charles. She thought of a pond in the woods. . . .

Henry VIII was there, with two of his wives, Catherine Howard and Anne Boleyn. Tarzan was there, keeping close to the heating ducts. Frankenstein was there along with Count Dracula, Lucrezia Borgia, Cardinal Richelieu, Scarlett O'Hara, Marie Antoinette, Rasputin, George Sand, the Hunchback of Notre Dame, Nero, John the Baptist, the Queen of Sheba, Alice in Wonderland and the Mad Hatter. Over a hundred and fifty costumed guests were dancing in the huge ballroom at Thrax Hall to the music of a London rock group that was imitating the style of that sensational new group from Liverpool, The Beatles. When Charles, in his red Devil's costume replete with pitchfork and tail, came into the room, he paused to drink in the fantastic scene. The blaring twentieth-century music in the elegant gilt-and-gray eighteenth-century ballroom was bizarre enough contrast, but the costumes ranging across thousands of years of fact and fiction gave the scene the appearance of a time warp.

Then he spotted Clara Bow dancing with the Scarlet Pimpernel. Sylvia and her diamonds shimmered like a distant star. Charles took a flute of champagne from a passing waiter and sipped the Laurent Perrier as he continued to watch his sister dance.

It all depended on Sylvia.

Ten minutes later, the rock group was replaced by a conventional orchestra that began playing vintage Noel Coward. As the sweet strains of "I'll See You Again" slurred out of the saxophones and clarinets, Sylvia made her way through the crowd toward her brother, the huge Blood Moon Ruby dangling above her cleavage like a bicycle reflector.

"Hello, Charlie," she said, kissing his cheek. "How was your flight?"

"Bumpy."

He set his champagne glass on the green marble top of a chest made by André-Charles Boulle in 1716 (which Ronald had recently re-insured for £250,000).

"How are your legs?" she asked. "Feeling spry enough to dance with me?"

"I think I can manage a fox-trot."

He led his sister onto the dance floor and she felt him press her body against his.

"Charlie, I know why you're here," she said. "You're being very foolish, you know. Father will scream bloody murder when he finds out."

"Let him scream. All I'm trying to do is save Ramschild from going down the drain."

"Well, you'll be wasting your breath trying to get me to go in with you. I'm not going to antagonize Father."

"You haven't even given me a chance to . . ."

"There's no point in listening to you, Charlie. Ronald's against it and so am I."

"And who told Ronald? Eddie?"

"Yes. He phoned."

"I figured as much. Eddie's such a self-righteous bastard. Anyway, what Eddie doesn't know because I don't *want* him to know is that I've got support outside the family."

"Who?"

"They'll remain nameless for the time being."

"Don't you trust your own sister?"

"I don't trust Ronald. Anyway, it's roughly another million and a half shares that will back us in a showdown. We can win if we all stick together!"

"But win *what?* Control of the company? Who wants it? I'm happy the way I am. And I certainly don't want to turn against my own father."

"Sylvia, we're not turning against him!"

"I'd like to know what you call it."

"We're saving what he built up in his lifetime. That senile old man sitting on his yacht is not the same Nick Fleming who built Ramschild Arms from a hunting-rifle company into Fleming Industries! If Father were sixty instead of seventy-five, he'd be selling everything in the factories, including the pencil sharpeners, to the Pentagon! All I'm doing is trying to save him from himself."

"Do you *really* think he's gaga?"

"Of course! No sane man would turn down telephone calls from the President of the United States begging him to sell to the Pentagon. No sane man would refuse hundreds of millions of dollars' worth of orders. He's gone soft in the head." He hesitated, looking at her. Then he added, "You look very beautiful tonight."

"Mm. Thanks."

"And I'm crazy about that perfume."

"It's something Ronald gave me for Christmas. It's called *Nuit d'Amour.*"

" 'Night of Love.' I like that."

"Speaking of love, how's Daphne the bitch?"

"Don't talk like that. Daphne's nice."

"She's a pill, and you know it. I never could understand how you married her. I thought you had better taste in women."

"Once I had excellent taste in women," he said softly, looking into her eyes. "When I was young." He pressed her a little harder against his body. "Once I had the best woman in the world."

She felt her heart race.

"Charlie, don't talk that way."

"I'm all alone over at Audley Place," he whispered in her ear. "Come be with me tonight."

A vision of a naked young man stretching beside a wooded pond flashed in her mind.

"I can't," she said nervously. "And don't hold me so tight. It doesn't look right."

"Don't tell me you don't enjoy it."

She didn't answer.

"Come with me to Audley Place. No one will miss you in this crowd."

"You're disgusting."

488

She pushed him away and started off the dance floor.

Charles smiled. He knew she was tempted.

Sylvia went into the billiard room where a bar had been set up. She was suddenly hot and nervous. She needed something stronger than champagne.

"Give me a whiskey, please," she said to the bartender. She was trembling. When he handed her the glass, she took a gulp of the single-malt Scotch, which gave her a strong jolt. Ronald, looking dashing in his Scarlet Pimpernel costume with its red-and-gold coat, came up to her.

"Well, so far no one's fallen down drunk," he said, adding to the barman, "A whiskey, please."

"Yes, everyone seems rather well-behaved tonight," she said.

"Of course, it's still early. Are you all right? You look a little flushed."

"It's the whiskey, I suppose. I got a little dizzy on the dance floor. I feel better now."

"Are you sure? Can I get you something?"

"No, really, I'm fine." She hesitated. "Darling, would you mind awfully if I went over and stayed with Charlie at Audley Place tonight? He tells me he feels so lonely there. You know the house is full of memories of Mother, and . . . well, I know what Charlie means. Is it all right?"

"Yes, I suppose. But you'll have to be back by lunch. We have a houseful of guests to feed."

"I'll be back."

"Has he mentioned the stock?"

"Oh, yes. I shot that down in flames."

"Good girl. Well . . ." He finished off his whiskey and set the glass down. "Once more into the fray."

And he returned to the ballroom.

Oh, Sylvia, she thought, you're going to regret this.

CHAPTER 55

B Y five in the morning, the last of the buses were gone. Sylvia should have been exhausted, but her adrenaline was pumping. She threw a nightgown, a toothbrush and a day dress into an overnight bag, put on her sable coat and joined Charles and Ronald in the Great Hall.

"You really do look silly in that Devil's outfit," she said as she came up to them. She turned to Ronald. "Good night, darling. You must be exhausted." And she kissed him.

"Yes, I am, a bit."

"Then go on up to bed. I'll see you later in the morning."

Taking her brother's arm, she started across the marble hall where, so many years before, her mother had seen her father for the first time. But Sylvia wasn't thinking of the past. She was thinking of *now*.

"There's snow forecast," called Ronald as she opened the door.

She turned to look at him. He's so *good*, she thought, so kind. Don't do this to him.

But God, I can't back out now.

Outside, it was bitterly cold. Charles's chauffeur hurried up to take Sylvia's overnight bag, then helped the two into the back seat of the Rolls.

"I know what you're trying to do," said Sylvia after the car had started up. "You're terribly obvious, you know. Romancing me because you need my stock votes. It won't work, you know."

He reached over and took her hand. "I don't care if you back me or not," he said.

"And pigs have wings. Oh, Charlie," she sighed. "You're so devious. Basically, you're a *rotten* human being."

He smiled. "We're both rotten," he whispered. "That's why we love each other."

She closed her eyes. She wondered if he was right.

By the time the Rolls pulled up in front of Audley Place, it had started snowing lightly.

"Mother loved this house so," she said as she walked with her brother to the front door. "I come over here every once in a while just to be with her. Not that I believe in ghosts, but memories can certainly haunt a house. Mother's memory is in every brick of this place."

"She was a wonderful woman," said Charles.

"How did she ever have *us?*" Sylvia asked as she opened the front door.

Charles didn't answer.

Inside, a fire was still burning in the living-room fireplace, albeit low. After Charles took off his coat, he put on a log and stirred the embers. Sylvia was looking around the long, low room that once, centuries before, had been a dairy. She was almost obsessed by her mother, remembering Edwina so vividly, torn between her physical desire for her brother and her guilt.

Charles slipped the hood of his Devil's costume off his head and began unzipping the back. Then he stopped. He had spotted a telegram on one of the long tables. He went to the table, picked up the telegram and opened it.

"It's from Diana." He began reading aloud. " 'Your father has suffered mild heart attack . . .' "

"Oh, my God!" Sylvia interrupted.

". . . 'due to shock at your treachery.' She doesn't mince words, does she? 'You are discharged from your present duties at Fleming Industries and your office locked. Your father being flown to New York Doctors Hospital.' "

He crumpled the telegram and threw it into the fire.

"All right," he said softly, "it's open warfare. Good."

He looked at Sylvia, whose face was chalk.

"It's a sign," she said.

"What is?"

"Father having a heart attack. It's a sign from Mother! I *knew* it when I came in here."

"Knew what? What the hell are you talking about?"

"I knew it was *wrong* for me to come here tonight! Oh, Charlie, I want you. I suppose I've always wanted you ever since I was old enough to know what sex is. I don't know *why* . . . it's like some evil seed inside me I can't get out of my system, some poison . . ."

"It's not evil, and it's not poison. It's something beautiful between us. It's a private, secret love. I don't give a damn what the rest of the world calls it!"

"The rest of the world calls it *incest,* Charlie," she said quietly. "Now I'm going to bed. Alone. In the morning I'm going back to Thrax Hall. And if you're smart, you'll get back to New York and start making your peace with Father."

"To hell with Father!" he shouted. "He's had his turn. It's my turn now! All my life I've been known as Nick Fleming's son—even in the R.A.F., when I was a fucking *hero,* I was still known as Nick Fleming's son! To *hell* with Nick Fleming! He's a feeble, senile old man now, with a weak heart! Fuck him! He discharges me? I'll discharge him!"

"Charlie," she said softly, "he's our father. I feel sorry for you."

She started toward the stairs.

"You come here!" he roared.

"I'm going upstairs."

"You'll do what I say! Come back here! I'm going to fuck you right here on the floor in front of the fire. I've been thinking about it all night!"

"I'm not going to do it!" she yelled. "Now shut up about that!"

"You"—he started limping toward the stairs—"come here . . ."

She started running up the stairs screaming, "Charlie, *stop* it! I'm *not* going to do it!"

"You'll do what I say! And you're going to vote your stock the way I tell you!"

"No, I won't!"

He was climbing the stairs as fast as his weak leg permitted.

"I'm the head of this family now," he was saying, "and you're all going to take orders from *me.* If we vote together we can get the old man *out.* Then I'll make millions for all of us—billions! I'll fill every Pentagon contract I can get. And I've got plans, Sylvia, secret plans! The Pentagon wants missiles—they've got billions to invest in missiles!—but Father wouldn't bid for those contracts. When I take over the company, I'll build those missiles for the Pentagon. I'll build them whatever they want! It's perfect, can't you see? The Pentagon will go on forever because they've got Russia to use as a threat to scare the shit out of the public. And we will be the manufacturing arm of the Pentagon, so *we* will go on forever, getting richer and richer. It's so beautifully simple, don't you see? But Father's standing in the way. That's why we have to get rid of him!"

He had reached the top of the stairs, panting from his exertions.

She was standing in one of the bedroom doors at the end of the hall.

"I may be rotten," Charlie," she said, "but I'm not sick and you're *sick,* Charlie. You're sick like Chester Hill was sick, but he didn't want to blow up the whole world, for Christ's sake! I'm glad we've had this little 'talk'—if you can call it that. Now I see what's *really* going on in that twisted brain of yours. You're a menace, Charlie— a real menace. For the first time in my life, I'm beginning to see what a great man my father is. And if you think I'm going to help you get him out of Fleming Industries, you're not only sick, you're stupid. So good night. And I'm locking this door."

She stepped inside the room and slammed the heavy wooden door, turning the iron key in the elaborate antique iron lock. *That* will keep him out, she thought. My God, he's a raving lunatic! Or is he drunk? Whatever, Charlie was telling the truth tonight. Hadn't Eisenhower called it the military-industrial complex? Hadn't he tried to warn America? The military-industrial complex is my bloody *brother!* she thought. And that must be why Father's refusing to sell to the Penta-gon—*he* must see it too!

She turned on a lamp and looked around the low-ceilinged guest room, unchanged since Edwina had furnished it back in the thirties. Everything was warm and cozy and comfortable and unpretentious. With its chintzes and its big four-poster Queen Anne bed, it was a terribly English room. Sylvia felt safe in it. Kicking herself mentally for not having remembered to bring up her overnight bag, she began removing her jewelry. She placed the valuable—one could almost say "invaluable" in the case of the Blood Moon Ruby—stones in a white china dish on the mantel. Then she turned down the bed, which had a thick, soft *duvet.* That should keep me warm, she thought. She sat on the bed and removed her silver pumps, then stood up to take off her dress and stockings and panties. Dropping them over the back of a chaise longue, she hurried across the rug to the bed, shivering slightly since she was now naked. She slipped under the sheets and the heavy quilt, pulling them up to her chin and relaxing as the heat of her body began to warm her.

THUD!

She screamed as she saw the ax blade chop through the wooden door. Then it vanished.

THUD!

"Charlie, stay *away!"* she shouted.

THUD!

"Charlie, please . . ."

THUD!

"Oh, my God. . . . Charlie, *stop* this!"

Riiip . . .

There was a crash, and a hole appeared in the door. As he pushed the splintered plank through, it clattered to the floor. Then she saw his arm reach through, groping for the key. The red of his Devil's costume galvanized her. She threw back the *duvet,* got out of bed and ran across the room to the door, grabbing an antique silver buttonhook off the top of a lowboy on the way.

"Billions!" she heard him saying. "We'll make billions, Sylvia! Think of the power we'll have! The missiles we'll build will protect America! We'll put them in silos in every state of the Union. And someday we'll blow Russia off the face of the earth."

His hand had found the key. Gripping the buttonhook, she jabbed it into the back of his hand, then ripped it down, tearing open the skin. He screamed in agony, but didn't let go of the key. Blood was pouring out of his hand as he pulled the key out of the lock. She kept jabbing at him as the hand and key vanished through the hole in the door. She backed away as she heard the lock turn. The door was opened, and there stood the Devil, the ax in his left hand, the key in his blood-dripping right.

Slowly, he came into the room.

"You shouldn't have locked me out, Sylvia," he said softly. "You want me as much as I want you. That's why you came here tonight."

She was backing away, staring at the ax.

"Charlie, please don't," she whispered. "Don't do anything stupid."

He tossed the key and the ax on the floor.

"I wouldn't hurt you, if that's what you're thinking. I love you, Sylvia. I'd never hurt you." He began taking off the Devil's costume. "You don't understand. I'm doing this for *us*. The family. You and me. We've always been special ever since we were children. Special friends, special lovers."

He tossed the costume on top of the ax. He was in his shorts now. He started pulling them off, the blood from his hand dripping on his legs and the floor.

"We'll make love, Sylvia," he went on. "Then you'll help me. Now you see how important it is that you help me, don't you?" He was naked now, naked and blood-spattered. "Remember by the pond all those years ago? Remember how beautiful it was? You're the only woman I've ever *really* wanted, ever *really* loved. I've made love to hundreds of women, but the only woman I've ever loved is my sister. You'll help me, won't you? My darling Sylvia . . ."

He came to her, hands outstretched in a pleading gesture. She

494

looked at his hard body and marveled how much she hungered for it. Yes, she *did* love him. She had always loved him. She adored him and hated him and now even feared him.

In one lightning-swift gesture, she swept the buttonhook up and plunged it into his left eye. His scream-howl filled the room as he staggered back, his hands over his face. She ran around him, out the door, down the hall to the wooden stairs, down the stairs, his screams chasing her. Grabbing her sable coat, she threw it over her nakedness and then ran to the front door. "Sylvia, Sylvia," he was crying. It broke her heart, for there was no rage in his voice, only anguish and hurt.

She opened the door and ran outside. It was snowing hard now, and the snow bit into her bare feet, but she didn't care. She ran down the long, dark wing of Audley Place toward the kitchen and, beyond, the servants' quarters where the caretaker and the chauffeur were sleeping. One window was already lighted, and another blinked on. They must have heard the screams, she thought.

Oh, Charlie, my Charlie, I'm sorry, forgive me, but I had to do it. . . . I had to exorcise you. . . .

You *are* the Devil, Charlie. Someone had to stop you, or you'd blow up the world. . . .

THE splendid antiques and fine art had been replaced by hospital furniture and a tacky landscape on the white wall, but Nick didn't care; he was still alive, and the doctor had told him that very morning he could leave the hospital by the end of the week.

"I guess they can't bury me yet," he said to Diana, who was sitting next to his hospital bed.

"The doctor tells me that if you take good care of yourself, you'll be around a long time. And it's *my* job to see that you do."

He looked at her and smiled. "I've been a lucky man," he said. "I've had two wonderful wives and only one clinker."

"Whom we'll forget about. You know, Nick, I was thinking about my life, which has not been exactly humdrum. . . ."

"Hardly." He smiled again.

"And I came to the conclusion things worked out for the best after all. If I'd married you when I was young, we would probably have divorced. When we were young, we were both too headstrong to survive each other. No, I think it's better that I married you later. I'm wise enough to appreciate you now."

He held out his hand and she took it.

"And I'm wise enough to appreciate *you,*" he said. They smiled at each other a moment. "Do you think the doctor would let me take a cruise on the *Seaspray?*"

"I'm sure he would. What could be more restful?"

"Then why don't you tell Captain Grant to take the yacht over to the Mediterranean. When I get out of here, we'll fly to Rome and meet him at Ostia. Then we can cruise the Mediterranean for a month. There's an island off Tunisia called Djerba that I want to take a look at. I've been approached to invest in a resort hotel there."

"Sounds lovely. I've never seen Tunisia."

"Good."

He released her hand, looking for a moment at the television on the wall, where a soap opera was spinning its endless web of intrigue with the sound off.

496

"I've been thinking about Charles," he said quietly. "I've never understood how a man who's been as successful in his life as I have could have been such a disaster as a father."

"You haven't been a 'disaster,' darling! I think Eddie's a marvelous human being."

"Yes, he is, isn't he? Oddly enough, he was the one I had the least hopes for, but he's turned out well. But I'm talking about Charles. He and I have never hit it off. There was a truce for a number of years, but I always had the feeling that behind his mask there was a tiger ready to pounce. Well, now he's pounced and it cost me, among other things, a heart attack."

"It cost him an eye."

"Yes, the score's almost even, I suppose. The sad thing is that there has to be any score at all between us. Why should a father and son be competitive?"

"Because you're sort of a king. And he used to be the crown prince. Read your history—crown princes were always plotting against their fathers because *they* wanted to be king."

"Well, he's not the crown prince anymore. I'm not going to do something dramatic, like write him out of my will. Charles will inherit his share, but he'll never work at Fleming Industries again. I think that's punishment enough, don't you?"

"Yes. I think you're being wise and very fair."

"But Charles had a point about Ramschild. It's wrong to own an armaments company and refuse to sell its products. We're having to lay off hundreds of workers, and it's unfair to them. What would you say if I sold it? Would it bother you? I mean, your grandfather founded it."

She thought a moment. "No," she finally said. "When Grandfather founded it, wars were bloody, but at least they could be won. Now war is unthinkable. As far as I'm concerned, I'd be delighted to get out of the arms business."

"Good. Then we'll sell it. It'll be a relief to me to get out of that business too." He looked rather sad for a moment. "I used to be proud of it," he said. "But then I used to be proud of America. I'm not so proud anymore."

"But I'm proud of you," said Diana. She reached out her hand and he took it.

"I really *am* lucky," he said softly.

She smiled. "So am I."

They were really very much in love.

The nurse came in with his lunch tray.

"Lunchtime, Mr. Fleming," she chirped cheerily. "And dessert today is lemon Jell-O."

He made a face as she put the tray on his lap.

"Put on the sound, will you?" asked Nick, who was watching the TV. "There's a news announcement."

"They're always interrupting the good stuff with news," grumped the nurse as she turned up the sound.

"Today," said the newscaster, "the Pentagon announced a new series of atomic tests to take place in Nevada. The new hydrogen bomb is reported to be one thousand times as powerful as the bomb dropped on Hiroshima in 1945."

The video switched to a desert. There was a blast of light, a rumble that became a roar, and then a terrifyingly familiar mushroom cloud began taking shape.

Nick stared at the horrifying spectacle, the end of the world in dress rehearsal.

He knew he was right to get out of the arms business—it was perhaps his last and best gift to the world.

But it occurred to him he might not have gone far enough.

Charles was ushered into the impressive, paneled Pentagon office on the E-Ring, and Lieutenant General Bruce Vanderkamp came around his desk to shake his hand. Behind the desk stood two flags: the American flag and the standard of the Department of Defense.

"Good to see you, Charlie," said the beefy General, pumping his hand. "I heard about the accident with your eye. Sorry about that. What was it, a fishhook?"

"Yes. I was fly-casting in England and the hook caught in my eye."

"Must have been painful. Take a seat. I hear your father's put Ramschild up for sale."

Charles, who was wearing a black patch over his left eye, eased himself into the wooden chair in front of the big wooden desk.

"Yes, and that's why I'm here, Bruce. I want to buy it."

"Well, we'd be damned pleased if you did, Charlie. It's no secret we've not been happy with your father. We *need* Ramschild—need it badly. Those goddamned slopeheads in Nam are giving us a lot more trouble than we expected. We need more guns, bullets, tanks . . ."
He hesitated. "But will your father sell to you, Charlie? We hear there's bad blood between you."

"I'll take care of that problem," said Charles with quiet terseness.

"The point is, you'll never have any trouble with Ramschild once *I'm* in total control. I'll build you anything you want."

"Oh, we know that, Charlie. We have every confidence in you."

"I think you'd agree with me that Ramschild is a vital part of America's defense?"

"Of course. A *very* vital part. That's why we're so upset with your father."

"Then will you loan me half a billion dollars? The price Father's put on Ramschild is a billion dollars. If I can borrow half a billion from the government, I can raise the rest of the capital privately."

The General didn't even hesitate.

"The loan can be arranged, Charlie. No sweat."

Charles smiled as he stood up. He reached across the desk to shake the General's hand.

"Then we're in business, Bruce?" he said.

"We're in business."

The office was on the fifth floor of a sleek glass-and-steel tower in Geneva, Switzerland, overlooking the lake. The title on the reception-room door read *"Société des Travaux Internationaux,"* or International Works Organization, and the decor was expensive office chic. Charles was led down a hall by a Swiss secretary to a door marked "Mehemet Bey Ali." She opened the door, and Charles entered a large office whose window walls gave breathtaking views of Lake Geneva and, beyond, the snowy Alps. Behind a kidney-shaped modern desk stood an impressively tall and solid-looking middle-aged man with sleek black hair and an Adolf Hitler black moustache. He wore an expensive dark suit with a pinstripe in it that was a shade too loud. On the fourth finger of his right hand, he had a big diamond-and-gold ring. As the secretary left the room, he and Charles shook hands.

"Delighted to meet you, Mr. Fleming," said Mehemet Ali in English slicked with the pomade of a Turkish accent. "Please, take a seat." He gestured to a leather sofa in front of one window wall. Charles sat down. Mehemet Ali picked a silver cigarette box off a marble table and removed the lid. "A cigarette? The finest Turkish tobacco."

"No thanks. I don't smoke."

"Ah, a wise man. If only I could break the habit. But the pleasures of nicotine . . ." He shrugged. "Do you mind if I smoke?"

"Not at all."

"Thank you."

He removed a slim cigarette from the box, replaced the box on the table, then lit the cigarette with a platinum lighter, exhaling luxuriantly. Then he sat down in a leather chair opposite Charles.

"You are correct, Mr. Fleming," he said. "I have checked the family files. In 1922, a certain Diana Ramschild—who is now your stepmother, I believe?"

"That is correct."

"Yes. In 1922, Miss Ramschild made an . . . agreement with my grandfather. The sum she paid was one thousand pounds sterling."

"A sizable amount of money in 1922. Probably the equivalent of twenty or thirty thousand dollars today."

"Yes."

"However, the agreement was never carried out. It wasn't my father who was killed. It was a movie actor named Rod Norman who happened to look like my father."

"That is correct. A mistake, but an understandable one. Your stepmother wrote a letter to my grandfather complaining about the mistake, but my grandfather's attitude was that the job had been done. Besides, the Turk who went to Los Angeles to do the job stayed in America, opening a restaurant in San Diego, so"—he shrugged— "what with one thing and another, we forgot about it."

"Do you think that was fair business practice?"

Mehemet Ali shook his head. "No. My family has high standards. We should not have allowed such sloppy work to be executed. But in those days it was difficult getting from Turkey to Los Angeles, and then there were wars and . . ." He spread his hands. "We were wrong."

"Then it seems to me you still owe someone an assassination. It seems to me you should arrange the death of Nick Fleming."

The Turk's black eyes widened. "He is your *father*," he said.

Charles nodded. "Correct. At the end of this week, his yacht will be anchored off Djerba, an island off the coast of Tunisia. There are two guards on board at all times when it's at anchor, but my father would be reasonably accessible then."

Mehemet Ali sucked on the cigarette. Then he tapped its ash into a marble tray.

"You had better say your farewells to your father, Mr. Fleming," he said.

Charles stood up. "I already have."

CHAPTER 57

DIANA stood on the deck of the *Seaspray* looking through her binoculars at the man on the beach who in turn was looking at her through a pair of binoculars. Now he lowered his binoculars. I've seen that man before, she thought, lowering hers. But *where?* He was about six feet tall, trim, with almost white-blond hair, which gave him a German or Nordic look. *Where?* she thought. Now the man turned and started walking up the beach.

A crewman came up to her.

"The helicopter's ready, Mrs. Fleming."

Diana put the blond stranger on the beach out of her mind. "I'll just run in to say goodbye to Mr. Fleming, then I'll be with you."

"Yes, ma'am."

She went inside, through their study to their bedroom. Nick was sitting up in bed. The heart attack had forced him to rest more than usual, and he was showing every day of his seventy-five years, which saddened Diana. Nick, her love of so many years, was an old man. Ironically, Diana, who was six years younger, looked many more years younger because of her skin transplants.

"You'll be back tomorrow?" he said as she came to the bed.

"Yes, unless he can get everything done today, which I doubt. The last time I was there he told me he wanted to do some gum work the next time I came in. Anyway, I've booked a room at the Hassler for tonight." She leaned over and kissed him. "How are you this morning?" she asked.

"I feel fine. But I'll miss you."

"And I'll miss you, darling. But I won't be gone long. When can we leave for Malta?"

"Tomorrow, as soon as you get back. I've seen all I have to see here."

"Good. I've never seen Malta." She squeezed his hand and smiled. "Goodbye, my love. Till tomorrow."

"Goodbye, my love."

She went to the door and turned to take another look at him. He

501

was holding up his right hand and his fingers were crossed. That simple, silly, secret love "signal" they had shared over so many years never failed to give her a surge of pleasure and affection.

She crossed her fingers, blew him a kiss with them, then left the room and went to the fantail of the ship where the helicopter was waiting to fly her to Tunis.

It was shortly after one in the morning when she sat bolt upright in her bed in the Hassler Hotel in Rome.

Werner Herzer!

The name had come to her in her sleep, the name that connected with the face of the man she had seen on the beach that morning, the man who had been looking at the *Seaspray* through his binoculars. Lieutenant Werner Herzer! How many times had she seen him during the war sitting drinking beer at Semiramis, grinning lustfully as he watched the naked show girls. Werner Herzer, the man in charge of Fritzy von Stoltz's execution squads, the man who enjoyed his work.

Why was Werner Herzer looking at the *Seaspray?*

Then she knew, and the panic began.

Turning on the light, she grabbed the phone.

"Room eight," she said to the hotel operator. "Hurry!"

She almost screamed with impatience and anxiety as she waited for the phone to be answered.

"Yes?" Gregory Hardwick's voice was sleepy. He was the Scots pilot of Nick's private jet who had flown Diana from Tunis to Rome that morning.

"Greg, it's Mrs. Fleming. Get dressed and meet me downstairs as soon as possible. We have to fly back to Tunis immediately."

"But . . ."

"No questions! Just do as I say!"

She slammed down the phone and leaped out of bed. Diana, who was normally easygoing with her employees, was too afraid to be civil now. She ran to the bathroom, praying that she was wrong.

But she knew why Werner Herzer was studying the *Seaspray*.

When they reached the private jet at Fiumicino Airport, Diana said, "Call Captain Grant on the radio. See if anything's wrong, and if not, tell him I think there may be a professional assassin trying to board the yacht and he should alert the guards."

"Right."

Diana paced the carpeted interior of the luxurious jet, which could seat twelve, as she waited for Greg to raise the *Seaspray*. When she heard the radio operator's sleepy voice, she hurried back to the cockpit.

"Who is it?" she asked.

"It's Gordon."

"Tell him to get the Captain—no—just have him check Mr. Fleming. See if he's all right."

She was so panicked, she wasn't thinking straight. Keep calm, she told herself as she returned to the cabin to continue her pacing. Keep calm.

"Mrs. Fleming!"

The shocked sound of his voice told the story. She ran back to the cockpit. Greg Hardwick's face was white.

"Something horrible's happened," he said. "Mr. Fleming is dead."

She didn't scream or cry out. She slowly clenched her fists.

"How was it done?" she asked softly.

"He was shot in the head. One of the guards was killed too. Do you think it was one of the crew?"

She shook her head.

"No. There was an assassin. Tell them to leave everything as it is till we get there. When we're airborne, radio Interpol in Paris. Tell them to look for a man named Werner Herzer, who was a lieutenant in the Wehrmacht during the war. He's about forty, with blond . . . blond hair and . . ."

Now the tears began. She pulled a handkerchief from her purse and wiped her eyes.

"Can I get you anything?" asked Greg.

"No . . . I'll be all right. . . ."

She went back into the cabin and strapped herself into a seat as Greg started the engines. The realization that the great love of her tormented life had just been murdered began to hit her. By the time the jet roared down the runway and into the air, she was sobbing.

When the helicopter landed on the fantail of the *Seaspray*, it was dawn in Djerba. Captain Grant and a quarter of the crew were on deck to greet Diana. The copter rotor slowed and Diana climbed out. She looked around. A few feet away from the swimming pool lay the dead guard, his body covered by a tarpaulin. She walked to Captain Grant, a gray-haired Londoner who had worked for Nick since the yacht was commissioned. He saluted Diana, then took her hand.

"I'm terribly sorry, Mrs. Fleming," he said. She nodded wordlessly, trying to keep her emotions in control. "The police from Djerba have dusted for fingerprints and taken photos," the Captain went on, "but they haven't removed Mr. Fleming's body, per your instructions."

A breeze flipped the brim of her white hat. She put her hand on it.

"Which guard was killed?" she asked.

"Niko Theodoropolis."

"Have you notified his wife?"

"Not yet."

"When you do, tell her I will send her a check for one hundred thousand dollars. But don't tell her I'm sorry her husband died. If he had been doing his job, both he and my husband would be alive. Fire the other guard."

"Yes, Mrs. Fleming."

"Now I'm going to see my husband. I don't want to be disturbed for an hour."

"Yes, Mrs. Fleming."

The crew watched as the magnificent-looking woman in the blue suit and white hat walked to midship, where she vanished inside. She went through the study, putting her purse and hat on a chair, then paused before opening the bedroom door. Might there be some miracle? Might Nick be sitting up in bed smiling to welcome her? Had this all possibly been a nightmare?

She opened the door and went in.

All was still. Everything seemed normal. There was no sign of a struggle. Slowly she walked toward the bed.

There he lay, peacefully, it seemed, as if he were asleep, until she saw the bullet hole over his left eye and the blood on his pillow. Her love for this man had dominated her life. She had had his love, lost it, then fought to regain it. And now he had been snatched from her.

"Nick," she whispered, "my darling, my love, I'll pay him back for this outrage, this . . ." She put her clenched fists to the side of her head as she came closer. "It's *my* fault. I should never have told Fiona I hired an assassin once to kill you. She told the whole family and gave him the idea. . . . But I never *dreamed* . . . Oh, Nick, oh, my God . . ."

She took his dead hand and began weeping. "You were my life," she sobbed. "You were everything to me. How can I go on without you?"

She released his hand, wiping her eyes on her sleeve. Then she leaned down and kissed his face. "Remember that day," she whis-

504

pered, "so long ago when you made love to me in that empty house by the Sound? You said our love would be forever. It is, my darling. It is."

She smoothed his hair. Then, still choking with grief, she walked aimlessly around the stateroom, not knowing what to do, not wishing to leave him.

Suddenly, her grief gave way to rage.

"CHARLES!" she roared. "You'll pay for this! You'll PAY!"

Screaming like a banshee, she grabbed the curtains over one of the portholes and tore them off their hangings. Then she began tearing the yellow linen to shreds as she continued to scream.

Outside, the startled crew wondered if Mrs. Fleming had gone mad.

Daphne Pierce Fleming was not the "bitch" her sister-in-law Sylvia claimed. Daphne was too dull to be a bitch. Pretty, the daughter of a wealthy stockbroker, Daphne had gone to all the right schools, but no great idea of Western man ever excited her imagination and, in fact, few Western men set her on fire until she met Charles Fleming. She fell in love with Charles, but she was more than half in love with Charles's father, and the rift between Charles and Nick had upset her tremendously.

The assassination of her father-in-law destroyed her. She wept copiously until her husband turned on her and snarled, "Would you shut up? Your tears aren't going to bring the old bastard back!" With which he slammed out of their Fifth Avenue duplex.

Daphne was amazed, but she never really had understood her husband.

Four days after Nick's memorial service, Daphne was dressing to go out to dinner with Charles when her butler, Yates, knocked on her bedroom door.

"Mrs. Fleming, is Mr. Charles in there?" called Yates, who was a Barbadian. Daphne finished clasping her pearl necklace as she crossed the bedroom. She opened the door.

"He's in the shower," she said.

"Mrs. Fleming senior is here to see him. She's in the living room."

Daphne, a honey blonde with a weight problem, looked startled.

"Oh. Well, I'll tell him. Did you offer her a drink?"

"Yes, ma'am. She didn't want one. She said she'd just wait. She said she wanted to see Mr. Charles alone."

"Oh."

Yates lowered his voice. "She's a real tough lady, isn't she? She looks *mean*."

Daphne stiffened. "Mrs. Fleming is a very *nice* lady, Yates."

"If you say so, ma'am."

"You can go home now."

"Yes, ma'am. Good night."

"Good night."

Daphne closed the door, then walked across the room to Charles's bathroom and knocked on the door.

"What is it?" he called.

"It's your stepmother, dear. She wants to see you."

Charles, who had just dried himself, looked at his reflection in the steamy mirror. Diana? Jesus Christ, did she suspect . . .

Ten minutes later, he walked into his living room. Only one lamp was on. Diana was standing at the end of the long room looking out the windows at the spectacular view of Central Park. Across the park, the lights of Central Park West twinkled merrily. The lights of a jet sailed sleepily across the Hudson. Charles could barely see his stepmother in the darkness.

"It's a bit inky in here," he said, reaching for the light switch.

"Leave the lights off," she said. It was an order. Then she added, "I like to look at the park."

"But I can't see you."

"I lived behind veils a good part of my life. One learns to like being invisible. Sit down, Charles. We have something to discuss."

Uncertainly, he came around the table with the lighted lamp on it and sat in a chair next to it.

"I loved your father with all my heart," she said quietly. "He was a fine man. Oh, he made mistakes in his life. He hurt people. He hurt me once, long ago, and I thought I'd never forgive him. But I did forgive him because I loved him. Do you know anything about love, Charles?"

He hesitated. "Well . . . I suppose I know as much as anyone. . . ."

"You love Sylvia, don't you?"

"Of course. She's my sister."

"I had a long talk with Sylvia after the memorial service. She's devastated about her father, you know. She broke down and cried. She told me all about that peculiar evening at Audley Place. She told me what you said . . . and did."

He tensed. "Sylvia lies. She's lied all her life!"

"Oh? And you told the truth?"

"Whatever happened between Sylvia and me is *our* business, not yours! And I don't have to sit here being attacked by you!"

"Am I attacking you, Charles?"

He swallowed hard. "Well . . . I wish you'd turn on a light!"

"Very well."

He watched her move from the window to a lamp. She turned it on. She was wearing a black dress under a mink coat.

She was holding a gun.

He started out of his chair.

"Don't move!" she said. "And don't make a sound, or I'll blow your head off."

He was sweating. He eased back into the chair.

She came around the table and walked toward him. "An offer of one billion dollars has been made to us for Ramschild," she said. "The offer comes from a syndicate headed by a certain Lester Keating, a Texas oilman. But I think Keating's a front, Charles. I think the syndicate is you. Am I right?"

He was staring at the barrel of the gun.

"I don't know what you're talking about. And I'm going to call the police. . . ."

"You're not going to do anything," she interrupted. "Or I'll kill you."

"Please, Diana."

"Shut up. You're a despicable toad, Charles. What you did to your sister was depraved."

"Look what she did to me! She put my eye out!"

"Too bad she didn't simply kill you. At any event, whether you are the syndicate or not is irrelevant because Ramschild is not for sale."

"What?"

"Sorry to disappoint you, Charles. But your father wanted out of the armaments business. It's a business of death. It always has been, but now the death is of the planet. That doesn't bother you, but it bothered your father, who was a decent man. And just before he was killed, he told me he had made a mistake. The mistake was to put Ramschild up for sale, because someone else would simply continue making the missiles of death for the Pentagon. Nick told me, 'We'll keep Ramschild, but we'll convert it to peaceful purposes. We'll convert it to making heavy machinery.' And that's just what we're going

507

to do, Charles. We're beating the sword into a plowshare, so to speak. Maybe we'll be an example to other arms companies. I doubt it, but it's worth a try."

The sweat was pouring off him. She was standing directly in front of him now, the gun pointed at his forehead.

"The last question remaining is, who killed Nick Fleming? Who killed my love?"

"Diana, for God's sake, put that gun away."

"Why? You want to sell guns, Charles. Don't you think you should experience what guns are all about?"

"You can't just shoot me. . . ."

"Oh, yes, I can. I'm a very tough lady, Charles. I love fiercely and I hate fiercely. Someone ordered the execution of my husband. Sylvia thinks it was you. Edward thinks it was you, though he admits we'll probably never be able to prove it. And I've thought it all over and come to the conclusion it was you, Charles. Am I right?"

"Of course not. Father and I fought, but I wouldn't *kill* him! It was *you* who tried to kill him! *You're* the killer, Diana."

"You're so right, Charles," she said softly. "I'm the killer. I'm squeezing the trigger, Charles. Very slowly."

He started crying. "For Christ's sake, show a little mercy, Diana! I'm innocent! Oh, God, you can't kill me in cold blood!"

"I'm killing you in *hot* blood, Charles. I loved your father with my very soul, and you killed him."

"I *DIDN'T!*" he screamed. "Daphne, help me! *DAPHNE!* Oh, God, don't . . . don't . . . Oh, my God . . . PLEASE!"

She put the gun against his forehead. He felt the cold steel on his skin.

"DAPHNE!" he screamed.

"Goodbye, Charles."

Click.

She stepped back. Trembling, drenched with sweat, he opened his eyes. She tossed the gun in his lap.

"There were no bullets," she said. "But the next time . . ." She smiled slightly. "I hope you're a sound sleeper, Charles," she said. "Because you'll never know how it's going to happen to you, or when. Every time you see a stranger watching you, that may be the man who's going to pay you back for killing my love."

"Charles, what's wrong?"

It was Daphne, who had appeared in the doorway. Her husband jumped out of the chair.

"She tried to kill me!" he exclaimed. "She scared the shit out of me!"

Diana was at the door. "Just remember, Charles, you'll never know when or how or who."

And she left the apartment.

No, Nick, she thought as she went down in the elevator, I won't kill your son. But *Charles* will never know it. Let him sweat out every miserable moment of his miserable life. Perhaps that's his worst punishment. But I couldn't kill him. There's been enough of that.

She walked out of the lobby onto Fifth Avenue. It was a cold night, with gusty winds. Her limousine was waiting for her, but she wanted to walk a while, to be alone with her thoughts.

"Follow me," she told the chauffeur, who was new on the job.

"Yes, Mrs. Fleming."

Mrs. Fleming. She had wanted to be that for most of her life, and she had finally become it. As she walked down the sidewalk, she remembered the brash, cocky young man she had met in Connecticut so many years ago. Nick, my darling, my love, she thought, forgive me for all my faults. Forgive me for once hating you. Thank you for giving me the sweetest treasure of my life. Thank you for giving me love. And I'll carry on your fight, Nick, your fight against war and annihilation, your fight for peace. . . . I'll do my best, darling. But, oh, how I miss you!

The chauffeur, moving slowly beside her in the long limousine, wondered why a woman who had everything in the world was crying.